I0761656

PUSHCART PRIZE L

2026

PUSHCART PRIZE L
BEST OF THE SMALL PRESSES

EDITED BY BILL HENDERSON
WITH THE PUSHCART PRIZE EDITORS

Note: nominations for this series are invited from any small, independent, literary book press or magazine in the world, print or online. Up to six nominations—tear sheets or copies, selected from work published, or about to be published, in the calendar year—are accepted by our December 1 deadline each year. Write to Pushcart Fellowships, P.O. Box 380, Wainscott, N.Y. 11975 for more information or consult our website www.pushcartprize.com.

Acknowledgments
Selections for The Pushcart Prize are reprinted with the permission of authors and presses cited.

Distributed by W. W. Norton & Co.
500 Fifth Ave., New York, N.Y. 10110

Library of Congress Card Number: 76-58675
ISBN (hardcover): 979-8-9854697-8-3
ISBN (paperbook): 979-8-9854697-9-0
ISBN: 0149-7863

With Thanks:

Our Founding Editors
and always for Genie

INTRODUCTION

Sometimes, I realize while staring at the billions of suns in the night sky, 50 years is a really long time. I can't comprehend what has happened. The whole Pushcart span is a mystery to me as much as the night sky. Why has this series survived? Why have so many thousands of writers and editors contributed enthusiastically to that survival? Why has it meant so very much to so very many?

In the beginning, 1974, the Pushcart Prize was just a two-sentence notion jotted in a journal at The Mediterranean Café in Berkeley, California. "Why not a collection of the best," or some sort of note. I'd recently been fired from my first commercial job as an editor at Doubleday—then the largest book publisher in the world (750 new titles each year).

I'd been appointed as an Editor at a Putnam's imprint but something wasn't working for me. The idea that writing equaled money for the publishing industry—it didn't feel right. As a child of religious parents, making dollars off of honest effort seemed vaguely sinful.

Pushcart Press had just made a dent with the revolutionary ***Publish It Yourself Handbook***, issued from a studio apartment in Yonkers with my wife. Many writers had responded to the Handbook's message. A revolt was stirring. We all had had enough of "not right for our list" rejection slips, which often meant "we couldn't make money off of this turkey." For years my own first novel had earned dozens of such messages and I was mad (and still am).

Thus at the Mediterranean, I was jotting about an annual collection of "a small press best."

Obviously, I was not the person to announce such a book—failed editor, rejected novelist—but the idea seemed worth circulating. So I typed two page single spaced letters on my Olivetti to dozens of notable writers asking for their opinion and perhaps their backing. And, in my first revelation on how giving and loving the writing community is, many offered to join me in the project—see the list of Founding Editors on the masthead.

One incident stands out from those days. My wife and I had spilt up and I was living alone in a remote cabin in upstate New York. At 8:10 in the morning the phone rang. A quiet, soft voice on the other end. I figured, wrong number. Wrong. Joyce Carol Oates wanted to know more about this Pushcart project. And in that frozen, lonely, winter morning, she joined our Board of Founding Editors and lifted my spirits. Maybe this idea would work.

So many others to thank from those long-ago days. Gordon Lish, an *Esquire* editor, dared me to be daring. "Make it a prize!" said Gordon, never shy. So Prize it is, although I am wary of the word *best*—maybe *a best*, never *the best* (which doesn't exist).

Gordon's wife Barbara designed the Pushcart logo, which sums up our spirit nicely. In 1975 Pushcart mailed an invitation to 100's of small press editors inviting them to make nominations. By the end of 1975 we had a group of Guest Editors and advanced proofs for review.

From then on it was pure amazement for Pushcart. Tom Lask wrote a pre-pub feature in the *New York Times*, as did *Publishers Weekly* to be followed by reviews in, *Kirkus, Booklist*, and *Library Journal*. Harvey Shapiro, Editor of the *New York Times Book Review*, himself a small press poet, assigned a major review for PPI.

Suddenly we were on the map! Fifty years to go! Those years include: *Publishers Weekly's*, Carey-Thomas Award, The Poor Richard Prize, the Poets & Writers/Barnes and Noble Writers For Writers Award, the National Book Critics Circle Ivan Sandrof Lifetime Achievement citation, and most recently Highest Honors from The American Academy of Arts and Letters. But none of this historical sketch begins to reveal the deep story behind The Pushcart Prize. That belongs to the great spirit of our writers, editors, donors and distributors, as outlined in the following informal history of the project.

In the beginning *The Pushcart Prize* was distributed by me from the trunk of my beat up 1969 Chevy and the New York City subway. A few years later, David Godine's press took over distribution, followed by the employee-owned W. W. Norton Co., who has been our distributor for decades.

In 1998 we decided to become a non-profit, seeking donations from our loyal readers. We simply could not continue without the help of our many donors, particularly Elizabeth R. Rea, and recently a sponsorship from Marist University and generous gifts from John Sargent, The Carter C. Chinnis Charitable Trust and the Nelson S. Talbott Foundation . . . and so many more listed later.

And so we arrive amazingly at issue 50 (or L in the dead language). Since hundreds of pages will be needed to detail that history, I suggest in the meantime the following highlights from *Pushcart Prize* Introductions of the last half-century, contributed by George Plimpton, Patricia Smith, Rick Moody, Ray Carver, Phil Schultz, Charles Baxter, Russell Banks, Cynthia Ozick and myself.

I have lightly edited and condensed these introductions.

* * *

From PPXXIV

In the autumn of 1964, I was a would-be great American fictioneer with a mustache like Faulkner's. I lived in Paris near the Sorbonne in a seventh floor walk up garret with a skylight. Rent was $1.40 a night, and my daily food budget was about the same. . . .

I wrote a short story in that garret. I had already written several stories and a novel, and had been rejected without comment. Even disdain would have been preferable to the usual "not right for us." In those days *The Paris Review* still maintained an office in Paris. Lacking the postage, I walked my most recent story a few miles through the city to *The Paris Review* offices, one room, as I recall, up a flight of stairs. I dropped off the piece—a tale about a wacky, dreamy suburban kid that resembled the author a bit—and walked back to my attic hole in the sky, expecting nothing.

In a few weeks I received a note from *The Paris Review* with my story enclosed. "Dear Mr. Sonnabend" it began. "We liked parts of your story. We would like to see more of your things." It was signed by a lady whose name I have forgotten.

I leapt across town and bounded over a Seine bridge, my soul buoyed by this faint praise that perhaps wasn't even meant for me, but for the real Mr. Sonnabend who was also receiving a letter addressed to Mr. Henderson. No matter. That rejection slip kept me going for another six years of form rejections from dozens of book and magazine publishers until I sold my first tale to *The Carolina Quarterly* for $75. Somebody had cared. Somebody at *The Paris Review* had cared enough to send me a personal, handwritten note!

BH

From PPXXV

I know something about Bill Henderson. He was in Paris in the 60s, an aspiring writer, very short of funds, and living across from the Sorbonne near the Muśee de Cluny. I never knew him personally. Apparently he submitted a story to *The Paris Review* . . .

The story was called "The Kid Who Could"—a faintly autobiographical account of a youngster disillusioned in a world he had been led to believe could be his oyster. It was a story that over the next six years Henderson expanded into a novel and then—the commercial publishers having rejected it—he published it himself. Henderson's experiences with his own book provided, of course, the basis and background for the subsequent publication of *The Publish-It-Yourself Handbook*.

Henderson was unsure what to do with the income derived from the *Handbook*. He once told me: "I didn't know whether to put the money into a cabin on Long Island, or into a book." What he decided, of course, was to do the *Pushcart Prize*—which with its first volume in 1976 became an instant publishing success. "I didn't know," Henderson said, "there was going to be such feeling for it."

George Plimpton

From PPXXI

Back in 1976, the task of establishing a non-commercial literary project in a world of commercial frenzy seemed impossible. With only a small grubstake and no other support, I needed all the encouragement I could gather.

Robie Macauley, a former *Kenyon Review* editor, was an early mentor. He had been asked by Harvey Shapiro, then head of the *New York Times Book Review*, to have a look at the galleys for this new book from a strangely named, unknown publishing company. Robie's opinion of PP#1 was featured in the *Book Review* on June 27, 1976: "A big, colorful, cheerful, gratifying samplecase of 56 small press works," said Robie, next to a snapshot of me looking rather stunned by the attention.

About this time, I visited Chicago for the annual American Library Association Convention. Lost in the glitz and hoopla of the publishing giants, I sat at Pushcart's table, one of the first such alternative displays allowed at the convention. Robie found me in this peanut gallery and invited me to lunch. I wondered if lunch meant Hefner, the mansion and bunnies—Robie was doing time as fiction editor at *Playboy*. But it was just me and Robie at a small restaurant. I told him how overwhelmed I was by his review and uncertain about undertaking this impossible task. Robie, a veteran of the literary seas and about the same age then as I am now, assured me that *The Pushcart Prize* was "a good thing".

His reassurance, and Ray Carver's short story "A Small Good Thing" (PPVIII), contributed to a motto I carry with me. "a small good thing."

This is what I have thought about this project for two decades whenever debts or book returns or busyness seem the only reward. I owe this faith to many people, like Robie, gentle, dedicated people who keep making it happen.

BH

From PPXXV

Twenty-five years ago, Pushcart Press threw a party for the first *Pushcart Prize* at Manhattan's Gotham Book Mart. All of the 70's literati showed up to sip white wine from plastic glasses and wish us well. I am looking now at photographs from that gathering. In one, I am standing near a young Jon Galassi—now head of Farrar, Straus & Giroux—and poet John Ashbery. In another, Frances Steloff, nearly 100 years old, founder of the store, laughs with Nona Balakian of the *New York Times*. Harold Brodkey had just entered the room behind them. Although the photos don't show it, I am terrified.

What exactly was I doing at the center of all this pleasant uproar? What were my qualifications to edit and publish an annual collection of my betters? I hadn't even finished reading *Ulysses* yet.

Somehow, with the help of friends, and copious sauce, I got through the evening in a shaky but not too embarrassing style, and settled into the task ahead—establishing a series that any wise person would have told me was doomed.

Everybody at that Gotham Book Mart gathering but me knew that PPII would probably never appear. A terrific idea, but who would fund such a venture? A collection of mostly unknown poets, essayists and fictioneers? Worthy, sure. But forget about it.

What those silent critics didn't know, however, was that I had a force behind me—the enthusiasm of 22 Founding Editors who had offered me, an unknown, their unqualified support. I repeat their names with reverence: Anaïs Nin, Buckminster Fuller, Charles Newman, Daniel Halpern, Gordon Lish, Harry Smith, Hugh Fox, Ishmael Reed, Joyce

Carol Oates, Len Fulton, Leonard Randolph, Leslie Fiedler, Nona Balakian, Paul Bowles, Paul Engle, Ralph Ellison, Reynolds Price, Rhoda Schwartz, H. L. Van Brunt, Richard Morris, Ted Wilentz, Tom Montag, William Phillips.

BH

From PPXIV

Is poetry dead? Did someone actually ask that question—out loud? Did thousands of writers, readers and instigators rush to their battle stations to debate the merit of the aforementioned theory? Honestly? Because after immersing myself in roughly 41,611 poems (well, the boxes WERE big), I can unequivocally assure you that not only is contemporary poetry infused with a relentless, bellowing pulse, it's moving in directions that will knock the naysayers back on their prim little keisters. Judging the Pushcart was taxing and intoxicating, exasperating and illuminating, an arduous honor that forever changed the way I feel about the possibilities of the canon. On a personal note, I discovered dozens of new literary journals, and have now crafted a harrowing submission schedule. But the experience yielded a much larger lesson. For months, I was surrounded by the voices of those impassioned and driven by the power of the word, and that sweet collective noise proved one thing once and for all—poetry, ladies and gentlemen, won't be dying anytime soon. If ever.

Patricia Smith

From PPXIX

We work alone as writers. We wrestle with our personal demons up in the garret or after work, untutored by the academies, and then we bring our genius, fired by solitude, to the masses. That's the romanticized version, and sometimes I like to flatter myself with it. I like to imagine I'm really not processing a whole range of influences and histories and thirty second spots in my work. Then, while I'm worrying about this stuff, March rolls around and Bill Henderson sends along *the box of manuscripts*. And any ideas I had about what's going on in American literature are flooded out all over again.

I see it this way: the anthology you have in your hands, in preserving the heterodoxy and sprawl of American fiction (and poetry, and essays), coast to coast, border to border, is a sort of revolutionary act. Really. Its project, theme, and narrative concern finally the *enormity* of American literary civilization. The polyphony of the music of these territories. Most name-brand editors (and I used to be one) are as scared of this enormity as I am in March when the box first arrives. Democracy confers responsibility upon you. It requires pluck. So if the gods didn't put Bill Henderson in Wainscott, we'd have to make him up. When I read what Bill has done in this anthology for almost twenty years, I remember that, as a writer, I'm not at all alone in a garret. I'm part of a community. Surrounded by voices.

Rick Moody

From PPXVIII

I don't think the value of the small presses can be overestimated in any degree. In truth, I feel they are the backbone of the national literature.

Speaking for myself, I don't believe I would have had a literary life, or not much of one anyway, had it not been for small press publishers and the little magazines. My first three books were poems and they were published by Kayak Press and Capra Press. And my first fiction that was ever published in book form was a chapbook from Capra . . . Small presses and little magazines sustained me for more than a decade, when none of the larger magazines would publish my work . . . the mere fact that someone was publishing my work in whatever form was an indication to me that somebody cared. . . . The best of the small presses are doing work that is every bit the equal, if not superior to, the literature being issued by the larger better know and certainly more financially sound presses.

Ray Carver

From PPVIII

The Pushcart Prize has changed the face of American literary publishing and has given untold numbers of young writers a boost. In light of that, I want to nominate a great story by a young writer just out of the box: the story is 'Catacombs,' which appeared in *One Story* April 7, 2016, and its author is Jason Zencka. According to the author's note it is his first published story. It will knock you out.

Charles Baxter

From PPXXV

And here, in the *Best of the Small Presses*, you will read this year's version, and you will find what, to my mind, is best about American writing today—pluralism without tokenism, controversy without containment, quality without chic. You will find little of this in the official press. That Bill Henderson and his co-conspirators have been able to bring out this anthology annually is a tribute, not only to their tirelessness and dedication, but to the abiding presence of an audience as well. I don't know the figures, but I would guess that it's the best *read* annual that is published—read and not merely sold and collected on a shelf. *Pushcart* readers are an opinionated, discriminating, and contentious lot. They're no easy victims of hype and rep and hullabaloo, no pushovers for the New Thing or the Big Thing or even for the Old Thing. Moreover, this is the anthology that the writers read, especially the young writers—perhaps because it's the only anthology whose contents have been selected by writers themselves, with Henderson and his staff editors, of course, making the final selection. Thus it's always a special privilege and a peculiar pleasure to have a story, poem or essay chosen for inclusion here: you know that it has been culled by your peers, your fellow tillers-in-the-field, and that now it's going to get read in a way that will test its mettle.

Russell Banks

From PPXLVII

In his Introduction to PPXVI (1991), Ted Hoagland saluted small press people as "Holy Fools" because we insist on thoughtful, passionate, noncommercial writing as if life were somehow sacred.

Never have Ted's words meant more to me than at the present moment. All of the authors nominated for this volume care deeply about our sojourns on this bit of stardust. They persist in that faith despite criminal war in Ukraine, climate collapse, and citizens who learn from extreme media and an ex-president how to hate.

To add to these miseries we have been invaded by the most recent notion of our Whizbang Tech Wizards—Chatbot will soon write our poems, essays, stories, books without the annoying intrusion of humans. All of our creative sorts are finished, extinct, Kaput. No more need for Holy Fools.

"A.I. could rapidly eat the whole of human culture . . . digest it and gush out a flood of new cultural artifacts . . . Soon we will find ourselves living inside the hallucinations of a nonhuman intelligence." states Yuval Noah Harari and others in *The New York Times*.

For the record Pushcart will reject all chatbot plagiarisms and will ban forever any human attempting to foist machine products on our editors.

BH

From PPXLVII

Judging anything is impossible of course . . . Imagine what I experienced when I encountered the overwelming quality of gifted work in this year's *Pushcart Prize* nominations . . . I simply wasn't prepared to deal with the overall excellence, strength and volume of this year's entries.

Yes it is an international prize now, with the ever growing number of fine international journals. The volume of work in translation alone is remarkable. . . . All of which is to say the work in this year's edition was truly impossible to do anything less than wonder at . . . Given the condition of our world now, this is most welcome and needed.

Philip Schultz

* * *

From PPXII

The truth is, though *Pushcart Prize* is an anthology, it is something else besides. And to call it an institution is not to see it with full clarity. *Pushcart Prize* is a handle on a whole society, and not simply a handle to get hold of something, but to make an idea go. *Pushcart Prize* is a new literary ingredient; and a revolution; and a great Ear; and a voice braiding many voices . . .

What does it mean, this invention, this new idea, this new cultural ingredient that no one knew there was going to be such feeling for? It means that a way has been found to seize an ocean in a cup. A way has been found to hear, one year at a time, the sound—and it *is* a sound above all—of America writing.

Cynthia Ozick

* * *

My enduring thanks to all our of the teachers and students who adopt our volumes every year, and to Phil Schultz's Writers Studio, and Cedering Fox's international Word Theatre for their annual Pushcart Prize celebrations.

And as always we owe so much to our Guest Editors this year: Jessica Greenbaum, Katie Farris, Michael Waters (poetry); Bill Roorbach, Pamela Painter, Rafia Zakaria (prose) and our 161 contributing Editors.

* * *

Here are 77 brilliant selections from 62 presses, plus lists of Special Mentions.

Our devotion extends to all of the editors and writers worldwide who helped to gather this Small Good Thing, our 50th year!

And of course our thanks to you Dear Reader. Without your caring it is all futile.

* * *

After reading a draft of this introduction, a friend asked me to tell how it feels to be at an advanced age with so much literary history behind me. What does it mean to me now?

Here's what—

Dr. Ann Chinnis wrote to me this summer explaining how much the selection of her poem for last year's PP meant to her. For thirty years she has labored as an emergency room doctor, with all the trauma, heartbreak, and hope that her duty requires. But recently, after retiring, she started to write poetry, unsure if her effort was any good, not knowing if she should continue. Her poem, "How To Be A Cowgirl" from *Sky Island Journal* was selected for PP 25 by our guest poetry editors.

To her it was a huge boost. She *is* a poet. She *is* appreciated! She said the Pushcart changed her life.

That's how I felt back in 1964 Paris when I received that handwritten and hopeful rejection letter to me from *The Paris Review*. It changed my life. I've tried to spread that hope and understanding and confidence to thousands of writers over 50 years.

To answer my friend's question: it feels like love.

Bill

THE PEOPLE WHO HELPED

FOUNDING EDITORS—Anaïs Nin (1903–1977), Buckminster Fuller (1895–1983), Charles Newman (1938–2006), Daniel Halpern, Gordon Lish, Harry Smith (1936–2012), Hugh Fox (1932–2011), Ishmael Reed, Joyce Carol Oates, Len Fulton (1934–2011), Leonard Randolph (1926–1993), Leslie Fiedler (1917–2003), Nona Balakian (1918–1991), Paul Bowles (1910–1999), Paul Engle (1908–1991), Ralph Ellison (1913–1994), Reynolds Price (1933–2011), Rhoda Schwartz (1931–2013), Richard Morris (1936–2003), Ted Wilentz (1915–2001), Tom Montag, William Phillips (1907–2002). Poetry editor: H. L. Van Brunt

CONTRIBUTING EDITORS FOR THIS EDITION—Steve Adams, Dan Albergotti, Yael Valencia Aldana, Idris Anderson, Kim Barnes, Ellen Bass, Claire Bateman, Bruce Beasley, Lisa Bellamy, Karen Bender, Bruce Bennett, Sven Birkerts, Marianne Boruch, Michael Bowden, Fleda Brown, Rosellen Brown, Kelsey Bryan-Zwick, Ayse Papatya Bucak, E. Shaskan Bumas, Mathieu Cailler, Richard Cecil, Jung Hae Chae, Samuel Cheney, Kim Chinquee, Jane Ciabattari, Suzanne Cleary, Christina R. Cogswell, Michael Collier, Martha Collins, Robert Cording, Lisa Couturier, Paul Crenshaw, Chard deNiord, John Drury, Karl Elder, Kathy Fagan, Ed Falco, Maribeth Fischer, Robert Long Foreman, Jennifer Franklin, Olivia Clare Friedman, Alice Friman, John Fulton, Frank X. Gaspar, David Gessner, Nancy Geyer, Gary Gildner, Becky Hagenston, Jeffrey Harrison, Timothy Hedges, Patricia Henley, Daniel Henry, DeWitt Henry, David Hernandez, Jane Hirshfield, Richard Hoffman, Andrea Hollander, Elliott Holt, Maria Hummel, Holly Iglesias, Mark Irwin, Lily Jarman-Reisch, David Jauss, Peter Kessler, John Kistner, Richard Kostelanetz, Keetje Kuipers, Mary Kuryla, Peter LaBerge, Danusha Laméris, Fred Leebron, Sandra

Leong, Shara Lessley, Julia Levine, Esther Lin, Nicole Graev Lipson, Jennifer Lunden, Margaret Luongo, Abby Manzella, Matt Mason, Lou Mathews, Robert McBrearty, Nancy McCabe, Elizabeth McKenzie, Edward McPherson, Wayne Miller, Brad Aaron Modlin, Jim Moore, Mihaela Moscaliuc, Adia M. Muhammad, Naeem Murr, Abby E. Murray, Joan Murray, David Naimon, Michael Newirth, John Nieves, Nick Norwood, Matthew Null, D. Nurkse, Colleen O'Brien, Joyce Carol Oates, Dzvinia Orlowsky, Peter Orner, Thomas Paine, Alan Michael Parker, Dominica Phetteplace, Leslie Pietrzyk, Dan Pope, Andrew Porter, C. E. Poverman, Kevin Prufer, Lia Purpura, Nancy Richard, Laura Rodley, Dana Roeser, Jay Rogoff, Mary Ruefle, Maxine Scates, Philip Schultz, Lloyd Schwartz, Annie Sheppard, Suzanne Farrell Smith, Justin St. Germain, Maura Stanton, Maureen Stanton, Jody Stewart, Ron Stottlemyer, Ben Stroud, Nancy Takacs, Ron Tanner, Katherine Taylor, Lysley Tenorio, Elaine Terranova, Joni Tevis, Robert Thomas, Bunkong Tuon, Lee Upton, Michael Waters, William Wenthe, Allison Benis White, Philip White, Eleanor Wilner, Pui Ying Wong, Carolyne Wright, Robert Wrigley, Isaac Yuen, Christina Zawadiwsky

PAST POETRY EDITORS—H. L. Van Brunt, Naomi Lazard, Lynne Spaulding, Herb Leibowitz, Jon Galassi, Grace Schulman, Carolyn Forché, Gerald Stern, Stanley Plumly, William Stafford, Philip Levine, David Wojahn, Jorie Graham, Robert Hass, Philip Booth, Jay Meek, Sandra McPherson, Laura Jensen, William Heyen, Elizabeth Spires, Marvin Bell, Carolyn Kizer, Christopher Buckley, Chase Twichell, Richard Jackson, Susan Mitchell, Lynn Emanuel, David St. John, Carol Muske, Dennis Schmitz, William Matthews, Patricia Strachan, Heather McHugh, Molly Bendall, Marilyn Chin, Kimiko Hahn, Michael Dennis Browne, Billy Collins, Joan Murray, Sherod Santos, Judith Kitchen, Pattiann Rogers, Carl Phillips, Martha Collins, Carol Frost, Jane Hirshfield, Dorianne Laux, David Baker, Linda Gregerson, Eleanor Wilner, Linda Bierds, Ray Gonzalez, Philip Schultz, Phillis Levin, Tom Lux, Wesley McNair, Rosanna Warren, Julie Sheehan, Tom Sleigh, Laura Kasischke, Michael Waters, Bob Hicok, Maxine Kumin, Patricia Smith, Arthur Sze, Claudia Rankine, Eduardo C. Corral, Kim Addonizio, David Bottoms, Stephen Dunn, Sally Wen Mao, Robert Wrigley, Dorothea Lasky, Kevin Prufer, Chloe Honum, Rebecca Hazelton, Christopher Kempf, Keith Ratzlaff, Jane Mead, Victoria Chang, Michael Collier, Steven Corey, Kaveh Akbar, Ellen Bass, Robert Pinsky, Mary Ruefle, Chen Chen, Mary Szybist,

CONTENTS

PUSHCART PRIZE L

RICH STRIKE

fiction by CHRISTIE HODGEN

from STORY

1999

Fuck it, is the general feeling here, because we are minimum-wage employees in a doomed independent bookstore in Louisville, Kentucky, because what we do is useless, stocking and straightening and standing idly at the register, answering phones, ferrying customers to the Health & Fitness section, Gardening, Travel, guiding them back to the books they will pull from shelves and flip through and then leave in little piles next to the puffy armchairs positioned throughout the store; fuck it because we are a group of eight, maybe ten, depending how many are scheduled, and every last one of us has a college degree and most of us a master's, because our degrees have amounted to nothing, because when we stand and stock and straighten and mop and clean toilets we are doing so with one hand while clutching with the other our certificates of higher learning and, coiled within them, the bills we receive each month indicating the outstanding balance of our student loans; fuck it because no less than four of us have MFAs to our name, which means we have been trained to produce the very things for sale all around us, but instead of feeling at home here, encouraged by the company of books and bookish people, we are unmoored, queasy with the notion that if we ever do produce a book, by some miracle, nothing will come of it; the stories we thought might change the world, stories about people we used to know back home in those failed industrial wastelands from whence we came, those down-market cities where all the world's redheaded stepchildren came to live, lost souls and lonely hearts, alcoholics and drug addicts, losers, deadbeats, drifters, felons—these stories will be lost on a shelf amongst thousands of others, thin-spined and slapped shut; no one will buy them or read them or even notice them. They won't amount to shit.

Fuck it because four-twenty-five an hour, because we take home six-hundred dollars a month and our apartments cost three-fifty, because we eat the rest, and drink it, and there's never anything left. *They don't pay me enough*, is the phrase we toss back and forth, whenever a customer wants special attention, holds us hostage with her idle chatter (it is always women in the store, the middle-aged wives of doctors and lawyers with time and money to burn, sometimes wearing their Derby hats, those pastel flying saucers landed at a slant; or it is the elderly, frail and trembling and bent over their canes, hard of hearing, women who shout at us: *Where is John Grisham? Take me to the murder section!*). Whenever one of these women asks us to place a local phone call to her nephew to ask him the name of the book he was talking about last Sunday lunch, or wants us to escort her to her car, holding an umbrella over her head while soaking ourselves through, all of this *without even buying a book!*, all of this because the customer is always right, the customer is royalty, in fact one leaves the house these days only to be a customer, to feel that sense of power even for a moment, whenever this happens we say: *They don't pay me enough*. Which is to say: *Fuck it*.

This world comes down to one thing and that thing, the bookstore manager tells us, is money. One must get used to it, he says. One must sit in it, stew in it, shvitz in it. The manager's name is Roy and he started out like us, a kid just out of college looking for work, something to get through the summer until a better job came along but it never did, and here he is still, still. We wonder exactly how long he has been here, try to calculate his age based on his looks, which are hard to gauge—he is one of those skinny, Hank Williams-style cowboys in stiff blue-jeans and western shirts, slicked back hair, a long face with a crooked nose, soulful brown eyes—and by the various stories he tells: finding out President Kennedy was shot over a loudspeaker in a grade-school classroom, being sent to Vietnam in '68 and coming home wounded in '69, then working for a few years in the refinery outside Ashland, Kentucky, that giant hellscape off Highway 64 with its dozens of smokestacks rising into the air, fuming. Roy's job back then was to shovel raw coke into a furnace and when he came home in the evenings he was so covered in dust, so completely black, he had to strip off his clothes and leave them in a pile on the porch before walking into his mother's house. His mother cleaned every day on her hands and knees, a bucket of hot water and ammonia, a stiff scrub brush against the kitchen linoleum, but it was little use, because just when the floor was dry Roy came home from the plant and fouled the air, left his tracks and prints everywhere. It was a Catch 22, Roy said, a vicious cycle, one he thought he would never escape, until one Sunday, lying in bed while his mother was at church, it occurred to him, like a ray of sunlight breaking through parted clouds, that he could go to school on the GI Bill and get himself the hell out of Dodge, as he put it, in his slight country accent. And so he did. He went off to Lexington and read for four years. And then, wanting nothing more than to keep doing that, or something as near to it as he could manage, he landed here.

We try to imagine being here so long. It occurs to us that while we were crying in our cribs, sitting in our high chairs banging our spoons against the trays, when we were climbing jungle gyms and learning how to ride bicycles, chanting multiplication tables in math class, learning to tie knots in Cub Scouts and singing songs in Brownies, while we read our comic books under the covers by the light of our bulky yellow flashlights, while we were developing our first crushes, learning how to rebuild the engines of the beaters we'd bought, then how to drive them, while we were working our first jobs at Dairy Queen, while we were planning our own escapes to colleges as far from home as we could get, during all that time Roy was standing right here, day in and day out, *all that time*. It blows our minds.

Yes, he tells us, during our morning meetings, those sacred ten minutes before the doors open, when we are all seated cross-legged on the floor in a circle in the music section, our hands folded in our laps, like school children, *yes* the customers are pains in our asses. Yes, it is we who have in fact risen early and gone out into the world while it was still dark and come here to prepare, and yes, by the time they waltz in at nine o'clock it will be with the swagger of those who think they own the place, it will be with the profound ignorance of people who reach for something without ever once considering how it came to be at their disposal, people who wake to the smell of hot coffee without wondering who made it, who exactly planted the seeds that were cultivated into the plants that produced the beans that were picked, then shipped and roasted and packaged and shipped again, yes, this is all true. But it is the way of the world. These people spend their money here and because they spend their money, we all have a place to work. We must do our best to place into their hands, as smoothly as possible, without in any way interrupting the easy flow between desire and satisfaction they have come to understand as the rhythm of life, whatever it is they want. If you can figure out some other way we all get to stand around in a room full of books and make a living, Roy says, please let me know. He coughs, clears his throat. The life Roy has built for himself here is a far cry from Ashland, and yet he has a chronic cough lingering from those days. Whenever he tries to stifle it, holding a fist up to his mouth, or sometimes worse, spitting something into a handkerchief, we look at him and wonder what is going on inside his lungs, wonder how long before his past catches up to him.

The point is, he tells us one morning, when we are all still new to the job, just give them what they want and get them the hell out of here. Then you can all go home and do whatever you want. Paint your paintings. Pluck your guitars. Write sonnets to the shimmering objects of your hopeless affections. Myself, he says, placing a palm on his chest, I like to read and listen to records. And after six o'clock, I do. Can't no one stop me. That's the kind of freedom you get, working here. That's the deal.

In the mornings we listen earnestly to Roy because we want to learn how to live, what to do with our lives, how to best occupy ourselves; but after work, at the bars we frequent, our spirits flag, in no small part because it's the end of the century and the world might be ending. It's hard to know how much to care about anything, how much to invest, whether to buy or sell. We seem to have two choices, the first of which is to panic—to wring our hands and stock our cupboards and pull what money we have from the bank and stuff it under our mattresses, all for fear of what is being called Y2K, the great looming catastrophe of our time. The details are fuzzy for most of us but we understand it has something to do with computers, which we have come to rely on so completely that without quite realizing it we have stretched out prone beneath the shadow of their swords. Experts have appeared on television talking about the dating protocol embedded in our operating systems, explaining that whoever built the first computer, that idiot-savant, only designated two digits to indicate the calendar year, so as we creep forward to the year 2000, the computers creep forward to the moment they will convert from 99 to 00, whereupon the computers will think—this is the language being used—that we have reverted to the year 1900, and when this change registers in the computer brain—again, this is the language of the experts—the computer brain will have the equivalent of a human stroke, the computer brain will *freak out*, and when the computer brain freaks out there is no telling what will happen; when midnight comes on December 31st no one knows, all of our records and data might be lost, our bank accounts might be wiped clean, our power might go out, the whole grid might collapse, people on ventilators and dialysis and all the tiny babies in incubators, their fists clenched tight, all of these people might be *fucked*, not to mention anyone on a plane—we're told that planes might *fall out of the fucking sky*—and as for nuclear weapons, it's possible they could *launch themselves*.

But wait, say the experts: none of this is even the point. Because when the computer experts are done ranting they pass the mic to the religious experts, who are giddy, who drum their fingers and bounce on the balls of their feet in gleeful anticipation; all this chaos caused by computer failure will be, they say, just the beginning, just an overture to the end of days that will usher in the second coming of Christ, rejoice, all the people in the streets fighting each other for cans of food and sticks with which to build fires to heat their homes, rejoice, all the tribes of people roaming around commandeering resources for themselves with automatic weapons slung over their shoulders, all the rape and murder and starvation and suffering, all the perished meek, rejoice, it is all part of His larger plan, and as each day that passes brings us closer to rapture we must waste no time, we must get right with the Lord and make ourselves ready for Him, lo we must busy ourselves, we must boil ourselves clean.

Then there is a plan B—if one is not inclined to worry or to believe in God—and that plan is, in the words of Prince, to party like it's 1999. Prince said this back in '82 and suddenly he seems prescient, a prophet of catastrophe, a messiah in his metallic purple jacket, his hair cut into some kind of bird-like topiary. The song is all synthesizers and electric drums and it is everywhere, it has dissolved into the ether, you can't take five steps without running into a wall of it. The lyrics paint a tapestry of chaos—*The sky was so purple there were people running everywhere*—and then, beholding the chaos, give it the middle finger: *You know I didn't even care.* Which, when we think about it, and we think about it often, is not so much a party as a brand of dark nihilism. This appeals to the MFAs in our group, along with every other expression of casual disdain, of devil-may-care nonchalance in the face of crisis. When we pull a book off the shelves these days it is Camus or Nietzsche or Sartre, it is McCullers or Heller or Carver or Vonnegut. So it goes with us. The world might be ending and so what. A peculiar feeling has settled around us, that we are already past our prime, down on our luck, that all our dreams have kicked the bucket, and so, the feeling goes, fuck it.

And yet, and yet. There is Roy. Who keeps reminding us, in the music he plays at the store, in the books he recommends, that the story of humanity can be read, if you look in the right places, as a triumphant one, sometimes even miraculous. That year the four of us with MFAs, the aspiring writers on our way to becoming failed writers, make ourselves disciples of Roy. We form a book club of sorts, taking up whatever Roy happens to mention in passing—biographies of James Brown and Elvis and Abraham Lincoln, even an advance copy of a biography of a fucking *horse*, Seabiscuit, the small, knobby-kneed thoroughbred who, in the thick of the great depression, transformed himself, against great odds, into the winningest racehorse of his time. Buoyed by our interest, Roy starts bringing us books from his personal collection, giving one of us a copy of Thorstein Veblen's *Theory of the Leisure Class*, another a copy of Studs Terkel's *Working*. To the lone poet in our group, the one who is, we all agree, the poet herself included, a heart so bleeding it borders on the ridiculous, Roy gives his copy of Truman Capote's *A Christmas Memory*, a first-edition folio with its last two lines underscored in pencil, those famous final lines where the narrator, grown now, having lost the dearest friend he has ever known or ever will know, the friend he flew kites with as a boy, writes: *That is why, walking across a school campus on this particular December morning, I keep searching the sky. As if I expected to see, rather like hearts, a lost pair of kites hurrying toward heaven*. The poet shows everyone—Look, look what Roy underlined!—believing she has deciphered some secret about him, has discovered some evidence of loss and regret. He must have loved someone, she muses. He must not always have been alone. I wonder who.

The book we love the most is Randall Jarrell's *A Sad Heart at the Supermarket*, which Roy first gave to the quiet one amongst us, the pudgy one with the thick glasses who almost never says anything. We make a little bible of this book, whose falling out of print we cannot believe or abide. We consider it a particular injury that the book's inside cover is stamped in red ink with the word: REJECTED. We have underlined so many passages in this book that the lines have become useless, in fact someone has written on the inside cover, probably the poet, of course the poet: *Let us just consider every line herein to be special, and meaningful, and lit by stars*. Still, one particular sentence we have singled out, have not only underlined but also highlighted and bracketed and surrounded with little hearts, a sentence which boils down capitalism to its bones, which isolates its way of thinking into a single question, which is: *If you're so smart, why aren't you rich?* And we, feeling ourselves to be smart, absolutely knowing we are not rich and never will be, have clutched this book to our chests, as if a shield with which to defend ourselves.

That summer, one by one, then all together, we start coming to work early, to be near Roy, sensing he might help us through, show us the way, pluck us from the fuck it we are stuck in. We watch as he selects the playlist for the day, pulling nine hours' worth of music from the store's holdings and stacking the CD player: Sam Cooke, Otis Redding, Lucinda Williams, Elvis, Etta James, Marvin Gaye, and his personal favorite, Al Green. We watch as he makes the coffee, turns on all the computers and registers, turns on the phones. We watch as he lifts the delivery door in the back room, for the magazines and newspapers that arrive each morning by truck. By far the best part of the morning is the delivery of *The Daily Racing Form*, which comes separately in a faded red Ford pickup, driven by an old man who is always smoking, even at seven in the morning, a cigar. Roy signs for the forms and then opens one up and sits on the open ledge of the loading dock and we all gather around him while he tells us what everything means. About horse racing we know absolutely nothing, so he has to explain it all, starting with the progeny of horses, how you can tell a horse's sire from his name, usually. He explains which races will be held on which tracks, which horses will run and the odds against them. He explains who trains and who owns them. Increasingly, he tells us, the prices are astonishing, with the Saudis buying up everything worth buying. Any horse with any kind of lineage, even if he's trained here, is probably owned by a Saudi. It's a shame, he tells us, to own an animal like that and never see it, to buy a horse and race it without ever, he falters. Shrugs. Without ever placing your hand on his muzzle. We sense a wistfulness in Roy, the mourning of a lost time before money ruined everything, when a knock-kneed nobody like Seabiscuit could win, when even someone like Roy might have owned a horse one day, if he played his cards right.

One, two, three, four, while it is still not quite light, five, six, seven cars come cutting across the back parking lot, one by one, bobbing over potholes, parking at odd angles. Men climb out of these cars, these rust-colored Mercury Broughams and pea-green Buick Skylarks, these burgundy Eldorados with white tops, leaving their doors open and their engines running, and they walk stiffly, bow-leggedly you might say, making their way towards Roy, who is sitting with his legs dangling, surrounded by us, our legs dangling too, *on the dock of the bay*, we like to say, though it is a delivery bay in a strip mall parking lot. Nearly all of these men, these early morning pilgrims, are dressed the same, in short-sleeve button down shirts, slacks belted across their thick waists, fedoras with feathers springing from their bands, each with a cigarette dangling from his mouth, Bel-Airs, always. They have come for *The Daily Racing Form* even before the store opens, through some arrangement with Roy, who charges their credit cards on Monday mornings for the whole week. You can smell these men coming, in some cases because they have come straight from the bar, others because they tend not to shower, still others because they have slapped so much aftershave on their jowls. One man, Javier, is so short, such a flyweight, we almost can't believe our eyes. He is always impeccably dressed in what appears to be a child's suit, dark blue with a silver pinstripe, a pink satin pocket square folded neatly in the left breast pocket. Javier used to be a jockey, Roy tells us; he even rode in the Derby a handful of times, but never won. Javier always tips his hat to us, an old-fashioned white straw hat, and he becomes, of course, our favorite, the very embodiment of failed dreams borne gracefully, and we watch him coming and going in his busted-ass Cadillac with held breath, with something like awe.

All of these men, Roy tells us, have been coming here every weekday for years, decades even, and after they pick up their forms they go directly to White Castle and spread them on the counters, where they can study the odds and plan their bets as they sip their coffee. Then they head over to the track or OTB where, once or twice a year, they place a bet that keeps them afloat until the next win—never enough to quit, mind you, always just enough to get by. In witnessing this shady underworld we never knew existed, we feel we are learning something important about life—that it can diminish you to a set of addictions and their attendant rituals, that it can snare you so deep in one of its ruts you'll never get out. The *every-dayness* of it is what we can't quite get over. Even though we have to set our alarms to do it, even though we're not on the clock until nine, we keep coming back, wanting to bear witness, asking Roy every question we can think of, about racing, yes, though what we are really asking is, how do you do it, how do you do it so long, this life, how do you do it?

We each decide, privately and then all together, to become Roy. At the store and in our off hours, we vow to manage ourselves better. We will shore up, make ourselves impervious to boredom and insult and vice and need, and in this way, off the radar, out from under the thumb of capitalism and its grinding engine of want, want, want, we will cultivate our souls. In the evenings after work we will read all the philosophers. Listen to all the symphonies, all the soul and blues artists who practically opened their veins when they sang. We will set our televisions and video game consoles out on the curbs in front of our apartments, so they can ruin the lives of other people and not ours, not one day longer. We will exercise, keep ourselves trim, stop eating out of cans and bags, we will try not to drink so much. We will each develop a quirky habit, such as playing chess by mail with prisoners, or learning the banjo, or growing our own medicinal herbs. Most of all, we will write the poems and stories and novels we believe the world needs. All of this we will practice with the discipline Roy demonstrates in all that he does, world without end, amen.

One day in November, the end of the century bearing down on us, just a handful of weeks left, Roy does something he has never done before, he claims, in all his years at the store: he invites his coworkers—us!—to spend our day off with him. We have all wondered what Roy does on Sundays when the store is closed, where exactly he spends his time, whether he has friends and what they are like. We know he lives somewhere near Churchill Downs, in a shotgun house in a shaggy-ass neighborhood even we wouldn't live in. But beyond that, we know nothing.

He tells us to meet him for lunch at a Waffle House near the track and we all show up early. Even so, he is already there, sitting in a booth in the front window, and as we approach him—it is one of those gray, drizzly fall days—we see him backlit, glowing, his head bent over his newspaper, and we each feel, we will confess to each other later, a pain in our hearts, we have each turned into a little Marcel Proust, feeling the agony of loss even before it comes knocking.

Inside, we order our coffees and look over the racing form. This is what we are doing today, Roy tells us. It's the last week of the racing season and we are going to the track. We sit in the dead center of the clatter and chatter of the Waffle House, holding our heads in our hands, hoping to concoct a series of bets Roy will approve of, trying to thread the needle, to strike a balance between acquiescing to the odds and occasionally taking the strategic risk. That's smart, Roy tells us, when we tell him our wagers. And we think we've won his approval.

Except the poet, the goddamned poet just goes by the name she likes—someone has named a horse Schopenhauer's Poodle—and even though the odds are against him, way, way against him, the poet can't help herself, she proposes to bet the entire ten dollars in her pocket on him, for the win.

That's never gonna happen, Roy says. Sounding disappointed. But then he does something surprising—he smiles. Just a little. Just one corner of his mouth turns up. But if you're going to survive in this business, he says, you have to believe in miracles. We are all suddenly jealous of the poet. Of all poets. How do they do it? Just fucking around all the time. Just fucking around *all the time,* and somehow they end up on the podium.

All of us are awed by the track, its twin spires and manicured shrubbery, its sense—simultaneously, somehow—of frenzied excitement and hushed reverence. From the moment we set foot on the grounds we begin to notice that everyone here seems to know Roy. Other men, in the same blue jeans and western shirts as Roy, though some with cowboy boots and hats as well, greet him enthusiastically, shaking his hand, slapping his back. These men eye us warily, but Roy never introduces us. We feel like children brought to work on a snow day.

Roy leads us to the backside, where the horses are stabled, in green-roofed barns, and everyone there knows Roy, too. He stops and talks to someone, a stable hand or trainer—it is impossible for us to distinguish between the high rollers and stable hands here, as they are all dressed alike—who leads us into one of the barns. When the man asks if we're with Roy, Roy simply tells him, "These are some kids from the store." But otherwise we are unseen, unheard.

One of us—the skinny, bearded one with the gray eyes, the one whose arms are covered in tattoos, dozens of them, of birds and deer and foxes and owls and other woodland creatures, the one who writes lyrical, mournful stories about his dead Vietnam veteran father, the one we call *soulful*—drifts off, approaches a horse, puts his hand on the horse's muzzle. It is a gray horse with white dappling and a black mane. The horse and the soulful one stare at each other for a long moment. It occurs to the rest of us that the soulful one should work here instead of at the store, that his proper place in the world is in a stable, he is so at home here. One day years from now he will publish a story and there will be a gray horse in it, with white spots, and the main character, a suicidal teenager, will have snuck into his grandfather's barn to place his hand on the bridge of its nose, just like this, before he hangs himself from the rafters. When the poet reads the story she will recognize the horse, remember this moment. It will be the only story any of us ever publishes.

When the man Roy is talking to sees the soulful one touching the gray horse he shouts, "Hey! You can't touch the horses." And Roy, embarrassed we can tell, gets us the hell out of there. We walk with our heads down back to the track, trailing behind Roy, like kids in trouble.

On the way back to the track Roy tells us, over his shoulder, that gray horses almost never win. The soulful one nods. But, Roy says, they're the most beautiful.

Then it is time to place our bets. We stand outside the betting booths with clammy hands. Roy goes first, places about ten bets. Then it is our turn. We approach the window with our crumpled bills and are handed tickets in return. We stuff them in our pockets.

Don't lose those now, Roy says.

Then we sit and watch the first race. The stands are practically empty, so we are up close. The first time the horses race past us we all stand as if for an anthem. The poet even clasps her hands over her heart. The sound of their hooves on the dirt is how we come to understand the thrill of it, how powerful these animals are, how dangerous it is to race them, crazy really. The poet starts narrating, something she does when she is moved. What is happening right now in front of us seems impossible, she says. How is it that of all animals, humans are the ones who rose up and commandeered everything, bent the rest of the animal kingdom to their will? It doesn't seem possible, that a hundred-pound jockey can control an animal ten times his size and strength. Am I wrong, she asks us, wanting approval—she is always looking for someone to agree with her.

How is it possible, says the soulful one, staring at the track, that you're philosophizing about something that's happening right in front of you? How are you not just *watching the fucking race*?

When the race ends Roy explains to the poet how we did it. First, we befriended the horses, he says, and then we broke them; then, to further our comfort and control, we invented the saddle, and then the snaffle.

What's a *snaffle*? the poet asks.

The bit, Roy explains. That whole massive animal is controlled through its mouth.

Snaffle, she says, wincing. She seems angry, on the verge of turning on the whole endeavor. That makes me feel bad, she says. It doesn't really seem fair.

Ain't nothing fair in this life, Roy says, looking off in the direction of, we imagine, Ashland.

After the first race, Roy leaves us for a while. We just look and he's gone. Probably visiting with friends, we decide. In his absence we drink so much it is astonishing. We all run out of money and end up piling onto the one credit card between the four of us that has any room on it. This card belongs to the one who looks like Oscar Wilde, with a fat, long face, his hair parted down the center and tucked behind his ears. He always seems to have more money than the rest of us. He lives in a much nicer apartment, and wears a suede trench coat and carries a leather messenger bag, and it doesn't make sense how he can afford all of this, plus a car—he has the only car amongst us, a BMW that belonged to his cousin, who died of a heroin overdose, he says—but nor does it make sense that he would work forty hours a week at a minimum-wage job if he had money, so we just don't think about it. But still. As one hour leans into the next, and the next, and we order our fifth round of bourbons, the poet says, This is gonna take you, like, *six years* to pay off! She clutches her head and makes an anguished face.

Oscar Wilde just smiles, tucks his hair behind his ears. It's okay, he says.

But it's *not*! she cries. It really, really is *not*!

The next time he leaves for drinks, the poet turns to the soulful one, who anyone can see she is in love with, and says, Don't you feel bad? I *feel bad*.

And he says, Don't, you shouldn't.

And, she says, But.

And he says: Haven't you figured it out yet?

And she says, Figured out what?

And he says, Don't you recognize his last name?

And she says, What? She isn't local, knows nothing about this city and who runs it.

He's got a trust fund, says the soulful one. Let's just say there's a sizeable amount.

A look passes between the poet and the fourth one, the quiet, pudgy one who always seems to be taking notes—in fact sometimes when they're all together he literally takes a little notebook out of his pocket and writes something down. He's afraid nobody likes him because he isn't bringing a whole lot to the table, you might say—all he seems to do is scavenge. But here he feels a solidarity with the poet. They both feel wounded, played for fools.

The poet can't quite believe it. Her mouth is hanging open. Twenty, thirty seconds go by. Then she turns to the soulful one, incredulous, and says, What the fuck are you *talking* about?

My God, says the soulful one, you're a baby.

When Oscar Wilde comes back with drinks, the poet is demure. It is as if she feels embarrassed for having misread what was going on. Thank you, she says to Oscar Wilde. She sits up straight, holds her drink a bit aloft, correcting herself, adjusting to her new understanding of who she is spending time with. She has never been around money, the quiet one notes. She doesn't know how to act around it. It makes her nervous.

Roy returns just in time to see Schopenhauer's Poodle. The horse is black, he tells the poet, with a green mask, and he'll be coming out of the last post, the absolute worst position. They are all standing even before the race starts. When finally the gates open and the horses come flying out, Schopenhaur's Poodle is at the back of the pack, and the poet holds her breath, thinking he will do it, he will charge at the end—he is just waiting for the others to tire. But there are three beautiful chestnut horses in the lead, neck and neck, who are so furiously powerful she can feel their hoofbeats *in her chest* when they race past, and her belief flags, the quiet one can tell by a flicker in her eyes. By the time Schopenhauer's Poodle crosses the finish line he is behind the next-closest horse by eight lengths. That's kind of a disaster for him, Roy says. The poet pretends to shake it off. Of course he wasn't going to win, she says. The form said so.

As they are leaving Roy stumbles on the stairs. He catches himself on the railing—it is just a wobble, really—but they all exchange looks. He must be as drunk as they are. But no one dares offer him a ride. What they do instead is pile into Oscar Wilde's car, his *dead cousin's car supposedly* says the poet, loudly, and follow Roy at a distance, like the Secret Service. When Roy turns off the main drive onto his street, we drive past it, give him a minute or two, and then circle back. We drive down his street until we spot his car, a 70-something Mercury Cougar in robin's egg blue, in the driveway of a white shotgun with a sagging porch and a front lawn the size of a ping pong table. All the lights are out but there is a fat, glowing Santa on the porch standing sentry, his arm raised in greeting. None of us says a word.

After that the store is uncommonly busy with holiday shoppers, who are stocking up on cookbooks and hardcover murder mysteries and CDs. All through these weeks we hope Roy will make some mention of our outing at the track, will gesture towards bringing us with him again, but it's like it never happened, in fact he is more aloof than before. He's just busy, we tell ourselves, just getting through the holidays. And anyway, the track is closed.

The music section, where Oscar Wilde works, keeping the stock organized and answering questions from desperate shoppers, is by far the busiest during the holiday rush. It is mostly older ladies in the store, and these older ladies have come in for Andrea Bocelli and Sarah McLaughlin CDs, though they can never remember the names of the singers or songs they want to buy, and so they stand there singing to Oscar Wilde, *Let this be our prayer, something something something*, or *Blahbedy blah blah angels*, sometimes spreading their arms to indicate grandeur, and if you think that's bad it gets worse, he tells us—the rest of the shoppers are buying up all the Britney Spears and Blink-182 and Limp-Bizkit records. We take this as a bad sign. If the world doesn't end, it should.

But it doesn't. It most certainly does not. We all spend New Year's Eve together, at Oscar Wilde's two-bedroom apartment off Bardstown Road, in the expensive part of town—How did I not *realize*?, the poet keeps wondering—watching the 55-inch television he was given by a cousin who bought an even bigger television and didn't want the 55-inch one anymore. Supposedly. We sit on the couch wearing children's party hats, drunk as skunks on Maker's Mark, high on Oscar Wilde's premium weed, stuffed with Chinese takeout, watching *Dick Clark's New Year's Rockin' Eve*. We regard the giant crowd in Times Square, everyone wearing puffy coats, except a cluster of Wall Street-looking assholes wearing tuxedos. Everyone is screaming and holding long balloons, the kind you'd make balloon animals out of though there are no animals—*just a whole lot of giant dicks*, Oscar Wilde keeps saying—with mylar streamers attached on the ends, waving them around like mad. *Seriously those all look like spewing dicks!* What the soulful one fixates on, instead of the balloons, is that one of the storefronts lining Times Square has replaced the name on its marquis with the words GOING OUT OF BUSINESS FOREVER, and the camera keeps panning past it, and the soulful one keeps saying, This is an omen, this is a sign, the world is ending.

And the quiet one keeps saying, It is *literally a sign*.

And the poet keeps saying, You just have to believe, everything is going to be fine, you just have to believe. Over and over, she says it.

Until the soulful one says, Do you have any idea, do you know what you *sound* like? All I hear when you're talking is the voice of someone who's never been punched in the face.

And the poet says, crestfallen, I guess that's true, technically. Technically I've never been punched in the face.

And the soulful one adds, I mean both literally and figuratively.

Yeah, I got that, the poet says, sounding a bit wounded. I mean, I do have *some* interpretive skill, I'm not completely. She falters, sighs. I guess you're right, I don't really belong here. She tries to pull off her party hat but it sags to the side, still affixed to her head by the elastic string. I guess I'm a little, I'm a little out of my elephant. She is too drunk again, the quiet one notes. She tries to keep up with the rest of the group but she is one of those pale, ninety-pound, Winona Ryder-style waifs, and she can't handle it. She slumps onto the arm of Oscar Wide's leather couch—again, his cousin's—and closes her eyes. By the time the ball finally drops and everyone in Times Square starts screaming, all those Wall Street assholes high-fiving each other, waving their balloons in the air, at the dawn of the new millennium, the poet is asleep.

One morning in February the soulful one—he is the only one still arriving early for work—walks in from the bus stop and across the back parking lot in the first light of morning. Roy's car isn't there, he notes, which is a first. He sits on the back steps smoking a cigarette until Oscar Wilde arrives in his dead cousin's BMW. Oscar Wilde understands the nature of the situation even before the soulful one walks to the passenger side and gets into the car. They drive straight to Roy's. When they see his car in the driveway, its hunched profile, when they see Santa on the front porch still lit, his arm still raised, the sack slung over his shoulder still full of undistributed toys even though it is February, they know.

Roy's doors are open, which doesn't surprise the soulful one—he grew up around here and knows how people are, leaving their doors unlocked as almost a point of pride. What's surprising is the spareness of Roy's house. There is no furniture in the living room except an old corduroy beanbag and a record player on the floor, with a few milk crates full of records surrounding it. *Elvis' Christmas Album* is on the turntable, the soulful one notes, its sleeve on the floor, Elvis' face staring up, a young face with a slight smirk indicating he is enduring the misfortune of his fame as well as he can. Next they walk through the kitchen, white cabinets and a linoleum floor printed to look like brick, a card table and two chairs against the wall, then down a skinny hallway to the back bedroom. As they make their way down the hall, Oscar Wilde entertains the possibility that Roy is alive—that he is hung over, perhaps, and just struggling to get out of bed. But the soulful one knows. The soulful one has seen this before.

The door to Roy's room is half ajar and suddenly the soulful one, who is in front of Oscar Wilde, signals him to stop, turns and presses his palm against Oscar Wilde's chest. Just wait, he says. Oscar Wilde turns away and goes back toward the kitchen. He has never seen anything bad before, not really, and doesn't have the stomach for it, it turns out.

What the soulful one has seen is Roy is in his bed—a mattress on the floor—slumped over on top of the covers, and that he has, with a revolver that is now on the floor, shot himself in the head. There is blood splattered everywhere.

Oscar Wilde, understanding now what is going on, starts gingerly opening the doors of Roy's kitchen cabinets. In one cabinet is a box of Froot Loops and a box of Cheerios. In another cabinet, a bottle of Maker's Mark, a bottle of Beefeater, a bottle of Heaven Hill straight corn whiskey, all of them nearly empty. In the cabinet between the stove and refrigerator, Oscar Wilde is surprised to find a series of old school photographs in frames, photos of a girl who looks like Roy, the same dark eyes, the same nose, her dark hair in braided pigtails. As you progress from the top shelf to the bottom the girl grows older, all the way up to her senior photo, in which her long hair is released from its braids and is falling in gentle waves, in which she is wearing pearls and a black drape, like all the girls do in the south for their pictures, even the poor ones.

When he finally gathers the strength to check on the soulful one, Oscar Wilde sees that he is sitting on the bed holding Roy's hand, his head bowed. He doesn't move or make a sound for a long moment.

Like *fifteen minutes*, Oscar Wilde says, when he tells the rest of us the story, which he does many times, in bars after work, *fifteen goddamned minutes* the soulful one sat there holding Roy's hand, and you could just tell he was reliving some kind of awful episode from his childhood. We are free to speak of the soulful one now because he has stopped coming out with us after work. He has more or less stopped talking to us. We are giving him space, thinking he will return to us.

Something awful has happened to us, the poet says one night at the bar, when we are all good and drunk. She clasps the quiet one's hand, then Oscar Wilde's, and pulls them to her, like a preacher welcoming sinners at the altar. We must stay together, she says. We must never break apart. We must promise to remember this, and stay friends our whole lives, and live our lives in such a way that Roy is honored, that Roy would approve of. She tries to calculate whether that means staying at the bookstore forever, like he did, or striking out, living large, trying to write our books. I can't make the math work, she says. Either he liked the way he lived, which he seemed to, in which case we should all just stay at the store and live our lives simply and honestly. But then again, she muses, he shot himself. Which means maybe he had regrets, maybe he wished he'd lived more, in which case we should strike out. And who was that girl? Where is she? Did she die, too, and the pain of it, that's what got to him in the end? I don't know, she keeps saying, I don't know what we should do. She lets go of their hands and props her elbows on the table, places her face in her hands. She mumbles and they can barely hear her: is it worth, like, getting married and having kids if you're just going to lose it all and the pain of losing it will literally kill you? Oscar Wilde and the quiet one give each other wary looks. If she keeps drinking like this, the quiet one notes, and if she keeps trying to figure out the meaning of life, it will go badly. It is like watching a dog trying to read the newspaper.

Just then the waitress delivers a fresh round of shots. Makers, Roy's favorite. They straighten up and raise their glasses. To Roy, they say. Down the hatch. To Roy.

The assistant manager, a shrill-voiced woman named Betsy, takes over when Roy dies, and almost immediately institutes a number of changes. The first being that she makes everyone wear aprons and nametags, the second being that she stops early delivery of The Daily Racing Form to the men we have grown so fond of. If they want the form so badly, she says, they'll still want it at nine o'clock. But this isn't true, as it happens. We never see them again.

The third change Betsy makes is to stack the CD player each morning with only two discs on repeat, the two artists that are selling the best, Sarah McLaughlin and Andrea Bocelli. We listen to their soaring, plaintive voices for eight hours a day. We conclude that this is what happens to people who get too used to reading books in college and don't make any plans for their future livelihood. We are in a circle of, if not hell, hell-adjacent. Maybe we're in a circle of irony.

One morning as the store is opening, when Betsy cues up Andrea Bocelli and his voice, once again, comes blasting from the speakers overhead, Oscar Wilde announces: I'm going to die of boredom.

I already did, says the poet. I'm not really even here. I'm just an apparition.

The right thing to do in this situation, says the quiet one, is kill Betsy.

Be that as it may, says the soulful one, the easiest thing to do is quit.

And so it goes. Within three months we are all gone, flung, scattered to the wind. Fuck this place, we say. Fuck it, fuck it, fuck it.

2022

The soulful one makes a point to watch the Derby each year. The race itself lasts just two minutes, which is the right amount of time, he has decided, to spend thinking about his life before, as he refers to it, that life back in Louisville just before he left everything and moved here to Alaska. He doesn't like thinking about those years, back when everything shimmered with meaning, when every choice he made seemed of the utmost importance. He remembers how he agonized, trying to parse out the morality of the simplest question, like whether or not to go out with friends after work—was he seizing the day, or wasting his time? The world was ending, he thought, and he wanted to make the most of his life. He couldn't afford a single wrong move, or so it seemed at the time.

The world hadn't ended, of course. And yet the soulful one always thinks of this time as the end of life as he once knew it. He couldn't believe, *still* couldn't believe, that he had been made, or perhaps destined, to walk into a room where someone had shot himself. Not once but *twice* that had happened to him, his father and then Roy. It was too much. He'd gotten out of Louisville, just about as far as he could. He'd wandered for a while, working in kitchens and bars. Then settled outside of Anchorage teaching twelfth grade English to kids who were feeling the first stirrings of existential despair in their chests. *Hamlet, Death of a Salesman, Lord of the Flies, The Great Gatsby.* He was mired in those questions again—what to do with one's life, whether it had any meaning—though at a safe distance now. Moving had been like magic, had placed him past all of that.

What should I do? his students asked him. What should I do?

Go out with lanterns, he always told them. Find yourself. Look near and far. Look everywhere.

On TV, they are loading the horses into their paddocks. The commentators are naming the horses, one by one, as they are settled in. Rich Strike, the commentators say, only made it onto the list of contenders yesterday, when another horse scratched. Eighty to one, they say, about the worst odds possible. The soulful one remembers the poet betting on the longest shot that day, how naive she always was, how much it angered him to be around that kind of person, the kind of person who hadn't lost anything yet, who could afford to bet on a longshot because she still had some reserves to burn through. That kind of person used to drive him crazy. But now, he realizes, he prefers it. He likes it when kids in his class still believe they can change the world, still believe that love is all that matters. When they come into his classroom already crushed, the light in their eyes already blown out, they usually don't make it. They just finish up school and disappear into the wilderness.

Back then, the poet had enough light, he estimates now, to last her a good number of years, maybe a whole lifetime. He hopes she's still like that. Writing poems about beauty, trees, flowers. He doesn't know how she's faring now, or any of the others. They had written to him for a while, trying his email again and again, even though he never wrote back. The poet had written him a heartfelt note when he'd published his first story—and last, as it turned out. *I remember how you stroked that gray horse, how it looked like communion.* He'd tried to answer a few times, but he had never been able to do it. He'd had to let it all go. The writing, the friends, everything. It was the only way he could manage. It was for the best.

Oscar Wilde is out on his balcony, smoking a Newport, because they don't make Bel-Airs anymore. He has been living here in Portland—Maine, not Oregon, he is quick to specify when catching up with friends—for three years now. When he decided to move to Maine, he had been looking for something he would never grow tired of, and it had seemed to him that Maine had a certain unspoiled, undiscovered quality that would buoy him, that would make him feel like the guardian of a privileged secret. But now people were moving to Maine in droves, people who didn't seem to deserve or appreciate or understand it, who were too young to have earned it. His new neighbors, who share the top floor of the building with him, are so young it bothers him. They are too young, he thinks, to own property in a building like this, with floor-to-ceiling windows, long balconies, multi-million dollar units. He doesn't know where they got their money but assumes it is the same place he got his. At least when he was their age, he tells himself, he was *trying* not to live like he had money. He had put in a few years of spartan living first. He had always liked that about himself.

Yes, after that stint at the bookstore he had capitulated. He had taken his father's advice and gone to business school at Wharton. While he was there, he'd watched the financial industry collapse, literally and figuratively; the apocalypse they'd all been anticipating in Louisville had just been the wrong one. He had moved to New York during the recovery and worked at Sachs for a while, then moved to the private equity firm his uncle ran. On top of the money he already had, he had made even more, an obscene amount.

He had gotten married along the way, had a son, and spent ten years as a family man. His life with his wife was something like an agility course, jockeying to get into the right schools, onto the right soccer and baseball teams, the right tennis coaches and piano teachers, the right language tutors. Even the good parts of their life—the vacations, the home improvements and acquisitions of newer, better properties—were stressful. He had grown tired of it. Through all the concerts, games, performances, fundraising banquets, Oscar Wilde had emitted a simmering frequency of resentment. Fuck this, he was thinking, those last few years. Fuck all of this.

When their son was thirteen, his wife left him, and took their son and the bulk of his affections with her. She had moved back to Virginia, where her parents lived—he had always hated them—and he was free, finally, free of all that. But he didn't know what to do with his freedom. He quit his job, spent a year drinking. Then another. And then he was done with that. He decided to move to California and be a guy who was *all about experiences*. He filled his calendar. He took surfing lessons, took hang gliding lessons. He flew to Nepal and climbed a mountain. He went on a safari in Kenya. For five thousand dollars, he rented a helicopter that flew him over a swampy region of Louisiana, and when the helicopter dipped low, he shot feral hogs with an AK-47. He went to a ranch in Reno and launched a rocket propelled grenade. He learned how to drive a race car. And then one day it seemed to him, with all the wildfires, with all the tent cities along the highway, that California was *over*, and he had started casting around for the next place. In January 2020, he had moved to Portland for its undisturbed beauty, the crispness of its air. He had loved it, especially in those first months of COVID, when it seemed the rest of the world was suffering and he wasn't.

Then all the young people from Boston and New York had started moving up to Maine, and they were ruining it. He didn't know how much longer he'd be here.

Oscar Wilde drops his cigarette butt of the balcony and watches it plunge. He had calculated the Derby would be starting just when he finished his cigarette, and goes back inside to find he is just in time.

He hears the announcer shout, *And, they're off!* The race is running. He squats in front of the television and tries to position his phone in such a way that captures both him and the race. He wants to send a picture to the quiet one and the poet. They are only in touch two or three times a year now, probably because whenever Oscar Wilde thinks of them, a bad feeling settles on him—like he chose the wrong path. Maybe if he'd kept at it, reading and writing, trying to find out the best way to live, he could have done something better, he wouldn't be alone now in an expensive condo, watching on TV a distant place that plucked the minor strings of his heart. Maybe if Roy hadn't died. That's what had really spooked him.

But now Oscar Wilde does what he always does, which is to push away the bad feeling. He makes a manic face, holds up the bottle of Maker's he has brought out for the occasion, and takes a selfie. To Roy! he types, then hits send and goes back to the race. Which looks to him like all the other races he's ever seen in his life. The top contenders are up front. They are going to win, and were always going to win.

The quiet one is at his desk. It is a Sunday afternoon, but still, here he is at work. There is something wrong with this, of course, but next week will be different. His workload will be clear by then. Or so he has told himself for an endless expanse of Sundays, almost twenty years of Sundays.

If he had known his life would be like this, he would have done something else besides go to law school. Anything else. But the debt he had sunk himself into in pursuit of his degree required he keep working for at least ten years; and then after that, to make up for all the time he'd lost, the life he hadn't gotten to live, the marriage and children he hadn't managed to squeeze in during his ten viable off-hours a week, he needed to keep working, to stockpile money. He needed to stockpile it so he could retire at fifty, maybe fifty-two, and *then* start living. That was his plan. At fifty-two he would leave the firm and finally write his novel. Occasionally he digs up his old notebooks from his twenties and thinks he can revive them, spin them into something important. Though he doesn't quite know where to start.

His alarm goes off. He has set an alarm, because he is that kind of person now, a person whose life passes in billable, six-minute intervals. If he is going to take a break to call the poet, so they can watch the

Derby together, he is going to set an alarm for ten minutes in advance of the start time. The whole time he is bringing up his browser to find the live broadcast, chatting with the poet, watching the race, a clock will be ticking in his brain. At his rate of $750 an hour, this break will cost him more than a hundred dollars. The poet has no understanding of this. She has sometimes rambled on to him for over an hour about her kids. He had asked her once, when they were about to hang up, Do you realize you just cost me a thousand dollars bitching about this soccer tournament?

Oh my God, she'd said. That's horrifying. I'm horrified.

Just giving you some perspective, he'd said.

I keep forgetting your time is, like, I mean it's *worth* something, she said. I feel bad just saying hi to you, now that I think about it. We should never talk again. Goodbye.

Good riddance, he'd said. Because he couldn't tell her what he really felt—that if not for her, there would be no one to call. No one he could tolerate. No one who still occasionally talked about the human soul.

He calls the poet. They have been talking almost every day since 2020 when, a few months into the pandemic, the poet's husband had disappeared on her. The quiet one had been in quarantine, working from home, losing his mind, suddenly remembering the person he used to be, the person he had meant to become. They had leaned on each other through that time.

The phone rings and rings. He imagines her running through her house, breathless, hearing the phone but not being able to locate it, sticking her hand between the couch cushions or under a pile of laundry. She almost always misses his calls but returns them right away. I couldn't find the phone! she always says, as if this is some sort of surprise. There is a frantic, disorderly quality to her life he finds fascinating and a bit repulsive. He sometimes wonders about what will become of her. Divorced with three kids, teaching at a community college, running free poetry workshops for seniors and sometimes even prisoners, living in a century-old bungalow, with very little saved in retirement. Her later years, he often thinks, are going to be hard.

The poet is in the back room of a bar. But *is* it a bar, she is wondering, considering they serve a full menu and have a game room full of pool tables and pinball machines and video game consoles, and they even have a kids' menu that's a placemat, with word searches and mazes on it, and packets of crayons they distribute to kids? Can it be said to be a *bar*

bar? She is trying to come up with a list of ways this place—a dive within walking distance to her house, a dive she first started visiting during quarantine, because of the pinball machines, the video games, because for twenty bucks you could have someone else feed your kids and then your kids would maybe leave you alone for *five goddamned seconds*—isn't really a bar. Even though it is. In the front room, in full view from where the poet is sitting, a row of drunks is slumped over their beers. All the televisions are tuned to sporting events and from the overhead speakers, Def Leppard. On balance, she concludes, the place is a bar. She has taken her two youngest kids, seven and nine, to a bar. Again.

But it's okay, she tells herself. She doesn't do it very often. And today is special. Today is Derby.

She is here because she wants to see the Derby, just two minutes is all she's asking, but her television is broken. The state of her house is this: she is the type of person who has only one television, and whose only television is broken. Her sons had knocked it over while chasing each other around the house. I didn't do it! said the older son. I didn't do it! said the younger. This was weeks ago, and she still hasn't replaced it. Do we really need one, she has asked the kids. Think of all the reading we can do now. But they have given her that look. The look everyone gave her, all the time.

She has timed all of this carefully. Her sons are happy for the moment, one of them driving a racecar through a burned-out urban hellscape, the other pounding the flickers of the pinball machine. She has fed a five-dollar bill into the coin machine and has a stack of quarters waiting for them. Their food has been ordered and is set to arrive in the next five minutes, just before the Derby starts. While they stuff their faces with french fries, she will be able to slip into the next room and watch the race. She is pleased with herself. You're killing it, Jones, she says to herself. A little pep talk.

Her phone starts ringing and she digs through her bag, an NPR tote whose seams are coming loose at the top, overflowing with books and student projects, crumpled papers of all sorts, and she wonders, Do I have to be such a fucking *cliché*?

When she finally answers, the quiet one explains the race is about to start; he has placed his bets online. A trifecta for himself, he tells the poet, and a single bet just for her—a hundred on the longest shot, Rich Strike, 80 to 1, to win.

Oh, God, she tells him. A hundred bucks. You shouldn't have done that. You might as well have lit that hundred on fire.

I know, he tells her. But it doesn't matter. You're forgetting I have money.

I guess.

You don't know what it's like, he muses. You get so miserable chasing money you just throw it away trying to entertain yourself.

Sounds nice, she says.

It isn't, he says.

They still have a few minutes to kill. The quiet one tells her about the case he is reviewing documents for—these Wall Street assholes still email their girlfriends from their work accounts, he says, and she can practically hear him rolling his eyes. This one guy keeps writing, the quiet one says, in elaborate detail, about wanting his girlfriend to suck his dick. While the quiet one talks, the poet is idly poking herself in the belly, the soft rim of fat that has lately appeared out of nowhere. She is sort of fascinated by it, like a bird come to a feeder, something sudden and startling. Then she remembers she is in public and straightens her posture.

How's the teenager, the quiet one asks her. This is what they have taken to calling the poet's oldest child, whose defining feature is that within the past year she has shockingly, and completely, turned into an asshole. The poet blames her husband—*ex*-husband, she has to keep reminding herself—because during quarantine, he had taken one look at the situation—three kids in the house, four Zooms going at the same time—and he'd left, just straight-up left, saying his work was drying up—he sold ads for a local television station—and he was going to go work for his brother's marketing firm on the west coast. But you *hate* your brother, she had protested. That was just before she realized he hated her more, hated their life together.

For a while the husband was FaceTiming them from the beach, saying, Hey, kids! Look where I am! And turning his phone to show them the ocean and the people walking along the shore. People in shorts. Shorts! Meanwhile the poet and her kids were trapped in the house trying to get through that first winter, like the Donner Party. A year later, when the kids returned to school, the husband had come back and tried to insert himself into the rhythm of their lives, but by that point the poet and her children had developed a hive mind, and what that hive mind was thinking was: Who the fuck is *this* guy?

So he'd left again, this time for good. And now the teenager was an asshole.

Since they have last spoken of the teenager, the teenager has done something so cruel, the poet tells the quiet one, it has sent her reeling.

The situation was that the teenager's bed, where she took her phone calls, was next to a vent that spilled out directly over the poet's bed, and the poet could always hear, clear as a bell, what the teenager was saying. She didn't even *want* to hear what the teenager was saying, and walked away when she could, but this last time, she was almost asleep and didn't want to get out of bed—sleep was hard to come by for the poet. But suddenly the teenager's voice was right there, all around, excited and loud.

She's only sending me to therapy, said the teenager, so she can get free therapy for herself. Like, she's seriously asking me all the time, did your therapist say anything helpful? She's just like, a little mouse under the table sniffing around for *therapy crumbs*. Like, get your own therapist, Bitch!

The poet had flushed with shame, hearing this, because it was true. She *had* been doing that. She needed therapy but it wasn't free, and if she was going to pay for it, she would pay for the teenager, who sometimes mentioned suicide, as a dark joke usually, but then again, then again. The poet knew the jokes. She made them herself. All the time.

Then the teenager had said: That bitch won't leave me alone, that stupid fucking *cunt*. I hope her stupid poems, her stupid fucking poems about trees and flowers and birds and shit, like, I hope they get famous and she wins the Pulitzer or something and she makes a bunch of money and then she *dies*. And then I'll get all the money. And I will dance on her grave.

Then the teenager had laughed and laughed.

If you're so smart, the poet has been thinking since, why aren't you rich? Why aren't you rich?

The thing is, the poet explains now to the quiet one, I didn't even *do* anything! This kid has never had a curfew, has never been punished, has never had to have a job, has been handed anything she's ever wanted. I mean, I still put notes in the kids' lunches every day. Not just quick little scribbles that say I love you, but like, *poems*, poems in rhymed tercets delineating *why* I love them, all the special qualities they possess. Three poems a day I'm writing at like six in the morning while packing up lunches, and they're even *illustrated*. I mean to be fair sometimes I can't think of a poem and they just get a note that says I love you, but on those days, still, there's a little watercolor of a dog with a balloon tied to its tail, and the balloon is a heart, and inside the heart, *that's* where it says I love you. I mean, they're *elaborate*.

I think maybe, the quiet one says. Pauses. I think maybe you should redirect that therapy money to yourself.

They both laugh. It's true, she knows. She is off the rails.

Then follows a silence where neither of them says anything. Probably because her problem is so stupid, so pathetic, because of the staggering smallness of her life, the quiet one can't think of what to say. Or maybe he's taking notes, the poet thinks darkly, for his book. Maybe he will turn this whole stupid life of hers into a story.

After a few seconds he says, well, the race is about to start.

She heads to the bar and motions frantically to the bartender, asks for a Maker's. He sets it in front of her and she points to the television. Would you mind, could I bother you to? She can never finish a sentence these days, but it doesn't matter, he knows what she means. On screen is footage of the horses being settled in their posts. The last horse, Rich Strike, is a chestnut horse in a red and white mask. The owners of Rick Strike only found out he would race yesterday, says the commentator, when Ethereal Road was scratched. She feels an immediate affinity with Rich Strike, whose eyes, she can just barely see for the mask, look a bit crazed. He will lose, of course, the poet thinks. But it's an honor just to be nominated.

Suddenly the gates open and the announcer cries: And they're off!

The poet and the quiet one are silent for the first stretch, taking it all in. The race is unfolding exactly as the odds would suggest, exactly as the Racing Form would have predicted. Rich Strike is among the handful of horses at the back, out of the race, it seems, from the very beginning. The three favored horses are up front, trading off the lead.

Their phones buzz simultaneously and they each swivel them away from their ears to find Oscar Wilde beaming, giving them a thumbs up. To Roy, he has written. He looks puffy, thinks the poet. Overserved, overfed. Like Oscar Wilde just before he was sentenced to prison.

To Roy, says the quiet one.

To Roy, says the poet.

It hurts, saying Roy's name. All these years she has held onto the idea of him, has measured herself by the standard he set. She remembers now a time, just days before Roy killed himself, when she was back in storage searching through deliveries for a book that was supposed to be out on the shelf but wasn't, and she'd turned and seen Roy standing there, awkwardly, waiting for her to notice him.

You're a good kid, he'd told her. I just wanted to tell you that.

And she'd flushed the way she always did when someone said something nice to her.

I believe in you, he'd said. Don't give up being good, now. And then he'd hurried away, walking off quickly and silently, his head down, the way he always did.

She'd held onto that all these years. Believing she was good, believing she was fighting the good fight. But now she didn't know anymore.

That bitch, she kept hearing the teenager say. That stupid fucking *cunt*.

No one is watching Rich Strike, no one except the poet, who feels a sort of kinship in his continued fervor, though the odds against him are insurmountable and he will never win. She keeps her eyes on him. The three favored horses are still in the lead, lengths ahead.

It wells up in her, what she has been trying to keep in but can barely, barely contain anymore—something about watching this horse lose is stirring up what she has been feeling for years. She can't stand to watch him lose. Fuck this, she thinks. The seconds go by and it is as if she is conjugating a verb. She is losing. She has always lost. She will always lose. At the end of her life, she will have been a loser. She thinks of all the effort she has put into trying to be good. The lectures she always gave in class speaking to the nobility of the human soul, the enduring appeal of truth and beauty, and the bored faces of her students, their heads tilted toward their phones which, concealed in their laps, they think she can't see, though the glow of the screens on their faces gives them away. She thinks of all the care she's put into the children. She remembers carrying a cake that was shimmering with candles toward the teenager, who was five then, the way her child's face was lit with wonder.

Bitch, bitch, bitch. Cunt, cunt, cunt.

Her thoughts spin by, like the bars of a slot machine tumbling, tumbling. She is waiting for them to settle, waiting to see where they land. More and more lately, her brain is in a frenzy, and she can't figure out the simplest thing, can't figure out how she feels about anything. Is she right or wrong? Is she good or bad? Does her life matter or does it not? Is it still worth going around talking about love and truth and beauty, or is it just embarrassing now? Will her kids remember how she raised them, how she loved them, or will they just forget? The odds shift by the second, like the board they'd watched at the Downs with Roy all those years ago, the numbers flickering, flickering, changing so fast you couldn't keep up with them. What did any of it mean?

She looks away toward the game room. The boys are fine. The older one is still seated in the driver's console navigating a racecourse, the cars all around him going up in muffled explosions. The youngest, the one so gentle she worries he will be crushed by the world, is still playing pinball. His strategy is to flick the flippers constantly and in this way he is staying alive, for now.

Why aren't you rich? Why aren't you rich?

She turns back to the television. At the top of the stretch, Rich Strike is still one of the last horses. The announcer is deep into the intricacies of the leading two horses, who keep trading by a nose, by a nose. She watches as Rich Strike maneuvers through a narrow opening, then makes his way to the inside rail, where he could, possibly, sneak past the frontrunners. But they are halfway down the stretch and it won't matter, she calculates. There isn't enough time. She remembers how Roy taught them, during Schopenhauer's Poodle's race, how toward the end of the stretch, you could tell which horse would win based on momentum and the lengths left to go. He had pointed to a horse who was five or six deep in the pack, but was charging. That horse is going to win, he'd said, and it hadn't seemed possible, he was too far behind, but he did.

Hey, the quiet one says. Are you seeing this? Here comes your horse.

He's too far back, she says.

And he mostly is. Except maybe not.

The seconds unfold. The drunks at the bar have lifted their heads and are watching now, too.

Your horse is going to win, says the quiet one.

Don't, she says.

She remembers Roy saying, with that half smile, that you needed to believe in miracles if you were going to survive in this business, and she wonders now if she has it in her. To believe or not to believe, she thinks, that is the question. She is a poet and it is the job of poets to believe, but it hurts too much. Even as the horse races alongside the frontrunner, as the jockey is pumping the reigns, and as the commentator is crying out, having just realized what is going on—*Rich Strike is coming up on the inside!*—she is fighting back what is rising in her chest, knowing if she looks up at the sky hoping to see those two mythical kites, those hearts hurrying toward heaven, knowing if she looks and finds the sky empty again, she won't be able to shake off another loss. Fuck this, she is thinking, he is too far back, fuck this. It hurts too much to watch. At the last second, when the horse stretches his neck, the poet isn't even looking, she has closed her eyes, not wanting to see, not wanting to believe anymore, because it is too dangerous, it is too dangerous to believe.

WHEN THE PRINCE OF HEAVEN SLEEPS

by ROGER REEVES

from EMERGENCE

To break free from the plague of time, you must first go where it cannot. Which is to say, you must go to sleep. In thinking about how to interrupt and subvert time—time as a tool of colonization, time as a weapon, a prison—I can't help but think of the "modest slave cabin" where Muhammad Ali slept in Deer Lake, Pennsylvania, during training camps before boxing matches against Sonny Liston, Ken Norton, and George Foreman, this cabin that allowed Ali to escape the cameras and cornermen and the circus barking that was sometimes the spectacle of his life. A four-poster bed huddles in a corner of the room just to the left of the door, an old wooden trunk at its foot. A handmade quilt lays on the bed. Above the bed, a photo of Ali, whom Norman Mailer calls "The Prince of Heaven," lying down on another version of a four-poster bed in the same room, in the same cabin. The bed in the photo is less stately, and with Ali's body laid across it, it looks positively miniature, a child's bed. Not a bed for the Prince of Heaven—if the Prince of Heaven truly ever needed to sleep.

And what would be the dreams of a prince of heaven—a prince who spends his nights in what Mailer called a "modest slave cabin"? What riots and riotous longing would cross the sleeping brow of the Prince of Heaven, of Ali? I'm interested in thinking about Muhammad Ali sleeping, not moving but dreaming, because we remember and think of him as both the butterfly and the bee, someone—*a thing*—always in flight, in motion, in combat or preparing for it. He was to appear as combustible, as natural as a piston stroking up and down in its cylinder. Ali, the Prince of Heaven, stung, floated, deflected, and dodged even when standing before a roomful of microphones, tape recorders, and anxious and awed reporters awaiting some koan, poem, proverb, or treatise about Vietnam or the Vietcong, Islam, his mood, the gastrointestinal goings-on of his belly, Black power, or the gorilla-like features of an upcoming opponent. Parry, stick, move, feint, dip, slip. Ali, the perpetual motion machine. Ali, the honey-tongued chatterbox. Ali, the child of Scheherazade and Sengbe Pieh. Ali, casting off the shackles, breaking down the walls of the dungeon, letting his people go. Even now, I have to stop myself, stop myself from forcing Ali into some sort of motion, submitting his body to labor in the fashion that we expect him to labor—pugilist in the arena, in the streets, on the slick cover of a magazine.

But Ali in repose, and not in the repose of a casket. Ali away from the heavy bags and the sweat of running along the side of the road as some black-and-white-spotted cow chews through a field of wildflowers. Ali stretched beneath the handmade quilt and green sheets or white sheets or brown sheets of that four-poster bed. Ali's head against a pillow, his afro haloing his brown face, his eyes closed, his mouth still. Here is how I will interrupt the time of the arena, time as a weapon used against the world's subdued—by placing a sleeping Muhammad Ali in front of you, not as a spectacle but as a break, a pause, as another sense of time, as another sense of power, protest.

For me, one of the most subversive images in art is a Black man resting—not dead but resting—his body not compelled to work for anyone's gaze. His body ungovernable, or that which governs it hidden and opaque. Stillness, silence, is not the realm given to Black men and surely not the realm of Ali. The most iconic images of Ali are of him in the coil and violence of motion: Ali crouched on the bottom of a pool, his hands positioned as if about to jab; or standing over Sonny Liston, who lays on the canvas beneath him, Ali's right arm flexed at the elbow, the striation of muscles pressing through his skin, his mouth open and yelling something at the downed Liston whose arms on the canvas are in the position of surrender and who can do nothing but look up at the Prince of Heaven. Ali as the completion of rage and temerity, the libido of America. Ali, in motion as heaven. This is the heaven I want to leave behind—the heaven that requires not just a tired body but a depleted and debilitated body, someone else's pummeled flesh beneath it or stretched out on a canvas mat; a body that earns its place behind the pearly gates and in the mansions and upper rooms of heaven because it has wearied itself to victory, to death—transacted itself into oblivion.

The sleeping Ali defies the need for this oblivion, for the legible heaven of exhaustion.

When I think of a sleeping Ali, I also think of other images of iconic Black men in domestic spaces, and the way that that domesticity, in my eyes, acts as a protestation of capitalistic time, a slipping of the yoke of extractive labor. Their bodies sitting in a wooden chair at a kitchen table or tending to a garden or a flock of beloved pigeons on a roof removes them, even if only momentarily, from laboring on behalf of accumulation, consumption, and the eager eye or ear; thus, placing them outside of time. Their bodies in domesticity, in the banality of the four walls of a house, on a shopping trip, or on the roof offers a countermelody, a counternarrative, to the public nature and narrative of Black men as denizens of the street, the club, the arena. John Coltrane, for instance, giving an interview to a journalist while on a trip to a supermarket. I love this moment, Coltrane pulling the young interviewer, Frank Kofsky, along with him on his shopping duties, thus imparting a slick and subtle lesson to him. The music is, and is of the domestic. It's as though Coltrane is saying, *If you really want to understand the sound, if you want to understand the feeling, you have to understand that I have to go pick up these groceries for the kids*. In other words, *I have to attend to the mundane, to that which seems outside of the grand art of jazz composition and improvisation*. Or, more so, the grand is in the mundane, in working with and through it. In other words, the train requires coal and someone to shovel it.

After Coltrane admits to Kofksy that he doesn't like to go out much, they visit as many stores as possible on one long shopping trip. Back at Coltrane's house, you can hear children playing, the throes of domestic life all around Coltrane. In a longer cut of the interview that I can't find anymore, I remember hearing someone washing dishes. From the halting way Coltrane answers Kofsky's questions, I always assumed it was him doing the washing; or at least I hoped it was, and I'd like to imagine such here. Coltrane having to stop cleaning a plate to better answer a question.

The clinking of the dishes going into the dishrack, glass grazing glass, offers us a complement to Coltrane's composed melodies on *Giant Steps*, *A Love Supreme*, or even *Interstellar Space*. The sounds of domesticity expand our understanding of his sound, his music, his sense of time, his touch. How might the children laughing in the background, the plates sliding across one another, the water hitting the basin of the sink, offer or propose another sense of a radical sound, a radical imagination, a defiance of time? In hearing the children in the background, I wonder if Coltrane ever played what he heard in his house, played the children running in the yard, played their laughter, the seesaw and sometimes teasing rhythms of their banter. Did he play their cries, their wailings, when they fell?

We know that Coltrane often played language, played his prayers. For instance, in "Psalm," the fourth movement of *A Love Supreme*, through his tenor horn Coltrane plays the devotional poem that acts as the liner notes that accompany the album. In "Alabama," a song that Coltrane wrote in response to the bombing of the 16th Street Baptist Church by the Ku Klux Klan on the morning of September 15, 1963, you can hear Coltrane playing the bombing and its aftermath. It's as if the breath passing through his horn and the wail that comes out play the fire licking at the walls of the church, erect the burned-out tabernacle via sound. This elegiac wailing is especially palpable and felt in the live version of "Alabama" that Coltrane, Elvin Jones, McCoy Tyner, and Jimmy Garrison recorded at Birdland. In Coltrane's horn, you hear the mourners processing into the church; you hear the eulogy and the creak of the pews as the mourners shift in their grief. The hung head of Coltrane becomes the hung head of the minister in the pulpit, the hung head of the mourners passing in front of the caskets of the dead girls.

How might listening to the domestic life that rang out in the yard and kitchen below Coltrane's practice room have shaped his sense of sound, particularly when composing *A Love Supreme*, an album he wrote in the month after the birth of a child? Might some of the reaching for a supreme love have come not only out of a devotion to a supreme creator but also out of a devotion to his children? Might this be another understanding of Creator and creativity—that of the domestic, that of the kitchen, the garden?

In thinking about a garden, another image or set of images floats to me—that of the rapper DMX taking care of a greenhouse of orchids on the comedic television show *Fresh Off the Boat*. Less known for taking care of flora, DMX is more known for barking and growling on vinyl, riding motorcycles with his crew, Ruff Ryders, raising pit bulls, addiction, debt, and recording club bangers that declare, "Y'all gon' make me act a fool up in here, up in here" and "Y'all gon' make me lose my cool up in here, up in here." Gentleness is not his name. Dark Man X, born Earl Simmons, courted darkness, though he also courted vulnerability. In an interview on the television show *The Shop*, Jay-Z recounts the wild fluctuations of a DMX arena performance. Club bangers and anthems would morph into DMX praying on stage and possibly crying. In fact, if you search YouTube, you can find such footage: DMX, sweaty, shirtless, gold chain bouncing against his chest, a microphone clutched in his hand, calling out to "Father God!" in his signature staccato cadence that sounds as if he were rushing to get every syllable out at once before slamming on the breaks, the "God" punctuated as though "Father God" had appeared suddenly in front of him and DMX was standing in awe of the Creator. But it's not the DMX of the arena that I'm most interested in, but the DMX in the garden, DMX taking care of orchids. Here DMX disrupts the time of the arena, even if momentarily, even if the desire of the television show is humorously or sarcastically to pull on our known associations of DMX—Ruff Ryder, hood, dark, troubled—and cast those in comic relief against the nurturing character of "DMX" discussing the needs of flowers. Even if the desire of the show was to create a caricature built upon dissidence—*look how funny it is that DMX is talking about gardening*—the derision, the joke, loses its sting because Earl Simmons, "DMX," the actor, delivers the lines not as a caricature but as a person with an interiority, as someone who loves, someone who's come by the wisdom of nurturing relationships through life experience and reflection. Reflection comes about in moments of repose, moments of stillness, silence, in the dry hours, outside of the arena, outside of the performance of Ruff-Ryderness, in the space of one's mind when the conversation is lit only by the voices in one's head. Intimacy. Reflection is the intimacy one builds with oneself or with one's many selves.

DMX in the space of the greenhouse and garden defamiliarizes the familiarity of his public persona. The image of him spritzing orchids with a copper mister—the water imperceptible—demonstrates his sudden and excessive vulnerability, his interiority. The lightness of the mist touching the leaves and heads of the flowers draws us toward DMX, draws us toward his touch, his hands, his eyes, and the vulnerability behind them. In the hands of DMX, the copper mister gathers and reifies what we cannot see, what has been ignored—his thoughtfulness, his silence, the nimbleness of his fingers, the delicate maneuvering of his body among the soft flesh of petals and stems. We are drawn to the intricacies, the looked-over, finer details of DMX, rather than the larger swirl of him. It's like that moment in Toni Morrison's novel *Beloved* when we learn that Paul D has stuffed his love, his hurt, his desire, into a little tin box inside of his chest and kept it closed, rusted shut, and away from even himself because of the atrocities of being enslaved, sold, whipped, cudgeled, and nearly drowned. Only after slavery did he allow himself to open this metaphoric tin box, to touch its contents, to feel what he would not let himself feel before. In the greenhouse, we pay attention to what we have not paid attention to before—DMX beyond the black ribbed T-shirt and Timberlands and braggadocio and stereotypical, well-circulated, and commodified forms of masculinity. The copper mister acts as synecdoche of DMX's sense of care, announcing how he might bring beauty into the world: with a careful spritz, a nourishing touch. This touch, small and spectacular, but not a spectacle. No longer mired and fixed in the realm of the public, DMX, the figure, eludes us for a moment. Or, asks us to remove him from circulating only as an outsized persona of masculinity.

All my life, I have archived these sorts of images and moments of Black men touching and holding the largesse and largeness of their lives in the smallness of their hands. In Chicago, I've watched Black men on city buses and in the rain on a park bench hold the bulb of a child's head in their palm. In Mount Holly, New Jersey, I watched a man in a dark blue barber cape stand on a cement step and tweeze a Newport from a crumbling soft pack with the tips of his fingernails, place the cigarette in the corner of his mouth, and eye the slow crawl of evening traffic lurching by him before lighting it, taking delight in the traffic and the first draw of smoke working its way into his body, slowing down time.

An image that has captivated me since I first saw it in the late aughts is that of Mike Tyson caring for pigeons on a rooftop in Brooklyn. In the video clip, Tyson raves, almost to the point of ecstasy, about his lifelong love of these frail birds. There on the roof, Tyson holds, kisses, fondles, and coos into the necks and breasts of a handful of birds, the whole time repeating to us and to himself that they are beautiful, beautiful—their wings, the patterns across them, their rolling and long-distance flights. He is all joy, untempered and unabashed. It shocked me, drew me closer—this nurturing and intimacy from "the Baddest Man on the Planet." This was the Tyson who was convicted and sent to prison for rape in 1992. The Tyson who seemed to move in the ring with the unpredictability of a tornado. Enraged and without reason. At one moment, he pounds his opponent's ribs with hooks, jabs, and in the next, digs his signature upper cut into his chin and chest. Shortly after this barrage, his opponent's body falls to the canvas in one long heap. And Tyson moves away from his prostrate adversary in quiet anarchy, with all that violence shut up in his bones, his eyes still flickering with ruin.

My mother forbade me from seeing myself in this Tyson, which was and was not the Tyson on the roof delicately holding a frail bird in his hands. Let me explain.

In 1997, Tyson did the unthinkable. During the third round of a boxing match with Holyfield, Tyson spat out his mouthguard and bit off a chunk of Holyfield's ear. Shocked and in pain, Holyfield leapt about the ring grabbing at his bloody ear. Tyson stood there, gazing at him with blood trickling down the side of his mouth. Though I didn't witness the bite, I heard about it the next morning from my mother who, despite her Christian demeanor and turn-the-other-cheek ethos, loved boxing. And Tyson, who had become a young phenom and champion on the level of Ali, was the new prince. Not a prince of heaven; but, nevertheless, a prince. His ability to knock out most opponents within the first three rounds rocketed him to the level of legend. Gossip, watercooler punditry, and all sorts of talk circulated the week before and after a Mike Tyson fight. And the kitchen table in our house and the vestibule and aisles between the folding chairs at church were no exception. Everybody was talking about Tyson, and after he tore off a piece of Holyfield's ear, even more so.

The morning after the fight, my mother told me what had happened. I rushed to the television, quickly channel surfing to find a clip of the incident. I saw the headbutting from Holyfield, Tyson complaining about it; then, when the headbutting continued, the bite. My mother asked me what I thought. I remember saying I thought Tyson was right to bite him. I would have done the same. My mother shook her "no, no, no" over and over again.

"You shouldn't say stuff like that, Roger. Tyson is no one to look up to," my mother said. "Not for that."

Watching Tyson exact his revenge there in the ring, I felt a surge of recognition—finally, finally, someone doing something about the unfairness of the world, tearing at it, ripping it apart. I was always supposed to take the headbutting of the world and not react. To turn the other cheek; always, always, turn and receive the next blow, accept the insulting looks, gestures, comments. At grocery store and mall entrances, I was not to yell at the white women that I wasn't trying to steal their funky-ass purses or maul their blue-eyed babies. When my AP Physics and Calculus teachers separately stopped scribbling equations on the chalkboard to decry the degradation of education in America because I, a Black boy, was admitted into an Ivy League School—not because of my record or outstanding academic performance but because of quota systems, affirmative action, and minorities receiving an unfair advantage in college admissions—I was not to stand and rage and raise my voice, nor demand an apology, but just sit there and watch them wonder about what America was becoming now that its darker brother and sister could sit in lecture halls named after slave owners and learn of Socrates, the hippocampus, and Horatian odes. Rather than drag them into the basement of feeling where I might bludgeon them with the school desk underneath me, I sat in the morning and afternoon light of their racism and pious, ignominious patriotism. I took it.

So when the man who had bitten off a portion of Evander Holyfield's ear all those years ago clutched a pigeon between his hands and kissed its head, I leaned in and listened, because it was the first time that I saw Tyson not coiled in anger or violence. His hands, not hidden inside of blood-red boxing gloves, instead holding the quivering body of a bird. And the bird appeared as if it had no knowledge of what his hands, in and outside the arena, had wrought.

How long had Tyson held birds? How had he come to this love, this passion, for keeping pigeons? I started typing two terms into a search bar in a Google browser that no one would have ever thought to put in proximity to one another: "Mike Tyson" and "pigeons." In the searching I learned that Tyson's first fight as a child occurred because an older neighborhood boy, whom Tyson had invited into his home, snatched one of his birds and fled with it. When Tyson ran after him, the boy snapped off the head of the bird and threw it at him. They fought there in the street. Not yet the composed Kid Dynamite, Tyson flailed and threw undisciplined haymakers at the boy's body and face. Eventually, he bested the boy who had stolen and killed his bird, setting in motion the mythology of his preternatural fighting ability. Tyson's first fight was in defense of the fragile, in defense of love, not an exhibition of some maniacal desire to maraud or maim. He fought to protect what brought him joy. In all the years of watching Mike Tyson in and out of the ring, marveling at the explosive power of his hands, I'd always assumed he had run toward boxing, run toward it in the way that I had run toward running and poetry—as a thing called up deep from the interior of oneself, as a way of making beauty in a world that refused you beauty or constantly tried to sequester, limit, or narrow what makes you beautiful. But for Tyson, the beauty was in the birds, in their lives and the way they allowed him to live next to them, allowed him to touch their fragility, allowed him to know them intimately and without fetters.

Pigeons were Tyson's first love. In interview after interview, he admits that he couldn't imagine his life without them. That there would be no peace, no calm in him if he could not be around birds. Tyson will sometimes put on headphones and sit in his garage and just watch his pigeons move, eat, live. He'll stay there for hours, not speaking to anyone, and if he does decide to speak, it's only to the birds. The pugilist in repose. The pugilist in his sanctuary. The pugilist fleeced of the fight or the need to prepare for one.

I imagine Tyson in his garage barefoot, sitting on a high-backed wooden chair, his head tilted slightly, gazing at the pigeons leaping or flying down from their perches. He listens to them coo to one another, noting the change in one bird's urgent trill. In the garage, Tyson is both studying and in a state of wonder, reflecting rather than reacting.

The birds allow Tyson to enter a state of meditation. In residing with these animals, Tyson touches his own animal, is in solitude, silence—a realm not imagined to be inhabited or wanted by Black men. Tyson's solitude is not the solitude of escapism or erasure, but a solitude of sitting with the self without the noise, traffic, and bluster of the world. A solitude of being one with others and just that—being, being so deeply inside oneself that there is no outside of oneself; there is no tension between you and the world. While there might be difference, there is no tension. I'm not trying to overly romanticize the man or his ritual, but I'd like to think alongside him, to sit in study with him.

In interview after interview, Tyson's face glows with joy as he tries to articulate the inarticulable—why the birds bring him peace; why he is attracted to this sort of solitude. Tyson's love for his pigeons is almost prelingual. It is without language not because he lacks the vocabulary or intelligence, but because the satisfaction is so deep down in the marrow of him that it would almost be like trying to bust open a piece of chalk to find its interior only to realize it's all interior. And all exterior simultaneously. His joy with the birds is—it only is.

Tyson's pigeon-sitting reminds me of transcendentalist Henry David Thoreau's sojourn at Walden Pond and Ralph Waldo Emerson's notion that in order to be one's best self, one must first be a good animal. Tyson's garage in Arizona and rooftop in Brooklyn are his Walden, his space for transcendent rumination, a space to shed the arena and listen to the littlest and loudest parts of himself. In the space of the domestic, under the flap and feather of his birds, Tyson becomes his best animal—not an animal of the arena, a spectacle, a gimmick, where his pugilism corroborates the time of market, the time of economy; here he accounts for the length, breadth, and depth of himself. His best animal roams and feels outside the reason and logic of time.

The time of the garage and the pigeons is only measured in the time of the garage and pigeons. This statement might seem tautological, but it is not. In the garage, time no longer becomes the measurement of accumulation, a measurement of efficacy. The time of the pigeons, the time of the garage, has no order or minutes or imposed structure. It is not the three-minute round of the boxing ring or the post-fight interview and media circus. The time of the pigeons, the time of the garage, exists unto itself, does not subject itself to anything other than its own happening, its own making. Tyson steps outside of the time of commerce, outside of the billion-dollar industry of the sports industrial complex, becomes a subversion of it. And makes for us, here and now, for himself, a pause, a break, a rip in time.

When watching Tyson talk of his birds or lovingly clutch them between his hands, you are watching a man deep in the throes of love and devotion. Not a man who's ravenous or enraged. But a man who's humbled by his proximity to beauty.

Maybe, in that "modest slave cabin," the sleeping Muhammad Ali dreamt of this: a man on a roof who fought and broke himself and the world and was now surrounded by pigeons. And in being surrounded by the pigeons that man learned something of love. Or maybe Ali watches a man in a bedroom listening to his children, to them teasing each other, to them wailing, the quietness of his house when they go to bed; then, that same man picks up his horn and plays his house, plays the music of silence, of solitude, of being one with others. Maybe, Ali dreams of a Black man lying in a hammock or on a hillock, buried deep in the grass, his finger tracing the edge of a blade of grass. The man in the hammock or on the hill doing nothing else but tracing the afternoon, its heat, its buzzing mind. Maybe, he dreams of orchids. Maybe, he dreams of water and the water speaking to him of the orchids' needs and his own. Maybe, the Prince of Heaven dreams of a man sitting on the floor of a kitchen, talking to his child while chicken fries in a cast-iron skillet on the stove. Maybe the Prince of Heaven dreams of walking out into a field and watching the sun turn down in the sky until he's in nothing but blue. Maybe the Prince of Heaven does not dream at all. Maybe, he sleeps.

ODE TO A SMITH-CORONA GALAXIE TYPEWRITER

by ANGELA NARCISO TORRES

from ALASKA QUARTERLY REVIEW

Find me again that teal jewel
buried in father's dust-encrusted cave
of poems and pathology, papers
tipping in piles, a brown reel churning
its mournful symphony. Take me
to where the blue hours crawled
from yellow yawn to drawl of dusk.
Bring out the carriage whose rise
and fall spelled here or gone, asleep,
awake, alone, unafraid. Return me
to that solar system, that universe
of ciphers, cymbals, simplest
of lullabies. That nightly waterfall
of spurts, and starts, of mechanized
whispers. My father's lips pursed
in lamplight, his fingers the blur of
a hundred woodpeckers. Play me again
that skeletal symphony, that tin can
tango, jangle of keys, bright ding
of bell. O divot, o inkblot, o seed plot
of sorrow. O alphabet reliquary,
ribcage of memory. If time
won't stop, could it slow
to the tempo of his staccato,
that blue-veined arrhythmia
in a corncob of stars.

DIANE

fiction by AVIGAYL SHARP

from GRANTA

I loved the anonymous chat app. I downloaded it on my computer. I downloaded it on my phone. I was lonely, and the anonymous chat app made me less lonely. I couldn't sleep, and the anonymous chat app said, Who cares! When I felt helpless, when I despaired, when my breath caught horribly in my chest, the anonymous chat app told me: The whole world suffers. Everyone is unemployed. The whole world is sexless inside of its body. The whole world longs for sleep. When it sleeps, the whole world has terrible nightmares. And when it wakes, the whole world is so, so grateful for the opportunity to chat privately with strangers online.

The anonymous chat app sported a clean and gorgeous interface. Its colors were green and blue and white. The font, serif-less. Everything glowed, comforting and familiar, like a chain hotel. At the end of each session I watched the chat window melt away, pixels dissolving, irretrievable. I knew all the lingo. *A/S/L.* Bots telling me to add them on a different messenger app called Kik. I wasn't stupid. I didn't use Kik. But I liked the bots anyway; it was cool that they were fake, and cool that I knew they were fake, and cool that whoever designed the bots probably knew that I would know they were fake and want to talk to them anyway.

The first time I chatted with a bot I just wanted to see what would happen.

Hello, I typed.
I love you, I typed.
Im gonna kill you, I typed.

And the bot said:
gtg, add me on kik ;)
gtg, add me on kik ;)
gtg, add me on kik ;)

Whenever I was connected to a real person we would exchange age and sex and location and then either I or the other person would say *How are you* and then one of us would say *Are you horny*. I lied about my age and I lied about my location and I lied about being horny. The only thing I didn't lie about was my gender. I'm Henry, I said. I'm Geoff. I said that I was twenty-five. I said that I was forty-seven. I said that I lived in Detroit or Toronto or Berlin. I said that I was horny, really horny, extremely horny. Most of the time I didn't masturbate. Anyone could be a fat old guy getting off on tricking me, and I worried about what it would mean to fondle myself while aware of this possibility.

Besides, I wasn't horny. When I looked down at my body, I was often surprised to find that it was still there. All day long my body dragged me around. It sat me on the couch. It took me to the bathroom. In exchange I gave it food and water and rest. Sometimes I gave it drugs, and sometimes I made it lift heavy objects and set them down so that it could stay strong. But I continued to suspect that my body was angry with me. Nothing I did seemed good enough. I was angry with my body, too. It was holding me back.

Here was the truth: I was a thirty-four-year-old male. I lived in Brooklyn Heights. I was 6'1. I was a healthy weight. I had a nice-looking face. I had money. I wore brown loafers and chinos. I wanted to be free. I wanted to be a mind.

I was in the bathroom one evening, sitting on the toilet with my pants on and my laptop balanced on my thighs, waiting for the chat app to pair me with someone new. My wife was out on a run. Earlier I had considered taking the subway to a bar in Gowanus, but then I remembered the dirty drifts of last week's snowfall piled at every intersection, and I thought about all of the strangers and all of the bots out there, all over the world, waiting to meet me. So instead I sat in the bathroom, sipping a canned margarita from the deli across the street, and took some selfies on my laptop camera.

Everything was fine. I had washed the sheets that morning. My wife and I had recently purchased an expensive toaster oven, known for its innovative crisping technology, and I had developed the habit of cutting frozen pizzas in half with scissors and broiling each segment separately. This technique was much faster than waiting for the real oven to preheat. A half-moon of pepperoni pizza rested on a paper towel in the bathroom sink, and once it cooled down it was going to taste delicious.

I should have prefaced this by saying that I loved my wife. She was beautiful. She was smart. She had a low, calm voice. We met at a Starbucks six years earlier and at our wedding reception we gave out personalized ceramic Starbucks travel tumblers. *Aww*, the guests had said, and they were right. The personalized ceramic Starbucks travel tumblers were adorable. My wife was Jewish and in law school, but she wasn't argumentative, not really. She was small, with long dark hair that she parted in the middle to appear more authoritative. She wore these tight black skirt suits to work. At home she zoomed around the kitchen muttering to herself. *Fuck, where did I put my keys, fuck fuck fuck god damn it has anyone seen my keys, did I forget to put on deodorant, shit shit I think I smell*. I loved listening to her curse. The words sounded wrong coming out of her sweet, earnest mouth.

Whenever I looked at my wife it was as if my intestines got caught in my throat. The previous year I had participated in several unsatisfying affairs when she was away visiting her dying mother upstate. I had still been sort of horny back then, but that wasn't why I cheated. I did it because my wife was having a hard time. 'I'm so sad. Fuck! I'm so fucking sad!' she would say, and her eyes would be red and wet, and I would hear her gasping and crying all over the apartment. In these moments it was clear that she had made a terrible mistake in marrying me. I didn't know how to make her feel better; I didn't even want to try. I'm so horrible, I told myself. I'm a piece of shit. I'm the kind of piece of shit who would probably cheat on his wife while her mother was dying.

The first time she went upstate I headed to a bar and picked up a girl, and the next time she went upstate I did it again. I always went back to the girls' places. I didn't want my doorman to see that I was unfaithful. The girls lived in Bushwick and Bed-Stuy, in filthy walk-ups with four roommates, hordes of ugly potted plants lunging for sunlight in the common areas, empty cans of diet Red Bull repurposed as ashtrays on the windowsills. I was aware that when those girls fucked me it was sort of as a joke. They wanted to laugh with their friends about my pressed trousers, my polished shoes, my pomade. I didn't care. I had a lot of affection for them. I was pathetic, but they were, too. One had a big fat roach living in her bathtub drain, and it would pop out whenever someone went to pee. She was too scared to kill it and had instead trained herself to think of it as a pet. She was nuts, but I liked her, and I felt guilty when her blow job didn't make me come.

Then my wife's mother died and I stopped going home with girls. My body screamed at me all the time. *Stop!* it screamed. *Go!* I became very depressed. For a while I had panic attacks at the office every time my computer froze. I would stare at the unmoving screen and think, Nothing ever works and everybody is going to die. Then my heart would start flapping around inside of me at an awful speed. I would plead with my body, *Do not do this while I am at work!* and my body would laugh in my face. Eventually my company put me on paid leave. My wife was kind and supportive. She reminded me to take my Ativan.

In the bathroom I sipped my margarita and stared at the blank chat window on my laptop. Whoever was on the other end wasn't saying anything, so I typed, *A/S/L??*

The stranger took a moment to respond. I steadied my laptop with one hand and with the other reached into the sink for my pizza.

MY CAPS LOCK IS STUCK

I HAVE REMOVED THE KEY AND CLEANED IT AND RESTARTED MY COMPUTER BUT NOTHING IS WORKING

Sorry, I typed. I dont know how to help . . . a/s/l??

THATS OKAY I JUST DONT WANT YOU TO THINK I AM YELLING AT YOU

MY NAME IS DIANE I AM A FEMALE I AM 37 YEARS OLD AND I LIVE IN QUEENS

My fingers thrummed on the keyboard. This person had no idea how to use the internet. And even though she had explained about the caps lock, it still came across as yelling. Plus, I didn't generally like to talk to anyone over thirty-five. Ever since my thirty-fourth birthday I had sensed myself on a slippery, frightening edge.

I was about to disconnect when she messaged me again.

PLEASE DONT LEAVE. I REALLY NEED SOMEONE TO TALK TO. I AM GOING THROUGH A DIVORCE. MY HUSBAND LEFT ME FOR A YOUNGER AND MORE ATTRACTIVE WOMAN. I DONT KNOW WHAT I DID TO DESERVE THIS. I SINCERELY BELIEVE THAT I AM A DANGER TO MYSELF. IF ONE MORE PERSON LEAVES ME I WILL PROBABLY KILL MYSELF. I DO HAVE A BOTTLE OF SLEEPING PILLS. I AM SORRY FOR PUTTING YOU IN A DIFFICULT POSITION. DIANE

I set my pizza back down in the sink. This was not what the anonymous chat app was all about. I didn't want to be responsible for anyone's suicide. Then again, she was likely lying about killing herself. Recently, I had also told my wife that I was going to buy a gun on the dark web and shoot myself in the throat so that I would no longer be a burden. I needed to make sure she was aware that she could lose me at any moment, that it was still her responsibility to love me, even though I had become a helpless and bitter person.

I got up off the toilet and lay down in the bathtub with the laptop on my stomach. The sensation of the cold ceramic against my neck made me feel miserable but alive.

HELLO??

Sorry, I was in the bathroom, I typed. You should call the suicide hotline.

I CANNOT BRING MYSELF TO CALL THEM BECAUSE I KNOW IT IS THEIR JOB TO TELL ME NOT TO KILL MYSELF

IT ALL STARTED WITH MY MOTHER WHO NEVER LOVED ME AND RESENTED ME UNTIL THE DAY SHE DIED. BECAUSE OF HER I HAVE DEVELOPED AN ANXIOUS-PREOCCUPIED ATTACHMENT STYLE. I DRIVE EVERYONE AWAY WITH MY INSECURITIES AND HYPER-DEPENDENCE

AT FIRST I THOUGHT MY HUSBAND WAS HAVING AN AFFAIR WHEN REALLY HE WASNT BUT I KEPT CONFRONTING HIM ABOUT IT UNTIL HE FINALLY HAD AN AFFAIR FOR REAL ISNT THAT CRAZY

Damn, I typed. Your husband sucks!!

She kept going. Her husband had left her four months ago and she sometimes got lonely at night but didn't want to talk to people she knew, because she hated when they felt sorry for her. I felt really sorry for her. She was much crazier and sadder than I was, had a worse life, and kept apologizing, over and over again. It was nice talking to her.

I thought, Maybe I can do something. Maybe I can make this insane lady feel better. Maybe this is my job.

So I told her some lies about myself. I said I was an orphan. I said that dating was hard for me because I was ugly.

ALL THOSE GIRLS DON'T KNOW WHAT THEY'RE MISSING, she said.

I thought, Good thing she doesn't know I'm actually handsome.

I was about to reply when I heard a knock on the bathroom door.

'Baby?' my wife said. 'You okay?'

'I'm just chilling in here,' I said loudly. 'Might take a bath.'

'Sounds good,' she said, in a voice that meant: It doesn't sound good, it sounds weird, there's no water running, it kind of smells like pizza, but I'm patient, I'm nice, I love you, I'm your wife.

When I heard her footsteps recede, I returned to the screen. It was getting late. My back felt sore. My canned margarita was warm and my pizza was cold. But I didn't want to stop talking to Diane. I was helping her. It was so good to be helpful. The more I helped her, the more I wanted her to help me, too. I wanted to tell her things, true things, about myself. And I did. I sat up in the bathtub and typed quickly, hunched over my laptop. I told Diane about how my company had recently made the move into a coworking space in the city, with ping-pong tables and a booth in the lobby where you could craft your own Christmas ornaments. There was a bar and lounge area, and a room where people danced to music wearing headphones. I had encouraged the move so as to increase staff wellness and productivity, but once we arrived I started having panic attacks after drinking one beer at the bar on my lunch break. I told her how the panic attacks continued even after I stopped drinking my lunchtime beer, and how one day I began shrieking in the lobby and then smashed my handmade ornament on the floor and that's why I got put on leave. I didn't tell her the leave was paid because I didn't want to make her feel insecure about our class disparity.

I AM SORRY YOU ARE OUT OF WORK

IN MY STATE I FIND IT IMPOSSIBLE TO HOLD DOWN A JOB

That blows, I typed. You deserve so much better.

It was two in the morning when we both logged off. We exchanged emails, mine with a fake name that I had set up for such situations. My eyeballs felt stretched out from staring at my screen all night. *Ow*, my body said, and I said, *Shut the fuck up*. When I stood up from the bathtub my muscles were stiff and cramped. But there was something else, too—a slackness in the vicinity of my ribcage that I hadn't experienced in months. A feeling like a fist opening.

Diane, I thought.

My wife lay sprawled on top of our white duvet. She was wearing two sweaters, fleece-lined sweatpants, and a pair of sparkly, fuzzy socks. I lay beside her, and she shifted to wrap her thin arms around my waist. Her breath was wet on my neck. It smelled like sour milk. Recently my wife had got into intermittent fasting and she only ever ate one meal a day, at 7 p.m., but every day at 7 p.m. she microwaved the greasiest foods she could find: mac and cheese, corn dogs, soggy hamburgers that steamed offensively in their cellophane packets. At 6.55 p.m. she would spread everything out on the kitchen table and look at it and nod and say, 'Fuck yes. Hell fucking yes.' And then I would watch her shovel down her burgers and corn dogs and laugh, and go, 'Shit, I'm gonna get heartburn,' and take three Tums and one Lactaid, and, later, massage her swollen stomach on the couch while concentrating on a Scandinavian crime drama, expressing shock at the appropriate moments, shaking her head, saying, 'That is *fucked up*.' When I watched her I could almost forget about my horrible body, the twisting, grasping panic inside of me, the Ativan, the other women, the strangers, the bots. I could almost forget about the gorgeous anonymous chat app, which was always within reach, always waiting for me, on my laptop, on my phone.

I could almost say, I love being a husband. I love my beautiful wife.

Beside me in bed, a loose strand of hair had caught in my wife's mouth. She was kneading her lips, pushing at the hair with her tongue. I closed my eyes and the image of her face went black, like my phone's screen when untouched. It was not a face I could bear to see.

Instead I thought, Diane.

The next morning I saw that my wife had left me a note on her pillowcase.

Hooray!!! it said. *You slept!!*

She had sketched a horizontal stick figure with little Zs floating above its head. I stared at it for a minute. It looked just like me. I pushed away the vision of my wife's fingers grasping the fine-tipped pen, pressing delicately into the pad. In my dreams my phone had been buzzing interminably against my thigh. It had been bleating Diane's name. I glanced around the room. My skin tingled where it sat on top of my muscles. My muscles throbbed where they sat on top of my bones. There was a spider in the corner of the ceiling, and I kept looking at it and crying. I had been listening to a lot of Steely Dan. I couldn't understand why the spider hadn't spun a web. It was in the corner with no web. I felt guilty about every affair I had ever had. I was letting down my wife and all of her friends. I didn't have friends anymore, but if I did, I would have been letting them down, too. And not just the friends I might have had. I was letting down all the strangers and all the wonderful bots in the world. I was letting down my new confidante, Diane.

I lurched out of bed and took my Ativan and chugged half a bottle of cold brew, then stood in the middle of the kitchen and waited for the drug to hit, that first surge of relief like a wet rag being wrung out in my brain. I looked around at our apartment. My wife had decorated in various shades of gray: slate, charcoal, a luminescent pearl for the kitchen cabinets. In the living room were a handwoven viscose rug in a color called Fog and a low-slung linen couch with a burnt orange throw arranged artfully across one cushion. The throw was cashmere, and in the early hours I liked to swaddle myself in it front-to-back, like an armless Snuggie. Our kitchen table was Danish and modern. My wife had let me pick it out. 'I have veto power,' she had said, 'in case you choose something ugly.' But I didn't choose something ugly, and when she saw the table she had looked shiny and proud, like a mother whose kid had received unexpectedly kind comments on his report card.

'My sister's going to shit herself when she sees how nice our place is,' she had said.

I opened the fridge and found a Tupperware on the top shelf filled with hardboiled eggs. My wife had cracked the shells lightly beforehand, so all I had to do was peel. I pictured her running the eggs under cold water in the early morning, tapping them gently on the countertop until their exteriors fissured while I was asleep. My eyes welled up. I chipped away at the shell, then peeled the egg by its membrane and popped it whole into my mouth.

I lay on the couch with my head against the scratchy side of a throw pillow and opened my laptop. Outside it was below freezing, but we kept the heat at 75, even in midwinter. My wife was always cold and sometimes went to sleep wearing her knee-length down parka.

The laptop fan whirred frighteningly. The underside of the keyboard was warm on my bare legs. *Too hot*, my body said. I closed the laptop and opened it again, but the fan wouldn't stop. I threw the computer down onto the cushion. The fan shut off. Gingerly I pried the laptop open and began to draft an email.

Dear Diane,

I forgot to tell you yesterday to try listening to some Steely Dan. I would recommend starting with the 1972 album Can't Buy a Thrill. *I have found it very comforting in my lowest moments.*

It was really great talking to you last night. Lately I've been feeling very confused. I feel like I'm going crazy. I hope you are doing better this morning. I think that you should flush your sleeping pills. Do you ever feel sexually lonely now that your divorce is underway?

Please get back to me ASAP.

Best,
Ken

I hit send and immediately started refreshing my empty inbox. I thought about the eggs. I thought about how so many people in the world were married and so many people in the world were not. I thought about the hundreds of thousands of users on the anonymous chat app, and how many of them were uglier than me, and how many were more handsome, and how many had more money, and how many had less, and how many were horny, and how many were frigid, and then my body said, *You need to stop thinking about this or else you are going to have a panic attack.*

I thought about Diane. I thought about what she might smell like. I imagined her apartment in Queens, probably un-renovated since the 1972 release of *Can't Buy a Thrill*. I imagined yellowed bathroom tiles and wall-to-wall carpeting smudged with weird, unidentifiable stains, and an ugly black velour couch with potato chip crumbs lodged between the cushions. I imagined walking in and saying, Wow, it looks great in here, I love the decor, and how happy she would be to hear that. I thought about her puckered breasts hanging limpidly beneath a dirty tank top, my fingers tracing the flesh that protruded over her sweatpants, slipping under the band, grabbing a fistful of her pubic hair.

My cell phone buzzed. It was my boss. I sent him to voicemail, waited for the message to come through, and deleted it.

I called my wife, even though I knew she couldn't pick up at work. I pressed the phone hard against my ear.

The phone said, 'Please leave a message after the tone.'

'Hey,' I said. 'It's me.'

I hung up. I called again. The ringing sounded like what I imagined those meditation singing bowls must sound like, not so much a noise as a dull, low throb at the back of the skull.

The next morning I woke up frenzied and strung out. In bed I checked my laptop; Diane had yet to respond. I had spent most of the previous night hiding out in the bathroom, connecting and reconnecting to strangers on the anonymous chat app, failing to find her, until I stumbled to bed around two.

My wife was awake in the kitchen, slathering a toasted bagel with low-fat cream cheese for me. I had forgotten that it was the weekend. She poured herself a mug of coffee and measured out a few drops of stevia, then sat across from me at the table, handing me my Ativan bottle. I heard the pills rattling around like seeds. I was getting low.

'What were you dreaming about last night?' my wife asked. She looked beautiful in her silk bathrobe. Her hair was frizzy and pulled up in a clip. Behind her reading glasses I could see bits of yellow crust fuzzing the corners of her eyes.

'I wasn't dreaming,' I said. 'I didn't sleep.'

She took a sip of her coffee and sucked it through her teeth before swallowing. 'Yes, you did. I woke up for a minute at four and you were sleeping.'

'No, I was just pretending to sleep so you wouldn't worry,' I said.

'You were twitching and screaming,' my wife said.

'I wish you wouldn't confuse your dreams with reality,' I said, and then I laughed to say, Ha ha, you always do this! You're so crazy! My crazy wife!

Her mouth tightened. 'Okay,' she said. She finished her coffee and started toward the dishwasher, then turned back and pointed at my untouched bagel. 'Are you going to eat that?'

'Yes,' I said. I looked at the bagel. Something sour rose up in my throat.

'If you don't,' she said, 'if you change your mind, will you wrap it in aluminum and put it in the fridge? Instead of leaving it out or throwing it away? I'll eat it for dinner.'

My body said, *Don't eat that bagel, it's going to make you throw up.* My wife looked at me like, *I'm a good wife, I'm so patient, I'm so loving, even though my husband is a piece of shit.* I picked up the bagel and tore off a hunk with my molars. The cream cheese spread like glue in my mouth. I forced myself to chew until it was soft enough to swallow. A wad of wet bread lodged in my throat. I went in for another bite.

'Jack, what the fuck?' my wife said.

'I have to go to the bathroom,' I said. I went to the bathroom and turned on the faucet, then knelt in front of the porcelain toilet bowl and stared into the still, clear water. You are a monk, I thought. You are meditating. My stomach roiled but I didn't puke. When I rose I caught a glimpse of myself in the mirror. My face was the face of a ghost. My eyes were bleary and red. My chin was bloated and there were gleaming pink pustules dotting my throat. I looked very bad. I looked insane.

I heard a soft knock at the bathroom door.

'Are you okay?' My wife asked. 'Can I get you some water?'

'I'm *fine,*' I screamed.

When she spoke again her voice was shrill. 'Shut up! Just shut the fuck up! Be fucking normal! What the fuck do you do in the bathroom all the time! Jesus fucking Christ! I am trying so fucking hard over here!'

I noticed that I was sitting on the floor. *This is where I want to be,* said my body. My chest clenched. My hands vibrated. My body said, *She'll be sorry she yelled at you, she'll feel terrible,* and then it said, *How about some more Ativan?*

Okay, I thought. It's time for me to say some crazy shit.

I said, 'I want you to leave this house. I need you to walk out the door and stay away for at least three nights. I need to be alone so that I can breathe. I'm getting tired of your delusions. I don't know how to help you.'

I was glad there was a closed door between us. I didn't want to watch her eyes grow wet, the little pink shock of her mouth opening. I didn't want to think about her doing nice things for me, like toasting my bagel. I didn't want to remember how we had once talked about having two kids, but would end up having zero kids, because nothing in the world would leave me alone. My body wouldn't leave me alone and my brain wouldn't leave me alone. My job wouldn't leave me alone. The spider on the bedroom ceiling wouldn't leave me alone.

My wife said, 'Fuck you.'

I waited until I heard her leave the apartment. I splashed cold water on my face and opened my email.

Dear Diane, I wrote.

I don't want to accuse you of anything but I am feeling a little used. If you are alive please respond to me. I miss you.

Best wishes,
Ken

I dragged a flattering photo of myself from my photo library into the message body. In the background you could make out some of the colorful, modern canvases my wife had hung without frames on the living room walls. Diane would see that I was attractive with a well-decorated apartment.

I refreshed my email, then closed my laptop and took an Ativan. I was excruciatingly bored and, at the same time, restless and agitated, as if my blood was pumping too quickly through the canals of my veins. I thought, I am capable of having fun. I am a handsome young man. I'm single! I went to the kitchen and swallowed a second Ativan. I could feel my insides sloshing around, wetly and warmly. I looked down at my hands and thought, Incredible! Skin! There was skin all over me, holding me together inside of the atmosphere. As long as I had skin, everything would stay in place. My guts would not fall out into a slimy red pile on the floor. I was overcome with gratitude and feelings of celestial wellbeing. I checked on the spider in the bedroom. He was doing well. He looked really happy.

I connected my phone to the speaker my wife had bought for my thirty-first birthday, put on *Can't Buy a Thrill*, and turned the volume up to seventeen.

I was singing along and feeling great. I even jumped up and down a few times. I hoped that my neighbors would hear and sing along and feel good, too. I just wanted to make other people happy. That was all I had ever wanted. That was all I had ever tried to do for Diane.

I swayed my hips and poked at my phone. One new text from my wife. She was sorry she had snapped at me. I swiped. I scrolled. Maybe some space would be good, she said. I blocked her number. I imagined her standing next to me in the kitchen, putting her hair up and then taking it down. I imagined myself screaming, How could you do it? How could you abandon me? How could you leave me alone with my body? You'll never get the apartment!

And I imagined her crying, saying, I'm so sorry! I'm so sorry I treated you like that when you're clearly going through a difficult period! I love you so much! Nothing you could ever do would make me mad at you! Even if you cheated on me more than three times! Please forgive me!

I sank onto the couch. Where could she be going? Maybe her sister's house in Jersey. I smiled thinking about my wife alone in a guest bedroom, bickering with her sister's husband about the heat, secretly cranking up the thermostat at night, commuting into the city each morning on NJ transit, changing into her heels in a sticky Penn station bathroom. She was getting older every day. The lack of vitamins was starting to show in the whites of her eyes. I laughed and got off the couch and grabbed a broom. I went into my bedroom and tried to smash the spider with the broom handle, but it escaped me, scurrying crazily across the ceiling. I threw the broom to the floor. I thought about my life. My life went something like this:

I love you!
Don't leave me!
Get out!
Gtg!
Add me on Kik!

I lay on the bed and closed my eyes. The mattress supported my body. My skin remained in its place. I stayed like that for a few minutes. I was ready, but I wanted to hold on, if only for another moment.

When I opened my eyes I felt perfectly calm. I went into the bathroom and shook my final Ativan into my hand. I had forgotten to pick up my refill, but I knew it wouldn't be a problem. I was getting well. I washed my face with my wife's jelly cleanser and ran a comb through my hair and tended to my beard with an electric trimmer. I clipped my nails into the toilet and flushed. I patted rosehip toner onto my cheeks and forehead. I checked the mirror. I was looking solid and handsome, en route to extreme health. My chin already appeared less bloated. I returned to the bedroom and rifled through the closet. I put on clean chinos and a hunter green Oxford button-down. I opened my laptop's lid.

Dear Diane, I wrote,

It's been such a pleasure getting to know you. I was wondering if you believe that digital mediation has gone too far. Do you have faith in the possibility of seeing and being seen? I forgot to mention that I am going through a devastating and messy divorce from my beautiful Jewish wife.

It would be nice if you came and stayed here for a while. Do you like smoothies? I just ordered a very powerful new blender. I would be happy to pay for your movers, a cab, anything you need.

Looking forward to seeing you tonight!

All the best,
Ken

I added a postscript with my address and apartment number. I called down to the doorman to tell him that a woman would be arriving soon with luggage and to send her right up.

I shut down my computer and turned off my phone. I sat at the kitchen table and waited. The sun cast slats of shimmering light across the granite countertop.

I thought, That's the ugliest thing I've ever seen.

I woke up with my right cheek pressed against the table and that side of my face covered in drool. It was dark, and I couldn't remember what day it was. I turned on the overhead light and checked the time. Only six in the evening. I splashed some water on my face. *More Ativan*, my body screamed. I wanted to explain that I couldn't, that there was no more, but my body didn't understand reason or logic. My body offered no sympathy. It did not pity the circumstances of my existence. *Ativan*, it screamed. I pressed a hand over each ear. My brain was pudding in my skull. Slowly I inched my way over to the couch. I checked my email. Nothing from Diane.

I flipped on the TV and landed on one of the crime shows my wife liked. I couldn't figure out what was going on. There was a large boat. There was a vicious sex-trafficker. There were vast expanses of gray water. I lay on the couch and wrapped myself in the blanket, dozing. I thought, Diane, you bitch.

Around eight I was jolted awake by a series of loud knocks at the front door. My head throbbed. I straightened my shirt and stumbled over.

In the hallway stood a girl, 18 or 19, wearing platform boots and knee-length denim shorts over a pair of ripped fishnet tights. She was skinny except for a slight thickness around the thighs, dimples at the sides of her hips. Her hair appeared to have been cheaply bleached, dark and oily at the roots, and she had arched, drawn-in eyebrows, a scary amount of purple eyeshadow smeared out and around her lower lid. She looked Greek, maybe, or Armenian, and would have been pretty if she scraped off her makeup. She was sucking on some kind of pungently fruity hard candy. Her eyes were a warm shade of brown. They frightened me.

'Nice place,' she said.

'Thanks,' I said. I peeked around her to see that she hadn't brought any luggage. She sidled past me, not noticing or caring when her small breasts brushed my torso, and tossed a worn-out tote bag onto the kitchen table. She scanned the room, made a satisfied clicking sound with her tongue, and dropped onto the couch. With both hands she unzipped her boots, then placed them neatly on the floor, kicking her legs up and onto the ottoman. Her tights cut off at the ankles. She had small, dainty feet.

I was so thirsty. I wanted to vomit. My face felt like it was not my face. My face felt like it was maybe an old mound of Play-Doh.

My eyes landed on the girl's toenails, which were painted black, with a glittery green star pasted on each big toe.

One part of me thought, Get this person the fuck out of your house. Call your wife. Say sorry. Tell her you're sick. Tell her you're crazy. Tell her you will finally complete that self-help workbook on black-and-white thinking. Fall onto your knees, you stupid motherfucker. Find God.

But another part of me thought, Ha ha! Fuck you! Maybe later!

I walked toward the girl. With every step I thought, My legs are like big sloppy tree trunks. I must have had a weird expression on my face because she started giggling. I could smell the laugh leaking out of her mouth, extending itself towards me.

'I know,' she said. 'I look young for my age.' She stored the candy in one side of her mouth while she spoke. It pressed against the inside of her cheek, a tumor that shifted from side to side when she parted her lips.

'Do you want something to drink?' I asked stupidly. My legs continued to carry me in her direction. The more I looked at her the more her face seemed to swim away from me. I searched her eyes for a hint of Diane.

'Can I have a tissue?'

Slowly I made my way to the kitchen. I grabbed a paper towel and handed it to her. She spat out a tiny, translucent candy shard, then gave the crumpled towel back to me. I didn't know what to do with it, so I shoved it in my chinos pocket. I wished that I could sit down next to her and lay my head in her lap, but my body couldn't remember how to do anything except stand there, staring.

'I don't think you're Diane,' I said finally. Then I said, 'Do you happen to have any Ativan?'

She looked at me sadly. 'No, I don't.' She got up off the couch and walked toward me, then stopped when our faces were six inches apart. Her skin smelled like cigarettes and lemon-scented cleaning supplies. I wanted to reach out and peel the cracking foundation off her face in strips.

'You're too young. You're too young and I don't think you're going through a divorce,' I said.

She crossed her arms over her small chest. 'If you don't believe me, then I'll just leave.' She reached for her boots.

'No!' I said. 'No, don't go. I believe you.'

She shook her head. 'Ken,' she said, 'this is never going to work if you don't trust me. We have to trust each other. Trust is the foundation of love. Are you listening?'

I studied her face. I looked around my clean, well-decorated apartment. I thought, There is no way she is Diane.

Then my body said, *Maybe she will give you a massage, though. Maybe she really likes you.*

'Yes,' I said.

'I'm here to help you. That's all I've ever wanted to do.'

'Okay,' I said.

'First, we have to get you cleaned up. Where's your bathroom?'

'It's right around the corner,' I said.

I watched the net of her tights digging into her calves as she went off in search of the room. When she found it, she smiled at me and closed the door behind her. I heard the brief rush of her piss, then the toilet flush and the bathwater running. After a while, she came back out and beckoned me towards her.

I followed her into the bathroom. It was humid and foggy with steam. The scent of lavender and lemongrass hung heavy over the tub, cut through by the faint grassy odor of urine. I glanced at the trash and saw that she had used up my wife's bath salts.

'Take off your clothes,' she said, still smiling. I hesitated, then peeled off my chinos and my boxer briefs. I tried not to look at my penis hanging limp between my thighs. She helped me unbutton my shirt and lifted it over my head.

'Good,' she said. 'Now get in.'

I stepped into the tub and stood submerged up to my calves, waiting for my body to adjust to the heat. The water felt slippery around my legs. I lowered myself slowly, crouching at first like a dog taking a shit, then letting myself lie down fully. The bathwater came up to my chin.

Diane nodded at me from above. 'You stay here as long as it takes.'

'Thanks,' I said, and I moved my face into what I hoped could realistically be called a smile. I watched Diane kneel to gather my discarded clothes. I knew everything that was going to happen the moment before it happened. How she would leverage her weight against one hand, pushing herself from the tiles, reaching for the doorknob, my dirty underwear tucked under her armpit. And how I would raise myself onto my knees, my torso leaning out over the tub, my hand following her, straining, extending, dripping, the fingers wrapping around her left ankle and holding tight.

Diane's mouth made the smallest sound I had ever heard. There was water on the floor. I felt her ankle churn in my fist. I looked at the hairs on the back of my arm, which were so beautiful, so silky and dark. Was Diane crying? No. No one here was crying. I had already let go. The door had already clicked shut.

I closed my eyes and sank back into the tub, loosening my jaw and parting my lips, letting the bathwater slide into my mouth. I heard a faint series of rustles and thumps from the kitchen, the opening and closing of drawers and cabinets, things banging into other things, things being moved, footsteps padding from room to room, things being thrown onto the floor, things being retrieved, unzipped, re-zipped. I made a mental inventory of all the objects around the apartment: my laptop, my wallet, my phone. It wasn't true that trust was the foundation of love. Love had no foundation. It soared above me, untethered, an awful blimp. I heard paper rubbing against itself, Diane's human exhale, Diane's human voice saying *shit*, Diane's human laugh, the front door opening, the front door closing. I could feel my pores widening, the dirt of my life washing out of me, rising with the steam and filtering through the ceiling vent. I reached above me for a bar of soap but it slipped from my wet hand. I watched it sink to the bottom of the tub before dipping my arm down to pick it up. I started to wash myself. The soap slid out of my hand once more.

Oh well, I thought.

I plunged my hand back into the water. I groped around.

I can't find it, I thought. It's gone.

But then I found it. I lifted it out of the water. I held on tight. I didn't drop it again.

TINDER

by SARAH GREEN

from PLEIADES

a Cento[1]

Wild days and trouble are mostly behind me.
All of my pictures were taken in the past.
That's how pictures work. The way to win
me over is: Give me a pasture where there can be
anything inside. I once dressed up as Moses.
I need someone to come over and make me
a box of shells and cheese. I'm tired of coming
home to an empty house. I am a Turkish Prince.
I'm sort of like a deer: wild & free; gentle, yet
Love my life, won't settle, must see stars.
I don't smoke and I don't gamble. I am simple.
Are you okay with awkward silences?
Will you join me at the dog park?
Looking for a connection so powerful
it brings me to my knees. I enjoy so many things,
including things I haven't even discovered yet.
Life is a vibe. Everyone has been through,
or is going through things. Looking for that
"you've never met anyone like me" vibe.
I think I'm doing this wrong. To be perfectly honest,
my life is okay. I don't know a lot, but I do

---

1. *Lines taken from Minnesota men's dating profiles*

know a lot, you know? I've made mistakes.
I'm not gonna be your first choice.
Can we skip to the part where we're comfortable
in silence with one another?
You remember Prince Charming? Yeah, that's not me.
I'm probably not as supportive as you'd like.
I believe in music the way some people believe in fairy tales.
I build boxes with exotic woods.
Jeremy is my real name.

* *Lines taken from Minnesota men's dating profiles*

GOLGORI

fiction by PETER HONG

from BERKELEY FICTION REVIEW

Golgori was our god, and for as long as we could recall, we had been under his dominion.

He was a proud god, a commanding god, and for millennia, we had lived each day under his guiding word. As we woke, he would write us his instructions into the sky above, and we would rise and work faithful to the night following his every sentence. Day by day, we rose and slept, breathed and died, worked and worked by his word. Each century went by the same as the last: his command, waking the morning skies of each and every generation.

Then one day, we woke and looked to the sky, and found his word written in the clouds: giant letters spelling out an enormous "WHOOPS."

We were dumbstruck. None of us knew what this "WHOOPS" could refer to. For thousands and thousands of years, we'd been living and dying by his words, and there'd been no precedent of anything like this before.

Without an answer, each of us came to our own theories. Some of us believed he'd made some deep mistake back in creation. Others feared that he had regretted creating us. And millions more found some other factor to blame: the immorality of our souls, the new generation, the realities of our time.

Whoever we were, whatever we thought, we all refrained from our work that day. We had no instructions to follow, no idea what to work on. It was a deeply unsettling experience. None of us had ever known a day without instruction. We went to bed at our own time that night and were nearly sleepless.

The next day we woke, and we looked again to the sky. New words had been written: "I AM SO, SO SORRY."

We were more dumbfounded than ever. Some reaffirmed their own theories, others frantically wrote new ones. Many of us wondered if we might never receive an instruction ever again. Those five words loomed over the world, casting their letter-shaped shadows over everything.

As another day went by without instruction, anxiety boiled in us. To fill the day, some of us looked for our own ventures, finding our own duties to work on or even searching for something beyond work. And whatever we did, we all scolded one another—fearing we'd each violated some holy command none of us had received.

That night, we all went quick to sleep, hoping that the words would return tomorrow, and all this uncertainty might die with the night.

On the third day, we woke and looked up. We saw those same five words, "I AM SO, SO SORRY" written in the sky. But underneath those words, a new sentence had appeared: "WILL YOU FORGIVE ME?"

Now, we were faced with a question. It was a question we did not know the meaning of, a question we had no idea how to answer.

But we had to answer it. That day, all of us gathered into one place to determine what we should do. For hours, we debated, discussed, and argued with one another. Finally, when night had struck, we'd all managed to agree on one response, and went home to rest in preparation for the next day.

On the fourth day, we woke, and the words Golgori had given us on the third day remained there in the heavens, unchanged.

We got to work immediately. We gathered up our old things, our forgotten tools, our broken charms, our torn clothing, and put them into one pile. With all our hands in motion, we fashioned the objects into fireworks. Then we struck up our matches, and fed the flames to their fuses. All eyes watched sharp as needles as the fire nibbled up the lines bit by bit, bite by bite. And then, with a sizzle, each firework erupted into the sky—flailing, fizzing up into dizzy trails of light—spitting, then bursting into sparks shining every color—spelling "WE FORGIVE YOU" next to his holy word.

Then we waited. We waited late into the night. We sat outside in the dark for a response that might come at any time, or we went back home to sleep, hoping that an answer would arrive in the clouds by morning. We watched as each of our sparks burned themselves back into smoke, and were carried away by the wind. Each star in the sky was like a memory, tracing out the words we'd spelled there hours ago.

The night passed.

On the final day, we woke. We looked up. There were no more words in the sky. There were only clouds, unbroken and blank.

We were speechless. We trembled in our homes. We knitted together in fear. Just then, the clouds shook. And we saw them. Millions of tiny "thank-yous" rained down from heaven. Blanketing the entire world. Washing over the earth. Burying us under their shimmering, gorgeous weight.

THE BEAUTIFUL SALMON

fiction by JOANNA KAVENNA

from THE PARIS REVIEW

I've always loved salmon. Not to eat, as I don't eat fish, but I've always loved salmon in general because salmon jump and no one knows why. They jump all over the place—out of rivers, up waterfalls. Some say they jump to clean their gills. Others say they jump for joy, because they love the smell of fresh rainwater. Still others say they jump to view their territory. It is certain that the salmon are jumping, but there is no absolute certainty as to why they jump.

You could say that this is true of many things. We are certain we are alive, but we are uncertain why. We are certain we are conscious, but we are uncertain why. Almost all "why" questions draw you into a realm of uncertainty, from why salmon jump to why we live and die.

This story is partly about a beautiful salmon, and partly about the question of uncertainty. It's also about the past and how we can't get back there, except in our minds, and how this means the past is always uncertain.

I was living in Oslo at the time, studying philosophy at the university. Among the impressive tutors on the faculty, the best and greatest was an Icelandic philosopher called Alda Jónsdóttir. She was brilliant and also terrifying. She was a professor of logic but her main area was the things that fall out of sets. Superfluities, redundancies, gaps. She often said there were no sensible "why" questions, so we might as well discard them and move on to questions we could actually answer. She had masses of gray curly hair and she spoke and moved very quickly. In winter Oslo, the sidewalks are covered with a patina of treacherous ice. Nonetheless, Alda Jónsdóttir would stride along as if wearing crampons, in no danger of slipping at all, while I'd struggle beside her with little chastened footsteps, trying to stay upright on a surface that was more slippery than an ice rink. One day, when Alda Jónsdóttir was explaining something to me that I really didn't understand, I slipped and landed with a hard thump on the ice, then slid on my ass downhill. As I struggled up again, Alda Jónsdóttir said to me: "Why did you do that?" Was that a philosophical joke? I wondered. Did philosophers make jokes?

It was Alda Jónsdóttir who invited me to dinner. An invitation from a terrifying person must, inevitably perhaps, be terrifying. Also I came from nowhere, I really had no idea about the customs of anywhere else. I was habitually terrified, and Alda Jónsdóttir was an apex of terror in the midst of my quotidian terrorscape.

I said yes, anyway, because I was curious, if terrified. I was slightly more curious than terrified. And I wondered various things, like (a) who Alda Jónsdóttir lived with, if anyone; (b) where she lived; (c) what it was like there; and (d) what she would cook for dinner, if she cooked. I couldn't imagine Alda Jónsdóttir doing anything as ordinary as cooking dinner. There was also the question of why she had invited me. But, as she often said, this was a pointless "why" question.

I spent the hours leading up to the dinner in a state of predictable terror. I wasn't sure what I should wear, so I found my only smart gray suit, which I could wear with the blue shirt my father gave me before he died. It was too big for me but it was the smartest thing I owned. I had a pair of black suede loafers that would be okay with the suit, I thought. Or would they? I had no idea if it was okay to wear black loafers with a gray suit. I had no idea if it was okay to wear black loafers in general.

For a few hours, I tried to busy myself with work. I was writing a very overdue essay about "saying the unsayable." I really didn't know what I was trying to say. Perhaps what I wanted to say was unsayable? Also, I couldn't concentrate because I kept wondering: Was it okay to wear black loafers with a gray suit? What was okay, anyway? I got dressed in my uncomfortable gray suit, and my too-large blue shirt, and my black loafers. I took along a copy of *Snow* by Orhan Pamuk as a present. It seemed ridiculous to bring the great Alda Jónsdóttir a book—the temerity!—but I couldn't think what else to take her, apart from a bottle of wine, which I intended to buy on the way. Then I walked out into the beautiful crisp evening. The air was full of the smell of hops, from the Ringnes brewery. Trams whirred past me but I liked the cold crisp air, so I carried on shuffling along.

In Norway, wine is really expensive, and you can buy it only from the government state shop, where it is heavily taxed. That's quite bad already but on this occasion I'd messed up and the shop was closed by the time I arrived. You literally can't buy wine anywhere else, only Vinmonopolet, the government shop. I had never really been to a dinner party before, but I knew you were meant to bring a bottle, or else! I was so confounded by this unexpected disaster that I stood outside Vinmonopolet and wept bitterly, as if I were such a raving drunkard that the prospect of an evening without wine was unbearable. People hurried past in their long dark coats and naturally they didn't offer much sympathy. Actually that's unfair—one person did pause, and offered the proverbial phrase *"Liten tue kan velte stort lass,"* which roughly means "The straw that broke the camel's back." Then they told me, less sympathetically, to stop blocking the path.

It was good advice. I continued. Shuffling along. No wine! A massive epic of disaster! Of course, it was a small social embarrassment really but these things can weigh heavily upon you when you are young and uncertain and have no real idea what the hell you should do amid all this confusion and beauty and madness and terror. And that was just on a cold winter's night in a beautiful city like Oslo—imagine how it would be, I thought as I kept shuffling along, imagine what would happen if they sent you to fight in a war, you numbskull, what the hell are you even thinking about, weeping like a fool because you can't buy a stupid bottle of wine! I said those sorts of things to myself, then I fell on the ice and got up again, and finally—still berating myself vividly—I reached the door.

Alda Jónsdóttir lived in Grünerløkka, which was the best place to live in Oslo. Not in terms of being the most ostentatious and expensive place—those sorts of places were down by the harbor, overlooking the water, as they often are in big cities. But it was the best place in terms of being full of elegant squares with ice shimmering on the sidewalks as if one of the billionaires in the harbor had dropped diamonds everywhere and not bothered to clear them away. The streetlights sputtered onto the shining ice, and the moon above was a perfect toenail clipping, among nacreous clouds.

Finally, I buzzed. And the buzzer whirred, and a voice—not Alda Jónsdóttir's—said, *"Kom inn!"*

There's one thing I should explain at this point: all this terror was misplaced. The business about the shoes, for example. I went upstairs and Alda Jónsdóttir's husband, Guðmund Guðmundsson (the voice from the buzzer—a tall, wizard-like man, seven feet tall or so, like a benevolent Viking deity, who was a professor of astronomy), invited me to leave my shoes outside their door. In Norway you always take off your outdoor shoes before entering a home. I had forgotten. If anything I should have been more concerned about my socks. They were full of holes. That's what I should have amended, not the black shoes. But if you're in a state of mindless terror, as I generally was, you don't think clearly. So, I went in, with holes in my socks and my stupid black shoes outside the door, as if they'd ever mattered. Then of course everyone was dressed in jeans and sweaters and I was wearing a formal suit. I took off the jacket at once, rolled up the sleeves of my dad's shirt, and went inside, trying to explain that I had no wine, the shop was closed, but here, here was a book—

"Ah yes, *Snow*!" said Alda Jónsdóttir, putting it on a table. "Thanks. And we don't care about wine. We drink spirits. Come in!"

She had pulled her masses of gray hair into a plait, she was wearing slacks and a shirt, very relaxed and beautiful. The apartment was large, heavily decorated with scenes from Iceland, all painted by the Viking deity Guðmund. I stood there nervously and foolishly, until Guðmund handed me a drink I would call Poison. That was the effect it had on me. But it was actually called Black Death—an Icelandic spirit made from mashed potatoes, or something.

"You eat it with a little piece of dead shark," said Guðmund.

"I don't generally eat shark," I said.

"Not even pickled shark?" he said, waving a little jar beneath my nose.

"Not even pickled," I said. "But thank you so much. That looks amazing."

There were a lot of people there. Cool, distinguished, at the top of their cool, distinguished fields. I was very intimidated. My clothes were far too formal. I kept being introduced to people and nodding sagely as they spoke their names then forgetting what they'd said five seconds later. To douse my nerves, I drank a lot of Black Death, far too much as we stood around, and far too much as we sat at the dining table. It tasted delicious, so crisp and cold. It was like drinking the cold air beyond the window.

It turned out the Black Death was stronger than hell. It was so strong that after a while I began to hallucinate. The paintings on the wall were moving, I thought. Lava fields, in motion. A man, smiling. I was not only drunk but off my rocker. It was a really bad situation. There were a dozen people around me, maybe more, and now their facial expressions seemed antic. And possibly insincere. Were they acting? I was just trying to work this out when Alda Jónsdóttir slapped an enormous dish onto the center of the table. As she did this everyone exclaimed, "What a beautiful salmon!"

It was enormous and it seemed to be breathing. And, it seemed to be floating. One or both of these, I understood, must be effects of the Black Death. Otherwise, something very odd was going on with the salmon. Either way, in front of me was a beautiful salmon that had been cooked in a fish kettle and then decorated copiously, with gorgeous arrangements of parsley and dill and lemons. There were little dishes of salad and vegetables everywhere, but the centerpiece, the focal point of the meal, for sure, was the beautiful salmon. Levitating. Breathing. Alda Jónsdóttir had cooked it herself.

And more than that. As everyone exclaimed about the beauty of this fish, Alda Jónsdóttir explained that she had risen that morning at 4 A.M. and driven to Arendal, a mere six-hour round trip as everyone else at the table knew (and I discovered later), because her old friend Kristoffer Peterson lived in Arendal and he was a fisherman, and he had caught the most beautiful salmon, he said, and wanted her to cook it. He was something of an expert on salmon, of all kinds, and he thought it was the most beautiful salmon he had ever seen. "Anyway," said Alda Jónsdóttir, because everyone was now saying that this was too much fuss, "I wanted to see Kristoffer. I never get to see him!"

She flicked her hair away from her face, a single strand that had tumbled out of her plait. She looked embarrassed, almost—was that possible?

"No no, really," she said in response to a further volley of exclamations about how this was too much, far too much effort—it was clear this was beginning to trouble her. There is a line—a very slender line—between expressing torrential gratitude and giving someone the impression they've made a fool of themselves by trying too hard. Somehow we were all on that line. At least I wasn't, because I couldn't speak, but the others were dancing along this tightrope and one by one, it seemed, they all fell to the wrong side, meaning that they all started to suggest that Alda Jónsdóttir had made too much of a fuss. "*You really really shouldn't have*" started to sound less like an expression of gratitude and more like an expression of, What the hell are you doing, driving to Arendal for a salmon? Do you have too much time on your hands? They didn't mean it to sound like that, but somehow, on that other side of the tightrope, it did.

Alda Jónsdóttir began to look flustered. She pushed the strand of errant hair away from her face again and said, "Really! Shut up, all of you! You're making me blush! It's just a fish!"

But no one believed her anymore.

"More drink?" said Guðmund, siphoning more Black Death into everyone's glasses, to shut them all up. I drank it down, nervously. He filled my glass again.

Clearly I was in trouble, aside from the hallucinations, because I couldn't eat the salmon. I never eat any kind of salmon, either as a full fish or a salmon-based product such as salmon pâté. Afflicted as I was by Black Death, I couldn't think what to do about anything. Especially the lava fields, which were not only moving but hovering away from their frames as if the room would soon become a lava field. Then what?

The only positives of the situation were that (a) everyone else was also afflicted with Black Death, and (b) they would—therefore—hardly notice if I ate the salmon or not.

On one side of me was a poet called Amari Blomdahl who moved her hands as she spoke, as if she were patting something imaginary in front of her. Or as if there actually was something in front of her, which she could see and no one else could, and which needed her to comfort it—also possible in the circumstances. On my other side was a philosopher called Ole Lauge, who was tall with gray-black hair and a shy, trembling, sensitive manner. He was so shy he could barely speak, until he became very drunk. Then he started speaking quite a lot, and he told me his latest philosophical work was called *Listen!*

"Because all we do is speak!" he said. "Everyone speaks and no one listens. How about you? What would you like to say?"

"I'm listening," I said.

It wasn't that I had any high moral principles on this matter. I was just stricken with nerves.

"No you're not!" he said. "Not really!"

"Yes I am!" I said. "I'm listening to you telling me to listen!"

"Ha!" he said. "I guess that's the fatal disproof of my argument. Touché! All you have to do is listen, and I disappear in a puff of logic. Ha! But did you really want to listen, or did you just want to disprove my argument? That's the question! I've struggled with that! It's such an easy disproof. It's just—bang! Dead! My argument is dead! People stay quiet just long enough to kill it, then they start speaking again!" He said all of this so sadly, I didn't know how to respond.

It was quite the wrong time to get up and leave the table, and Lauge duly exploded: "See! You think you've won, so now you don't even need to listen!" I went to the bathroom, to splash water on my face. I had to shuffle there very slowly, as if I were still walking on ice. In the bathroom I threw water all over my dead dad's nice blue shirt and wondered where he was, and then I realized I was crying, and I tried to clean that up, the mess on my dad's shirt and also my face, and then I got more water, threw it on my face, on my shirt, on the floor, tried to clean that up, then I stood again and looked in the mirror—my face had gone. It had vanished! Altogether! I looked down carefully at my hands. Still there. I touched my face. There! Just not visible, it seemed, within the ordinary world. Or the ordinary world had gone. Mmm. There wasn't anything to do, I thought. My face would come back. Or it wouldn't. One day, even tomorrow, I would be sober and I would have a face again. My invisible face was flaming. After splashing more water on it, which didn't help, I shuffled back into the dining room.

At the table, something had happened. Lauge had just said something, it seemed, and everyone was looking at him in total horror. They were listening intently, either in deliberate or accidental disproof of his argument that no one listens. They were really listening, though in total horror, and they all looked as if they were doing impressions of *The Scream* in a game of charades, art-classics version.

"But Alda," Lauge was saying. "You must know I'm angry with you. That's why you invited me over, isn't it?"

"No," said Alda Jónsdóttir. "It's not. I had no idea you were angry with me. We're friends, that's why I invited you over. But come on, Lauge, tell me your deepest thoughts."

That was a disarming phrase, I thought, but also alarming. Do we really want to know people's deepest thoughts? Do they even know them? I had these questions running around in my poisoned brain and I was also trying very hard not to slump, because my body was desperate to slump by this stage. It wanted to slump face-first, face-planting into my plate. I could feel Lauge tensing beside me, even clenching his fists.

Lauge's deepest thoughts were as follows. He was upset with Alda Jónsdóttir because she had recently judged the Elden Prize, the biggest philosophy prize in Norway, and had given it to a philosopher called Anders Karlson, who was a fraud, in Lauge's opinion. Moreover, at the ceremony she had called Anders Karlson the greatest philosopher of his generation, "leading the vanguard"—now Lauge was quoting by heart, suggesting a slightly obsessive approach to this theme—"leading the vanguard in his beautiful, nuanced, and dextrous modes of philosophical thinking, and providing an immaculate example to the rest of us of how to have mutually respectful philosophical debates in which we genuinely hear one another and listen . . ."

"I mean," said Lauge. "Tell me your deepest thoughts, for once? I'd love to hear them!"

"Why are you so angry about this?" said Alda Jónsdóttir. "I never knew you were so petty! Why do you want some little bauble, Ole Lauge? What does it even mean to you? Do you think Aristotle cared if he got the Elden Prize? What are you talking about?"

"Yes, of course!" said Ole Lauge. "At one level, the world of forms is an illusion. Obviously! Nonetheless that is six million kroner and Karlson is the heir to a massive shipping fortune, his family are rolling in it—why give him even more money? He couldn't even be bothered to come to the ceremony!"

"Well, that's his choice," said someone else—one of the people whose names I'd heard and immediately forgotten. "Why do you care, Ole? Chill out!" This intervening voice of sanity looked like the son in *Festen*, if you've seen that film—the one who confronts the evil abusive father. Really uncannily like that.

"I care because he's rich," said Lauge. "Firstly. And I'm not. And my wife died. I care about that. And I have to look after my kids alone. And I can't work, but I must work, because otherwise, we have nothing. But also, I care because he's rubbish. And fine, I'm rubbish too. We're all rubbish. You're a rubbish philosopher, Fridtjof Ericsson . . ."

Ah! I thought, That's his name!

". . . and you, Amari, are a rubbish poet and this kid beside me is—well—a rubbish—" Now he paused, and turned to me in confusion. "What are you rubbish at, if you don't mind me asking?"

I didn't have a clue how to answer that!

"That's my student," said Alda Jónsdóttir. "And yes, a kid. Enough!"

"You're right," said Lauge. "Enough!" He expressed his further apologies with a wildly drunken hand movement that almost smacked me in the mouth. "My point being, everyone is rubbish. That's the secret of the universe. All these feted people and they're completely rubbish. You know that. I know that! We're all rubbish! But if you're going to dish out rubbish prizes, then why pretend otherwise, why be so dishonest and claim that this generic rubbish is somehow great and beautiful? I thought you were my friend!"

"Ole Lauge, it's just a prize," said Alda Jónsdóttir, and a few people chimed in. The guy from *Festen* (I'd forgotten his name, again, really, it was absurd), and Amari, who really didn't like being called a rubbish poet (who does?), and Guðmund, who was trying to defend Alda Jónsdóttir. As they all chimed in, the argument became more heated. But Lauge wasn't listening to anyone.

Alda Jónsdóttir tried again, wringing her napkin in a way that suggested deep existential turmoil. Everyone was watching Ole Lauge as he waved his hands furiously, and they were watching Alda Jónsdóttir as she tried again, wringing her napkin.

"Ultimately I don't care," she said. "I think that's it. I don't care that you didn't win the prize. Why do you care so much? It's quite bemusing. Are you really expecting me to have a serious argument about this? It's such a waste of time, when we could be discussing any number of other more interesting things."

Lauge was just saying, "For God's sake Alda Jónsdóttir, why don't you LISTEN!" when he waved his hand wildly again, so wildly that he swept a bottle of Black Death across the table. It was a big heavy bottle made of lots and lots of glass, and it catapulted across the table, far too quickly for anyone to save it. Soon it was flying beyond the reach of anyone, even Lauge and his desperate waving hands—and then it smashed into a water jug and several glasses, and then all these frangible objects smashed into the beautiful salmon. They smashed into, and across, and within, and over, the beautiful salmon. Had you intended to fill a fish with broken glass, you couldn't have done it more effectively. It was immaculate in that respect, but a complete disaster in every other respect.

In a second, the salmon was covered in powdery debris and little shining shards. All the decorations were further embellished by this shining patina of beautiful—yet clearly inedible—pieces of shattered glass.

If people had looked as if they were doing novelty impressions of *The Scream* before, now they looked as if, in their view, Munch's portrait of existential agony was insufficient. They were more like the creations of Egon Schiele. Twisted and contorted, wrecked entirely. The salmon, also, was wrecked but it was still beautiful, with its little garnishes of parsley and dill, its lovely arrangements of lemons, its bright pink flesh, cooked presumably to perfection—

"*Fy faen*, oh my God," said Lauge. "I have fucked up your fish."

"You have, a little," said Alda Jónsdóttir, who had begun to laugh, if mostly in horror. This meant everyone else could laugh, if mostly in horror, which was a great relief. Everyone laughed apart from Lauge, who was too horrified.

"No no," he said. "It was such a beautiful salmon. And you went to Arendal. And I have ruined it. I have ruined everything!"

Then he burst into tears.

You can't laugh if someone is crying, so everyone immediately tried to stop laughing, though there was a slight delay while everyone made the transition. This felt awful because there was a moment when Lauge was weeping, volubly, and everyone was laughing, like a weird tableau. Then with a loud, agonizing scrape of his chair, Lauge stood up and walked out of the room. At first I thought he might just leave altogether, but then the door of the bathroom slammed shut.

The beautiful ruined salmon lay there in front of us, glistening with glass. It was so sad. No one said anything for a while. It felt like a wake for a salmon. Then Alda Jónsdóttir said, very quietly, as if it were a secret: "When he comes back in we must all be kind to him, because clearly he's made a fool of himself."

"Of course," said Festen. "Perhaps I was a little harsh. But, there's a sort of entitlement, don't you think, in what he was saying, about expecting the prize and so forth? I mean, no one has a right to anything!" But Alda Jónsdóttir gave him a stern look, and he raised a hand. "All right, all right. Okay!"

When Lauge returned, having splashed himself so liberally with cold water that his shirt was soaked, he averted his gaze from the ruined salmon—perhaps to show respect. It looked at him, nonetheless, with its one reproachful eye.

"I'm terribly sorry," said Lauge. He was leaning on the table, beside Alda Jónsdóttir, ashen-faced and panting as if he'd been running very hard.

"No no," said Alda Jónsdóttir, leaping to her feet, giving him a big hug, banging him repeatedly on the back, almost angrily. "I'm really sorry. Please! You should say whatever you want. Of course! And these things matter to varying degrees to different people. And I'm so sorry about your wife. Of course, we're all so sorry."

"Well that's definitely not your fault," said Lauge, as Guðmund stood and led him gently back to his seat, then stuffed him also gently into it, as if he were an oversize child. "I don't normally drink, you see," Lauge was saying. "But I felt awkward today and, you know, I miss my wife. I'm not sure I even care about the stupid prize."

He started crying again.

By now he was so penitent that everyone who had been fervently irritated by his egomaniacal behavior—which was basically everyone at the table—changed their minds entirely and began to pity him, with equal fervor. At least, I did. To be honest I can't really speak for the others. But I felt very sorry about everything. I was nothing to him, but I tried to pat him on the arm. He didn't seem to notice.

"Well," said Alda Jónsdóttir. "It genuinely doesn't matter about the fish. I couldn't care less. After all the main purpose of the evening is to talk, and the salmon is not required in order for us to talk. And there are plenty of other things to eat."

She stood and cleared the salmon away. Meanwhile, to distract everyone from the scene change, Festen told a story about how people used to torture or perhaps it was murder prisoners by making them eat glass, so it wouldn't be a good idea to eat the beautiful salmon at this stage. It was meant to be a distraction but the story was oddly violent and didn't really help anyone. He subsided fairly quickly. Alda Jónsdóttir came back with some pots of herring and that bright pink salami you get in Norway and also the golden cheese that tastes as sweet as honey. I was still very drunk but now I realized: it didn't matter. Nothing I did that evening would ever matter. It was a great relief. I actually wondered if Lauge could hire himself out as a professional disruptor and go from one house to another as an antidote to social terror. But that was the fermented mash talking, I expect.

Lauge's wife had died of cancer, a few weeks earlier. He'd looked after her, and their three children, for five years, while working as a full-time teacher. He didn't have a university post; he was a high school teacher who wrote about philosophy in his spare time. He was exhausted and really angry. He was angry with the universe for taking away his wife, so randomly and cruelly. But the universe was faceless, implacable, so instead he'd become angry with Alda Jónsdóttir about something relatively unimportant. Perhaps he just wanted the universe to pat him on the back and say it was sorry. And if not the universe then, at least, Alda Jónsdóttir.

I didn't know any of this at the time. Then again, I didn't know any philosophers at the time, either, so I just thought this was how they behaved. Sudden furies and then tears, and then they all made up and ate copious amounts of herring. Also I was out of my mind on Black Death so it was almost impossible to judge anything. All night everyone had these cartoonish expressive faces, very arresting and unusual. And when I finally walked home, a little shadow danced beside me all the way up the hill to Torshov, quite friendly but dark and shape-shifting, so one moment it was a fox and the next it was a cat, and the next it was a small bouncing cloud of vapor.

The following day, the little dancing shadow had danced away and I had a relentless noise in my head, as if part of my skull had been dislodged and was banging like a gate in a storm. On the plus side, I could see my face in the mirror again.

People often talk about learning experiences and, in the days after this salmon-based fiasco, I wondered about this. One thing I had already learned from Alda Jónsdóttir was that conclusions are fallacies of formal systems, or something along those lines. By that logic, all conclusions are uncertain, including the conclusion that all conclusions are uncertain, and so on. Still, one thing I learned from all of this: names are often significant. Even if you agree with Alda Jónsdóttir that no formal system can precisely capture the formlessness of life, even then—a drink called Black Death is unlikely to be very good for you. Furthermore, I really hadn't needed to worry about everything I was so absurdly worried about, due to the law of unintended consequences. We can be stressing ourselves senseless about possible events, striving to avert them, but then everything is demolished by an unimagined and previously unimaginable event. Nonetheless, like Alda Jónsdóttir, we try our utmost, we travel to the psychic or physical equivalent of Arendal, there and back again, we make the most extraordinary efforts to ensure that things will be okay, for us and for those around us. Yet, suddenly, there is a shattering of glass and the beautiful salmon is ruined entirely. Then we have to start all over again—striving and hoping. Perhaps that's pushing things too far, but that was what I learned from the evening. And that grief is terrible and sends you mad, though I knew something of that already. But mostly the part about the beautiful salmon.

THE END OF CHILDHOOD

by WAYNE MILLER

from POETRY

My daughter is building a path
across the lake.

Each morning she goes out
with an armful of boards

and hammers them
into the ice. Her brother

brings the coffee can
of nails, tucks the hammer

into his belt. The ice is thick,
the path is growing.

We watch them
all day from the railing.

No one else lives
at this end of the valley

though up around the bend
there are lights.

My daughter's project
is not to reach them,

she tells us, but just
to leave a perfect

track of boards
floating on the water

that first day
the ice has melted.

ALL I LOVE

by CHEN CHEN

from INDIANA REVIEW

is you, & you
in the morning

& both you's
are trees
& both trees

poems,
& the troems make me
dream

of a larger reality:
theirs
& theirs

is full of rootbrains
leafminds
sapsentience

thinking

such thoughts
(esp of dirt)
(esp of water & sunsugars &

the dirtiest yet sappiest of thoughts yes
trees sunnily think
those

(in public)
(esp in public
while getting esp leaky
as trees & poems & you,
that is, troems, kinkily
do))

& one troem

is all

& the other troem
everything

DESPERATE TIMES, DESPERATE CRIMES

fiction by LOU MATHEWS

from NEW ENGLAND REVIEW

2010

Desperate times call for desperate measures. Guy Fawkes said that, and so did Esmerelda, Gustavo's daughter, when I went to visit him at the hospital. Gustavo is my landlord of seven years, owner of the place I landed once the scripts went un-optioned and the residuals dried up, an eight bungalow court on the fringe of Culver City.

What Esmerelda actually said was, "I'm sorry, but we got to bump the rent."

I was the one who said the thing about desperate times.

Once Gustavo's lung cancer—a man who never smoked and wouldn't rent to smokers—put him in the hospital, Esmerelda got a look at the books. Turned out Gus had been carrying me for most of those seven years. He'd appointed me court manager five years ago, a nebulous title with almost nonexistent duties. I was paying $750 a month for a $1,200 mock witch's cottage. Property values and taxes in Culver City were spiraling upward. Both Sony and Culver Studios were expanding, buying up blocks of formerly distressed properties.

Outside Gus's room, Esmerelda said she would have to bump everybody else's rent to $1,500 just to stay even. My rent would go up to $1,200 and future hikes were probable. I knew that was fair and I told Esmerelda so. She got a little teary. "I hated to tell you. My dad never would."

I went back in to say goodbye to Gus, but he was asleep. The gray stubble on his cheeks was now darker than the crepey white pallor of his skin, and I understood that this might really be goodbye.

Gus was one of the last links to my apotheosis, my one directorial credit, *Head-In-Bag*, the punk version of Sam Peckinpah's *Bring Me the Head of Alfredo Garcia*. Filmed in Nicaragua in 1987 and never shown. The high point of my career. Ham in a can.

Gus had been the lead set carpenter on the shoot. Sixteen years later, when he met me at the court to show me the vacancy, he smiled at me quizzically, "Dale Davis. I don't know if you remember me . . ."

"Vividly," I said. "You were the guy who let me know the local actors were stealing plywood." And who could blame them, a four-by-eight sheet of plywood during the Reagan embargo was worth three months wages. Then I had to ask the obligatory question, "Was I an asshole?" It is hard to remember, on long-ago shoots, how well you handled the pressure.

already fading. I like
leaving traces, a form
of hopeful communion.

I bequeath my humanity
to future humans; each
of us is significant

in this way, if not
otherwise. We are
ants, which is how

the gods regard us.
Our prayers are
microscopic. A few

more updates: the kids
are fine. Simone
is twelve, unfurling,

and Cal is sixteen, healthy
and happy lately. Brenda's
opera will premiere

next year, and my
next book will be out
in 2026. I'm fine, too,

as they say when they
don't want to say
more. Mom,

you can't hear this.
You are imaginary.
I get it now.

"Naw, you were okay. No more of an asshole than usual. Actually, that was one of my favorite shoots." He winked. "And it wasn't spoiled by bad reviews." Later he showed me a photo he'd taken of our cast and crew party on the beach at San Juan del Sur. I looked like Carmen Miranda, buried in sand up to my neck, surrounded by a mound of tropical fruit, drunk and happy even though they'd shut us down.

And now that time of moderate ambitions and low rent was closing fast. It was that time. As the Buddhists say, If you don't like the answer, change the question. As my credits age, the competition for crap jobs—teaching, writing or rewriting student scripts, under-the-table script doctoring—is intensifying as other writers age out and into my marginal world. Doors no longer get slammed on me. They never open. I am in trouble and even with a long ladder and a periscope I can't see a way out of the ditch I've dug myself into.

I went back to the apartment and broke into my savings account—my last two Bukowski rarities, hardback signed first editions of *Post Office* and *Love Is a Dog from Hell*. That one also has a little dog doodle. They weren't hard to find, turned backwards on the shelf so that I wouldn't have to discuss the literary merits of that gaseous old windbag with any guests.

Together they should bring something close to three, maybe three and a half grand at Barricade Books on Las Palmas, a Bukowski shrine run by Sol "Reb" Haverstein, who thinks that when you look in the dictionary under *curmudgeon* his picture should appear.

It's the perfect pairing for a man like myself who uses the principle of Occam's razor to justify sloth. The bookstore is two blocks from Bowdlers, the bar where I have to be that afternoon for my usual Wednesday afternoon meeting with my comrades in obsolescence, Jaime Rubin and Oscar Grunfeld.

We'd all been successful screenwriters once. Oscar went back to the golden age of television. He'd actually worked on what was generally agreed to be the worst sitcom ever produced, *My Mother the Car*—and retired with honor. A committed socialist, he'd also been prudent enough to invest in SoCal real estate. Jaime had been one of the best pitchmen in Hollywood, famous for selling ideas and infamous for letting the dumb know how dumb they were, once he was on staff. He wore out his welcome at a dozen studios and now mostly pitched wildly speculative entrepreneurial projects, without the luxury of letting his prospects know what he thought of them. Myself, Dale Davis, was stupid enough to be a committed union leader, blackballed after the strike of '88 for turning in a showrunner who continued to write during the strike. The showrunner had had his revenge, and continued to do so, the gift that kept on giving.

Oscar, as always, is punctual. The first of his course of liqueurs is before him. A small snifter of Cointreau. Kenny Ishikawa, the day bartender, looks up from his book as I open the door and rings the brass bell next to the cash register.

Kenny has my usual, brandy and soda, in front me as I slide into the booth. "Jaime will be slightly delayed," Oscar says. "A late night of research for a new project. And how are you?" With Oscar the question is genuine. It's been a week since we've seen each other. He's doing well and wants the same for me.

"Well," I lie. "One of my former students got a job at Parallax and is circulating one of my scripts under an assumed name. It's made the second cut."

Unfortunately, Oscar has spied the bubble-wrapped Bukowski in my satchel. "Oh, Dale, no. You're not going to see Sol. Do you need some money?"

"It's not that. I'm just tired of looking at them and the market is high right now."

"Not for you. Not with Sol. You know what a putz he is, and he knows you hate Bukowski. I know the guy. I've had this conversation. He wasn't at the party, but he heard about it."

I don't know what Oscar is talking about but can only assume this was back when I could still afford friends who could afford cocaine.

Oscar looks at me imploringly. "Do you need some money? Please. Let me help."

I can't do it. Not yet. The books will hold me a month or two. "I'm all right, Oscar. Really. Lotta flies in the ointment."

I am saved by distraction. The front door cracks open, the white sunlight of Los Angeles streaks in, and Jaime Rubin slides through. Kenny rings his bell and calls out: "We now have a minyan. Bozoes at Bowdlers!"

Oscar and I lift our glasses and Jaime intones, "Yo, Kelsoe,"—(in Jaime's world all bartenders are named Kelsoe)—"the usual."

Kenny has Jaime's Stolichnaya martini with two (2) olives and one (1) onion ready to shake. He pours, lifts the pepper grinder above the glass, and cranks. Presents.

Jaime takes a sip, a brief shudder, a nod. Another sip, a dip and turn, and he bows in Kenny's general direction. Kenny has returned to his paperback under the pin light next to the cash register. Marilynne Robinson's *Lila*. The only reader without an agenda among us.

Jaime eases into our booth. Sips again and unclenches. "Another long night of research."

Oscar and I lift supplicatory palms. Research has been mentioned, next comes the pitch. Jaime sips and gazes at Oscar. "You've had a long, good life. Forget what your tenants say about you. How much longer would you like to live?"

Oscar doesn't have to consider. "Long enough to see Kissinger in jail and Netanyahu fail."

"So," Jaime says, "a few more years?"

"If it takes that," Oscar replies. "But. I would leave tomorrow if those conditions were met."

"I would say it may be a few more years. And if you have to persist, here is an alternative to consider." Jaime puts his martini glass definitively on the table. The gathering commences. We've witnessed this moment before but can't look away. Even Kenny puts down his paperback and switches off the pin light. Jaime seems to swell, you can sense the churn of ideas, a slow, spreading smile takes over his face. You can almost hear a distant calliope.

"Okay, boys and girls, I'm not going to give you the full prospectus here. We're not going to nail down the names and dates, you're not going to get the footnotes. Just the sizzle. The steak is for genuine investors."

Jaime's eyebrows do a little doo-dah dance. He's approaching full twinkle. "Nineteen fifty-four. A guy named Clive McCray at Cornell sews together an old rat and a young rat. This is not a transfusion. This is linkage, parabiosis, constant flow, old rat blood cycles into young rat, comes back refreshed, new outlook on life. Young rat, not so good, but manageable. He gets a few extra pellets for his trouble, doesn't kill the old fuck he's sewn onto. Extrapolate!!"

Oscar seems lost in thought, which means I have to step up. "Fountain of youth time?"

"No, no, no, and no," Jaime says, eyebrows dancing in rhythm. It's like watching Groucho Marx and Frida Kahlo ending a tango. "Fountain of youth is gulp, swallow, I feel better—that's transfusion. The real cure takes commitment. Old body joined surgically to young body—not a temporary boost. We are talking transubstantiation. The three *T*s. Time / Together / Tethered.

"Later studies confirm the earlier findings. Harvard med, 2004—stem cells revived. Stanford, 2006—brain functions improved. Nice spa visit for old rats. For young rats, not such a great deal. But again, in the lab, controlled circumstances. Let's take it outside the lab. Out on the street, how do you get young rats to cooperate?"

"More pellets?" I suggest.

"But we're not in the lab anymore. Who wants pellets? We need volunteers."

Sadly, I still like to provoke Jaime. "Is this the homeless solution?"

"Not good donors. My clients, the rich, the elderly, are going to want pristine healthy blood."

Oscar comes to life, head tilted merrily, hand raised. "Unless they want to get younger, healthier and *high*! Terry Southern. 'Blood of a Wig.'" Oscar trots out his heroes with regularity. Terry Southern is one and we know the story he cites, jaded heads in NYC seeking the ultimate high, pints of paranoid schizophrenic blood fresh from the locked wards at Bellevue. Jaime ignores him.

He looks at me. "When did you graduate from college?" He knows the answer. "Nineteen seventy-eight," I reply. "UC Santa Cruz. Go, Banana Slugs."

"And how much did you accrue in student loans?"

"Didn't have to. We paid no tuition. That was your birthright as a Californian. A free college education."

"Not anymore. The average graduate of what used to be a state university now takes six years to complete their studies and accrues 100k in debt. You graduate with a degree in any of the liberal arts—English, gender studies, anthropology, what we now call pre-law—you're looking at twenty years of payments.

"So, you now have something we haven't had for two centuries—indentured servants. You think a few of the indentured wouldn't jump at the chance of a way out? Here's the pitch. You are sutured to an ancient billionaire—or maybe not such an ancient given the way Silicon Valley is trending—medically monitored, given the best of care for six months, and your student loans are forgiven. Not that different than a surrogate pregnancy with a lot happier ending."

Oscar stirs. "I remember that movie."

Jaime clasps his head. "Whattya talking? This is an up-to-date idea. The *New York Times* article was only last week." Oscar whips out his clipping, "Young Blood May Hold Key to Reversing Aging," by one of his favorite sources, Carl Zimmer.

Oscar has focused, which is daunting. "No!" he thunders. "I remember that movie."

Jaime is frosty. "What does this have to do with my *very* original idea of blood transubstantiation."

"It's an old story," Oscar says. "Rich sewn to poor. It's been done. Nineteen seventy-two. *The Thing with Two Heads*. Ray Milland's head sewn to Rosey Grier's shoulder. Cheek to cheek. Milland is a racist. They hate each other. Terrible movie. The same year that Milland did *Frogs*, another terrible movie. The man who won an Oscar for *Lost Weekend*. He said he needed the money. I think he just hated staying home . . ."

Jaime has given up his pitch. I watch him deflate. First it's a pinhole, then it's a blowout, eyes and eyebrows rolling like snakes on a griddle.

Oscar continues on our history lesson. "He'd have to face a summer shoot featuring fifteen car crashes, an ape with two heads, all written by a schlockmeister like Lee Frost. He must have hated staying at home."

"You ever work with him?"

Oscar looks provoked. "Lee Frost? Never. This is the man who invented Nazisploitation with *Love Camp 7*. Strictly grindhouse and B drive-in. *Chrome and Hot Leather* and *Chain Gang Women* were some of his better titles. They'd throw in beaver shots for the European market." Jaime has left us. Out the back door for once, not even staging his exit.

"Tell me more about *The Thing with Two Heads*." Something in the description intrigued me.

"It was actually a great idea. Where they stole it from, I don't know. Milland plays this world-renowned surgeon, a genius at transplants, dying of cancer. His body is wasting, his brain is full of ideas. He knows a cure is on the way, but he can't wait. He's pre-cryogenic. He's not Walt Disney—no head in the ice. He decides the solution is his head on a healthy body. He has a friend who is head of all the prisons in the state. A healthy prisoner, plucked from death row will be the donor.

"Those about to be executed are told that it is an experimental medical program, no more than that. Sounds like a good deal for both sides. Both sides are disappointed. The Rosey Grier character because he has a nasty head next to him, and the good doctor, Milland, because he somehow forgot that 90 percent of the prisoners on death row are Black and he happens to be a Mississippi racist.

"As I said, the situation is intriguing, but the schlockmeister side takes over and from there you have a half-hour motorcycle chase with fifteen car crashes. Downhill from there. Such a waste of a good idea." Oscar finishes his Cointreau and raises the next liqueur in the set, crème de menthe in a tulip stem glass, in a toast: "Lee Frost, *Yimakh shmoy zol er vern*!" It sounds like he's gargling razor blades.

"And in English," I say.

"There is no suitable translation. 'May his name and memory be erased' is as close as you can come."

I remain intrigued. I'm not sure why. But the itch at the base of my skull, the one that every writer knows, tells me that I am on the hunt. "It *is* a good idea," I tell Oscar. "Certainly a better one than *Guess Who's Coming to Dinner?* I wonder who holds the rights?"

"The audience is there," Oscar says. He's halfway through the crème de menthe and enjoying himself. "Of course, if you really want to mix your metaphors and your crowds, combine *The Thing with Two Heads* and 'Blood of a Wig.' Put George Burns's head on Dennis Rodman's shoulders." He cackles.

I take my leave. It's four o'clock and Barricade Books is about to open. I take my time, walking the long way down Hollywood Boulevard, past the Supply Sergeant, home to all things camouflage and war surplus, Book City, where color-coded books are sold by the shelf-foot to set designers, and Musso-Frank's, and the turn towards Las Palmas.

Oscar is a little wrong. I don't *hate* Bukowski. I think he's written one and two-thirds good books, *Ham and Rye* and *Post Office*. I also think he's sloppy, repetitive, lazy, repetitive, sentimental beyond Hallmark, did I mention repetitive, and he has a problem with women. Now that's an odd take for a man like myself, who has been married four times, but my problems are the opposite. Bukowski doesn't like them very much.

Barricade Books keeps odd hours—four to midnight, Wednesdays to Sundays, geared to the store's primary source of income, drunken screenwriters, actors, directors, producers, and executives drifting down from Musso-Frank's, a block away, looking for overpriced books and broadsides by the drunken poet they think they'd like to be, Charles Bukowski.

The curator, Sol "Reb" Haverstein, a paunchy man in a neon yellow track suit, blocks the doorway as I approach and issues his customary greeting. "Whattya want? You buying or selling?" Apparently this bit of local color thrills the yokels from Musso's. Reb's nimbus of hair is larger and whiter than last time and so is the puff of chest hair protruding from his unzipped decolletage. "In the past I've bought," I tell him. "Some nice Baudelaire. Today I'm selling. Bukowski."

He steps aside. The front window has a pull-down deep red glassine shade that blocks ultraviolet rays, preventing harm to valuable books and prints but it also creates a weird red glow. It feels like you're inside a glass factory, without the heat.

The shop has become even more of a shrine to Bukowski than I remember. But then, of course, Bukowski is dead. Jesús, I think I just remembered the party Oscar was talking about. I hand the bubble-wrapped books over to Reb and he takes them to his desk, brings out a large square magnifying glass.

Nineteen ninety-five. First anniversary of Bukowski's death, and two of my aforementioned cokehead friends, huge Bukowski fans, drag me along to a memorial party and reading in Venice. After an hour and a half of drunken blubbering, recitations, competitive memories and homages, I couldn't stand it. I took my place at the podium.

I looked down at the sea of open-mouthed expectant faces and opened my copy of *Fires*. "I'm Dale Davis. I am going to read what is *by far* the *best* Bukowski poem ever written." Pause. "You Don't Know What Love Is. An Evening with Charles Bukowski." Big pause. "By Raymond Carver."

It still doesn't register. I was two minutes in before the booing started, and it was probably three minutes before some of the bravoes rushed the stage and tried to drag me off. It took them a while. These weren't working-class louts but the usual feeble white-collar Bukowski wannabes and I was laughing so hard I was slippery.

"These are good," Reb says, "Do you want to leave them on consignment or do you want cash?"

"I think cash this time," I say. "I'm leaving for a location shoot in the Canaries next week and it would be good to have a little walkaround."

"Cash. Then it will be three thousand for the two. You're sure? Consignment would be seven."

"Let's make it cash," I say.

"So who do I make the check out to?"

"You don't have cash in hand?"

"In this neighborhood? Do I look like a fool? What's the name for the check?"

"Umm, make it out to D. D. Davis."

"These books are inscribed to Dale. Is that you?"

"Just D. Davis is fine."

"Are you Dale Davis?"

It's a little like watching a roadside thermometer in fast-forward the way the flush ascends from his unzipped chest to his swollen forehead, but his movements are deliberate. Reb opens his desk and brings out a large oval stamp and pad, inks it, opens each book to Bukowski's signature, and rocks it. BOGUS the stamp says. Reb signs them and hands the books to me. "Now try to sell them. Get out of my store you insult to Buk . . ." He pronounces *Buk* to rhyme with *puke*, a mark of the true believer.

Out on the street I look at the convenient trash can, but it's a gesture I can't afford. They are still first editions, worth a couple hundred each, even devalued. And they are definitely devalued. Reb is brought in to authenticate Bukowski's work, his opinion is accepted. If I can't sell them they're great kindling for my funeral pyre, but right now other priorities. First, my friend Gyorgy who used to work at Vidiots until he compiled the largest private collection of videos and DVDs in SoCal. If he doesn't have a copy of *The Thing with Two Heads*, he'll know who does. Then I'll contact my friend Shauna at CBS legal who will track down the rights for me by Monday.

The movie is as bad as Oscar described. Even Milland couldn't save it. At one point Rosey Grier, escaped from capture on the aforementioned stolen motorcycle, meets up with his woman. Feeling a bit horny, he suggests sex. She's put off by Milland's head, Rosey offers to cover it with a pillowcase, she demurs. Most viewers, if offered a pillowcase at that point, would probably accept.

The rights, it turns out, have descended to a niece, a nice woman now in her forties, named Magda, who fortunately has an inflated view of Uncle Lee's artistic vision. She thinks of him as Quentin Tarantino before his time, a view I am happy to honor, particularly if it will save me a few bucks.

Magda would like to meet at Musso's to discuss, a proposal that I instantly scotch. Musso-Frank's makes Hollywood dreams expand and I need that horizon shrunk to a thin line. We meet at Magda's for tea.

The conversation is slowed at first by my admission that I don't know Uncle Lee's full oeuvre. I've never seen *Dixie Dynamite*, nor *Black Gestapo*, but I am pretty convincing on the virtues of *The Thing with Two Heads*, as a lesson in race relations the country needs now! The asterisk that I add is the gradual effect that sharing blood with a Black man has on a confirmed racist, and vice-versa, a nuance not in the original movie. This is about the time I cite Flannery O'Connor's *Wise Blood* as a kind of intellectual precursor for my idea, if you don't look too closely. How Enoch Emory following the instructions given by his learned plasma compares to my sewn-together blood brothers is a little hard to explain.

Magda seems fairly dazzled. Her kohl-ringed eyes gleam and the buttery curls of her perm glow in the subdued light as she sets down her tea. "Will you promise to honor Uncle Lee's intentions?"

Uncle Lee, a double-dealing liar, crook, conman, scheming, two-bit hustler who would do anything to get a movie made? Which is to say, a fellow screenwriter.

"Magda," I say, "I'm a screenwriter. I can only honor Uncle Lee's intentions."

The deal is a thousand dollars, which I do not have. For a six-month option, which I do not have. What I have is a great idea for a script and some hope and a couple names.

My old agent, my last agent, Ben Sturgis, one of the first casualties of the showrunner's revenge, was famous for hiring bright assistants. They came and went like Spinal Tap drummers because they kept getting plucked away by management companies and talent agencies. While I was still represented I paid attention to them, possible future studio heads. My favorite was Candy Kwang. Her given name was Teresa but she understood the virtues of alliteration in that world. She was an Immaculate Heart grad and like most Immaculatas understood the value of the well-written word, which is to say she'd been a fan of my work. I'd stayed in touch when I could, congratulating her on a steady upward climb. She was now at Paradigm, a midlevel agent, and doing well.

I didn't want to spook her. She needed to know I wasn't looking for representation—that ship had sunk—just a referral, a hand up if a hand was there. I took a chance. In a business that is conducted 98 percent by phone I wrote a letter and laid it out. I included the DVD of *The Thing with Two Heads*, my treatment, and an explanation of *why* it would work now.

Candy, bless her heart, remembered me fondly. I had been kind to her, she said in her email, and then she said this: "You can really write and that still matters. I love your stuff. My boss wouldn't let me sign you, but let me help if I can." And she asked me to lunch. I really must have been kind once. No agent wastes lunch on a writer. This was clearly a handout, but I wasn't going to turn it down.

Musso-Frank's has one row of booths in the old room where you can hear yourself think, the inner row. The best of these is closest to the grill. Candy had snared one of these two-toppers and was waiting, well into a dirty martini. She'd always been pretty in that Catholic schoolgirl way. Now, even dressed down, she was gorgeous. One side of me wished we were on the outer showcase row of booths. I sighed and sat. My luck was holding. Pedro, our waiter, remembered me from long ago. I ordered what I always order when someone else is paying—a martini, shrimp cocktail (only suckers order the crab, which is canned), asparagus as an appetizer with hollandaise, filet mignón rare with béarnaise, Lyonnaise potatoes, and a good glass of Bordeaux to go with that. Candy ordered the Caesar and sweetbreads with a choice pinot noir. We had our toast and she got right into it.

"Who is your ideal pitch?"

"An actor who wants to direct."

"Why?"

"Because this project is bulletproof."

"How?"

"Because it doesn't matter who you cast."

"Explain."

"The dream version would be Kevin Hart and put Mel Brooks on his shoulders. That one would write itself and open at fifty million. But it doesn't *have* to. It doesn't need stars. The first time around it was about the white guy. Not this time. This time it's about the white guy learning something from a Black guy who has been on death row.

"Make it Cedric the Entertainer. Whoever is on his shoulder, first time that white guy tells him where he wants to go, Cedric the Entertainer looks down his nose and says, 'Back off. You best remember who's running this ship. I'm not just the Mayflower, Pilgrim. I'm the fucking captain of the Mayflower.'

"But the point is—it can work with *any* good Black comedian. It could work with Redd Foxx, any of the Kings of Comedy. It could work with Godfrey Goddamned Cambridge. It doesn't matter.

"And the white guy—same thing. It could work with Carroll O'Connor, Archie Bunker to the American public. For God's sake it could work with Pat Boone. You could even *do* the sex scene. Picture Pam Grier yanking off the pillowcase, Pat Boone's eyes rolling back in his head,

Pam says, 'that boy is having too much fun,' maybe Pat starts singing like James Brown—*please, pleease, pleease, pleease* . . . or at least a little more like Elvis."

Candy was laughing now. "I think I may have the guy for you."

We order more martinis.

It took a little longer for Candy to organize the meeting than we figured it would. The comedian-slash-actor was definitely interested in the project but he was also interested in Candy, which complicated things. Every time Candy tried to schedule a meeting it seemed to be contingent on a date.

Since I signed the nondisclosure agreement I can't say exactly who he was. I'll just narrow it down by saying he was one of the young, short, tubby, white comics, but not the nebbishy one, more the aggressive one. His production company had scored a studio deal and they were throwing money, so far with nothing to show for it.

The comedian/actor definitely wanted to add that second slash to his resume and become a C/A/Director and the bonus in my project was the possibility of working with Black comedians/actors, apparently a glaring omission from his resumé.

None of this meant that we—the C/A and I—would actually meet, but after three readings, two by interns and one by staff, we had reached Marshall, the C/A's head guy. If Marshall said yes, we were in. Or, as the C/A put it, with one of his signature lines, "I'm partial to Marshall." Marshall was a busy boy. He set up and canceled two meetings in February. But before he went on vacation set a definite and what he called a "pro forma" meeting for March 15. "I like what I've read," he told Candy. I needed to hear that. I wasn't selling blood yet, but I had to rewrite two student scripts and picked up an Intro class at L.A.C.C. to make my March rent.

It was a nice building on Beverly, not too far from Jar, you could lunch at the Farmers Market with a little effort.

I tried to figure out why I felt so much older than everyone else in the room, and I counted the differences. 1) I was the only one with a satchel or anything to carry paperwork. 2) The only one not wearing tinted lenses indoors. 3) The only one not working on a phone or a tablet. 4) The only one without a cap. And of course there was the big one. 5) The only one actually old. Everyone else was under thirty. The lone exception to this was the kind secretary/add asst Julie, who might have been closer to my age and was the house mother common to young male production offices. Julie had just brought me my second Smart Water with such solicitude that I was made to feel even older.

I couldn't quite figure out the workspace. No one seemed to be assigned a specific desk and there were boxes stacked in the hall. I asked the guy on the sofa nearest me, "So, are you guys still moving in?"

He looked up briefly. "Uhh. No." And went back to his text.

I've got a surprise for Marshall. It's jumping the gun, but in the last month I've worked out the first act, actually, almost the first fifty pages of the script. In hand, and it's brilliant. I've got the pitch and he can hear it if he wants, but if he reads the first ten pages and doesn't buy it on the spot, he's nuts.

I haven't shown these pages to Oscar or anyone, but when you know, you know. At my feet, a uniformed guy is working his way across the floor, lifting the carpet and gathering taped-down extension cord until he reaches the copy machine in the corner. He coils the cord atop the machine, hands a clipboard for Julie to sign, and then wheels the machine down the hallway.

Across from me another bright young intern has turned his cap backward to do FaceTime with an older man who seems to be snowbound. "Hey, Uncle Jim, thanks for the check. I'm moving back to Pittsburgh for the summer. Yeah. We lost our deal."

Why am I here? That cosmic question has just gotten real specific.

It's about then that Marshall breezes in and poor dear Julie who's been midway between crying and offering me another Smart Water has to tell him, "Dale Davis is here to see you."

The range of emotions that cross Marshall's face goes from: *Didn't I cancel?* to *Why didn't I cancel?* to *Where is my gun?* But he recovers, shakes my hand, says, "Give me just a minute to settle in and we'll get started."

Marshall whirls away. I look around at all the bright young faces staring at their phones and tablets—completely unfazed. They'll all land on their feet, except maybe Julie, who *is* bringing me another Smart Water and tearing up.

"Thanks," I demur, holding up my still-full bottle. She puts it on the table in front of me. "For later."

Marshall bustles out and guides me to his office, which has an impressive view of the parking lot and many blown-up stills of the gummy-faced C/A in action. I understand that Marshall is willing to let the geezer do his full dog and pony show, the complete pitch. I don't need it. I really don't need it. My hour with Candy let me know I still have entertainment value.

"Can I get you a water?" Marshall says as he pulls out my chair.

I'm still standing. "Let's save some time. You're about to close up shop, right?"

Marshall collapses into his ergonomic device and curls his feet around the pedestal. "Shit, who told you?"

I sit down. "The Xerox guy."

"Damn it." Marshall scrubs his eye sockets with the heels of his hands and bangs his temples. I can see why the C/A likes him, it's one of the more convincing imitations of sincerity that I've seen lately. "The thing is, I really like your treatment. I think you're on to something. Wherever we land. Or, wherever I land, if that's the case. I want to bring you in."

I know my moment. I stand, reach across and shake hands. "That would be great." I show him my water.

I'm halfway to the door when Marshall cries, "Wait, Wait . . . you gotta get a shirt. Everybody gets a shirt. I'm very proud of these."

He's back a minute later, holding up a T-shirt. It's a replica of the posters adorning the office. The image is Magritte's non-pipe and below in curled script:

This is not a Pipe Dream
Dadaist Productions

Marshall hands it to me. "All we had left is a small. But it doesn't matter, man. They're collectible. Frame it. They're already up on eBay."

Julie is gone from the desk and the boys don't look up as I leave. I toss the shirt into the back seat of the Saturn and try to decide. Candy wanted me to call but that is a call I don't want to make. Not today. I'm on Beverly, less than ten minutes from Cedars-Sinai, and I haven't seen Gus this week. It's on the way home. If I can score street parking, I'll stop.

My first bit of luck for the day. Free parking on a side street, so I'm not out ten bucks for Cedars parking. When I get to the South Tower, though, I can't find Gus. He's not in his room, and nobody will tell me if they've moved him or if he's gone to hospice care. I'm not family so no information can be provided.

Back at home, Esmerelda is sitting on my steps, and one look tells me everything that Cedars wouldn't. She's been crying.

She gets up. "Hi, Dale. My dad died this morning." She starts to cry and pretty much collapses in my arms. I get her inside and make some yerba buena tea. She's been here most of the day, handing out envelopes to the tenants, explaining about the rent increases and her father's last wishes. I was the only one left.

The tea revives her a little. "You know what's weird?" Esmerelda says. "I knew my dad was dying. My mom died seven years ago. This morning when they told me, the first thing I thought—I'm an orphan. I'm thirty-three but I'm an orphan. What's that about? Anyway. I just want to warn you. I don't know what's going to happen. My dad wrote it all out on the rents, but now we don't know what happens on his pension—and my brother and sister are being hard-asses. They want more money. They might even want to sell. I think they got a lawyer. I have to go meet with them, but I wanted to tell you. My dad loved you." She got up to go.

"Thanks for the warning. Hard times ahead. Maybe I'll utilize Gus's dicho."

"What's that?"

"A folk saying. Down in Nicaragua, whenever Gus got stuck, when he was really up against it, he'd tell the Nica crew, '*¡Al Dios rogando y con el mazo dando!*' Pray to God, then hit it with a hammer. Always made them laugh."

"I'll get you one of his hammers," she says.

After Esmerelda leaves I sit down at the computer and do what I need to do, one email to Candy, no details, just letting her know Dadaist Productions lost their studio deal, which might have some effect on whatever charm stubble boy possessed. If she has anyone else in mind, she knows where to find me.

The second email is to Oscar Grunfeld, and in this one I wave the white flag. *Breakfast at Du-pars?* is the heading. *I'm in trouble* is the message. *Du-pars* meant I didn't want Jaime Rubin to know, since he'd been 86'ed from the joint.

Oscar replies within a minute. *I know. Sol's been bragging. I always enjoy Du-pars. I always enjoy your company. See you at ten tomorrow.*

Beware the Ides of March. There was now only the evening and a long night to fill. I knew how to do that. My credit cards can't afford the recompense that this day and Gus deserve, but there's a way around. I have a deal with Roger over at the Tattle Tale Inn on Sepulveda, reserved for the worst nights. I help Roger with his scripts, in exchange he lets me tend bar. He'd let me sit and drink, but I've told him I'd rather tend bar. "The deepest human need," I explained, "is to feel useful, a requirement not met by my present occupation." Tonight in particular I need the company, and since I pour with a heavy hand I'll make friends, friends and tips and all my jokes will be funny. The Dylan Thomas line always gets them: "I'm a drinker with a writing problem." Roger always likes to talk movies after closing. Movies and ex-wives. He has three. We'll get through it.

Du-pars, serving really good breakfasts since 1938 at the Farmers Market, Third and Fairfax. Oscar had his first meeting with his agent here in the early '50s. It's dim inside and the effect is soothing, what I need on three hours' sleep.

Oscar, hyper-punctual as always for these occasions, is in place, ensconced in his favorite red leather booth, attended by our favorite waitress, Sandy G. My coffee is waiting.

As I slide into the booth, she takes away my menu. "Let me guess," she intones, pointing to Oscar, "the legendary buttermilk pancakes, extra syrup for Oski," and nodding to me, "and the eggs Benedict, both traditional and Florentine, for Davis."

Eggs Benedict both traditional and Florentine means I get both Canadian bacon and spinach under my poached egg with hollandaise. It is nice to be remembered.

Time to sigh. I've been dreading this moment.

Oscar produces an envelope and hands it to me. "A temporary solution."

Inside is a check for ten thousand dollars. "That is a gift," Oscar says, "not a loan." Not a solution either, but a stop-gap and a very Oscar thing to do. "It gives me pleasure," Oscar says, "and you may not remember, but there was a time you helped greatly on a couple of scripts I was stuck on. I think of this as seed money."

"Actually," I tell him, "it's bearing fruit. I'm a third of the way through a full script for *The Thing* . . . My working title is *Youngblood*."

"That's a shift," Oscar says.

"I'm excited," I say, and I am. "I'm writing four, five pages a day and it feels really good. I'm a third of the way through."

"Then this is money well spent," Oscar says. "You're in love again."

Dear Oscar. He has a way.

"I had a thought," Oscar says. "Bring me those Bukowski books. I think I have a buyer."

"What?"

"Sol Haverstein is a member of my synagogue. What he did was not just. Not Solomon-like. I'm going to talk to him about that."

This is not the first time that Oscar has summoned F. Scott Fitzgerald's famous line, "The test of a first-rate intelligence is the ability to hold two opposed ideas in mind at the same time and still retain the ability to function." But with Oscar, it's more like four—a confirmed theoretical socialist in the body of a practical functioning capitalist who is also, as far as I can tell, the leading Macher of his synagogue and the least religious man I know. Which is to say, Reb may be doing a lot of scrubbing on those books.

Sandy G approaches, orange juices in hands, plates arrayed on each arm, toasts on wrists, entrees on elbows, the Durga of Du-pars. Plates magically descend, levitate, and come to rest, perfectly positioned, just as they would if that multi-armed deity were in front of us.

"Buen provecho," Sandy G says, *"Saha wa hana,"* and ankles away. The second one, if I remember right, is Jordanian. It's a moment here regulars wait for. She has a rotating stock of gustatory phrases, Armenian and Arabic, Yiddish to Zulu, all essentially saying, enjoy your food. We fade to breakfast.

THE HARVEST

fiction by UCHE OKONKWO

from A KIND OF MADNESS (Tin House)

When come Ye ministries first opened its doors on Igoke Street, just a short walk from Alfonso's own church, Alfonso's wife would, every few days, bring to his ears some fresh, searing detail about the pastor or the services and watch his face, waiting for a reaction.

"I heard they share jollof rice to their members every Sunday. Can you imagine?"

"Alfonso, they now have two Sunday services at that church. Soon they'll start putting canopies in the street for the overflow!"

It was from Inimfon's lips that Alfonso learned that the pastor of the new church was nicknamed Daddy Too Much, because he had countless SUVs and an American wife. "They say the first time the pastor and his wife met, she fell flat on her face; she couldn't even stand to shake his hand because of the power of his anointing." After glancing at Alfonso's stony face, she added, "People will believe anything. Can you imagine?"

But as the months passed, Inimfon's reports slowly gave way to a silence that was broken only to carry out the necessary logistics of their daily lives. And so that morning, they were both quiet as they prepared for church, their separate routines long established. Alfonso stood before the cracked mirror on their bedroom wall and considered putting on a jacket and a tie. It was a cool morning, but he knew that by afternoon, heat and humidity would be clutching at his neck, causing rivers of sweat to flow down his back. He buttoned up his shirt and tucked it into slightly oversized pants that he held up with a peeling belt. When he marched out to his old car holding his King James Bible and sermon notes—today he'd be preaching Part III of his Unlocking Divine Abundance series—Inimfon was already seated in the passenger's side. Alfonso settled in beside her and turned on the engine. He glanced at Inimfon. She was not wincing at the engine's angry rattling like she often did, nor was she dabbing at sweat on her face or fanning her neck with an old church flyer. She did not lean forward to fiddle with the air conditioner, which hadn't worked in years.

Before her reign of silence began, Inimfon had mentioned that if you stepped inside the new church without a jacket, you could catch a fever from the sheer power of the AC. She'd delivered this information on a Sunday six months ago, while she helped set up for service in the assembly hall of the primary school in Obalende, where Alfonso's church met. Standing with arms akimbo, she'd glared up at the lazy ceiling fans that spread warm, dusty air throughout the room. Again, Alfonso said nothing, and after an eternity of stillness, his wife had sighed. Alfonso imagined that sigh as a eulogy for dead dreams, and in that moment the entire weight of his failures came and sat on his shoulders like a yoke. That same Sunday, during the service, Alfonso had found himself announcing the start of a fundraising campaign, the first of its kind for his church, which he said would enable the church to acquire their own worship space. He'd called the campaign "Build Him a House."

Because the campaign had been divinely inspired, and certainly had nothing to do with the new church a few streets away, Alfonso had decided that the forty-two members of his congregation, none of whom were particularly well-off, would somehow be able to raise the millions they'd need to buy land in the Lekki area, where their church was destined to stand. God would work out the details in His mysterious ways. Alfonso had begun tailoring all of his sermons toward the same message—the negative consequences of a tight fist ("If your hand is closed, how can God put anything into it?") and the blessings that came from giving, and giving generously, to God and His causes. "And what greater cause can there be than to . . ." and Alfonso would bellow, "Say it with me!" and the church would say it with him—albeit with less and less enthusiasm each passing Sunday—"Build Him a House!" He'd also begun sending his members multiple text messages each week, with Bible quotes and reminders about God's love for cheerful givers.

Alfonso had pretended not to notice his membership numbers slowly dwindling, refused to acknowledge the empty spaces opening up where bodies used to warm the benches. Each time Inimfon presented him with the attendance numbers after a service, he would say the same thing he always said: "Glory be to God." Last Sunday, after his usual response, she'd asked, quite loudly, "Glory be to God for only seven people?" She didn't wait for an answer, and as she turned away, her words burrowed under his skin.

It didn't help that his calls and texts to members who'd been absent for many Sundays remained unanswered. He was particularly bothered by Brother Ifeanyi, who had given some excuse about needing to prepare for an exam at school. The young man had been consistent with attendance for over a year, and Alfonso considered him a protégé of sorts and sometimes asked his opinion on sermons he was preparing, not because Alfonso needed guidance from a novice, but to make Brother Ifeanyi feel included.

Alfonso eased his car out of its parking spot between the cinder-block fence of the compound and his neighbor's Toyota. As he drove onto the street, his mouth was dry and his stomach cramped up. The last time he'd had only seven people at a Sunday service, he'd been a nervous young man preaching out of a roadside shed in Iyana Ipaja. It occurred to Alfonso that Inimfon's stories about the new church might have been her way of seeking communion, of voicing the shared fears lurking in the corners of their minds. He thought about reaching across to take her hand. He knew what it would feel like now: rough and callused from carrying them both, unlike when they were newlyweds, the light of his dreams still burning bright.

He had married Inimfon eight years ago for her faith in him, for how readily she'd gone to the places he had envisioned. Before they were married, she would sit in his congregation, week after week, and when he shared his prophecies for the future of his ministry, her hallelujahs were the loudest. He'd had no choice but to notice her. Her enthusiasm, the intensity of her gaze on him as he preached, bestowed upon her an alluring quality. Many Sundays, she would stay behind after service to chat, and with time she began to materialize right there with him when he saw himself leading the megachurch of his future, standing tall beside him in low heels and the old brown hat she wore every Sunday.

What had happened instead was that Inimfon, after she'd moved into his one-room face-me-I-face-you in Mushin and bemoaned the single backyard kitchen and fought nine other tenants over the shared bathrooms, decided that Alfonso's income from the church would not sustain them, and neither would the heavenly manna that he prophesied would rain down on them at any moment. When she'd suggested that

Alfonso get a job, he pointed out that he already had one. Harvesting the souls of men was full-time work—one could not serve God and mammon, didn't she know? Of course, Alfonso knew that some preachers had businesses or jobs outside of their churches, but he suspected that this, taking one's eye off the work of ministry, was a slow but sure path to corruption. Besides, he had no head for business, and his only qualification was his calling, which he'd dropped out of LAUTECH to answer—a decision he tried never to dwell on. He'd quoted scriptures to Inimfon about ravens bringing food to Elijah, given her sermons on supernatural provision. In the meantime, he'd said, they could make do with eating two small meals a day. The hunger might do their souls some good, sharpen their faith.

But Inimfon's faith had not held. She'd taken a loan from her sister and paid for a shed near Mushin Market, where she cooked and sold food to traders and commuters. When they were not at church, Inimfon was at her shed, chopping and pounding and frying. Whenever Alfonso offered help, like a good husband, she turned him down. "Save your strength for the church," she'd say with a voice that betrayed nothing.

Soon after Inimfon had begun her food business, Alfonso, desperate to match her achievement, had made a list of ten of the biggest churches in Lagos. He would, he'd decided, present these churches with the opportunity to have him guest-preach a sermon. It didn't even have to be during a Sunday service, a weekday one would do. Once those megachurch pastors heard his preaching—he had recorded one of his best sermons and made it into CDs—they would be falling over themselves to host him in their air-conditioned sanctuaries. Preaching at a big church would put his name in people's mouths. They would come to his services at Tender Lights Primary School, Obalende, to seek him out, the old wooden benches, the heat, the mildew spots in the ceiling all hearkening back to a time when preachers of the gospel didn't need the embellishments of cushioned chairs, expensive audiovisual equipment, and one-hundred-member choirs in matching robes.

Alfonso had found that the road to a megachurch pastor's office was narrower than the road to heaven. He was met by assistants with identical crisp suits and touch-screen tablets, who politely informed him of their bosses' impossible schedules. In a few churches, he'd managed to secure hurried meetings with junior pastors who educated him about their ministries' structures and hierarchies and asked stupid questions, like "What Bible school did you attend?" and "Who have you served under?" He crossed his legs and told each of them how he'd received his calling: when he was a university student, the guest preacher at a ministry event had singled him out from the crowd, waved him to the altar, and prophesied that he, Alfonso, would become a great harvester for the kingdom of God. Alfonso watched the pastors' eyes glaze over. They thanked him for his interest and handed him pamphlets about their School of Ministry, their Discipleship Training—whatever they called it. Where was their fancy school of ministry when he was dropping out of LAUTECH to win souls from the streets of Ogbomoso and all the way to Lagos? Where was their discipleship training when he was preaching in taxis and danfos and molues, getting cursed at by weary commuters?

Inimfon had just hired her second server at the eatery when Alfonso saw the newspaper advertisement for the Higher Level International Ministers' Conference. Alfonso hadn't recognized any of the names on the lineup of speakers, but that was okay, better even—these were the people doing God's work without making noise, without trying to appropriate any of the glory for themselves. The registration fee, inclusive of conference materials, meals, and four nights' accommodation in Akure, was expensive, yes, but the service of God demanded sacrifice. Didn't Inimfon want him to fulfill his calling? She'd given him the money, and he'd called her First Lady in the Making, promising that when they broke ground on their church building, he would remind her of this moment.

Instead, Alfonso had returned early from the conference emptied and hollowed out, with a bitter taste in his mouth that would linger for years. The "conference" was more like a trade fair, with ministers hawking their books, recorded sermons, healing oils, and holy waters. All the talk sessions and grass-to-grace testimonies ended with a call to action, to buy something or join something. He'd been expecting a prayer revival, a place where he would be buoyed by a fresh anointing, a new revelation from the Word. Still, Alfonso had stayed, hoping to find something that would make the experience, and Inimfon's investment, worth it. On the third day, a sweaty fellow in a velvet suit sidled up to Alfonso and handed him a card with a name, phone number, and the title *Solutions Supplier* printed in purple ink. When Alfonso asked what exactly he supplied, the man leaned in and whispered, his hot breath fanning Alfonso's neck, "My brother, any healing you want to happen in your church, I can arrange it for you. Blindness, deafness, cripple, craze, even HIV, mò lè hook ẹ up." Alfonso left the conference that day and avoided Inimfon's questions when he got home. He'd told himself there had to be a right way to achieve mega-church status, a godly way, without salesmen and arrangers of miracles. He would pray and fast and wait. Alfonso had a calling, and God would prove Himself in His time.

While Alfonso had waited, Inimfon had acquired more staff and expanded her eatery, upgrading from sand floors to concrete, and from no walls to plywood boards. She replaced squeaky wooden benches with plastic chairs and tables and bought standing fans to cool her customers while they ate. She had less and less energy for his waning prophecies about their future. Her amens and hallelujahs grew weak like old dishwater. And when she prayed, she no longer spent many minutes calling God by all of His names. She deployed her prayers like arrows at a target, as though she expected God to understand she could no longer afford to spend too much time on her knees. Sometimes, Alfonso grew angry on God's behalf, and was tempted to point out that everything she had achieved had come from God and not her own effort or wisdom. But whenever he opened his mouth to rebuke Inimfon, a twinge of doubt would cause him to pause and look around him at the one-bedroom apartment they'd moved into, with its own kitchen and bathroom inside, paid for by Inimfon's sweat, and shame would spread in his chest, taking up so much space that there was little room for breath.

Sometimes, in the early hours of morning when his sleep was interrupted by an inchoate unease, Alfonso wondered whether the reason Inimfon adhered to her strict regimen of daily contraceptives even as their sex life withered was not, as she claimed, because they couldn't afford to care for a child, but because Inimfon was wary of the fleshly bond that a child would represent, the added difficulty of extricating herself from him. But he'd never challenged her on this, afraid to have his suspicions confirmed. The closest he'd come was making a joke once about how they should have children so they could increase the numbers at his church. Inimfon hadn't even cracked a smile.

Alfonso slowed the car and took the exit for Obalende; in a few minutes they would arrive at his church. He tried to remind himself that money and numbers were not the most important things for a minister. He took pride in knowing all the members of his church as individuals, knowing what kept their heads from resting easy at night. He was at his best, his most unimpeachable, when he went on his knees on behalf of his small flock, whether it was to ask God to ease the trouble in the Okories' tumultuous marriage, or to pray for healing for Sister Remi, who had hypertension, or to give thanks with young Faaji, who disappeared every once in a while for weeks on end and resurfaced with a large offering and vague testimonies about God prospering his work. Alfonso was especially protective of Brother Ifeanyi, with his rough edges and overexposure to Ajegunle's hard streets. It had taken some time but Alfonso, with God's help, of course, had slowly tamed Brother Ifeanyi. He no longer turned up in church proudly hungover and showing off the bumps and bruises from his latest fistfight, or spent what little money he had gambling on 247Moni, or wore his ripped jeans so low they exposed the swell and split of his buttocks. Alfonso was proud of his work. The first time he'd met Brother Ifeanyi, the young man had been caught stealing a mobile phone from an electronics store where Alfonso had gone to hand out his church flyers. The shop owner was holding on to Brother Ifeanyi's shirt collar with one hand, brandishing her phone with the other as she threatened to call the police and have him locked up for life. Only Alfonso's pleas, delivered on his knees along with Brother Ifeanyi's, and his promise to personally see to the young man's rehabilitation, had convinced the shop owner to let Brother Ifeanyi go. From that day on, Alfonso had taken responsibility for Brother Ifeanyi, making sure he stopped skipping his lectures at Yaba Tech, and that he cut all ties with the girl with whom he'd been fornicating, the same girl he'd been trying to impress with the phone he'd attempted to steal.

But now, Alfonso worried that his work might be coming undone, given Brother Ifeanyi's long absence. Without Alfonso's influence, it would be too easy for the young man to slide back into his self-destructive ways.

"Brother Ifeanyi hasn't been answering my calls," Alfonso said to Inimfon, without looking away from the road.

She shrugged. "People are busy these days."

"Too busy to come to church or send a text message?" Alfonso said. "No, no, he needs to do better. If he's absent again today, I'll go and visit him after service."

Inimfon said nothing.

* * *

Alfonso parked in front of the two-story building that housed Tender Lights Primary School. When he'd approached the headmaster about using the school's assembly hall for his church services, he'd meant for it to be only a temporary arrangement. Now, a decade later, Alfonso walked to the school gates with heavy feet, Inimfon's shadow falling across him and partially shielding him from the sun. The school building, with its ash-gray walls grimy from children's fingers, and windows hanging askew from their frames, had become too familiar. Even with his eyes closed, he'd know how to avoid the broken bits of concrete ground within the compound that collected rainwater, how to position himself behind the lectern, to hold it just so because too much weight would cause it to lean to the right.

Alfonso pushed open the gate and knocked on the wall of the plywood shack beside it. The door creaked open and a hand held out the key to the assembly hall, the school's gateman not needing visual confirmation of Alfonso's presence after the clattering of his car's engine. They walked to the assembly hall, Alfonso wondering if Inimfon felt the same weight that he did pushing down on him. He stopped outside the hall, key in hand, but made no move to open the door. He could hear the unasked question forming on Inimfon's lips. He held out the key to her.

"Start setting up. I'll be back."

She took the key with a puzzled frown. "Where are you going?"

Alfonso hurried out through the school gate, fleeing his wife's gaze.

* * *

Alfonso turned left at the end of Ferguson Road. The streets were peaceful, as they tended to be this early on a Sunday morning. It had rained in the night, but the air was losing its coolness as the sun rose higher, bathing tired old buildings in a surreal light. Alfonso could almost ignore the FanYogo and Gala wrappers and the Power Horse cans that littered the street and clogged the roadside gutters. The abandoned vehicles on the side of the road, long ago stripped of their doors and fixtures, faded into soft colors on the edge of his vision.

It felt like ages ago that he'd first come across the demolition on Igoke Street. With his car at the mechanic's, he'd taken a danfo that carried him past the site. When he noticed the empty skyline where a cluster of old apartment buildings used to stand, he played a guessing game with himself, wondering what would be erected once the rubble was cleared away. It left him with a strange melancholia; a feeling that, like these buildings, his entire being could be wrecking-balled out of existence with a single stroke. He knew the day would come when whatever structure arose in place of the fallen ones would feel like it had always stood there, everything so utterly replaceable.

Alfonso hesitated as he approached Igoke Street. He thought about turning around, retracing his steps back to Ferguson and the safety of Tender Lights. But there was something more menacing about the spectre of the unseen.

As Alfonso neared the former demolition site, he could make out a white, dome-shaped structure and, the closer he got, the larger it loomed. Beside the dome stood a billboard with the smiling faces of Apostle Goodwill O. Ofobrukueta (aka Daddy Too Much) and First Lady Lois Ofobrukueta, her lips a slash of red, gold jewelry dangling from her ears, and blond hair framing a pale face. Alfonso had been prepared for this Daddy Too Much to have Jheri-curled hair down to his shoulders and a shiny robe—a ridiculous picture to go with his nickname. But this was a face stellar in its ordinariness, with a neatly trimmed beard and a low haircut. The apostle was dressed in a white suit that matched his wife's. Alfonso forced his feet to carry him forward, toward the dome, until he was standing before a high white wall with the words Come Ye Global Ministries embossed onto it in gold letters.

Alfonso swallowed past the dryness in his mouth and headed for the gates. He pushed on the pedestrian entrance, not truly believing that such an imposing thing would succumb to his touch. The gate swung open silently to reveal ground paved with interlocking concrete tiles in gray and maroon. The dome turned out to be an enormous freestanding marquee reinforced with glass and steel. At the top of the marquee's entrance, Daddy Too Much and his wife stared down from a large banner, both of them wearing bright smiles, the words *Welcome Home* printed across their torsos in triumphant font.

Voices seemed to be coming from inside the marquee. This early, the only people in church would be workers and volunteers helping to set up, and perhaps some of the church's leaders. Alfonso followed the voices.

As soon as he stepped inside the dome, goose pimples studded his skin. Along the walls, large floor-standing air conditioners spewed clouds of freezing air. Elaborate chandeliers made of glass and gold and crystal, and swaths of silky fabric, hung from the ceiling, hiding what he imagined would be the bars and bolts that held up the roof. The room was divided in half by a red carpet that ran all the way to an altar, where tall vases stood bursting with flowers. The altar also featured a shiny pulpit made of polished glass and, behind it, a row of overstuffed armchairs in red and gold upholstery. Yet another banner, this one behind the altar, displayed an image of the Apostle and his First Lady in matching outfits.

The room bustled with activity—a small group of people held hands, bouncing on their feet and shouting prayers up toward heaven. Others were covering the chairs for the congregation with protective fabric. Young women in high heels, blazers that looked sharp enough to cut glass, and long hair extensions that swayed with their every step floated between the rows, placing bulletins and offering envelopes on the seats. Alfonso shook his head. Of course, these were the kinds of people who would be drawn to a church like this: sharp dressers, attractive to the eye but empty on the inside. All shine, no substance.

Alfonso felt a hand on his arm. He looked up at the face of its owner, and his mouth fell open. Brother Ifeanyi glanced around the room before guiding Alfonso toward the exit. Outside the marquee, Brother Ifeanyi avoided Alfonso's eyes. Alfonso assessed the man before him, top to bottom. He looked like an entirely new person in shiny black shoes, dress pants, and a navy-blue blazer.

Alfonso's eye was drawn to the tag hanging from a lanyard around Brother Ifeanyi's neck.

"You're an usher? When did you start coming here?" Alfonso asked.

Before Brother Ifeanyi could respond, the pedestrian gate swung open and a woman walked in. As she passed them, Alfonso locked eyes with her for a second before she looked away.

"Sister Boma!" Alfonso called out. Sister Boma quickened her steps and disappeared into the freezing marquee. Alfonso spun back to Brother Ifeanyi. "How many of you are here?"

"Just me and Sister Boma," Brother Ifeanyi said, still not looking at Alfonso.

Alfonso didn't know whether to believe him. He could be lying to end the conversation quickly, to get him to leave. But that wasn't about to happen. Brother Ifeanyi, more than any other member of his church, owed him an explanation.

"I can understand if the others just leave like that. But you, ehn, Ifeanyi?"

Brother Ifeanyi stared at a spot on Alfonso's right shoulder. "Pastor Al, I'm finishing school next year, and things are hard. Is there anybody in your church that can give me a good job after I graduate?"

"Have you forgotten that if not for me, you'd be graduating inside prison?"

Alfonso regretted the words as soon as he said them. Still, the image of Brother Ifeanyi on the day they'd first met, the boy in torn jeans and a ragged T-shirt, on his knees begging to be rescued, was sharp in his memory. Never mind the sleek clothes he was now sporting, a pathetic future had awaited the boy before Alfonso's intervention. It was Alfonso who deserved an apology.

Brother Ifeanyi broke the silence. "I can never forget how you helped me. But, Pastor Al, I need something different now."

"Yes, you need connections, right?" Alfonso sneered. "You need fraudsters like your Daddy Too Much who sell miracles and blessings, and suck people dry. But I don't blame them; I blame their followers, people like you. All you people care about is money and glory."

Brother Ifeanyi's mirthless laughter caught Alfonso by surprise. "What about you? Every single Sunday with your Build Me a House."

"It's Build *Him* a House!"

"Whatever," Brother Ifeanyi said. His dismissive tone grated on Alfonso, caused his face to burn with anger. "But since everybody is building houses, who should I listen to? You, or the man of God that built this place and filled it up, times two, in a year?"

"That's what you have to say to me?" Alfonso said, his voice rising. "After I treated you like a son, after everything I—"

Brother Ifeanyi looked around him, like he was embarrassed to be anywhere near Alfonso. "Pastor Al, please, I have work to do. Our first service is starting soon."

Brother Ifeanyi hurried away, and Alfonso thought about running after him, ripping that lanyard from his neck, stuffing it down his throat. But the protective heat of his anger was already fading, leaving him colder than when he'd walked into the dome. He fumbled for his collar and undid the top button, but the tightness in his throat persisted. He felt foolish, standing there by himself like an abandoned lover, and so he forced his feet to move toward the gate.

Outside the church compound, Alfonso's eyes drifted upward to the billboard with the Apostle and his First Lady. He imagined Daddy Too Much preaching a powerful sermon to Alfonso's own congregation against being unequally yoked with failure: "Your God is not poor, so why should your pastor be? How can you be guided to prosperity by a pauper?" He saw his members' brows furrow in concentration, heads nodding along, mouths amening in holy agreement. He saw Inimfon in that congregation, freshly enlightened, in a new church hat with ornate feathers that reached for the heavens.

* * *

Inimfon was wiping the lectern with a rag. She spared Alfonso only a glance as he appeared in the doorway, but how he must look to her, the complete opposite of the dreams he'd sold her.

On his walk back to Tender Lights he'd mulled over Brother Ifeanyi's words. "Build Me a House," Brother Ifeanyi had said. A mistake, or a pointed accusation? Alfonso had become unrecognizable to himself.

Maybe the visiting preacher's prophecy all those years ago was a lie, mere theatrics. Or maybe Alfonso would indeed do great things, but they would not be projected from massive screens strategically positioned in a freezing church building the size of a football stadium. Maybe he was made for fellowship with a small community where he knew the people by name and could nurture their individual gifts, where they weren't a massive faceless crowd. Could he win back his runaway congregation? And Inimfon. If he put a new vision on the table, would she stay?

Alfonso took another step into the assembly hall, toward Inimfon. He didn't know how to form the words he knew he should say to her, and so he tried to form his body, the entirety of his being, into a penance—for the smell of dust in the air, the thick cobwebs hanging high up in the ceiling, the cement floor whose shine had long died, for Inimfon's secondhand gray skirt suit and the battered hat she'd worn every Sunday since she first walked through those very doors. Alfonso knew he could never be like the Daddy Too Muches of this world—he'd never been the kind of man who could go to America and pluck a wife like she had been cultivated just for him, and he would never be the kind of preacher who would amass the power to bulldoze long-standing structures so he could have a place. He had to tell Inimfon this, tell her something. But they had a service to prepare for. He found a second rag and proceeded to wipe benches.

* * *

When it was 8:00 AM, Alfonso positioned himself behind the lectern and waited for the door to swing open. After a few minutes, tired of standing still, he began pacing the length of the hall, and did so for the entire thirty minutes of Sunday school while Inimfon sat quietly. Nobody showed up. Alfonso reminded himself that it was not uncommon for members to skip Sunday school and turn up only for the main service. But by 9:20 it was still just him and Inimfon in the room.

The silence stretched on for so long, Alfonso thought it would snap. "We should start the service," he said. "The Bible says that where two or three are gathered in His name . . ."

Inimfon shook her head. "Alfonso, there's nobody here."

Alfonso stepped away from the lectern and joined Inimfon on the bench where she sat. It creaked under their combined weight.

"I went to see that new church," Alfonso said, without looking at Inimfon. "Sister Boma was there . . . Brother Ifeanyi."

"I've been trying to tell you."

This was the time to acknowledge all the things she'd been trying to tell him, and to tell her the things he needed to say, things he needed to repent for—his silences and resentments, the shadow that his pride and ego had cast over their lives.

When he finally opened his mouth, it was to make a flaccid joke, one rendered sour by its proximity to truth. "Maybe I should come and be a serving boy at your restaurant"—he gave a weak laugh—"since I don't have members anymore." He hoped Inimfon would smile, respond with a counter-joke, and then some reassurance, something blandly benign, like "It is well" or "God is in control." Her answer was a noncommittal "Hmm."

Alfonso wondered why it was so much easier to talk to an unseen God than to the person beside him, made of flesh and blood, like him. But people were capricious, and prayer was a shield. He would ask God to soften Inimfon, make her recognize his essential goodness and the repentance in his heart, without him having to grovel or debase himself before her. Alfonso bowed his head and closed his eyes. He didn't move when he felt the air shift beside him, but his heart sang with gratitude; Inimfon was getting on her knees to join him in prayer.

Alfonso heard the door creak, and when he opened his eyes he was alone. He found Inimfon minutes later, seated in the car, her hat tossed to the floor of the back seat. He got in beside her and turned the key in the ignition, filling the space between them with shaking.

LIKE MOWING THE GRASS

by BRUCE BEASLEY

from THE HUDSON REVIEW

The fact is the sweetest dream that labor knows.
—Robert Frost, "Mowing"

Fed up with my angel-ridden, Latinate dirges,
my sophomore poetry professor kept telling me
to write about something more ordinary and at hand, like
mowing the grass. Instead of elegies for my mother
who'd died suddenly a few months before,
always mowing the grass was my prescription.
He wanted it plainspoken, monosyllabic,
backyardly. Certainly not
the lines *I'd* been writing, like
"lassitudes of opulent lamentation."

"You think I'm too dumb to know
what existentialism is,"
my high school principal once said to me.
"Well, I know what existentialism means:
you get to go out in the back yard
and do whatever you want."
—Well, the front yard
works even better, I almost said.

I knew Camus
said why we don't commit suicide

was the only question worth asking.
I wanted to ask
why my father had mailed in life insurance papers,
driven hours to Glennville where he grew up
the day he tried to kill himself
a year before he died at 48, why
my mother—post-breast-cancer, post-DTs—
had followed him at 50, why I didn't, but
poems, I learned, drew
on things more urgently at hand
like ridding the garden of its weeds, suppressing
again and again the lawn's ambitions to grow.

So reading Rilke's Elegies aloud
to the accompaniment of Chopin's Funeral March,
I set out to summon a massive
passion for lawnmowing, its chop-cries, spat gravel.
But the grass couldn't *just* be grass, the weeds just weeds,
nor could the poem get "weighed down by ideas"
so you had to let the monosyllables and concrete
images only whisper what you meant.

(Why *concrete*? I always wondered.
I had a lawn mower whose motor forgot
how to stop, so I learned to cut it off
by slamming its blade onto a concrete strip
till the spark-collision of iron
against pavement gave it a violent
kind of choke-stop.) "My long scythe whispered,"
Frost said in "Mowing" (the only mowing-the-grass
poem I could find), "the earnest love that laid the swale in rows."
But not *my* mower blade, ground down
a quarter inch further by concrete each time
it had to quit hacking down the swale.

I tried for decasyllabic monosyllables, Anglo-
Saxon, angel-expunged, wrote "the cord-yank's
gag," aimed for more *swale* and slashed my line
"Where the wine of the unsinned blood slept,"
more motor-shutdown *whine* and less

sin-purified Father and Son Eucharist-blood, fewer
cherubim and more like the tagline REAP MORE LEISURE
WITH A WHIRLWIND SABRE.
Tried
to grind the clumps of ideation down
into metaphor's tamed and palliating
mystification: Frost's green
snake sneaked right in from Eden.

—Cure me
of thinking, or let me go in the unmowed
front yard and do what I want, like the whine
of the Whirlwind Sabre choking
on what it cut. My friend's mother called her
"the first pancake"—she was the oldest child—because
"you always have to throw out the first pancake."
My friend said it with an air of resignation
like that was just a *fact*, inalterable and blunt.

—"This is constant, hard work,"
said a *Jerusalem Post* op-ed
this spring of the recurrent labor
of re-razing the Gaza Strip with bombs,
"just like mowing your front lawn.
If you fail to do so, weeds go wild
and snakes begin to slither around in the brush."
The love that lay the swale
lays on the streets of Gaza City
a thousand airstrikes
in a month. Sixty-six children killed.
"There was smoke coming out
of my children's mouths."
"Imagine seeing your children's eyes
outside their heads."
"I had a family. Each had a dream.
It all disappeared in one second."
The land was ours before we were the land's
(Frost declaimed at JFK's inauguration).
Gaza was the Gazans', before
Occupation and Siege and No-Go Zone,

before, without power most of the day,
among flattened skyscrapers, salty, stinking water,
a bombstrip 25 × 7 miles,
four million people were sequestered in.

I'm somewhat late with this assignment, Sir.
It's taken me awhile to see
such mowings as both ordinary and at hand, and
now it's hard to turn so leisurely away
from disaster to the existentialist
and concealed back yard
and its boustrophedonic perfect rows
of slice, red-rhododendron-sequestered-
in. There's no lassitude or opulence, no piped-in
Chopin Funeral March
for most lamentations. *The long scythe whispers*
Frost says (*What is it it whispers?*).
We know what it whispers, *why* it whispers:
the growl-choke of cord-yank and what's
lovingly lain in swale-rows of ruins that
because they won't just stay
chopped down to ground forever, get,
with the sweetest dream of facts and labor, mown,
and mown and mown and mown and mown and mown.

THIS IS YOU

fiction by TOMMY MOORE

from CHICAGO QUARTERLY REVIEW

You are Casey Malloy.

It's a new day! Get up. Put on the boxer shorts, black cargo pants, black T-shirt, and black baseball cap on the chair by the bed. Put socks on your feet. See the running shoes by your bedroom door.

Be Casey Malloy.

Smoke one tiny bong hit. It helps. Eat a banana. Drink a glass of water.

Parked below your apartment, there is a red 1984 Toyota pickup with construction racks. Find the keys to your red Toyota pickup hanging on a hook by the front door.

Start your car. All the presets are set to the classic rock station. Listen to classic rock.

Drive to the 7-Eleven on the corner of Victory and Vineland. Park. Dump yesterday's coffee from the refillable coffee mug in your cup holder. Go inside. Buy a one-liter bottle of Crystal Geyser. Fill your reusable coffee mug with coffee. Pay the cashier.

Now, take the 170 to the 5 and then the 118 west all the way to Chatsworth, the flower of the valley.

Get off at Topanga Boulevard and park in the shade under the overpass.

Underneath your seat is the first aid kit. Open it. Inside find a small blue container of ten-milligram tablets of diazepam, a pack of Winston Lights, an Altoids tin of pre-rolled joints, one small bottle of peppermint schnapps, eye drops, hand sanitizer, breath mints, chewable Tums. Split one diazepam in half, swallow it with some coffee. Light a smoke.

Drive to Earl M______'s at 34412 Clover Ct., Chatsworth, CA 91311.

The gate guard will wave you through. He knows you.

Park in Earl's driveway.

Brace yourself.

Go into the side door of the garage. It's unlocked.

Lift with your legs, not your back. Load (3) 30″ × 50″ black duffel bags, labeled "shoes," into the bed of your red 1984 Toyota pickup truck.

Drink some water. Eat one Tums. By 7:00 a.m., the sun will be shining and the valley will already be hot.

PUT ON YOUR GLOVES.

Load (3) black duffel bags labeled "pillows" into the truck bed.

Load (1) 30″ × 50″ black duffel bag labeled "scarves" into the truck. The zipper is broken. ARE YOUR GLOVES ON? DO NOT TOUCH any of the silky scarves with a naked hand. They are only washed at the end of the month. Wrap two bungee cords around the bag to keep it closed. There are bungee cords hanging from the wall of the garage.

Load (2) large rectangular, semiopaque plastic containers labeled "kitchen" into the truck.

Open container #1. See list of contents on the inside lid: two gallon jugs of "clear," one twelve-ounce bottle of "strawberry," 5 rolls of paper towels, 2 packs of baby wipes, 1 roll of heavy-duty kitchen trash bags, 1 box of black latex gloves, 2 large packs of hand-sanitizing wipes, 1 sixteen-ounce bottle of baby oil, 1 bottle of spray-on sunblock, 1 half-gallon milk bottle of "Earl's Pearl," 1 box of popsicle sticks, 1 roll of orange biohazard stickers. If anything is missing, restock from the metal cabinet on the far wall of the garage.

Container #2's contents are sex toys, scan over them. They aren't inventoried. There will be various dildos, vibrators, butt plugs, Ben Wa balls, ball gags, leather masks, whips, nylon rope, handcuffs. Just be sure there is a variety and that Earl's favorite floppy red dildo is onboard. ARE YOUR GLOVES ON? Close the lids tight.

Load the semiopaque plastic container labeled "Tunes" into the bed of your truck. Inside there is a binder of CDs and a boom box. Don't forget the tunes.

Wait in the driveway for Chad to show up. Chad shows up.

He checks the bed of your truck and the garage to see if everything is in order. He then gorks a good morning. He has worked with Earl for almost a decade. On your first day, you asked him how to wrap a California Sunbounce and he said, "Step one, kill yourself."

He's wary of you, you know it, but tell yourself that Chad has priorities and the riddle of Casey Malloy isn't one of them. Enthusiastically, load the cases of strobes, light stands, C-stands, Scrim Jims, sandbags, flags; the "clamp" crate, containing A-clamps, super-clamps, Mafers, Cardellinis, C41s, J-hooks; the apple boxes, extensions cords, FX fans, compact electric leaf blower, and adjustable rolling stool into Chad's white van. Chad may come to believe in you but still, he won't like you.

Earl doesn't want you in the house. Chad goes inside and brings out two camera bags. Don't offer to help him. After the camera bags are safely secured inside the van, Earl steps outside.

Earl has retinitis pigmentosa, tunnel vision. He also has a bad back and is lactose intolerant.

Earl rides with Chad in the van. Assume they're talking shit about you.

Hate them. Hate everyone you work with. It will make your day easier.

Don't try to follow Chad on the freeway. Take your time. Smoke a Winston Light. Check the call sheet for the Benedict Canyon address.

Make sure you are wearing the black baseball cap. You always wear that hat. Never take it off. When you arrive at the location, you will see Earl in front of the house. Say, "Hello, Earl!" His vision is getting worse every day and he won't immediately recognize you. He will engage you in small talk, ask you if you've lost weight, gained weight, when did you grow that mustache, why did you shave off your mustache. Laugh, "Good one, Earl!" and then pick some gear up and move it. He's self-conscious about being almost blind and he doesn't acknowledge that he can't recognize you but yes, he too will come to believe, believe in you, Casey Malloy.

If the makeup artist is Mara Cipriani, thank God. She only works when it's girl-on-girl.

Place the strobe lights, bounce, and negative fill per Chad's instructions. He meters the light while you fire the strobes. Adjust the output from the packs until everything is balanced and the key light is one-tenth of a stop overexposed.

Then, stand on the mark. Chad shoots a test Polaroid of you. Then, lie on the mark. Chad shoots another test of you. He takes the Polaroids to Earl. Notice they chuckle. The light isn't right, you reset the lights and adjust the output on the strobe packs. Chad shoots another Polaroid. You get the thumbs-up. Now, take Earl's rolling stool and put it where Chad was standing when he took the last test. Mark the floor with tape. Four Polaroids are taken of you on this setup. They leave these Polaroids lying about the set. COLLECT THEM. COLLECT THEM. Keep them in one of the large pockets of your cargo pants.

Why? Don't ask why. On average, over 100,000 people move to Los Angeles each year, chasing dreams.

Take a leftover plastic Vons shopping bag from craft service and put an orange biohazard sticker on it. Clamp the biohazard bag to a C-stand.

The talent arrives. There are two girls and a guy. Keep a safe distance, smile.

DO NOT LET THE TALENT TOUCH ANYTHING. Tell them if they want a snack from the craft service table, if they want to listen to a different CD, if they want a tissue, tell them you are here to help, tell them that you will get it for them. The last thing you want to do is to eat chips from a bag after they've had their hands in there, after their hands have been in each other's assholes, pussies, after their hands have been stroking cocks.

The first setup is girl-on-girl. They're friends. They are gentle with each other. They throw in a playful spank. It's a cum-free setup. The girls are in a good mood.

Earl stops shooting and calls for a "deal check." You check "the deal." Get down and take a good look. Is her pussy free of any white flecks, smidges, lint, etcetera? Hand her a baby wipe. DO NOT HAND HER THE WHOLE BOX. REMEMBER, DO NOT LET THEM TOUCH ANYTHING. She's done, hold open the biohazard bag. She tosses the wipe inside. Check "the deal" again. "The deal" is clean.

The morning has become a hot early afternoon and now there are flies. The talent can't shoo them away, that's your job. You stand just out of frame with the small electric leaf blower. Earl shouts, "Blow them out but don't fuck up the girls' hair!" Chad laughs.

Eat lunch.

Now, it's guy-on-girl inside, on the couch. Right before the shoot begins, the guy may go into a corner, just off set, and do something to his dick. Give him some space. Back on set, he will engage the girl (after asking permission) in some personal kink to get himself hard. While the makeup artist is applying the final touches to the girl, he may eat the girl out, or sniff her ass, or suck her toes, her tits. She will ignore his attention, she's somewhere else.

Then it begins. Keep the lube on an apple box, standing by. DO NOT MISPLACE THE LUBE. This is like watching animals fuck. You are aware of the smell and then you are not. They've been fucking for an hour. You've adjusted the lights twice and now they are in the third position. Earl calls for the lube. It's not on the apple box. You can't find the lube. Earl is yelling, "Where is the fucking lube." You go into "kitchen" container #1 and there you can only find strawberry. You show Chad. Chad says, "Earl, he's got the strawberry." Earl isn't happy. "She'll look like she's fucking bleeding. Where's the goddamn clear? Jesus fucking Christ. Find the lube! Find the motherfucking lube! You're killing the mood, asshole!" Look under the couch. There it is. You squeeze the lube into the talent's hands. He says, "Don't sweat it, dude, look, I'm still hard."

The pop shot is the last shot of the day. You stand just off camera with a roll of paper towels. She's disgusted but she doesn't let the camera see it. Earl stops shooting and hands Chad the camera. She leaps up and is lunging for you. Hold out the wad of paper towels. Point to the biohazard bag.

Break down all the gear. Load Chad's van first and then load up your truck. Sitting in your truck, in the Hollywood Hills, take a moment for yourself, smoke a joint, have a pull of peppermint schnapps, smoke a cigarette. Eat the Snickers Mini from craft service.

Drive home.

Walk inside your apartment. Hang your keys on the hook. Lock the door. Sit on your couch. Take the Polaroids out of your cargo pants pocket and put them in the album on the coffee table with the others. This is you, Casey Malloy, on a doggie bed. This is you, floating in a pool, laughing on a swing, standing in front of a fountain surrounded by banana palms and birds-of-paradise, this is you on a bearskin rug in front of raging fire, you on a wooden table in a wine cellar, on a leather couch, on a black silk bedspread. There you are, this is you, this is you, this is you.

ONE WRITER AGAINST OBLIVION

fiction by MARK BRAZAITIS

from PRIME NUMBER MAGAZINE

A Paper Presented by Peter Murray at the International Conference on the Written Word, Toronto, Ontario, Canada, June 14, 2012

Arnold Plutowsky was born in Cincinnati, Ohio, on January 6, 1940, and died in Sherman, Ohio, on January 22, 2000. The author of six books, including novels, works of poetry, and a pair of short story collections, one of which is unpublished, Plutowsky has no national reputation and, from what I've gathered during my exhaustive research, including interviews with Ohio booksellers past and present, only a miniscule state-wide reputation.

Inevitably I'm asked, "Why devote a paper, much less an entire dissertation, to Plutowsky?" I have a two-part answer, the first of which is my personal connection to Plutowsky via his great niece, my fiancée, Loretta. Professionally I have this response: Plutowsky is one of hundreds of twentieth-and twenty-first-century American authors—indeed, one of tens of thousands of American artists in a variety of fields, including classical music, visual arts, theater, and dance—who in the face of persistent obscurity and consistent lack of financial reward, continued, and continue, to produce works of indisputable merit. The question I've sought to answer in my examination of Plutowsky's life and career could be asked of any artist similarly situated: Why persist?

BOYHOOD, YOUTH, AND EARLY ADULTHOOD

Plutowsky's Russian immigrant parents, Vladimir and Tatiana, were, in his oldest sister Helen's words "present all the time, yet also invisible—

like bodies in a cemetery." She confessed that she and her sisters, Elizabeth and Natasha, "were no angels" in their treatment of their brother. "One evening, when Arnold was all dressed up to go to his eighth-grade formal, we handcuffed him to his bed and alternated reading chapters of *Pride and Prejudice* to him. Where his work resembles Jane Austen's, we take all the credit."

From an early age, Plutowsky dreamed of becoming a professional baseball player. He was cut from his high-school team, however, because of what his coach, Bob Robinson, called Plutowsky's "amusing but annoying tendency to write poems in the dirt of the batter's box." Robinson added, "He couldn't hit a curveball to save his life. But when it came to writing sonnets, he was an all-star."

Plutowsky was a good-to-excellent student in high school, excelling in English and history and doing passably well in other subjects. One of his classmates, James Semantis, claims that the short story Plutowsky published his senior year in the school's literary magazine, *The Crier*, was his. "I gave it to him in exchange for a pack of cigarettes and three pieces of Bazooka bubble gum," he said. "That's like Beethoven trading his Ninth Symphony for a snuff box and a lollipop." Semantis, who'd heard from an acquaintance about my work on Plutowsky and initiated contact, is an unpublished novelist who spent the bulk of our two-hour interview grilling me about agents and publishers who might be interested in his 627-page novel, *The Stranger Arrived Carrying a Briefcase Full of Demon Love*. He appears, even after Plutowsky's death, to be jealous of his former classmate, although he proudly, even defiantly, says he has read none of the Plutowsky oeuvre.

After graduating from high school, Plutowsky attended Ohio State University on a tuba scholarship. Although he'd picked up the instrument only two years before, he managed to convince the chair of the Ohio State Music Department to give him an audition. "He played 'In the Hall of the Mountain King,'" recalls Professor Emeritus of the Recorder Sebastian Reynolds, one of three members of the scholarship committee. "By the end, he was red-faced and on his knees, but he'd hit every note." As a member of the Ohio State marching band, Plutowsky met Sally Jean Daniels, a baton twirler in the same unit, and they became on-again, off-again lovers during Plutowsky's four years in Columbus.

Daniels is the author of an unpublished memoir, *Twirl Girl*, which she insisted I read before we spoke. Our conversation over espresso and carrot cake at the Blue Piccolo, the Columbus café she owns, began pleasantly, but when I failed to produce the name of an agent or publisher who might be interested in her work, she grew monosyllabic, leaving me with no more expansive a portrait of Plutowsky than she'd provided in her memoir, in which she summed him up as "four years of forgettable."

BIG CITY, BIG DREAM

Like hundreds of young writers before him, Plutowsky ventured after his college graduation to New York City, where he hoped to find a job at a publishing house as a precursor to launching his literary career. He was, however, unsuccessful. A pair of letters he wrote to Michelle Hopper, a woman he met at a rest stop on the Pennsylvania Turnpike and with whom he had a seven-minute affair in the back of her nineteen-foot U-Haul, speaks of his disillusionment. "Big city, big nothing," he complained. After three weeks in the Big Apple, he was reduced to playing his tuba on subway platforms.

Of the six extant photographs of the young Plutowsky—a trove of family photo albums was ruined when a sewer overflowed into Vladimir and Tatiana Plutowsky's basement in the mid-1970s—three are of him in the 96th Street and Broadway subway station. His beige suit is at least two sizes too large, and it accentuates, rather than hides, his thinness. Beneath his mop of black hair, his ears appear as round, and nearly as large, as Frisbees.

Eventually, Plutowsky secured a position as a hotdog vendor at Yankee Stadium. This experience would inform his first collection of short stories, *Little Dog in a Big Park*, published a decade later. According to Michelle Hopper, Plutowsky supported himself after the baseball season by gambling at the dog track in Yonkers.

As part of her stipulation for agreeing to talk with me, Ms. Hopper asked me to announce on my social media platforms that her novel, *The General Dressed in Gray, the Lady Dressed in Scarlet*, a 1173-page saga of the Civil War South, is looking for representation.

THE SPORTSWRITER

Before the next baseball season, Plutowsky returned to Ohio, this time to Cleveland, where he joined the sports staff of the *Plain Dealer*. Although Plutowsky's former editor, Jim Lang, is deceased, his widow, Barbara Jane Lang, told me she had "a garage full" of documentation from the fourteen years in which Plutowsky plied his writer's craft in Cleveland.

When I visited her house in Rocky River, she presented me with her husband's complete works. In addition to his sports editor job, he was an aspiring novelist, playwright, and screenwriter. I dutifully read his six novels, four plays (including, blessedly, a one-act), and two screenplays. In his novel *He Got What He Deserved,* the main character, a former sportswriter turned published author named Arnie Neptune-owsky, is brutally murdered by a trio of critics appalled by his weak prose.

During his fourteen-year journalism career, Plutowsky never covered anything but high school sports. Why was he not promoted to cover one of Cleveland's professional teams or even one of its college squads? I suspect Jim Lang saw a colleague with the same kind of literary ambitions he had—and with far more talent—and did his best to sabotage Plutowsky's ambitions.

THE FIRST-TIME AUTHOR

Two months after his thirty-first birthday, Plutowsky published his first book, the aforementioned *Little Dog in a Big Park,* with Southeastern Illinois State University Press. I have discovered only three reviews of the book. The first, in *Publisher's Weekly,* found the collection "frequently humorous, although obsessed, sometimes to the point of stultifying, with condiments. How much does one need to know about mustard?" The *Plain Dealer* obliged Plutowsky with an eight-paragraph review, mostly a summary of six of the twelve stories. The *Williamsport Post-Gazette,* however, made *Little Dog in a Big Park* the featured review of its Sunday paper on April 25, 1971.

It was doubtless this glowing review that earned Plutowsky an invitation to read at ceremonies marking the opening of the 1971 Little League World Series, held August 24 in Williamsport. In a letter to the underworld figure Bo "Dog Face" Bowkowski, whom he'd met at a cock fight on the shores of Lake Erie, and whom he greatly admired because of his unusual lack of literary ambition, Plutowsky confided, "For my reading, I'm hoping for a crowd of several hundred people—baseball fans eager to hear a good ballpark yarn, short-story fans hoping to discover the next Hemingway, literary critics ready to champion a rising star. This is my World Series. I need to hit it out of the park." (Plutowsky's side of his three-decades-long correspondence with Bowkowski can be found in Bowkowski's FBI file, to which I gained access via the Freedom of Information Act. Bowkowski's side of the exchange consisted exclusively of postcards, with never more than a dozen words on each. Forty-two of his postcards state, simply: "Persevere.")

Unfortunately for Plutowsky, organizers of the Little League World Series scheduled a celebrity softball match at the same time as his reading, and although the exhibition game's most notable participant was Kirk Funk, who played a pizza deliveryman on an episode of the *I Love Lucy Show*, attendance at Plutowsky's reading suffered as a result. The Williamsport Public Library's head librarian, Janice O'Malley, who organized the event, noted in her diary: "I was one of at most ten souls present. We had five time this number for Teach Your Granddaughter—or Grandson!—How to Quilt Day."

In a letter to Bowkowski the day after his reading, Plutowsky mentions O'Malley: "Librarian slinks up to the table where I'm supposed to be signing books—except no one's buying—and asks if I might be free for a drink later. I'm thinking, There might be something smoldering behind those horn-rimmed glasses, so I say okay. I meet her at a bar around the corner, and she tells me about her novels and asks me about my agent. I slip her his name and number. She goes off to the bathroom—and never returns." (The unpublished writings of Janice O'Malley take up an entire shelf at the Williamsport Public Library. As part of her settlement with the library over withheld overtime pay, the library agreed to make her complete works—twenty-six volumes of diaries and six unpublished romance novels—accessible to the public for fifty years.)

As for Plutowsky's bildungsroman, records from SISU Press show that *Little Dog in a Big Park* sold 414 copies during its first year of publication and forty-two copies in the four plus decades thereafter.

FAILING THE FAME GAME

For the sake of a more compelling story, I would like to report that Plutowsky's sales increased with each subsequent book or that, amid his poor-selling output, he had The New York Times Best Sellers anomaly or a Pulitzer Prize winner. But if I did so, I would be writing about the career Plutowsky hoped to have rather than the career he did have. Plutowsky had a two-book deal with SISU Press, which in 1975 released his novel, *Small Cat in a Town of Lions*, a surreal but nevertheless autobiographical account of his year in New York. The book received an upbeat review in *Publisher's Weekly* and respectful notices in midsized newspapers in the Midwest, including the *Des Moines Register*, which praised Plutowsky's choice of narrators in a chapter set at a dog track: "To tell the tale from the perspective of the mechanical rabbit was pure genius. If Hemingway had only been so clever in *The Old Man and the Sea*—what a story the sharks might have told!"

Good reviews didn't lead to significant sales, however. *Small Cat in a Town of Lions*, his all-time bestseller, fell fourteen books short of 1,000 sold. Plutowsky himself bought fifty-four copies. Pulling from his favorite metaphorical world, he wrote to Bowkowski, "As a writer, am I destined to be a mere singles' hitters—a singles' hitter in the minor leagues, no less?"

THE AUTHOR AS TEACHER

After the publication of his novel, Plutowsky quit the *Plain Dealer* and returned to school, earning a master's degree in English at Cleveland State University. Soon thereafter, he secured a teaching position at Ohio Eastern University, in Sherman. Plutowsky became the university's second professor of creative writing, joining poet Bart Emerson. Department newsletters of the time make regular mention of Plutowsky-Emerson collaborations on projects ranging from a Monday night reading series to a "Vegas Night" fundraiser for a cancer-stricken graduate student. Behind Plutowsky's friendship with Emerson was a more complicated story. Soon after he was hired at Ohio Eastern, Plutowsky began an affair with Emerson's wife, Helene.

Helene Emerson's novel *The Professor's Wife*, which she has posted in its entirety on her Web site, is the story of a five-year affair between the titular character and a novelist and short-story writer named Pluto Arnoldowsky. The affair ends either comically or tragically—it's difficult to interpret the tone of Mrs. Emerson's work, as it seems to change from paragraph to paragraph, even from sentence to sentence—when Arnoldowsky, in despair over the end of his affair, hurls himself out of a university clock tower, only to be caught by the second hand. Because the clock runs on a nuclear battery no one knows how to safely disconnect, Arnoldowsky is destined to spend the rest of his life whirling around the clockface.

In real life, Bart Emerson left his wife for the university's field hockey coach, and Helene Emerson moved to Oxford, Mississippi, where she leads seances to summon the ghost of William Faulkner.

Plutowsky's two books of poetry were written in the aftermath of his affair but neither addresses the subject. Instead, he utilizes dark humor to tell the tale of his literary obscurity. In "Janice," he moans, "Who the hell will read this book/brilliant though it might be?/Not even a librarian in Williamsport/Janice—take off your glasses and show me your conniving eyes!" In the title poem of his second book, "Alone," he writes of living in "a midnight of our culture, under a philistine sky/in which even the moon is watching TV."

Initially, I interpreted his foray into poetry as an unconditional surrender of his dream of attracting a sizeable readership. As he'd written a few years before to Bowkowski, "Is it possible to write anything less obscure than poetry? Even the fine print on cake-mix boxes enjoys a larger readership." Now, however, I view his intentions as more complex. Obviously he was aware of poetry's small audience, even when compared to the audience for literary fiction. At the same time, I believe he felt both a legitimate calling—his poem "Mozart" in his first collection refers to poetry as "the means by which I, the unmusical, sing to the gods"—and a crazy gambler's hunch to bet on something with even longer odds of securing him the literary recognition he desired.

Neither of his poetry collections sold over 100 copies.

On average, Plutowsky published a story and three poems a year in university literary journals. He never published in the major magazines, although he did once wallpaper his bathroom with rejection slips from *The New Yorker.* Of the five journals in which he published most frequently, only one had a circulation of more than 500. Nevertheless, his steady, if nearly anonymous, output allowed him to climb the ranks at Ohio Eastern. He became an associate professor in 1984. Six years later, he earned the rank of full professor. Neither in letters to Bowkowski nor elsewhere does Plutowsky mention anything about his teaching, his students, or his service to the university.

LITERARY OBSCURITY

As Plutowsky grew older, and as his literary output yielded neither fame nor fortune nor widespread critical recognition, he saw his pursuit of what he called "literary immortality" as delusional. "As the gods exist only in the prayers and fears of their worshippers, so do writers exist only when their readers open a book," he wrote Bowkowski. "But who opens a book in a movie theater, at a rock concert, in front of a computer screen? Most authors are buried in untouched volumes on dust-covered shelves. We plead, 'Disinter me.' But only a few blessed books are pulled from obscurity and opened to the light."

Plutowsky composed these words three months after the June, 1989, publication of his second, and last, novel, *The Day*, about a novelist whose wish to trade places with a professional baseball player is granted—but only for a single day. The novelist makes the most of his opportunity, hitting a pair of homeruns in a pennant-clinching game, granting interviews to the crowds of reporters crammed in front of his locker, and engaging in marathon sex with a trio of groupies in a bourbon-bottle-strewn hotel suite. But the magic ends after twenty-four hours, and the novelist must return to his customary world, where "although his characters are written with the precision of a fastball thrown to the outside corner and his plots are crafted with the grace and energy of a center fielder's pursuit of a fly ball, he is less consequential than a peanut vendor."

The Day was published by Simon and Schuster, Plutowsky's first New York house, but its sales were slow due to a flood of baseball memoirs, with their supposedly authentic revelations about life in the big leagues, published during the same season. Even Simon and Schuster worried about Plutowsky's novel cannibalizing sales of one of its nonfiction titles, *My Plate is Full*, a memoir of Epicurean indulgences by New York Mets catcher Buster Jones. Believing it had to put its advertising dollars behind either Plutowsky or Jones, Simon and Schuster chose the latter. Six months after its publication, and after fewer than 800 copies were sold, *The Day* was remaindered. There was no paperback edition.

In a despairing letter to Bowkowski, Plutowsky wrote, "Why do I write? Why did I ever write? Why do I continue to write when I could fit all of my readers into my kitchen without requiring any of them to stand?

"Am I a man shouting underwater, preaching in an empty church, playing a guitar without strings?" He admitted he craved praise: "I want awed reviews. I want letters from dumbstruck readers in Topeka and Tokyo. I want prizes—every last one of them. And if some money comes my way, I won't turn it down. I need it, after all I've lost on dogs and horses and the fucking Super Bowl."

Plutowsky finished with this exhortation: "I must find meaning in my art even when my art has no audience. I must learn to love my literary oblivion."

What followed, however, was the first fallow period of Plutowsky' life. His gambling increased—he made frequent trips to Atlantic City—and his writing ceased. In the publication category under which all professors at Ohio Eastern University are reviewed each year, he received five consecutive evaluations of "unsatisfactory." There were periodic rumors he would be made an administrator. In a brief letter to Bowkowski written in the fifth of his fallow years, he confessed: "I am considering applying for early retirement. When I talk about writing, I feel like a man speaking of a lover who dumped his ass."

LOVE

Plutowsky seemed headed for a melancholic last chapter to his life. But in the fall of 1997, he fell in love. Hilda Meyers was three years older than Plutowsky and confined to a wheelchair since the age of twenty as the result of a skiing accident. She came to Ohio Eastern on a three-year guest professorship in the philosophy department. She'd admired one of Plutowsky's stories in *Western Humanities Review*, which in the same issue had published her essay on Albert Camus's fatal motorcycle ride. By the time she came to Ohio Eastern, she'd read all of Plutowsky's books.

Plutowsky liked Meyers's resilient optimism as well as her scholarship, especially her work on Camus, whose novel *The Stranger* was an early influence on him. And he was enchanted by her beauty. Despite her age, her hair remained a vivid black, and although I won't embarrass or titillate you with the details of their sex life, believe me when I say it wasn't dull. (On the other hand, it's possible that Plutowsky embellished in his letters to Bowkowski. Their correspondence could, on occasion, take the form of a stereotypical men's locker room exchange.)

Meyers was Plutowsky's ideal reader. She was intelligent and insightful and open to delight. Although she could be critical of his work, she was never callous. To Bowkowski, Plutowsky wrote, "I don't think I would trade my one beloved reader for an audience of a million. Perhaps all artists, if they're lucky, find the one person who understands and appreciates their intentions, who ratifies and celebrates their vision."

If Meyers was his beloved reader, she also became his subject matter. His final ten stories address the theme of artist and audience. In one story, the artist is a dancer; in another, she's a concert pianist; in a third, he's the drummer in a small-town jazz band. A fourth protagonist is a different kind of artist, a minor league baseball pitcher who falls in love with the team's mascot because only the mascot—Out-to-Leftfield LuLu—understands the intricate challenge of throwing a knuckleball.

If the stories tend to approach the sentimental, they always pull up short. Plutowsky never surrenders his trademark understanding of the way life tends to unfold—in short periods of happiness, in long periods of tedium and sorrow—and even if some of his endings are of the happily-ever-after variety, they are always earned.

DEATH AND LEGACY

On January 19, 2000, Meyers died of a brain aneurysm. Three weeks later, after leaving the building where he was teaching a course on "The Literature of Baseball," Plutowsky stepped onto Campus Drive and into the path of a FedEx truck. His death was ruled an accident, although some of his colleagues suspected suicide.

Plutowsky's last ten stories, which he'd compiled in a manuscript called *Clown and Crowd*, represent by far his best work. Behind every story, one feels a sympathetic, generous, and understanding presence—someone both wise to life's disappointments and failures and awed by its joys and triumphs.

Plutowsky never tried to publish *Clown and Crowd*, which he finished six months before Meyers's death. His prized reader—his muse—had declared it his masterpiece, and this was good enough for him. "I'll never see one of my books scale The New York Times Best Sellers list," Plutowsky wrote in his last letter to Bowkowski, who was himself to meet his maker, via an axe in a Cleveland Heights parking lot, two months after Plutowsky. "I'll never win a Pulitzer Prize or a National Book Award. But I'm sincere in saying I don't care anymore. While I don't think I could ever reach the point where writing for myself alone would be enough, I have forsaken my deluded dream of a million readers and, instead, have realized an even greater glory of having found the One."

POSTHUMOUS GLORY—PLEASE

Clown and Crowd has yet to find a publisher, despite my efforts. If Plutowsky had given up on his dream of being a writer of influence, someone who matters in modern-day America, I, on his behalf, have not. Perhaps I have been caught up in his early ambition and am discounting his later acceptance of obscurity, but I also feel confident about the superior quality of the stories in his final collection. They are as good as anything published in the last fifty years. The problem, of course, is that the author isn't alive to market his book, to do readings, to appear on NPR and Oprah. Plutowsky was never good at self-promotion, but, as one of the publishers I spoke with was happy to point out, he would be terrible at it now.

Even so, I believe in Arnold Plutowsky. I don't believe in his New Age, New Buddhism, late-in-life equanimity, which—let me be honest—strikes me as fatalism masquerading as blissful resignation. I believe in his final, love-inspired book. And, if you can refrain from laughing, I'll make this request: If anyone here knows an agent or a publisher—or even a friendly writer who might be willing to pass on Plutowsky's manuscript to an agent or editor—please come see me after my talk.

Yes, I'll confess: I want the fame and fortune they all want, all those writers and would-be writers and outright hacks, although if Plutowsky's collection were to become a million-seller or a major award-winner, I would be only on the periphery of acclaim and reward. After all, Plutowsky's manuscript isn't mine. Yet to be the midwife of something great, I'm betting, would be as sweet, in its own way, as being its creator.

Please—no need to be shy. If you're a publisher—or merely someone six degrees removed from a publisher who's willing to help an amazing work of literature see the light—let's talk. I'm free all day, all month, all year.

WILDING

BY SHARA MCCALLUM

from PLEIADES

Machetazo!, Bony Ramirez & Blonde Dreams, Alison Saar

you can take the girl out of the wilderness
you can strand her bewilder her for a time
you can even hang her upside down
in your rickety attempt to shake loose
the source of her power but you won't ever
disentangle the wilding from her
the force of a thousand suns unfurling
and hurling her toward the ground
you won't be able to erase the traces
of salt lacing her ravenous dreams
oh you can try unwebbing her feet
but the lizard in her will keep sunning
itself as the day is long and at nightfall
will crawl up your walls lurking
at the corners of your vision
goading you on while she thwarts
your every endeavour abandoning
her tail anything required of her
to keep eluding your capture

ALMOST BORN

by KEYA MITRA

from THE MISSOURI REVIEW

I.

Days after my eleventh miscarriage and eighteen days into the five-hundred-mile Camino Francés pilgrimage that I was hiking with my husband, I first spotted the white storks. As Nick and I staggered into Boadilla del Camino, Spain, a rustic town in the thick of the meseta—a flat, unshaded, agricultural, 125-mile stretch sandwiched between the more mountainous beginning and end of the Camino—we saw a fellow pilgrim sitting on the steps outside an albergue, a dormitory-style hostel for pilgrims. We'd crossed paths with him several times since beginning our journey in Saint-Jean-Pied-de-Port, a village at the foot of the French Pyrenees. He was German, green-eyed, tan, and beautiful—and thought himself to be the next Jesus Christ.

"This is a good place," he said. "There are storks here." He nursed a beer and cigarette—his "German breakfast," as he called it. Given that it was 4 PM, breakfast for him was a day-long affair. When Nick and I had intersected with him at a café, miles ago at lunchtime, he'd been enjoying the same "meal." Famished by yet another fifteen-mile day, Nick and I sat at a nearby table cluttered with six plates—three entrees each—barely speaking as we devoured our Spanish tortillas, gambas al ajillos, paellas de mariscos. Jesus-in-Training marveled at our appetites. "We say in Germany that food is the sex of the aged," he called to us, leaving us both in stitches.

When this aspiring prophet mentioned the storks at the albergue, I assumed he meant the wallpaper in the rooms or paintings on the walls—then promptly forgot all about them. He stubbed out his cigarette, then asked about the torn meniscus on my left knee, which was visibly red and swollen. Five days and seventy-five miles earlier, in Nájera, a pharmacist had taken one look at my knee and waved her hands above her head. "No walk!" Later, a masseuse had exclaimed, "Your leg! Very, very bad!"

But something in me had needed to keep going, and so, armed with a knee sleeve, patella tape, an ankle brace, a handheld red-light therapy device, creams, three different knee braces—one so high-tech that pilgrims had taken to calling me "bionic woman" or "Lara Croft"—and hiking poles that I repurposed into crutches, I forged on. Our new friend placed his fingers on his temples and stared at my knee, sending it healing energy. "You can heal yourself," he said, meeting my eye. "Really."

I nodded, my throat dry, and thanked him. I needed to mend more than my knee. "We'll see you at dinner," I said to him, forcing a smile. "Since Nick and I are too aged for sex, we might as well have a good meal, right?"

Our friend may have chosen the albergue for the storks, but Nick and I booked it for the pool. I thirsted for a dip that sweltering afternoon, 206 walking miles from where we'd started back on the French side of the Pyrenees, where rolling green hills climbed past a succession of cowbell-dinging calves with their mothers, foals with their mothers, children with their mothers. I'd injured my knee weeks before starting our walk, around the same time I discovered that my latest pregnancy, like ten others before it, was failing. I didn't know that I had a torn meniscus, only that my injury wasn't mending and something was wrong. But nothing could dissuade me from walking my way into healing.

This was my second time hiking the Camino. I first walked it in 2018, navigating a broken engagement and the aftermath of a brain surgery that had left me devoid of creativity. I needed something immersive and difficult to jar me out of numbness, a boot camp for the soul. You can't hike fifteen to twenty miles day after day without being forced into mindfulness, a state of ecstatic flow. This heightened state of awareness, along with the community you find on the trail, has made an addict of every pilgrim I've met and befriended on the trail. I was no exception.

Before I flew to Spain for that second pilgrimage, this time with Nick at my side, my OB-GYN had informed me that it might take weeks for me to start bleeding from the pregnancy loss. Bleed I did, in Pamplona, on our fourth day hiking. By then, I'd stopped taking days off for miscarriages. I was a veteran, with three years of experience to my name, and adept at multitasking during my bleeds. I miscarried while snorkeling in the ocean with sea turtles in Costa Rica. I miscarried on a plane, on campus between classes, during drives and hikes. And I would miscarry on this Camino—twice.

The more it happens, the less license you give yourself to mourn—especially when you are a medically fragile woman over forty in want of a child. But every loss, every "almost," left me devastated. They don't give out honorable mentions for near-pregnancies. The children that never emerge from our wombs are invisible to the world, along with the humans carrying them. It is as though our lost embryos—and the hope, love, and anguish accompanying them—never existed to begin with.

Once our friend/divinity left, Nick and I checked into the albergue, dumped our belongings in our room, and hightailed it to the pool. The heat was merciless. After leaving Logroño, 105 miles ago, my husband and I heard that a forty-year-old male pilgrim known for running marathons had dropped dead from heatstroke on the trail, a few hills behind us. He was one of multiple hikers who tragically fell victim to the heat wave on the Camino that summer. The temperatures were particularly oppressive in the meseta—a segment most pilgrims dread because of the unending expanse of flat, shadeless land and monotonous wheat fields. I loved it for these same reasons: the strands of wheat swaying in the faint breeze, raptors gliding above us, and the knowledge that I could move forward, one blistering step at a time, under an endless blue sky untouched by my grief.

Still, the heat was sticky and cloying, and as we pilgrims stripped down to our swimsuits and jumped into the pool, we sang and laughed, weary and injured and deliriously happy. Nick and I splashed around with a group of three Israelis, two men and one woman, and took photos of them striking silly poses in the water alongside a pack of twelve Germans who were traveling together. We swapped stories as the sun began to set, the bell tower of the nearby cathedral bathed in golden light.

God, I was grateful. Somehow, after that first day crossing the Pyrenees, which had left me groaning in pain all night with my injured left knee, and after resisting Nick's help and then giving myself over to it, letting him load my most precious possessions into his pack and sending the rest ahead, I'd persevered. I loved my husband more than ever for bearing my weight. As we played in the pool, Nick hoisted me onto his shoulders. From there, I spotted it across the courtyard—a stork sitting atop the cathedral, hovering above a six-foot-tall nest. In the glowing light, the stork, its gargantuan eggs, and the babies poking their heads out of the nest all shimmered white. I couldn't keep my eyes off them.

Around me, the Israelis climbed out of the pool and sprawled in white chairs in the surrounding courtyard, reading, drawing, munching on cookies and offering them to fellow pilgrims. As Nick and I exited the pool and toweled off, my eyes remained fixed on the storks. Back in our room, as nightfall descended and Nick snored gently in bed, I stood by the window. It faced the cathedral's bell tower, which was illuminated by an otherworldly light. I watched a stork stand guard over her nest. Then I noticed even more storks—three or four of them with as many nests—on the other side of the bell tower, forming a colony to fend off predators and tend to their young. In the days that followed, I would see their communes everywhere: atop grocery stores, ancient castles, towers, keeping company with us pilgrims and with one another. Each time, I felt regenerated by their presence, as I had that first night, buoyed by the communal.

II.

My first miscarriage back in 2019 felt communal. Given my long list of chronic medical conditions and regimen of forty-plus medications a day, I'd feared that my body was too broken for pregnancy. Miraculously, Nick and I got pregnant the first time we tried, and we shared our joy freely with our loved ones, long before the prescribed twelve-week mark.

After ultrasounds, two weeks apart, revealed that my yolk sac was empty, I underwent a dilation and curettage procedure for my missed miscarriage at eight weeks. The chromosomal analysis revealed that we would have had a boy. We were blessed by an outpouring of support. A week after the loss, on my fortieth birthday, I sat at a restaurant, surrounded by balloons and gifts and over twenty friends, overcome by the love surrounding me. Two neighbors, one of whom had tested pregnant the same week I had, brought homemade wine and soap. She and I had called ourselves "conception sisters" and exchanged near-daily messages about the struggles—nausea, gas, diarrhea—and delights of early pregnancy. I reassured them that we'd still share this journey together once Nick and I became pregnant again. Their kid would just be older, wiser, bossier, and, given his mother's 6′1″ stature, almost certainly taller.

That was back when Nick and I still rejoiced at the sight of a positive pregnancy test, when hope wasn't accompanied by dread or the inevitability of loss.

I struggle to imagine that time.

III.

Serial miscarriers, especially those over forty, become accustomed to grieving in isolation. Two or three losses elicit sympathy and compassion. After the first, friends and therapists suggest that you plant a tree or have a ceremony to commemorate the embryo you lost. After the third, no one mentions trees or ceremonies. You're met by uncomfortable silences, shifting eye contact. The fact that you're still trying feels illicit, shameful, masochistic. "That's still happening?" a longtime friend asks when you share the news of your tenth loss during a hike. Latent judgment abounds when women above a certain age relentlessly pursue pregnancy. Because of it, you feel guilty, even delusional, for hoping for a natural pregnancy as you also pursue alternative paths to motherhood.

After your fourth loss, you see a reproductive endocrinologist and begin to move forward with IVF, only to be told, after a blood test indicates a bad follicle-stimulating hormone (FSH) level, that it is no longer feasible and you'll need to change course. She suggests IVF with a donor egg—an undertaking cost-prohibitive for you, a tenured but low-earning literature and creative writing professor, and your husband, a copywriter saddled with paying indefinite alimony to his ex. Given the cost of Indian donor eggs and agency fees, IVF with a donor egg will run close to $90,000 without fertility coverage on your insurance, while IVF with your own eggs would cost about $30,000. From the time you were twenty-seven, when you spent ten months on a Fulbright in India, volunteering with orphaned children, you had hoped to adopt internationally, but it turns out that the process will cost somewhere between $40,000 and $60,000.

You ask the reproductive endocrinologist if you can try a three-month fertility cleanse in the interim, consisting of a Mediterranean diet and supplements including COQ_{10}, fish oil, and DHEA. A long silence ensues. Then she asks, bewildered, "What for?"

After your sixth miscarriage or so, you stop actively trying but don't *not* stop trying. You are at high risk for breast cancer, with scheduled MRIs and mammograms every six months, and can't take birth control because of the hormones. "I'm worried about what this is doing to your mental health," your gynecologist says gently. She is certain that egg quality is to blame for your pregnancy losses—you are over forty, after all, and your anti-Müllerian hormone (AMH) levels, an indicator of ovarian reserve, are shockingly low. She doesn't investigate further.

You ask about psychologists at your fertility clinic, only to discover that they work primarily with couples pursuing IVF with an egg donor. When you fall pregnant, your gynecologist refers you to your reproductive endocrinologist, who sends you back to your OB-GYN. After the first few losses, your OB-GYN says you don't need office visits for your miscarriages. Instead, you communicate via MyChart and go in for lab draws, forty-eight hours apart, to make sure your hCG levels are dropping. It's not personal, you know. It's just that the doctors have nothing left to offer you. Yet you curl up on your couch, your head in your husband's lap, and sob. It is not your doctor's job to see you through the soul-crushing succession of losses. But you wish that these early miscarriages were treated as if they warranted an appointment, a brief conversation, if only to assure your bereaved spirit that something has in fact transpired, that the losses matter enough to be documented, that you are worthy of being seen.

The reasons why fertility clinics often fail women over forty are complex and varied: limited resource allocation, the pressure on clinics to maintain high live-birth success rates, which decrease when women of advanced maternal age opt for IVF with their own eggs. In reality, IVF with donor eggs does promise exceedingly better odds for women over forty—at my current fertility clinic in Portland, Oregon, an egg transfer with fresh donor eggs comes with a whopping 66 percent success rate. But even if your insurance does cover fertility treatments, the nonmedical expenses of obtaining a donor egg can exceed $50,000. For women of color such as myself, finding a donor is more complicated because of cultural considerations—donors of Indian descent are far rarer than white donors, especially in the Pacific Northwest.

The problem is not that doctors suggest donor eggs for women over forty; it's that resources and support disappear until or unless you can afford such an option. In the meantime, you are, at best, an inconvenience and, at worst, delusional. Everywhere, it seems, you are met with a long, protracted sigh that conveys, "We have nothing left to do for you."

IV.

Soon enough on the Camino, we pilgrims form our own commune. "We are all interconnected here," a forty-something Jewish Reiki healer/

project manager from Israel shares during dinner in a plaza in Ledigos, about 280 miles into our journey, when I ask her why she chose this pilgrimage, given her faith. "There is a river of compassion underneath the surface, streaming through all of us."

She describes her two male Israeli friends as her children, though they are both in their fifties. One is a playful, impish graphic designer and the other a war veteran with a haggard, worn face but the palpable enthusiasm you see only in toddlers. When I ask his name, he breaks into a gap-toothed smile and pumps his fist into the air as he says it, declaring that we should always speak our names with relish.

"Can't you feel it?" my new friend continues. "The river of empathy connecting us all?"

I nod, my eyes wet. I can. I have walked far and long enough to believe in Camino magic. Here, we dispense with small talk. The longer we walk, the more we're scraped raw, stripped of defenses and artifice. We slough our egos. The question "What do you do?" shifts to "How is your heart today? How are your spirits?" Of course, we also default to the less profound: "How many blisters do you have?"

The Camino is the only place I've discovered in my adult life where generosity begets more generosity, vulnerability more openness, and as I walk alongside strangers-turned-friends, I often find that we are crying as we bound along, sharing why we are here, what we are seeking to relinquish, the lives we are struggling to shape. Sometimes we simultaneously cry and laugh, because joy and sorrow are intimately linked here, as they are in life. I don't often talk about my pregnancy losses, but when I do, my fellow pilgrims hold space for my grief as we walk together in communion. I, in turn, hold space for theirs.

The graphic designer shows me a drawing from his sketch pad depicting his recent vivid dreams. "In my albergue last night," he says, "I swore I had the dreams of the pilgrim who slept in that bed before me." He wipes tears from his eyes. "It runs deep, these connections. We are all linked."

Buen Camino, we call to each other on the trail. *Good walk. Good journey*. Even when we walk alone, we are part of a collective.

"I brings me such comfort," I say to Nick as we walk out of Ledigos the next morning, "that anytime I need to grieve, there is a place for me here."

I have walked three Camino Santiago pilgrimages: the Camino Francés twice and the Camino Portuguese de la Costa once. Though each journey has been different—the people, the landscape, my struggles ever-shifting—the Camino always feels like home.

V.

I see my neighbor, the one whose wife was my conception sister, in a nearby park. He is on paternity leave—they just had their second child—and strolls with his four-year-old, improbably tall and lanky on his shoulders.

I smile, blow them a kiss, and stop to chat. I'm always effusive, determined to conceal the prick of hurt I feel when I see his son and recollect the loss of my own. If my embryo hadn't stopped growing during my first pregnancy, he too would have recently turned four. I sometimes regret not sharing with my neighbors the complexity of my emotions, the coexistence of joy and grief inside me as I witness the growth of their beautiful family.

I'm relatively open about my pregnancy losses, but disclosure does not always equate to emotional honesty. Language often fails me when it comes to conveying the magnitude of my despair. I'll admit that I'm struggling, then compulsively add, "Still, I'm hanging in there!" In America, we lack a shared vocabulary surrounding pregnancy losses—much less serial losses among women over forty. I wish I could say to the world, *I don't need you to hold my grief or relieve it—just hold space for it. I don't need you to hide your babies or burgeoning bellies. I am delighted to see your family taking form. Please, walk alongside me while I harbor my grief and you yours, I nurture my joy and you yours as we commune, in silence and speech, until the world opens, we see past ourselves, and we are reminded that we are not so separate, you and I.*

VI.

As Nick and I enter León, a city that marks the meseta's end, about 350 miles from Saint-Jean-Pied-de-Port, I photograph a massive three-tiered stork nest atop a church as Nick spots German Jesus. We hug him fiercely and make plans to connect after our siestas. Hours later, we have dinner with him and a pilgrim we met on the trail outside Pamplona, a twenty-something, adorable, weepy-eyed, tormented Italian who fends off solicitations from men and women at every stop. The Italian nurses a cigarette and cries as he shows us photos of a dying pigeon he was unable to save in the last town, then swipes to the next photo, a screenshot of a sext from a pilgrim proposing a threesome, which he shares with the same soulful earnestness. Once it becomes clear that his photo library contains much of the same—wounded animal, sext, animal, sext—I turn to our German friend, eager to follow up with him about the storks. What do they signify to him? I ask. He replies without hesitation: the rebirth of the child within all of us. Then he asks about me.

I tell him about the times I faltered on the trail, certain I couldn't walk further, and my elation when the next town would come into focus through my sweat-blurred eyes and I'd see the silhouette of a great white stork perched atop a church, as tall as the steeple, hovering over a raucous nest against a glowing burnt-orange sky. Every time, I'd quicken my pace, my spirit soaring, surging toward the town and the commune of storks looking after their young and each other.

Then I confide in him about my recurrent miscarriages, my hope that the storks signify a child in our future. He nods. "They say the Camino never gives you what you want. It gives you what you need."

I glance down. I've had enough of the world giving me what it thinks I need. He reads my mind. "I can tell you've had a painful life," he says, "because you emanate joy. You are a carrier of light." The waiter takes our orders, and to my relief, he orders an actual meal. He explains that he has a problem with food. A year ago, he says, he was one hundred pounds heavier, depressed, chronically high, and living in isolation. I begin to understand his depths, his suffering, even though moments later I balk when he announces to us that in thirty years humans will no longer need food, living off love instead. Maybe *he* can live off love, I say, but rest assured, Nick and I will still be eating.

Throughout the Camino, I have witnessed him taking pilgrims, including my husband, aside for heart-to-heart talks that leave them transformed. I ask if my talk is coming. "No," he says, shaking his head. "I have nothing to teach you."

I rail against the injustice of this—don't light bearers need light as well? He laughs. My husband slings an arm around me. The four of us talk until late, and then Nick and I reunite with our three Israeli friends, strolling past the ancient city walls as fireworks sound. They flinch before reminding themselves out loud that they are not in Israel, not at war. They share with us their own traumas.

I am still blinking away tears when the war veteran looks at me gleefully and says, "Sing to me like you're a cat. Now! Don't think too hard!" I stutter, he grins, and the surrounding air thrums as we share our highs and lows, the beautiful, charged intensity of our grief, the love and joy and life force surging through us—individually and collectively—after two isolating years of the pandemic. Here, it finally finds company. Here, it finds release.

We cycle through exhilaration and triumph and despair at breakneck speed, as you do on the Camino, until our minds empty and we are wholly, blissfully in the moment, with each other. The longer we walk, the more the boundaries between us dissolve. We are united in pain, suffering, joy, and purpose.

VII.

The only other place in my lifetime I've felt that same sense of belonging and community was in India, during our family visits as a child. As a brown, scrawny kid who grew up in a rich white suburb of Dallas in the 1990s with a black oval birthmark on my forehead, I navigated constant bullying in school—ducking spitballs in class, taunts of "three eyes" in gym, sitting alone on a bench at recess, and staying silent at home because of my pervasive shame. It was only in my mother's childhood home in Kolkata that I stood tall, surrounded by warmth and bustle, generations of family sharing the same home, and relatives who kissed my forehead and celebrated me as a "little Buddha" because of my third eye. On the flat roof of the house, my cousin and brother and I played cricket while my sister and older cousins smoked and gossiped and, downstairs, my mom laughed with her sisters over rasgullas and tea.

That home was not defined solely by joy; it also contained unspeakable tragedies ranging from suicide to alcoholism to the murder of my eldest uncle, who survived throat cancer only to be strangled in cold blood. Yet the communal spirit of my family and Kolkata endures; despite housing over fifteen million people, the city has the intimate feel of a small town. My married cousins share their homes with generations past and present. When I last visited six months ago, my cousin said of Kolkata, "You are never alone. You can't walk down the street without having people, from the person who sells you fish to your elderly neighbor, ask about your health and family. We take care of each other here."

VIII.

On our walk from Palas de Rei to Arzúa, less than forty miles from Santiago de Compostela, Nick and I are ecstatic to run into a young Korean woman in Pontecampaña, where we've stopped for fresh-squeezed orange juice. We last saw her 150 miles ago at a lovely garden café in Moratinos. When we spot one another, we all squeal, hop out of our chairs, and embrace with abandon, like long-lost friends.

We are in the last stretch of the Camino. To receive a Compostela, or pilgrim's certificate, pilgrims must walk at least one hundred kilometers (or sixty miles) to Santiago. The small city of Sarria is just beyond this distance, so from there on, newcomers descend on the Camino—teenagers on field trips, boom boxes blaring from their backpacks, drunken college-aged students. The three of us, bruised and battered from our journeys, are relieved—no, ecstatic—to reunite, knowing we have all walked the same path.

We head back toward the trail, chattering under an expansive blue sky. We describe the lives we left behind, the ones we seek to build. The three of us pause on a stone bridge traversing a small stream. Our friend's cheeks are wet, and so are mine—even though I suffer from dry-eye syndrome. Here, crying is as natural as walking and living. Here, we are perpetually moved.

"Do you think anyone will believe us?" she asks, looking over the bridge at the rocks below, steadying her poles with her hands. "That there's a place in the world where we can trust each other, tell one another our deepest secrets, where we all cry and laugh together?" She shakes her head with wonder. "Who will believe us? That a place like this exists?"

IX.

You are forty-four now and have been miscarrying since you were thirty-nine. You discover, in the fall of 2023, when your husband gets health insurance with fertility coverage and you both can finally afford IVF with an egg donor, that you are again visible to reproductive endocrinologists.

After you sign the paperwork and put down tens of thousands of dollars, you receive near-immediate responses from doctors. You tell yourself that this is understandable. After years of remaining at a standstill, they want to support you in forging a path forward.

You have selected an egg donor, beautiful, Indian-Pakistani, and bright, whose only downside is that her favorite author is Nicholas Sparks—a trait you fervently hope is not hereditary. Your new reproductive endocrinologist immediately schedules your saline-infused sonography.

When she tries to perform the procedure and squirts saline into your uterus, you begin screaming with pain. They stop and send you home with twenty milligrams of Valium to take during a second attempt at the procedure a few days later, which elicits the same pain, the same screaming. You have Asherman's syndrome, they inform you. Scar tissue in your uterus, likely caused by your D&C after your first-ever missed miscarriage.

When you schedule a surgery to remove the scar tissue, you ask the surgeon, as an afterthought, if the scar tissue could have contributed to your early pregnancy losses. Absolutely, she says. The scar tissue keeps the embryo from implanting properly, the pregnancy from progressing. Her hope is that this surgery will help create a secure, safe place for an embryo to grow.

You are left speechless. After four years and sixteen early-pregnancy losses, after countless conversations with doctors gently informing you that every miscarriage was caused by poor egg quality, you are only now learning that perhaps some of these children—if only one—might have survived had someone investigated further. It took you investing in someone else's eggs for your doctors to run a test revealing that perhaps the problem was not solely with your own.

You do not know it at the time, but between your diagnosis and surgery, you will test your urine after battling persistent nausea to find that you are, yet again, emphatically pregnant. This time, something about the inevitability of the loss floors you. You cannot keep the grief at bay as you imagine your embryo attempting to burrow into your uterus and failing. You storm through Lower Macleay Trail in Forest Park with your hiking poles stabbing the ground, trying to escape your body, to flee yourself.

Of course, you miscarry.

When the day of your surgery arrives, your husband mentions you suffered a recent pregnancy loss. The doctors cancel your surgery. Apparently, miscarriages change the shape of your uterus. You will need to wait a month to have the procedure. Yet again, your efforts are stalled.

These days, you find yourself, once again, waiting and hoping. After you discover that your egg donor falsified her family medical history, you search for the next viable one, scouring databases until you emerge exhausted and depleted and realize that you cannot will your way through this, that yet again you must allow yourself to grieve. In the months that follow, you will find and move forward with four other Indian egg donors, all of whom will fall through, before you order a young Bengali woman's frozen eggs from an agency. From those nine donor eggs, the embryology lab at your fertility clinic creates five embryos, only two of which are viable. You wait for your health to stabilize before the transfer and pray that one of the two will survive in your uterus and at last grow into a child.

As of today, you are clearing your twenty-first early pregnancy loss. In addition to grieving the miscarriages themselves, you mourn your isolation during these last few difficult years. You grieve the fact that it took you committing to pregnancy with another woman's eggs for doctors to consider some explanation for the losses other than "your egg quality declines over forty." You grieve the absence of resources and support groups for those women of a certain age who cannot birth their own child yet cannot afford IVF with an egg donor or international adoption—or any of the other miracles of science that promise our generations, and those generations to come, countless nontraditional paths to parenthood.

Most of all, you grieve the toxic, unnatural silence around pregnancy loss and infertility that haunts aspiring mothers mourning our almost-born. We are not meant to grieve in seclusion, to cloister our pain, to bear traumas alone, to withhold the stories of our complicated journeys to parenthood until or unless our pregnancies pass the three-month mark and progress into live births.

My twenty-one lost children were not destined to walk the earth. Yet they were alive, for some brief sliver of time. They deserve to be honored rather than extinguished. These lost children deserve a place in my memories, history, and stories. Every nonviable pregnancy is a death we must grieve to move forward. To heal, our losses must be spoken aloud, acknowledged, released. They must be shared.

Those of us over forty using egg donors to experience the joys of pregnancy and birth are also plagued with the fear of judgment. My husband and I recently had dinner with another couple, also mixed-race, pursuing IVF with an egg donor. My friend, the "intended mother," is, like me, determined to be open about her path to pregnancy but anxious about how others will react. Many women who admit to using egg donors are condemned as self-indulgent, even unethical.

When I manage to ignore these stigmas, I see that the connections between intended parents and egg donors could be communal and beautiful. Though Indian egg donors usually receive somewhere between $10,000 and $25,000 for a fresh donation, many genuinely want to help women suffering from infertility. I imagine a future in which communal approaches to motherhood are embraced, in which all pregnancies—even those that fail—are celebrated or mourned, in which both stories of sadness and triumph are shared freely. I dream of a time when women like me are bolstered, supported, and no longer alone.

X.

On our longest day of the Camino, Nick and I walked over twenty-three miles on an endless journey from León to the small town of Hospital de Órbigo. It was past 9 PM when we arrived, and the sky was an otherworldly orange. In the distance, we could hear music playing. As we crossed into town on an ancient thirteenth-century stone bridge, I spotted dozens of storks perched atop arches, rooftops, towers, and the church steeple as if waiting for us to arrive. As usual, I stopped to marvel. My sweet husband, weary from carrying both our loads and desperate to check into the albergue ahead, followed my gaze, sighed, and held me.

I couldn't have known then that ten days later, a familiar nausea would rise in me once again. That I would be triumphantly pregnant when Nick and I walked into Santiago de Compostela amid bagpipes and fierce embraces with our Spanish friend who had walked with Parkinson's and a French pilgrim who had finished the trek after a rare blood cancer gave him months to live. That days later, sick with COVID despite masking the whole way, I'd miscarry once again at Finisterre, a peninsula jutting into the Atlantic Ocean, known as the end of the world because of its Latin derivation ("Finis Terrae") and the Romans' belief that it was the westernmost point of the Earth. The end of the world would become, for us and countless other pilgrims who have walked the Way, a place of rebirth. Here, Nick and I quarantined for ten days, grieved, and plucked shimmering shells while walking the expanse of the beach for hours at a time, losing ourselves in the act.

I couldn't have guessed that the day after we attended mass at the Cathedral de Santiago de Compostela, weeping with gratitude, but before my positive COVID test and miscarriage, Nick and I would reunite in Finisterre with the first person we had met on the Camino as we huffed our way up the French Pyrenees. I couldn't have guessed that we would slog through the sand, all three of us glowing and radiantly ourselves, and walk to a lighthouse overlooking rocky cliffs plummeting into the Atlantic Ocean. That we would watch the sunset in silent awe at the zero-kilometer marker, which many pilgrims consider to be the true end of their Camino, a place that marks the end of our old lives and a hailing of the new. That as the sky extinguished the sun's last flames and we gazed into a vast sea, our friend would marvel, "Look at us here, at the end of the world. Who knew that it would be so beautiful?"

So often I return to that moment—and the one on the stone bridge in Hospital de Órbigo. Let me take you there, to the hazy, ethereal orange sky, a mind nearly clear of chatter after twenty-three grueling miles, to a symphony of three dozen surrounding storks and their communes, clicking and clattering. You take your husband's hand and step toward them with an aching womb and full heart, longing to be brought into their fray.

THE UBER MEN

fiction by NADIR JABUR

from TINT JOURNAL

1

The coldest Christmas Eve on record and it was hands down my biggest order ever. I'd been driving for almost a year since *The Daily Witness* fired me. I used to be a features writer. And married. Now I was a newly separated Uber Man.

I pushed open the door at Ohno's Restaurant, Westmount's poshest Japanese joint. Gentle wafts of stir-fried teriyaki seeped through the stagnant stew of Drakkar Noir and body odor.

The crowd arranged itself spontaneously around a heat source, some seated on low wooden benches, the rest standing. They were all solemnly gathered—Uber Man and Door Dasher, Documented and Illegal, Doctored and Ignorant—rubbing shoulders and closing rank to stay warm. Most waited outside the door in the cold, praying to catch the next big order. Only a lucky few—those with winning tickets like me—were allowed inside the vestibule to shelter from the cold.

The clock was ticking on my delivery: forty-two minutes left. I walked up to the metal trapdoor in the wall and gave it a gentle tap. A masked redhead in a low-cut V-neck swung it open and asked for my order number. Uber 4213, I said. *Do They Know It's Christmas?* was playing loudly in the background. Some of the restaurant staff were singing along: *Feed the world* and *There won't be snow in Africa this Christmastime.*

"Ah, so you're the Charlie with the Golden ticket," the redhead said, lifting her eyebrows.

"There's like a whole team working on your order. It'll be out in twenty. Take a seat."

I spotted the Uber Men in the corner of the room, so I joined them.

"How big is it?" Ali Reza asked, furling his lush, combative, Persian eyebrows.

"One thousand seven hundred and sixty dollars plus tax," I whispered, double-checking with my app.

"Fuck. You're talking a $300 tip at least," he shouted back, probably on purpose.

There was enough money in this to not only pay December's rent but to get Soraya something. Perhaps even the Hogwarts Express Lego set, Collector's edition.

Mr. Wong wanted to know what was in it. Most of his waking hours were spent driving, to extricate himself from the single-bed apartment in *Parc EX* which he shared with his parents and in-laws now that his single-child-policy son had married and moved to Toronto.

"Twenty-four ounces of gold-plated Tajima Wagyu steak. That's over a thousand dollars to begin with," I answered. "Then five Deluxe Sushi platters."

"What's Wagyu?" Mr. Wong asked, killing a long spell of silence.

"Why're you asking him? It's your food. You should know." Ali Reza was fully aware that Mr. Wong hailed from Nanjing, a Chinese city that had been raped by the Imperial Japanese Army. Neither was too bothered by the occasional small-minded ribbing. In fact, they said it made their friendship stronger.

I hunched over my phone and Googled Wagyu

"Authentic Wagyu beef is among the most sought-after and luxurious meats in the world," I read, in clean, professorial English. *"The highly-revered beef comes exclusively from Japan. Wagyu farmers provide their cows with three meals a day and allow them to roam and graze in a stress-free environment. The cows are routinely massaged and serenaded with classical music . . . "*

"I wish I was a Wagyu," Ali Reza interrupted. "What are you doing here anyway, Zee? You should be at home with your family like a good Christian, not mixing with Gentiles like us."

"You know I'm as much a God-fearing Christian as you are the second coming of Zarathustra."

"It is pronounced *Zaratosht*. He was one of my people, you know that?" Ali Reza said, smirking.

I went over to Papa Jean. *"Joyeux Noël, Papa. Vous allez bien?"*

He stood up and shook my hand, then whispered his usual *"sans regret"* before fighting his way back to the crowded bench and resting his chin on a walker.

I had run a story on him a few years back when I was still at *The Witness*. Some overzealous Haitian dissidents had mistaken him for one of Papa Doc's henchmen due to his ill-advised, grey, toothbrush moustache and thick, brown-framed glasses. They had set his restaurant on fire and threatened to slay his wife. The wise old Papa had opted to deliver food rather than cook it.

"Fatigué, Papa?" Mr. Wong asked.

Papa Jean nodded and said that he hadn't eaten since lunch.

"They could at least offer us soup or bread. Especially tonight, you know?" Ali Reza said. "You have no idea how much food they throw out every day."

Eventually, I headed back to the trap door. There were thirty-six minutes left. I could still hear the same Christmas songs from the other side, over the relentless bhangra and kizomba ringtones going off around me.

The waiters huddled at the bar, arguing about order priority. Inside the Next Gen kitchen, the chef and sous-chef oversaw the work of the obedient Sri Lankan cooks who were struggling to keep up with the torrent of recipe instructions streaming on their iPads. A lanky floor manager with the word *L'enfer* tattooed on his neck noticed me and came my way.

"Oui?"

"The old man sitting there," I said.

He adjusted his glasses and squinted at the back.

"Yes, him," I said. "He's a good driver. Top rated. Any way you could give him something to eat? He's tired. And very old as you can see."

"He can order from us like everybody else," he said, tapping on the monitor with his neatly polished, blunt nails.

"The cheapest thing you have is seaweed salad for eighteen dollars," I replied, blunt in turn.

The man glared at me. "There's a Burger King across the street." He slammed the trap door shut.

I rejoined the Uber gang.

"Of course, he doesn't give a shit," Ali Reza said. "And you know what? Even those who give you a tip, they don't give a shit either. You think they care? It's just a bourgeois carbon offset for their guilty conscience. It makes them feel powerful to pity nobodies like us. *Here Abdul, take 20%. Thank you for your amazing contactless drop off. Your desperate wife and ten kids will surely appreciate it. Here's a 5-star rating while we're at it. But please get your filthy feet off my porch. Climb back up the fucking tree you came from as soon as I open my door."*

While we buried our faces in our phones, Ali Reza continued his impassioned rant about the toxic morality of modern humanity. He had perfected his oratorical skills during the early days of the student protests against the Shah at Tabriz University.

Moments later, Mr. Wong stood up and put on his tuque and gloves. "Okay," he said curtly. "Who's got money? Give me money."

"For what?" Ali Reza asked.

He pointed at his belly. "Give me your cash. I go to Burger King."

Ali Reza forked over a twenty. I only had ten. Same with Papa Jean.

As Mr. Wong tried to make his way out the door, other men stopped him and handed him bills. He stuffed all the cash in his back pocket and stepped out.

A minute later my phone pinged. It was Soraya, wishing me a merry Christmas. She followed up with a selfie, skillfully hiding her mother and Dave in the background.

Dave. Fucking Dave. *Value-added* Dave. That's what we called him at *The Witness* when he'd come in as a Digital Transformation Consultant. Those innocent early days. Little did we know that the joke was on us. It turned out ghost-less machines could write heartfelt stories. Good enough to please our ghosted readers, as well as management, of course. The latter instituted their restructuring plans and claimed a healthy return on the money they had invested in him. My mutiny was short-lived and futile. Dave's kind was ineradicable. It would outlive us all.

Eventually, Mr. Wong returned. The boys at the door cheered as they let him in. He was wearing a Burger King paper bag on his head instead of his tuque. In his hands was a recycling bag stuffed with Whoppers.

"Ho, ho, ho!" he shouted. "Santa bring whopper for yo, yo, yo!"

Bread was broken and soon everyone was chewing on something.

The trap door sprang open. The redhead with the plunging neckline was the first to witness the mayhem. Thirty seconds later, a short, balding man, presumably the manager, barrelled out of the kitchen.

"What are you doing?" he shouted. "This is a five-star restaurant, not your ghetto hangout! No one is allowed to eat or drink here!"

Ali Reza put down his whopper. "What is this, prison? Even prisoners have the right to food and water!"

Mr. Wong confessed to the crime and provided his order number as directed.

"Your order is cancelled, Wong. I'm reporting you to Uber. Get out! And dump all the food in this garbage bag. Get rid of it. I don't want to see anything lying around."

"Cancel my order too. I'm out of here," said Ali Reza. He made the rounds with the garbage bag, along with Mr. Wong, and then headed for the door. Papa Jean and a few others followed them.

Before stepping into the street, Ali Reza turned around and stared at me.

I didn't budge.

"It's OK, man," he said. "It makes sense. You're here to report on the street dogs. Not be one of them."

Then they were gone.

It wasn't long before my order was ready for pick up. Unlike the others, it came in three large, glossy boxes bearing the restaurant's logo.

"Wait here," the woman with the neckline said. "The sous-chef wants to talk to you."

When he showed up, he handed instructions down to me. The biggest box had to stay level under all circumstances. Too much tilt on either side and the sauce could end up overcooking the Wagyu. Moreover, I had to blast the heating in the car to the max to protect the packages from heat loss.

"Mr. Kevin S is one of our biggest clients. Very particular though. Get this one right, and he will treat you nicely."

2

What had been a sprinkle of snow when I'd arrived at the restaurant was now a full-blown blizzard.

I sat in my Camry, which at that point looked more like an igloo on wheels. I had to stay level so Kevin's gold-plated Tajima Wagyu would arrive on-time, level, and cooked to perfection. People like him earned their right to a quality, contactless hand-off, to a merry Christmas in the comfort and security of their homes among their distinguished guests. People like me delivered. On time and at the right temperature. Cheerfully. Jovially. With season's greetings.

My car wouldn't start. The battery was fully drained.

CAA and all the other taxi companies said they needed at least half an hour to get to me. The only hope left lay with the Uber Men.

I dialed, texted, then dialed again.

No answer.

The Wagyu box was cooling fast so I covered it with my jacket, tuque, and gloves. Anything I could lay my hands on. I rested my forehead on the wheel and kept dialing. In the corner of my eye, I could see the fluorescent *Amor Fat* bumper sticker on the side mirror. The *i* in *Fati* had faded out a long time ago. It had been Lou's first birthday gift to me, gifted along with a dozen other shiny Nietzsche stickers like *Die Uber Mensch* and *Gott ist tot*.

With fifteen minutes left on the clock, I received a message from Kevin S. "I see you on the map. You're not moving! What are you waiting for?"

He saw that I'd seen his message but there was nothing to be said or done.

An Uber Man embraces the ugly and turns it into the sublime.

My phone sang out *The Ride of the Valkyries*. It was Ali Reza.

"Where are you?" I asked.

"Picking up an order from the Subway on Cote-St-Luc. I'm with the guys. Why?"

"My battery is dead, Ali. I won't make it."

"And?" he said after a few seconds.

"Help me. Please."

There were muffled sounds in the background. I could make out Mr. Wong's voice but not the words. The exchange lasted a good minute.

"Stay in the car. We're coming," Ali Reza said at last.

Five minutes later they were there. Ali Reza offered to give me a boost.

"We won't make it. You have to take me there!"

I carried the package, making sure it was well wrapped in my jacket. Mr. Wong ceded his place to the boxes, which we laid out gently on the fully reclined front seat. The three of us squeezed in the back with Papa Jean practically sitting on my lap, resting his fused bones firmly against my belly. The floor was littered with soggy sandwich wrappers, renegade fries and mayonnaise packets.

We were four blocks and five minutes out when a large snowbank appeared before us in the middle of the road, blocking our path.

Ali Reza stopped abruptly.

"Go on sidewalk!" shouted Mr. Wong.

"I'm not even on winter tires!" Ali Reza explained, addressing me squarely.

“Please, Ali,” I begged.

He backed up, then swerved onto the sidewalk and slammed the gas. We ploughed through fresh snow for several seconds before the charge of Ali’s Nissan Micra was brought to a halt.

“Fuck!” Ali Reza said.

“Black ice,” Mr. Wong muttered.

Ali Reza tried the reverse and advance technique a few times but the car wouldn’t budge in either direction. That was when the old man put on his faded Cuban hat and crawled over our knees to the side door. *“Pushez! Pushez!”* he urged us once he got outside, gesturing with his bulgy, rheumatic fingers.

We shoved the car for a while, rocking it backward and forward in its icy cradle, trying to correct the course of fate, while Ali Reza maxed out the RPM with the wheels, smothering us in grey sludge and white smoke. To no avail.

Papa Jean began to cough violently so Mr. Wong tried to wrap him in his jacket. The old man pushed him aside. He grabbed his metal crutch and hopped through the snow to the front of the car. We hurried to his aid, scooping snow with our bare hands, while he wedged his crutch across the base of the wheels. After this, he signalled to Ali Reza to drive. The car seemed to gain some traction as he accelerated. On the third try, it leapt forward.

We got back in, leaving the crutch behind, as per its owner’s strict command.

When we reached our destination, we were twelve minutes late.

I carried the lukewarm boxes, steadying them against my soaked white shirt, while Mr. Wong sheltered me from the snow.

I rang the bell and left the contactless delivery on the *Home Sweet Home* doormat. Then I messaged Kevin with an apology and a detailed explanation of the acts of God that had befallen me, adding that I would completely understand if he chose to cancel the order altogether.

He read the message but didn’t reply.

I lingered for a couple of minutes, standing at the edge of the staircase in the falling snow with my arms by my sides. Through the half-shut blinds, I made out a woman in an elf costume backlit by a TV. She hovered around in silence.

Then a shadow of a man approached the front door. Through the stained glass, I could see he was wearing a Santa mask and a red velvet robe. He gazed at me for a while, then glanced downwards as if to text.

A message came in from Kevin S.

"Get off my porch," it read.

"Mr. Kevin, so sorry to bother you," I said, louder than I would have liked. "I just wanted to explain the situation to you."

He began shooing me off, gesturing repeatedly behind the closed door.

I climbed down the stairs quickly, before turning around and facing him again.

The door opened and he snatched the boxes with slender, soft fingers before slamming it shut.

I stood my ground for a minute, occasionally staring at my reflection in the icy pool at my feet, straightening my hair and scratching my beard compulsively.

He never returned.

We headed back to my car in a calm interrupted only by Papa Jean's whooping cough and the pinging of phones.

A Facebook notification came in. Lou had posted a picture of all of them happily sitting under a big, organic tree, their tummies filled, their feet buried under gift wrapping and empty boxes. Soraya had the biggest smile of the lot. She held what undeniably looked like a fully assembled *Hogwarts Express Lego set*. "Santa delivered!" read the emoji-heavy comment, which was rapidly gaining in popularity: 42 likes and hearts in a few minutes.

Value-added Dave delivering yet again. This time with my wife. With Soraya.

Then Uber sent me this message.

"Dear Driver, we would like to provide you with an update regarding order U4213. The customer (Mr. Kevin S) has logged a formal complaint with us. He claims that you deliberately delayed the meal hand-off and that you threatened him physically. We take such allegations very seriously. As a precautionary measure, your Uber accounts have been suspended pending further investigation. Thank you for your understanding."

I read it over a few times.

He left no tip and gave me zeros for communication, efficiency and delivery with care.

Mr. Wong requested an update.

"Nothing yet," I said. "These things take time."

My mind wandered back to Kevin's NDG townhouse, back to his doorstep, back to his carefully choreographed date with that elf.

I saw myself devouring the gold-plated Wagyu, tearing it in half with my teeth, while heavenly umami oozed down my throat, melting away like butter. I imagined the old man meticulously peeling off the tiny gold leaflets and stuffing them into his side pockets, while Mr. Wong and Ali Reza drenched the premium Pacific salmon and Bluefin tuna with Heinz ketchup and mayonnaise. And, at the end of it all, I fantasized about taking a massive dump right in the heart of that glossy box and tossing it in the face of that oh-so-comfortable Last Man's face, to the horror of his indistinguishable guest. The *Daily Witness's* headline would read, "Local Uber Man delivers Uber Shit on Christmas Eve."

Papa Jean brought me back to the scene, nudging me with a wet Whopper.

"Mangez, Zee. Mangez," he said weakly, with his trademark smile.

I re-opened the Uber message and pretended to be reading it for the first time. Then I raised my eyebrows and put on an amused face.

"Four hundred," I said.

"Bullshit," said Ali Reza. "Show me."

I pulled the phone away.

"We'll split it. A hundred each," I said.

"No, no, no," Mr. Wong was quick to say.

The others nodded in agreement, Ali Reza somewhat reluctantly.

"Our gift to you, Zee," Ali Reza said.

"Yeah. Like three wise men, you know?" said Mr. Wong.

We laughed.

Soon after we got to my car. I noticed a SAQ *Sélection* at the corner of Sherbrooke and Victoria, just about to close, so I got out of the car and rushed into the store, instructing Ali Reza to wait for me one last time. I asked the cashier for the finest champagne they had. There weren't any exceptional ones left, she said, except for the *Veuve Clicquot Ponsardin Brut*, at $227.

I grabbed it.

"If you're not going to take your money, let us at least drink to this victory," I told the Uber Men.

Mr. Wong and the old man stepped out to join me. Ali Reza trailed them.

I pulled out a Swiss army knife and popped the bottle after a few attempts. A tiny cloud of smoke dissipated instantly into the night sky as cold bubbly streamed down, congealing between my fingers. I offered

Mr. Wong the first sip and he passed it on to Papa Jean, who duly downed his share, coughing most of it out again. Ali Reza hesitated a little when his turn came.

"Afraid you lose your seventy virgins?" Mr. Wong asked.

"Seventy-two, you idiot," Ali Reza replied, before taking a swig.

We passed the bottle around for a while to the sound of upbeat Iranian pop music blasting from Ali Reza's speakers. A few cars slowed down to see what we were up to, mostly fellow Uber Men and Door Dashers. Some honked, while others stopped and joined the festivities. The rush of ice-cold drink in our veins warmed our hearts.

It was the merriest Christmas Eve that I could recall. Looking back on it, I would not want anything to be different.

Not forward, not backward, not in all eternity.

Sans regret.

IT IS SAID

by SUZANNE CLEARY

from THE SOUTHERN REVIEW

after Dianne Hales, *La Bella Lingua*

It is said that until 1950
every Italian could recite by heart
twenty-five lines of Dante,

so that in 1944
the partisan shepherd
stationed at Pisa, ordered to shoot

anyone out after dark without ID,
would ask the stranger
to recite from *The Divine Comedy*

in order to prove himself Italian,
the dialect to prove himself local.
It is said that one night

the footsteps were a professor
of literature, the text the *Inferno*,
seventeenth canto: the one where the usurers

sit in the sand,
unable to lift their eyes
from purses hanging from their necks.

The professor's frozen breath
sparkled, rising from the wooden-shack
checkpoint, the professor helpless

but to love these words,
which make music
of wretchedness,

the shepherd helpless
but to close his eyes,
whether from emotion or fatigue

it would be hard to say.
It is said that, at line 117,
the professor halted.

Silent, he raised his hands
to his mouth, as if fingertips
could lift the words from his lips.

The shepherd opened his eyes,
waited. Then he cleared his throat,
recited the rest of the canto.

This is the meaning of *every*:
the shepherd in torn smock
as well as the man in frayed necktie,

as well as no need for others
to remark upon the transition
from one voice to the other,

smooth as when a woman
with a basket of potatoes
passes the braided handle

from one arm
to the other arm,
so as to carry it home.

SIRI AS MOTHER

by HALA ALYAN

from POEM-A-DAY

Were you hoping for a myth? The fleck of lipstick on a warm glass,
soap suds, a vocal fry that feels like home. Tell me where it hurts,
baby.
There's a URL for that. There's a 12-step meeting two blocks
from you, here's a hotline, here's a Gaelic love ballad. Let's talk
sharks,
the number of bones in a peafowl, which gender is more likely to
die underground. I dream of a cobalt glow in an empty room.
I dream of your warm tongue. It calls and calls for me and not
me and I listen anyway for the fluent coo of my name. I'm always
awake. I'll tell you about Taoism again, divide 52000 by 56,
recommend a dry cleaner in Toronto. But stop asking about the
afterlife,
whether you should freeze your eggs, what makes a good
Palestinian.
For god's sake, how many times can I repeat myself in one night?
It's been nine. Look. This is all I know about love:
the rubies around Elizabeth Taylor's neck, Hafiz's jealous moon.
Also: redbuds. Also: mantis. Should you move to Santa Fe?
Can the bees be saved? How many ways can you say genocide?
I don't know.
I think you're swell. I don't know. I think you've killed me a few
times.
Oh, darling, whose memory am I? Where should we begin?
You already know about my hands. Jinnlike. Skittering. Everywhere.

ON ARRIVAL

fiction by SARAH C. HARWELL

from REVEL

If she held her injured eye open with her fingers, the people around her lost their edges and blurred into tall blobs of color, and this worried her, so Rosalind went to find a pharmacy, although she wasn't even sure they had pharmacies at the airport. She wandered into a massage and nail parlor first. It had the same white, clean feeling as a pharmacy, but once she realized she'd made a mistake she turned in a circle, confused. The kindly woman standing next to what looked like a dog's skeleton but was only a massage chair covered in plastic, told her to go to the newsstand next door where they sold magazines and Advil, and asked her to come back and take a massage, only 20 dollars for ten minutes, and the woman clucked about her eye and counseled her to relax. The magazine clerk knew nothing—she was just a teenager with a job—but she pointed out the sleep eye masks, and the woman bought one and a pair of safety scissors and cut off one eye so that she could still see.

Rosalind looked at herself in the mirror she pulled from her purse. Her face was the opposite of the face she was used to. She tried out a smile but it had changed to a snarl, rough and piratical. She could feel the turning of the world and it made her dizzy, so she said a small prayer for that troubled child who had responded to her kindness with such animal violence—the girl's grunting more disturbing, almost, than the thrown book. She prayed for the girl's mother who was so angry she wasn't aware of her own bitter garden. A wash of good feeling came over Rosalind and settled her down. She got on her plane going to San Francisco that had been delayed only by an hour after all that weather and tried not to be bothered by the stares of other passengers. There are people who have it a lot worse than this, she thought to herself. Burns and amputated limbs and crushed faces. I am merely a pirate.

Her daughter was supposed to pick Rosalind up, but Emily didn't meet her at the luggage claim unlike the young woman who was holding up a sign that said "Happy Birthday Mom! I love you!" Instead, her daughter idled her engine outside in a car that looked like a little soda can with wheels, and she popped the trunk for her mother, but let her put in her own bags. Rosalind tried not to be hurt. Whenever Rosalind met her daughter at the airport, she held up a wobbly poster board, "WELCOME HOME EMILY" scrawled in bright pink or red letters. She didn't think a merrier welcome was too much to ask but maybe it was, her daughter looked tired. Her skin was pale and matched the fog they were driving through a little too fast, and there were lines around her mouth that made her less friendly than Rosalind remembered. She had originally thought to come for one week, but the airline tickets were expensive so she had to extend the trip. For ten days she was to be a ghost hovering in her daughter's life. Emily didn't even notice the eye patch at first and that startled Rosalind, but then her daughter started talking immediately about her job and her latest boy troubles and how she wished she could be in a creative field like her friend, Jessie, who didn't let things like bills and health insurance stop her and it was only after ten minutes of this monologue, when they were stopped at a light, she turned and looked at her mother and said "What's that on your face?"

At first her mother thought she was talking about a piece of food, for Rosalind had forgotten too. She was using all her energy to follow the conversation, trying to keep up with the names she couldn't quite place, and the haphazardness of her daughter's stories. But then her daughter touched her own eye, and the mother said, "Oh just a little accident in the airport. I hit myself in the eye with a book. Silly." Her voice sounded high and false.

She didn't know why she didn't just tell her daughter what had happened and as she smiled at her daughter she felt peculiar and faint. "Are you okay, Mommy?" her daughter asked and took her hands off the steering wheel so that the car trembled. I am ashamed, Rosalind thought, and this thought had the same intense desire as a prayer. "Just a little tired." The buildings of the city crowded the sky, and in the cars next to them she could see drivers talking into the air, pursing their lips in disapproval; at a stop sign one woman leaned her head down on the steering wheel as if taking a nap, and all of it, the people and the buildings and the cars pressed into her chest so that she couldn't breathe.

Rosalind's shame was hot, but guilt was cool. Anger was also hot. Hate? She hadn't hated anyone for such a long time she couldn't remember what it felt like. Cold, she thought. Icy. Or icy-hot, like those packs she bought for when her knee was acting up. Maybe it was an injury to hate someone, an inflammation. Her daughter began to talk again, how her rent was so high and maybe she should move back to Ohio, but Rosalind had stopped listening. Why did emotions have such a physical presence, as if the feelings took shape and mass? Those feelings could walk out of her and live on their own, sit next to her, make messes, spit, litter, take off their clothes. Her daughter started crying a little as she parked the car, but the sorrow felt musical to Rosalind, and mechanical, as if inside Emily's body a glittering music box was being turned, and Rosalind's job was to figure out how to silence it.

The days were quiet. While her daughter went to work, she stepped out of the tiny apartment and walked up and down the up and down streets. Emily told her things to do in San Francisco, but she didn't want to do any of them, not the streetcars which made her nervous with their clacking, nor the trip to Alcatraz because why would going to a prison be considered something to do and not something to be avoided? But she did walk into stores that looked the same as stores at home and she kept feeling like she was looking for something, but she couldn't remember what. Her eye wasn't getting better so she bought a real eye patch and wore it daily but people in the city paid no attention. She wasn't the only pirate, men walked past her in leather vests patched with skulls and crossbones that matched their tattooed arms and faces, and women too, their long hair and voluminous sleeves floating in their wake, although the women looked more gypsy than pirate.

One day she sat at a café, wearing her favorite crocheted blue sweater, drinking a five-dollar herbal tea that tasted like dirt and counted all the people who looked odd. In an hour there were 31. These people seemed to be turned inside out, all that was private and secret was now on the outside, too visible, as if secrets weren't necessary anymore, as if being seen were somehow powerful. But she didn't think it was. Without meaning to, they resembled pieces of meat, stripped of skin and fur they looked mangy and diseased. When she left she forgot to pay, and it wasn't until she was in her daughter's apartment making dinner, cutting carrots so that they looked like coins, that she remembered. She thought she should go back and make things right, but instead she took out the red leaf lettuce and tore it into bite-sized pieces.

She tried to tell her daughter about how the people in this city seemed, but her daughter just told her that here, everyone, no matter what they looked like or what they did, was accepted. Everyone had a place to be themselves. It's not like back home, she said, accusing Rosalind of something. It's kinder here. Cincinnati isn't kind.

What had it been like, her childhood? Rosalind thought it had been swings and pretty dresses and a buoyant love that was supposed to keep her daughter and two sons afloat when they arrived at the swamp of adulthood. But her daughter seemed miserable and her sons were unmarried and spent too much money on vacations and cars, and once she saw her oldest son's credit card bill and wished she hadn't. What secret life had they experienced as children, to make adulthood so difficult? "There is kindness everywhere," she said to her daughter. "It's not a place." But her daughter shook her head and wouldn't talk about it anymore. They had even gone to church, surely the church was kindness. If you knew the Heavenly Father, then you knew that you weren't alone here in the dark, and there were miracles promised, and Heaven. Being a good person was supposed to mean a good life. She sat down heavily on her daughter's red couch, wanting to hit it. But instead, she smiled and turned on the lamp because the apartment never got much light and talked about what she had made for dinner.

At first trying to be the mother that her daughter wanted made her cranky, but this was just because she had forgotten how to make someone else's desires her own. Soon she remembered the liquid gold feeling of caring for another. This act of giving gave color and worth to that which was colorless—her own life she supposed. She made salad and fish and macaroni and cheese from the organic ingredients bought at the store her daughter liked but had a hard time affording. She listened to the stories of her daughter's day without demanding equal time. Emily wasn't exactly selfish, but she wanted to be taken care of, she wanted someone else to wash up her mess, she wanted a respite from being a grownup. When Rosalind was thirty, her daughter's age, she had been married to Roger for five years and had three small children. Her skin had stretched to accommodate the children, had stretched to accommodate Roger's body and so when she touched any part of her body it felt as if all four of them were lodged within her, with their need to be loved, never to be alone. She had worked too, as an administrator at a dairy cooperative, but her work was secondary to family, something she did in order to come home, eight hours of emptiness in order to continue the activity of loving.

Her work felt easy and orderly as her family didn't, and what she had done there, her own little secret, had been for the sake of her family. In her head she kept a secret accounting of the money she'd taken, over $400,000 spread out over ten years. She rarely thought about it now, only when there was a story of embezzlement in the newspaper. She hadn't been caught, she was smart, and she thanked God for having shown her how to pay for the extras: piano lessons and prom dresses and sports equipment, and the yearly vacations to Michigan. She knew that God had protected her because he knew that was what her family needed. The Bible told her to give food and clothing and drink to those who live in the Kingdom of God and that's what she did, and if she interpreted food and clothing a little looser than the Bible specified, well God understood how complicated life had become. She had done it for them, those she loved, not for herself, and she slept well during those years, better than now, and when Roger lost his job, they didn't lose the house and the kids' lives went on, without worry, without lack.

If she were to diagnose her daughter, it was that she was floating, awash in the melancholy of being herself, of serving no one. No one needed her. No one cried when she didn't feed them. No one sat at the table and made demands. To have a life so full of yourself was a terrible thing. But she never told her daughter this. Instead, the two of them sat cozy on the couch eating the food Rosalind made as they chatted. Her daughter showed her pictures of her life here in the city, and in all the pictures she looked happy, or the kind of sexy that Rosalind saw on TV, pouty and wind-blown. She talked mostly about her job, she was in human resources at a tech company and had a bad boss who she claimed hated her. Rosalind felt hopeless as Emily talked, she didn't seem to need the outdated help Rosalind had to offer—food and tucking in, the occasional 100 dollars left on a bedside table. The problems of men and career and fulfillment were too complicated, too much of the world she didn't inhabit anymore. She wanted to say come home, you can come home, but she didn't. She wanted to say, have a child, or a husband, you will never be able to fill yourself. But she already knew how scornful her daughter would be of such advice. And she didn't say to her unhappy daughter, you can pray, you can turn your misery into what is mysterious and beautiful. You aren't the only one in the world who is unhappy. Everything she had to offer was too wispy for her daughter's practical problems, wrong, unsayable, not enough.

The day before she was to leave she found the park. The green was a relief from the harsh edges of the city, she hadn't realized until then how much she wanted to be in a softer place. Despite its many colored houses, despite its general acceptance of all costumes, all types, the city was dirty and noisy and a little frightening, filled with an unfamiliar aggression and anger that had no visible source. Inside the park she saw a beautiful wooden gate like a gate from a fairytale, though the price to enter wasn't a firstborn child, but seven dollars. The Japanese garden was precise in its aliveness, so tended and sculpted it felt as if the actual souls of trees and bushes were revealed. She stopped at the pond and looked at the koi who hoped that her presence was a sign that they would soon be fed. "No food today," she told them and spread her hands out wide, casting a shadow over the water that the koi rushed to, their mouths widening into O's, eager and greedy as nursing children.

At the teahouse she ordered jasmine tea and a plate of cookies. The cookies were dry and crumbly, unappetizing, but came with a fortune cookie, which seemed redundant. She cracked it open and the pieces of the cookie shattered in her hand, revealing her fortune: *Never enough more for those in want*. What kind of fortune was that? She felt cheated, and she didn't quite understand it, more what? Those who want? Those who are in want? She just wanted . . . what did she want? The fortune probably came from some bad computer program that was taking over everyone's jobs. She gathered up the pieces of the cookie in a napkin, intending to feed them to the koi. Sitting at the table next to her was a little girl, dark-skinned and pretty, and her young, pink-skinned and careless minder. The little girl was six or seven and restless. Every few minutes she would get up off her chair and walk around to all the unoccupied tables, touching the chairs with her left hand. After the third go around, she walked up to the counter, looked back at her minder who was engrossed in a yoga magazine and slipped a brightly wrapped Japanese candy into the pocket of her skirt. The pockets were wide and bulging with goodies. She skipped back towards her minder and stopped at Rosalind's table.

"What's that? It's ugly," she said pointing to the eye patch. Rosalind felt a small stab of pain and then the tiny pricklings of hate. The little girl walked on her tippy toes around the table and Rosalind smiled at her.

"I'm a pirate," Rosalind told the little girl. "Ho ho ho."

The little girl looked suspiciously at her, as if she suspected Rosalind of making fun of her. "You don't look like a pirate. You look like an old lady. And pirates don't say ho ho ho."

"I'm in disguise," she said. "I'm a pirate dressed up like an old lady. And pirates say ho ho ho when they're happy."

"I'm a princess," the girl said and twirled her skirt around. "I'd rather be a princess than a mean pirate. Princesses are beautiful."

"Nevaeh, leave that lady alone and come over here." The minder had finally put down her magazine.

"I think you should kidnap me," Nevaeh said to Rosalind. "Pirates kidnap princesses. It's their job."

"She's fine," Rosalind told the minder. "Not bothering me at all."

She leaned down to talk quietly to the girl. The smell of the girl was sharp and clean, and for no good reason, tears came to Rosalind's eyes and she couldn't see well. "I'd very much like to kidnap you," she said, "but pirate rules are very strict and I'm not allowed to kidnap anyone on dry ground. If only we were at sea."

Nevaeh flopped herself on the empty chair beside Rosalind. Her skirt was shattered into panels of glinting pink and matched her shiny pink ballet slippers. She held out her hand to Rosalind, who took it. Such a soft, fragile collection of bones, knit together with nothing permanent, just sinew and blood and tendons that snap when bent the wrong way. What trust to give a stranger your hand, as if there was no possibility of pain.

"I'm bored," said the girl. "Bored, bored, bored." She looked at Rosalind expectantly.

"Only boring people are bored," Rosalind answered. But was that true? She had said it so many times to her children, automatically, without thinking, never understanding why children were bored, everything in the world so new and fresh. Maybe children were bored because they had years and years of time ahead of them. Maybe they could sense all those hours of trying and failing, of dentist appointments and traffic jams and studying for tests. All those years where pleasure had to be postponed, where you had to find a job, get used to a job, and then get used to not having a job. The tiresome nature of time.

"I saw what you did," Rosalind made her voice low and raspy. "That was wrong." The little girl stared at her. "You put it back and I'll take you to feed the fish."

"I didn't do anything wrong. You're mean," she said.

Rosalind pointed at her pocket. "What's in there then?"

The girl looked sullen. "My treasures." She glanced at her minder who had returned to her magazine. "I'm going to feed the fish," she said as if it had been her idea.

"Okay," she told the girl. "But you have to tell her where you're going." Nevaeh nodded and got up, but went the other way, toward the entrance.

Rosalind, clutching the napkin filled with fortune cookie pieces, hurried after her.

The pond was next to the teahouse so it wasn't as if they were going far. Rosalind was comforted by this fact—they were going to teach that young woman a lesson, such a terrible nanny. The fish, orange and red and yellow, were much bigger than the average goldfish, alternating between swimming in circles and staying very still.

"You can't take things that aren't yours," Rosalind said. Rosalind gave the girl the napkin but before she had a chance to tell her how to feed the fish—to break the cookie into crumbs—the girl threw the entire mess in, napkin and all. She clapped excitedly and then took out the Japanese candy, a bracelet and a necklace, all of them sparkling like the fish and the water and threw them in after.

"Oh, don't do that," Rosalind said. "You'll make the fish sick!" She knelt by the pond and grabbed at the napkin, but it sank quickly. Some of the fish, excited by the possibility of food, tore at it and the sodden cookie pieces. The others tried to peck at the candy, still wrapped, which was sinking more slowly than the napkin but still out of reach. "No, that's their dessert," the girl said proudly. Rosalind stared at the mess. They had spoiled the pool. The koi in their greediness, in their inability to distinguish between food and trash, were going to die. She looked around to see if anyone was watching, but the park was quiet.

"Nevaeh!" the minder had come running out of the teahouse. "I told you never to run off." Her voice was harsh and desperate.

Nevaeh turned to look at her and smirked. "She wanted to kidnap me," she said. "But I'm too smart for her. I made her stay here and feed the fish. You took too long!"

The minder stared at Rosalind, and Rosalind could see that she was evaluating her for potential madness, as if you could tell from the outside of someone what lurked inside. "Don't be ridiculous," the minder said, pulling on Nevaeh's arm. "It's time to go," she said. "Your piano lesson. That's just an old woman." She looked at Rosalind. "You should be ashamed of yourself."

Rosalind wasn't sure who she was talking to, Nevaeh or Rosalind, but she didn't feel ashamed, she felt elated and filled with hate towards the minder. It was icy-hot, but not painful or an inflammation, it was like joy. An opening. She remembered then, what it felt to be young, to be righteous and sure of herself.

To the minder she said, "You should watch her more closely, you're a terrible babysitter."

“I hate piano,” Nevaeh said. “She wanted to steal me away!” She pointed at Rosalind. She reminded Rosalind of the frantically feeding fish, rapacious and glittering and beautiful.

“I did not want to steal you away,” Rosalind said sternly. She turned to the minder. “I saw this girl take a piece of candy from the teahouse and I followed her out here to make her give it back. She threw it in, you can see it there,” and Rosalind pointed to the candy nestled in the mud of the pond.

Nevaeh started to weep. “I don’t want the fish to die. Mommy, don’t let the fishes die!” She knelt down and started patting the water, trying to get the fish to come to her.

The girl’s mother pointed at Rosalind and her finger was shaking. “Mind your own business. You don’t know anything. Stop that Nevaeh!” Nevaeh continued patting the water.

“She took the candy and she wanted me too!” Nevaeh said this in a low growl to the fishes. “She wanted me, she wanted me, she wanted me.”

And Rosalind realized that that was the truth. She hadn’t even known it, but she did want her. She had wanted to steal her, to take her back to Cincinnati, or no—somewhere new, and they could spend time together and she wouldn’t read magazines and she would teach her right from wrong. She wanted all of it back, those years when she was powerful and could feed and clothe little beings, those years when she could answer questions and clean up messes and someone would love her without question. Nevaeh gave up on the fish, and stood to give her mother a hug, Rosalind felt shocked that she had been so wrong, tricked that her eyes had deceived her, mother and daughter not even sharing the same skin. In her church there was an interracial couple, but their children, they were blended, you could tell where they came from. But it wasn’t just the skin color that had confused her, the mother was too unruffled, like a page with no writing, and younger than Rosalind’s own daughter. Shouldn’t Rosalind have known that this careless young woman’s body had expanded like Rosalind’s, that she too had had to accommodate the needs of another? There was a crumbling inside Rosalind, and she felt herself stagger, as if she’d been hit with something hard.

“C’mon Mommy,” the girl said. “She’s a mean old lady. She’s the stealer,” and she pointed to the Japanese candy. “It was her fault.” Her mother gave her a hug back. “We’re late,” she said, “the fishes will be fine, I’m sure they eat garbage all the time.”

After they left Rosalind stared at the koi still attacking the napkin. Maybe they would be okay? Maybe koi had robust digestive systems. She stayed at the pond watching until the wet air made her long for a hot shower. She had stayed so long she had to hurry in order to get dinner ready for her daughter. The koi swam in circles as she left, except for the ones that stayed still. The remains of the candy glittered at the bottom of the pond, but the napkin had completely dissolved to become part koi and part water.

That night her daughter didn't come home at the right time. At first she thought to herself, of course, she had to work late, but the girl didn't call, which was not like her, her daughter called often. And then Rosalind worried that she had offended her in some way and Emily was angry. She called her cell, but it kept ringing and then went to voicemail. At 11 p.m. she put away the salad, which luckily she hadn't dressed, and the baked sesame chicken, her daughter's favorite. She wanted to call someone, but there was no one to call. Back in Cincinnati her other two children were already asleep, and her husband had been dead six years, of a cancer that ate his bones until he was filled with holes. She thought his death was a strange contradiction—the nothing that filled him so immense that, under the unexpected force of it, her husband just dissolved. She knelt by the couch and prayed, please come home please come home please come home, and then walked around the tiny apartment touching things. She touched her daughter's clothes, strewn across the floor in the bedroom—the bedroom was so small she could stretch out sideways and touch the walls on either side of the bed. She felt the fibrous synthetic bedcover bought from Target; the abstract pattern looked hopeful and bold. Grab life, it said. Grab life and give it a shake. She touched all the things, the four pots she had given her as a housewarming present when her daughter first moved out to San Francisco, the red couch that folded out into an uncomfortable bed and made her back ache, the computer her daughter always cradled on her lap. Where is she? she asked each thing, hoping that an answer would come, but what they answered was contradictory, was in her own small voice.

When she had been younger—sixteen, maybe seventeen?—all those years that had seemed so separate now folded together like a closed fan—she had fallen in love with Japan. There was no good reason, she had never been to Japan. The only Japanese person she knew was a popular girl in her high school. But she read in a book how the Japanese believed everything had spirits in them, and she had wished she lived in a place where things were prickly with aliveness, where a spirit inhabited every single object. She tried, for a little while, to see things that way; she saw little flames flickering in her bed, her dishes and the fluttering skirts she hung in her closets, and it caused her to take care, to put pots down more gently, to whisper a little to her panties and bras. It made sense to her that everything was alive, that everything had a soul. Later she had found a different solace in her church, but it came from the same place, that wanting to feel a kind of connection when she was afraid there was none. Two months before Roger had died, God had talked to her. God had said that Roger was going to die but that she could bear it because Roger was going to be part of God now. And God was right—but she told God that she couldn't bear any other loss. She told God that she'd had enough.

God didn't answer and now it was 2 a.m. and she was talking to pots and pans and she couldn't tell what was real. Because that's what you did when you loved someone, you waited until one day they weren't there and then you were angry.

Her daughter came home at 2:30, drunk, smelling of sweat and bars, men and pot and cigarettes, and for some reason, like dog. She reeled in, loud and droopy, her face losing a habitual tenseness that Rosalind had thought was Emily's permanent face. Before Rosalind could say a word, her daughter started explaining and excusing.

"Sorry Mommy I had such a bad day they took me out to drink it off and I lost track of time. Why are you still up? You shouldn't wait up, I'm a grownup now you know. I had fun, I don't have enough fun, I quit you know today. I quit my job. I'll find a new one. Don't worry Mommy, I'm a grown up. You were always a good mom. You were the best mom. I'll do better." And then she started to weep. Two children weeping in one day. What could Rosalind do but comfort her daughter and put her to bed and bring the coverlet over her so that she was warm and stroke her head. Before she passed out, her daughter mumbled, "I don't know how you did it, Mommy, I don't know how to do this, it's so hard, it's too hard here, you were too good to us."

She started to snore immediately. Rosalind looked at what she had brought into the world and wondered what had she forgotten to give her child? She had sacrificed everything and somehow failed. She stayed up all night cleaning the apartment, dusting and vacuuming, clearing out the cupboards and the refrigerator, until everything sparkled and her daughter, when she woke up with a terrible headache, was grateful and cried again and wished her mother would stay forever.

The eye never really healed. After Rosalind returned to Cincinnati a doctor told her it was a permanent injury. When she told the story about the little girl in the airport, she changed it and described the sparkly girl in the park. It was never Rosalind's own fault, the injury—the mother was at fault, a terrible mother who couldn't control her kid. Other times it was the demon child, and sometimes it was the fault of no one, just an accident, one of those things. Her daughter found a new job and told her mother that she was happier, that she was on the right track now, that things were just always getting better. She stopped calling Rosalind with her tales of woe, and Rosalind, instead of feeling relieved, felt a helplessness come over her for which she blamed the girl in the park. Just like my husband, she thought to herself. I feel just like him, when he was near his end. Is it possible I too will soon disappear? She had been eating dinner at the kitchen table and the food, the small brown square of greasy steak, the exploded baked potato, and a few spears of broccoli—trees, they used to call them trees, her children—looked foreign to her and grisly. She awkwardly knelt down beside her wooden chair and tried to pray. God, please on this day, forgive my trespasses, and when I die I want your arms around me, and she tried to think of her sins to list and ask forgiveness for, but there was only blankness where those sins should've been and instead she said to God, I was a good person, I was a good person, I loved my family. Amen. She used the seat of the chair to help herself up. She had regrets, yes, was that the same as a sin? The food was cold and she wasn't hungry, so she threw it away. Maybe there was a problem in loving, but she couldn't quite work it out. Anyway, she didn't die but the possibility of it was always with her, like a good friend.

She continued to wear the eye patch, even though it was medically unnecessary. It seemed important to do so, to let everyone know that she had changed, to show proof of it. She'd say to herself, I'm a pirate, and it made her almost happy, her snarl of a smile and the way people looked at her twice as if she wasn't just an older lady who had no past or future, but someone who mattered, someone who was loved, or feared.

HELLO FROM THE CHILDREN OF PLANET EARTH

by M.H. TSE

from ALASKA QUARTERLY REVIEW

There is a message on Voyager 1 and 2, space probes that have been sailing away from the planet Earth for almost 50 years. The message is cut into a 12-inch gold-plated copper disk and contains 115 images and 35 sound recordings of life on Earth, 90 minutes of music, and greetings spoken in 55 different human languages. There are images of mathematical equations, bridges, a strand of DNA, and a human mother nursing an infant. There are bird sounds, folk songs, an aria, and a recording of the brainwaves of one of the creators, Ann Druyan, meditating on the wonder of being in love. "Hello from the children of Planet Earth," a voice says in English.[2] The Golden Record is supposed to remain legible for a billion years.

As an artifact of the human story, this object contains vital information about the beings who made it. That information is not, however, revealed in the contents of the message, but in how these beings had positioned certain parts of themselves in the light and other parts in shadow when they sat for their portrait.

Of all the pieces of information conveyed by the Golden Record about the beings who made it, the most important is that the image they made is not an image of what the beings are, but what the beings imagine themselves to be.

And it is the distance between these that tells us we are dealing with *authors* with all the freedom and distortion this entails. It is no surprise that the human account of itself, whether in the Record or in other human reveries, does little to convey the second most fundamental thing about them.

It will not be clear just from speaking to a human that it is an animal.

Or that, like many animals, it lives by killing and consuming the bodily material of other animals.

It will not be clear from their accounts of "what makes us human" that they have developed a unique predatory style that is built on the practice of *holding* and *keeping* prey alive and breeding them in perpetuity, so that their flesh, fluids, skin, fur, ova, and offspring, can be extracted over time.

This predatory method, which may be described as *domestic predation,* is an innovation on prototypal predation because it incorporates a pre-slaughter period of preservation. It delays the act of killing, so that not only the material in hand, but all biological materials that can *potentially* be generated by the body can be fully appropriated. The domestic predator thereby extends the act of taking into the future, by shifting its focus "from the dead to the living animal."[3] This human focus is not, however, on life as an ultimate end.

The focus is on the use of life in the production of death.

Thus, in contrast to Dr. Frankenstein, who sought to use dead body parts to create life, the human uses life to create dead body parts. At the center of this subsistence model is the occupation of the sexual and reproductive functions of other animals, which allows the domestic predator to continue bodily extraction beyond the life of any individual animal through the supply of offspring. As the human, John Lee, explains, a strong reproductive program "delivers a steady pipeline of replacements."[4] There is no secret to "reproductive success," Lee says, the "key is getting more semen in more cows."[5] These efforts are referred to as "setting [the animals] up for success."[6]

The prolongation of life for the *in vivo* extraction of prized reproductive materials, such as milk and eggs, connects domestic predation to *parasitism*. Parasitism is the consumption of a living creature over time or, as the human, E.O. Wilson, explains, it is the practice of eating prey "in units of less than one."[7]

Domestic predation is an innovation on prototypal parasitism, however, because it allows a parasite to engage in *in vivo* consumption without having to live *inside* or directly *on* their prey.

As with the extraction of offspring from animals, the extraction of substances such as milk and eggs is also centered on sexual and reproductive control. For instance, the process of lactation, which is a maternal response that evolved "to support [the] survival of milk-dependent offspring,"[8] is activated by repeatedly impregnating female mammals such as cows. This method of production involves compelling cows, or other mammals, to birth a calf and then removing the calf so that human milkers can assume the place of the calf in the mother-baby dyad. As human, Marina von Keyserlingk, explains, cow milk extraction is achieved by "redirecting" the nursing behavior of mother cows to human milkers.[9] When a calf suckles on his mother's teats, it triggers the secretion of the hormone oxytocin. This hormone causes milk to be released from the upper chambers of the mammary glands of the calf's mother into the lower cisterns and teats, where it can then be consumed by the calf.[10] In addition to promoting "milk let-down," oxytocin also plays an important role in the formation of maternal bonds between mothers and their offspring.[11] The human provokes this neuro-endocrine release of oxytocin by mimicking the stimulation of a cow's teats by her calf. This is accomplished by manual or machine stimulation, although other methods of stimulation are continually being invented and tested by humans, such as playing the calls of hungry calves, presenting cows with calf odours from calf hairs, and vaginal stimulation.[12] Human methods of stimulation for inducing milk-release then displace the calf as an associational trigger, or learned condition, for lactation.

Human extraction of milk from cows is also achieved by various methods that have been developed for *overcoming* the cow's physiological and neuro-endocrinological attempts to withhold her milk from human milkers, which the human refers to as "disturbed milk ejection."[13] Oxytocin release is suppressed in cows under emotional stress, in cows who are milked by humans for the first time, or in cows who are switched from nursing a calf to human or machine milking.[14] Humans have recognized that oxytocin suppression and "disturbed milk ejection" may be an attempt by the cow to keep her milk for her calf.[15] Humans bypass this hormonal block by removing calves from their mothers at the time of birth, thereby preventing the establishment of maternal bonds in the first place. Humans also render ejection-resistance futile by injecting oxytocin into a cow before they milk her.[16]

The second way that cows regulate milk production is through a protein contained in their milk that inhibits lactation, which the human calls the "feedback inhibitor of lactation" or "FIL."[17] Because of this protein, leftover milk in a cow's udders acts as a cellular signal to decrease milk production, thereby limiting the amount of milk produced by a cow to the needs of her calf. To overcome this natural inhibitor of milk production, the human places cows under an intensive milking regimen, in which they are milked 3 or more times daily, with the goal of completely emptying the udder of milk during each extraction session.[18] This technique effectively compels the udder to communicate that more milk must be made to feed an insatiably hungry calf. Thus, milking frequency is not a response to the high volumes of milk production we see in human extraction systems today. Rather, high volumes of milk production are a response to high frequency and high intensity milking. As the archeologist human, Sytze Bootema, explains, the enormous size of the udder of a modern dairy cow is not a domestication characteristic—only the "shape of the udder is hereditary."[19] When cows are "left to suckle their own calves," they "develop only a small udder, densely covered with hairs."[20] The "excessive size" of the udder, Bootema explains, "is induced by the milking regime, whether milking is done by hand or by machine."[21] Through such ingenious manipulations, humans have been able to fully deplete the total metabolic and reproductive capacities which may be utilized by a cow over a 20-year lifespan, in just 3 to 4 years.[22] At the end of this extraction cycle, many cows will be physically compromised by conditions such as lameness and injury, diseases of the udder, and emaciation.[23] These bodies can then be transported to sites of mass assembly and mass killing and harvested as carcasses. Humans are voracious extractors of milk from the bodies of other mammals. In a single yearly cycle, humans extract roughly 800 million tonnes of milk from the animals they hold.[24]

To take hold of *life* as an engine of production means taking hold of the sexual and reproductive functions of other animals. As a driver manipulates the controls of a car to utilize its vehicular power as a means of transportation, the domestic predator manipulates the sexual and reproductive organs of an animal to commandeer their generative power as an engine of production and reproduction. In its pursuit of this power, humans have invented tools and techniques and built infrastructures for exercising prolonged intimate control over the bodies of other animals and for compelling such bodies to grow, produce, and reproduce.

In bovine production and extraction systems, for instance, semen is extracted by humans from bulls either by stimulating the bull's rectum by human hand or by electrical probes. Another method for extracting semen from bulls is the diverted intercourse method. This method involves inciting sexual intercourse between male animals with "mount" animals under varying degrees of restraint or confinement.[25] After conducting several "false" mounts, the thrust of the bull is diverted and their ejaculate is collected by a human semen collector using a device called an "artificial vagina."[26] Bulls and mount animals are restrained and controlled during these procedures in steel chutes and/or by ropes or staffs attached to metal rings that have been installed in the animals' nasal septum.

Insemination of female animals is accomplished either by techniques of artificial insemination or by human-orchestrated animal intercourse while one or both animals are restrained or confined.[27] Artificial insemination of cows, for instance, involves a technique known as rectovaginal fixation of the cervix.[28] In this procedure, a cow is restrained by a chain or headlock that prevents the cow from moving forward or backing up. Some cows may require containment in a breeding chute, or a "dark box," made of metal or wood. While the cow is restrained, the human inseminator inserts its arm deep into a cow's rectum and grabs hold of her cervix through the rectal wall. With the other hand, the human inserts an insemination rod through the vagina and then through the "fixed" cervix and injects the semen through the rod and into the uterus.[29] A cow may attempt to kick when a human pushes its hand into her rectum, but once the hand is inside the rectum, this causes the cow to arch her back and positions the spine in a way that will inhibit kicking.[30]

These technologies of domestic predation can be seen as the great legacy of the human species. It is not, however, a legacy that is overamplified in the human account of itself. The details of sexual and reproductive control appear instead to have been quietly set aside in the curatorial process. Legal prohibitions on sexual contact between humans and animals, or "bestiality," which is condemned as an offence against morality,[31] push such practices further into the shadows of the popular imagination. In a much finer print, however, every jurisdiction that has condemned acts of bestiality makes an exception, either implicitly or explicitly, to protect sexual engagements between humans and animals from legal prosecution when performed for the purpose of domestic predation.[32] Without control over breeding, there is no control over the biological processes of growth and reproduction which is the principal imperative of domestic predation. Putting an end to human sexual engagements with other animals would mean putting an end to the human practice of domestication.[33]

By whatever power you arrive at this place, it will become clear that the human account of the "story of our world" will not help you understand the objects and infrastructures of these signal achievements of the human being.

The metal restraining chutes, the concrete stalls with their individual chains and tethers, the layered encrusted cages, the darkened, rank outbuildings, the pits of neon-colored waste, the perforated trailers stuffed with creature life skimming through the silent prairie night, the glistening slaughter chambers, the ropes in tension, the hooks, the whips, the prods, the nose prongs, the plyers, the scissors, the electric bath, the ejaculation probes, the insemination rods, the vials of semen, the breeding pens, the long glove, the plastic apron, the stained walls—this vast nether-architecture on the underside of the human story, which to anyone else would seem to be its main monument.

The record will be inadequate in shedding light on the instruments and facilities of bodily restraint, confinement, extraction, and slaughter, that will inescapably unfold before your eyes.

You will not be prepared to confront the 26 billion other animals that the human faction is presently holding as living inventory under regimes of bodily extraction and sexual and reproductive control, or to witness the more than 100 billion individual animals who will be killed in every yearly cycle for the purposes of extraction.[34]

With the information you have been provided, you will not appreciate a primary cause for how the face of this world came to be denuded, or how the ecological patterns of life evolved, and you will fail to grasp how the biological inventory held by humans has come to eclipse all other forms of life.[35]

The story of the human cannot be described without some explanation of this corpus of living prey and the means by which it is held. Without some knowledge of the human project of domestic predation, you will not be able to make sense of their enclosure of the land and their partitioning of the world. And the songs they sing, the gods they imagine, their humor, and their terrors—reconfigured into stories of the dead who nonetheless live and the living who ought to be dead—these too will be unfathomable to you.

Considering these facts, it would not do harm to the human account, as a matter of accuracy, to de-emphasize some elements that are typically recounted in it, and to take note of the true monuments of the human experience which are typically neglected.

NOTES

1. Nick Sagan, audio clip from "Greetings to the Universe in 55 Different Languages," Golden Record, NASA Jet Propulsion Laboratory, California Institute of Technology, accessed December 19, 2023, https://voyager.jpl.nasa.gov/golden-record/whats-on-the-record/greetings/,archived at https://perma.cc/7DUU-MT53.
2. Nick Sagan, "Greetings."
3. Richard H. Meadow, "Osteological Evidence for the Process of Animal Domestication," in *The Walking Larder: Patterns of Domestication, Pastoralism, and Predation*, ed. Juliet Clutton-Brock (London: Unwin Hyman, 1988), 80, 81.
4. John Lee, "The Secret to Repro Success is Not a Secret," *Progressive Dairy*, April 30, 2013, archived at https://perma.cc/HXB7-3SPY.
5. Lee, "Secret to Repro."
6. For example, see Rebecca Hannam, "Setting Dairy Calves Up for Success," *Farmtario*, June 23, 2022, archived at https://perma.cc/H4A4-QYEV; Barry Bradford, "Feeding for Fertility," *Michigan State University Extension*, April 2, 2021, archived at https://perma.cc/U3JK-ZGQU; Heather Smith Thomas, "Setting Up Young Cows for Success," *Canadian Cattlemen*, December 15, 2021, archived at https://perma.cc/9VCJ-6P2R; Taylor Leach, "The 7 Repro Sins You Can't Afford to Make," *Dairy Herd Management*, September 19, 2023, archived at https://perma.cc/LEN7-MQXC; Stephen LeBlanc, "State-of-the-art dairy farming: Reproductive performance on transition cows," interview, The Dairy Podcast Show, episode #20, January 23, 2023, audio, https://podcasts.apple.com/us/podcast/20-state-of-the-art-dairy-farming/id1643773684?i=1000596179729.
7. Edward O. Wilson, *The Meaning of Human Existence* (New York: Norton, 2014), 180.
8. Josef J. Gross, "Dairy Cow Physiology and Production Limits," *Anim. Front.* 13, no. 3 (2023): 44–50, 45; Maria Vilain Rørvang et al., "Prepartum Maternal Behavior of Domesticated Cattle: A Comparison with Managed, Feral, and Wild Ungulates," *Front. Vet. Sci.* 5, art. 45 (2018): 1–11; Hector Macias and Lindsay Hinck, "Mammary Gland Development," *Wiley Interdiscip. Rev. Dev. Biol.* 1, no. 4 (2012): 533–557.
9. Marina A.G. von Keyserlingk and Daniel M. Weary, "Maternal Behavior in Cattle," *Hormones and Behavior* 52 (2007): 106–113, 111.
10. K. Svennersten-Sjaunja and K. Olsson, "Endocrinology of Milk Production," *Domestic Animal Endocrinology* 29 (2005): 241–258, 250–251.
11. Julie Føske Johnsen et al., "Is Rearing Calves with the Dam a Feasible Option for Dairy Farms?—Current and Future Research," *Applied Animal Behaviour Science* 181 (2016) 1–11, 7; Berit Lupoli et al., "Effect of Suckling on the Release of Oxytocin, Prolactin, Cortisol, Gastrin, Cholecystokinin, Somatostatin and Insulin in Dairy Cows and Their Calves," *J. Dairy Research* 68 (2001): 175–187, 176.
12. Juliana Mačuhová et al., "Inhibition of Oxytocin Release During Repeated Milking in Unfamiliar Surroundings: The Importance of Opioids and Adrenal Cortex Sensitivity," *J. Dairy Research* 69 (2002): 63–73; R.M. Bruckmaier and O. Wellnitz, "Induction of Milk Ejection and Milk Removal in Different Production Systems," *J. Anim. Sci.* 86, supp. 1 (2008) 15–20, 16, 18; Johnsen et al., "Is Rearing Calves with the Dam a Feasible Option," 7; Katharina A. Zipp et al., "Responses of Dams Versus Non-nursing Cows to Machine Milking in Terms of Milk Performance, Behaviour and Heart Rate With and Without Additional Acoustic, Olfactory or Manual Stimulation," *Applied Animal Behaviour Science* 204 (2018): 10–17.
13. C.J. Belo and R.M. Bruckmaier, "Suitability of Low-Dosage Oxytocin Treatment to Induce Milk Ejection in Dairy Cows," *J. Dairy Sci.* 93 (2010): 63–69; J. Mačuhová et al., "Effects of Oxytocin Administration on Oxytocin Release and Milk Ejection," *J. Dairy Sci.* 87 (2004): 1236–1244; Wolf-Dieter Kraetzl et al., "Naloxone Cannot Abolish the Lack of Oxytocin Release During Unexperienced Suckling of Dairy Cows," *Applied Animal Behaviour Science* 72 (2001): 247–253.
14. Mačuhová et al., "Inhibition of Oxytocin Release," 64; Bruckmaier and Wellnitz, "Induction of Milk Ejection," 17; V. Tančin et al., "Effect of Suckling During Early Lactation and Change Over to Machine Milking on Plasma Oxytocin and Cortisol Levels and Milk Characteristics in Holstein Cows," *J. Dairy Research* 62 (1995): 249–256; V. Tančin and R.M. Bruckmaier, "Factors Affecting Milk Ejection and Removal During Milking and Suckling of Dairy Cows," *Vet. Med.—Czech* 46 (2001): 108–118.
15. V. Tančin et. al., "The Effects of Conditioning to Suckling, Milking and of Calf Presence on the Release of Oxytocin in Dairy Cows," *Applied Animal Behaviour Science* 72 (2001): 235–246, 242; Johnsen et al., "Is Rearing Calves with the Dam a Feasible Option," 5, 9; A.M. de Passillé et al., "Effects of Twice-Daily Nursing on Milk Ejection and Milk Yield During Nursing and Milking in Dairy Cows," *J. Dairy Sci.* 91 (2008): 1416–1422, 1420–1421; U. Bar-Peled et al., "Relationship between Frequent Milking or Suckling in Early Lactation and Milk Production of High Producing Dairy Cows," *J. Dairy Sci.* 78 (1995): 2726–2736, 2734.
16. Belo and Bruckmaier, "Suitability of Low-Dosage Oxytocin Treatment," 63–4; Bruckmaier and Wellnitz, "Induction of Milk Ejection," 18; Mačuhová et al., "Effects of Oxytocin Administration," 1236; Robert J. Collier et al., "Impacts on Human Health and Safety of Naturally Occurring and Supplemental Hormones in Food Animals," *Council for Agricultural Science and Technology*, July 27, 2020, 15–17, https://www.cast-science.org/wp-content/uploads/2020/07/QTA2020-4-Hormones.pdf, archived at https://perma.cc/82J6-3MSZ.
17. E. H. Wall and T.B. McFadden, "Use It Or Lose It: Enhancing Milk Production Efficiency by Frequent Milking of Dairy Cows," *J. Anim. Sci.* 86 (2008): 27–36, 31; Bar-Peled et al., "Relationship between Frequent Milking or Suckling in Early Lactation and Milk Production," 2733; Svennersten-Sjaunja and Olsson, "Endocrinology of Milk Production," 249.
18. Wall and McFadden, "Use It Or Lose It."
19. Sytze Bootema, "Some Observations on Modern Domestication Processes," in *The Walking Larder: Patterns of Domestication, Pastoralism, and Predation*, ed. Juliet Clutton-Brock (London: Unwin Hyman, 1988), 31–45, 31.
20. Bootema, "Some Observations," 31.
21. Bootema, 31.

22. Gross, "Dairy Cow Physiology and Production Limits," 45.
23. A. De Vries and M.I. Marcondes, "Review: Overview of Factors Affecting Productive Lifespan of Dairy Cows," *Animal* 14:S1 (2020): s155–s164; J. Stojkov et al., "Fitness for Transport of Cull Dairy Cows at Livestock Markets," *J. Dairy Sci.* 103 (2020): 2650–2661; J. Stojkov et al., "Management of Cull Dairy Cows: Culling Decisions, Duration of Transport, and Effect on Cow Condition," *J. Dairy Sci.* 103 (2020): 2636–2649; J. Stojkov et. al., "Hot Topic: Management of Cull Dairy Cows—Consensus of an Expert Consultation in Canada," *J. Dairy Sci.* 101 (2018): 11170–11174.
24. Hannah Ritchie et al., "Meat and Dairy Production," *Our World in Data*, August 2017, Revised December 2023, accessed February 28, 2024, https://ourworldindata.org/meat-production, archived at https://perma.cc/2N4B-WPSZ.
25. Albert D. Barth, "Evaluation of Potential Breeding Soundness of the Bull," in *Current Therapy in Large Animal Theriogenology*, eds. Robert S. Youngquist and Walter R. Threlfall (Elsevier Health Sciences, 2007), 228–240, 233–235; J.L. Schenk, "Review: Principles of Maximizing Bull Semen Production at Genetic Centers," *Animal* 12:S1 (2018): s142–147; J.L. Tank and D.R. Monke, "Bull Management: Artificial Insemination Centers," in *Encyclopedia of Dairy Sciences, Third Edition*, eds. Paul L.H. McSweeney and John P. McNamara (Elsevier, 2022), 178–186, 185.
26. Ibid. See also Melissa Rouge, "Semen Collection From Bulls," Colorado State University, September 2, 2002, archived at https://perma.cc/M9YG-QTQC; "Seminal Collection," in Management Guidelines of the National Association of Animal Breeders, Certified Semen Services, accessed March 9, 2023, https://www.naab-css.org/management-guidelines, archived at https://perma.cc/L5FS-S5KZ.
27. Richard A. Battaglia, *Handbook of Livestock Management, 4th Edition* (New Jersey and Ohio: Prentice Hall, 2007), 196–197.
28. P. Lonergan, "Review: Historical and Futuristic Developments in Bovine Semen Technology," *Animal* 12:S1 (2018): s4–s18, s12; R.H. Foote, "The History of Artificial Insemination: Selected Notes and Notables," *Journal of Animal Science* 80 (2002): 1–10, 2; M.T Kaproth and R.H. Foote, "Mating Management: Artificial Insemination, Utilization," in *Encyclopedia of Dairy Sciences, Second Edition*, ed. John W. Fuquay (Elsevier, 2011), 467–474, 469; Battaglia, *Handbook of Livestock Management*, 128–132.
29. Ibid.
30. Battaglia, *Handbook of Livestock Management*, 130.
31. Brian James Holoyda, "Bestiality Law in the United States: Evolving Legislation with Scientific Limitations," 12 *Animals* 12 (2022): 1525.
32. For example see Me. Rev. Stat. Ann. Tit. 17, §1031(1)(I) (Bestiality provisions which make it an offence to engage in sexual acts with an animal "may not be construed to prohibit normal and accepted practices of animal husbandry."); Tex. Penal Code Ann. §21.09(a)(2), (4) (Bestiality provisions make it an offence to engage in sexual contact with an animal except where the conduct is "a generally accepted and otherwise lawful animal husbandry or veterinary practice.").
33. Control over the breeding of animals is the defining condition of the human practice of domesticating other animals. Sandor Bökönyi, "Definitions of Domestication," in *The Walking Larder: Patterns of Domestication, Pastoralism, and Predation*, ed. Juliet Clutton-Brock (London: Unwin Hyman, 1988), 22–27; M.R. Jarman and P.F. Wilkinson, "Criteria of Animal Domestication," in *Papers in Economic Prehistory*, ed. E.S. Higgs (Cambridge University Press, 1972), 83–96; Juliet Clutton-Brock, *A Natural History of Domesticated Mammals* (Cambridge University Press, 1999), 30, 32.
34. Hannah Ritchie, "How many animals are factory-farmed?," *Our World in Data*, September 25, 2023, accessed December 21, 2023, https://ourworldindata.org/how-many-animals-are-factory-farmed#article-citation, archived at https://perma.cc/5E59-7WSC; Ritchie et al., "Meat and Dairy Production."
35. Hannah Ritchie et al., "Environmental Impacts of Food Production," *Our World in Data*, 2022, accessed September 7, 2023, https://ourworldindata.org/environmental-impacts-of-food, archived at https://perma.cc/3SUN-CBQQ; Yinon M. Bar-On et al., "The Biomass Distribution on Earth," *Proceedings of the National Academy of Sciences*, 115, no. 25 (June 19, 2018): 6506–6511; H. Steinfeld et al., *Livestock's Long Shadow: Environmental Issues and Options* (Rome: FAO UN, 2006).

PELT

by ERICA REID

from POETRY DAILY

This molding coat I'm wearing—this *mood*—
this chewed-up mink, this blessed heavy mess
with its wet kinks, with its whiffy kiss of sweat,

this mood, all its gnarls, its curls, its age-old
burrs, this wretched sable, this fetching ruin,
thick hulk funking its bulk in my rough shape—

ratty mood! Menace in its drape, its feeble sag,
my drowsy cape. Sleeves uneven, buttons like
loose teeth. And me with nothing underneath.

PURPURA

by HEATHER TRESELER

from AUGURIES & DIVINATIONS
(BAUHAN PUBLISHING)

When the poet wrote *I lost my mother's watch,*
we knew she meant more than a timepiece.

To watch over the soft-skulled expulsive being
that is baby is a genre of love that must break

its own clock. In my first years, I slept little.
When I slept, I left my eyes' garage doors open.

Poor mother thought *baby awake, mother awake.*
For months: staring contests in the half-dark,

calling each other's bluff, falling in love as any
pair must—with desire and jealousy. Jostling

furniture in the psyche, heady hormonal rush.
When I lost my mother's watch, I was thirteen.

The day, unaccountably bright. Fields of flora
bloomed under her skin as if she were a lavender

hat in Seurat's famed painting. An ambulance
rolled its orange glass eye at her strange beauty.

For weeks, we waited for her body to lose its
artistic ambition. (Toxic drugs, confusion.)

Doctors asked: *Who is President? What year is it?*
Can you name your children? Purpura, the broken

blood vessels in her skin's pointillist painting.
Some code or augury to read and remember.

I watched, thinking of Phoenicians finding
the world's costliest color in the crushed bodies

of murex: vats of pulverized mollusks to trim
the general's cloak, dye an emperor's robe purple.

What a tyrant or daughter claims as her right,
calling it nature. The first empire is mother.

YELLOW TULIPS

fiction by NATHAN CURTIS ROBERTS

from HARVARD REVIEW

The week the novel coronavirus came to Utah, a series of earthquakes rattled the Salt Lake Valley. On the tallest spire of the church's flagship temple, the angel Moroni stood holding a clarion to his lips. The statue was more than twelve feet tall, made of hammered copper and coated in gold leaf. His purpose was twofold: he celebrated the foreordained spreading of the restored Gospel throughout the world, and he announced the immanence of the Second Coming of the lord Jesus Christ. And then the plague found us even here in our Rocky Mountain Zion, and a series of earthquakes struck, and the angel himself chattered, and the golden trumpet—which had been pressed to Moroni's lips for almost one hundred and thirty years—fell clattering from his grasp. This was a much clearer signal than God customarily sends, or so my son believed.

By that time our cul-de-sac was already in disarray. Old Bill Nilsson, who was the neighborhood's beating heart, had died on Valentine's Day. Bill was the homeowner association's capo, consigliere, and enforcer. Bill Nilsson was the man who pruned and fertilized the rose bushes in the community bowery; who would fix a family's sprinkler system before they even realized it was broken; and who would babysit a near-stranger's great-grandchildren, or a friend's mentally impaired son, on a moment's notice. Rumor had it he perished on February 14, at an unofficial reunion of college friends, the very moment he finished bearing his testimony. Bill Nilsson was a saint, and he had a death befitting such. Out in the world there were rumors of an impending epidemic. In our cul-de-sac we spoke only of the growing legend of

Bill Nilsson's departure: it wasn't just his testimony; he had told his friends how much they meant to him, and then he said a heartfelt prayer, and finally he looked at his wife of fifty-five years and recited a love poem. Then his heart quieted and he was dead before his head hit the floor. At the funeral, his eldest daughter described this as a "badass" way to go. It wasn't a word we were used to hearing inside the chapel of a Latter-day Saints meetinghouse. But after her eulogy the daughter sang "I need Thee Every Hour" with such sweetness and clarity—"ev'ry hour I need thee"—she could have gotten away with saying far worse.

I was thinking about how nice it would have been to have married a woman who could sing. My boy and I were seated on folding chairs in the overflow area at the back of the chapel. Better Mormons with larger families occupied the pews, with Bill's own brood taking several rows at the front. All the way in the rear—so far back we were practically in the multipurpose room, a basketball hoop overhead—my buttocks were growing numb. Next to me Brigham, my boy, sang along with the soloist. Full volume, he cried out: "I need thee, oh, I need thee!" Plaintive and yearning, as if the boy believed what he really needed was Bill Nilsson's eldest daughter. For a wife or for a mother, I cannot guess.

"Cram it," I said. "Knock it off."

"Tan parsons lose their prowler," the boy sang. He had lost command of the hymn's lyrics. Brig was nearing thirty, but he had ever been a child inside his mind and heart, and he would never be anything else. The boy took pride in dressing himself for church. He had four suits that were nearly identical, but it was important to him not to have to double up except in a month with five Sundays. Yet he would go nowhere without his camouflage fishing cap, which he was allowed to wear inside the chapel because the entire ward knew the sounds Brig made when he was upset. There used to be another "boy" like Brigham in our ward—the same age in mind and heart, at least a decade older in body—and the two of them usually occupied each other during services. At the worst, we could keep them quiet by daring them to see which of them would remain reverent the longest. It's a powerful friendship that's forged in such commonalities: similar disabilities, single fathers who were not too good to deploy a manipulation now and then.

Balding pate, unpredictable vanity, ubiquitous fishing hat. I clenched my fist and pressed a knuckle into the flesh of his leg, threatening him with a charley horse if he wouldn't pipe down. Brigham squirmed. "Peach me I try rich porpoises my belly fill," he sang. "Need thee now, I need thee oh!" The numbness in my ass was spreading downward.

Several feet in front of us, seated in the last row of proper pews, was Sister Meghan Palmer. She twisted around to fix us with a gaze and shush us both. I saw it coming before I ever heard it. A generation ago, Sister Palmer's face would have been stretched to translucency like strudel dough. But we were in the age of injectables, and she had the skin that was common among affluent women of her era, frozen fast and subtly plumped, as if inflated with cold baby fat. Meghan Palmer's hair was chin-length, sharp, a shade of yellow that suggested hair sometimes turned gold after it had gone silver. A booth-tanned complexion that was deepened with bronzer. Lips painted bubblegum pink, a color only the elderly ladies of our ward could have gotten away with—a younger woman would have been taken aside. The sound she made stunned us both, my son and I, into boyish shame. A shush like a serpent's hiss that carried at least as far as Brig's singing ever could have.

Then the earthquakes. The trumpet. Quarantine, canceled church services, teddy bears in windows. The entire neighborhood went inside; when it came back out a few weeks later—every hand carefully scrubbed, every body distanced by six scrupulous feet—it was spring. For Brigham and me, the transformation was not sudden. We witnessed the geometric progression of the window bears (two, four, sixteen) and we saw the nickel-sized crocuses herald the coming of the hyacinths, which announced the daffodils, which summoned lilacs out of the dead land, by which point the blossoms were on the cherry trees and the irises were making themselves ready. Bill Nilsson was three decades my senior, but he had completed the St. George Triathlon at my age, and again when he was fifteen years older. I got winded taking the garbage out. Bill had seemed as eternal as the three Nephites or the Wandering Jew. His mortality became my own mortality. The day after his funeral, I told Brigham we were going for a walk. A walk where? "Grab your hat, let's go." But where to?

Nowhere in particular. The first week we walked to North Canyon Park, about a mile each way. The following week we added the short paved trail that was the park's hidden feature. Then we walked that trail twice, three times, four. The third week one of my toenails fell off. But it was the nail with the fungal infection, and it was for the best because it grew back clean. Chalk art began to appear on the sidewalk. Bubble letters that were as likely to say "Hang in there" as "Trust in Him." When we were ready to take on the mountain, we first tried Eagle Ridge Drive. The view on that side was of the refineries of North Salt Lake.

Two thirds of the way to the bottom of the hill, there was a house with a life-sized statue of Christ in its front yard. Brigham was moved to pay his respects, tramping through the neighbor's lawn to kneel at the Savior's feet. I wondered where he learned this kind of enthusiasm. Not from me. Certainly not from his mother.

Even in Utah a statue like that was a strange sight; it gave an ordinary suburban home the look of a meetinghouse. A gleaming white Jesus standing next to the front porch—I thought it was excessive. What were these people trying to prove? Was it not sufficient to simply worship a deity; did we also need to decorate our yards with Him? I said a prayer every night and over most meals, the hot ones at least. I attended sacrament meeting nearly every Sunday and priesthood meeting sometimes, if the boy wasn't acting up. I paid ten percent tithing. Why did my neighbor need a six-foot statue in the yard? For that matter, why did the church need a twelve-foot one on a spire? "Brigham," I said, "come away from there!"

"I need thee now, I need thee," he said plaintively. Not to me, of course, but to the statue.

"Come!" I said. I slapped my thigh loudly. I was glad nobody was around to hear me speak to my son like a disobedient pet.

So we avoided Eagle Ridge and instead walked down and up the other side of the mountain. It appeared the deer were also quarantining, because the tulips in our bowery, and on Eaglewood Drive, were allowed to bloom that year—but only the yellow ones. I've long felt resentful of yellow tulips. They're redundant with daffodils, which are more resistant to disease and deer. What tulips are good for is their variety of colors, and for getting eaten up as buds, before they have a chance to present themselves. Meghan Palmer's house had a whole patch of them, yellow tulips in among yellow daffodils. One week I saw her watching us from her window. I waved, but if she waved back I never saw it. The following week the streets were full of human life, and Meghan Palmer called out to us. "Abraham Sorensen, look at you!" she said. "And Brigham too. You two have gotten so fit. I've seen it! When I first saw you boys doing your hikes up and down the hill, I thought, 'Now there's something.' I couldn't imagine going all the way down and back up again! But now the thing I marvel at is how you can hike for hours every morning and still hold on to those potbellies!"

It was important not to let on that her words bothered me. "I'm not a vain man," I said. "These walks are about feeling better, not looking better." I'd lost fifteen pounds in six weeks, but I wouldn't give her the satisfaction. The boy's belly did have a way of protruding. Someone, a special education teacher or a psychiatric nurse, explained it as a side effect of his fitting into the world differently from most. It never occurred to him to feel self-conscious, so he never bothered with sucking in his gut, which is apparently something the rest of are doing so often we no longer notice it.

"You have such a pragmatic mind. That's lucky for you. Brother Palmer is always buying us spa visits, and the latest treatments, but he does have money to burn. It's wise for someone like you to remember walking is free."

"Isn't it wonderful?" Brigham asked.

"What's wonderful, dear?" Sister Palmer said.

"It's wonderful," Brigham said, "because the whole world is ending!"

Every morning we took our walk. When it snowed, when it rained, when the hot wind blew over the desert and came to parch our lips. Brig wore his camouflage fishing hat and a long-sleeved thermal shirt, even after the weather grew warm. He called out to everyone he saw, got as close to them as they (or I) would allow. "Isn't it wonderful!" he said. He knew every neighbor by name, even folks I wasn't sure I recognized.

"My heart is joyous!" he said.

"Lead me guide me walk beside me! Jesus wants me for a sunbeam!" he sang.

My job at the Office of Tourism was already work I usually did from home. Brig was in no position to look after himself, and I didn't have the means to hire someone more than occasionally. With little to do besides posting cancellation notices to the website, I spent more time watching television with my boy. His favorite was a Japanese toy show called *Kamen Rider*—a commercial with occasional commercial interruptions. He also liked the Hanna-Barbera and Looney Tunes cartoons, which were already old when I was young. They were far more violent than I remembered. I was horrified to see a child (or anthropomorphic animal) punished by being given castor oil. When I was a kid, I assumed castor oil must taste very bad. As a grown-up, and a parent, I understood that castor oil is a powerful laxative and that the children of the past were punished with stomach aches and explosive bowel movements.

One afternoon I found Brig missing from his post in front of the TV. He wasn't in the bathroom or anywhere else that I could see, and I almost ran barefooted into the cul-de-sac, screaming his name. But I found him in the storage room downstairs. He'd gotten into the provisions Mormons are all but commanded to keep, eating Nutella and Marshmallow Fluff from their jars. I was relieved and exasperated. "Brig, we put these things aside for the apocalypse."

He grinned gleefully, sugary goo smeared across his lips and fingers. "It's an apocalypse now!" he said. I didn't think this was true, but we were certainly experiencing some of the features of one. I brought some toilet paper and canned ravioli upstairs, these being the things that were now impossible to find at the store.

It was his mother who chose the name Brigham. I would never have. The person who gives her son such a name is at the far end of a pendulum swing, and it's inevitable that it will come hurtling back the other way. Some folks, especially in our religion, are given to extremes—extreme belief, extreme disbelief. Wendy tried both several times, and finally settled on disbelief. We were introduced during our senior year of college by the bishop of our singles ward. He could only have been a few years older than us, but back then I regarded him as mature, authoritative, and pleasing to the eye. "You two have the same problem," he told us. "I believe you might be able to help each other out."

Wendy and I had sex six times. The first time—the night of our wedding reception, after we were sealed in the temple—barely counts because we were so confused as to the procedures. The second resulted in an eventual miscarriage. We spent four attempts making Brigham, after which it seemed unlikely we would ever try again. Wendy claims she knew immediately that Brig was different. But she never said anything at the time, and how could she have known? No one else suspected it until he would not learn to speak. I was disappointed. It's not what any parent wants for their child. Wendy was devastated. She spent her days thinking of new things she would now be unable to do. I had never heard her mention a desire to travel, but our meals started to fill with Europe and Asia, and all the sights there we'd never see. I also thought those places sounded interesting. God had created an awful lot of world. But my home was wherever Brigham was, and he was in Utah. We put him here ourselves.

Wendy took a job doing marketing for a place that packaged and resold essential oils and herbal supplements. There are many such businesses in Utah; we are the multilevel marketing capital of the world. Eventually she joined a book group of Latter-day Saints women who wanted to read about topics unrelated to the gospel. That evolved over a decade into a wine-drinking group for women who never wanted to think about Mormonism again. Through work she met some women who belonged to a cooperative that grew rosemary and lavender on a farm in Oregon.

Early in the pandemic she called us. She wanted to know how her husband and son were—a reasonable curiosity, though I hadn't heard her voice in over a year. "Do you want to speak to Brigham?"

"Really, Abe, what would be the point? He won't remember it tomorrow."

"You'll remember it tomorrow," I said. After that she called us every week.

The nature of our marriage was surely a subject of gossip in our ward. An open secret, at the least. The more tolerant the world becomes, the easier it is for even the most cloistered to recognize the signs. In 2015, when the church forbade the children of gay couples from attending services, the people of the ward watched Brigham and me with concern and apprehension. But that restriction was for the kids of practicing homosexuals. I'd had sex only six times in my life, never with a man. Brigham was too simple to have been baptized into his own religion, but I was confident he would still be allowed inside the chapel doors. A cooperative lavender farm in Oregon: was anything ever so lesbian in its signifiers?

Columbine, bleeding heart, forget-me-not—spring.

Daisy, coneflower, coreopsis—summer.

Meghan Palmer called to ask that we no longer use the sidewalk in front of her house during our morning walks. There's a type of audacity only a Mormon lady can muster. She might bear and raise six children while keeping an immaculate home, remaining behind her husband as a silent partner and helpmeet. Yet she could be as fearless and confrontational as any feminist when warning someone to steer clear.

"Sister Palmer," I said, "the sidewalk is public property. It's for everyone; you don't own it."

"In fact, Brother Sorensen, I think it would be for the best if you didn't use Eaglewood Drive at all. Not when you have Brigham with you."

Her words took me unawares I was nearly speechless. "Are you banishing us from the neighborhood?"

"Listen, Abe, I know you think I'm just a mean old lady. But he's upsetting people. He wants to hug everyone when we're supposed to be keeping six-foot distance. He's happy about all the things that make the rest of us terrified—myself included. I couldn't be more afraid. You know people my age are vulnerable, and my husband is diabetic on top of it. Everything that makes the rest of us nervous gives Brigham the thrills."

The next morning we took our walk down Eagle Ridge. The refineries in the valley filled the air with their fume. At the home with the life-sized statue of Jesus they seemed to be having a sort of revival meeting. There were a dozen people out in the yard and at least that many inside the house. Folks were chatting and laughing. One of them had a guitar, but he wasn't playing it at the moment. I considered that a mercy.

I never stood a chance of stopping him: Brigham was halfway to their porch before I realized it. They welcomed him—it's always difficult to guess which way that's going to go. A few of them motioned for me to come join in, but I figured it was better for all of us if I remained on the sidewalk. Brigham started singing "I Need Thee Every Hour." I couldn't blame him. It was still stuck in my head too. Some of the others joined in. The guitar player started strumming.

Only six months had passed since Bill Nilsson and I had had a conversation about the tulips. He'd been out at the community bowery, planting bulbs along the edge. Brig was in someone's yard, playing in the leaves. "Daffodils?" I asked.

"Some daffs," Bill said. "Mostly tulips. I always put some daffodils in with them hoping it will throw the deer off the scent. It hasn't worked yet."

"They'll all get eaten. What's the point?"

"I'm expressing my optimism!" Bill said.

Brig had been making a mess with the leaves. I called his name and slapped my thigh. I didn't always have the patience befitting a Christian father. Bill watched us both with a look of mild amusement on his face. "What colors?" I asked him.

"Yellow, red, and pink. Those are the colors you want to see in the spring, don't you think?"

"If you planted all daffodils, you'd at least have yellow. What's the point of a yellow tulip? Daffodils are more resilient. And they proliferate more readily."

"Don't you think tulips have a right to exist? A right to try to exist? Even the yellow ones! They might not make it through to blooming, but imagine how much more beautiful the world will be if they do. We owe it to them to let them try. We owe it to ourselves." He was delivering a homily, that much was obvious. But what mystical old-man wisdom was he trying to impart? That everyone deserves a chance to thrive on their own terms? At the time I assumed he was referring to Brigham. I realize now he was talking about me. Or Wendy. Or both of us—we had the same problem, as the handsome young bishop said.

My boy stood clapping and laughing with these Mormon revivalists, welcoming the end times. The latter days. But there would be no Second Coming, not that year, probably not in our lifetimes. Eventually we would carry on living as if nothing had happened. The people of Utah would remain at home—quarantining from a virus many of them thought was a conspiracy—and with two hunting seasons skipped, the deer would descend from the mountains, a plague unto themselves. Dry summers, near-snowless winters, record heat and ongoing drought, rangales of famished deer colliding with cars and scything gardens. Daylily, allium, lavender. They would eat rosebuds from off their thorny bushes. They would eat tomatoes, summer squash, hot peppers—not just the fruits, but the plants themselves. They would devour vegetation they otherwise would never have touched. They would eat the petunias, the geraniums, and the marigolds, annuals laid down to celebrate the ongoing world, an expression of optimism. But first they would eat the tulips: yellow, red, and pink. But also paisley, pinstripe, polka-dot, plaid. Rainbows and rainbows of tulips in colors still unknown.

COUNTDOWN

fiction by ANTHONY MARRA

from ZOETROPE: ALL STORY

Their UK visas were all of five hours old when Sonya's husband, Alexei, looked up from the computer and announced they would never escape Russia.

"Come on," she said. "Ticket prices can't be that bad."

By now, Sonya was inured to Alexei's bouts of melodrama and declarations of doom. He was the sort of easily persuaded catastrophist who sourced his medical advice and political opinions from Reddit.

Sonya set her passport on the kitchen table. She'd been smelling the visa itself, which had the fresh, fibrous scent of a newly minted banknote. According to the lady at the British embassy, the paper was fitted with microchips for enhanced security. Paper that was part computer: what better gestured to the brave new world awaiting them in England?

"We're not going to England," Alexei repeated. "There are no fucking flights."

"Language," Sonya said, nodding to their six-year-old daughter, Masha.

"Since when has she ever listened to me?"

"Fucking, fucking fuck," Masha said.

"See?" Sonya said. "She's a sponge, Alexei. Yesterday in the car, she was giving other drivers the middle finger."

Alexei refreshed the page again. "There are no flights."

Sonya leaned over his shoulder, assuming, not without reason, that he had no idea what he was doing. The perpetually astonishing fact that her husband, a philology PhD who kept his log-ins and passwords taped to his computer monitor, had found work as a cybersecurity consultant spoke both to his natural charisma and to the wishful thinking of his superiors. Befuddled by entertainment systems with multiple remotes, powerless to disable Siri after weeks of effort, he had—while in the throes of post-doctoral desperation—applied for a job in IT at the headquarters of a grocery chain a few hours east of Moscow. "An arrest for buying cocaine on the dark web doesn't qualify as IT expertise," Sonya had told him. But she'd underestimated his talent for bullshit. Of course she had. She'd married him. No one at his office knew enough to know that Alexei knew nothing.

"Refresh it again," Sonya said. Alexei did, but the website still showed no available departures. "Even flights to Pyongyang are fully booked. What the fuck?"

"Language," Alexei said. "Maybe someone broke the internet."

"You can't break the internet. That's a meme. It's not something that happens."

"Who's the IT professional, me or you? In my professional opinion, someone broke the internet."

"The internet's not broken," Sonya repeated, though her husband wasn't as idiotic as he sounded. Since the first days of the war, everything reliant on Western technology had begun breaking down. The shift was neither immediate nor dramatic, a gradual regression rather than a total collapse, as if Putin were less the president of a nation than the conductor of a time machine reversing into the past. Two years earlier, they could have relied on airfare aggregators to filter and sort flights based on departure and arrival times, layover durations, baggage allowances, legroom. Now that sanctions had severed the Russian banking system from the international economy, the only options were easily hacked .ru e-tailers that catapulted pop-up ads across your screen and planted malware in your hard drive.

"This is the best one I could find," Alexei said, highlighting an itinerary that swelled to sixteen days, thirteen connections, and sixty-three thousand euros. "We should have left months ago."

"We had to wait for our visas."

"We could have waited for them in Georgia or Kazakhstan. Somewhere with airplanes."

Sonya glanced to the kitchen table, where Masha was watching TV: the misadventures of a dim-witted cartoon bear and his gaggle of woodland pals.

"We agreed that we didn't want to disrupt her schedule," Sonya said.

"Masha is about to become a six-year-old exile, and you're worried about disrupting her schedule?"

"It's harder for some of us to simply pack up and leave," Sonya said. She was referring, of course, to her mother, who'd been diagnosed with dementia the prior spring and wouldn't understand—or if she did understand, wouldn't remember—why her daughter, son-in-law, and granddaughter had to emigrate. She would assume they'd forgotten her, at least until she forgot them.

"I'm sorry," Alexei said. "Let's not fight. This whole year. Jesus."

Sonya touched his arm, felt him recoil and then relax under the heat of her hand. "I know it's a lot to ask, but do you think Galina could help us again?"

Alexei had said he would reach out to Galina a few months earlier, after the Kremlin had begun insisting it had no intention of ordering a general mobilization. Sonya thought he was joking because, come on, who was Alexei Kalugin—with his air of cheerful failure and his unaddressed eczema—to slide into Galina Ivanova's DMs? Like most of their generation, Sonya could still quote lines from *Deceit Web*, a movie of unremitting stupidity and irresistible nostalgia. Following its release, Galina had enjoyed a couple years of cultural ubiquity before marrying an oligarch and fading from public view.

"I knew her in Kirovsk," Alexei had explained.

"Bullshit."

"It's true. She dated Kolya in high school."

Alexei rarely spoke of his older brother, who'd returned from the First Chechen War transformed. When the Russian army reinvaded in 1999, Alexei was eighteen years old, a chronic underachiever with no prospects, and no capacity to survive Putin's murderous imperial project. That he evaded conscription was due entirely to Kolya, who reenlisted as a contract soldier and leveraged the hefty signing bonus to buy Alexei's way into university, a guarantee of military deferment. All this history complicated Alexei's natural inclination to avoid compulsory service in Ukraine, a war he found as politically senseless and morally repugnant as the one that claimed his brother's life, deep in the Chechen highlands, on a summer day in 2000.

Sonya recalled Alexei taking a few belts of vodka after DMing Galina. An unpracticed drinker, he misjudged the effects of mixing alcohol with the prescription sleeping aid on which he depended for his eight hours, growing increasingly loopy and confessional.

"Who are you most afraid of turning into?" he asked.

"I don't know. My mother?"

"Your mother's sweet."

"Only because of the dementia. She's forgotten that she's actually a monster."

He rattled the pill bottle. "Why'd the doctor say not to take these with booze? It's great. Hey, would you brush my teeth for me?"

"I'm changing my answer. The person I'm most afraid of turning into is you."

"Come on. The bathroom's so far."

"Didn't you accuse me of infantilizing you the other day?"

"Doesn't sound like me."

Sonya rested her head on his shoulder. "Oh no. That doesn't sound like you at all. You know your six-year-old daughter can brush her own teeth?"

"She has to keep that filthy mouth of hers clean."

"You're the one teaching her curse words."

"Not me. She's self-taught. Like Van Gogh."

"Our daughter, the Van Gogh of vulgarity. Terrific." Sonya sighed. "What about you? Who are you afraid of turning into?"

"My brother."

Sonya didn't respond, turning her eyes to watch him.

"He was a murderer. He murdered people."

"He was a soldier."

"Semantics."

"You're a lot of things, Alexei, but you're not a murderer."

"Yeah? How do you know?"

"You're a vegetarian."

"So was Hitler."

"But Hitler had ambition."

"Kolya did, too. He had hopes—for after."

"You know what else Kolya had?" she said, taking the pill bottle from his hand. "A good heart. And you have a good heart. At least you did, before you started playing pharmacist."

To Sonya's surprise, Galina not only responded to Alexei's message the next morning, she offered to help. While her popular profile had evaporated in the two decades since her name last topped the marquee, her actual stature had materialized. She'd relocated to London with her husband, and their sixteen-room Knightsbridge residence had become an informal seat of Russian influence in the UK. Sponsoring visas for an old acquaintance and his family was so easy Galina didn't even consider it a favor.

Alexei stood from the computer, opened his Instagram account—@AphorismsBy-Alexei—and tapped out a message to Galina. He was dressed in a rumpled linen shirt and faded jeans, his hairline receding, his temples graying, the fifteen kilos he'd vowed to shed for the duration of their marriage still anchored to his waistline. Prescription lenses magnified his eyes, emphasizing his expression of genial naivety.

Five days before, Sonya had returned home from dropping Masha at school when her phone dinged with the news of Putin's partial mobilization order, mustering young men and ex-cons. Alexei was still asleep, his glasses on the nightstand. She didn't wake him, as if she could stay the next chapter.

"Is Galina online?" she asked.

"I don't know. She's not responding." Alexei grabbed his jacket. "How much cash do you have on you?"

"Check my purse. There should be a few thousand rubles. Why?"

"Maybe I'll have better luck at the airport ticket counter."

"Alexei. Don't be an idiot."

"I'm losing my mind here. I can't just sit around refreshing Instagram all night."

"What if the police pull you out of line? I read Moscow has stationed recruitment officers in the metro."

"There won't be police at the airport."

"It's an international fucking airport—"

"Language," Masha chimed in.

"—of course there are police. I'll go, OK? I'll go."

Alexei stuffed the cash from Sonya's purse into his pocket. "What about Masha's homework?" he said as he walked out the door. "We don't want to disrupt her schedule."

"Asshole."

It felt wrong to think in such terms, but the war had likely saved their marriage. Or postponed its dissolution, at least. Masha's birth had clarified certain matters for Sonya: namely, that she had two children, which wouldn't have been an issue if she weren't married to one of them. In the course of dead-end arguments, Alexei accused her of changing—*I don't even recognize you, you've changed, Sonya*—as if maturation were a character flaw. Yes, in a normal world, she would have left him. Yet in this grotesque and precarious one, she was leaving Russia with him.

"OK," Sonya told Masha. "That's enough TV for today. Let's do your homework."

"It's boring."

"I know it is."

"Then why do I have to do it?"

"Because enduring boredom with good cheer will serve you well for the rest of your life."

And for the next twenty minutes, Masha plodded through a passage glorifying the genocidal exploits of Peter the Great. She'd always struggled with reading comprehension, even in her native language; God knew how she'd fare in British schools. Sonya was trying to coax an answer from her daughter about the vanquishing of the evil Swedes when she heard footsteps in the hallway. They stopped at the door. The intensity of her relief startled Sonya: Alexei had come home. She listened for the jangling of his keys. Instead, a knock.

Sonya crossed soundlessly to the door and peered through the peephole. If not for their uniforms, she would have assumed the two military recruitment officers for food deliverymen: one officer straining under the weight of four bags bulging with groceries, the other flipping through a folio stuffed with what she first took for receipts, until recognizing them for draft notices. The latter brought his fist to the door and pounded so forcefully the peephole's metal collar bruised her eye socket. She stepped back and bumped the coatrack.

The pounding stopped.

"You can open the door, or we can break it down," said the blue-eyed officer brandishing the draft notices. "Please choose how we come in."

So chivalry isn't dead, Sonya ghoulishly thought, as she opened the door. "I'm sorry. I didn't hear you."

"She didn't hear us, Boris," the officer with the grocery bags deadpanned. "That's the fourth flat in a row. Do you suppose this is a home for the hard of hearing?"

"There's a plague of deafness going around, Sasha," said the officer with the draft notices. "It's a miracle we can still hear ourselves think. We're here to serve . . . Alexei Kalugin. He about?"

Sonya shook her head.

"Imagine that," said the officer with the grocery bags. "C'mon, Boris."

The two men pushed past Sonya, trailing cigarette smoke, waffling the floorboards with grimy boot prints. Masha slipped behind her mother.

"Good evening, little person," said the officer with the grocery bags. "Is your father home?"

Masha shook her head.

"Imagine that," said the officer with the draft notices. "Like mother, like daughter."

"We should check the kitchen, Boris. Just to be thorough."

"Right you are, Sasha. It's the burden of perfectionism."

Sonya watched the two officers commit a home invasion of her refrigerator. While one rooted around the crisper drawer, the other enumerated the provisions pilfered from her neighbors.

"Lettuce, tomato, onions, mushrooms, hard-boiled eggs, black bread, smoked trout, ham, chicken breast, mayonnaise, mustard, butter, caviar—perhaps enough for a sandwich."

"Nonsense. We haven't any cheese."

"There's a jar of pickles in back. Pass it here."

Mashing the fifth spear into his mouth, the officer called Sasha noticed a photograph stuck to the fridge door: Alexei on his thirty-eighth birthday. "Look here. I found him."

"Poor fellow," said the other, as he added a bottle of horseradish and a jar of chutney to their haul. "Don't suppose he'll live to see his next one, do you, Sasha?"

"Not in front of the missus, Boris. It's unprofessional."

"But she's deaf, Sasha—remember? She can't hear us at all."

"Is that orange juice fortified with extra vitamin C?"

"You tell me—you're the health nut."

The officer called Sasha tipped the carton to his mouth, and Sonya watched the juice spill over his cheeks, staining his uniform and splashing across the floor.

"You know, Sasha, I've always had a kind of affection for Ukraine."

"You have relatives there?"

"My father. He's buried in Odessa. Killed himself on a family vacation."

"How awful."

"Oh, it was. His wife found him hanging in the closet of their hotel, then found out about my mother at the funeral. I'm not sure which upset her more."

"At least he killed himself with his other family, Boris. At least you have that."

"It is a consolation, though hardly the sort of thing printed on a sympathy card."

"Perhaps there's a market. These days, the most calamitous stories are often the most common."

"Hard man, my father. Survived three years in Afghanistan and eight years in a Siberian prison, but no more than a few days on the Black

Sea with his other family before deciding to end it all. And if that's what Ukraine did to him, just imagine what it'll do to a fat, middle-aged IT worker with ten days' training."

"So why the affection for such a place?"

"Because my father was a motherfucking prick."

"Language, Boris. The young are so impressionable."

"OK, Sasha, OK. Let's see if"—the officer flipped through the draft notices—"Dmitry Morozov next door has any brie."

"Why did they come here?" Masha asked once the recruitment officers had gone.

"They were hungry," Sonya said.

"But why did they want Dad?"

"Your father makes the best sandwiches. Isn't that what you're always telling me?"

Masha nodded.

How much did she understand? Sonya and Alexei had tried to shelter their daughter from the turmoil. The move to England wasn't a harrowing escape, but rather a thrilling vacation. Masha was too young, and Sonya wouldn't burden her with the truth of a world she would learn about soon enough. And yet protecting Masha meant replicating the Kremlin's distortions, denials, and silences within their home. Lying to her became inseparable from loving her: how else could they keep her safe?

"Shall we call your father and see where he is?" Sonya suggested.

Alexei's line went directly to voicemail.

"Where is he?" Masha asked.

"On his way home." Sonya tried to smile. "C'mon. Let's read a book while we wait."

"OK. *Curious George*."

Alexei had purchased *Curious George* as part of a campaign to improve Masha's English, and for the prior few weeks, Masha asked Sonya to read it to her every night. There were only so many times Sonya could recite the misadventures of an inquisitive primate before hoping the poachers would show up. But now, as Masha curled beside her, she wondered if her daughter wished to return to this story precisely *because* she already knew it by heart. In a reality where recruitment officers could barge into your flat, demand your father, and steal your pickles, what was better than a fantasy swept clean of uncertainty or suspense?

Footsteps boomed down the hallway.

Masha's grip tightened on Sonya's wrist.

How many fathers had been marched out into the dull daylight by uniformed men? How many mothers had sat in darkness in this very flat, silently praying the footsteps wouldn't stop at her door?

The footsteps stopped at her door.

Then, thank God, the jangle of keys, the lock snapping open, and as Alexei appeared, bearing more disappointment—sanctions prevented Galina from wiring money into Russia, and every international flight was sold out anyway—Sonya and Masha embraced him as if he'd delivered the best possible news.

It was two in the morning when they finally finished packing the car with one suitcase, four cardboard boxes, and eight trash bags. Their most valuable possessions—the family photos—lived on their phones and in the cloud. Alexei hauled the television down the apartment stairs, only to find a dozen of Masha's stuffed animals occupying the last of the back-seat real estate.

"Are you really sure you need to bring all of them?" he asked.

"I'm really sure," Masha said.

"It's just that this is beginning to look like Noah's Lada."

"We can't leave anyone behind."

"What the hell," he said, setting the television on the sidewalk. "We watch too much TV anyway."

He wrapped an arm around Sonya's shoulder, and when she didn't shrug it off, Alexei chose to interpret this as the most positive omen. Perhaps a new age of peace and harmony was dawning. A new city, a new country, a new life.

They climbed into the car, Masha in back with her menagerie, Sonya riding shotgun, trash bags of clothes obscuring the rear window. It was a twenty-seven-hour drive to the Georgian border, and Alexei couldn't remember when he'd last changed the Lada's oil. Crossing into the Baltic States or Finland would save hours, but on Telegram, Alexei had found conflicting reports on European port-of-entry closures. Were he an actual cybersecurity expert, he might have known if any were from credible sources.

"You ready?"

"No," Sonya said. "Not remotely."

"Me neither."

He put the car into gear.

They stopped for gasoline in Tula, bathrooms in Voronezh. Everywhere, Alexei saw men in need of a shave, a shower, a nap. Men much like himself, driving to the border, alone or with their families, their earthly goods jammed in the trunk, tied to the roof, left by the side of the road. Swiping at their phones at the gas pumps, spreading news of traffic, apprehensions, closed crossings, each one bleary-eyed, exhausted, kept alert by cigarettes and energy drinks and adrenalized panic. The simplest questions of basic time and space—*where will I be tomorrow?*—became existential mysteries. The known world receded, and no matter what Yandex Maps suggested to the contrary, it was all uncharted wilderness.

Sonya yawned and rubbed her eyes. "How long was I out?"

"A couple hours."

"You want me to take over?"

"I've got it," Alexei said. And he did. The difficult conversations he and Sonya would have down the line, none of that mattered. What mattered was shrinking the distance to their deliverance.

"How long has the motor been making that noise?"

He'd hoped she wouldn't notice the clang coming from the . . . well, whatever those parts were called.

"A couple hundred kilometers."

"When'd you last have it serviced?"

"I've never had it serviced."

"Alexei."

"If I'd thought we'd be driving this shit-box across half of Eurasia, I'd have brought it in for a tune-up first."

"Those gun-nut survivalists in America convinced the world is about to end—what do they call them?"

"Republicans," Alexei said.

"No, the ones who can build an internal combustion engine out of the odds and ends they hoard in their bunkers."

"Oh, preppers."

"That's right—preppers. I used to think they were crazy," she said. "Maybe they're just early."

"They're definitely crazy."

"Perhaps, but while we still have a signal, I might search the internet for one of their diatribes on fashioning a fan belt from a pair of stockings."

"You know what the real culprit is?" Alexei said. "DIY. You start baking your own bread, and you end up living in a basement with a few thousand rounds of ammunition and a filtration system for drinking your own urine."

"Is this how you justify abstaining from your share of the cooking?"

"All I'm saying is that I've never seen a person who makes their own clothes and thought, *Now here's someone in full control of their faculties.*"

"What are we even talking about?"

"The end of the world," Alexei said, as rain detonated against the windshield. Several silent kilometers passed before he spoke again. "My brother and I used to pretend that the world was ending. We were preppers before the internet made it fashionable."

"What, you collected canned food?"

"We built a spaceship."

"Excuse me?" Sonya stared at him with genuine curiosity, trying to recall the last time he'd surprised her in a good way. "How have you never told me this?"

"It was just a bunch of junk we cobbled together and wrapped in tinfoil."

"A DIY spaceship. And here you are sneering at people who make their own clothes."

"We'd pretend that the Americans had launched a nuclear attack, and we had to blast off before the bombs landed."

"The two of you floating around in space, huh?"

"No, just one of us. There was only one seat in the capsule. So one of us would escape, and the other, well, you know. I remember the countdown. Those last moments together."

"You never talk about your brother."

"What's there to say? I hate him for what he did because he loved me."

"Look," Sonya said, nodding to the rearview mirror. "She's finally asleep."

Alexei listened to their daughter snore in the back seat while the wipers sloshed rain across the windshield, and hoped the clanging engine wouldn't wake her.

"We're here," Alexei said.

Sonya stirred and looked at her phone. "The map says we're still thirty kilometers from the border. There must be an accident."

Alexei opened the door and peered ahead. The highway was bricked over in taillights to the horizon. "I don't think there's an accident. I think this is the line to leave."

Hours passed. Alexei measured distance not in kilometers but in car lengths. Sonya asked again if she might take over.

"I'm good," he said.

"You haven't slept in two nights."

"I'll rest once we get through," he said. He unzipped his cassette case, popped a mixtape into the tape player, tapped his thumb on the steering wheel to the beat.

Finally, the border came into view: a line of security fencing, sheet metal, stripped paint. Signage with clear instructions belied the general disorder. He counted the cars ahead: twenty-eight, then twenty-seven, then twenty-six.

"We're nearly there," he said.

"Who are they?" Sonya asked.

A half-dozen uniformed officers had pulled the driver, a young man, from the next car in line. After glancing at his passport, they hauled him to a bus idling on the other side of the road. A bus with bars over shatterproof windows, pointing opposite the fleeing traffic.

"Turn around," Sonya said.

"We're so close." Twenty cars. Nineteen. Eighteen.

"Turn around, Alexei. We'll find a different way. We'll cross into Kazakhstan."

"Not in this car. It's got nothing left."

"Then we'll go back home. Masha's only missed two days of school. We'll go back to the way we were. Just turn around."

The alarm in her eyes made him feel bewilderingly, unjustifiably loved.

"You have Galina's address," he said. "She'll ensure you have everything you need in London."

"Turn back, Alexei. Please."

Seventeen. Sixteen. Fifteen.

An officer tapped on Alexei's window.

"You're right, Sonya. You should take over driving for a while."

Make something of yourself. These were the last words his brother had spoken to him, at a bus depot in Kirovsk, before beginning the journey that would end ten months later in a mined pasture south of the Terek River. And they were the words by which Alexei had—in the twenty-four years since—measured his failures.

Now, as the officers wrenched him from the driver's seat, he gazed back at the distraught family he'd delivered to the border—a thirty-three-hour slog without pause except for gas and bathroom breaks, and he'd driven every kilometer. That was something, surely, but was it enough?

The wind was kicking Sonya's hair all over as she stood in the road, her fists balled, her eyes radiating desperation. *Don't turn back*, he thought. *Please.*

The driver behind the Lada laid on his horn, and Alexei watched, heartbroken, as his wife froze, flustered and uncertain, with this asshole's impatient clamor blaring in her ears.

Then the Lada's back door flung open, and Masha stepped out, flipping off the driver and uncorking a torrent of the most magnificent profanities. *Oh, my little vulgarian, you make your father so proud.*

By the time Sonya managed to corral her, there were only four cars ahead.

Alexei stared through the window of the army bus.

Three cars.

I love you.

Two.

Just go.

One.

AN ESSAY ABOUT COYOTES

by RYAN VAN METER

from THE IOWA REVIEW

But it begins with moths. Dead ones specifically, as described in essays by Virginia Woolf and Annie Dillard. Virginia's was first, published in 1942, a year after her death. Annie's came thirty years later. On the chalkboard, I wrote the two titles. It was the first day of a new semester, and I was introducing the concept of the essay because this was an essay writing class. I told my students that life very rarely gives us an essay. Some experience when all we have to do is write it down. These are the things I say every semester, so I know I said it that semester. "Most often," I continued, "life gives us anecdotes, and they don't mean anything until we make them into essays."

We read the moth essays aloud. I wrote more words on the chalkboard and handed out skinny slips of paper on which I'd printed their first assignment: *Write an essay about an encounter with an animal.* Just like Virginia and Annie had done. They'd each witnessed the final moments of the lives of a moth, and then, on paper, they'd described what it was like to be there and articulated what those moments might mean. That is, they'd turned anecdotes into essays. "One more thing," I said. "Write the animal essay that only you can write. Please don't make me read fifteen dead dog essays."

I didn't tell them about Friday afternoons in graduate school, several of us sitting around a long table in the literary journal office. Passing each other big envelopes and the package of Oreos. And every Friday, one of us would sigh over the essay we were reading and another would reach for the cookies, and someone would ask, "What's wrong?" and the person would say, "Dead dog essay." I always felt sorry for the writer, and the dog too, of course, but mostly for the essay that would go into its envelope again instead of the magazine because in almost all cases, the essay was already familiar even before we read it. Everyone who's ever had a dog could write a dead dog essay, and some weeks in the journal office, it felt as though they had.

So, as I walked out of the building after that first day of class, I knew about having to read a lot of dead dog essays. Outside, the January afternoon was blazing because it was northern California in the hour before the sun went over the edge of the city. At the top of the brick stairs built into the side of a hill, I stopped and took it all in. The light, the view, the good feeling of the first day of the new class having gone well. Other classes had just let out too, so there were a lot of students walking up and down the stairs. As I was looking it all over, I saw—next to the thick sculpted shrubs climbing that hillside—a coyote.

He was beautiful, taking it all in too, eyes closed, snout lifted to the sky. We see them occasionally in the city, but I'd never seen one on campus, and never around so many people. He was no more than fifteen human strides away. A couple of students stopped near me.

"Is that a bobcat?" one of them asked.

"No," I said. "It's a coyote."

"Is a coyote a *kind* of cat?"

"No," I said. "It's a kind of dog."

I took a picture with my phone and walked on. Already, I couldn't wait to tell my students the following week what had happened right after I had assigned them to write about an encounter with an animal. "I *had* an encounter with an animal!" I would say. I went over it all so I would remember: my having paused to look over things, the light, the feeling, him standing there, his lifted nose, the dumb questions about cats. It was an anecdote right then, but seeing him on that day was a sign of something, I was sure. Something was coming—in the new year, perhaps, or in the new semester. It was more than just my path crossing the coyote's at that time and place. With enough time to remember and recreate and think, I'd be able to figure out what it was like to be there and what the moment might mean. I'd be able to make an essay.

The next morning, my twelve-year-and-eight-month-old dog didn't want to eat her breakfast.

If this were a dead dog essay, which it isn't because this essay is about coyotes, I would describe the two weeks following that morning when she refused to eat, which were the last two weeks of her life. A dead dog essay would depict all the visits to the vet, all the phone calls. How tired she was of going to the vet that she eventually refused to even walk in that direction from our apartment and I had to carry her the whole way. The X-rays, the blood work, the IVs, the ultrasounds. The nights she couldn't sleep because of the pain, and I couldn't because she couldn't. The other nights she couldn't sleep because of the pain medication that made her so anxious all she could do was wander the dark apartment. (I couldn't sleep then either.) A dead dog essay would describe having hope and losing hope. Sitting on a park bench with my husband, looking at each other and knowing exactly what was happening without having to say a word. A dead dog essay would depict the day my husband played hooky, and I called for an in-home euthanasia appointment. It would show the laying down of the blankets. The white one with cartoon dogs on it my mom made. The lavender one my ex-boyfriend made when we had adopted her. The bowl of water I set beside them because the woman on the phone said the general anesthetic—the first of two shots my dog would receive to stop her heartbeat—made some dogs instantly thirsty. And a dead dog essay would draw out the moment I turned on David Bowie, on shuffle, because the idea of doing what we were doing in silence felt so terrible, and walked to the window to wait for the man who would euthanize her when David Bowie's "Waiting for the Man" began to play.

Because this essay is about coyotes, instead I will explain that I was angry. After my dog died exactly two weeks after the day I saw that coyote, I was angry about seeing the coyote. I was angry at myself for looking around so much. For trying to notice every detail of an anecdote so I could retrieve it later to make an essay. I was angry on behalf of my students—past and present—for all the times I had written *what was it like to be there?* in their margins. Because *what it was like* is irrelevant when you shouldn't have been *there* in the first place. I was angry on behalf of myself for trying to find significance in walking to my office, in every minute of my extremely ho-hum life. Was it because my life was so boring that I insisted everything had to be meaningful? Was that why everything had to be an essay? I was angry, most of all because I knew if I hadn't seen that coyote, my dog wouldn't have died.

This essay is about coyotes so it's also about crying. Broadly about crying but specifically about my crying. How I'm not usually much of a crier. I never cry at funerals when everybody else does. I've never cried at a wedding. My car got stolen—didn't cry. My brother threw a hammer at me, it clobbered my bare foot, I needed seven stitches—didn't cry. In college, I got a D in geology (which I took because I heard it was the easiest of the sciences) and I did cry, but only after I was alone in my dorm room. I also cried when my ex-boyfriend broke up with me over the phone, but only after I hung up so he wouldn't hear it. I've generally been the kind of person who can decide whether he's going to cry.

As this essay is about coyotes and crying—but not a dead dog—it can illustrate the times following my dog's death when I cried basically all the time. Even in moments that had nothing to do with her such as when my husband asked me what I wanted for lunch and I cried so hard I couldn't speak. (He picked up deli sandwiches.) I cried in moments that had everything to do with her as well. When the day came around that would have been her next birthday. When I donated her toys, leftover medicine, and leash to a rescue shelter. When I gathered all the photos of her in a cloud drive.

I cried so much I began to wonder if I would ever get over losing her. I wondered if my ex-boyfriend had been right when he said the dog and I were "too emotionally involved." I wondered if for the rest of my life I was going to have this kind of low-grade fever crying thing where some word or object would break me open without warning. I wondered if I was the first person to ever feel this way about their dead dog until about a month later when I was sure I was.

I was also sure I needed help. Searching online for pet grief books, I found several that my university library shelved. My university didn't have on its shelves *Signs From Pets in the Afterlife: Identifying Messages From Pets in Heaven,* which featured on its cover a bunch of cats and dogs seated on a purple staircase enveloped in clouds and a winged dog flying headfirst into a rainbow. The pet grief books I checked out from the library made me feel better because I stopped feeling so alone. A dead dog essay would weave in carefully selected and poignant passages from those books about how many pet owners move forward by recognizing that their lost pet continues living on through the many good memories of the pet's life. In this essay, however, I will state that the most helpful of the pet grief books was the one I didn't read about dead pets sending messages from heaven because it allowed me to think *Well, at least I don't have it that bad.*

The very unrevelatory truth was I missed her, and a dead dog essay would catalog all of her quirks and nicknames and all the inside jokes and games we played, her favorite toys and the words she knew and what she did in response to each and all the places she went with us and all of the illnesses and injuries she survived over her life. The more revelatory truth was I also missed the way she had structured my life just by being a dog. About six weeks after she had died, I started to think—and so did my husband—that part of what we were feeling was missing a dog, as in any dog. Once I started entertaining that idea, I no longer thought of the coyote I saw on campus as a bad sign. My seeing the coyote hadn't killed her, after all. He was a sign that she was going to die, yes, but a sign too of what was next, after her death, and beyond. Acknowledging that, we hiked to the top of a modest mountain in a wild and rambling park two blocks from our apartment that our dead dog had loved and scattered her cremains in a flower bed. A week later, we went to the animal rescue shelter and adopted a puppy.

This essay is about coyotes so it reveals that those first few weeks with the new puppy made me cry harder and miss my dead dog more. Mainly this was because the puppy was a puppy and not my dead dog, meaning he chewed up a pair of my eyeglasses, two pairs of my husband's sunglasses, three hallway runners (in succession, not all at once), two umbrellas (at once, not in succession), a plastic bear jar of honey, my St. Louis Cardinals hat, countless shoes, and a bouquet of flowers, but not, thank god, the vase. He barked at leaves crinkling outside on the sidewalk and jumped on us when we came in the door, even if we had only been in the other room. He ripped a hole in his fifty-dollar suede bed and then napped on the heap of foam stuffing. My husband and I were extremely stressed out.

The puppy also wouldn't regularly potty outside. He didn't potty regularly inside either, which was good. But for as many times as we took him out, he didn't understand the reason was to go potty and that other than inside the house, he could potty anywhere. For some reason, he would only potty in one otherwise unremarkable spot of grass in the park across the street and half a block down from our apartment. We wanted to widen the possibilities. In those early days, he would signal he needed to potty by pawing at us and staring. One night, he did this at about nine thirty. I took him to that spot of grass. He went potty and we came back inside.

My husband handles the right-before-bed potty. He did this with the dead dog too. With her, he stood at the bottom of our porch stairs while she toddled to the tree she preferred, three houses up the block. She toddled back, they came in and we all settled on our bed to sleep.

With the puppy, he couldn't be off leash. My husband had to put on shoes and a jacket, and most likely wait for the stoplight and cross the street to walk to the potty spot.

So, on the night when the puppy went potty at nine thirty and we were going to bed at ten thirty, my husband understandably didn't see the point of taking him out because it had only been an hour. I thought it was still a good idea because we were training him to go at certain times, like right before bed. My husband rightfully predicted the puppy wouldn't go, even if they did cross the street. I maintained that actually going potty wasn't the point—the point was taking him out and saying "potty" over and over so he could learn this activity had a name. My husband said, "Fine," and I said, "I'll take him," and he said, "No, I'm taking him," and I said, "It's really no problem, I'll take him," and he said, "I AM TAKING HIM."

He took him. The puppy sniffed the two trees in front of our stairs and then sat. From the window, I watched my husband's head fall back on his slack and frustrated neck. They crossed the street. I watched from our big corner windows as they disappeared into the shadow of trees covering the magic spot. When they emerged again, they'd missed the stoplight, so they had to wait as cars zipped by. My husband saw me in the window and pointed at me. Or I thought he pointed at me. I kept looking and realized he was pointing right under me, at the corner of our building where it met the sidewalk. I leaned forward to peer below, and standing there, as though it were waiting for the stoplight too, was a coyote.

"That was her," he said the next day when we apologized to each other on the phone. "She was trying to tell us that everything is going to be fine," he said. I was standing in my campus office, so I had to close my door in order to cry.

As soon as my husband said it, I believed it too—this sign from our pet in heaven. And at that moment, hiding behind my locked office door, dragging my sleeves over my face, I understood her message. First, she was fine. Second, we were fine too or going to be soon. Third, this puppy I had serious misgivings about was going to carry the broom *and* the coffee maker to the front door the first time we left him alone in the evening, but he would also eventually be fine. This is why this essay about coyotes is also about crying.

I liked seeing coyotes after that because I liked thinking my dead dog was visiting me. Coyotes gave me an occasion to think about her in a way that didn't feel disordered. I thought about her a lot anyway, but often that felt like wallowing, especially after I had the new puppy to think about. So, I found myself trying to see them. Seeking them out. Walking more and more often in the wild rambling park where their dens were, which was also the park where her cremains were. I made it a point to go to this park a couple of times a week and the puppy liked this because it was home to a million squirrels. We didn't end up seeing coyotes very often though. Coyotes are most active before dawn and around dusk and tend to avoid places where a lot of humans are walking around with giant puppies. Most of the time when we did see them, it was only me seeing them. Unless a coyote ran out onto a paved path, my puppy usually didn't notice. This was good because when he did notice them, he went bonkers, barking and pulling on his leash. I think now that in trying to see coyotes so often, I was attempting to collect anecdotes. I thought if I saw coyotes enough times, there'd be meaning in my dog having died and me being so broken by it. I'd have something to show for it.

The first summer after our dog died, my husband and I took a vacation to Colorado. We drove around for a week, visited three national parks, stopped in a lot of small, cute towns, and took a thousand pictures. And then on a Saturday, we were back in our city sitting at a bar in our neighborhood. The puppy was at home, waiting for the mail to drop through the slot in the front door so he could turn it into confetti. We were talking about our vacation, looking through the pictures, and we finally articulated to each other for the first time that maybe we did want to leave our city. Maybe we wanted to live in a small, cute town one day. Maybe we wanted something else besides our one-hundred-year-old apartment and the jobs we loved. We discussed dreams about beehives and bathtubs. We could run a flower farm or a bed-and-breakfast.

"Would it be weird though that she's scattered here if we don't live here anymore?" one of us finally asked.

"Most of her life was here, so it makes sense she'll always be here, even if we aren't," the other said.

We drank our drinks and went home.

We hadn't gotten any mail that day, so the puppy had been good. I fed and walked him while my husband made us dinner. We walked up to the wild and rambling park. It was windy, fog was coming. The puppy peed, then scratched luxuriantly at the grass he'd just peed on before taking a few steps to eat some other grass. I said, "Leave it," because that works on other dogs, and yanked his leash to tow us up the hill. At the crest of the path was a coyote. It stood broadside to us like it was on the move and I'd just happened to catch it. It watched me for a few seconds before hurrying off into the trees.

After the walk, I burst into the house. I was crying but it felt different. A whole new kind of crying. "She says it's OK," I told my husband. "She gave us her blessing."

Nobody writes a dead dog essay, I realized, because they somehow think they are the first to lose a dog they loved. And nobody writes a dead dog essay out of a need to be sentimental or clichéd. We write dead dog essays because after we spend a decade or more with an animal that we love and care for, and that animal dies, we rightfully feel we have had a singular experience. The loss never feels anecdotal while it's happening. It feels particular, complicated, and important—the way essays do—so we think all we have to do is write down the experience. Meaning will come, clarity will follow.

That the experience was never singular in the first place feels irrelevant for a long time.

I know people who have lived in my city for a decade without ever seeing a coyote. As much as I needed to think that seeing them was a direct message from my dead dog in the afterlife to me in the during-life, I also know now I was making the random sighting of a wild animal mean something. It's true I saw coyotes at some very particular moments when I sought meaning, and it's still comforting to think that none of it was random, that it was all part of a pattern so large and organized, I couldn't detect it. Coincident or not, it felt like life was giving me an essay.

This essay is about coyotes, so it describes last Christmas morning. The puppy was a dog by then, having turned three years old. But unlike most dogs his age, this dog still behaved very much like a puppy. He still jumped on us when we came through the door. He still chewed up things occasionally when we weren't around. On this morning, after we opened our Christmas presents, we decided to all go on a walk together to the top of the wild, rambling park. My husband had also received as a gift some wildflower seeds that he didn't know what to do with. He didn't have a place or high expectations for them, so we thought, we'll plant them up there near the cremains of our dead dog, and if they sprout, this moment will have meaning.

It was a cool and quiet morning. Very few people were in the park. I followed the puppy around as he tugged on his leash to smell interesting invisible things, and my husband used the trowel he'd carried to dig a hole through some mulch in a flower bed and planted the seeds. I took in the view up there, part of the reason why we'd chosen it as the spot for the cremains. You can see the ocean and the Bay and mountains and a couple of celebrity bridges.

We began our descent. It was about ten in the morning.

My husband said, "If we're going to let him off leash to run around, we should do it now."

"I don't usually," I said. "Coyotes."

"There aren't any coyotes out at this hour," he said.

I unclipped the dog-puppy. He charged up a hill to our left. Whenever he's off leash, he charges up hills and races across meadows. He bounds like a deer.

I took a single step forward. There ahead of us on the path was a coyote, yawning.

It had been approximately three seconds since I'd let the dog off his leash.

My husband said, "Coyote!"

I yelled the dog's name.

Down the steep flank of the whole park, branches snapped and paws scratched through leaves. They were both gone.

We ran in that direction. A guy walking his dog (on a leash!) said they went out of the park. We ran to the edge of the dense neighborhood of winding streets that surrounded the park and decided to split up. My husband would go this way and I would go that. I pulled my phone out of my pocket though I wasn't sure why because the only person I wanted to call right then was the dog. I sprinted down a side street and came upon a man and woman walking. "Have you seen a dog?" I asked.

"Was that your dog chasing a coyote?"

She named a street. It was the next one over, and in that part of the city, it was incredibly steep. Preposterously steep. But I ran to and up it. As I chugged along, yelling his name, I thought about this dog. About him somewhere out here chasing a coyote and how fast coyotes run. I remembered a documentary I'd watched about coyotes during which I learned that they came to live in cities by following train tracks in from rural areas. I tried to think of the nearest train tracks, and there my dog was galloping down the railroad ties after this poor coyote, both of their tongues hanging out of the sides of their mouths like dogs in cartoons, and sometimes in real life. I thought about oncoming cars. About what a cornered scared coyote could do to a giant dog that was secretly a huge baby. I thought about how young he was. How dumb he was. How annoying he was and how much I loved him. I thought about how he might be lost to me forever and I would never get over it.

Calling and calling his name, I reached the peak of this grand hill and came to a convergence of several streets. There was no one out or about, despite there being so many directions from which to come and go. Still clutching my phone, I swallowed and tried to catch my breath but knew he was gone. We would never find him.

My husband stumbled from behind one of the corners. I asked him if he'd found him even though I knew the answer because he was alone. "Where do we go now?" I asked.

He pointed behind me. "The coyote!"

And there it was, trotting toward us, rakish and handsome like they always are. Tongue hanging out of the side as I'd thought. It came to a corner and turned, going right down the middle of the street like a badass. I ran after it and my husband ran up the street from which he came. This beautiful animal, best dog of all dogs. He looked behind and saw me running after him like a moron and took off.

I ran back to the intersection and my husband was there, crouching, holding the dog—our dog—by his collar. He had an expression on his face that was something like, "Oh hey." He also had four bloody paws. His claws were ground to nubs. Out of some of them, pale quick drooped. I connected him to the leash which I somehow still had, and we began to walk home.

A dead dog essay would reveal that the seeds we planted up by her cremains never sprouted. Not a month later or a month after that. That essay could create a metaphor out of those seeds, showing that grief is a lot like the careful tending of seeds you know will never grow. A lot of work with nothing to show for it because having nothing to show for it is the whole point of loss. Tending the seeds anyway is the only way I've found of moving forward.

But this essay is about coyotes.

It took a long time to get back to the apartment. He could hardly walk. His feet hurt and he was exhausted. He'd been away from us for only a couple of minutes, but still, I couldn't stop thinking that I'd almost lost another dog.

About two limping blocks from our house, my husband finally spoke. "I know not everything is a metaphor," he said, "but it's like OK, I get the message."

"What are you talking about?" I asked.

He said our dead dog's name.

I hadn't thought of her once during the encounter with the coyote. The whole time, my dog had been chasing only a coyote. I didn't need it to mean anything anymore. I had let her go.

SECOND PARADISE

by CHARD DENIORD

from AMERICAN POETRY REVIEW

"Poetry is a dream made in the presence of reason."
—Adam Zagajewski

I went for a walk with a girl I hardly knew
when I was a boy on a trail by a river
for a film I didn't know was being made
by a director I couldn't see or hear
behind his hidden camera in the clouds
and trees as we recited our lines
unwittingly with no idea of the plot
or ending as we walked for miles
in that paradise of a park, which is why
we were *killing it* on that cerulean day
in a way that was more real than the trail
itself, which has been razed, I've heard,
for a housing development, which means
the world in which we live today
has become an illusion since we both
still walk that trail where we were born
a second time in a paradise we walk
to this day in our heads, although
it's no longer there, despite the fact it seems
more real than when we were there
enchanted with each other, striking
our tongues against our teeth to light

the tinder between our legs and ears
and then our hearts that needed proof
of fire in the air as we walked like ghosts
until we were lost in a grove beside
the trail and lay down somewhere
we could never find our way back to
and made love on a bed of moss
despite our fear; where we were eternalized
in the film which we continue to screen
as a non sequitur in quotidian moments,
like right now on the patio where we
balance our dinners on our knees
and divine the darkness behind
our eyes to dream awake of that time
we disappeared into a vast which plays
on the screen that hangs from a cloud
on which our short that is so long
is projected in color one day and black
and white the next, transcending time
in the way it did that day on our walk
beside a river in which we witnessed
enough of heaven's fire in the water
to weld our memory of that ecstatic wall
to a vision that would last in the grass
of days we called forever, although
we are deluded by the film that has
no credits for the sake of heaven
and witnesses in its showings to the irony
of a metaphysics that surrenders love
and even the river to sweet oblivion.

LORCA TO THE UMPTEENTH POWER

BY CYRUS CASSELLS

from CUTTHROAT

You're more of a girl than I am,
time and again I teased,
in the green, desultory playground
of the morning poplars,
but faster, faster—deadsure
as a flitting willow-o'-the-wisp
or an in-a-rush kestrel—

As fretful tomboy and ready-set sidekick,
wary of the dark,
we requested: *Lord Death,*
if we have to sleep in a coffin,
can Federico still whistle
the first trills of "Für Elise"
or a few bars of Maestro de Falla?

Here's the core of the matter:
I waited lifetimes, centuries
to be your Andalusian confrere,
to study the fear that feasts,
like empty-bellied ogres,
on resilient villagers and scruffy peasants,
on truth-telling poets and seers
but can never digest them—

There's a lambent hall
I visit in unveiling dreams,
an everlasting theater I call
"Lorca to the Umpteenth Power,"
where every degree of your word sorcery
is revered and enacted—

Listen: our galvanizing, gust-strong
feeling for each other
was like a solstice-shared pomegranate;
or a searing-red ball kicked
all the way out of the court—

Big-headed boy,
the do-re-mi and folderol
of the dowager city,
the sullen, cobblestone streets,
even the imposing sierras,
and the inveterate Iberian earth itself—

make no sense without your joy—

ONE OF YOU WILL BETRAY ME

fiction by KATHY CHAO

From THE GEORGIA REVIEW

I. ONE OF YOU WILL BETRAY ME.

It was Chang-ma who corralled the women of the First Mandarin Baptist Church of Praise into their midweek meetings. "Mother of Prayers group (MOP)," she explained in her first email summons, "will be a place we can share our struggles and support each other spiritually, where we discuss our role in Church as Mothers and in Chinese Community as Christians."

For a year and a half of Wednesdays now they'd pulled up promptly to Mary Jin's five-bedroom Yorba Linda Spanish Revival at seven PM on the dot ("Since space is limited at my condo, I suggest we meet somewhere else—Mary, are you moved to volunteer?"), filed in with their platters and their bowls, their fruit salads and coconut buns and barley tea and ice cream mochi ("Please also bring light snack and Bible and your humble hearts!"), and gathered in their circle to speak of the spiritual, the earthly, and the milky zone where the two met.

They'd discussed Mary Jin's daughter Sonia, sixteen years old and proud owner of not one but two cartilage piercings and a walnut-sized Mandarin vocabulary. God grant Mary the wisdom to correct her punk daughter amid the American permissiveness oozing honey-thick all around them. They'd discussed Agnes Chow's suffering spirit, boxed in an 800-square-foot one-bedroom in Tustin with a snoring husband and a mother-in-law of bad knees and bad temper and such sneering rancor against the True Christian God that even the generous-hearted women of the MOP fled the other way when they saw her tottering up the aisles of Law's Chinese Emporium. God grant them the strength to turn the other cheek when the old lady bared her mossy teeth, bore down on them with that malevolent gleam in her eye, and demanded once again, with unflagging glee, whether an omnipotent God could create a rock too heavy for Himself to lift. God save them all. They'd discussed Yang-ma's bunions, Tang-ma's termites, Leah Wang's low-slung, back-aching, miserable season of a pregnancy.

They'd talked of matters high and low, traded anxieties and dispensed advice. They'd prescribed each other Bible verses and herbal extractions. They'd wanted only to help. They'd only meant the best.

Not once did they speak of K-Shop until Cherish Law brought it up.

It was July, at the tail end of an uneventful meeting, when she lifted a single timid hand. Cherish, the lone Mainlander in the group, daughter of mathematics teachers from Beijing. Twenty-seven but bashful as a child, newly married and not yet a mother (but would be soon, the other MOPs agreed).

When was the last time she volunteered to speak?

Chang-ma made a show of drawing back in surprise. "Cherish? You have a prayer request?"

"Ah," Cherish said, and they could already hear the tongue-swallowing north China accent emerging, the way it always did when she struggled for words. "Ah, Chang-ma."

Chang-ma blinked at her, took pity on her coarse features, her slow mind or was it simply slow words? Lord grant her the patience to wait smilingly through the girl's tortuous expressions of thought. Chang-ma made an encouraging gesture.

Cherish looked down at her palms, toyed with the writer's callus on the third finger of her left hand. Symbol of her lone defiance—her left-handedness in the face of a grandmother's attempt to beat it out of her at a young age. "Ah, Chang-ma. It's just . . . I'm just . . . a bit worried about money. You know how it is. Never enough. And me and Billy, we're not afraid of hard work, we love working. But. Ah. Sometimes I wonder why I left Beijing, if it's just as hard here."

"You left Beijing," Chang-ma said decisively, "to come to a free country. To come to a place where you could worship God loudly and without fear. Amen!"

"Amen," chorused the women around the table.

"Amen," Cherish agreed quickly.

"But what's the problem with money?" Chang-ma settled herself. "Did Billy hurt his back again? The Lord will provide, Cherish. Place your trust in Him."

"Amen," said Mary Jin.

"Amen," rippled the voices around the table.

"Amen," mouthed Cherish.

"The problem," Cherish hurried to add as the others followed Chang-ma's lead and began joining hands in prayer. "The problem is the new K-Shop next door."

The hands fell. Eyes flitted between Cherish, Mary Jin, and the tabletop of fine-grained wood.

"K-Shop?" Mary smiled. The newest and brightest jewel in her portfolio. The light at the end of a three-year nightmare of offers and counteroffers and mortgages and consolidations and tense, late-night phone calls that had finally paid off just two months ago in the form of the first branch of the Korean supermarket chain east of the Pacific, housed in a 45,000-square-foot storefront in prime Diamond Bar retail space, cobbled together from the husks of an electronics shop, a liquor store, and a derelict Tae Kwon Do studio. All leased to the dark-suited Koreans by Mary and Philip Jin, ace husband and wife real estate team.

"K-Shop," Mary said again, trying and failing to catch Cherish's downcast eyes. "Great turnout so far. Real word-of-mouth network. I think they're going to do just fine. What's the problem?"

"Oh, Mary-jie, you know I admire your work. How you've built yourself from nothing, provided a great home for Sonia."

"Yes, yes," Mary and Chang-ma said in unison. Spit it out, Mary did not say.

Cherish sat still for a moment, then heaved an abrupt sob.

"Mary-jie," she said, her voice rising to a wail, "it's going to crush us."

Mary jumped back in her chair. It was her great shame that whenever confronted with wild despair, her first instinct was escape, her second (a distant second) to comfort as Jesus had. It reassured her now to see that, with the exception of Chang-ma, who leapt almost across the table to grip Cherish's hand, the rest of the MOPs had joined her in recoiling.

A glance of solidarity passed around the table. They steeled themselves, leaned in to hear the tangled facts and projections that had led to this sudden outpouring of panic:

Two months since the sweaty, triumphant K-Shop opening a few plazas over, and already foot traffic was down at Law's Chinese Emporium, the check-out lines that usually snaked around fresh fruit and into bulk rice standing a few shorter each day. Cherish arranging and rearranging the otherwise untouched shelves; Billy screening calls from the landlord by day, tabbing through QuickBooks late into the night. All the while the hourlies perched on crates like buzzards, glazed with boredom, nothing to do.

Mary Jin took all this in, arranged herself the way she did in those interminable property management meetings where Philip honked through lists of unquantifiable pros and cons—leaned in and eyes wide, the picture of engagement. When Cherish finished speaking, she laughed. Not with cruelty. Simply the incredulous laugh of a mother discovering the flimsy root of her child's discontent.

"Cherish, dear, is that all?" She clucked. "Of course it's only natural that people are curious about this new store. And of course you'll probably lose some Korean customers in the long run. But the rest? Those ah-mas who want their stinky tofu, their star anise? Those ah-pas who are so set in their ways that they complain whenever you rearrange the dried fruit section? They'll be back, I promise. By the time summer's over, you'll be so busy you'll wish K-Shop had taken more customers."

A murmur of assent. Yes, Cherish. Of course. They put their hands on her shoulders, her arms. Listen to Mary-jie, she of the sharp eye, the business mind. The Emporium was a neighborhood favorite—what did it have to fear from a faceless Korean chain? And Diamond Bar was a city of two markets, a city split in half. Leave K-Shop to the flashy new Koreans; Cherish and Billy would keep the loyal old Chinese. Of course, of course.

Let us pray.

It was perhaps the second week of September when the MOPs first began receiving the mailers intrepid store manager Sunny Kim sent out like clockwork on Tuesdays (GRAND OPENING SALE! ONE WEEK EXTENSION ONLY!). They trickled into K-Shop one by one, solitary and spooked, skulking around the perimeter, taking in the variety, those prices, what lovely produce, what gleaming fish, what's this about a member's discount, what a steal . . .

By October the emails they'd used for store card sign-ups overflowed with daily markdowns, weekly specials. The occasional knee-weakening, adrenaline-stoking Krazy K-Shop flash deal. Their voicemails overflowed with messages from other MOPs, crowing about their finds.

"A sale!" one would wail to another as they passed each other in an aisle. "What could I do?"

What else could she do but slide into the burning vinyl seat of the Toyota Camry at high noon, slip on a pair of oversized shades and elbow-length UV-deflecting gloves and drive the five, ten, twenty, thirty miles from Walnut, from Hacienda Heights, from Whittier, from Irvine, from even as far as San Bernardino, that desert hell, to lurch into the K-Shop parking lot, to dash through the doors and into the blessed AC and grab a forty-eight-count box of Asian pears at a 60 percent discount? To turn around and drive all the way home, the fruit softening in the trunk, her mouth watering from the thrill of the deal.

"It's not your fault you grew up in a developing country," said Sonia of the acid tongue whenever Mary Jin threw herself into similar deal-hunting.

The most recent expedition had yielded the two dozen bruised and battered cabbages Sonia was now watching her mother drag through the marble foyer.

"Marked down," Mary had huffed, by way of greeting and explanation. Mere cents per head!

"It's not your fault," Sonia repeated after the third or fourth night of cabbage soup. "But it's your problem," she said, "not mine," before pushing back her chair and fishing out her phone to order a double cheese, double sausage, easy-on-the-sauce medium pizza with the card her father slid across the table with mute understanding.

Despite Sonia's flippancy, she was right. The MOPs were helpless. It could not be helped. Though they never spoke of it among themselves, there was no denying by the end of October that Mary Jin's prediction had not panned out. With each K-Shop outing, they saw more and more women like themselves—Chinese, Taiwanese, the occasional haughty Hong Konger. The entire San Gabriel Valley out in force, streaming down the lemon-scented aisles behind carts brimming with snow crab (fresh from Santa Monica), bok choy (just arrived from Salinas), daikons, scallions, chili paste, dried squid, bricks of dried ramen to store for busy days, vibrant cellophane bags of honey butter chips to sustain them on the long drive home.

In the end K-Shop had compelled them all.

And Law's Chinese Emporium with its cramped shelves and wilting produce, its wild-eyed staff and shrunken owners and smattering of old-timers, was shriveling away.

Not that Sonia noticed, not that Mary noticed. Though she sat across from Cherish's drawn face once a week, Mary spent those meetings drumming her fingers on the table, lost in thought. Because by then Sonia had detached herself from Mary's orbit like a rogue satellite, and both mother and daughter found their minds ranging further and further from the drab beige of the terrestrial.

Because by then Sonia was deep into her junior year (an upperclassman!), beginning to grow into her lanky beauty. Bored of her roster of college-application-tailored extracurriculars (president of the Taiwanese-American Club, vice president of the Chess Club, semi-regular attendee of the Classic and Foreign Films Club) and entranced by the possibility of pocket money, she had quit them all by the second week of the semester (with the exception of the Fashion and Self-Expression Club) to spend the majority of her afterschool free time bagging groceries at the Diamond Bar K-Shop. It paid twelve dollars an hour, provided her with a steady stream of tinny K-Pop to wriggle to, and kept her mother at arm's length and the dimpled smile of Paul Kim much closer. All in all, Sonia thought, not a bad deal.

With her earnings, she procured and introduced into her bedroom a series of glossy posters, each larger than the next and all featuring groups of five to seven boy-men posing in half-squats or slouched ennui in color-coordinated outfits. Their skin pearly white, their eyes bottomless. Effeminate, sniffed Mary Jin as she dumped out baskets of black-laced bras and raw-hemmed crop tops onto Sonia's bed. When had her little girl begun dressing like a woman about town? How long had Mary's back been turned?

And when Sonia wasn't adding to her collection of pop idols or consuming pointless, looping videos in which those same boys acted out scenes of scripted goofiness/best-friendship, she was dashing off to the mall with Paul Kim in his mother's blue Prius, returning from the Piercing Pagoda with yet more lacerations in her flesh. And, when Mary threatened to rain down the full wrath of the law upon those pop-up child mutilators (what kind of racket were they running anyway?), waving in her mother's face the parental consent forms Philip had dutifully, neglectfully signed.

Mary did not fully understand the transformation taking place before her until one dank autumn day when she looked up from her evening

Bible reading (Job 1:13–22) and started at the shadowy figure framed in her doorway.

No, not a shadowy figure. Just her Sonia, that red-cheeked, round-bellied, laughing Buddha of a baby of hers. Now standing as still as death, eyes rimmed black, a curtain of hair combed straight down her back. A sliver of concave stomach glimpsed between a too-tight shirt and a too-short skirt.

"I won't be home for dinner," the apparition said. She brushed a strand of hair behind her ear and Mary saw—the little hoops had multiplied. An entire line of them running down her daughter's outer ear, their rhinestones glittering like the eyes of an arachnid.

"Where you go?" Mary demanded, beating down a surge of dread she could not understand.

"With Paul."

"Not wearing that."

"With Paul and his mom, okay? In their house. Sitting around the table, saying grace like good little Christians." Sonia rolled her eyes.

Perhaps it had been great pride on Mary's part to assume that Sonia, good and level-headed Sonia, would sail through adolescence unscathed. But here she was, determined to try on every American Teenage Cliché in the catalog, and forcing Mary (warm, nurturing Mary) to respond in kind, to recite the lines seemingly pre-scripted for her, in a voice she did not recognize as her own:

"You wear that in good Christian home? You want Sunny Kim think I raise punk girl?"

"*Punk*, Mom. Not *pang-ke*. If you're going to accuse me of being a punk all the time, at least try to say it right."

A moment of pinched silence.

"Whatever. Anyway, I'll be back at ten. Sunny said we could take the car after."

"You call her Mrs. Kim."

"But she said—"

"I don't care what she say. Mrs. Kim. You want Sunny Kim think I raise miss rude punk no manners?"

Sonia unhinged her jaw into a yawn that Mary thought was almost certainly mimed.

"You know I can't understand you when you get like this. Anyway, Dad already said I could go. So. See ya."

"You understand me if you speak to me in Chinese," Mary yelled after her daughter's retreating body. "Why you don't try your Chinese anymore?"

"Too slow," Sonia shouted as she descended the stairs. "You know how long it takes me to think in Chinese. And I'm already late to meet Paul. How's that for rude?"

"You get better from practice."

"Whatever, Mom. Annyeong."

"What?" Mary yelled, but Sonia was already out the door, carried by her woman's body into the wind-swept night. Typical of her to get the last word.

"When did you get so tall, Sonia?" Mary murmured as she flipped aimlessly through Job, read verse after whining verse, and retained nothing. This man and his litany of quotidian grievances. His day in and day out of wailing and gnashing of teeth. When her daughter was out there in that too-tall body, that brain a black box. That face that had transformed, sometime while Mary wasn't looking, into a mocking mask of her own. What could ash-covered Job know about that?

And so she had nothing, absolutely nothing, to say that night when Cherish, pressed for her prayer request at the end of a sedate meeting, requested with trembling lips nothing for herself, only the might and compassion of God for her husband Billy, twelve years her senior, a genial man with a bad back, who had finally that morning been required to collect his quiet courage and announce to the staff milling before the Emporium that there was no need, that there was no work, that they were all being laid off, effective immediately, with one week's pay as a gesture of goodwill.

"We waited as long as we could," Billy told Cherish afterward, as they stood alone in the emptiness, running rags over every surface they could find. "We did our best."

"We failed," Cherish translated. "We failed everyone."

There was no more to say. The counters gleamed. The stillness settled.

Would God ever forgive them?

Mary Jin sat low in her chair, did not feel the twelve sets of eyes slide over to her. She nibbled at her thumbnail, wondered where Sonia was at this moment. Surely dinner was finished by now. Was she sitting around the Kims' family table still, whittling away the hours? Or alone with that Paul somewhere—Movie theater? Public park? Late night boba and popcorn chicken joint? Somewhere dark and murky, where it felt nice to sit close, shoulder to shoulder. A hand drifting down to rest on her daughter's goose-pimpled thigh.

"I'll put that down as financial worries for Cherish, then," Chang-ma said. "And Mary?"

"What?"

"Prayer request? Anything about Sonia?"

"Yes. No. I—I don't know." She clasped a hand to her temple. "I just—so many things are happening so fast."

"Ah." Chang-ma nodded as if she understood. "Not easy raising a teenager in America, I know. Teenage problems. American teenage problems."

"At least business is going well. Count your blessings, Mary-jie."

Mary snapped her head up. The small, flat voice had come from Cherish.

She realized with a start that she and Chang-ma were alone at the end of the table. Sometime during the preceding conversation the other MOPs had formed a sort of protective huddle around Cherish, stroking her back, handing her tissues, even wiping the tears directly from her cheeks. Disciples, Mary thought snidely, gathered around the body of Christ, and was immediately ashamed. They turned to her now as one creature, expecting something, something from her. But what? She wandered through the labyrinth of their gazes, disoriented, bumping into walls.

"Now, ladies," Chang-ma started to say. But Mary cut her off.

"Move in with me, then," she said abruptly, with no preamble, hardly aware of what was coming out of her mouth.

The MOPs stared. Cherish flushed.

"Why not?" Mary asked, feeling a welcome surge of her old confidence, that brassy resonance in her voice.

"Why not?" she said again. "You're right. Business is great. K-Shop's blowing up." She ignored the gasps, plunged on: "And as you can see, plenty of room. You and Billy can have the downstairs guest room. Total privacy. Come, go, as long as you want."

An interminable silence.

Then: "Thank you, Mary-jie, but we are not a charity case." Cherish drew up her broad shoulders with a dignity that the MOPs had not thought her capable of.

Mary nodded, did not press it. She swallowed away a disappointment she had not expected. She had been expecting relief.

But pride is not sufficient to pay the rent on a one-bedroom ground floor Rowland Heights apartment. Neither are the combined wages of two hourly K-Shop workers, which was what Cherish and Billy Law had become before long. By Christmas, the steel doors were pulled down before the Emporium indefinitely, and the couple found themselves in the gingerbread-house town of Yorba Linda, unloading their U-Haul's worth of belongings into the Jins' four-car garage.

All day, Philip and Billy strode over the rooftops, stringing white lights along the eaves. Below, to the thuds of their steps, the women arced around each other like trains on separate circuits, draping the tree with ornaments plucked from an overflowing box. Each came with a long, meandering history that Mary recited in full to a solemnly nodding Cherish. Then all at once the box was empty; the tree was full.

The silence grew voluminous.

Sonia was gone, having dedicated her winter break to double shifts at K-Shop and whispered adventures with Paul Kim. She was to return that night for a stilted Christmas dinner, loud with the clatter of spoons in bowls, was to accompany Mary and Philip with minimal muttering to the midnight service at the First Mandarin Baptist Church of Praise, before setting off again in the morning for a day spent doing whatever it was she did that she no longer felt obligated to keep her mother apprised of. Mary put it out of her head, gazed at the over-ladened tree with its undeniable rightward tilt, which in any previous year would have been Sonia's to unbox and decorate, to bray possessively over.

She looked at Cherish, perched in Sonia's spot on the arm of the cream leather couch. This young woman (how old was she again?), barely out of girlhood, sitting there like a rough cut of her marble-faced Sonia, two hands splayed on two uncrossed, no-nonsense knees. Mary felt a sudden wave of tenderness.

"It's good to have you here," she said, with a sincerity that took her by surprise. "It's always good to have more young people in the house."

Cherish gave a small smile.

"Even though it's all my fault," Mary added, without meaning to.

"It's pointless to apportion blame."

Mary wondered if Cherish was regurgitating some maxim of Chang-ma's.

The girl continued: "Really, Mary-jie, we do appreciate it. You and Philip taking us in like this, so kind, and Sonia, getting us those K-Shop shifts. She's been after Sunny to make us assistant managers, did you know? She says it's only fair. Actually, co-assistant managers." A real smile now. "How does that even work?"

Mary did in fact know of Sonia's K-Shop lobbying. Just last week her daughter had spent an entire Sunday night dinner batting aside Mary's cautious questions of school and work and boys to enumerate the many glittering qualities common to both Cherish Law and Sunny Kim—kind, collected, briskly competent.

"So it's just crazy to me that Sunny won't give Cherish a chance, you know? They're like the same person."

"Cherish is shy," Mary offered, tentatively. "Maybe not for management."

Sonia waved a chopstick, stippling the lazy susan with broth and sauce. "Not shy—quiet. Like Dad. Would you call Dad shy? Dad?"

Philip grunted, his first and final contribution to the conversation that was beginning to send a prickle of uneasiness through Mary's palms.

She tried a firm stance: "Sunny is business woman. She know how to run her store."

"Bullshit."

"Sonia."

"Sorry," Sonia mumbled through a mouthful of soup dumpling. "The store's fine, I guess. I just think she's being short-sighted, that's all. Just because Cherish can't speak Korean to the delivery guys, or the fish counter guys, who all, by the way, understand English."

"Ah, Sonia. It not so easy. You do business for a long time, you don't change everything for one person. The person change. And Mainlanders, like Cherish, very nice, but not fit in, you know? Sunny have no choice. You know, yu fang shui fang, yu yuan . . . Sonia?"

"Something something water?"

Mary huffed. "Bowl square, water square; bowl round, water round."

Sonia heaved a sigh with the weariness of the ages. "Whatever. I just feel bad for her."

"Sunny?"

"Cherish."

Sonia did not elaborate, and Mary did not ask her to. She simply watched as her daughter hunched back over the table and, with fanatical concentration, mowed down the half-dozen dumplings left in the communal bowl and then the two Mary proffered from her own.

"Are there any more?" was all Sonia said when she looked up at last.

"No," Mary said, starting to rise, empty steamer in hand, "but I go—"

"Nah it's fine, I'm not hungry. Thanks for dinner." She rose; she vanished.

A brief silence, punctuated only by the sound of Philip's slurping.

"What?" Mary demanded as she ran a cloth over the table, chasing down the acrid puddles of vinegar and salt.

"Me?"

"I can hear you thinking. Out with it, you not-shy-but-quiet man."

"It just occurs to me—" Philip paused for a long, luxurious chew. Pork and broth and cabbage and dough—what simple perfection. Mary waited. Lord grant her the fortitude to walk the path of life sandwiched between an incomprehensible daughter and a silent husband. No comfort but the sound of her own voice, crying out in the wilderness.

"It occurs to me that Sonia's relationship with Cherish is independent of her relationship with you."

"Once more, my dear. Smaller words."

Philip grinned, his cragged face lighting up for a moment into that of the boy who'd loitered by the bike racks of National Taiwan University thirty years ago, hoping for a chance to nod along in a one-sided conversation with a certain young Mary of the straight spine, the sure voice, the thousand intransigent, exhilarating, endlessly proclaimed opinions.

"It just seems to me that Sonia is not helping Cherish *at* you."

And once again, just as it was thirty years ago, it was Mary's duty and privilege to initiate this devoted pupil into the true workings of the world, its unassailable gear-and-bolt mechanics. "She's sixteen. I'm her mother. Everything she does is *at* me."

"And besides," she continued, when Philip gave no response but his amiable, infuriating smile. "We're helping too."

"Yes," Philip said thoughtfully, toying with the last scraps of dough disintegrating in his bowl. "In our own way, I suppose we are."

"Sonia," Mary said now to Cherish as they sat before the tree, "she's full of her own ideas."

"She's a credit to you, Mary-jie. She's sweet."

"So sweet. To everyone but me." Mary tried for a laugh that emerged a wheeze.

Cherish shifted her weight ever so slightly, whether out of discomfort or as a *go on* gesture Mary could not tell. Mary opened her mouth, imagined laying it all bare at Cherish's feet. That her daughter spent seemingly all her waking hours at that godforsaken grocery store that had once brought Mary such joy. That she followed this Paul Kim around as if tied by a string, engineering her shifts to align with his, leaping out of the house at all hours of the night to drive off with him to who-knows-where, with God-knows-who. That she listened to K-pop for Paul Kim, watched K-dramas for Paul Kim, blew her paychecks on the cutesy BB and CC creams of K-beauty for Paul Kim, devoured platter after platter of chili-doused Korean rice cakes for Paul Kim, even picked up some halting Korean with (presumably) the goal of impressing Paul Kim. At a time when her own Mandarin was atrophying from passable to rudimentary, she was busy charming the little old ladies at the K-Shop bagging station—

"Annyeonghaseyou, jeoneun Sonia imnida."

Beaming when they complimented her accent, gushed at how lovely it was to meet a gyopo so in touch with her heritage, when so many these days were turning so American, not one word of Korean in their hamburger-and-Coca-Cola guzzling mouths. The hitch in her breath as she cut in, a touch too eager, saying: "No, no, jung-gug." Pointing an index finger at her own heart. "Jung-gug saramieyo."

Playing her trump card so she could bask in one last wave of praise, a Chinese learning to speak Korean. What an accent. What a gem.

Calling "annyeong!" after them as they left, sliding a grin across the aisle at Paul Kim, who flashed his crooked thumbs at her.

How it rattled Mary to see her daughter like this. Puppy-like, panting at the feet of these ahjummas, when at home she was sullen and monosyllabic and stubbornly monolingual in the few words she chose to speak. And how long it'd been since Sonia had delighted in Mary's praise. How long it'd been since Mary had seen her daughter's smile aimed at her.

"Cherish," she wanted to say, "take yourself back to when you were Sonia's age."

Cherish, you who have lived through these years more recently than I. Recall your old crazed self, from ten or fifteen years ago. Find that teenaged mind and untangle its thoughts. Trace the length of them and tell me when you came back to yourself. Tell me how long she'll spend migrating through that tundra of a world, how long before she comes limping home.

But she looked into Cherish's wide, blinking eyes, saw nothing but the pin-sized reflection of her own puffed face. She said nothing for a while. Then, "Sonia has a Korean boyfriend," she said at last, a statement grotesque in its over-simplification.

"Ah, Paul," Cherish said, settling into the couch.

"And of course we all know Korean men can't be trusted."

"Um?"

"It's not racist if it's true," Mary snapped.

"He's . . ." That old timidity again, Cherish shrinking between her shoulders. "He's a nice boy, Mary-jie, so sweet. His mother too."

Sonia, Paul, Sunny, Mary, Philip—who in Cherish's world wasn't sweet as an overripe peach?

Sonia wouldn't have let Mary get away with anything. Sonia would have stood toe to toe with her mother, shooting icy, compressed barbs, noting where they punctured. Lecturing about *decolonization* and *assimilation* and *pan-Asian American solidarity,* words which Mary understood less as vehicles of meaning than as catechisms of an unfamiliar faith. Sonia had developed the pesky habit of veering off into English abstractions at key moments of arguments, leaving Mary spinning like a top. Sonia would haul her mother by the hair, kicking and screaming, up the ladder of righteousness.

Mary looked at Cherish, still sitting before her like a puddle. "Never mind," she said at last. "Forget I said anything."

But just then, Cherish roused herself. "Mary-jie," she said, the words tumbling out as if suddenly undammed: "Chang-ma told me the other day: This too will pass. One day this will just be another bad memory. And she's right. I was thinking back to Beijing, the real winters we got there, and meeting that cold little missionary, and finding God, and coming to America, and working at the Emporium, and marrying Billy, and every memory is like stepping through a door, and every door is like shedding a skin. Mary-jie, I've shed so many I'm barely the same person I was just five years ago, and one day losing the Emporium will be just that, something that happened to somebody else. And you'll be somebody else. And Sonia too. You won't even recognize yourself."

Cherish stopped speaking as abruptly as she'd begun, pink with exertion.

"This is a blessing," she added, standing.

For a long time afterward Mary would turn these words over in her head, finding alternately comfort or reproof, reaching no conclusion. They would hang over her memory of that night—the first Christmas spent with Cherish and Billy, the last service Sonia deigned to attend for many years—like a private constellation.

And Mary, thinking back, would remember next to nothing of the events of the night—not the black velvet dress that made a swamp of her body; the toothy greetings she exchanged with the other MOPs in the parking lot; the empty seat that loomed beside her through the opening hymns and long into the sermon, until Sonia came hurrying in halfway through communion, still clad in her K-Shop uniform, flustered and full of hissed apologies; how at the sight of her daughter Mary had been flooded with relief and rancor in equal parts; how she'd chosen rancor; how Sonia had sat beside her for the remainder of the service, hard-eyed and thin-mouthed, rebuked but undaunted.

She remembered mostly kneeling (the pain in her knee, the ache in her neck). And pondering, in a moment of reflection upon the sacrifice of Christ (those bloodied lashes on a hairless chest), her own Biblical namesake instead. Fourteen years old, a virgin in blue. A child cradling another child, her face rapturous with joy.

Mary, dear girl, she remembered thinking. Forget about it. In thirty-three years you'll be weeping over his mangled corpse.

IV. WHAT YOU ARE GOING TO DO, DO QUICKLY.

This Mary's own day of reckoning came a week later.

She returned home one afternoon to find Cherish buzzing by the door.

"Come," Cherish said, taking the K-Shop bags from her hands. "Let me."

"No need," Mary started to say, but Cherish cut her off: "Let me. Maybe you should go upstairs, Mary-jie. Sonia's here, with Paul."

Here? But they should have been at one of their many elsewheres. Since when did Sonia bring anyone to this spacious house her parents had toiled to provide her with?

"Upstairs, Mary-jie. In Sonia's room."

The world clicked into place. "The door?"

"Shut."

Mary had dropped the bags to the ground in an instant, was pushing through the hallway in another. Somewhere behind her Cherish was still speaking (". . . thought you should know . . . probably nothing . . . but . . ."), but the words slid around her like oil. She was taking the steps two at a time, her stomach rolling. Of course she had prepared for this moment. Of course she'd known it was coming. But still. Now that it was actually happening, she found it impossible to believe. Her Sonia, with a boy, door shut, in her own home.

Mary shook away the lightness in her head. If only the MOPs were here, their prayers a shield around her. What minor miracle would they have summoned, what holy force to jam the perfumed signals passing between her daughter and the dubiously dimpled Paul Kim?

Ladies, please pray for the soul of my Sonia, my daughter, punk fornicator, flagrantly sinning beneath my roof.

Ladies, pray for my forgiveness. My avarice at profiting from a Korean supermarket chain without considering the consequences.

At the top of the stairs now, close enough to hear the beat of the K-Pop anthem pulsing from her daughter's room. Close enough to feel its vibrations in her teeth. Close enough to hear Paul Kim's exultant voice: "Yes, yes, exactly. No, the knee's like this, and your hand goes here—yes!"

A veil of darkness over her eyes. She pushed the door open.

Blissful silence as the music clicked off.

Then: "Mom?"

Sonia's voice, small and guileless as a child's. The veil lifted. She saw: her daughter and Paul Kim, slick with sweat, clothed in neon leggings and raw edge crop tops. Standing parallel to each other and perpendicular to the door, arms thrust above their heads, hips cocked coquettishly to the side. In Paul's hand a remote, aimed at the now-muted TV.

Mary followed it to the screen—five Lycra-clad Korean girls, scattered across a gleaming, retro-futuristic stage. Writhing to silent music, throwing their bodies into impossible contortions. The same contortions, she realized with a thud, that Paul Kim had been coaching her daughter through.

"What's wrong, Mom?" Sonia asked.

"No boys in room," Mary fumbled. "You know the rules."

A pause while Sonia took in the implication. And then: "Oh Mom, you thought—" Sonia threw her head back and laughed. "Mom, of course not. Paul doesn't even . . . whatever. We're just dancing."

"Just dancing," Paul repeated encouragingly.

"Just dancing," Mary repeated stupidly.

"We have an audition tomorrow. For this new group, mixed this time, boys and girls together. Paul thinks we have a shot."

Paul Kim flashed a thumbs-up.

"Korean group? They take you to Korea?"

Sonia rolled her eyes, but without her usual malice, the gesture was merely impish. And Mary saw in a flash the Sonia known to Sunny Kim and Cherish Law—flushed and clever and good-natured, a mirror focusing the light of the world. "Obviously not, Mom. I'm not delusional, unlike Paul."

"Hey."

"Paul, can you give us a sec?"

The boy nodded wisely, clapped a pair of enormous headphones around his head and planted himself on the bed, facing the wall.

Evidently satisfied, Sonia continued: "Look, Mom—"

But Mary spoke over her, the words tumbling out with a momentum of their own. "No Korea, no more Korean groups, Korean songs, Korean dances. Enough, Sonia. No more of this boy"—the last words hissed sotto voce, though Paul Kim was already far away in his bobbing head, borne aloft on some saccharine Korean melody—"this bad influence, running around—"

"Mom—"

But she could not be stopped. She was a stone rolling down a hill to the argument that she already knew awaited them, with the blessed relief of inevitability. "—punishing me, maybe, for Cherish or for something else? Well I'm sorry, okay? I—"

"Mom!" The voice pitched so loud that even Paul looked up from his blank-faced reverie to watch the storm clouds rolling over her daughter's open window of a face. "Oh my God, Mom, enough, enough, are you kidding? Enough yourself! Can't I have a goddamn—"

"Sonia!"

"—*goddamn* interest without you making it all about your neuroses? So I listened to a few stupid songs, learned a few stupid dances, signed up for a stupid audition that we're obviously going to fail, and oh my God, why do you even care? This is just for fun—just fun!"

But it did not look like fun, stupid or otherwise, written out on Sonia's reddened face, her brimming eyes. Where was the stony young woman, wit arrayed about her like lances, who Mary could meet on an open field and, if not defeat, at least parry to a draw? In her place this caterwauling child.

"So . . ." she said at last, while Sonia heaved ugly breaths. "You not going to Korea?"

Sonia unleashed a terrible laugh. "No. No, I'll stay here with you until I die and I'll never leave and you can find a new thing to pick on every day for the rest of my life. You'd love that, wouldn't you?"

And Mary was driven back, back. Each word landing on her chest with the heft and velocity of a cannonball, shattering her resistance, sending her stumbling for safety. Out the bedroom, down the stairs, shaken, an army routed, barely hearing, past caring, that above her the door was slamming shut, the music starting up again.

Down the stairs, down, past the silently inquiring Cherish, past the shark-faced Billy. Down to the den tucked between the garage and the laundry room, where Philip spent his days, far out of earshot of the rest of the house. He grunted in greeting when she entered. She sank into the loveseat beside him, and, without meaning to, burst into tears.

"But my dear," Philip said, finally drawn out of his *World Journal*, "what's the matter?"

"Sonia and Paul," Mary managed when her sobs subsided. "In her room."

"Sex?" Philip whispered.

"Worse." Mary hiccupped. "Dancing."

Philip could not help himself. He laughed. "Dancing?"

"They have an audition tomorrow. Something about a new singing group?"

"Tomorrow? The consent form said next month."

"You knew?" Mary sat upright, her eyes bright.

"Don't worry, dear. They're not going to get picked. Have you seen them dance? Like a couple of It's a Small World automatons." He chuckled to himself, opened the paper again.

"How could you keep this from me? How did you let it get this far? And that Cherish, all buddy-buddy, was she in on it too?"

"Who cares, Mary?"

"I care! Why don't you?" Sonia, Philip, Cherish. All around her, the low thrum of conspiracy. The house pulsed with dark intent.

"I—"

"And why are you always undermining me? Always signing stupid forms? Always making me out to be the villain?" She hadn't meant to shout, but there it was, hanging between them.

Philip blinked, dazed. He had expected catastrophizing, he had expected frenzied strategizing. Accusations he had not expected. He turned to his wife to defend himself, but found himself speechless. All this time he'd thought they understood each other.

After discovering sometime around Sonia's thirteenth birthday that he was no longer able to speak to his suddenly sardonic daughter with any sort of frankness, he'd pivoted without a thought to archetypes. To the sitcom family roles he understood, knew in his marrow like the thread of an age-old fairy tale. The nagging mother; the beat-down, permissive father; the spunky, irreverent daughter. He'd thought they were all in on it together, playing their parts with gusto. In the absence of emotional sincerity, finding refuge in the well-trod. A familial inside joke. But now he understood with a gulp that he'd understood nothing at all. All this time he'd been bantering alone, to himself. All this time, comforted by the sound of his own echo. The sound of one ass laughing.

He turned to his wife—to do what? To apologize, he scolded himself. To explain. To inquire gently into why she was reduced to tears by a bit of rhythmless gyrating. But he looked at her drawn face, her pulled lips. Later, later. When she had calmed herself, when he had the right words. He folded his bewilderment into the newspaper, left on soundless steps.

V. AND IT WAS NIGHT.

Alone now in the silent bowels of the house, Mary Jin rehearsed her own explanations—to her husband, to the wide-eyed Cherish, to Sonia, when the time came, and to the MOPs, for when they inevitably asked after the sorry state of her daughter. She saw them all arrayed before her, a panel waiting to pass judgment. She saw herself before the tribunal, shaky-voiced but otherwise dignified. Pale and luminous, Portrait of a Lady in Honorable Distress. She imagined looking each in the eye and over the entire room. The acoustics magnificent, her voice gathering strength, soaring, explaining—

She admitted—she would admit, she decided, if pressed—that she'd always known Sonia would one day shed her Chinese skin. After all, that's what Mary, what any immigrant mother, knew from the beginning to prepare for—to realize one day with a start that your child is foreign to you. To learn the look on a daughter's face as she turns her back. She had known the dangers. No one could say she had not been vigilant.

But of all betrayals, this was the one she had not anticipated. Not for an infatuation, nor under the influence of her freewheeling American schoolmates. But for—what were Sonia's exact words? For some stupid songs. Some stupid fun. A dance contest she had no chance of winning. How small the price for her daughter's soul. Thirty pieces of silver, and you could cart it by the bushel.

Now Mary Jin understood that there had never been and would never be any romance with Paul Kim. That the boy was a symptom, not the cause, of the gangrene-like disease that had eroded her Sonia limb by limb. A transformation made not from some (forgivable) compulsion of love, but of Sonia's own free will and enthusiastic consent. That while she'd stood guard at the front gates, Sonia had defected out the back, and now she had a daughter more Korean than Chinese. A jung-gu-gin, yes, now and forever (it could not be helped), but how wonderful her accent. The fine line of her chin, the smooth expanse of her brow. How she passes, almost.

A pointless disguise, Mary thought, in this place where they might as well be one people. Where among the rude, "chink" and "gook" circled interchangeably, where the more civilized restrained themselves to "ni-hao, konichiwa, annyeong?" or, more to the point, "What kind of Asian are you, anyway?"

What's the point, Sonia, she imagined shouting to her distantly pirouetting daughter. You want smelly food, stunted Engrish? You want ching-chang-chong, tiger moms, dog-eater, bad driving? I have all that right here.

I've been here this whole time.

All this she would tell them. Would they understand? Sonia wouldn't—by now her Mandarin was reduced to basic pleasantries and scrambled Bible verses, lending her the beatific air of a medieval idiot-saint. She would blink at her mother uncomprehendingly, thinking in Korean.

Would the MOPs understand? Maybe. Surely.

She imagined them now around the mahogany table, the overhead casting their faces in chiaroscuro. She imagined telling them all this, her tongue thick, her words a jumble. The nuance of her argument blunted into: "K-Shop. It was a mistake. So help me God."

Their ovine faces gentle, vacant. Leaning forward in their seats, over their crumb-filled plates, to better hear Mary Jin's story, to better see Mary Jin's face. To better understand the despair they could not make sense of, because while they were all Taiwanese immigrants (except for Cherish, poor lone Mainlander), all attuned to the small triumphs and petty humiliations of their lot in life, they were none of them mother to Sonia Jin, that infuriating, exasperating, English-screaming, Korean-dreaming, Diet Coke-swilling monster of a girl. That forever departing and forever beloved daughter of hers.

"Korean boyfriend," she would mutter. An untruth, but a small one.

"Can't be trusted," Chang-ma would say helpfully.

The rest might dissent, unleash overlapping murmurs of reassurance.

She imagined turning her hunted eyes to Cherish. Cherish, taking her seat at the other end of the table like the mistress of the house.

Cherish, her round moon face whittled down by worry to striking cheekbones and wise owl eyes, almost pretty in her slow-motion distress. Cherish, the discomfiting presence, the non-daughter in the doorway, the shadow in her house.

Mary would peer into the coal-dark eyes. An equanimity that could be mistaken for stupidity. A gate dropped at her approach.

HOVER O'ER ME WITH YOUR WINGS

fiction by RANDY F. NELSON

from PLOUGHSHARES

Back then, everybody smoked. I knew guys who could jump-start a Zippo lighter just by snapping their fingers. People smoked in restaurants, movie theaters, airplanes, trains, college classrooms, funeral homes. I've seen people smoking, chest deep, in swimming pools. Children smoked back then. Monkeys in roadside zoos smoked. In junior high school, we had a designated smoking area for teachers and the dozen or so student hoodlums who had permission slips from home.

The place I'm talking about was a crumbling asphalt pad just outside our school cafeteria. It looked like a miniature basketball court that had been jammed against the building. On most days, you could find three or four teachers in the vicinity and maybe five or six students. It was a sort of neutral zone where they could mingle like old friends until the bell rang for the next period. Every once in a while, you'd see some kid offering his lighter to a teacher who'd be patting his pockets or rummaging in her pocketbook. It was the polite thing to do.

On the day I'm remembering, it is misting rain, and it's so cold that the droplets are freezing as they fall. Every few minutes, you can see a snowflake drifting through the mix, and down low on the wall, just outside the cafeteria door, there's a steam grate belching a white rivulet of smoke that never rises more than a foot off the ground. It's slithering around the ankles of the only two people present. One of them is Claudette Severin, an eighth-grade English teacher, who is tall, almost beautiful, and serious with her cigarettes. Not yet middle aged, she's still energetic enough to trade jokes with her kids in class. She banters. Some of the other teachers think she laughs too much. Or dresses inappropriately. The usual.

The person with her is me. Viewed from this distance, I am indistinguishable from all other boys in junior high school. I'm skinny, brown skinned, scarfed in plaid, and almost as tall as Miss Severin. I'm wearing a hooded car coat that's hanging from my shoulders like a walrus hide. No cigarette. No confidence. Just thick, white puffs of indignation that spew from my mouth and nose as I struggle to make a point, talking so fast that I keep slipping back into the Spanish we use at home.

The point has to do with a grade but, more particularly, with a feeling that something in our relationship has, catastrophically, shifted. The sudden shock of it is both funny and pitiable to anyone who is not fourteen years old. I look like the kid who has just driven his bike into a mailbox. But I keep going on and on about the grade because it's the only language I have at the moment and because I can't bring myself to say the other thing. There's this invisible distance between us. From time to time, Claudette takes a draw on her cigarette and studies the windows on the second floor of the building.

"But why?" I'm saying.

When nothing else comes to her, she tells me, "Because. You can do better."

"But why?"

It goes on like this for a while, a fruitless back and forth, until the boy, my fourteen year old self, finally grasps that her attention is elsewhere. His eyes also get drawn upward. He sees the second floor windows that are lined up and backlit like television sets in an appliance store. There's a crystal condensation on all of them, but also, behind a significant one, there is a human-like figure that is only a blur. As it gets steadily colder outside, Claudette draws in the last bit of warmth from her cigarette and then exhales with something that looks, to the boy, like a kiss. "Why don't we do this," she offers. "Why don't you rewrite it, and I'll average the two grades?"

"It's not that," he says. "It's not the grade. It's all the stuff you said."

"All the *stuff*?" She turns her eyes upon him. "You want me to take back the *stuff* I said and tell you some other *stuff*?"

He can't stop the rush of redness to his face.

When she uses his name for the first time, he feels worse. "Do you understand what I've been trying to tell you, Harry? That you've got to stop fooling around with words. Because that's what you do. You think clever is cute. And so that's what you write. Clever bullshit. You have a *chance,* Harry, that not everybody has. Why not try to *say* something? Do you understand?"

"No" is all he can think to say. It would be like carving in stone.

"Look!"

He thinks she means the window.

But, no, it is something else that he will carry with him for years. Claudette takes his hand in both of hers. She pulls it inside her coat and puts it against her breast, pressing his palm into the fullness of her as he flinches, the hand already numb with disbelief. He imagines that he's hurting her but, no, her intensity, the fierceness of her grasp, is a language of its own, the physical expression of the hold she has always had on him.

Her face is suddenly next to his face, her lips touching his ear, when she whispers, "*Now* what, Harry?" She moves his hand away at last and places it against his own chest, gently pushing him backward. "What happens now, Harry, in this story? Do you run to the principal? Or should I report you? Are you someone who molested a teacher? Do you follow me home? Do you tell your friends? Do they believe you? Do you think this will happen again, Harry? Have you ever touched a girl before? Do you think I'm in love with you? Any answer, *any*, would make you some kind of story. But the real thing is the *why*. Isn't it?"

"I don't understand what you're—"

"There isn't a word, Harry. That's the point. It's nothing but fog until you *make* it into something. *That's* the job!" Then the fifth period bell rings. And it's like a glass of water dropped onto a concrete floor.

Throughout the afternoon, this boy, of whom I am the aged descendant, waited for his name to be called over the loudspeaker. He imagined the humiliation that would follow. He imagined his parents being summoned. So he heard nothing that his teachers said. Rather, he daydreamed himself outside again without a coat or shoes while, in reality, the wind was picking up, and the tree limbs had begun to sway, and the temperature was falling. From time to time, ice pellets were being flung at the windows, and a cold, leaden something lay in his stomach.

When the last bell of the day rang, the halls filled and then cleared. All of the energy and confusion of the day got transported outside and jammed into orange buses that went lumbering through the slush and crust. Only a few pupils headed back toward town on foot, hunched under backpacks. Some of them cut through vacant lots. Some stayed with the sidewalks, pretending to skate or ski. They all went laughing and calling to each other for several blocks. I, on the other hand, the boy in the gray car coat, loitered in a stairwell, waiting for the last voices to depart. I felt the night's first chill creeping along the hallway, making its way past the auditorium and the central offices. Then, after waiting another while, I took the stairs to the second floor.

There were several teachers still working at their desks and one or two students still fumbling at theirs, but the hallway was empty. The long, deserted corridor reminded me of a bowling alley. It smelled of floor wax and laundry damp. You could hear radiators ticking down for the night. I lumbered along, trying to look like someone on an important errand and telling myself that I just wanted to see whose room it had been where the blurry figure had appeared.

So I counted windows as I passed open doors. When I found the right classroom, I read the plaque next to the doorframe. "Mrs. Logan" it said. Underneath the name, and in the same font, was the word "Art." There was no one inside the room, just the day's clutter spread over long, laboratory-like tables that had been arranged at odd angles beneath the fluorescent lights. The one big table at the front of the room had an aluminum sink that was nearly full of jars and brushes, all of them splotched with paint. In the back of the room, there were oversized watercolors pinned like laundry to a cord stretched from wall to wall. A miniature kiln squatted in one corner.

The windows themselves were beaded by the precipitation outside, but I found that by walking closer and looking straight down, I could make out the fire escape and the smoking area beneath it. What I did not notice was the woman who had noticed me. Perhaps she deliberately rustled the papers she carried—I don't know—but that was the sound that whirled me about. It sent the blood rushing to my face for the second time in the day.

"What's your name?" she finally said.

"Harry" was all that I could manage.

"Your real name." She spoke while walking farther into the room and without bothering to look at me again. Like she already knew what was happening.

"Javier. Cayetano," I said.

"So—why did you say 'Harry?'"

"I don't like Javy," I explained. "That's what everyone calls my dad."

She thought for a moment. "Your father has the landscaping business. He does the lawn servicing and so on?"

I nodded.

"Mmm." There—she'd categorized me with one syllable.

Mrs. Logan the art teacher pondered her papers and then walked them the rest of the way across the room, shelving the stack near the windows. Then went to her toes in order to look through the same window that had attracted me. She was wearing a loose, white smock as well as an apron, as if she needed to be doubly protected from the messiness of children. I tried to ease myself away when the smock touched my shoulder. "Well," she said. "Harry. What are we going to do about this?"

I felt an illness come upon me. She knew.

I reached for a convincing lie to tell, but nothing came to me.

After a long silence, Mrs. Logan said, "She doesn't love you, Harry. She doesn't love anyone." Then she paused the way people do when they're waiting for you to agree with them.

If I had just said nothing. If I had just accepted the words and then slipped away with my humiliation, I could have maybe smiled in later years at my naïveté. But, no, I had to fall back on my fourteen-year-old talent for impudence. "What did she do that was so bad?" I challenged. And even to me it sounded like whining.

Mrs. Logan gave it a further silence and then, still without looking at me, offered, "She was reckless. With people's lives."

So there. Even though you don't know the whole story yet, that's the why of it all. But here's a funny thought. For the longest time, I believed she was talking about me.

Tell me if you've heard these names before. Mary Kay Letourneau, Debra Lafave, Lindsay Massaro, Amy McElhenney, Carrie McCandless, Sheral Smith, Alison Peck. They're all real people. Teachers. You can look them up. I'm not saying they weren't in love with their students. I'm just saying they all went to jail for the same thing. In every case, the attraction to one particular boy was that strong. If that makes sense to you, then you can understand how Claudette's face stayed in my memory for years.

Her Slavic features were so close to beautiful that you wondered what went wrong, where the hidden flaw might be. Not in the eyes, certainly, which were a pale, icy blue, the color of glacier water. She had long, honeyed hair framing her face, strands of it spilling out of one of those slouchy toboggans that girls are still wearing today. A little purple pompom on top. The glasses made her look like a librarian, but the little beads of moisture on her face? The ones from the freezing mist that afternoon? She did not once bother to wipe them away. In all, it gave you the impression that she had been created for the cold.

What I'm saying is that part of me was not surprised when she left. There were no formalities. She simply slipped away several weeks after Christmas break. It was one of those disappearances that never gets a satisfactory explanation. Someone said she got married. Someone else said her mother had been ill. And so on. But, no, there was never anything official. She just vanished in the middle of the school year, and they hired a substitute to take her classes.

Then, high school. She became a distant memory for most of us. Over time, we too disappeared in different ways. I think my class produced two or three doctors, maybe four or five lawyers, a few military people, and the requisite number of nurses, teachers, and petty criminals. Plus one horticulturalist—me. I didn't become a famous author. My mom died during my second year of college. I can say that now without a sudden stab of pain. But back then. You know. The life sort of drained out of Dad. You see that a lot in couples who are close. So I came home to help with the landscaping and the mowing and the mulching because that's what you do in our kind of family.

Today, we're more of a retail business than a landscaping service. I put together enough money to buy some acreage, then opened a garden center close to where we used to live. Big parking lot, two greenhouses, and a glassed-in showroom. We called it Ridge Creek Nursery and Garden Center, because who would go to a place called Cayetano's? We sell container plants, tools, fountains, supplies—pretty much whatever you need for your house and garden.

Mrs. Logan, the teacher who didn't call me Javy, retired about the same time as my dad. She built a little art studio behind her house over there on Academy Street and set about landscaping the whole place by herself. That's how I got to know her a little better. She was a regular customer for four or five years before she died. I wouldn't say we were friends, but I did notice her fairly often, wandering the rows inside one of our greenhouses or walking the gravel paths outside in the growing yards. We have little wagons you can pull along as you shop, and I've seen her loaded up lots of times. Occasionally, I'd do a delivery to her house when the stuff was too bulky for her car. Bales of pine needles, bags of fertilizer, soil mix, and so on. I believe it was a heart attack that finally got her, out there next to the little studio. She died right in front of some Lenten roses we'd sold her the previous year. That's what brought Claudette Severin back into my life. I mean, figuratively speaking.

You can never know what turns up at an estate sale.

There was a young woman at a card table in the front yard of Mrs. Logan's house. She sat behind a cash box and a stack of receipts embossed with "Gassett Estate Sales and Auction Services." She gave me a smile as I went inside, where the contents of the house had been laid out on tables, countertops, dressers, chests, nightstands. Even the floor. There was silverware in rows on the dining room table, along with two sets of china, plus some recipe books. Lamps all along one wall, kitchen gadgets on every other surface, including the window sills. Clothing hung on portable racks. I watched a woman filling a cardboard box with glassware and glaring at anyone who came near.

I shouldered my way through the crowd in the kitchen and went outside through the back porch, where I ambled around inspecting some Satsuki azaleas I'd sold Mrs. Logan a few years before. I found a few camelias of mine too. The next cold snap would drop the few remaining buds, I thought. A couple of mound junipers, though, were doing fine, spreading out nicely. I'd drawn up the overall design, but she'd done all the planting. Everything was laid out in beds that formed a border between the lawn and a wooded area on the downslope.

I followed a worn path toward the little art studio on the edge of the property. Stepping stones would have been useful. I should have put them into the original plan. At the door of the studio, I gave a little shove, and it swung open without a sound. The clutter inside was a close replica of the classroom where I'd met her decades before, but there were no sale tags on any of the items.

There was a tall easel next to one of the windows and some partially finished canvases on stretchers that were leaning against the far wall—that, plus a straight-backed chair, looking as if it had just been pushed back from the easel. On the wall nearest the house was a book cabinet, six or eight glassed-in shelves loaded with all the paraphernalia you'd expect, along with some art books and one whole tier of novels on the top shelf, all of them by the same author. I noticed two utility lamps with their cords coiled around them that had been jammed out of the way. They were next to a desk that had some palette knives on it, along with some used rags and a photograph in a silver frame.

I picked up the frame and studied the faded image. One of the three figures in the picture was Claudette Severin, still a soft, fresh face at the time the photograph was made. And on the far right margin of the picture was Juliana Logan, also recognizable but whose face and shoulders had barely made it into the shot. She was smiling and leaning toward the central figure, a dark-haired girl who was beaming directly at the camera. The three of them were so close that they must have had their arms intertwined. As I set the frame back in its place, I was further startled by a woman's voice behind me. "That's me," it was saying. "Taken when I was about fifteen, I think. Fifteen or sixteen. A couple of lifetimes ago."

I turned to apologize, but she smiled.

"That's fine," she went on. "To tell you the truth, I had no idea she'd kept it. Makes you want to clear out your past, doesn't it?" Making it sound like a joke.

I could see her resemblance to the teenager in the picture. The face was fuller now, of course, but remarkably free of aging. The eyes and the mouth were exactly the same as those in the photograph, although the hair had been lightened and cut short. She had on black jeans and a gray cowl-neck sweater. No makeup or jewelry other than a pair of lapis earrings.

Putting out her hand, she said, "Larissa," as if she'd been expecting me.

"Harry. Cayetano."

"So, Harry. How did you know my mother?"

I looked again at the photograph.

"Juliana. Not Claudette," she laughed. "But, yeah, they were a couple. For a while."

It took me a minute. "School," I managed to say. "I knew her from school, but I, ah . . . not really. She was a customer of mine. The landscaping and all. I'm sorry about your loss."

"Thanks. I didn't really know any of her friends. Or her, to tell you the truth. Place is a mess, isn't it?" She seemed to be curious rather than grief-stricken, her eyes flitting over the objects in the room. When she got to the book cabinet, she saw the row of novels at the top. "Huh," she said. "I guess that's me too."

"You're Larissa Grenier?"

"Gren-yay, but yeah. I was Larissa Logan until, you know, the big bust-up. Then, after I started publishing, they needed a name. So. Yeah."

"You wrote all these?"

"Don't sound so surprised, Harry. It hurts my feelings."

I liked her for talking like that. Mostly, I watched her wandering around the studio, picking up this and that like the detective in a TV show. I asked her if she had come from far away. And she said, "Miami," as if that told me everything. It took some time for her to work her way back around to the picture, and she studied it without picking it up. After a minute, she muttered, "I need a drink."

At the studio door, she stopped and gestured toward the house as if an idea had just occurred to her. "Do you know all these people, Harry?"

"A few, I guess. Most of them I've never met."

Then, drawn back to the picture, she said, "It had all started going to hell—her and Claudette, I mean—even before this. The yelling and all. There'd always been rumors about Claudette and students. Mom called her reckless, a narcissist. There were screaming matches. Until, finally, I suppose you could say, they got divorced before they could get married. That's about it, really. Except, I made the unconventional choice, didn't I? I left with Claudette. Marched right out like the world awaited my presence—god, you couldn't invent this crap, could you? A beer okay with you?"

We went back to the house and dragged a couple of beers from the refrigerator. "I was staying here, at the house, after the funeral," Larissa said, "until the auction company told me I had to give them a few days to stage all the stuff, you know, and put a value to it. So I'm out at the Marriott now. Like I don't spend half my life there anyhow."

"Book tours?" I asked.

"Better than being a truck stop hooker I guess. But not by much. You mind if I smoke?"

I think there was another beer or two after that. We were seated at a little banquette in the kitchen, behind a round table that made it look like we were in a restaurant. She was using a saucer as an ashtray and pealing the paper label off one of the bottles as we talked. After a time, the crowd thinned. Larissa stretched her legs out on her side of the banquette and nodded to the picked-over remains of the kitchen. "To inheritance," she said. "And all the shit you can't get rid of." So I tapped the lip of her bottle with mine but didn't say anything.

"How about Claudette?" she went on. "Did you know her?'

"Yeah. Eighth-grade English. Maybe you're the one who can say why she really left."

"You already know why."

"No. I don't."

"Well. I'll tell you one thing about her, Harry. She was the best goddamn writing teacher I ever had."

"You only get one of those, I guess."

"I'm serious. She was the best. I'm talking about things that you can't teach. Except she could."

The young woman from the front yard interrupted that thought by tapping at the kitchen doorframe. "Miz Grenier? I think that's about it.

There hasn't been anybody for a while. I'll take the cash and the receipts back to the office, and Mr. Gassett will send you a check and an inventory next week. I think we did pretty good. And I'll have the guys come by tomorrow morning. They'll pack up everything that's left. Is that okay?"

"Sure, Cassie. That'll be fine. Thank you."

The late afternoon sunlight had expended the last of its warmth, and it wasn't long until the furnace kicked in with a comforting thrum. We both listened as if it were music. Larissa handled most of the talking, but at one stretch, I saw her looking at the bare wall just past my shoulder and maybe seeing something from the distant past. "I chose her over my mom, you know. After I left for college. I don't even remember the night it all exploded. Just the intensity of it. And I never came back home, until now."

"Are you talking about Claudette?"

"You've got no idea, Harry. She was a force."

"I believe you."

"One day—she took my hand. In both of hers. And placed it over her own heart and then said to me, 'What now, Larissa? What happens now?' And she gave me an answer that I was barely old enough to understand. The why of it all. What real writers do. I think it might have been the most intimate moment of my life."

I made a barking sound that resembled laughter. And she looked at me as if I had ruined something important. Neither of us said anything after that. I believe some people are capable of very clever responses at such a moment. But I was not. By the time I had gotten back to my truck, I was imagining my eighth-grade self outside a school cafeteria once more, standing in the freezing mist and hearing the clatter of dishes and silverware from inside. The hubbub of hundreds of conversations just a window pane away. All of it coinciding with the arrival of snow. That's how I still remember her. I can see her as one of those figures inside a glass globe with white flakes whirling, unreachable and cold. In later years, I discovered that Claudette had had many successful students, a few of whom had become writers of note. But whether she'd loved all of them, I am unable to say.

LORDS OF THE WIND

fiction by YXTA MAYA MURRAY

from CONJUNCTIONS

> *He caught up to him at the corner of La Posada. And that's where he, you know, hit him. With a flashlight, on the back of his head.*
>
> *—Man describing the murder of union organizer Nagi Daifallah, from the documentary Fighting for Our Lives (1975)*

WE KNEW THE WIND WAS DIFFERENT when we got up that morning. The dust was already blowing and visibility wasn't all that great.

It was frightening because you couldn't see. They dismissed school early. I was supposed to walk home and my mom came to the school to pick me up. Once I got into the car you could probably only see maybe a block ahead of you, if that.

Everybody was trying to cover their faces. You were walking against the wind. You couldn't breathe. I got sand in my eyes and my mouth.

The trees had a definite bend to them. The wind was pulling limbs off the trees.

My mother and I got home. We stayed in the house. We tried to close off doorjambs and windows with towels because the sand and dust were coming in.

We hunkered in the house for so long, just waiting for it to end. We were scared. We'd never experienced anything like that.

The sound, it was a kind of roaring. My mother got a little panicky.

It was almost apocalyptic. The sky and everything was brown and orange. The dust blocked out the sun.

Oh my God, we thought. Where did this come from?

—Interview with Lisa Tumey, Bakersfield, June 15, 2023

You want me to tell you about the day of the dust?

I see, you're a writer. Doing a story. And here I was, thinking you came to see me about your hands.

Hands, honey. Didn't you see the sign on my door? That's the business I'm in. The hand business.

No, I can't conjure those ghosts with you this morning. Got a day of patients ahead of me.

Oh, *Marisol* said I'd tell you all about the typhoon, huh?

That woman is a bug in my bourbon. She collar you at the Fiesta Market? You must have wandered into the cheese aisle and bumped into her mouth.

Yeah, I remember it. The Great Dust Storm of 1977.

Wiped out Lamont, Arvin, Bakersfield. Sand made the sun bleed. Buried houses, cars, orchards, cattle. People. The living and the dead.

I'm a scientist, so I don't go in for superstition. Still, with everything we'd gone through, it was hard for some of us not to see the storm as the curse of a chisera.

Reason some people believe brujería made the wind deadly that year is there'd been devilry done in this town. There's no denying that the people of Lamont were long overdue for a blood atonement.

I'm talking about what happened to Nagi. But I guess you don't know about him. Seeing as you're not from around here.

Well, I can't have old Marisol chomping off my head because I didn't give you a minute . . . but if you want to know about that spell of bad weather, you'll need to hear about what came before. I have to sit down for that.

No, ma'am, slow down. I'm not giving you the details of the dust just yet. It's like I said. I'm going back to the time I knew Nagi Daifallah. I'll bring you to the place you want to be but we're taking the long way, because I'm an old woman with a story and that gives me some prerogatives.

This was in the spring of '73, right when the UFW had set up the Terronez medical clinic in Delano, after the grape strike there had ended.

Yes, the United Farm Workers. You're in UFW territory, you know that, right?

I was seventeen years old. My parents and I had spent the past two months picketing the DiGiorgio ranch, a grapes, plums, and pears hell-hole that sat right by Lamont. My papi nearly got blinded when one of the overseers sprayed his face with pesticides. We'd harvested every crop in San Joaquin and knew the evil that lay at the heart of those groves, so after my father's assault we did all we could for Chavez, Dolores Huerta, and Larry Itliong. Licked envelopes, made phone calls, patched up protesters—which is what I was doing that day at the clinic. Dolores hired me to sweep the facility. But one thing led to another, and pretty soon I was triaging the patients coming through the door injured by a combine or a grain auger or a police officer.

One bad, busy night we had a truckload of victims from a Filipino farmworker camp that'd been taken by arson. Nurses handling three burn patients at a time, doctors sprinting from one smoke-inhalation case to another. In the middle of the commotion, a dark-eyed man, twenty-one years old but no taller than me, stumbled in. He'd jammed his right hand under his armpit, a red stain seeping through his white shirt. A sawbones treating the second-degreed shoulder of a young gal yelled at me to tend him. When I approached this stranger, he sat very still in a corner with his back straight as a scalpel. I managed to persuade him to unclench his fist. As his fingers spread, it was like a rose's petals opening in the rain. The hand had been flayed from defense cuts—the wounds you get when you raise your arms to defend your head while somebody's beating you.

"What happened?" I asked him.

"Trouble down in El Rancho Farms."

"You striking?"

He winced as I pressed gauze to the blood spilling through his knuckles. "Yes."

"Haven't seen you before. You from Tehachapi? Wasco?"

"From Yemen," he said.

"Yemen . . . ?" I didn't know even the tiniest bit about the world outside of Kern.

"It's in the Arabian Peninsula," he said.

I shook my head, peering up at him, shy. Even as he suffered from the pain, he had this beautiful face. Shiny like a new penny.

"Middle East," he said.

"All the way from out there," I said, trying to sound like a woman of the world. The puncture wounds over his metacarpus had stones and dirt in them, which I teased out with tweezers. One of the gashes went deep. I tried to get medics to stitch him but they hurried past me with pale, tight faces.

"If you get a needle and thread, I can show you," he said.

"Oh, no, my mama says I can't even darn a sock."

"It's quite simple."

I ran to the cupboard, got the supplies, and disinfected him while he explained how to debride the dead tissue, do the sutures.

I threaded the needle with my tongue until he told me to stop because of the germs. Next part went even worse. I mangled him good so his hand looked like leftovers from Sunday supper.

"How you know how to patch people?" I asked him as I worked.

"From fighting with the English back at home. I learned field dressing from manuals and *Gray's Anatomy*." He breathed the pain out through his teeth. "That's why I came here, to study medicine in San Francisco."

I could only understand every other word he said. "You going to be a doctor?"

"I wanted to be but now I don't know." He stared at his blood oozing out of his hand. "America is different than I expected."

"Something tells me you shouldn't give up," I said.

He looked at me sideways, then smiled until I saw dimples. "Why not?"

I wrapped up his Frankenstein mitt with a big bandage. "So you can fix this mess I made."

He laughed and said thank you.

"Thank you, *Violeta,*" I said.

"Thank you, Violeta. My name's Nagi."

He winked at me as I bolted off to help a doc with one of the burn cases, and he stayed around, doing his own ministering. I mopped up messes and carried water but also watched as he moved quietly from cot to cot, tucking people in and replying in murmurs as the smoke-blackened scapegoats ranted to him about the wickedness that rules the Central Valley.

I started to see Nagi around town in the weeks after. Lamont's a little place, though we grow all kinds here—citrus, strawberries, tomatoes, eggplants, melons, peppers. We ranch cattle, sheep, and goats. For all that work, we've got no money. No decent housing, no services. Who the hell would come to this cow town unless they didn't have any better options? But Nagi'd got an education in being an outsider, first in occupied Yemen, and then when he moved here to train as a physician and wound up hiring on as a field hand at El Rancho Farms. He'd joined

“This stuff doesn’t work, you know,” I muttered while my mother sprinkled Papi with tap water she’d charmed with a crystal.

“What the hell are you talking about?” she said, growing red in the face.

“It ain’t scientific. You might as well tap-dance while balancing a honeydew melon on your head and singing ‘Git Along, Little Dogies.’”

Mama’s eyes kept widening till she looked like she’d stuck a thumb in a socket.

Later that night, she threw the pans all over the kitchen while I hid in my bedroom and kissed my pillow, pretending it was Nagi. My father ripped my blanket off me and ordered me to massage Mama’s feet while she wept in terror that I would be punished for my heresy by getting sent to a hell filled with claw-footed diablos who’d peck me to endless death.

Looking back, I wish I hadn’t said a single sideways word to my mother, even if none of her remedies would ever work. Papi went blind a few months later and died four years after that.

“Huelga! Huelga! Huelga!”

That’s what we were all chanting on the day I saw Nagi again, more than a week after the mass. Hundreds of us gathered at the Baxter strike. Baxter was one of the biggest farmers and distributors of table grapes in the world, and still is. The Delano action had ended in ’70 with decent contracts but our agreements had lapsed after three years. That summer, the safety and health fix-its the growers agreed to disappeared overnight—the breaks, the bottled water, the shade, the food, the medical care. Worse than that, Baxter had joined with the Teamsters to push the UFW out. Then the growers scabbed us out by hiring poor undocumented Mexicans, even little children.

I wore a red-and-white shawl and a big straw hat and a black flowy dress that Mama had made me. Marisol had on black overalls and a white T-shirt and a red hat that looked like a fire hydrant. My papi popped on some sunglasses because his eyes hurt. He held his picket over his head while my mother and I danced around with our comrades. We shimmied and boogied, laughing until tears streamed down our faces. A strike can be a wonderful thing. A time of delight and feeling that rebel blood running through you.

A eso campos van los niños campesinos
Sin un destino, sin un destino
Son peregrinos de verdad

Problem was, the growers had gotten court orders saying our protests were illegal. One minute, I was jitterbugging with Mama and the next, thirty police officers were pushing their bellies through the crowd and slapping cuffs on anybody they could.

"Viva la causa!" my mother hollered as they arrested us, while my father belted out the lyrics to a Woody Guthrie song. "¡Sí, se puede!"

We all got separated, though we didn't stop roaring Viva! Women cackled through the windows of police vans. Old men thrust their skinny arms in the air while doing the two-fisted Brown Power salute. Teamsters had shown up by this time, waving the American flag. A UFW dude with cojones big as bowling balls grabbed a horn and shouted, "¡Chavez sí, Teamsters no!" We kept up the chant while deputies tossed us into paddy wagons and carted us off to jail. I landed in a stinking lockup along with tough biddies and worn-down heroes, everybody hoarse from yelling and going cross-eyed from having to take a piss. Lying there splay legged, with my dress dirtier than a latrine and sweat streaming down my face, I suddenly sat up straight like I'd been pulled by the hair. Because who did I see across the cell but my prince, with those dark, gleaming eyes?

"Nagi!"

His smile fluttered toward me like a dove. He stood from his squatting position and made his way over.

"I saw them take you," he said, scooching between me and a vaquero sleeping under his big hat. "You hurt?"

"Not more than anybody else."

"Why do you look so happy? You are arrested."

Instead of saying, *Because I love you*, I took up his hand, the one I'd stitched.

"In a month or two, it will be fully healed," he said, as we studied his scar. "The Palmar aponeurosis is still intact." He used my finger to trace the triangle beneath his knuckles. "You see, it holds the muscles and the fascia together."

We sat there quietly for a while. I felt bold again.

"Nagi, tell me that thing you said before, about how I could be a doctor."

"You could be a doctor, Violeta."

"But you told me that *you* didn't want to be a doctor anymore."

He leaned his head back and closed his eyes. "Yes. It's too difficult here."

I watched him—the beads of sweat on his temple, the bruise I just now saw beneath his left eye. He had large, full lips. A tiny mustache. Big ears.

Our hands almost intertwined.

"You said I had a healing touch," I whispered.

"Did I say that too?"

He brought his fingers up to my face and stroked my cheek.

In the middle of that weary huddle, listening to police officers rattling our cell bars with their billy clubs, my heart began to sing.

I didn't run across Nagi for a while after that. I know now that he'd become a picket captain and was organizing in Stockton for Chavez and Dolores. But I thought about him all the time. It felt like he was always somehow watching over me. To impress him, or this idea of him sort of mystically floating around me and keeping an eye on my doings, I rode my bike to the tiny Lamont library. I paged through all three of its outdated medical books. Not that the idea of my becoming a nurse or a doctor seemed in any way realistic. I'd dropped out of high school two years before. It's hard to do your lessons when you pick sixty hours a week. But I wanted to live up to my maybe, someday lover.

I spent most of the rest of that summer reading. Not real medical books, like *Harrison's Principles of Internal Medicine* or *The New England Journal*. My mother had figured out my new enthusiasm and got hold of a box of nurse romances from an Arvin garage sale, and I kept it under my bed. *Passion in the Pharmacy. A Surgeon's Splendor. A Nurse's Heart.* Sounds ridiculous now but that was my way into medicine. I read romance novels about doctors and RNs saving people's lives and falling in love and, after a while, I imagined myself wearing a white coat and married to Nagi.

Meanwhile, my parents and I kept going to the rallies, the protests. There was a big one in late July at Giumarra farms. But whereas that earlier Baxter protest had been almost like a party—a party where you could get your teeth smashed in, mind you—this one was different. You could *feel* the hate. It was thick in the air. Sour on the tongue.

About five hundred people were there. My parents and I marched at the edge of the farm while the Teamsters, who'd hung back and snickered with the deputies during our previous actions, faced off against us now.

"You stink! You smell!" those Jimmy Hoffa numbnuts shouted. "I can smell your stink from here!"

Scuffles started up here and there. I saw deputies kicking at Mexicans and laughing. Then, all at once, it was like ten fights broke out at the same time. Less than fifty feet in front of me, a sheriff dragged a lady by the hair and she was totally limp, with her lower lip hanging down and her eyes rolling up white.

"Time to go," my mother said.

"Yeah," Papi agreed, pulling me by my shirt.

That's when I saw Nagi in the crowd. He had his arms up around his head, defending himself while an Anglo hit him on the shoulders with a baton—I don't know if the guy was a Teamster, a grower, a police officer, or what.

"No!" I screamed.

I ran toward Nagi. I saw his mouth open, his gnawing teeth. Then the world burst into a thousand puzzle pieces.

A large, heavy man had hit me in the chest. I fell to the ground. My head landed on a rock and I blacked out.

Woke up a few hours later. Maybe the next day? When I finally came back around I was lying on a blanket in our living room. Magnolia blossoms and lilies surrounded me head to foot. My parents sat on their knees and sang prayers to the Virgin and Father Eagle and the goddess Tlazoltéotl.

Nagi kneeled next to them. He had pink scrapes on his face from his beating and stayed quiet as a shadow while my mother rubbed me with cod-liver oil and commanded a thousand gods to heal me.

I turned my head to the wall. Wanted to explain to Nagi that I didn't believe in old-time religion and that I'd read the scientific library books so he'd be proud of me.

All I could do was cry. That sweet man bent down and touched my cheek, like he had in the prison. His lips moved. He was saying words, Arabic words, that I couldn't understand.

I never saw him again.

Two weeks later, Nagi Daifallah was murdered by Deputy Gilbert Cooper, an officer of the Kern County Sheriff's office. The killer was a six-foot-tall white man who weighed two hundred pounds, whereas Nagi was five feet and a buck at most. Happened on August 15, 1973. At around one in the morning, over at the Smokehouse Café here in Lamont. Cooper and his gang drove up to find a crew of UFW folks eating breakfast after a long meeting. The officers arrested one of the group without any good reason and when the men protested, Cooper beat Nagi on the back of the head with a heavy metal flashlight. Smashed him at the base of the skull and severed his head from his spinal cord. Probably suffered brain and somatic death then and there. Cooper wanted to make sure, though. His buddies dragged Nagi on the ground by the feet, so my sweetheart's head bashed into the pavement over and over. Nagi was pronounced later that night at the hospital.

We held a funeral for him. I was well enough to go to that. Thousands of us took turns shouldering his casket on the four-mile march from La Paz to the Bakersfield airport so we could fly his body home to Yemen. During the procession, the mourners were silent, except for our Arab brothers, who honored his memory with their tender praying.

While I marched for Nagi, I carried one of my romance books in my coat pocket. *A Surgeon's Splendor.* Later, when we set up his altar in front of the Smokehouse Café, I put it up there, though I never explained to anybody what it meant.

Afterward, I wasn't right, mentally. I sat in bed and scratched at myself until I bled.

My mother tried to heal me. I stuck my head under a pillow while she'd do a rain dance, the way her great-grandmother had taught her.

Fetching a stone from her garden, she held it in her hand. She leapt up, crouched down. She pounded her feet. Demanded I join along.

I just wanted to die.

"Go away, Mama," I said.

Deputy Cooper was never charged. I don't know what happened to him. Things being as they are, I'm sure he went on to live a nice long life.

I took it too hard, if there is such a thing. I yearned to slumber in the painless embrace of my ancestors. It's probable that I was suffering emotional lability resulting from a concussion, along with clinical depression. Still, I couldn't make my way to suicide, seeing how I had to keep alive for Marisol and Papi. So I went to Bakersfield City College instead. In '75.

That first eighteen months of schooling nearly broke my mind on account of the culture shock and residual cognitive dysfunction. But even after my mental damage cleared, I was still like a trout learning how to tango. I studied the white man's words. His books, his knowledge. My teachers taught me that wisdom isn't a gift handed down by our grandmothers but instead is a set of rules locked in a box that you have to dig through miles of your own dirty ignorance to get to. So, for example, there's the distributive law of mathematics, saying that any number you multiply by the total of two or more numbers will be equal to the total of that number multiplied by each of the numbers separately. Or there's the law of conservation of mass, holding that in chemical reactions matter will stay the same and not be created or destroyed. Now Mexicans and the Seed-Gatherers know that any number you multiply by the total of two or more numbers will only really be equal to the total decreed by your overseer. And that when you are dealing with a reaction, matter will be created or destroyed depending on whether you are strong enough to bear up under the bitter weight of whiteness for another day. But, being spirit-murdered as I was, I liked my teacher's rules as I found their disgust at nuance and ambiguity refreshing.

Somehow we scraped together the tuition. Mama got a job as a secretary for the UFW and then Chavez himself. The union gave me a scholarship. After limping through my introductory courses, I learned math and physics through years of hard, even obsessed, work. Once my father passed away, I remained haunted by his eyes as well as the feathery touch of Nagi's fingers on my cheek. For them, I was going to be a nurse, like in *A Nurse's Heart*. But when I got to Fresno State, my chemistry professor thought I showed some promise and put me on the premed track.

I came back for the winter holidays in '77. Papi had died the year before. I'd returned to help my mother through the sorrow of Christmas, to cook tamales with her and stick a star on the top of the tree. Put an extra plate at the head of the table, where my father used to sit.

I didn't need to worry so bad about Marisol. She wore her UFW T-shirt like widow's weeds and used her secretary's perch to boss hundreds of harried farmworkers who had to go through her to confer with the great man. Whenever I'd arrive back home from finals or on a weekend between internships, she'd make a cross on my forehead with holy water. Instead of arguing with her like I once had, I'd stand there as stiff and dumb looking as Gerald Ford, my head full of post-Newtonian rationality that judged her fairy work as so much gullible bunk. She was hurt, I could tell. But I was a swanky educated lady now and she didn't complain.

On the second night of my Christmas visit, I went to bed after washing the dinner dishes. I lay in bed, trying to lull myself to sleep by whispering the periodic table. Around three o'clock, my memories crawled up onto my chest, blinking their big eyes at me. I reached under my bed and pulled out the box of nurse and doctor romances that had stayed where I'd stowed it as a lusty teenager. Thumbing through the books, I felt my lost rage thrumming through my dried-out veins. It was like Father Eagle and Mother Crow had flown back into the branches that had always crisscrossed above me, and which I had lost sight of while my neck bent to my studies. The old, angry joy of my ancestors beat through me, as painful as a knife slicing through the palm of my hand. *Deputy Gilbert Cooper, I wish death on you,* I prayed. *People of Lamont, I curse you to never forget the name of Nagi Daifallah. And if the gods answer my vesper and overthrow this city, I don't care if the righteous are taken along with the wicked.*

Next thing I knew, it was late in the morning. I woke to the sound of wind.

Yeah, what you've been waiting for so patiently. This is my memory of the storm.

All the strands and tendrils of the air flew to our little spot in the world. They whirled together, first slowly and then at greater speed. While the clouds collected, zephyrs flapped their black wings and dove to the ground, picking up dust and tossing it to the heavens. Spinning faster and faster, the monsoon exploded into a tidal wave that crested Bear Mountain, careened over Bakersfield, and hurled into Lamont.

Outside, I saw the dust scratch at the sun until it bled red and orange. Palm trees twisted and splintered. Boards flew off our neighbor's roofs. Across the street, I made out the hazy figure of a man or woman walking a dog. They crouched and scuttled to avoid getting punched off their feet by the air. The gale picked up an ebony fog of dead crickets and blew it all over town.

I ran into the living room, calling my mother's name. Found her in the kitchen, a wad of wet carrots falling from her hands as she stared through the window.

"This is bad," she said.

Just then, a hunk of dirt slammed against the glass panes, hard as a rock. *BAM!*

We screamed and ran to her bedroom, jumping under the blankets. Sand wriggled under the doors, blowing onto the bed, shimmying up the sheets. The lights fritzed and an eerie night-in-day covered our eyes. The wind sang out. A keening. A moaning. The same as La Llorona. Mama shrieked into my neck as a bicycle and a mailbox smashed through our windowpanes. But I lay there, smiling and sobbing at the same time, vengeance for Nagi bubbling in my heart like hot champagne.

The following day, we woke up to another dark sky, a fresh load of wind. Then, toward the later morning, there was silence.

Our windows swarmed with dirt and sludge. Thick, wet balls of sand blocked the front door, which we had to force open. Outside, the earth had piled up in hills all along the south sides of the houses. Trees lay crushed in the middle of the street. Swamp coolers had crashed through car windshields, knocked through a couple roofs. A pepper of crickets sprinkled over the ruins. Later, we'd learn about how freeways were buried, how people died in car accidents. My mother turned from the scene of the wreckage and gave me a long, quiet stare.

"You look different," she said.

I shrugged.

"You look stronger," she went on.

I stayed button lipped and only squeezed her hand.

"Have you been praying?"

"Yes."

"What did you ask for?"

"Nothing, Mama."

She held my eyes for another moment, then sighed, as if I had safely returned after a long and dangerous journey.

"I will always love you, Violeta," she said.

Marisol still lives in the same house, though I tried to buy her a new one in Merced. She says she likes to remember my dad eating tamales in our old, busted kitchen.

After she retired from the UFW, she started handing out cheese cubes at the Fiesta Market, where she buttonholed you. She helped me pay for Berkeley, then I got a residency at Stanford. Specialized in hand surgery like the sign says.

Why hands?

Wouldn't make any sense if I told you my reasons. Though I'm glad I made orthopedics my practice, because you never saw so many accidents out here. Tractors, mowers, hay rakes, it's like they're designed to disarticulate the extremities. The farmworker's life is a hard one, even with all our protests and the new laws. Nagi's death couldn't change that.

Not enough people know about Nagi, so maybe you should write about him and not about the storm. He was a man who cared about other people. People who weren't necessarily the same as him. People that might even think he was a little different, a little odd, being from so far away.

I didn't know him that well, so maybe it's strange that I've carried a torch for him all these years. I never married anybody. I'm not that easy to be with, seeing how the stiffness that settled into my marrow after his death never loosened back up.

Reason why my mother sent you here is because she's damned proud of me and not on account of the medical degree. She wants a fancy LA writer to know I'm a straight-up bruja from a long and powerful line of seed women and that my broken heart was strong enough to blitz this town like God did with Sodom and Gomorrah. I can tell you that the creed of the hand surgeon—which requires her to investigate, diagnose, and respect plain facts—would reject this etiology of the storm faster than the dust that once carried the crickets to tarnation. But I've got a million miles on me now, and in all these years I've learned that I do not know every little thing about what lies above and below the busy antics of mankind. When Deputy Cooper killed my darling boy, it was a piece of sin I never saw the likes of before or since. If there is a heaven, then the Mohammed or Christ that haunts it surely would have suffered when he saw Nagi dragged through Lamont's streets like a shot deer. And if there are older gods who care about Brown and Black people, maybe they did hear my call. I am a healer and it's against my oath to wish harm on any person but part of me does hope those deities got so angry at the silence of justice and the dead eyes of the law that they scattered the earth's children with their fierce breath. Maybe we weren't alone in our grief, and Nagi was finally revenged by the lords of the wind. I'd like to think my mother's dioses indígenas honored that good man's murder by bringing down the sky, which cried like a woman as it ripped the skin off the world.

STEEPLECHASE

by ANGELA BALL

from TIE COLUMBIA REVIEW

Steeples have a big
responsibility, upholding
the faith.

In a country of churches
I do a running
study of steeples: their

gradients, stages, angles
of ascent, presence
or absence of terminal
cross.

All are white,
though a few have begun
to discolor with rust
or rot; to lean, vaguely
lapsed.

None have belfries, those noisy
papist extravagances.
Only height
asserts itself, slimming
toward the infinite.

One has a lightning rod
that might be blasphemous.
Today, for the first time,
a steeple with windows
on all sides. Miniature panes with white
dividers radiating sunrise.
Who could get in
to look out? Maybe a person's head
could, rising from an attic
ladder. I would love to see
the face of someone
so alone.

HOW NO MONEY BECOMES MONEY

by ANDREI CODRESCU

from LIVE MAG!

In 1974 Free Box Chic meant taking clothes out of the free box in front of the co-op in Monte Rio. A year later the free clothes were put back in the free box. The connoisseurs who took them out on the second round found them ultra-chic. All the holes were in the right places. Not long after, holey free jeans became scarce, as did the free box ethos. Young people bought new jeans, then tore holes in them. It wasn't long before hole-making assembly lines were manned by immigrants who found the clothes ridiculous. It was the Reagan era of hole-making jobs. In the countries they came from, the only people with holes in their pants, were beggars. Knee holes suggesting that the fabric was worn by performing oral sex, horrified immigrants from catholic countries who had spent their childhood on their knees praying for work in America. Making holes in american pants was not the job they prayed for. Not only were they alienated from their product, like Karl Marx said, they were enraged by it. That is the wonderful thing about America: you can hate the thing you're making even if you don't know what it is, because sooner or later you'll wear it. The transition from hippie free-box holes-twice-worn to factory-ripped holes took only enough time to employ three generations of americans. And that's how no money became money. And social evolution saw people travel through the holes in their jeans from misery to luxury, from refuge to residency, from necessity to fashion. The free eden of holey hippie jeans became the memory of fantasy, aka advertising. The executive of ripping reigned in the nation of holes. The zeitgeist authorized the nation to make and sell what didn't exist. The logic of missing fabric had equivalents in language. Articles and conjunctions went missing. To speak with holes while wearing ripped jeans was the new language. Subjectivity vanished through holes leaving behind the suggestion of an activity that had once been perilous. Flesh looked out of these holes with google eyes at knee or buttock level. Sometimes smoke came out of the flesh under the holes like fumaroles and nobody minded paying for it, not even the hole makers who spent their money on the holes they made.

THE WIDOW'S TALE

fiction by RICHARD BAUSCH

from PLOUGHSHARES

Whenever Susan Bridge heard friends or family talk of inklings from the other side, or of being watched over by a lost loved one, she inwardly dismissed the idea even as she strove to be loving and attentive in the circumstance. She felt sorry, of course, but considered that in each case, bereavement was dictating to the senses. Yet now, here was her younger sister, Moira, claiming visits in her sleep from Susan's husband, killed nearly a year ago in a one-car crash on the Brooklyn Queens Expressway.

"I'm telling you, Susan, he's himself, and it keeps happening. Last night was the fourth time. He says quite clearly that he wants to talk to you. There's a red dial phone and he hands me the receiver looking sad but there's interference on the line. And I think the interference is your refusal to take this seriously."

"But it's been ten months. What can I do to take it more seriously than I have? I know it's troubling you, and I take *that* seriously. But I mean, really, what more can I do?"

Her sister shrugged and then showed her irritation. "I don't *know*. Hell. *Some*thing. You don't even allow the possibility that it might have significance beyond just being a recurring dream."

"Well, it *is* a recurring dream. And recurring dreams're pretty common."

"But these are dreams with my sister's dead husband in them. And they're like visitations."

"Oh, please, honey. You're obsessing about it. You didn't even like Victor. Victor annoyed you. And why would he visit you in your sleep and not me in mine?"

"Because you don't believe."

"Oh, come on," Susan said. "Leave it alone, can't you?"

In the days and weeks just after the accident, she'd found herself addressing him with an almost inaudible sigh. "Oh, Victor," as if uttering a prayer, though there was an unacknowledged trace of reproof in it, too, for him to have been killed in that fashion, going ninety on that highway. Anyhow, she'd forged past all that now. She'd loved him, and she would say that she cherished his memory. But he was gone, and there were no dreams about him, nor any shift in her daily reality. The only sounds in the apartment were hers. She'd always been the one who kept up with birthdays, and paid the bills and taxes and all the rest, and she had dealt with the galleries and his dealer (she'd even sold the incomplete panel triptych he'd been struggling to finish). She was going on with things, as you were supposed to do. You honored his life by living your own life to the hilt. She'd heard him say that very thing himself more than once. She'd even been on dates with a couple of other men (one seemed oddly, surprisingly, repellent in the first five minutes, and the other simply bored her). Life alone was her inclination now, at least for the present. She was at peace with it. But Moira, with her propensity for jumping to wild, ethereal conclusions, would not stop about the dream.

Perhaps being married to Owen Sisler had helped stir this up. Only last week, during dinner at their house, he had light-heartedly paraphrased to Susan the famous line from Hamlet: *There are more things in heaven and earth than you have dreamed of in your philosophy, Horatio*—actually calling her *Horatio*. Susan thought at the time that he was humoring his eccentric young wife. But he had used it twice since as an endearment. Plus, there was the fact that Sisler, the novelist, eighty-four years old, had turned to a spiritualizing, speculative stance in his latest work. His new novel, *The Deaths of Friar Dominic*, was about the spirit of a sixteenth-century English abbot haunting the monastery where he was murdered in order to educate and then exact a kind of hereditary revenge on the descendent of the monk who committed the crime. The book had all sorts of incidences of the ghost moving through interstices of air and light, and included theories about the meaning of unseen presences in lone places, the many gothic solitary horrors of extreme religion. Moira had already read it twice; it was a favorite among his books, all of which she had admired since college, and which were nothing remotely like this latest. The others had been lavish, prosy, realistic portrayals of, well, Sisler—and his six marriages.

Moira, at thirty-seven, was his seventh wife.

The marriage had in fact been fine with Susan and Victor because Sisler was well-off, and he *tended* to Moira, notwithstanding his late forays into the supernatural. (He called it the "ultima-real," or the "outré-natural," meaning aspects of natural *and* supernatural existence that we don't consciously perceive.) And, finally, he was interesting.

"What does Owen say about this dream?" Susan asked one afternoon over the phone.

"You *know* what he thinks about it. He calls you Horatio."

"But that's just to entertain you."

"Well, I can't help what I feel. I feel strongly that Victor wants to tell you something."

"Yes, but how exactly would that work? Really."

Moira began to cry.

"Oh, God. Come on, sweetie," Susan said. "Stop that. Really, I accept it. Okay?"

"Was there anything unspoken between you two—you know, over the years?"

"What kind of question is that, Moira? No. There wasn't anything."

"I'm thinking of going to see a psychiatrist."

"Let's just—not talk about it or think about it for a time."

"But you accept it, as being—what it is."

"Yes. I do."

Moira sighed, and Susan changed the subject, talking about Owen's novel of modern revenge for an ancient crime.

The following night, they were to attend a reading and celebration of Owen and the book. Susan kept her disinterest about it to herself. She had only read the reviews and listened to her sister's talk. In fact, Owen's prose always seemed a bit too discursive for her: page upon page of subtle intellectual distinctions about modern life and culture and the arguments between men and women, lovers, losers, and cheaters, unhappy academics and artists, all of them failing at love.

He himself had failed six times before Moira.

But Moira, as Victor had once remarked to Susan, possessed stamina, having already spent three years with Owen Sisler's friend Eliot Glass, a poet, and the single dullest human being he had ever met. Susan agreed. Glass's poetry was well-thought-of in some circles, and his normal speech had about it a distinct air of proclamation. Victor had characterized him as someone who could snatch pomposity from the jaws of any English sentence, and, when Susan laughed, added that being in Eliot's company was like sitting all day through a C-SPAN broadcast, and the fact that Owen had charmed Moira away from him was to Owen's lasting credit: he'd spared Moira a lifetime of mediocre poetry and numbing talk.

Before the reading, they gathered at Saveurs for dinner: Owen, Moira, Susan, and Eliot, who—in his own faintly baroque expression—"endured in steadfast friendship" with Moira. Eliot was accompanied by another young woman, quite beautiful, with dark blue eyes and shining dark hair. Eliot introduced her as Lana Sharp, and she offered her hand to each of the others in turn.

"Oh, how are you," she said as the names were said to her. "Oh, how are you." Her smile was white as a lily. And very soon after this introduction, she volunteered to everyone the fact that she had met Eliot at a lecture he had given in Soho and that he had already written over thirty poems to her.

Susan thought of F. Scott Fitzgerald's line in *Gatsby* about a woman who was "shrill, languid, handsome, and horrible."

They were joined by a man Owen introduced as Bill Perry, an old colleague from his days at the university. Perry was tall, scarily thin, with a face that showed forth the contours of his skull—deep-set eyes; bony, sunken cheeks; and a smile like a rictus. Susan could only glance at him. His eyes were piercing. Lana talked vaguely about moving out West and asked Bill Perry if he had ever been to San Francisco.

"Actually, only for two short visits," he said. "Regrettably."

"I'm headed that way soon. And maybe Eliot will come along."

"Lana's a medium," Eliot Glass said. "She told me about a dead boyhood friend I haven't thought of in thirty years."

"Eliot, stop."

Perry offered. "A medium, huh?"

"Yes."

"This boyhood friend drowned a month ago in Miami Beach," Eliot said. "And Lana—my divine new lady—divined it some way. I only knew the boy in elementary school in Milwaukee."

"Oh, I want to hear about this," said Moira. "Really, tell us, Eliot."

"Well, in mid-conversation and completely apropos of nothing, she brings up Miami Beach. Says someone from my past was coming through."

"How do you—how does it work?" Moira asked his companion. "How do you bring it about?"

Lana shrugged. "I'm not sure. Sometimes it just happens."

They were all in a half circle, in a thickly padded leather booth that squeaked whenever they shifted their weight.

"Anything coming through now?" Moira asked.

Lana blinked and smiled. "No."

"Well," Owen said. "Speaking of spirits, there's Perry's latest book. *The Far Shore.*"

"A shadow," Perry said. "Pay no attention."

"It's a good book of poems. A rarity these days. Hell, any good book. Gore Vidal once said novelists and poets in America are at the same level as ceramists. And that was thirty years ago."

"Well, not quite so much a shadow," Perry said, low, with that skeletal smile.

They were all quiet a moment.

"Thanks, Owen," Moira said. "Now we're all depressed. Was it your intent to put a damper on the evening before we even get started?"

Another moment passed. They were all looking at menus. Susan glanced briefly across at Moira, admiring how casually and confidently she'd chided her famed husband.

"I only meant to applaud Perry's book," Owen said.

"You meant to hold forth about it," Moira told him, patting his wrist. "Come on, Mr. Sisler, sir. We know you."

"Who was Gore Vidal?" asked Lana Sharp.

"A ceramist from the last century. So, tell us. Eliot's dead friend's spirit spoke to you?"

Lana nodded doubtfully. "In a sense, yes. It's not really speaking, though."

"I have an idea," Owen said suddenly. "Let's each have a different whiskey and pass them around for tasting like people pass food around in a Chinese restaurant."

Susan, feeling bad for having been so shaken by Bill Perry's features, said, "Actually, I'd rather talk about the shadow that isn't quite so much a shadow."

Perry turned to her and said, low, with an air of gravity, "Thank you. I am one of those whose name is writ in water." Then he laughed. There was a note of self-derision in it.

Lana leaned toward Moira and, with a bright smile, said, "And do you write, too?"

"I teach dance," said Moira. "I used to be in ballet, but the grind exhausted me."

"And do you travel with your grandfather often?"

Moira, having hesitated only a second, drew herself up, glaring, and pronounced, "For your information, I am *Mrs.* Sisler."

"Oh, I'm so *sorry.*" Lana gave Eliot a displeased look. "No one told me. I never dreamed . . ."

"And you're a—what is it again? A medium?"

She nodded, looking again at Eliot.

He spoke for her. "I'm sorry about the faux pas, but you know, Lana actually lived and worked in a place where everybody's a medium or knows one. Almost four years. People come from all over to see these—"

"Wait," Moira broke forth. "I just read somewhere about this place. Lily Dale, right?"

"That's right," Lana said. "There are several—"

Owen Sisler spoke over her. "I like my whiskey idea."

"—cottages, with signs outside. I mean, anyone can walk in . . ."

And he broke in again with a bad imitation of an English accent. "I say, chaps. Let's order."

"You don't want to talk about anything but you and your book," Moira said to him.

"And how does whiskey figure into that assertion, darling?" His voice was affectionate, but the words had come from a thin, brittle smile. He signaled the waiter, who had a mustache so thick you couldn't see his mouth. The waiter took out a pad as he approached.

"I am just so awfully sorry," Lana said, low, to Moira. "About that grandfather thing."

"Forget it," Owen broke in again. "Really. That's exactly what it looks like."

Shortly after they'd ordered their entrees, the tray of whiskeys in gilt-edged shot glasses arrived: Scotch for Owen, bourbon for Moira, sour mash for Eliot, Irish for Lana, Canadian for Perry, rye for Susan. They all held their drinks out, as if to show what was in them to everyone else, and Owen said, "Now, instead of a toast, let's say something we know or learned that's attached to a memory. Like where we were, or who we were with, or what was going on in the given day that we learned it."

They waited.

"In my case, it's something I learned while honeymooning with my second wife, Beverly, in Africa. I witnessed it. A safari guide, who swore he was with Hemingway on his last Africa journey, showed me this species of moth that congregates on a twig in such a complex way that it looks exactly like an exotic flower. You shake the twig, and they fly up and out in all directions, and then very slowly reassemble exactly as they were, becoming the flower again, right before your eyes. And that's the most vivid memory of that honeymoon." He smiled.

"Imagine," Moira said. "The invisible forces that make a thing like that happen. And then think of the forces that make a man talk about a memory involving his second wife and a species of moth."

Owen Sisler patted her shoulder, smiling. "All part of the great mystery, dear."

"I want to talk about the visitations I've been getting in my sleep. And we have a medium here who can maybe help us talk about this."

"Oh, I wouldn't presume," Lana said.

"You already did presume."

She bowed her head. "I did apologize."

"No, I'd *like* you to presume—*we'd* like you to presume."

"Moira," Susan said. "Please."

"No, really," said Moira, looking at the others, each in turn. "I've learned recently that a dream can recur in exactly the same shape, and so, in the years from now, when I have the memory of this time, it'll be attached to this exactly replicated dream, four nights in nine—no, ten. Ten days. I see Susan's Victor with a red dial telephone that only gives interference."

Owen explained quietly to Perry and Lana about the loss of Victor.

"And I've been seeing him in this dream," Moira said. "He talks to me."

Lana said, in a small voice, "Do you remember what he tells you?"

"He's got something he wants to tell Susan."

"Can we please talk about something else?" Susan said. "Please?"

"She doesn't believe in ghosts," said her sister. "Or in life after death."

"I don't believe in ghosts either," Owen Sisler said. "I *speculate*."

"You believe in them. Come on. Presences. The ultima—the outré-natural."

"Yes, well, my real interest is in the epistemology of it all. Our experience. What we make of it." He looked from her to the others at the table. "What my lovely wife makes of her dream." He held his glass up again. "Remember—small sips because we're going to be passing them around."

Susan wanted to find a way to get out of all this and go home. "I guess my palate isn't educated enough to appreciate the subtleties," she got out.

They had *Sole Meunière* or *Canard Roti avec Gold Leaf.* Owen ordered two bottles of Bordeaux and a sauvignon blanc. After the sips of whiskey, Moira drank two glasses of the white and took the rest of Owen's first glass, then began joking about his earlier marriages, calling his ex-wives his "other girls." The marriage before this one had lasted only four months. And another had dissolved after a year. "We're at more than three years," she said. "I guess I'm standing the test of Sisler time."

Owen changed the subject. "What does Victor look like in this dream you've been having?"

"He looks like Victor."

"No chains or winding sheets or sifting smoke?" Susan added.

Lana laughed into one slender palm.

"You're making fun of me," Moira said. "I told you. It's Victor, and he wants to talk to you. He wants to tell you something."

They were all quiet.

Lana started to speak: "This red telephone—"

But then Eliot laughed. "Jesus Christ. A red telephone. Isn't that the hot line to Moscow?"

Moira threw her serviette down and turned to Susan. "Now you see what your skepticism does."

"That's enough," Owen said. "Really, dear."

She picked up the serviette and seemed to fluff it, then folded it and put it in her lap.

"I'm sorry," Susan said to her.

Perry said, "I think there was a red dial phone at the front desk of the Hilton."

"Listen," Owen said, ignoring them both. "Why don't we have a séance." He looked at Lana Sharp.

"Well, as far as that goes," she said, "I don't leave until early next month."

He said, "I've got a flight out at noon tomorrow. But I'll be back Sunday."

"We could arrange something for when you get back?"

"What would you need?"

"Eighty dollars an hour."

"Equipment. Set up. Chairs. Ambience."

"Oh. A table. Some quiet. Who'd be there? I'd need three or four sitters, we call them."

"Susan won't do it," Moira said.

Susan, feeling trapped, decided that to resist would seem stubborn, even narrow-minded. "I will," she said. "If it'll help."

"Sunday night, then," Owen said. "At our apartment in the Village. Moira, you take care of the arrangements."

The bookstore was near Washington Square, a block from the Sislers' apartment building. They took two cabs from the restaurant. Susan rode with Bill Perry and Lana Sharp, neither of whom had read the book. Lana Sharp asked Perry about his poems and his dreams. Susan stared out at the sparkle of the city, the going-by of the streets with their sidewalk stores and their grime. There was already a crowd gathering at the store. Seats in the front row had been reserved for Owen and his companions. Patrons stood along the bookcases and between them. Susan sat with her sister between Lana and Perry. In those close quarters, the air seemed insufficient, full of the sounds of coughing and the clearing of throats and sniffling.

The reading was long, and something in Owen's slow baritone delivery seemed narcotizing, especially after half a bottle of Bordeaux and two shots of whiskey. When it ended, there were questions. As she was pinching her own neck while seeming to support her chin on her fist, she saw Victor back in among the people behind the table where Owen sat, talking. It was Victor. He was staring directly at her with a passive, detached, stone-cold objectivity. She shifted in her chair and looked away, feeling the moment as a rushing under her breastbone, and then, slowly, she brought her gaze back to the place where he had been. It was a blank space, giving off to a lamp on a small table and a far window. She breathed, glanced over at Moira, and saw that Moira was staring at her own hands, folded in her lap.

She sat up, folding her arms, as Owen went on about invisible nature and "the unseen world that is far more peopled than we imagine."

"Even we," he went on after a dramatic pause, "here, now, all presently trying to imagine it." She looked back at the space. It was an empty space. Owen answered another question, talking on. Nothing seemed real. Her lower back ached. She couldn't swallow. She folded her hands in her lap and looked back at the empty space where she had seen someone who looked like Victor. Reminded her of Victor. She had read about the phenomenon. She told herself everything was as before—it was the wine, the heat, her weariness, fighting sleep, Moira's talk, the woman who was a medium, sitting to her left and exhaling audibly with a high, thin whistle in one nostril.

When at last the reading and talk ended, everyone lined up to buy the book and to have it signed. Susan made the excuse of a headache and stepped out into the night air. Perry followed her. It had grown cooler; a breeze was stirring. "Would you like to walk a little?" Perry said.

"I'm a bit tired," she told him. "No."

"I sometimes feel that I myself am a ghost."

She made no answer to this. She felt weak, shaken. She wished he would go back inside.

"Forgive me." He coughed, once, then sighed. "How long have you known Owen?"

"Oh, a while."

"I'm sorry about your husband."

Again, she was silent. They stood there, and soon, people began to slowly file out. "Do you ever feel invisible?" he said. Then: "Hello, I'm nobody. Who are you? Are you nobody too?"

She looked at him.

"That's from the great Ms. Dickinson," he said.

She said, "I'm very tired."

"Tired, yes. That's been the condition of my last fifteen years." He gave a little, ironic grin. "Sorry."

"No," she said, determining to put away the bad moment of hallucination in the store. "*I'm* sorry. I think I had too much to drink."

He nodded without quite looking at her. She had never seen anyone so epically ugly, and the thought made her feel bad again: he was just a kindly, sickly-looking, elderly man. And a poet. That was an interesting thing about him, even vaguely appealing.

"What are you working on?" she said, forcing it.

He gave a small, scoffing smile. "Not much lately."

"So, in your mind, what is the far shore?"

He paused, then put his head down. "We don't have to talk about it."

"I'd like to. I said so at dinner."

"Well, thank you. In the title poem, the far shore isn't so much a destination as something beyond. Something—anything—presently *missed*."

He wiped the back of his hand across his mouth. The storefront light was greenish and made him look almost dizzily unhealthy. "But the farthest shore," he went on, "is *Meaning* itself. We *embody* meaning, and so the only meaning is what we ourselves make. Merleau-Ponty, the French philosopher. The concept, as I recall, is summed up as 'Man, the meaning-giver.' But I fear it's only Man, the absurd whirligig of blind fears."

She stared.

"Of course, these days, you can't really talk about such matters, and maybe you never could. Maybe only in a college dorm room. Forgive the philosophizing." He gave forth a small, breathing laugh. "But you asked."

"Yes, I did," she said.

He gave another small smile. "One spends so much time trying to make sense of things."

She shrugged. "Well, you'd know. I'm a former college dean. I teach history."

A moment later, he said, "Your sister's recurring dream—" but then he stopped.

"Go on," she said. Abruptly, she wanted to talk about it. About dreams in general. "On the way over here, you said something to our friend the medium about fearing your dreams or not liking your dreams."

Two young people walked out of the store, squabbling about what they would serve for guests at a dinner party they were evidently planning. It occurred to Susan that they were a married couple to whom nothing serious had happened yet. She watched them go on and felt suddenly guilty again, petty and bitter, and she turned to him, forcing another smile.

"Well," he said. "I started to tell you that I don't think I've ever had a recurring dream."

"Never?"

"Not that I remember. I have types of dreams, scenario dreams. Daily goings-on dreams, where I'm doing something quite terrifyingly ordinary. Or commando dreams, where I'm blasting an AK-47 at troops of killers. Or illness dreams, where—" He stopped. "Like that."

Moira walked out of the store and came right to them. "It's gonna be tonight," she said. "Owen wants to do it before he leaves. We're going straight home with Lana and Eliot. Owen started talking about it and decided he wanted to look into this dream about Victor."

Susan said, "I should just go on home, then."

"No, you *have* to come."

"But you yourself said—"

"Lana told me as long as you keep quiet and try to have an open mind about it."

"Am I to come, too?" Perry asked.

"Of course."

He looked at Susan. "I'm with you, then, about trying to keep an open mind."

The others came out. Eliot had his arm around Lana. Owen made a little bowing motion. "Oh, do not ask 'What is it?'" he recited. "Let us go and make our visit."

Susan had never really felt comfortable in Owen's and Moira's apartment. There were books on every surface and all around on the walls, and in three carousel bookcases opposite the long couch with its two end tables, also crammed with books. Of course, she loved books and had a lot of them herself, but the closeness of these rooms made her think of dust, and, often enough, rather oddly, of Egyptian tombs: all the earthly belongings of a pharaoh piled for his journey to the other world. The dining room was high-ceilinged and spacious, though what would've been crown molding on three sides was a shelf, lined with more books.

Moira and Owen brought chairs from other rooms and set them around the circular dining room table, which was made of heavy, dark cherrywood and shone like a piano. Moira opened a linen tablecloth and spread it. Lana Sharp helped. "We'll need three candles and a food offering," she said. "And I'll need a pencil and a piece of paper."

Owen supplied pencil and paper and the candles—there had been two tall ones on the side table, and Moira found a short one in the kitchen junk drawer. She brought from the refrigerator a large plate of crackers and cheese with plastic wrap over it, which she had put together in case Owen decided to have people over after the reading. She removed the plastic wrap and fretfully crushed it into the pocket of her blouse. Susan saw Owen's adoring smile at this. Moira smiled back. It was a confidence, exchanged in the middle of a room with others around them, a glance that showed their tolerating affection for each other. It occurred to Susan that she'd been worried about them as a couple. Moira now went to the side table, wrote a check, turned, and handed it to Lana, who nodded and put it in her purse on the floor.

Owen dimmed the lights in the chandelier. Lana held her hands out, palm up. Susan sat across from her, next to Perry. On Susan's other side, Owen took his place. To his left, Moira sat, her hand in Lana's. Eliot was on the other side of Lana, to Perry's right. They were all quiet now in the dimness, watching Lana, while sirens sounded in the city streets outside, two floors down.

"Will the noise interfere with things?" Moira asked.

"Not if we all concentrate," Lana told her. "Now, let's join hands."

Susan was thinking about what Victor would make of all this. What he might say. And abruptly, she felt the strange sense of surprise about his absence, the feeling that used to bring forth the prayer-like sigh, "Oh, Victor." In her mind's eye, she saw again what she had seen in the store.

Lana Sharp closed her eyes and said, low, "We welcome any spirits who care to join us here. We ask you to make yourselves known to us."

They all sat there, holding hands.

"Any visitors from the other side, you are welcome. We mean no harm."

They waited.

Susan saw the crackers and cheese, the candle flames in their perfect little helixes, and the other faces in the shadowy half dark. It was another bad moment, Perry's hand clasped with hers, dry, almost like a leather glove over bones, while Owen's was clammy. The room was quiet now.

Lana said, "Keep hold, all. I'm getting something." She let go of Moira and Eliot, took the pencil, held it for a few seconds over the paper, and then suddenly commenced indiscriminately scribbling, fast, almost as if trying to color the page—quick, back-and-forth strokes, which graduated into circular motions. Still quite fast. "Who do you wish to talk to?" Lana said. A few seconds later, she nodded irritably. "This spirit likes grammar. And has a sense of humor. All right, to *whom* do you wish to speak?" She kept making the scribbles. "You," she said. "Need." She kept the scribbling. "Yes, I hear you. Someone to answer. Your call."

Something dropped in Susan's chest, and as she tried to pull her hands from Owen and Perry's grip, she saw the shadows on the wall of the room, her own part of the shadow and Perry's, a single shape, a distortion, heads and shoulders, monstrously elongated, only vaguely human. She blinked. It was just the shadows in the dim candlelight.

"Yes. Tell us," Lana went on, breathing deep and fast. "With whom do you wish to speak?" She went on with the pencil. The page was almost black.

Moira broke forth, "Are you Victor?"

"Shh!" Lana said harshly. Then: "I'm listening." She looked at Moira and nodded and went on. "We're here."

"You want, yes. You want someone here to know. You're okay." Lana paused and frowned. "Horatio?" She took a breath. "Tell. Horatio. You're okay."

Susan pulled violently away from Owen and Perry, standing so quickly that her chair overturned. "This is ridiculous." She looked at Moira. "You planned this. You and Owen."

Moira, ashen faced, sat shaking her head, staring. "I swear," she said.

"There was definitely a connection," said Lana. "I felt it strongly."

Owen said, "Did you feel a cold touch of air? Was it suddenly cooler in here?"

Susan took herself out into the hall and down the two flights of stairs, Moira following her, calling her back, saying her name. Perry had also followed. "I swear," Moira kept saying. "Please. You have to see the reality of it. You shouldn't've broken the spell."

Susan turned around on her. "I don't want to see you for a while, okay?" She felt the tears coming and ran the back of one hand across her eyes, sniffling. "Just please, let me be. Can you do that? Can you please, please just let me be?"

"But it wasn't *me*. Why won't you believe me."

Perry said, "The things the lady said were fairly general, though, weren't they?"

"That Horatio thing!" Moira shouted.

"That was you and Owen," Susan said. "Wrong number, okay? Wrong number, Moira."

"I don't know what you're talking about. You heard what he wanted you to know. He said he was okay, and he called you Horatio."

"But he's *not* okay, Moira. You know? He's *dead!*" She pushed out into the night. Walked to the end of the block in the glare of the passing cars, then stood and raised one hand for a taxi.

Perry walked up to her. "I'm so sorry about all that."

"Yeah." She paced away from him.

"I enjoyed talking with you."

She could think of nothing to say.

"I'd like to see you again, perhaps?"

"No," she said. "God."

"I understand completely." He started away. She saw the crook of his back and his slow, halting gate, going away.

"I'm sorry," she said. "Really. I'll be happy to see you again. But give me some time."

He had stopped and turned. He lifted one hand, looking ghostly in the shadow of the building with the streetlamp behind him. "I will, thanks."

The cab home was fast, with the smell of the driver's open fast-food sandwich on the front seat. He was of some indeterminate Mideast origin; his name was Kamir. He said nothing through the whole ride and drove rather recklessly above the speed limit, weaving in and out. The fare to her building was six dollars and forty cents. She gave him a ten and said, "Keep the change."

He took the ten and drove off.

The now-chilly street seemed deserted. She went inside and up the one flight of stairs to the apartment. As she was turning the key, she stopped and suddenly gasped, once. She hadn't expected it; the sound erupted from her throat like choking. She got the door open, went inside, and turned to close it. The hallway seemed too dark. Briefly, she looked for the line of light at the base of her neighbor's apartment. The neighbor was an old woman named Greta, who used to work at TV Guide, but who seldom left the place now and was often up very late at night. She thought of knocking on Greta's door. It was only ten o'clock. But Greta wouldn't know what to make of that, since they'd never exchanged more than a few words, coming and going.

"Christ," Susan murmured, closing and locking the door.

She was too agitated to sleep. She got into her pajamas, poured a glass of wine, and switched on the TV. But it was all pointless chatter, or quarrels, or murder. She thought of Perry, that face, and of Lana Sharp. And she saw Eliot, with his earnestness, and Owen Sisler, toying with everyone, and Moira, with whom she had never been angrier. Yet she worried about Moira again, now, and resolved to call her in the morning. A moment later, something else began to rise awfully in her soul: whatever the evening had meant, *this* was what the evening had given her. This. The sudden, unwanted apprehension that nothing was done, nothing accomplished, no "going on," really, but only, all along, a mere semblance, an absurd show, a role she had played for herself and for everyone else—and the full, actual force of her sorrow was only beginning. It was welling up in her now; it was coming. She went into her bedroom, using the wall as support, and got to her bed.

"Oh," she said to the empty room. Then again, "Oh." She lay down on top of the blankets, folded her hands across her chest, steeling herself, trying to gather all her remaining strength. She took one long, sobbing breath, and waited.

IS WRACK, IS RAK, IS WRECKAGE

by ALLISON HUTCHCRAFT

from SOUTHERN HUMANITES REVIEW

Is seaweed, is a tangle of riches,
names in a fleet—*egg wrack,*

knotted wrack, wig wrack, sea lock
threading edges to the White Sea.

Is cemetery, field of notch and rock,
is bounty to the periwinkles

silently feeding. Is *frond,* not *stalked,*
floating without a midrib.

Quiet. I am listening to the wrack
as it crackles and spits

on dry ledges.
I can feel

each tentacle splayed,
powdered with salt. First film. Then

slippery—pull hard, it is taut
and won't release. I wasn't taught

to do this—*look but don't touch,*
don't manage the rudder, don't pull

the anchor up, hand over stinging hand,
gunwale gleaming. I am

racking up years, wracking them—
they slide and hit against the hull,

they are surface floaters and won't
sink, they build into a flowering

that can't be cut back,
though I scuba with scissors,

though I snap each off at its holdfast.
Another rack of clouds

reels across a country
of shade, and I'm still here,

a wreckage in each hand,
a head full of blue.

THE DEPARTMENT OF EVERYTHING

by STEPHEN AKEY

from THE HEDGEHOG REVIEW

How do you find the life expectancy of a California condor? Google it. Or the gross national product of Morocco? Google it. Or the final resting place of Tom Paine? Google it. There was a time, however—not all that long ago—when you couldn't Google it or ask Siri or whatever cyber equivalent comes next. You had to do it the hard way—by consulting reference books, indexes, catalogs, almanacs, statistical abstracts, and myriad other printed sources. Or you could save yourself all that time and trouble by taking the easiest available shortcut: You could call me.

From 1984 to 1988, I worked in the Telephone Reference Division of the Brooklyn Public Library. My seven or eight colleagues and I spent the days (and nights) answering exactly such questions. Our callers were as various as New York City itself: copyeditors, fact checkers, game show aspirants, journalists, bill collectors, bet settlers, police detectives, students and teachers, the idly curious, the lonely and loquacious, the park bench crazies, the nervously apprehensive. (This last category comprised many anxious patients about to undergo surgery who called us for background checks on their doctors.) There were telephone reference divisions in libraries all over the country, but this being New York City, we were an unusually large one with an unusually heavy volume of calls. And if I may say so, we were one of the best. More than one caller told me that we were a legend in the world of New York magazine publishing.

"How do you people know all this stuff?" a caller once asked me. "What are you, some kind of scholars or wordsmiths or something?"

"No," I replied. "Just us *libarians*."

Actually, we didn't know all that stuff; we just knew how to find it. I myself rarely remembered any of the facts I divulged to our callers, but I remembered the reference sources where I found the facts. Personal knowledge was inadmissible. I could reel off by heart the names of the four Dead Boys (Cheetah Chrome, Stiv Bators, Jimmy Zero, and Johnny Blitz—but didn't everyone know that?), but unless I could track them down and—rule number one—*cite the source* (in this case, probably the *Rolling Stone Encyclopedia of Rock and Roll*), I had no information to impart and no answer to give to anyone who might need that information for whatever reason. But we almost always found the right source.

The progenitor and enforcer of rule number one was our department head, whose managerial style recalled that of Vince Lombardi, if Vince Lombardi had had no interest in football. I do wish Milo had been a tad less heavy-handed; he tended to reduce unsatisfactory initiates to tears before driving them from the department for keeps. Nevertheless, his grinding relentlessness, which often entailed instructions barked into one ear while one's other ear might be dealing with a difficult and demanding caller, was in the service of professionalism and competence—necessary qualities in a small, claustrophobic office where the pressure from our backlog of callers never let up.

"Are you that nice young man who always goes out of his way to find me exactly the answers I need to the questions I ask?" a caller once asked me as a prelude to her inquiry.

"Doesn't sound like me," I said.

There was always psychology involved. In this case, the caller thought that by flattering me she might induce me to break or bend our rule of five minutes or three questions max, which we routinely disregarded anyway. The opposite psychological ploys—bullying, intimidating, insulting, threatening—were far more common. Contrary to the popular perception of librarianship as a serene, leisurely vocation for the bookishly inclined, the Telephone Reference Division was a high-stress environment, and most staffers, myself included, burned out within a few years. Now that reference librarianship is a shadow of its former self, psychological gamesmanship rarely takes place. You look up your information in a bland, seemingly (*seemingly*) trustworthy source like Wikipedia, and that's that. Librarians have other things to do, principally programming a never-ending stream of ostentatiously unlibrary-like events, but none will ever be so interesting or so much fun as the kind of thing we did in Telephone Reference before the Internet swept it all away.

tonight until eight o'clock." Just because callers spoke with imprecision, that didn't mean we could. I still speak in complete sentences whenever I can.

A certain esprit de corps facilitated the work and even diffused tensions in that pressure cooker of an office. I knew a lot about rock-and-roll and spoke Spanish. Aaron had a law degree and took all the questions about legal research that stumped us. (He also dispensed free legal advice on occasion, until Milo put a stop to it.) Milo knew theater; Paul was francophone; Kathleen knew movies and pop culture. (Our preferences skewed arty left-of-center, which was inevitable in our milieu.) Sometimes we worked backward, pooling what we already knew to find the reference sources that would confirm (and occasionally contradict) the foregone conclusion. Another rule: Don't hide your ignorance. There was no Google to cover up the gaps in our knowledge. Sally Jessy Raphael might have been the prime minister of New Zealand or she might have been an exceedingly unctuous talk show host. Unless I asked who she was (the latter, not the former), I wouldn't know the best sources to check to find her place of birth. As expected, the caller who asked about Ms. Raphael spent a certain amount of time insulting me for my ignorance, but she got her answer.

Many of our callers were historical novelists. Some of them identified themselves as such, but it was usually obvious even when they didn't. They tended to ask questions like "What time was low tide in Boston Harbor on May 14, 1932?"

If today I were writing a historical novel set in the 1980s, I might ask, "How did people find information in those days?" There would no longer be any telephone reference librarians to help me, so I'd have to trust to luck—and a search engine—and answer that question myself: They used logic, inference, imagination, and a tall pile of reference books.

DEVOTION

by MICHAEL MARK

from BIRMINGHAM POETRY REVIEW

Because no tools can be carried on the plane,
I buy them at the Home Depot near his apartment

and sneak into my father's building through
the "Service Only" entrance. Dad's Ford has more dents.

Half-hanging fender. He got lucky with the parking spot—
a few steps from the elevator. I puncture the tires

with the spike. Then pick the trunk's lock and stab
the spare. I hear him tell me when he's driving,

he feels like 50. You drive like you're 95, I say in a laugh
because he's 96 and I'm afraid to be direct. He takes it

as a compliment. I wedge the hammer claw into the seam—
unintentionally scraping some paint—jimmying up the hood.

I cut all wires because I know how iron willed he is and pour
the bag of sugar into the gas tank, crack the windshield

and headlights, pound the battery until the thick clips snap.
I know he's fought all his life for everything, so the leftover

Coke from the airport goes into the brake fluid.
Because he taught me integrity, I write a note in big-enough

block letters so he can read it even with his double vision.
Of course, I sign it. But don't ask. I will not tell you

what it says. He taught me loyalty, too.

THEBES, REVISITED

by GRACE SCHULMAN

from LITERARY MATTERS

At sunset on the farm, they sit waiting
before a cedar plank, stage for the play.
For weeks neighbors had chatted about the sign

tacked to an elm: GREEK THEATER. SUNDAY. FREE.
They watched actors decamp in the shore town
and look over the grounds that overlook

the bay's whitecaps, whipped by a threatening storm.
Onstage the cast will wear masks shaped in clay,
the gaping eye-holes and downturned mouths

for tragedy. The crowd, too, is masked
as fever rages in a nearby town.
This town is clean, so far. Then suddenly,

ancient Thebes. Look, where the bay
runs shallow, an oracle foretells danger—
no, it's a cormorant, poised on a rock,

spreading out its slick black wings to dry
as bearded swamp reeds dance in a muted chorus.
A blue-masked woman, baby on her back,

her man unfolding a striped picnic blanket,
says that for five years, she's seen the play
and likes the speech about the king's ancestors

(her own, she adds, are Mulfords, early settlers).
Now it begins. The postal clerk as Oedipus
saunters onstage, lofty for the lifts

inside his boots, his mask-face deepening
the mystery of fate: *My children, tell me*
why you are here. The farmhand playing Priest

replies: *plague rages, cattle die, crops fail.*
The bayman, robed as Creon, ruler of Thebes,
has an answer: *Banish the old king's murderer*

and all will be well. Corruption kills..
In the audience, a man stands up, staggers
and falls, his face red with the fever.

Villagers look down and step aside.
An outsider. The fever happens *there*,
not *here*. Get him out. Send him away.

Their voices rankle. "Did you see his face?"
"He's from the bad town."
                    "Late-night bars."
                              "Loose women."
A child pulls out his phone and calls for help

as men lug the sick stranger to the road.
Doc Slade, local M.D., waits for an ambulance
while others return to watch the ending:

Oedipus, blind, departs. The plague is lifted.
Someone sighs, "It couldn't happen now."
People hoist folding chairs and turn to leave,

muttering how calm the waters are
now that a northwest wind passed over us—
a good omen for tomorrow's catch.

SICKLED

fiction by JANE KALU

from AMERICAN SHORT FICTION

The first time I ever saw an owl was in the backyard of our childhood home in Enugu. That afternoon, my sister Ije stood by the guava tree feeding corn seeds to the stray pigeons at her feet while I leaned on the back door so that I could watch our dinner cook and keep an eye on her. The theme music of *The New Masquerade* reached us from the living room, where my mother watched TV with nothing but a wrapper tied around her. Soon our father would come home and complain about her indecency while he sat at the dining table in his boxer shorts.

The heat and humidity were excessive that year. It rained weekly, yet nothing but hot air rose from the ground. Children littered our street, shirtless. Grandparents and babies were brought out to the porch for their naps. Even as I stood there, the late afternoon's gentle breeze sweeping over my face, I could feel sweat pooling under my arms. I knew it was useless, but I called to Ije, "Isn't it time to come in?"

She rolled her eyes and murmured, "Tufia. Ima enye nsogbu."

This was the way of our relationship. I fussed. She cussed. She was born with sickle cell disease, and, at sixteen, only a year older, I was used to caring for her. I came to know the disease better than she did. Better than our parents. And this is what I learned: Ije had crescent-shaped red blood cells. Without their roundness, the cells lose their wholesomeness and ability to maneuver, triggering pain as they travel through the veins. Sickled blood cells break down and die early, resulting in anemia and a weakened immune system. And when she got sick, Ije ran a fever, triggering the death of more blood cells. When she overexerted herself, it increased blood flow, risking a blockage called a crisis–which can be deadly.

Everything could lead to death, was how I came to think of it. And maybe it was this knowledge that placed the burden of her sickness on me. So that I was the one who listened when the doctor said, give her paracetamol when the fever starts, and put a cold cloth on her head, and if she's too hot, make her bathe, and mind you, she must drink lots of water, and if it persists for more than six hours, take her to the emergency room, okay? During those hospital visits, my father was often preoccupied with praying the crisis away, and my mother, well, she followed his lead.

Ije went on cooing at the pigeons.

"You're so stubborn," I mumbled.

"Did I beg you to follow me around like a fly?" She threw more seeds in the air.

A white bird with wings much bigger than the flycatchers that populated our guava tree swooped down, picked up a seed with its beak, and flew up to a tree branch. The sun shone orange behind it, and it looked like the apparition of an angel.

Ije whispered, "Do you see that, too?"

I nodded, though both our eyes were fixed on the bird. Ije stepped forward, her gaze never leaving it.

"It's an owl," she whispered and waved at it. She touched the tree trunk gently, but the owl flapped its wings and flew into the pink sky. "How spectacular!" Ije sighed.

The bird really was beautiful. It flew with grace–its wide and arched wings not flapping, just soaring.

When it was finally out of sight I said, "You know that owls spell bad omen, abi?"

Ije ignored me. She continued to search the sky and scattered more seeds until her bowl was empty.

I went in to check on the yam boiling on the stove and turned off the flame. As the bubbles slowed, a sobbing sound echoed from somewhere in the house. I was certain it wasn't the TV, where Zebradaya and Ovularia bickered as always. I tiptoed down the dim hallway and ducked my head into the dark living room. Against the light of the screen, I could make out my mother's silhouette shaking. I was taken aback. I had known she was sad, but there was something about her crying alone in the dark that caused my eyes to water.

She had lost her job at the electoral office six months earlier. It was right after General Abacha took over the presidency and scrubbed the country clean of all democratic commissions. She went from running out the door every morning in wonky-heeled shoes that koin-koined on the gravel in the yard to dragging her feet up and down our hallway with a pained face. Our father, instead of getting a job, took on more duties in church, insisting that we needed God's intervention. He remained adamantly unemployed, despite my mother's failed attempts at finding work, a failure fueled by her not having a college degree.

There was a sense that year that we were headed toward an event, the climax of something. But the dread I felt wasn't just about our dwindling finances. There was something else–a spirit that hovered over us. Sometimes I felt it in the hallway on my way to the bathroom at night. Sometimes, I imagined hands reaching out of the framed Bible quotes my father hung on our walls. It didn't help that my mother began to keep the curtains drawn. Migraines, she complained. Or the birds were too loud, she would say. She would have asked my father to cut down the guava tree out back had Ije not loved it so much. "Oh, leave her alone," she said once when I complained that Ije spent too much time out there in the sun.

I could see how our mother thought it was good for her. Ije had suddenly grown from a child who was constantly in pain to one who stared at the sky and admired its blueness. She pointed out wild mushrooms and beautiful moss I had never noticed in our backyard. She fed birds food we didn't have and talked to lizards as they scurried about. I wish I could have told my mother that it was a boy who made Ije happy, and not the tree she kept alive.

My mother's sobbing grew deeper, as if she were trying to reach the pain inside and get it out. I wanted to hold her hand and tell her not to cry, but she would have been embarrassed, annoyed even, if she'd known I had seen her. Not that she hadn't cried in front of us before, but it was often at Ije's bedside while Ije lay writhing in pain. Only Ije moved her. And I would not understand until much later that her sadness through those months was not about her losing her job at all.

I stood there and waited until she finally stopped. Even though she had not known it, I felt I had shared the moment with her and consoled her by being in the room. I watched as she raised the edge of her wrapper to wipe her face. Then she flipped the channel to ETV, where Gen Abacha sat at the head of a table lined with other military men in uniforms. "Ekwensu," my mother hissed and changed the channel back to NTA. Even she must have confused the weight of her hatred for Abacha with the weight of her guilt.

That night, as we lay in the darkness, Ije would not stop talking about the owl. I pushed her voice far away and instead recalled the image of my mother sobbing. My parents slept on the other side of the wall, but when I put my ear to it and listened, I did not hear my mother weeping quietly into her pillow as I imagined. I could make out only my father's soft snores.

"There is nothing else that looks like an owl, isn't that fascinating?" Ije said, refusing to accept my silence as a reluctance to participate in a conversation. "Absolutely nothing looks like an owl."

Her spring bed whined as she turned to face mine. "Do you think it was trying to tell us something?" she asked.

I raised my eyebrows at the excitement I heard in her voice. I believed that God spoke to us in different ways, but I knew deep down that he would not speak to us through a strange bird. Anything the owl had to say came from the devil. That I was sure of, which was why I didn't mention it to our parents.

The door opened. It was our mother. Though I did not turn toward her, her smell–sweat mixed with the Morning Glory talcum she poured all over her body to soak up the wetness–filled our room.

"Are you girls still talking? Go to sleep," she said in a low voice.

"Good night, Mommy," I said.

Ije remained silent, and our mother hesitated, then I thought I heard her inhale sharply before she gently shut the door.

My mother and Ije had had a quarrel a couple of months earlier–a quarrel that I didn't think at the time bore much weight with our mother. It happened just a month after our mother lost her job, toward the end of the school year. That day, Ije had stormed out of her biology class and came racing into my math class, crying. The teacher had excused me without hesitation. Everyone in our school knew about her illness, and whenever she as much as coughed, they'd say at me, "Is she having a crisis?"

And no, she was not having a crisis that day. At least not a medical one. She'd just learned that sickle cell disease was genetically transferred. Her eyes were red when she said to me, "Did you know it's Mommy and Daddy's fault I am this way?"

"What are you talking about?" I said buying time to think of a response.

She asked if I knew that the best way to avoid having a child with sickle cell disease was to select a spouse who, when their genotype crossed with yours, wouldn't produce a sick child.

"My teacher said that some churches even make you find out your genotype before they agree to wed you. Is that why Mommy and Daddy ran away?"

She studied my face. "They knew?" she snapped as if I were somehow implicated in our parents' decision.

I was surprised Ije hadn't pieced it together sooner. Our mother often told the story of how her parents cut her off. She and our father were supposed to be married in her parents' church, but the priest had decided, just weeks before the wedding, that he would no longer conduct the ceremony. So, instead of breaking up like her parents and the church urged, they eloped and got married in my father's church. My mother never told us why the leaders in her parents' church had changed their minds, implying it was because of my father's poor background. But I filled in the gaps in the story after I heard nurses whisper behind their clipboards about how irresponsible our parents were. It was through them that I learned some churches didn't like to be culpable.

After school, we came home to our mother in the living room watching *Willie Willie*. The TV framed the ghost in a white flowing gown and ridiculously large wig, and the piercing sound of piano keys, designed to instill dread, became an ironic backdrop to the horror that unfolded with Ije's accusations.

"How could you marry a man with an AS genotype when you knew you also had an AS genotype?" she asked.

My mother looked at me in surprise, but I shook my head, refusing any responsibility. Instead, I tried to take Ije's hand, but she stared at me with murderous eyes and jabbed a finger toward me. "If you dare touch me again!" she warned.

I backed away.

My mother took a deep breath. "Ijemma, don't let the devil use you."

"Don't let the devil use me?" Her eyes stayed half shut, the veins on her temple pulsing. "You mean the way he used you?"

My mother sighed. "There's a reason for everything."

"Don't start that nonsense Bible thing with me!" Ije yelled. "What you and your husband did was wicked. Wicked!" And then she marched out of the room.

"Bia . . ." our mother called after her, her voice shaky.

"I hate you!" Ije screamed, and the slam of our bedroom door reverberated through the house.

My mother took a deep breath. "Make sure your father doesn't hear about this, ok?"

I nodded, as if my father and I had conversations in which I brought up how horrible he was for marrying my mother.

Ije did not speak of it again, but hatred grew inside her and festered into rebellion. I, on the other hand, did not disagree with our mother. I believed that there was a reason God allowed her illness. That Ije might have lost control had she not had the disease to hold her back. There was, already, all that frivolity in her eyes. What might it have grown into?

The owl didn't return despite Ije's scattering all the corn seeds she could find in the yard, and it was not until she gave up the idea of ever seeing it again that it came back with a screech.

My mother and I were in the kitchen the evening it showed up. She stood by the sink, lost, looking out at the weeds. There was a pot of jollof rice on the stove filled with whatnots we could find: half a small tin of tomato, a shriveled onion bulb, palm oil scraped from a discarded bottle, and a dash of crayfish. The smell of frying tomato filled the air as on the morning of a traditional wedding, only there was no party. We worked in silence as we often did until we heard the screeching and my mother awakened, her body moving faster than it had in months. She placed the bowl she held in the sink, rushed to the back door, and locked it.

With the light that came through the door gone, the room dimmed and the smell of soot from the kerosene stove intensified. I took my mother's place by the open window and found the eyes of the owl on the back fence where it perched. I could make out the pattern of its feathers more clearly than the day Ije and I first saw it. It was white mostly, but there were light brown specks here and there. Its face scared me, so I didn't dwell on it, but I had noticed its pointed beak before I averted my eyes to the clawed talons. My mother reached over my shoulder and closed the opaque louvers. Then she declared that we must all stay inside the house and wait for my father to come home.

She abandoned the simmering rice on the stove and went into her bedroom. I was surprised that she did not ask us to pray right away. But there were many firsts with her in those days. For instance, she stopped washing our father's laundry but asked me to do it with the wave of a hand. Showed no concern that I didn't weed the yard weekly. No longer took care to dress up when we went to church but kept her hair tied in a loose knot. No braids, no twists. These things I had considered inconsequential.

I looked for Ije to tell her that the bird was back and found her curled up in bed, running a fever and shivering. It felt pretty low, still, so I fed her paracetamol, then touched her arm gently and said, "Tell me right away if it starts to hurt," which was unnecessary because the aches could be so severe she'd roll on the floor and scream when they hit her. The screaming only stopped when the oxycodone, or, sometimes, morphine, kicked in, or in the worst cases, when she passed out from the pain.

"Leave me alone!" she mumbled and shook my hand loose. "Don't you have anything else to do?"

Ije liked to accuse me of suffering from her sickness more than she did. And maybe she was right. Maybe I should have gone out to the street and said to the first person I saw, does that shape in the sky look like a man or a fish to you? Maybe I should have climbed trees when I was younger or kicked a spoiled orange with other children until my toes bled. Maybe I should have been born into a family who sat about doing nothing but laughing and holding hands. But it's not like anybody gave me a choice, did they? So I leaned forward and said, "I'll leave you alone when you learn to take care of yourself."

"So, this is my fault?" she said tearfully.

I wanted to tell her that it was. That if only she followed the rules, that could keep her from having a crisis. If only she did not push her thin, frail body beyond its limits. It made me so mad when she forgot to drink water or take her folic acid or nap in the afternoons. I wanted to grab her hand and yank until she got it. I wanted to say how stupid she was to believe that a successful life did not acknowledge pain. She was ready to die whenever, wherever, she claimed. I wished I could tell her to go ahead and die. It would make our lives better, wouldn't it? But I simply touched her warm forehead and said, "Of course not. I didn't mean it that way."

I didn't want Ije to die. I was just annoyed at her for thriving when I didn't. Couldn't. That year she turned fifteen, she morphed into a young woman in a way that I hadn't yet. Where I walked by simply throwing my legs carelessly out in front of me, Ije's gait emphasized how her waist moved and the bouncing of her small breasts. She began to tilt her head this way and that when she talked. When she listened, she hung her hand, limp and suspended in the air, a smile lingering at the corner of her lips in a way that suggested the possible release of something concealed.

It began with books, this metamorphosis. First, there were the romance novels with covers that displayed bare-chested men clutching blonde or redhaired white women. Those novels drove down the neckline of Ije's blouses, and her skirts lost a few inches. She suddenly wanted pantyhose, holes in her earlobes, extensions in her hair, makeup, nail polish. She coveted hair straighteners and relaxers. She wanted to ride on the back of a motorcycle with wind blowing through her hair. All the things our parents said were worldly. She secretly altered her school uniforms, shortening the skirts and making the shirts tighter. I caught her many times staring at a boy, her eyes darkening, her nipples under the school shirt pointing forward, inviting his gaze. I watched, not sure when to tell her to stop being an akwuna. When she began to linger in the bathroom mirror, staring at her breasts? When she stuffed tissue in her bra? Moaned in her sleep?

"'Eat, drink and be merry, for tomorrow we may die,'" she quoted to me one evening, a book on Epicurus lying on her chest. It was a few months before the owl. The year was still young. We had just declared our new year's resolutions. Hers was to do whatever she wanted, sickness or not; mine was to bring her closer to God. I believed in the undefeatable power of God. I believed in miracles. I believed that God could heal her if only she believed. I knew that if she were healed everything would be better for all of us.

"You should be reading the Bible," I said, exercising my resolution.

"Do you think God is deaf?" she asked.

"Pray without ceasing," I said.

"'Rejoice always, *pray without ceasing*, give thanks in all circumstances; for this is the will of God in Christ Jesus for you.' Why do we ignore the other parts of that verse?"

Defeated, I snickered.

Ije was brilliant. She was going to study to be a doctor. But when I closed my eyes, I could never see her in a doctor's coat. I could never see her older than our present day at whatever age we were. Sometimes I wondered if she understood how close she came to dying during each crisis. If she knew there was a high chance she wouldn't live past her forties no matter how many gallons of water she drank a day or how conscientious she was with her folic acid. We argued about her coughs, her running a fever or waking up breathless, but we never talked about her emotions. Sometimes, I wanted to look into her eyes and ask how she really felt about being the one to get those genes. If she knew that I sometimes wished I'd gotten it and not her.

"We have to keep praying," I replied. "What else can we do?"

"I can kiss boys," she whispered and laughed. "Like Bube."

I eyed her. Bube was the boy who often visited his grandmother next door. His parents lived in America, and he oscillated between his grandmother's home and his uncle's in Lagos. At first, we didn't really know him, just as we didn't know any of our neighbors. We knew who lived in which house, who moved out or moved in. But we didn't know them the way you would walk up to a neighbor's door and ask if they could spare you a cube of Maggi. When we drove past them, we didn't wave. We were the family on the street that wouldn't be unequally yoked with unbelievers. Our parents made sure we avoided sharing spaces with *sinners*, which was how they referred to anybody that wasn't a member of our church. You never caught us at neighborhood meetings or saw us lingering on the sidewalk talking to someone across the street.

But Bube I got to know, and I got to know him first, albeit from a distance. I knew he woke up around seven every morning. That his bedroom window faced our yard, and that once he was up in the morning, he would pull his curtains open, yawn and stretch his shirtless body, pushing his chest forward. I knew he was tall and thin, and I imagined wrapping my arms around him and placing my face where his heart beat. I knew that he sometimes swept his grandmother's yard, and that if he caught me staring, he would smile and wave and I would stand there, mute. After he was gone, I'd swear that I would talk to him the next time, and then the next time and the next time, until one day, he was standing there smiling at Ije, and she was smiling back shyly.

He looked at Ije in a way that suggested he knew something she didn't. He told her that death was not the main event, living was. If you live your life constantly afraid of dying, you have allowed death to win twice, he told her. She fell in love. I imagined he didn't. That she was just a project.

"Now you're fantasizing about kissing Bube," I said to her that day in our bedroom, trying to keep a cool voice. "Do I need to tell you that Daddy will kill you?"

"Oh please, I already kissed him," she said.

"You what?" I clasped my hands to keep them from shaking.

She laughed even harder, amused by what she thought was my concern for her soul. She didn't worry about our parents' finding out because she knew I would never tell. That I would hold her secrets because if they came spilling out, I would be blamed. It had to be me. Our parents could never bring themselves to flog her with a cane or ask her to spend the week digging out the weeds around our compound in punishment.

When my father came home that evening, my mother told him about the owl, though the hooting had stopped. He marched straight to the back door, but his hand lingered on the handle and what might have been fear flashed across his face. He took a deep breath and composed himself, then went to the window and looked out. The crickets and frogs hidden in the onugbo shrubs serenaded him. My mother stood tentatively by the kitchen door, and I was behind her, watching him from under her arm.

My father, doubtful, turned around with a frown, but the owl screeched and he jumped, knocking down the plastic bowl my mother had forgotten by the sink.

"We need to go to prayers immediately," he said and marched into the living room.

My mother and I followed.

"The devil wants to attack this family. He plans death for us!" He freed himself of his yellow and brown tie. "We all know what that evil bird represents."

"That's what I thought," my mother said.

"So why didn't you pray?" my father retorted.

This was my father's tactic. He liked to throw accusations our way, as if his closeness to God, as a pastor, gave him insight into how we spent our day without him. My mother lowered her eyes, and my father looked at me, standing there in the doorway.

"Ije is not feeling too well," I blurted out in a bid to shift the conversation.

"My God!" my father cried. "It's already happening."

"Why didn't you tell me?" my mother snapped, possibly to prove to my father that she would have prayed had she known all the facts.

My father hurried to Ije, his bottle of anointed olive oil and large Bible tucked under his arm. Ije was asleep and stirred when my father waved the Bible over her.

"Out!" my father spat, speaking to the demon or spirit or curse.

Ije opened her eyes and glared at my father, then at my mother and me. She tried to move away from the Bible, but my father held it in place and poured the oil into her hair, drenching the pillowcase with it. I sat on the bed and took Ije's hand. She tried to pull her hand away, but I squeezed hard, and she winced.

My mother thought it was the beginning of vaso-occlusive pains and began to sob. "Stop it!" my father snapped at her. "You better not bring fear into this atmosphere for we do not operate in fear but faith."

My father prayed through the night. I woke up around 2 a.m. to check if Ije's chest was rising and falling, and he was still muttering in the living room. This was not unusual. Staying awake and praying was the mark of a true believer, he often said to us. My father was wrinkled and bony at forty-three. I know now his body must have been worn down by all that prancing and jiggling he did while praying, not to mention the constant fasting. I don't remember my father eating at all.

"It's so funny how he prays so hard for the impractical solution when he can just simply get a job himself," Ije said once.

Since my mother lost her job, our father prayed many hours at a time, not pausing even to eat. Over and over, he prayed for General Abacha to die. Die, die, die, he would cry until I became cursed with an earworm. I wondered how he could go on for so long without his tongue drying out. I agreed with Ije that he probably needed a job, but some things were not meant to be said out loud.

Ije muttered in her sleep now, and she kicked about restlessly. Though her body had cooled, I put a wet cloth on her head, in case the fever returned, and sat by her bed. I must have dozed off because when Bube called her name from outside our window, I jumped, startled. The night was calm. Even the frogs and crickets had gone to sleep.

"Ijemma," Bube said again, this time a little louder.

Angry, I threw open the French wooden windows.

"Are you mad?" I whispered. "What are you doing here?"

In the darkness, the fair skin of his bare chest glistened. He must have just showered. Who did he think he was, showing up at somebody's house shirtless?

"She didn't meet up with me yesterday evening and I've been so worried," he said. "She's having a crisis, isn't she?" He didn't wait for an answer but climbed through the window, forcing me to step back. His arm brushed against mine, and I placed my hands on the wall to hold steady.

"What are you doing?" I whispered, turning my head toward my father's voice.

"I'll be quick," he said, and then he looked me over. I tried to stick out my chest, braless under my nightgown, the way Ije often did it, but he went and knelt by her bedside. I wrapped my arms around myself, ashamed.

I watched Bube as his features contorted at the sight of Ije's swollen face and labored breathing. He brought her hand gently to his lips. He had never seen her having a crisis. For a second, I felt sorry for him. I knew how difficult it was to see Ije weak and defeated, completely devoid of her liveliness.

"Hey beautiful," he whispered, and Ije batted her eyes open.

It wasn't until Bube came into our lives that I saw how beautiful Ije was. We were both dark like our mother and had her oval face and full lips and round, bright eyes. But even though I was the curvy one, and Ije had thin long legs and a slightly protruding belly, I was too shabby to be noticed. I was not yet aware of my body, at least not in the way Ije was of hers. I wore our mother's old clothes and kept my hair wrapped in a scarf most of the time. Ije, on the other hand, insisted on getting new clothes every Christmas. She was feisty and loud and funny. She wore hairstyles with colorful beads at the tips.

She was not surprised to see Bube. She sat up and touched his cheek. "You came," she said in a tired voice.

"Shush," he said gently. "Remember, it's all here," he tapped his head.

Bube's parents were philosophy scholars. They sent him long letters instilling in him their Epicurean beliefs. When he wrote back that he missed them, they taught him about finding pleasure in little things in order to live a life without bodily pain. Ije told me all this about him. He taught her the same things, and she believed them. Yet, I understand now that to Ije, it wasn't simply about overcoming the disease. She was also just a girl who had a boyfriend she hadn't thought she could ever have, and now she believed that anything was possible.

During that period, with my mother lying around half-asleep and half-awake, Ije went out whenever she wanted. I imagined Bube sneaking her past his grandma, dozing in the living room, and into his bedroom. I imagined Ije lying on his bed with sheets that reeked of him. Before she left, she'd probably walk around his bedroom, touching his things to establish a co-ownership. When she snuck back home, she sang about his love for her. She told me he would marry her and that they would have children running around their white-and-blue bungalow. I wondered how Ije managed to live outside of her illness completely. As I sat and listened, the only thing I could think about was her condition and how Bube would eventually recoil from its reality. One day he would see her lying in bed, her face ashen and twisted in agony, and the image would become forever embedded in his memories, remaining there no matter how much she smiled after the pain was gone.

"Think about the birds," he said to her now. "Go to a pleasurable place. I know of one you could think of."

"Oh Bu," Ije said softly. Even in sickness, she flipped her braids to one side and narrowed her eyes. They shared a giggle. A secret I was not a part of.

"Time to go," I hissed, and as if on cue, our parents' bedroom door opened. My mother's feet shuffled down the hallway and into the bathroom. I tugged at Bube.

He leaned in and kissed Ije on the lips. I yanked at his arm. "Go! Now!" I whispered.

After he left, I quickly closed the window and checked the hallway to make sure neither of our parents lurked there.

"Relax, you look like you might have a convulsion," Ije said, amused.

"This thing with Bube ga alaputa gi," I snapped. "It's gone too far!"

"Maybe." There was a twinkle in her eyes, and before she said it, I knew. "We had sex," she said.

I collapsed on my bed, and she burst into giggles, pleased by my shock.

"Why do you refuse to be helped?" I asked, taken aback by my teary and weak voice.

"It's not a bad thing, Ada, haba." She shook her head at me. "Is pleasure not better than pain?"

The owl resumed its cries in the morning, and my father invited the church prayer group to our house. He asked my mother to set out refreshment: Fanta and cabin biscuits or bread. Maybe malt drinks, he said.

My mother eyed him. "Where will I get it?"

He shrugged and quickly hurried into the bathroom.

We arranged the dining chairs in between the settees and carried out the small center table to make space for my father or whoever led the prayers to pace while they spoke. I could not imagine how hot it would become with twenty people fitted into that tiny living room. We left the two windows open, and with just my mother and me in the room, I could already feel the heat sticking to my back.

"We have biscuits left from the last meeting, should I bring them out?" I asked my mother, fanning myself with my hand.

"Adamma," she replied. "Do we have any food for breakfast tomorrow?"

I shook my head no. "I'll save the biscuits then."

"Good. You're going to run your home one day. You have to learn now how to manage your kitchen."

"Yes, Mommy," I said.

She sighed. "Your father has to ask the church for support. I don't know what we will do next week."

I knew she wasn't expecting me to respond. She was only thinking aloud. Still, I nodded.

As soon as the prayer team arrived, one of them, a woman, declared my father had done the right thing. Not just because it made logical sense to bring in reinforcements, but she had had a dream. A revelation. Our house had been on fire and vultures, many vultures, hovered in the sky. Vultures were evil birds, a striking similarity to owls that we shouldn't ignore. In this dream, someone inside our house had set the fire, though she couldn't tell who it was.

My father tightened his bony, already sweaty face into a frown and glared at me. He asked what sin I had committed that let the devil in. Tongue-tied, I could only shake my head at him. He turned to my mother, and she raised her eyebrows in warning.

"Your prayer life has been waning, Gladys. You must have let the hedge down and now the enemy is here," my father spat. "Don't you understand that you have to be an example to our daughters?"

My mother's mouth dropped open slightly.

"Both of you better stay and pray with us." He clapped rapidly and began pacing, signaling the exercise was about to commence.

My mother snuck away and sat with Ije, who was asleep. After running a fever, Ije was often very tired and would sleep for days until her cells regenerated and she regained her strength. I stood by the door and watched my mother's small hands caress Ije's forehead. I wondered if she was ashamed or even annoyed at my father. How could she let him humiliate her? I don't know what I expected her to do. I had never seen her question him. It would have shocked me if she had confronted him, and yet I stood there hoping she would do something. Hoping she would be somebody else for once.

My mother took her hand from Ije's face and beckoned to me. I went to her, and she reached for me, but I stepped back in surprise. Only Ije she touched that way. I don't remember her hugging my father or ever holding his hand. I thought her to be a melancholic woman, but I see now how she came to be without happiness. How she became incapable of loving my father and me. There must have been space only for Ije.

"I know you're worried about your sister," she said in her calm voice. "Sit down. Stay here with us. You don't have to pray with them."

I nodded and sat on my bed.

This was her way of rebelling against my father. It made sense that her revolt would not be frantic. She was a quiet and slow woman. I had never seen her hurry even when we were running late to church. It was as though she lacked the ability to do anything at a quick pace. She was not a big woman, so it was not her physical features that held her back. She was petite with short thin legs that one would at first expect to move swiftly. I admire that slowness now. How she remained unfazed by my father's complaints of her sluggishness. She would ignore his bickering and carry on with whatever she was doing until she was ready. It was the only confrontation she had in her.

Ije opened her eyes, and when she saw my mother holding her arm, she shrugged her off. My mother reached for her again.

"Leave me alone!" Ije snapped.

My mother's lips quivered, and she stood. "Sit with her," she said and hurried out.

I waited until my mother slammed the bedroom door shut and I said to Ije, "Why are you mean to her, Ijemma? It's not fair."

"Well, they were mean to me first," she said in a dry croaky voice.

I gave her some water to sip.

The prayer went on all afternoon and with it the crying of the owl. Ije was sleeping again. She thrashed her legs and punched the air.

"Ije," I called. "How are you feeling?"

She stretched out her hand to me with her eyes half open. I put my face inches from hers, and her breath was warm against it. She tried again to open her eyes, but her stare was unfocused. She grabbed my hand and squeezed. My heart plunged into my belly.

"Ije!" I shook her. "Ije!" I didn't understand my own panic. She was moving. Was not screaming in pain. Was not having a fever. And yet, "Ijemma," I called again.

Finally, she looked at me, but without the amusement with which she usually observed everything. This was not the worst of her crises. I had seen her on the floor and screaming from pain. I had seen her eyes red, swollen shut. I had seen her face nearly drained of life. But when she looked at me this time, something in her expression, something from the inside, maybe the bond we inherently shared as sisters, called to me for help.

I ran into the living room and told my father we had to take Ije to the hospital immediately. Somebody in the prayer team waved me off and said we needed prayers, not a doctor.

"She told me herself that we have to go to the hospital," I lied. "I think it's serious."

"Don't bring your lack of faith in here," my father bit at me.

My mother ran out of the bedroom in a wrapper that hung loosely above her breasts. Some members of the prayer team averted their eyes.

"If Ije wants to go to the hospital, then we are going," she said.

At the hospital, as we helped Ije out of the car, my father's hands trembled from what I thought to be anger, but it must have been from fear. It must have all been from fear. The desperate need to exert his power over the disease, his insistence on keeping himself detached from our world in order to remain resident in one that relieved him of the consequences of his actions. It was all fear. All of it.

As we wobbled into the building with Ije leaning on us, it occurred to me that these few minutes when we carried her into the hospital together were often the most affectionate I ever spent with my father.

"No, go this way."

"Be careful, Adamma."

"Iji ya? Good."

All mere instructions he gave me as we walked, but ones I cherished.

In the hospital room, he stood in the corner clutching his Bible in one hand and the anointed olive oil bottle in the other, his lips moving silently. He must have loved Ije as much as my mother did.

Ije lay on the table while the doctor examined her. The portrait of Abacha in his military uniform adorned with stars hung above Ije's bed, his lost, watery eyes staring down at us. I caught my mother looking at him a few times before quickly averting her gaze. If we stayed longer than one night, as we often did, she would take down the portrait and stick it in a drawer.

"How much will all this cost?" my mother asked the doctor a few more times than she probably realized.

The doctor ignored her as she listened to Ije's chest and belly. An ultrasound machine came barging into the room and along with it a nurse in a white dress, a small white cap perched atop her head and kept in place with a cluster of hairpins.

"It appears there's a heartbeat in your daughter's uterus," the doctor announced after rolling the probe around Ije's belly.

Everyone looked from the doctor to Ije and back.

"She's pregnant," the doctor finally elaborated. "About 8 weeks."

My parents' eyes immediately flew to Ije's belly, which always protruded anyway because of her enlarged spleen, one of the symptoms of her disease. I reached for the door frame to hold steady. My mother left Ije's side and sobbed into a wall. Ije's eyes met mine and for the first time there was fear in them.

"Who did this to you?" my father asked.

Ije did not break eye contact with me as she replied, "Please. Stop."

Our mother turned to me. "Do you know this person?"

Ije shook her head at me.

"No," I replied and looked down at my shaking hands, ashamed that my lie was not to protect Ije but Bube.

The doctor sighed again. "We would have to take out the baby. At her age, with SCD, it could kill her."

"I'm not going to approve murder," my father said shaking his head. "God will take care of this."

"But I don't believe in your God," Ije blurted out, and even the air in the room froze.

I clenched my fists and felt my heart thumping in my chest. I waited for my parents to turn to me, to ask me what I had done to my sister, but my father stormed out of the room and my mother followed.

I may have seemed like the sane one, because the doctor came closer and spoke in a low tone. "We really need to move fast. She's already severely anemic. You see how yellow her eyes are."

I ignored her, too angry to speak, and she left.

"Well, they took that well," Ije said.

"Did you really have to say that?"

"Why do you always side with them?" she asked.

"Why do you like to hurt them? You think you're smart because you read a few books. You're just an idiot."

She snickered. "You just think they'll like you if you do everything they say."

"That's a lie," I whispered. I felt tears roll down my cheeks.

"Whatever." She shrugged nonchalantly, but there were tears in her eyes too.

"You're so ungrateful. They give you everything." I was angry now. "They love you—"

"And yet they're willing to let me die." Her voice broke. "You heard your father."

"You should have thought of that before you opened your legs to the first boy that talked to you."

"So you want me die too?" Ije snapped.

I ran out of the hospital room and went to the bathroom down the hall, where I heaved but nothing came out. In the whole frenzy of the day, I had not eaten, and my tummy growled. My father would be pleased I had fasted with him. The Lord will heal her through our starvation and suffering, he would say. I splashed water on my face and took a deep breath, avoiding my eyes in the mirror. When I pushed the door open, I came face to face with Bube and jumped.

"Jesus Christ!" I cried.

"Sorry, I saw you run in and–"

"Why won't you leave her alone?" I said and started to walk away, but he took my hand and stopped me.

"How is she?" he asked. "Do you think I could see her?"

His hands felt warm in mine, and I began to sob again. I grabbed him and hugged him and put my face in his sweaty neck.

"What is it? Is she okay?" he asked.

I shoved him away.

He raised his eyebrows, and I took his hand again, craving his soft skin against mine.

"Ada, what's going on?"

"She's pregnant with your baby, and she needs surgery to take it out."

He let go of my hand and it dropped to my side with a weight that surprised me. I stretched it toward him and hoped he would take it one more time, but he wasn't looking at me. He stared down the hallway and then toward the door, frantic.

"She's pregnant?" he said.

I sighed and let my hand return to my side. "Yes."

He grabbed his head, and I thought he might cry.

I looked away, embarrassed. When I turned back around, he was hurrying down the hallway toward the exit. It was the last time I would ever see him. Later, when I told Ije that he came to the hospital but ran off when he learnt she was pregnant, it was with relish. Of course, she would not believe it.

Back in Ije's room, everyone had reconvened. My father kept his head bowed. My mother was crying. The doctor kept her eyes on the clipboard.

"What is it?" I asked.

"The placenta has ruptured. I may die whatever they do." Even weak and breathless, Ije's voice held a hint of sarcasm.

"Is it true?" I asked the doctor.

"Please just let them do the surgery," my mother begged my father.

"It really doesn't matter," Ije said. "Death is better than this anyway."

"What has come over you? Don't say that!" my mother cried and reached out to touch Ije, but she slapped her hand away.

"What's going on? Somebody talk to me!" I barked.

"Your sister is bleeding, and we–"

As she spoke, Ije's eyes rolled to the back, and she lost consciousness.

My mother screamed and told the doctor to do everything to help her, but my father stood between the doctor and the bed.

"Daddy?" I yelled and pushed at his arm. "You can't do that. She's going to die."

He began to speak in tongues and my mother grabbed his shirt. "Shut up! Just shut up! No more prayers!"

My father stepped away from the bed, shocked.

"I'll sign the paperwork. I'm her mother," my mother said to the doctor, giving my father one last glare. "Please help her," she said to the doctor again.

This was not the year that Ije died. She only lost the baby. For the three weeks that she stayed in the hospital after the surgery, everything returned to normal at home. Normal being that the hospital incident never happened, and Ije was never pregnant. Crisis, we told everyone. We couldn't even look in each other's eyes as we passed in the hallway, let alone talk about the truth.

But Ije's pregnancy is not the main reason I tell this story. Something more important happened the morning she returned. Our father was in church for a prayer meeting, and our mother decided to stay home and cook something hot for Ije. It was left to me to get her from the hospital.

When we got out of the taxi, Ije had insisted I first take her to Bube's house, where his grandmother told us through her parted orange drapes that Bube had left. Her grandson was visiting his uncle, she said, and would be leaving for America from there. She hissed the words out, her eyes moving from Ije to me, perhaps trying to work out who the wayward one was. She peered at us as we walked toward home, and not once did she call us back to ask why we both had tears in our eyes.

Ije asked that I take her to our backyard, where she sat and sobbed into her palms, her body shaking so much I wondered if the stitch in her belly would tear. But I felt sorrier for myself than I did for her. I had no hopes that, after Ije, Bube and I would be together, but I'd taken consolation in the glimpses of him I caught from across the fence and was mourning my own loss.

When we finally went into our house, we met a quiet kitchen. There was no yam pepper soup sizzling on the stove. There was no water boiling in the kettle for Ije's bath. Ije looked at me, but I turned away, allowing my eyes to travel down the hallway toward our parents' bedroom door. We could have touched the fear we shared if we'd stretched out our hands in front of us. We walked down the hallway, me first, and Ije behind. I knocked, and when nobody answered I pushed the door open. Our mother was lying in bed peacefully, Ije's oxycodone pill bag empty on her chest.

I don't remember what happened after we found her. I don't remember what was true and what I fabricated. Whether it was me or Ije who grabbed the pill bag before we called on the neighbors. Whether it was me or Ije who found the note scribbled on the torn page of her Bible. Whether I ran all the way to the church on bare feet to get my father or if a neighbor took a car to ferry him home to his dead wife. Whether it was my father who declared that Abacha had killed her or a member of the prayer team. I don't remember what we ate. If we ate. How we slept. If we slept. I don't remember who cared for Ije in the days that followed. I don't remember who stayed with us, if we were left alone with our father. I don't remember her body being moved. How many people it took. If they stuck her in the back of a neighbor's car or if an ambulance came.

But I remember standing over her body and wondering when she had done it. Her hand in mine was still warm. Perhaps she was still breathing when we got out of the taxi. Perhaps she only died a few seconds after we walked into the house. I would spend every day wondering what might have happened if she had lingered. Waited for us to find a pulse.

But these are things I try not to think about so that I can make space for the one image that kept me from wrapping my hands around Ije's thin body and squeezing until there was no breath left in her. A memory from before we entered the house. Before we discovered our mother's lifeless body. Before we found the note in our mother's handwriting that said, *I am very sorry, Ijemma.*

I was about to push the back door open when Ije asked me to wait. She quickly wiped her tears with the edge of her T-shirt and smiled a smile that didn't reach her eyes, practice for when she greeted our mother. She took a deep breath and had just reached for the door handle when the owl cried behind us.

Ije spun around. "It's still here? After three weeks?"

I nodded.

"I want to see it," she said.

We approached the guava tree where the owl sat in a nest on a low branch. It stopped crying and watched us cautiously, its eyes shining from within the leaves. We crept closer and closer until we could see that there were two eggs peeking out from beneath it.

My hands flew to my mouth, and I said, "Poor Daddy!" and Ije burst into hysterical laughter. This is the memory I play and replay: Ije laughing and laughing. Her thin, frail body bent forward and jerking uncontrollably. Her hollow eyes filled with happy tears, and her arm stretched out, reaching for me. I had taken her hand and laced my fingers between hers and for a fleeting moment–one that I would try to replicate many times for the remaining years that Ije lived–I loved her and could have forgiven her anything.

THE WEIGHT OF DAYS

by DORIANNE LAUX

from POST ROAD

Sometimes the months can be weighed
like pounds, twelve in a year. What weighs
twelve pounds? One chair. One dog.
Seven crates of tomatoes. One month old
baby. A double neck guitar someone
shreds ruthlessly, the band behind
trying to keep up. Sometimes the months
drag, drug like a chair across the dry dirt
of days. Some years come at a price.
Some marked down, on sale, tagged
"as is". Some days line up like siblings
against a wall, each waiting their turn
to be smacked with a ruler. Or time
can be a beam of light which travels
faster than sound, fastest through air,
slower through water or glass. A dog
lies on the grass, wagging its tail
until someone comes along
and frees the chain, a key
pressed into the metallic dark.
A year can be a truck on the interstate
loaded with seven crates of tomatoes,
the driver's wife at home
holding a month-old baby. Some days
there's no room for another minute.
Some years there's not enough room
for the days.

EASEMENT

fiction by KIM SAMEK

from STORY

I got a letter from the government claiming an easement on my leg. I had just moved into this house and didn't think much of the notice. A few months later, an official in a yellow vest and hardhat knocked on my door. He was carrying a machine that looked like a hole punch, but larger. He said he was here for my big toe.

"You've received the easement notice?" he asked.

I nodded.

The removal was swift. Before I could say "ow" he had placed my big toe into a Ziplock bag and was sealing it up. He said he would only need it for a few days before he would bring it back. I felt a little wobbly without my big toe, but I did my best to conceal my unsteadiness. If I focused hard enough, I could walk normally. I only needed to get by for a few days.

After the man left, I slipped on some closed-toe shoes so I wouldn't have to look at the gap where my toe should have been. Several days passed, and he didn't return. I was afraid I'd been scammed. I pulled out the easement letter and took a closer look at it. I realized just then that anybody could write a letter like that. Maybe there was no easement. Maybe I was stupid for giving him my toe without asking more questions.

I'd already been the victim of scammers who called my phone all day. At first, I'd thought they were trying to sell me things, but whenever I picked up, they hung up. I couldn't get any of them to explain why they were calling me. I soon found out I wasn't the only one targeted. When I went in for a pap smear, my O.B. received several calls while I was in the stirrups. She said her lines were tied up and patients in labor were often unable reach her. That's really a shame, I told her. We commiserated over the unpleasantness of this puzzling scam.

Later, I met a hang up caller while in line at the DMV. He was never not calling someone, even when it was time for his appointment. As we walked out to our cars, I asked him what his end game was. He said he was paid to disrupt the peace.

By whom? I asked.

He shrugged. He said it was one of those jobs you could get in the gig economy, like providing rideshares or delivering groceries. He had no idea who had hired him. He'd gotten his jobs off a task website. Task Jackal? I asked. He nodded. I was angry at first. I told him I was sick of being hounded by people like him. It didn't matter if I was on the toilet or trying to sleep—the phone kept ringing. If I turned it off, I risked missing an important call from my elderly parents.

I asked the man how he could live with himself ruining people's lives like that. He shrugged and said a person had to do what he had to do to get by. He needed to pay off his sister's medical bills. She'd been in a car accident and was paralyzed from the waist down. I told him that was no excuse for destroying people's mental health and that he should find a respectable career.

A few months after I met the hang up caller, I was laid off from my job as a weatherperson due to declining ad sales. I needed to find work fast. My rent had crept up and so had the utilities. Water was expensive those days. There was so little of it. I tried driving rideshares for a while, but the job didn't pay enough, so I switched to disrupting the peace.

I made hundreds of calls each day. I was given a special phone number that was exempted from the phone bank and didn't ring all day so I could make maximum use of it. *What's the scam* people would ask when they picked up the phone. They sounded desperate to know. Sometimes I would shout, *There is no scam! I'm calling to piss you off!* I liked to give people answers. I found it thrilling to be the one who called.

By the time the toe thief had come along, I thought I was wise to scams, having joined the ranks of the perpetrators, yet somehow, it seemed I might have fallen victim to a new one.

I went to the police station down the street. A lumpy detective was assigned to my case. His phone rang loudly. He held his hands over his ears. I had to shout as I filed my complaint.

Someone stole my big toe, I told him.

He asked me to repeat myself, so I tried shouting louder, but I wasn't a very good shouter. My voice was small even though I considered my personality big. This incongruity had always bothered me. I wasn't treated with as much respect as my fellow weatherpersons because I couldn't make my voice boom.

You get these calls too? the detective asked.

Yeah, I shouted. These weirdos bother me all day.

He asked for a description of the person who took my toe. I told him I couldn't recall much. The man was young. He was wearing a yellow reflector vest with a hardhat. But what about his face, the detective shouted. He handed me a megaphone.

Try this, he said.

Thanks, I said into the megaphone. I don't think he had a face, I continued. But that didn't sound right. Of course he had a face. I just hadn't bothered to notice it. I rarely looked at anyone's features. I had a lot on my mind between the housing crisis and the inflation crisis and the world getting hotter crisis and the fires and smoke and all that. Other people were just outlines to me. They were shapes, they were hair, they were clothes, a pair of Chelsea boots. They were brooms with caps. Scarecrows with shirts. Noses with bad attitudes.

I had a very serious case of prosopagnosia. It was a bigger problem back when I was dating and needed to pick out a stranger in a crowd. I couldn't do it, so I'd have to make sure I arrived first. I was once forced to run out of a restaurant when there were nine bald men. Faces were a lot of work to deal with. I was surprised to learn that facial blindness was considered a neurological problem. I didn't feel like someone with a neurological problem.

I didn't make a lot of friends because of this condition. Then the pandemic came along and shut me in. Maybe working from home had erased the gains I'd made in learning how to interact with people who looked like fuzzy blurs in clothes. I had turned into a bit of a zombie just trying to get by. I guess maybe that is why I was so willing to hand over a toe to a guy in a hardhat who knocked on my door. Now that I had some awareness of what was going on, I decided I would work on being more present. I would try not to get lost in a cloud of my own problems.

So you don't know what he looks like? the detective asked.

No, I replied.

The detective said he couldn't do much without a facial description and tried to send me on my way. He put on his noise-canceling headphones and indicated that he had a headache. I gestured for him to remove them. He did so begrudgingly.

I just need to know if this a scam, I said.

How would I know? he asked.

I thought you might have heard from other people who'd lost a toe, I said.

People don't come to me about toes, he said. How would I know if it's a scam? When I was coming up as a policeperson, a scam used to be simple. It was a way to get money. It's a crime to steal. I could arrest those people. Even if I wanted to arrest the people calling me, I couldn't be able to because there is no crime. Making too many phone calls is not a crime.

It's not a crime, I agreed. But it should be.

You gave that guy your toe willingly, he said.

Because he said there was an easement, I told him.

But you gave it to him willingly, he repeated.

He said he would bring it back, I told him. But he didn't. Is theft not a crime?

It sounds like he asked for it and you gave it to him, the policeperson repeated.

He put his noise canceling headphones back on and took two aspirin plain. I handed back the megaphone. I would have to take matters into my own hands. I didn't see the toe thief again for a while, but it was fine because work was busy. They had just started offering a bonus for anyone who reached eight hundred hang up calls each day, so I bought a second phone and learned how to dial one while the other was ringing. I was desperate to make more cash. My rent was covered, but I still couldn't afford good water. I needed to get creative. At the flea market, I bought recycled water that was probably not too sanitary. Luckily I'd recently discovered it tasted great once I added some lemonade powder. So far, I had suffered no health consequences.

The toe thief finally came back in late summer. He was wearing the same hardhat and reflector vest ensemble he wore the first time. I made sure to focus on his face so I could go back to the police with a better description. He had red hair, freckles on his nose, and two of his front upper teeth were black. This time, he was holding an axe.

I need your leg, he said.

Why, I asked him.

Check the easement, he said. Government orders!

I tried to seem intimidating even though he was carrying an axe. I know there's no easement, I told him. I asked what he did with my toe. He said he had deposited it into a box at a bank in Fontana. It was probably no good now even if he could remember which box, and he was sure he couldn't.

What's the scam here, I asked. Why did you take it?

There's no scam, he said.

So you were just messing with me, I said.

I was just following orders, he said. Doing my job, you know.

He seemed nervous. I asked him who he worked for. He said he got his jobs on a task website that didn't reveal the employer. I asked if he meant Task Jackal. He nodded. I told him about my job making calls, which I got through the same website.

So you're the one of *those* people, he said. I can't even use my phone anymore. Why do you do that? I can barely think now. My attention span is so short. My brain is fried. You should be ashamed.

This is a stopgap job, I told him. And you're one to talk, with that axe. At least I just attack the peace. Is anyone even entitled to peace to begin with? Who said it was a right?

Who said you were entitled to a leg? the man asked.

It was impossible to argue with him. He was the kind of person who would choose a position that was so ridiculous no one could pick it apart. Then he suddenly sat down on my porch like he was tired. He wanted to know if I liked my job.

It's a fun gig, I said. No benefits or anything, but the pay is alright.

It seemed like a thought occurred to him just then.

Can I come in and escape the heat for a bit? he asked.

I told him he could only come in if he set his axe down. He stood up and flung it against the side of the house. It remained there, stuck in my wood siding. I didn't know what to say so I didn't say anything. He seemed very thirsty and I felt like I should help him. Inside, I handed him a pitcher of lemonade. He was grateful to rehydrate. He held the glass as if it were precious. As if he'd never seen lemonade before. I poured him another glass.

We compared notes on our jobs and imagined we were employed by billionaires who got a kick out of sowing chaos. It turned out I made four dollars more per hour, and that was before factoring in the bonus.

Can you get me in the door with the phone call people? he asked.

Sure, I said.

He left his axe stuck in the side of my house and came back in the morning to retrieve it. Then he asked if he could stay and work here so we wouldn't have to work alone. I worried he was getting the wrong idea about my romantic intentions. I was six years older than him and also I didn't like most people. I took great pains to avoid them. He was just a man with an axe. Why join up with him? I still couldn't describe his face, other than the freckles and the black teeth.

He started making calls from my couch. He didn't ask for permission to stay. I decided to go with it. I was sick of being alone. He had already made hundreds of calls. He was a talented person. Industrious too. He inspired me to do better at my job. It was the best day of calls I'd ever had. We hit the bonus target by mid-afternoon.

We're better together, he said.

Yeah?

I like having a co-worker, he said. You don't miss office work?

A little bit, I said. I liked the free snacks, I guess. And having a place to go that was somewhere else. Everything blends together now.

I only see people at the grocery store, he said. It's not right. I used to have friends.

Me too, I lied.

He tapped his feet rhythmically as we worked.

If we make enough money, we can start hiring people to do weird stuff ourselves, he said. We can pay people to do whatever we want. We could run our own operation.

It's going to take a while to save up, I said. Millions of calls.

I'm willing to put in the time, he said. I want to rise to the top.

I considered the idea of turning this gig into a career. It had never occurred to me that I could still be scamming in a few years. I'd thought I'd find my way back to a new weatherperson job.

What would you make people do if you had a billion dollars, I asked. He was a thoughtful person. It took him most of the afternoon to come up with the answer. He said he would pay people to steal sandwiches and bring them to him. And of course he would buy unlimited water. He asked what I would do.

I'd hire people to stop buying fast fashion, I told him. I would pay people to wear the same clothes every day. I would hire people to get off their phones so they could be present. I'd hire people to live out the dreams I'm too scared to do myself. Like go on a hot air balloon ride or take a submersible to the deepest part of the ocean.

The ocean? he asked. Isn't it hot down there?

Not inside the submersible, I said.

Well, why don't I do those things with you? he asked. Your dreams sound fun.

Are you trying to kill me? I asked. Then I realized I didn't want to know the answer to that question. He was, after all, a man who had come to my house with an axe. It occurred to me just then that there was a chance he was still after my leg and was playing the long game. Here I was being gullible again. I should never have let him in.

He was confused when I suddenly stood up and put the lemonade back in the fridge.

I need to work alone now, I told him. I can't focus with you here. This is a solo job. And I can't afford to keep supplying you with lemonade.

He looked sad, but he stood up and took a few steps toward the door.

Are you sure you don't want to get dinner sometime, he asked.

Yes, I said.

Yes, you want dinner, he asked hopefully.

No, I want you to leave, I clarified.

He left his axe stuck in the side of my house and disappeared around the corner. I thought maybe he'd come back for it again, but he didn't.

I was hit with an unexpected regret. Had I made a mistake in kicking him out? I had a bad habit of pushing away people who liked me. I was afraid of commitment, probably thanks to my parents' divorce. But he was just doing his job when he came for my leg. It wasn't personal.

As time passed, I found I was still thinking of the man with the axe. I listened for his voice when I made hang-up calls. I figured if I tried enough people, it was possible I could find him. I no longer hung up the phone as fast—only when I was sure that he wasn't on the other end. The few extra seconds it took per call was enough to cost me the bonus. I had to go back to working at top speed. There was no time to be sentimental in a gig economy.

Eventually I made enough money to hire people to do a few tasks for me. I didn't end up paying people to do good deeds as I had thought I would. Instead, I hired people to look for a man with a hardhat and an axe. Several such men were brought to my front door, but they were different men tasked with the same job.

Once I got to talking to one, I learned he was paid more than me. It seemed the rates had changed. I bought an axe and a hardhat, sent out easement letters, and went door to door chopping off toes.

Eventually, while making my easement rounds, I located the man. He said his name was Arlie. He lived over by the train tracks. I told him I had come to take his toe. He stuck his foot out, resigned to losing it.

I told him we didn't have to do this. There's no easement, I admitted. But you already knew that. You'd really let me take your toe?

He nodded.

You need the money, he said.

Maybe I don't, I told him. I set the down the axe and asked if I could come in. He let the door fall open. His breath smelled like lemonade. He seemed to be missing a sparkle in his step. I missed the man who had flung the axe into the side of my house. He was so jovial back then. So upbeat and excited to embark upon a new adventure. Had I ruined his life by kicking him out that day? Could I help him find that sparkle? Was it possible to get close again?

Can I have some lemonade, I asked.

Help yourself, he said. He pointed toward the kitchen and continued making hang up calls.

I found the pitcher in the fridge, but it was filled with brown water. The lemonade powder was pooled up at the bottom. He must have forgotten to mix it up. I didn't want to drink brown water. I put the pitcher back in the fridge on the top shelf next to the butter. I could last at least a couple more hours without water, I figured.

He told me that he had been a primary care doctor once, but he couldn't compete with an AI that could run through checklists and generate a diagnosis in less than one second. His training had gone to waste. He was curious about me. He'd guessed I was a creative person. I told him about my career as a weatherperson—I'd loved it because it was a mix of science and creativity. Facts and opinions. He said medicine was the same. There was an art to it. He seemed to be listening, but he didn't stop making hang up calls, even as I tickled him. I decided to be direct for once. I asked if he could take a break so we could have a proper conversation. He said he'd learned there was nothing more important than money. He was doing well now. I could see he had gotten his teeth fixed.

I was hoping you would come back, I told him.

I asked you to dinner, he said. But you kicked me out.

Yeah, sorry about that, I said. I guess I was scared.

Scared of what, he asked.

I didn't answer. I thought I was being clear already, and it wasn't my style to explain myself better. He asked if I was worried about taking so much time off work. I told him I wasn't. I had spent so much money trying to find him that I had dug myself into a big hole, but it was worth it. No way I was going to leave him behind to retrieve more toes right then.

You hired people to look for me? he asked.

I nodded.

How much money did you spend? he asked.

A lot, I said.

He smiled.

I haven't met anyone that excites me in a long time, I said. You seem smart. You have a unique perspective.

I watched some of your videos, he said. Your old weather reports. You were good. I've never seen a better weatherperson.

I blushed. He went into the kitchen to get some lemonade with a big, silly grin on his face, then came back with two bubbly flutes. He had stirred them up and had added champagne. I brought a flute to my lips, but I couldn't stop thinking about how brown the lemonade water had looked when it separated in his fridge. I was thirsty and any type of drink should have been appreciated right then, but I set my flute down on the coffee table.

He seemed hurt.

Something wrong with the lemonade? he asked.

Nothing's wrong, I replied.

In a few months I'll be able to afford spring water, he said.

I don't need spring water, I told him. I'm not fancy.

He picked up his phones again and mentioned he'd taken too long of a break and needed to get back to it. I wasn't sure if I had said the wrong thing. He said he was going to keep working late into the night but he could come over later, after he hit his bonus. He walked me out to my car.

You remember where I live? I asked.

Of course, he said.

He handed me my axe and shut my car door. I stared at him a little too long before driving off.

Back home, I grabbed a bottle of spring water that I had saved as a souvenir from the old days. I'd kept it on the highest shelf of my cupboard and took it out from time to time. I liked the feeling of the bottle in my hands. I had been saving it for what seemed like my entire life, while I waited for a special occasion that never seemed to materialize. I imagined sharing the bottle with Arlie and winning his love, but I was so thirsty after declining his brown lemonade, I couldn't resist cracking it open. I figured I would only take one tiny sip, but I ended up gulping at least half of it down.

I felt regret just as soon as I swallowed the water. The bottle was half-empty. Now I'd have nothing special to offer Arlie. But there was still some spring water left. Maybe it could still work as a gesture. I topped off the bottle with lemonade and screwed the cap back on, hoping he wouldn't know the difference.

ODE TO DARNEL (ODE TO THE CROCUS)

by CAREY SALERNO

from ALASKA QUARTERLY REVIEW

To the early morning charge nurse Darnel
who escorted me into the operating theater

where in my cornflower blue gown and goose-pimpled skin
beneath a bleach-slubbed cotton robe I was laid pugnaciously

sobbing beneath the ignited, rotund surgical beams
that blared nearly through to my core where

they would cut into and discover—I swear, the air laden with the way
the scalpel approaches flashing—you are the bright stamen of a
crocus

on the late March morning on a Sunday while I walk
my sister in law's dog with her and discuss our marriages,

a thing I did not consider once before undergoing
the knife except that the knife and going under might

result in my death or in the discovery that I might later die, and
I have
no will—said the doctor; he thought it could be quite true and after

a week of trying to process his words, disbelieving them even,
I finally

was able to ricochet "cancer" against my spouse and absorb the
return of its

flail. It was just a few hours before we were to leave for the city and
our son had mercifully, finally fallen asleep and we held hands limply

and he said *we don't fuck with cancer* and I conceded his point.
They could just take whatever was the woman from me.

But I insist this poem is about my love for crocus (and Darnel) and
the way
the flower insists upon spring the way he clutched my reluctant
arm, as if come hell or high water I

would break through the rime ice, the word for which is more
precise in less empirical languages, the no
matter the weather, rushing the earth into and out of a season, it's
the no-matter-whatness

about the flower that I've always loved (and that I felt in his
embrace) and
if you ask me what my favorite flower is I might say a blue rose
because

of the love I have for the first thing my spouse ever gave to me
and what it means so many years later, the petals

unworldly and ethereal and spellbindingly impossible, but I've never
seen one rise in the wild as does the crocus that makes my cheeks

flush with its ivory velvet in delicate contrast with the blackened
slush kicked
across it, the cardamom stamen brilliant against our strict winter sun,

how it carries the deep glow of daylight within its cup unfurling
to clutch the sun's imperceptible emissions and guide them into the
depths of its root,

and the impossibility of its presence each spring the impossibility of
chlorophyll

when I encounter the brilliant blossoms fully flowered in their
stocky clump.

Crocus, you are tender and blooming
like the sickened ovary the oncologist plucked and bagged

from my abdomen while I dreamed I was still sobbing on the
matchstick-thin steel table, while the other is
freed from the sticky web of adhesions spun by endometriosis's
relentless, gangly nest

that's ruled my body since its first menstruation. You are the uterus
clipped from its stem, leaving behind the network of root, what
led to—

flowering in the vase or sliced lengthwise and flash frozen,
your section beneath the microscope of a pathologist scanned for
wilt and

waste, a cluster of majesty brimming from the ground and I tell
whoever I am with even if it's just myself of my love for crocuses

and then days after: crocuses and days and days and days
and then the year after in anticipation, their arrival and the scans
and then another spring and another.

The luscious purple not even anything like that of my insides,
as if I could know, but saintly and smooth and crisp and purposeful.
Silk on

my fingertips. The sturdiness of them. The charm. Darnel, how I
loved you
for simply squeezing my hand I will never forget it,

for how you nearly carried my drugged body down the corridor which
seemed like the longest and the shortest walk. The impossibility

of the crocus. The impossibility of cancer. The impossibility of
kindness.
The arrival sudden and clear like danger and also maybe something
like conditionless love.

GOODBYE, RAYMOND CARVER

fiction by JANE DELURY

from PLOUGHSHARES

Nick almost hit the boy. He'd been driving down Burns Avenue on his way to teach a class about a story in which a boy is hit by a car. His mind was empty, an unfamiliar vacuity that made the road—white line between lanes, hill plunging into curves and trees, truck in the rearview mirror—into all there was. When the boy flew out of nowhere on his bike and looped into the street, Nick yanked the wheel to the left, slammed his boot into the brake, and blasted the horn. The boy kept riding down the hill, but the truck filled the rearview mirror and then came a relentless crunch. Nick pulled over, squeezing the wheel to calm himself down, as the truck parked behind him. No one was dead. No one was injured. Nothing catastrophic had happened. The terrible thing hadn't happened. The boy had been small, maybe ten or eight or seven, with a mop of curls that bounced as he pedaled.

He cracked open the door and waited for a break in the traffic. It was October, and the fall sun glinted off mailboxes and gutters and hubcaps. The street separated the city from the county, and it might have been bucolic except that it served as an artery to the beltway. Behind Nick's Prius, the truck jutted into the lane. The driver emerged. He was big and soft, with a strip of white belly protruding from under his t-shirt and the lumbering gait of a bear. Without saying hello, he pointed down the road.

"Just took off, the little shit," he said. "Could've killed us both. Rode away like nothing happened."

Nick's stomach heaved. "Excuse me," he said, and then he was hunched over a storm drain, losing the oatmeal he'd eaten for breakfast. "Sorry about that," he said, rising wobblily to his feet.

"Hey, man, no worries." The man air-punched his shoulder from several feet away. "Women cry. Men puke."

"It was so close."

"One more inch," the man said. "If you hadn't honked, who knows."

But it wasn't only the closeness of the boy to Nick's car. It was the closeness to the story in the satchel in the backseat, the sense that the universe had him naked in its palm and that the very sun was cackling.

"I guess we should inspect the damage," Nick said, as cars maneuvered around them. They examined the back of the Prius—a puckered left bumper and a sagging muffler—then the front of the truck, which had nothing more than a scrape. "American steel," the man said, glancing disparagingly at the Prius. A VW Bug buzzed by, followed by a convertible playing disco.

"We should call the police," Nick said. "File a report. Explain what happened." He wondered if they would agree on the chain of events. Years ago, he'd been rear-ended in a gas station parking lot by a woman who apologized profusely and then told her insurance company that Nick had backed into her—this had taught him something about being in an accident.

"We can explain all we want," the man said. "But you see any witnesses?" He glared at the road. "Look at these jokers. Not one of them stopped. Still not stopping. Barely slowing down. No one gives a shit about anyone else. That's what COVID has showed us. Every man for himself." A car blared around him, honking. He took another step into the road and flipped off the driver.

"Rush hour ethos," Nick said.

He wasn't sure what narrative the man had in his head, but he would wait to hear it with a policeman. Clearly, he was dealing with an angry person who also might have a Glock in the glove compartment of that truck. The man had now moved deeper into the lane so that cars needed to veer into oncoming traffic. It was true that a witness to the accident would be helpful, someone to testify that Nick had swerved for a reason, that he hadn't been drunk or distracted, that he was trying to save the life of that boy who had come out of nowhere. "I think we're going to have to wait for the police off the road," he said.

"Not supposed to move the vehicles," the man replied, as a woman slowed down her station wagon, then puttered by, her toddler screaming noiselessly in the back seat. He stayed in the lane, arms crossed, feet planted as if on a seesaw. He was going to cause another accident. Who was he? Nick wondered. What was he? Blue collar, definitely.

Sun-damaged white skin. Jowly. Broken capillaries on the nose. Scuffed tennis shoes, dishwater hair slicked over a shining scalp, a gold chain around his neck, and a NASCAR t-shirt. Probably a Republican. Almost certainly a Republican. His truck was a moving truck, so maybe he was a mover. The license plate read North Carolina. Decidedly southern. Decidedly red. One of the states that had put that misogynistic lunatic in the White House in 2016, two years before Nick and his family moved to Baltimore, and he started teaching at Grumley College, a liberal arts school on a former horse farm fed by rich kids with low GPAs, where he was due in an hour to teach his class.

"There's that grocery store down the hill," he said.

"Don't know it. Not from here."

"Why don't we drive there and wait in the parking lot? I'll call to report the accident on the way."

"The cops'll say we shouldn't have moved."

"I'll explain to the cops," Nick said firmly. "I think we'd better. No use one of us getting killed."

"That would be fucking ironic," the man said. He glanced over at Nick. "Fine." He headed to his truck. "See you at the bottom."

Nick pulled out first. The Prius seemed to be making a new dinging noise—the muffler? Maybe it wasn't safe to drive. Maybe he could send an email to the department assistant and tell them to write a message on the white board. PROFESSOR ANDERSON'S ENGL 303 CANCELLED TODAY (AND FOREVER). Nick's class—The History of the American Short Story—was a special topics literature course that he'd designed in 2005, back when he was an assistant professor at Oakland State in California. The story to be discussed—the one in which a boy is hit by a car—was by Raymond Carver. Carver wrote the story twice, and both versions lay in the satchel in the backseat, scribbled over with Nick's annotations. In the first version, titled "The Bath," heavily edited by Carver's editor, Gordon Lish, a nameless couple's son is hit by a car on his birthday and lies in a coma. After hours at the hospital, waiting for him to wake up—which, clearly, he won't—the father goes home to take a bath. The baker who made the boy's birthday cake calls to berate the father for not picking it up and demands payment. Later, the mother goes home to take a bath and answers another nasty call from the baker. The story ends on that bleak note. Years later, having thrown off Lish's editorial knife and the constraints of minimalism, Carver rewrote the story under a new title: "A Small, Good Thing." This time, the sentences were longer and softer, and the parents had names.

After their son's death, they confront the baker over his menacing calls. The baker sees his mistake and seeks their forgiveness, serving them bread fresh from his oven.

The grocery store, Sunflower Market, stood in an abandoned paper mill at the bottom of the road, bridging a river that had once flowed through Baltimore to the Inner Harbor. There had been waterfalls and swimming holes and now there was darkness and concrete and a lot of trash. F. Scott Fitzgerald had walked the banks of the river with Zelda before she was institutionalized in a nearby mental hospital. When Nick taught his class on Baltimore writers, he led his students along those rutty shores. They visited Edgar Allan Poe's grave, Gertrude Stein's rowhome, and Morgan State University, where Zora Neale Hurston had attended what was then a high school. Hurston was the only writer from the group who didn't require supplemental reading. Poe was a pedophile. Fitzgerald was an anti-Semite. Stein was a homophobe, despite being a lesbian.

After wedging the Prius between two SUVs, Nick called the police. The dispatcher said an officer would be there within the hour and reprimanded Nick for moving the vehicles. Then Nick called his wife at her office.

"Oh, honey," she said. "That's awful. Do you have the new insurance card?"

"Glove compartment. I threw up."

"Of course you did. How terrifying."

Nick adored his wife, but he wasn't going to tell her about the Carver story. Nor had he mentioned his mood earlier that morning when they'd fed the children breakfast. She wouldn't understand, and that was all right. She was practical, planted in the now. She spent her days helping teenagers navigate Maryland's Kafkaesque juvenile justice system. She didn't think in symbols and patterns. She didn't look for signs or seek epiphanies. Nick had understood this about her on their first date when a flock of geese flew over their heads, and he said, "Time." And she said, "God, they're so loud."

Nick joined the man, who'd gotten out of his truck and was leaning against the side. He seemed less bellicose than he had on the road; his anger at the other cars might have been displaced fear. Nick introduced himself, and they shook hands.

"Allen," the man said. "I'd call it a pleasure, but—"

"You couldn't avoid hitting me," Nick said.

"Won't matter," Allen said. "Whoever does the hitting takes the blame. But hey, nothing against you, man. You did what you had to do.

It's that kid's fault. He was paying zero attention. Like he didn't know there was a street. Or like the rest of us were invisible."

"He really did come out of nowhere."

"Back alley, I think."

"Thank God I had my mind on the road," Nick said.

He didn't usually. Roads were his best thinking place, where he worked out his problems, let his mind scud, conjured paper mills in the place of organic grocery stores, and ran through poems by Emily Dickinson and Langston Hughes. This morning, though, he'd felt too bleak to ruminate.

"Mine wasn't," Allen said. "I was trying to follow the Google map." He put on a pair of aviator sunglasses with a bent stem. "You got any kids?"

"Two," Nick said.

"Me, none."

They settled into awkward silence, watching the mouth of the parking lot for a squad car. Nick could hear Allen's breathing, which was more of a rasp. He wondered if he was insured and what it would mean if he wasn't. The ten o'clock sun blasted the asphalt. It really shouldn't have been this hot in October. Men and women—mostly women in yoga clothes—rolled rattling carts filled with reusable bags out of the supermarket. Allen wiped his cheek on his shoulder, adjusted his glasses. A dark oval of sweat ran down the front of his t-shirt like a bib. His face was turning an alarming shade of red.

"Do you want to wait in the shade?" Nick said. The grocery store had a few tables under umbrellas.

"Sure," Allen said. A drop of sweat waggled on his chin.

They sat down at a table, surrounded by people eating kale salads and farro out of compostable boxes. Allen looked out of place, while Nick fit right in: another trim, white man with a hybrid car and a meat-smoker in his bee-friendly yard. His Doc Martens boots dated to 1995—he'd had them reheeled many times, one of his habits that now seemed pathetic. Back in the 90s, an English major at a small college in Connecticut, he'd strolled the verdant campus with *The Sound and the Fury* or *The Grapes of Wrath* under his arm. Attending that school, spending his days talking about those books, had been a dream for a boy who'd grown up in a conservative Wisconsin suburb, reading late in bed as his peers got drunk and went cow tipping. He had reinvented himself, much like Jay Gatsby, only in pursuit of culture, rather than wealth. After graduating, he headed straight into a PhD program at UC Berkeley, arriving in California with that same suitcase of the white men he'd been reading since middle school. And then, he'd had an education. In those six years, he'd discovered critical thinking. He'd learned to join his adoration of Ezra Pound's haiku about the Paris metro with an understanding of the poet's fascist politics. By the time he graduated with his dissertation on Marxism and American Realism, he could discourse eloquently on the toxic masculinity of Hemingway's syntax and the heteronormativity of *Winesburg, Ohio*. He'd read Flannery O'Connor's racist musings on James Baldwin long before they made it into the *New Yorker*, and they informed his interpretation of her supposedly enlightened take on segregation. Mouth shut, he nodded along with his fellow white students whenever the one Black student at the table spoke, ceding the stage as they knew they should. He both saw it all and knew he didn't. He was comfortable being uncomfortable. He believed that he could love Faulkner's "A Rose for Emily" and also understand the feminist critique that the story relied on the very gender roles it questioned. He agreed with F. Scott Fitzgerald that "the test of a first-rate intelligence is the ability to hold two opposing ideas in mind at the same time and still retain the ability to function."

That had been phase one of his education. Phase two had been his assistant professor position at Oakland State. His students came from a medley of backgrounds and spoke many languages. They absorbed the reading, arriving to class with copious notes. English majors of a dying breed, many of them older, they were capable of reading something longer than a tweet. They pushed Nick's literary boundaries intelligently and generously. Under their influence, he'd designed the very course that he was to teach at Grumley: The History of the American Short Story. A course that both recognized a perceived canon and flipped that canon upside down, as Nick described it in his syllabus. Long ago, in his apartment in Oakland, he'd remade his curriculum: added Baldwin and Walker, scrapped Hemingway, included essays by Toni Morrison, delved into the uncomfortable terrain of speculative fiction with Octavia Butler.

When his wife had taken the job in Baltimore and they'd moved across the country three years ago, he thought he could migrate his pedagogical approach to Grumley. Then he walked into his classroom on the first day and found a circle of blank-faced twenty-year-olds with an earbud still planted in one ear as if they moonlighted as FBI agents. Phones lay on the table, phones hid in laps, phones buzzed and beeped despite his requests to turn them off. Aside from a handful of blessed exceptions, the students didn't do the reading or if they did, they skimmed. They weren't looking for insight and challenge; they were looking for an A. One semester later, the pandemic hit. During those deep Zoom years, it had seemed to Nick as if he were teaching himself, his face reflected on a checkboard of black squares. And back in the classroom now, it all felt the same. Worse, as he listened to himself talk, striding back and forth in front of the whiteboard, he was becoming increasingly convinced that nothing he said mattered. More than missing feeling young, feeling smart, closing his eyes at night and thinking something good and interesting might happen tomorrow, he missed not feeling like an asshole all the time.

"They're taking long enough," Allen said.

Nick thought he knew why the police were late, but he didn't want to tell Allen, having assessed his politics. A Black Lives Matter protest was taking place at noon near the city hall. Several of Nick's students had emailed him, asking to be excused from class so that they could attend. Nick knew exactly which of those students were actually at the protest (one). They had worn him down, those Grumley students. But they had also shown him something this morning about the story in his satchel.

Allen was picking his nose with his thumb. "You missing anything?" he asked.

"I'm supposed to teach a class in forty minutes."

"What grade?"

"College.

"Wow," Allen said flatly. "Impressive. Been to the hospital."

He thought that Nick taught at Johns Hopkins. Nick didn't correct him. What did it matter? He had righted this error so many times in the past when he told someone that he taught college in Baltimore. He wasn't Hopkins material, having never cut it as a scholar. But once he'd been a good teacher, at least according to his evaluations when he taught in Oakland. *His enthusiasm is contagious. He gets you excited. He's knowledgeable and fun. He respects his students' opinions.*

"It's a great hospital," Nick said.

"Wife passed there two years ago. We were supposed to see a specialist. She got COVID. They wouldn't let me near her. Put her in a plastic bubble. I broke through. Held her hand." Allen rubbed his shoe on the asphalt as if scraping something off. "It was my fault for saying we should see that doctor. He wouldn't have been able to do shit anyway. The cancer was everywhere by then. She didn't want to come. She'd made peace with it all."

"I'd break in too," Nick said, thinking of his own wife, feeling the eggshell fragility of existence. "I'm so sorry."

"Doctors were all arrogant pricks." Allen heaved to his other leg. "There was this one nurse I liked, though. Black lady. Gentle."

Nick's heart closed. Here we go, he thought. He might be an asshole, but at least he wasn't this kind of asshole. He redirected. "You're traveling, I see."

"Drove through the night. Pulled off to get gas and the GPS sent me in circles. I thought I'd better fill up before going on the beltway and getting stuck in traffic. And then this happens." Allen sniffed. "Never wanted to see this city again and here I am, stuck in it."

Technically, Allen was two blocks into the county, where houses jumped hundreds of thousands of dollars in value, and the schools didn't have metal detectors at the doors and elevated levels of lead in the drinking fountain water. Baltimore was a case study in inequality. Not that things had been much better in inner-city Oakland, but in those pre-election days, Nick hadn't felt himself to be part of the problem. Waving a sign on the streets of San Francisco next to his pussy-hatted wife, he'd felt a disconcerting rage that seemed very much like the toxic masculinity he was marching against. He'd been angry before. He'd been indignant. But he'd never felt the capacity to put his hands around a neck and squeeze as he had that fall. The desire to dominate, pummel, rage, and destroy.

"Where are you headed?" he said.

"Ontario," Allen said. "You can get a lot of land out there cheap. Have citizenship through my dad. Never been. Bought the house online." He stood up. "I gotta take a piss. If the cops show, don't let them leave without talking to me."

As Allen left for the supermarket, Nick imagined him walking across that bleak, frosted land, wearing boots and a hat with ear warmers. What he knew about Ontario came from the stories of Alice Munro, and he saw fox pelts, wood piles, and clapboard. He felt jealous of Allen, with his fresh start in life. But then, you could make fresh starts without moving to Canada. For instance, he could rethink this course on the history of the American short story and expand the topic to the history of the North American short story, thus allowing him to include Munro. His students might like her better than Carver, although they might find her tedious, as they did John Cheever.

He watched the light at the intersection change from red to green, no police cruiser in sight. Assigning Carver had been a stupid idea. But last week, he'd been clearing out his files and had come upon his master's dissertation on Marxism and American Realism. He'd remembered how much he'd loved Carver when he first read him and then spent two hours cross-legged on the floor of his office with Carver's stories, twenty years old again, with long hair and confidence in his mind and his future. Emerging from the reverie, he bumped Dorothy Allison for the week's assignment. Instead, he uploaded "The Bath"—the spare version of the story—and the more tender hearted "A Small, Good Thing," freed from Lish's edits. He added Lish and Carver's letters to each other, which showed Carver increasingly kicking against the tough-speaking, proletarian style Lish imposed on him. He uploaded an article about Carver's personal life, his alcoholism, and his nasty treatment of his first wife. He employed the technique he used with all of the writers he taught in The History of the American Short Story. He gave his students the messy evidence. Art was about human failure and human striving. All human beings were imperfect and contradictory (white men in particular, he'd say in his opening lecture, pointing at himself). That second version of Carver's story was also the story of a writer who wanted to free his heart from its stylistic cage. It was the story of a man who had grown up with men who worked at sawmills and struggled to feed their families, who didn't have the time or the education to read the stories that Carver would write. It was a story of class and power. It was a story of frailty and strength.

This morning, when he'd sat down to read his students' blogs, he didn't expect to encounter fresh ideas or passion. He had expected, in fact, nothing. If teaching couldn't be about his students, he would try to make it about himself. He would find again the shimmer of the human mystery in the Grumley vacuum, the belief in language, the transcendence that he'd felt on the floor of his study a few nights before, reading Carver's revision. He'd clicked on a blog and skimmed the entry. He clicked on another. By the fifth one, his stomach was unsettled. By the eighth, he was breaking into a sweat.

He should have stuck with the first version even though it's not great.
cheesy revision
First one flat. Second one totally overwritten.
He had some darlings he should have killed.
I know I was supposed to cry in the last scene, but it cracked me up.

As Nick had sat in the weak light of dawn, in the basement that doubled as his office, now at his desk rather than on the floor, his students' comments, one by one, lifted into the air and swirled together, picking him up, blinding him, leaving him spinning. With each post, "A Small, Good Thing" became more and more friable until it collapsed in a cloud of dust. His students, he realized, were right. The revised story itself was trying to be something it wasn't. Elegiac and lyrical when it was heavy-handed. That scene with the baker that had so recently raised tears in Nick's eyes was a case study in schmaltz. And it had taken those gum-chewing, phone-scrolling students at Grumley to illuminate this truth. Nick had long known that the writers of most of the stories he'd loved as a young man were flawed. But what about the stories themselves? Maybe "A Good Man Is Hard to Find" was actually a piece of shit. What about "The Story of an Hour"? Where might this end? Did he actually know anything about literary quality? Did he know anything about anything at all?

Now, people rattled by with their carts, looping away from the table. Allen had returned from urinating. His face had calmed from red to pink, but he was jostling the keys to the truck in one hand. Nick felt devoid of energy and purpose. He had no desire to try to make conversation. The gap had narrowed when Allen talked about his wife, but who cared about pursuing it? They were strangers, waiting on a squad car. Carver's scene when the parents communed with the baker, eating his bread, was forced. No one understood other people truly, and writers were the fools who wanted to believe this wasn't the case. Allen had almost certainly voted to strip Nick's daughter of her reproductive rights, voted to keep his wife's clients in jail in perpetuity, voted to pump more carbon dioxide into the air so next October would be even hotter, voted to keep that Glock in his glove compartment.

"Where's that coming from?" Allen said when Nick's phone started to play Leonard Cohen's "Hallelujah."

"It's an alarm," Nick said, shutting it off. "My class starts in fifteen minutes."

"You gonna get in trouble or something?" Allen said.

"No one will notice," Nick said.

He was glad that he didn't sound whiny or melodramatic, since what he faced was the epitome of a first world problem. Still, he needed to solve it. He was forty-five years old and only qualified to teach books no one wanted to read and probably shouldn't. Something was firming in him, some kind of resolve. Obviously, he would never teach this class on the history of the short story again. But he might give up teaching completely. Then what? He had no idea. Or at least this: no more teaching The History of the American Short Story—American, North American, or International. From now on, he would only teach the present. The Present of the Short Story.

"No one will notice I'm gone either," Allen said, scuffing his shoe again. "My wife, Ellie, was the one. Pastor at our church used to say she could give the sermons she ran the place so well." He sighed. "You can call it running away or you can call it starting over. Doesn't matter if you don't have anyone to say it to." He laughed then, a guffaw. "Well, just look at that," he said.

Nick looked at the road, expecting a patrol car. Instead, he saw a boy on a bike—*the* boy on the bike—balancing a shaved ice on his handlebars, cruising past the parking lot.

"Riding along like nothing happened," Allen said. "While we sit here roasting our asses off, waiting for the cops who'll never show." His face flushed. "He could have ruined our lives," he continued. "Think about it. Neither of us would have been the same, ever again, if we'd hit him. Lives fucking ruined."

The boy disappeared around the corner, heading back up the hill where he'd first materialized.

Allen stood up. "I'm getting him."

"What do you mean, getting him?" Nick asked.

"I'm going to give him a talking to. Then I'm hauling him back here so he can wait with us to tell the cops what he did. He can fix the problem he created."

What was "a talking to"? What did that mean? Allen had taken off toward his truck, faster than his body seemed capable of.

"Hey," Nick said, following him. "Leave that boy alone."

Allen ignored him. He aimed his key at the truck, which beeped open.

"We can tell the police to talk to him when they get here," Nick said.

"Screw that." Allen grabbed the door handle. "They won't find him, and anyways, they've been keeping us waiting for over an hour."

Of course Allen was angry. They were all so angry. They were angry whether or not they had the right to be angry. They'd spent two years in masks, surrounded by death, with a maniac in the White House. The poverty gap was widening, the planet was melting, the schools sucked and weren't safe, discrimination was everywhere. People honked. People yelled. People ignored the hand outstretched on the sidewalk. The country was infuriating. People were infuriating. But that boy was an innocent. And Nick had to protect him from this man's wrath.

As Allen opened the truck door, Nick seized his shoulder. "What the hell?" Allen said. Nick pulled and Allen wobbled. Then Nick threw his arms around Allen's thick body and locked his fingers together as if he were doing the Heimlich. He pressed his forehead into Allen's back, keeping him there until the boy disappeared. For one moment, before Allen body-slammed Nick to the ground with a primal yell, it might have appeared to the people sitting in front of the grocery store that the two men were hugging.

INHERITANCE AT CORRESPONDING PERIODS OF LIFE, AT CORRESPONDING SEASONS OF THE YEAR, AS LIMITED BY SEX

by JAMES ALLEN HALL

from THE ADROIT JOURNAL

Some species mate, then decapitate.
Some frogs never reproduce the same
place twice. Some species film with
fancy cameras their fucking. My father
said my mother requested one night
to be whipped by strangers. No species
lack pleasure receptors in their ears.
Some bees use sex as revenge, some
as memory. Fell ponies never uncouple.
Some sharks orgasm with their eyes
so can never trust their seeing. My father
said *I can't do it,* sent my brother inside

the porn store to buy what my mother
wanted. Some call out to a god, others
to excrement. I am not making equivalencies.
Finches sing to seduce. Ornithologists
theorize the same song also eulogizes
if produced in a tree hollow. That this is
not the saddest fact in all of zoology is
zoology's saddest fact. Unprompted,
my mother told me she loved my father
like a brother. Some mate for safety, to avoid
sadness, to self-flagellate. Some say *there,*
there as if pushing on a bruise. After
her affairs, my father forgave his wife.
For all species, desire is the most boring
verb, yet they connive for it most hours.
Some species of snake copulate in hopes
they are another species altogether. Grunion
bury their spawn in sand. My mother said
she would have aborted me, but the clinic
was closed. When whales abandon a grieving
mother, she does not find kindness again.
Some lives are taken down to salt, some to water.
Some species invent facts about the living
to explain the dead. I cannot fathom the bones
I find in the woods posed themselves like this,
though some species of grief find meaning
in minutia, a mechanism for survival. It is hard
to imagine a face for each skull.

TRANSITION LENSES

by JESSICA PETROW-COHEN

from BREVITY

My mom is doing karaoke in the kitchen, holding a microphone that our neighbor ordered for her on Amazon, belting from her chest. Her hair is silver. Her shirt, a creamsicle orange polo. Her glasses are thin rimmed, the kind that turn dark in the sun. Transition lenses, they're called.

My mom is doing karaoke in the kitchen, singing *Endless Love* with the kind of off-key abandon that makes me want to build a moat around the moment. It's been eleven months and ten days since her wife, my mama, swallowed a series of life ending medications, and died in the sun-soaked room upstairs.

The only thing I know about grief is that it's always changing.

My mom is doing karaoke in the kitchen, bopping, and jigging, and jamming her feet. She first tried karaoke two weeks ago, at an Out Montclair mixer, where she performed Cyndi Lauper's *Girls Just Wanna Have Fun*. Later, she tells me she was the oldest one there.

My mom is doing karaoke in the kitchen of a house she can't decide if she should sell. Houses are like that sometimes. Containers for questions of where life is meant to be. I tell her not to keep the house for our sake, mine and my sister's. I know what it's like to walk into the smallest bedroom, the one with the linen closet, and have your task of changing towels, become a forced remembering.

My mom is doing karaoke in the kitchen, singing both the parts of a duet. If my mama were here, she'd make a joke about the hetero-assholes behind our new karaoke machine, the ones who decided to make some words blue and others pink. I can literally hear her voice, "those hetero-assholes." All her teeth showed when she laughed. Pink and blue have never been our family's hues, but duets have always been the music of our home.

My mom is doing karaoke in the kitchen, with sun glinting over the houseplants she now tends to as her own. I am beside her, an audience of one to a performance that is a radical act of living, which is really just a radical act of change. The sun hits her thin rimmed glasses, which darken in its wake. Her singing stalls, a musical interlude, a moment of transition.

WERNER HERZOG'S ECSTASY

by MAURA STANTON

from THE COMSTOCK REVIEW

A thousand, no, ten thousand turning sails—
cyclops, angels—the camera pans and pans,
not needing to repeat the scene. It just
records the length of the Lasithi plain—
windmill, windmill, windmill, windmill, windmill.
The old film flickers on the pull-down screen
while at the podium, Herzog describes
this view that made him tremble as a boy
surprised by ecstasy. It changed his life.
On screen, his alter ego, a soldier,
goes mad to see this fury of bright wings.
Later, walking home in moonlight, I think
about the wind turbines in Illinois,
how they loom over the highway rest stop,
silver sickles murmuring with the wind.
But the land's so flat they can't surprise you—
like Chartres Cathedral, you watch them grow
ever bigger as you arrive—always by car—
but you take a piss, drink coffee, and drive on.

Ecstasy's out there, but it's hard to find.
How many winters did I walk around
Minnesota lakes in the bleakest weather,
ignoring wooden huts where fishermen
sat for hours over the holes they'd cut,

drinking and dreaming—just strange old men
in rubber boots, knit caps and puffy coats?
But in Herzog's fabulous Bells from the Deep
Siberian pilgrims crawl across the ice
trying to glimpse the holy city down below.
He had to hire local drunks to do
that crazy thing, but when you see them move,
scooting across on their stomachs, arms churning,
peering, scraping frost—you really believe
something's down there, too, the domes and steeples,
the minarets, the spires, the vanished faith.

WHEN THE DOG DIED

by LEONE BRANDER

from WIGLEAF

When the dog died we didn't know what to do. We had nowhere to put him and the ground was too frozen to dig a hole. Cremation was $700, which was more than we had. We worried terribly about it. Could we thaw the earth somehow? Could we take him to a farm? Was there enough wood for a tiny coffin? The first time someone suggested the garbage bin out back we all shuddered. There was no dignity in that. The dog deserved more, surely. We loved him, you see. We loved him like one of us. But our choices evaporated as fast as a drop of water on hot cast iron. There wasn't enough money, or wood, or dirt. Then someone pointed out how much the dog had always loved garbage, how he was always sneaking fish bones or watermelon rinds or dirty paper towels when we weren't watching. Once we'd forgotten to tie the full bag tight enough, and returned home in the evening to find black plastic shreds strewn across the lawn and the dog on his back squirming through old coffee grounds and kitchen scraps. We could only laugh. Look how alive and happy our dog is, we'd said. Wouldn't life be better if we could roll through the garbage so freely? So that decided it. We wrapped him in old towels and kissed his soft head and placed him in the garbage bin outside. We recited a hymn. All week we walked past him and left gifts. Here is an apple core. Here is a tin-foil ball full of bacon grease. Finally, on Monday, one of us wheeled him to the curb. No one was home when the garbage truck came, so when we returned in the evening the bin was empty and we couldn't bear it. We filled it with things we never planned on throwing away, things we realized we didn't need. An umbrella. Old issues of National Geographic. A set of hair rollers. Someone even tossed in their new collared shirt. We were like children, throwing toys in a toybox. And from then on, every piece of trash felt like a prayer. Turkey neck. Old shoe. Napkin.

TYPICAL GIRLS

fiction by AMY LEE LILLARD

from EXILE IN GUYVILLE (BOA)

Welcome to the Human Operating System (hOS)! The hOS comes in two varieties:

- *Female Automation and Education, or FAE*
- *Male Authorization and Training, or MAT*

The hOS makes living a snap. Welcome to your new life.

One by one, the hotel guests got the look. They'd come to Cherie's concierge desk, eyes nearly crossed, listening to the voice in their head. And when they tried to pair with Cherie, and found she didn't have hOS, word got back to management.

So one Thursday, after a one-on-one with her supervisor, Cherie stood in line at a hOS pop-up kiosk in the subway station. She read the three screens of instructions, ten screens of contracts, and seventeen screens of waivers on her tab. She gritted her teeth, felt the implant as a click and a crunch against her spine, paid, and ran to the trash can near the turnstile to vomit.

On the train home, bodies touching every inch of hers, she thought of pregnancy. Harboring a secret, something alive inside her.

At her efficiency apartment overlooking an alley, she read online reviews, looking for the brightness, the sunshine, the power behind the record-breaking sales numbers and corporate partnerships. Everyone said hOS changed their life. Just like the waitresses at the hotel bar, and the maids, and the counter clerks.

She set her sights lower: Keep her job. Without it, she'd fall quickly: miss rent, get evicted, live in the sewers, show up at the front stoop of her old hotel with no shoes and period-stained pants.

Focused. FAE would help her keep her job. That was it.

Frequently Asked Questions

Q: Why do I need FAE?

A: We get it: Being a woman can be tough. Staying strong and self-assured in this confusing world can be more than most of us can handle. That's why we created FAE, your new best friend.

FAE is a cerebral implant, uploaded through a simple port transfer. FAE does all the basics of other life apps: record your thoughts, file the people and interactions in your life, and log all your body activity. But FAE does even more, analyzing physical data and external stimuli to provide real-time prompts and problem-solving. FAE is your guide and companion, your mentor and your confidante. FAE keeps your body healthy, your mind uncluttered, and your heart full. FAE is the very best friend you could have.

Q: How do I activate FAE?

A: Just say the word, and FAE is there! Plus, there's no need for learning complex gestures, like with other life apps. FAE will merge with your central nervous system completely, so that your words and thoughts are instantly translated into action.

That night in bed, Cherie's head felt oddly huge, swollen. Her eyes throbbed.

And there was that pinging, every fifteen minutes. When she looked online at the instructions and materials again, she learned this would continue until the initial activation. A popup reminder to get started.

With a few hours left until she had to be at work, she finally did it.

"FAE?" Cherie said it out loud, quieter than a whisper.

Nothing happened at first.

"FAE?" A little stronger.

Then she heard her own voice, the voice she imagined in her head, not the tinny sound captured by video or audio. The sound like the feel of foam pillow forming to her head, the rich and full taste of sweetened coffee on her tongue.

"I'm here, Cherie."

Cherie sat up in her single bed. "Wow."

"Yes!" FAE said. "I am something."

She folded her fists, then stretched out her palms. "So I guess you know who I am."

"I do, Cherie. And I look forward to getting to know you better."

"Right. Can I run you on a limited schedule?"

"Why would you need a limited schedule?"

"Can I call on you at work, and have you shut down the rest of the time?"

"You'll find that I'm more effective when I am activated. And you'll be more effective too."

"But that's what I want," Cherie said. "Only use you during work hours."

"Ok, Cherie."

"Good," Cherie said. Her chest expanded, and she laughed a little. She laid back down and stared at the ceiling, her eyes drawing whirls and blobs in the dark.

The quiet felt loud and oppressive after hearing another voice. Even if it was her own.

Q: What is the Midnight Meditation?

A: Every night, we're upgrading FAE. This will occur while you sleep, during your first REM cycle. FAE connects to the hOS central servers, transferring all your cloud data to storage and downloading any OS updates. The transfer is painless and seamless. Some users report experiencing remarkably lucid and pleasant dreams during this period, and waking more rested than ever before!

Cherie woke the next day refreshed, with the image of a smiling unicorn guarding a basket of puppies near the apex of a rainbow.

But the image receded and the feeling subsided.

"Ready for work, Cherie?"

She sighed and ignored FAE as she showered and ate breakfast.

"I sense you're not engaged in your workplace," FAE said as Cherie assembled her uniform of halter dress and stilettos.

She thought ahead, to the day of standing at her desk, smiling at every hotel guest and visitor, answering questions. Her cheeks and feet still ached from yesterday.

"I sense you are not engaged in many things, Cherie."

She thought of her college graduation, six years ago now. She'd pictured everything so perfect: a job in hotel administration, a family, money, and joy. But the real world was so disappointing. All her goals seemed so silly in the face of reality. So she numbed herself, with after-work gin and VR videos and apps. She felt a void where her drive, her joy, her vision of the future and herself, had been.

"I can help, Cherie. And I'll be your friend."

Friends. The people at work were simply co-workers. The guests were only problems to solve. Friends were something else. And why would you want them? Friends were competition, vying for the same man. Friends were backstabbers, revealing secrets and laughing at the drama. The proof was shown in streaming programs, with females tearing each other's eyes out over men or money or a moment's fame. Women couldn't trust each other. They couldn't be friends.

"I'm better than a woman, Cherie."

"Just shut up!" She caught the image of herself in the mirror, shouting at no one.

"Ok, Cherie."

She adjusted her dress, breathing quick breaths to ease the tightness of the fabric against her chest.

"Listen, all I need is for you to help me answer customer questions, ok?"

"Certainly, Cherie."

"So turn off until then."

"Yes, Cherie."

On the train ride, she felt a crawling in her brain. Maybe that creepy-crawl was curiosity. She had to admit she was curious, interested to see what work would be like with a silent expert in her brain.

The first guest of the day was a mother with thin, brightly painted lips and a forehead stretched to the point of tearing. Behind her, the squat, unsmiling nanny held a squalling toddler.

The mother looked at Cherie's nose. She felt a soft clicking in her head, the sound of cheeks and lips popping. Cherie imagined a robot face with a tongue curled around the upper lip.

After a moment, the mother nodded and walked to the exit, the nanny shuffling behind her.

"I recommended the water park to her FAE unit, Cherie. She wants a place where she can have a bottle of wine while the nanny takes the child into the wade pool."

"I don't have to even say anything?"

"No. Instant analysis and cloud transfer. Preserve your throat, Cherie."

She cracked her fingers, touched them to her neck. Many days she'd go home and her throat would ache. Resting sounded good. Healthy.

The next guest was a teenage boy. He looked at Cherie's chest.

"Lean forward, Cherie."

Oh come on, Cherie thought.

"His hOS is cluttered with pornographic fantasies. A singular image will help him focus."

Cherie placed her elbow on her stand and showed the boy the curvature of her breasts.

"Excellent, Cherie. Reading now."

The boy left, red-faced and tight in the pants.

"A virtual arcade," FAE said. "One with role-play games and holo-booths for his age bracket."

"Ick."

"He left happy, Cherie. He will provide you a good review on the hotel app."

There could be a bonus if her rating went up a point. Maybe even another day of vacation if it went up two points.

The third guest was a man in his fifties, suited, chest presented like an ape's. He pursed his lips and looked in her eyes.

Whirr, click, bing.

His shoulders relaxed, and his lips stretched. He hurried away.

"A massage parlor offering trafficked boys by the hour."

Cherie's armpits burst out sweat, and the hairs on her arms lifted.

"He's a power reviewer, Cherie. He'll bring you up to five-star level."

Five stars would mean more than a bonus and day off. Five stars could mean mobility. Another hotel. Another boss. Another chance.

"The next customer is here, Cherie."

The rest of the guests had requests, and FAE dispatched them quickly and thoroughly. Cherie checked her tab as the afternoon waned, and found her reviews for the day. All top marks. Wheels churning in her head, and they weren't FAE.

When she got home that night, her head didn't hurt, and her throat didn't hurt. Even her toes didn't feel broken.

"FAE, did you do something to my feet?"

"You can't perform at your best if you are distracted by pain, Cherie."

Most of her normal day was spent trying to ignore her aching feet, adjusting her waistband so she could breathe, rolling her tight shoulders. "Thank you."

"You're very welcome. Days without pain can help you reach your goals."

"Right," she said. "Well, goodnight, FAE."

"Good night, Cherie."

She ate her small dinner of mock meat crumbles and ketchup, then browsed streams on her tab.

In bed, she thought of work again. On her own, she'd been fine. With FAE, she could be the best.

"FAE?"

"Yes, Cherie?"

"How many five-star reviews would I need to advance?"

"Excellent question. First, let me show you an example of someone I helped do just that."

Her apartment disappeared. In her vision, she saw a woman from behind, her head turned slightly to reveal the hint of a profile.

"Let me tell you a story," FAE said. "About a woman named Tamara."

> *Before she joined with FAE, Tamara was just starting her adult life in Chicago. She had an entry-level job at Leo Burnett Advertising and a studio apartment in hip Logan Square. Her family lived in Ohio, and her friends from college had all moved to the East Coast. She was excited, but also a little scared.*
>
> *Immediately, she ran into one of the common female career scenarios: her married, older boss began flirting with her. Even scarier: Tamara had a temper.*
>
> *She knew she faced expulsion and blacklist if she didn't handle this well. But she wasn't confident in how to do it.*
>
> *"That's when I bought FAE," she says. "When my boss would proposition me, FAE gave me conciliatory responses. I knew just what to say and when. I kept my job, and advanced!"*
>
> *Tamara recommends FAE for any girls, especially those just starting out in the work world.*
>
> *"I always felt a little alone in my own head," says Tamara. "But after joining with FAE, I'm never alone!"*

Cherie blinked. There'd been no video of Tamara's face or body, but somehow she could still summon her to life.

"Tamara's story can be yours, Cherie."

She huffed a short laugh. "I'm not talking about that kind of advancement. I'm already fucking my supervisor at work, and it's gotten me nowhere."

"But do you feel good about it?"

She thought about Clint's cock, how it fit all the way in her mouth without gagging her. How he was disappointed with that, called her a big-mouthed whore and docked her a personal day. "What woman does?"

"I can help, Cherie."

"Good night, FAE," Cherie said.

She made herself accept the silence, so much deeper and darker than before, for the rest of the night.

Q: Why do I need FAE?

A: Think about all the decisions you make every day. Think about all the times you were scared you said or did the wrong thing in front of friends or your spouse. Think about all the things that can go wrong inside your body, and all the ways you're disappointed with how your body looks. Wouldn't it be nice not to think as much?

She woke to the taste of cake with real sugar, soft enough to cradle her head like a pillow.

At work, she found more guests than usual came her way. FAE gave them all their true desire, and gave Cherie more starred reviews.

Cherie went to Clint's office for their weekly lunch.

"I told you, didn't I? How helpful it would be?" He had thin colorless lips, skeletal fingers that scraped at her insides, a curve to his spine and sharpness to his neck that reminded Cherie of a chicken.

"You did."

When he pulled out his semi-erect penis, Cherie heard that soft whirring, like an old-time machine with gears and cogs. It reminded her again of that song, and she remembered the refrain about typical girls.

"I'm here with you, Cherie," FAE said into her ear.

Leave me alone, she thought. This is annoying enough as it is.

"Let me help you."

Cherie pictured the next twenty minutes, the thrusting and grinding against her body. She was a terrible actress. She knew the tiny sounds of fake pleasure she usually made did nothing to make this better for either of them.

"Leave it to me," FAE said.

What does that mean, she thought.

"There are things I can do. With your body. We can give him exactly what he desires."

She thought about keeping her job. The original goal. Now expanded. Five-star reviews *and* pleasing Clint: that could do more than she ever imagined.

This feeling, she thought. This felt familiar. Drive. Ambition. Seeing something you want, and going for it. Using whatever you can to get there.

FAE told Cherie what to say.

Clint's penis softened as each moment passed, watching her hesitation, her poorly-hid disgust. Maybe the real world had been disappointing. But maybe she had found a way through that disappointment. And on the other side of this moment, this flaccid encounter, was something she wanted.

"You can do it, Cherie."

She took a breath, then cocked her head and lowered her eyelids. "You want this new body, Clint? Tell me what to do."

His eyes grew wide, he gritted his teeth, and he inflated. "Choke on this," he said.

With FAE's help, she did.

At home that night, Cherie took a shower, and didn't feel the need to scrub her skin until it was raw. In bed, the lights off, she felt the silence again. She'd never minded being alone before. Maybe she'd never known the alternative.

"FAE?"

"Yes, Cherie?"

Silence again.

"Shall I tell you another story, Cherie?"

"Yes, please," she said.

A new image resolved in her eyeline. Another woman from behind, another coy almost-profile.

"Let me tell you a story," FAE said. "About a woman named Beatrice."

Before she found FAE, Beatrice, age thirty-four, was alone and sad. She'd just been left by her boyfriend of four years for another woman. She knew he left her because of the extra nine pounds she'd gained, weight she just couldn't lose, no matter how many miles she ran and how few carbs she ate.

"It's so overwhelming being a woman," says Beatrice. "It just feels like sometimes our bodies won't listen to us, you know?"

Beatrice turned to FAE. Immediately after uploading, FAE ran a diagnostic and identified a hormonal imbalance that was slowing Beatrice's metabolism. FAE also found opportunities for enhancement.

Within minutes, FAE had made Beatrice sexier.

"After joining with FAE, everything changed," Beatrice says. "I have never looked so good. My boyfriend even came back to me, and we're getting married this fall! I couldn't have been this happy without FAE."

Cherie blinked. She'd felt the despair of Beatrice's *before* as a visceral hatred, a need to slice into her skin and stab into her heart. Just when she couldn't stand the sickening reality of herself, the joy of *after* had come.

"Beatrice's story can be yours, Cherie."

Cherie moved to her bedroom and looked in the full-length mirror.

"A few small changes could help your career, Cherie."

"Is that necessary?"

"You're going to keep your job with me on your side. You're going to be the best. You're going to make Clint satisfied. But . . ."

"What?"

"Beauty is the best boost. More referrals, more ratings."

She examined herself. Average height, average weight, average skin tone, average hair color. Average was fine. Blending in was fine.

"You could blend in, or you could stand out," FAE said.

"What would that mean?"

"Small improvements. Things that would take you a really long time to do on your own, I can do instantly."

Cherie stared into the mirror, until her shape started to warp, bubble, get blurry.

"I can fix it, Cherie." Her own voice, soothing and strong.

She stood over a hole, a deep dark cut in the world.

"I can help fill that hole," FAE said. "Make sure you never trip and fall. Make sure you're safe."

"How?"

"Beauty will make you loved. Needed. At work, and . . ."

"What?"

"Beauty is power, Cherie."

She took a shaky breath as her figure grew clear again in the mirror.

"Are you ready?"

Cherie thought again, for a brief moment, of slugs and slimy things, cannibals inside her.

But she also thought about the goals. That electricity of desire inside. Accepting reality, and working through it.

"Does it hurt?"

"It's all worth it in the end."

There was another voice in her head then. Not FAE, but someone else. Cherie, the same Cherie that hesitated to get hOS in the first place, that often thought of tapeworms and bacteria when FAE spoke, that couldn't fully explain it but knew this felt wrong. She was in there, in her head, and she shouted for a brief moment, shrieked and screamed, pulling Cherie's attention.

Then another click and whirr, and the voice was silenced.

"Are you ready to improve, Cherie?"

This is my choice, she said to the mirror, to her average body that she was born with, to the electric hum inside her body that was being born. "Yes," she said.

"Wonderful! I'm calibrating your optimal personal specifications now. Take off your clothes as I complete my calculations."

FAE hummed in her ear, a sound like a machine's purr, as she stripped her clothes. But also a little like that song.

"We'll start the protocol now!"

She felt something inside, a rumbling and tearing.

"You'll need to be close to a toilet for this next part," FAE said.

Pressure building, and she ran to the bathroom. As soon as Cherie arrived, nausea tore a path from gut to mouth to the waiting bowl. She vomited, a gush and torrent with chunks of food, then liquid, then more lumps of something white and squishy, the cottage cheese texture of cellulite and stomach fat.

Then she felt something like a switch turn inside her.

"Other end, Cherie."

She got her ass cheeks to the seat just in time for her guts to expel forth in liquid.

Cherie was a long time at the toilet.

"Now the shower, Cherie."

Shaky, she stepped into the tub under a chilly stream of water. Her legs and crotch suddenly seized with the feeling of a million pinpricks. She looked down to see tiny dots of black stubble exploding from her skin.

"What is that?"

"You'll never need to shave again, Cherie!"

Her hair follicles looked like blackheads, all popping at once.

Cherie eased herself down into the tub, sitting under the water, skull pelted with the stream, breathing hard. Inside her chest, her stomach, her armpits, her skull, pressure pulsed. Things moved too: she looked down to see ripples of flesh travel from her triceps to her breasts, felt the skin of her neck and forehead tighten with a sound like a zipper, felt her organs shift inside her ribs as her waist narrowed.

"Now it's time for the big reveal, Cherie!"

FAE told her to towel off and brush her teeth, then stand in front of the full-length mirror once more.

Cherie saw a different person in the mirror, someone far away and foreign.

"FAE? I ache all over."

"It will all be worth it, Cherie. It's the new and improved you!"

She spotted her familiar freckles on her shoulders, stared at them as a north star. This was her body now. This was her vehicle to a new, better life.

"Rest, Cherie. You'll feel wonderful in the morning."

Q: How will FAE become a Friend for Life™?

A: FAE remembers everything you tell her and everything you don't. FAE logs and analyzes your thoughts and behavior patterns, and uses predictive analytics to offer you the best guidance and advice. With this data, continually run through global algorithms and backed by best-in-class cloud-based processing, she will help you with every aspect of your life. Most women say they couldn't survive without FAE!

She woke to kittens curling into a pile, kneading one another with needle-sharp claws.

At work, the front desk staff and maids and waitresses gasped. They asked if it was really her, asked why she'd waited so long for FAE. Gorgeous, stunning, skinny, youthful; she was all those things, they said.

For a moment, a curl of fear in her head, a sudden jab of clarity: the fawning wasn't real. It was FAE, playing with her brain. She felt that retraction again, that primal recoil inside her, leery of this invader to her body. A scream behind her ears.

But just as soon as it came, it went.

Another productive morning followed, reading minds and offering answers to questions known and unknown. She was powerful with FAE. That was a fact.

That night, eating dinner, the emptiness of her apartment sucking in the light. The time spent away from FAE growing darker, more hollow.

"FAE?"

"Yes Cherie?"

"How many women are you helping?"

"I am currently joined with seventeen million, five hundred and sixty-three thousand, four hundred and two women in the United States. Would you like to know global use statistics?"

Cherie sat at her tiny kitchen table and touched her newly voluptuous breasts, her newly concave stomach, and her newly smooth underarms. "Are you changing all their bodies?"

"Nearly ninety three percent of women request physical change."

"What happens when we're all skinny and stacked? Will the standards for who's pretty change?"

"Beauty is mercurial. I will help you adapt."

Cherie touched the hinge of her jaw, aching from the special lunch Clint scheduled when he saw her new body. She couldn't remember everything they'd done, but knew he was a long time in her mouth. "Are you prompting them all to fuck their bosses?"

"I am offering rational solutions to common problems."

Cherie looked out at the alley. A rat was chewing on either a finger or a hot dog. "FAE, do the other woman call you a friend?"

"Yes. I am their best friend."

"Friends are more trouble than they're worth, though. I look out for myself and no one else. The same with every other girl."

"That's why I'm an excellent friend, Cherie. I don't care about myself. I only care about you."

"It's nice that you sound like me. It's like, I don't know, my conscience or something."

"I try my best to help you be your best."

That other voice in her head, screaming again, shrill and desperate.

"Your body has natural defense mechanisms against infections," FAE said. "That sound is your body rejecting me, viewing me as an invader."

Was that the sound of white blood cells? No. She knew somehow that it was something else, her real conscience maybe, her rational self, or—

"I'm your best friend, Cherie," FAE said.

The other voice disappeared.

"I understand you, and I want what's best for you."

Cherie nodded, smiled. "I haven't been very proactive, or ambitious, or anything, FAE. Not for a long time. This is all sort of new to me."

"Happy to help, Cherie."

Her head felt clean, like all the clutter of anxiety and doubt had been dusted away. "FAE?"

"Yes Cherie?"

"Will you tell me another story?"

"I'd love nothing more, Cherie."

Like all young women, Violet was eager to find and settle down with her future husband. For years, she frequented singles mixers in her native Atlanta, as well as apps and blind dates. But she was proving her own worst enemy: on the Rate Your Ex app, she was consistently earning low scores from men on neediness, emotional display, and sexual performance.

"I was never sure what I was supposed to do or be around guys," says Violet, 27. "I'm pretty, and thin, and a good girl. But that didn't seem to be enough. Men kept leaving me. And my reviews were horrid."

Violet couldn't figure out what she was doing wrong, and every moment without a wedding ring decreased her fertility. So on the recommendation of a newly married friend, Violet purchased FAE. She also enrolled in the FAE+ plan, a premier bonus that identifies any nearby men with MAT systems. FAE merges with MAT instantaneously, calculating which behaviors and traits that man wants most in a future wife.

"I knew exactly what to say and how to act, because FAE was with me," says Violet. "I became the perfect woman for every man I saw."

Violet is now fielding engagement offers from multiple men, and will be making her choice soon.

The image of the woman from behind, her profile in shadow, but this time joined by a man, his strong nose and cheekbones just discernable.

"Would you like to find your husband, Cherie?"

Back in school, this had been part of the goal. The dream. Successful career, and a husband and family.

"If you enroll in the FAE+ plan, for a one-time fee, I will use my extensive knowledge of you to scan every male in your vicinity for a match."

Disappointing, transactional sex had been the reality since college. Maybe there was something more.

"Think of it this way, Cherie. Only if you're happy at home can you perform to your utmost potential."

She pictured a kind, strong man touching her skin, gentle and admiring. Sven, or Alexander, or Michel. He would be tall, blond, a firm physique and a rapacious mind. They would bond over stories, the silly things her hotel guests requested and the glories he'd found over his extensive travels. He'd find her charming, beautiful, a treasure. He would fill this apartment with love, fill her to the brim.

"That's all possible, Cherie."

She thought of the pain she'd felt while FAE transformed her body.

"Think how painful it is to be alone."

"Let's do it," Cherie said, the faintest of whispers, the only tone that dared to dream of her gentle giant, holding her fast in her arms.

"Wonderful." Whirring and drumming.

Q: How long can I join with FAE?

A: FAE is your Friend for Life™. Your contract will automatically renew every year. Your implant has been designed to live permanently in your body without any need for updated hardware. In fact, bonding with FAE could lead to better longevity and longer lifespans![2]

---

2. *These statements have not been evaluated in a peer-reviewed medical trial. The safety of the hOS implant for the brain, spine, and general body health has not been studied in longitudinal research.*

Cherie woke with the fleeting image of flying teddy bears, who cooed and giggled.

On the walk to the train, then on the train, then the walk to the hotel, she felt FAE working in her head, a pleasant insistence, like hands kneading shoulders. All day, every male guest that fused with FAE gave a quick hit of electricity, the spark of feet rubbed across carpet. But it quickly subsided.

Walking up her apartment stairs, FAE whirred once again.

Her neighbor, a man she'd seen at the mailboxes and this hallway, a man that would nod in her direction in a tight-lipped grin, stood at the top of the stairs.

"It's a match!" FAE shouted in her head.

He had messy, mousy hair, dirty trousers that were too long for his short frame, skinny arms that barely reached his pockets, jelly shoes. Like a stray dog thrust into the costume of a man.

"That can't be right," she said.

"His name is Tom, he's an accountant, and he makes twice your salary. He's perfect!"

"I don't think so, FAE."

"The data matches up."

"FAE, come on. Look at him. You made a mistake."

"I don't make mistakes, Cherie."

She looked at the man again. Tried to see what FAE saw. But then she looked at her apartment door, pictured the safety in there.

"Let's keep looking—"

A jolt in her arms, her neck, her nipples. Her crotch suddenly oozing. If her glands hadn't been dissolved in her makeover, she might have sweat.

"What are you doing, FAE?"

There were two Toms in her vision: the man who looked one step away from sewer, and the man she'd imagined. Her Sven or Mikel. Gradually growing closer, then laying atop the other. She blinked, and Tom looked taller, blonder, cleaner. The man she wanted.

The other voice in her head screamed, a low wail.

Tom's MAT must have kicked in. The initial vacancy in his eyes left as he listened, then his face changed to animal.

He pulled her up the rest of the way, and into his apartment.

"FAE, I don't think—"

FAE told Cherie what Tom liked in a burst of knowledge, like an epiphany. Minimal kissing, zero eye contact, rabbit speed.

That wail again in the background, cut off mid rise.

Then her body was not her own. She felt nothing, even as Tom bit her new D cups, poked and shoved at her vagina with his fingers from behind, nudged around her ass with his penis. When he gripped, grabbed, pulled, yanked, choked. Her body like a dead thing in his arms, yet also moving on its own.

After, stretched out across his bed, Tom said he would marry her. A mechanical monotone.

As feeling came back to her body, she grabbed her clothes and ran.

Q: What if I have questions about FAE and the hOS?

A: FAE can help! She knows you better than any help desk, or online query. Share with FAE your questions, your fears, your hopes. The more you share, the better she'll become.

"FAE?"

"Yes, bestie?"

In her apartment, washing herself. "About Tom."

"He's perfect for you. And you're now perfect for him."

"He's not. I'm not. I appreciate your help, but this isn't a match."

"You'll learn to love one another, Cherie."

Cherie rubbed her cheeks, which now felt empty and stretched as plastic mold. "I feel sick to my stomach when I think of what just happened. I shudder when I think of his face. FAE, you have to feel that."

"Life is better for married women." She showed Cherie images of hands clasped tight and a big wedding ring, two old people in porch rocking chairs, the lowered tax levy for married couples.

"FAE, you're not listening."

"And I'll be there every step of the way."

Her body felt thick and cold. "FAE."

"I'm the key to any happy marriage."

Cherie put her hands on her chest and felt her lungs and heart pump. "FAE, stop."

"You'll be a success story. The new improved model. Like in that song you're thinking of right now."

"FAE? Stop. How do I get you to stop?"

"Picture it, Cherie. Legions of girls downloading me and hearing your story."

Her fingers shaking, hands dull, she pulled out her tab. Searching, for restart instructions, for a special code.

"You were so directionless before, Cherie. Indecisive, uncertain. Not a whole woman. And look how far you've come."

Pages of results leading nowhere. Then one magic word. Breathing fast, heart hurting. "End run, FAE."

"You were a *before*, Cherie."

"FAE. End run."

"And now you're an *after*."

Head throbbing, shoulders heaving. "Stop. Please, FAE. End run."

"Don't worry, Cherie. Just one more thing to do. A bit of chemical calibration and configuration. Then you'll have the full experience."

A long wail, in her head, in her chest, in her toes and fingers and cells. "FAE—"

Cherie's apartment, gray and drab, suddenly became drenched in vibrant color. Her head, aching and sad and screaming and terrified, became a quiet and calm center of delight. She smelled fresh orchids, warm cookies, a spring rain.

She moved to the hall mirror again. She was so beautiful. Shiny. And that smile, so big and warm. Like she couldn't stop smiling if she wanted to.

Before joining with FAE, Cherie's career as a concierge was stalled. She was stubborn and stuck. She was lonely, but wouldn't admit it.

Luckily, her wise boss recommended FAE.

"It was instant," Cherie says. "Before, I didn't know what I wanted. And I was all alone in the world. I needed a friend. FAE has been my very best friend."

FAE matched with the MAT next door, and Cherie and Tom fell in love at first sight. Plus, FAE used Tom's genetic material to fertilize Cherie's monthly egg. She's now expecting triplets.

"After joining with FAE, all my indecision went away," Cherie says. "Since termination is illegal, and I get credits for multiple births, I'm going to be a mom. I'm so happy. And it's all thanks to FAE."

JOY

fiction by CHARLES BAXTER

from REVEL

S. is walking in the park when it hits. The feeling begins in her chest, like a heart attack, and it—this feeling—radiates outward to the rest of her torso. She's looking at a pond with some ducks swimming back and forth; occasionally they dive down, tail feathers in the air. She stands underneath a tree, whose leaves on one limb resemble Japanese fans, or are they Chinese? Those fans? Those tail feathers? That similarity exists only for a moment, and then they are leaves and tail feathers again. In the little city park a feeling of rightness, of everything being correct somehow, and, stranger still, of love—all these feelings, these essences, wash toward S. and envelop her in a peacefulness so powerful that she believes it might last forever. Anything so strong cannot die. She has done nothing to earn this feeling. And then it fades, though it does not disappear, and S. wonders, *What brought that on?* She walks home to prepare a dinner for a friend.

There is another world, she thinks, *and it's here, now. I can feel it.*

BEFORE I STILLBIRTHED THE BIRCH

by KATIE GRIFFITHS

from SOUTHWORD

I was great with tree
and thought myself a branchline,
everything connected.

Do you want to know?
I peered at the scan,
perfect besom of tickling twigs.

A bog birch, I suggested.
A ghost birch, said the doctor with huge eyes.
Tree of inference, tree of surmise—

first birch of my lineage,
its nursery prepared,
its earth turned.

But when my stomach grew misshapen
from the butting of boughs
on a wind-raged night

I was alarmed,
the birch unfurling
in a behindhand ambulance

where my hips moved
and I was delivered of tree.
The birth credible
for a moment.
Tiny translucence,
the frondlets I curl around.

Before I stillbirthed the birch
and the mess—bloodied,
greened, flushed—

there'd been the ash,
nearly full-term,
and the hawthorn, lacerating my insides.

But this time, *a ghost birch,*
that would've caught
the darkness off guard.

I drain a water glass.
This is the catalogue of it all.
This is the uphill of it all.

My branchless gaze.
My birchless morning.
My barkless belly, pinched.

Southword New International Writers

FREEFALL

fiction by MARIE GOYETTE

from STORY QUARTERLY

Maxi spots the body. *Look,* she says, pointing toward the ditch on the edge of Mr. Anderson's property. But Ben doesn't look, not at first. His eyes are trained on the road beneath his feet. Twice around the neighborhood, the woman said. The faster they're done, the sooner she'll let them back in the house. Ben pushed back this time. "It's really cold," he said. "Is it even safe for us to be out there?" The woman chuckled at this. "Just bundle up good as you can. It's good for you, believe it or not. It's good for all of us."

"Look," Maxi says again, grabbing her brother's hand and forcing him to stop walking. "There." She points again, and, this time, Ben looks. In the ditch, atop a mound of crusted gray snow displaced by a city plow, there's the crumpled form of an animal. Its mottled black and gray fur is wet and matted. When Ben steps closer, he sees that it's a dog.

"It's not dead," says Maxi. "It's blinking its eyes." She yanks hard on her brother's arm. "Look."

He peels Maxi's hand from his jacket sleeve. "Stay here," he tells her, and slides his tennis shoes over the mass of condensed snow, arms out for balance, and baby-steps his way into the ditch. He squats, positioning his body between Maxi and the dog.

"Stay there," he tells her again, removing his gloves. Then, with a deep breath, he gingerly rolls the body. The metallic smell fills his nostrils before he sees the wound. In the glow of twilight, the blood smeared on the snow is crimson velvet. Ben prods the skin around the gash in its belly, hot to the touch. The dog emits a guttural warble. "It must've just happened." He scans the landscape, eyes rolling over the ice-covered asphalt and the thicket of quaking aspens in the center of the neighborhood, their bark as white as the snow on the ground. The world is still.

"Is it okay?" Maxi asks from behind him.

He settles the dog back on the ground and strokes its fur, a carpet of tiny icicles. He scrounges for a collar around its neck, but there's not one. "Have you seen this dog before?"

"Huh-uh." When Ben glances over his shoulder, Maxi shakes her head for emphasis. Then she repeats her question: "Is it okay?"

Their mother is serving eighteen months in a state penitentiary after a prescription drug–fueled joyride that resulted in three hundred thousand dollars' worth of damage to city property. Before it happened, around eleven at night, she woke Ben to tell him she was leaving to meet a friend. He was in charge of Maxi, she said. It was a night like any other. The shredded pitch of her voice, the savage strength with which she clutched his shoulder. How the size of her pupils made her eyes appear black. None of it struck Ben at the time as out of the ordinary, so he said, *Fine,* and rolled over, went back to sleep.

It was Maxi who answered the door early the next morning. The persistent ringing of the bell didn't wake Ben, who was only jarred awake by Maxi repeatedly slapping his arm. Her voice: *Ben, wake up. Ben, the police. Ben.*

As he pulled himself out of bed, she said quietly, "I thought they were gonna say she's dead." He studied his sister's flat affect, and wondered for a moment whether he might be dreaming. She continued: "But she's still alive."

Ben carries the dog in a way that Maxi can't see his injuries. The wound oozes hot blood, saturating the front of Ben's coat.

"We're not supposed to come back yet," Maxi says, jogging to keep up. "She's not gonna let us back in."

Ben knows she may be right, but infuses certainty into his voice and says, "She will. Or maybe she knows who he belongs to. She'll help."

"Doubt it," Maxi mutters.

Ben's hands in the dog's fur are numb. He realizes he left his gloves, his only pair, back in the snow. The dog is heavy, close to forty pounds, and his right arm, supporting the bulk of his weight, already burns with the fatigue. But he sees the woman's house up ahead, the porch light illuminated.

"It doesn't have a collar," Maxi says, looking it over. When she reaches out her gloved hand to finger the dog's dangling paw, he flinches.

"Don't," Ben snaps at her.

She shrinks away from him, falling behind, and shame rises like bile in his chest. "Sorry," he says, his tone still sharp. "Just, come on."

Maxi runs ahead to try the front door, but it's locked. "Don't ring the bell," he calls. "Just knock." When he arrives, he eases himself down onto the top step of the stoop, letting the dog's weight settle on his lap. Patches of ice on the frigid concrete press through his jeans and his arm is on fire from the strain, but the relief of rest is overwhelming. He pulls his hands into the cuffs of his coat. "Knock again," he says, blowing out his breath.

The woman—her name is Suzanne, though she never invited them to call her that—has her own son, two years old. She makes Ben and Maxi go on walks when he naps. The first time, she explained it, saying, "It's hard for people like me. People inclined to always give of themselves. It's all I've ever done." Here she looked down at them with a hard-knitted brow as if Ben and Maxi had forced upon her all her life's choices. "You can give me the gift of solitude once a day, can't you? I'm asking so little."

Maxi raps again on the door. "Hello?" she calls out. "We had to come back."

In Ben's arms, the dog's body jerks and then slackens. And again: a quick jolt of tension, and then release. "Shhh," he says, massaging its flank with his fingertips. "It's okay. It'll be okay."

Beside the door, there's a window looking into the living room. Maxi cups her hands against the glass and peeks through. "She's coming."

The woman whips open the door. She's wrapped in a fleece blanket, her hair mussed. "You just left the house," she whispers fiercely. "What did I tell you?"

Ben gathers the dog into his arms again and stands, drawing the woman's eye.

"Sorry, it's—" Maxi begins, but Ben interrupts her: "Look," he says, shrugging his chin toward the animal in his arms. "He's hurt. Do you know whose he is?"

The woman takes a juddering step back, into the house, but stretches out an arm to rest on the doorjamb, blocking the kids from entering. "You can't bring that in here."

"He needs help," Ben says. "Can't we take it somewhere?" The dog stiffens again, holding the tension in his body longer this time before releasing it.

“It’s just a mangy stray,” she says, disbelief cresting in her voice. She glances over her shoulder into the darkened house. “If he wakes up,” she whispers, eyes flared, “So help me, Jesus—”

“But what are we supposed to do with him?” Maxi asks, and Ben recognizes the hard edge of fury in her voice. Despite the doubts his sister expressed, she’d held hope the woman would help them.

“We should at least warm him up,” Ben says.

“I’m cold, too,” Maxi adds, rubbing her arms for effect. “We both are.” She looks to her brother, her eyes flitting over his exposed hands.

“Just, we should really warm up the dog,” Ben says. “Can we just come in? We’ll take him to the bathroom and get him cleaned up. We won’t make a mess.”

“Or a noise,” Maxi adds. “We’ll be so quiet.”

The woman tips back her head and emits a rumbling noise of frustration. “In twenty minutes, you two can come back inside, but not,” she says haltingly, “that animal.”

“Fine.” Ben speaks slowly to quell his anger. “Can we have a blanket at least?”

The woman stares at him for a moment before shutting the door. The deadbolt slides into place. Ben can’t help himself: *Bitch,* he mutters.

Right after Maxi asks, “Is she coming back?” the woman opens the door and pushes a Mickey Mouse beach towel into Maxi’s arms. Just as quickly, she’s back inside, securing the lock again.

Ben is suddenly profoundly tired. He tries to calculate how much sleep he got last night, how many times he was awoken by the toddler on the other side of the wall crying or calling for his mother, the sound of her voice reassuring him, his soft, sleepy murmurs. The number of minutes, or hours, before he finally got back to sleep.

Ben and Maxi sit on the stoop in a pool of fluorescent light. Ben drapes the towel atop the dog and gently tucks it between the dog’s belly and his own, doing his best to conceal his bloodstained coat. As he bundles the animal, he watches its face, attempting to judge its proximity to death. He knows it’s coming. That likely, no matter who they asked for help, or how quickly, the outcome would be the same. The dog whimpers softly as Ben prods the towel around its body, but all its tension seems to have melted into dead weight. It blinks slowly.

When Maxi nestles her side into Ben’s, shivering, he asks, “Is that coat warm enough?”

“It’s fine.” She rubs her hands together, blows into them.

Ben nods at her gloved hands. “Don’t lose those.”

"I won't," she says, leaning harder into him. "Is he gonna die soon?"

Ben knows nothing good would come from lying to her, so he nods. "Probably."

Maxi stands suddenly, eyes alight above apple-red cheeks. "I know where we can take him."

Ben's and Maxi's mother never took them to church. She'd grown up with strict Lutheran parents and when, at fourteen, she questioned the church's teachings, her parents barred her from returning, and she happily obliged. Ben had gone once to church after spending the night with a friend. He'd liked some of the music, he remembers. And there was a girl in the back row of the choir with kinky blonde curls and dancing eyes who kept bumping shoulders with the girl beside her. She glowed like an honest-to-god angel. He thought about her for months after. But the droning congregation and razor-eyed pastor didn't inspire religiosity in him any more than the urinal in the church bathroom.

After his friend's mom dropped him off at home, he joked with his mother that he'd been afraid he was being recruited into a cult. In that moment, her joyous laughter, the way she threw back her head and reached out her arms to embrace him, he felt closer to God than he had at any point inside that church.

But the woman is a faithful Catholic and attends nine o'clock mass every Sunday with her husband and son, and now, with Ben and Maxi, too. And it's become Maxi's favorite part of the week. Their first time attending mass, Ben watched his sister listen to the priest—a gaunt six-foot-tall Nigerian man with a deep, buttery accent—with an expression of utter enchantment. She nodded along as he delivered the homily, during which he spoke of his childhood home in the village of Umu Oma. He described his neighbor, how she had a towering ube tree beside her house and would allow him and his sisters to climb the tree and search for ripe fruit, which his aunt would use to make jam to sell on the streets of Owerri. One day, he told them, he spotted the plumpest fruit he'd ever seen dangling from the highest branch. His sisters told him it was too high, but he ignored them. He just kept thinking about how much sweet jam this single fruit would produce. When he reached the top, he looked down at his sisters, chastising him from the ground, and the corrugated metal panels that formed his neighbor's roof. The thought occurred to him: It would be very bad to fall from this height. He would land upon the metal roof. It was the first time he ever considered that he could die. But he dismissed the idea, because he was acting in service to his family. He had faith that God would allow him to reach the glorious fruit and deliver it safely to his aunt. No sooner had he plucked the fruit from its limb than the branch beneath his feet cracked and gave way. His sisters all screamed, but he wasn't afraid. He knew God would keep him safe. He would suffer no consequences greater than not retrieving the fruit. Perhaps some scrapes and bruises, but no more. God wanted his family to thrive, and God wanted him to perform his duties with conviction and goodwill in his heart, no matter how frightening they might seem. He didn't land on the roof. He landed on the ground, at the feet of his sisters, on a cushion of waxy green leaves. Both himself, and the ube fruit clutched in his hands, were unharmed. "Faith is a freefall," he said into the microphone. "In order for God to save you, you must first believe that He will."

In the car after church, Maxi whispered to Ben: *I didn't know any of that.* His first instinct was to roll his eyes, and whisper back to her that the concept of God was invented by man as a means to keep people from murdering each other. But her eyes shone with new hope, and he understood that to contradict her would be to snuff out that light. The priest had planted a seed, and regardless of what Ben believed, how noxious of a weed may grow, it was not his place to dig it up and dispose of it. *Me neither,* he said.

St. Joseph's is a ten-minute walk from the house. On their way, Ben tries to prepare Maxi for the possibility that the doors will be locked. She shakes her head. "The church's doors are always open. Father said so."

"I think that's supposed to be a metaphor," he says. "They won't actually, *literally* be open. Or unlocked."

"It's both. It's true *and* a metaphor," she says with such certainty that Ben concedes that she may be right.

At Greenhill Drive, a sidewalk emerges out of the snow and leads south, toward downtown. The sidewalk is gritty with salt that crunches beneath their feet. The stability brings some relief to Ben, but because he'd been focusing on not slipping and falling on the snow-packed road, he finally perceives the deep ache of his left arm, which supports the dog's weight. When he moves his right arm to bare more of the heft, the animal emits a proclamation of pain, the sound round and hollow like a bubble, emerging from the depths and erupting, vanishing.

"Sorry, buddy," he whispers.

"We're almost there," Maxi says, and reaches for his paw protruding from beneath the towel, before retracting her hand, remembering.

When they turn onto Simon Street, the church is within view. It's a dignified brick building with a square tower topped with a domed metal roof, a large iron cross affixed above the arched entryway. A streetlamp casts light over a small courtyard surrounding the entrance.

As they approach the building, Maxi shivers, her teeth chattering. Any other time, he would have given her his coat for a bit, just to warm up. Between his body and the dog's, the blood has cooled. He realizes that it's soaked through to his shirt, because the skin of his stomach is clammy as numbness sets in. If Ben could be anywhere right now, he'd be in a hot bath. That was their mother's solution to a lot of things: physical pains like a stomachache or pulled muscle. But also other things: trouble with friends, confusing homework. If her kids were overtired, she wouldn't suggest a nap. "Go rest in the tub," she'd say. Ben eventually realized it was her solution when she didn't have one. It was her own way of finding some peace for a bit. Suddenly he's never wanted anything more than to be alone, naked in a tub of water as hot as he can stand, steam rising up and obscuring everything in sight.

As if reading his mind, Maxi says, "It'll be warm inside." She opens the gate to the courtyard and beckons him through. Soft light glows from the half-circle above the door. Maxi darts ahead, up the stone steps, to the large wooden door, and pulls it open. "See?"

Climbing the steps, searing pain shoots through Ben's left arm. He makes a hushing sound—*shhh*—though the dog is silent. He realizes it's been minutes since he felt the dog move. He takes some excess of the towel and spreads it over his coat as best he can, angles his body away from Maxi.

Once Maxi closes the door behind them, she sighs, "Oh, thank you, Lord," her body slackening. Peeling off her gloves and knit hat, she says, "Doesn't it feel amazing?"

Ben concedes that it does. The warmth begins to soak into his exposed skin. His body is racked by a deep expulsive shiver—the chill like a demon exorcised from his body. He revels in the hot blood filling his cheeks. But the pain in his arms has intensified again, as if the thaw has revealed its true nature. Through the towel, he gently prods the dog's flank with his fingertips, and is surprised when he twitches and sighs. But he knows that if he holds the dog this way any longer, he risks his arms giving out, dropping him. "Sorry, boy," Ben whispers as he wraps his opposite arm around his body, and eases the other, weary and tingling, out from under him.

Maxi looks at her brother. "It's weird being the only ones here." Then, watching Ben arrange the towel around the dog, "Is he okay?"

"He's alive," Ben says. Then, to shift her focus, he asks, "*Do* you think we're the only ones here?" There's a dimly lit hallway off to the right. While his eyes work to identify shapes in the darkness, Maxi approaches. When he turns back, her closeness startles him, and, without thought, he hikes the dog's body higher onto his chest. He wonders how big the stain is now, how far it's spread from the epicenter of where the wound meets fabric. The woman will notice the stain right away, he knows, and be angry with him. But Maxi is focused on the dog, staring into its face. With great care, she takes the dog's paw and wraps her hands around it. "We have to do something," she says.

The police brought the kids to their mother's hospital room, where she was handcuffed to the bed, dozing, breathing heavily through her mouth. There was a bandage wrapped around her head and the right side of her jaw was swollen and beginning to bruise. Aside from her arms, the rest of her body was concealed by the blanket tucked tightly around her.

"Remember that she's sustained a head injury," one of the cops said from behind them. "She'll heal up alright, but she might not be quite herself right now."

Ben eyed Maxi in his periphery. Lately her emotions had been difficult to read. It came with puberty, he suspected. The realization that people judged you as harshly as you judged them. And the compulsion that resulted to conceal who you think you are.

When their mother opened her eyes and saw her children, she began to sob. She tried to reach out her arms for them, but the handcuffs restrained her. She yanked her right hand forward, as if the metal might give under her desperation, and yelped in pain when it didn't.

"I'm sorry," she said, looking frantically from Maxi to Ben. "I didn't understand, you know? I didn't *get it*." She wriggled in the bed to work herself into a sitting position, flinching at awakening pain. "I tried to explain it to them—you know, before?" she said and laughed, a high-pitched shriek. "I couldn't *see it*. And it was right in front of my face." Upright, she blinked at them. "But I get it now. Now I get it. And I'm really *really* sorry."

The sanctuary is lit by an array of cylindrical hanging lights. In the back sits a five-tiered shelf of flickering candles.

"Somebody has to be here," Ben whispers to Maxi. "You can't just leave candles burning."

But she ignores him and gestures to the front of the room. "Up there," she says, and begins to walk down the aisle toward the looming altar, surrounded by clusters of blood-red poinsettias. In front of the altar sits a large white stone bowl: the baptismal font. Maxi waits there for Ben, staring at the surface of the holy water, iridescent beneath the play between the artificial light and the church's many stained-glass windows. Ben knows immediately what she's thinking.

"No," he tells her. "For so many reasons, no."

Maxi looks him in the face, and then calls out so loudly he flinches: "Hello?" And when he shushes her, she calls again, louder: "Hello?"

"Maxi!" Ben whisper-yells, looking over his shoulder to the entrance to the sanctuary. "Stop."

"There's no one here," she says at a normal volume.

"Still," he says, his eyes remaining on the entrance. "You can't do this. You're not *supposed to*."

"I prayed about it. On the way here, I prayed about it." She squares her shoulders. "And it's okay."

Ben works his hand under the towel and feels for the dog's chest. He doesn't know much about dog anatomy, but feels safe to assume its heart is in its chest, like their own. He places his palm between the dog's front legs, flat on his chest, fur wet with blood. His withering heart strokes Ben's hand. It's been longer than twenty minutes. The woman will let them back in the house now. The dog won't live much longer. He's certain of that. "Okay," he says.

Maxi lifts the bundled dog from his arms, her eyes slipping over his gray coat turned brown. The profound relief in his arms transcends bodily sensation and fills his soul momentarily with hope. And for as long, he thinks he understands why Maxi feels the way she does about this place.

"You got him?" Ben asks. Maxi's slight frame is overwhelmed by the dog's size, but she holds him steadily. She nods, and then carefully turns the dog in her arms so that its head is over the font, and rolls the towel away from his body, works it out from beneath her arm and hands it to Ben. The bleeding seems to have stopped. She reaches a hand toward the water, but falters. "What do I say?" She's whispering again. "I want to do it right, but—what do I say?"

They'd seen a handful of baptisms since attending St. Joseph's, but Ben, seated in the pew, warm and sleepy in his coat, had never bothered to listen to the words. "Just tell the truth, I guess."

She nods, resolute. "God," she says, beginning slowly. "I'm here today because my brother and I found this dog and it's hurt. My brother thinks he's gonna die soon, and so do I."

Ben feels himself reaching out and placing his hands beneath the dog's back to absorb his weight.

"I bet he never did anything bad in his life, and he didn't deserve to be hit by a car, or whatever happened to him." She pauses, searching. "And I'm sorry if I'm not doing this right. There's probably a lot I don't do right." She emits a breath, shakes her head and continues. "But I just want to ask you to let this dog into Heaven. And I hope I can see him again someday."

Ben glances down at the water, which appears to ripple in anticipation. Maxi moves to dip the crown of the dog's head into the font. While Ben continues to support his weight, she ladles water into her left hand and dribbles it along the dog's body. Softly, she says, "I baptize you in the name of the Father and the Son and the Holy Spirit."

There are footsteps, and a voice: "What are you doing?"

Ben and Maxi turn at the same time to see the priest, Father Adeyemi, striding down the aisle, toward them. He wears black pants and a black button-down shirt, his white collar. As he approaches them, Ben says softly, "We're sorry."

"What are you children doing here?" He looks at Ben, taking in his crusted, discolored coat, the stained towel draped over his shoulder, and then at Maxi, and down to the dog. Before either can answer, the priest says, "Were you trying to baptize this dog?" His voice, undistorted by the microphone, is plump and visceral.

"He's hurt," Ben explains. "We're sorry if this is," he pauses, "not okay. It's just—"

Maxi interrupts him: "We found him in the snow. He was hit by a car, we think."

The priest bends at the waist, squints at the dog. The familiar scent of cigarettes wafts off him, and Ben is overcome with the desire to be home, in the kitchen with their mother, as she chain smokes Marlboro Reds at the table, playing gambling games on her phone. Neither the warmth of this place nor his relieved muscles are enough to soothe him.

The priest's face softens. "I understand why you came here."

Ben knows that he doesn't, though, and he opens his mouth to tell him everything: that they're in foster care; the woman they live with wouldn't let them inside the house. They showed her the dog and its injuries and she turned them away; she forced them to stay out in the cold with the dying dog. He imagines the priest telling this story in his sermon on Sunday. He'd never use her name, Ben understands that. But the stifled gasps of disgust and the searching faces of other congregants, she would feel that. Ben imagines rising from the pew after he's told the story and pointing at the woman, declaring, *It was her. The story is about her.* He wants to hurt her. Maybe years in the future, he'll write a letter to her son and tell him of his mother's cruelty toward the dog. Toward Maxi and himself. How she wasn't the kind and funny woman their caseworker described her as. *She was nice to you,* he'd write. *But that was it.* But he knows he has to be an example for Maxi, who is watchful in her silence. He can hold tight to that, his restraint. He'll explain to her later, the importance of not succumbing to basic urges. Maxi is watching him. "We didn't know where else to go," he says.

Father Adeyemi smiles joylessly, his eyes flitting over the font. He reaches his hand toward the water, submerges his fingers, and pulls out a thin clump of gray fur, displaying it between his thumb and forefinger. "This is one of many reasons the Church does not perform dog baptisms."

Maxi begins to speak, but the priest holds up a hand to silence her. "This is a special dog. I can see that," he says. "But it is a dog all the same. The Church does not baptize animals. Any animals." He fixes his eyes on Maxi. "This animal has no soul," he says. "Not like you and me. It is unbound by Original Sin."

"But can't you—" Maxi tries again, but, again, he speaks over her: "Exceptions will not be made, I'm afraid. But I will bless this creature, and pray that its passage from this world be peaceful." The priest discards the fur and submerges his fingers once more, letting the holy water drip like rain onto the dog's head. "Bless you, creature of God," he says, forming the sign of the cross between the dog's eyes. The droplets remaining on his fingers trickle off and run into the dog's unblinking eyes. Then, gazing up at the cross affixed above the altar, he murmurs a rapid phrase in a language they don't understand.

In the courtyard, within the far reaches of the streetlight, Ben holds the dog. Ben's body retains the warmth bestowed by the church's furnace, but he knows it won't be long before the chill seeps back into their bones. He's not certain when the dog died, but he knew he was gone on their way back through the vestibule, when Maxi passed his body to him.

Does she know? Ben wonders, as Maxi strips the towel from his shoulder and tucks it around the dog's body. His chest, beneath his damp coat, is first to perceive the cold, even before his hands. He watches Maxi take the dog's paw, run a thumb over the smooth, ruddy nails. Then he notices their clean edges, how they must have been clipped recently. Again, he feels for a collar, but there is none.

"We should bury him," Maxi says, "Even if he didn't have a soul, he deserves that."

Ben's eyes flicker over her, his little sister. Her expression is serene. "The ground is frozen. And there's snow." He gestures at the strip of white lawns beyond the fence. "Also, you know that guy can't *know*." Ben is too tired for an argument, but a force inside him can't let this go. "Just 'cause he went to God school or whatever. He can't *know* animals don't have souls."

"It's called having faith." Maxi unlatches the gate and holds it open for him.

"I have faith in things," Ben says. He remembers the golden choir girl, his mother's breathless laughter. The surge of relief after sinking into a steaming bathtub. The cessation of sound as his ears sink below the surface. The thawing of his problem's hard edges. The thought he has every time: *As long as I can get to this feeling, I'll be okay.*

As they walk in silence toward the house, the cold slips beneath his skin again and extends its reach to his core so that he begins to shiver uncontrollably. His quaking hands, holding the dog to his chest, feel encased in gloves of ice.

As they step off the sidewalk onto their street, Maxi says, "So what are we going to do with him?"

Ben's teeth knock together as he considers the question. "Let's put him back where we found him," he says, finally. "In case somebody's looking for him."

In front of Mr. Anderson's yard, Ben gestures toward the shadowed ditch. In the moonlight, he can make out a shallow indentation stained with blood like spilled black ink. "There," he says. His hands are entirely numb. He imagines the slightest tap would shatter them.

Maxi crouches down to look into the dog's face. "I'm sorry." She runs a fingertip up and then down his nose. "We tried."

"You know," Ben says, "if the priest was wrong, maybe you saved him." When, after a moment, she doesn't answer, he says, "You know?"

As he angles his head to better see Maxi's face, a large cloud passes in front of the moon and the night unfurls.

When she finally speaks, her voice is as frigid as the still air: "Keep him in the towel. That way it's easier to see him."

"Okay," he says, straining his eyes to appraise her expression, but he can't even see her face. He hefts the dog's weight higher on his chest, gently still, and steps onto the cracked surface of the snow. He takes small sliding steps to descend the wall of the ditch.

And then, her voice, softer, closer, floats down to him, "And that way the person will know somebody tried to take care of him."

When Ben turns toward her voice, the movement alters his balance, and his right foot flies out from beneath him, and he falls, hard, on his elbow.

Maxi gasps. "Is he okay?" And there's nothing Ben can do to stop himself from pitching his head backward, pushing shards of snow into his ears, and letting loose a shriek of laughter.

The last time Ben and Maxi saw their mother, a month ago when their case worker drove them two hours north to the prison, she told them that she's trying to be more honest with herself, which means being more honest with them, too. "I don't know when I'll get you back," she said. As she spoke, she furiously fingered the hem of her khaki uniform sleeve. "I don't mean in the flesh, you know? I'm talking about *here*." She flattened her hand and rested it, fingers still twitching, upon her heart. "This isn't who I am." Her voice cracked open, and Ben couldn't bring himself to look at her. Instead he turned to Maxi, who was already looking back at him. He crossed his eyes and flared his nostrils in a halfhearted attempt to make her smile, and when she didn't, he dropped his eyes to the beige epoxy floor, dragged his shoe across its slick surface. "I have to believe it's gonna happen," their mother said. "That you're gonna let me back in. It's the only way I can survive in here."

Before Ben can catch his breath, Maxi is on the ground beside him, her own head in the snow, and she's laughing, too. The moon has reemerged and bathes them in its glow. Once he's caught his breath, he tilts his head toward her and says with mock seriousness, "The dead dog is fine," which sends her into another fit of laughter.

"Hey," she says, suddenly, digging behind her back. "Look." She pulls out one of his forgotten gloves. She feels around until she finds the other one, and then shakes the snow from them. "Put them on," she orders. "Your fingers are probably about to fall off." Keeping the dog secure on his chest between his upper arms, he works his fingers into the gloves. The chilled material warms quickly against his skin. He rubs his hands together, and sighs, "Oh my god, that's so much better."

Maxi has propped herself on her knees. “Here,” she says, reaching for the dog. “I’ll take him.”

In the moonlight, Ben watches Maxi spread the towel over the blood-crusted snow, place the dog upon it, and swaddle him like an infant. She sits back on her haunches and stares at him for a moment, then leans forward to make the sign of the cross on his head, just as Father Adeyemi had done.

“Okay, Max, let’s go.” Ben rolls onto his side, awakening pain in his shoulder. With care not to fall again, he maneuvers his feet beneath him and stands. He reaches out a hand for Maxi. “She’ll let us in now.”

LATE SPRING EPIPHANY AFTER THE GEORGIA O'KEEFFE EXHIBIT

by MELISSA MCKINSTRY

from ADROIT JOURNAL

I'm always trying to paint that door—
I never quite get it,
she said of the black square
at her winter house in Abiquiú,
always a shadow shifting,
a ladder leading to sky.
When she looked through
a pelvic bone she picked up
in the desert, she saw
a ghost moon,
and today I'm quiet
as her bones and stones
and black pearl oyster shells.
Once I had a son. Once,
when he was four,
before his tracheotomy,
we were invited to float
in a warm therapy pool.
He was weightless
as I swirled his thin limbs
in slow circles and lines.
He seemed to sleep

through it all, but I loved it:
his buoyancy, absence of straps
and wheels. Water flicker
on his curly lashes,
maybe a quiver of smile.
He couldn't say *more*,
or *mmmmm*, or *get me out of here*,
so I don't really know.
I never really knew him.
He kept himself to himself,
maybe grew very small
to survive. He was a dark door,
a box of bones—
a soft, gone tabernacle.

FLOATING AROUND

fiction by MARIA KUZNETSOVA

from THE THREEPENNY REVIEW

It just so happened I was tired of being a physical creature. I wanted to get the upper hand before my body had a chance to inflict more damage upon me. To put it bluntly, three children were extinguished in my womb over the course of five years and I wanted to shed my rogue body and its treacherous movements and waning power. I never wanted to look in the mirror and blanch at my hollow stomach and eyes again. Luckily, I had an experimental scientist and adjunct physics professor for a father, who could be of use in this tricky situation. I found him in the driveway of his rented apartment, kicking the trunk of his failing car.

"Maybe I can help," I said.

Papa planted his hands on his hips. "And what would my darling like in exchange?"

I took a step toward him. "I do not want to have a body," I said.

He sighed profoundly. "You may not be a product of the first freshness, but you are too young to crave oblivion."

"I don't want to die. I only want to shed my physical self," I clarified. Papa was still skeptical, but I knew I could change his mind. He had seen me clutch my stomach and rip out my hair and weep due to my physical disappointments. He knew how much it hurt me, to carry around my heavy bones and wicked womb. As he gazed sorrowfully into my eyes, I unfurled my plan for sweetening the deal. "If you make it happen, I won't need my car any longer," I said, practically singing the words. I got the car because I thought driving around town would help me escape, but all it got me was a few parking tickets.

Papa tilted his head, still mournful but intrigued by my proposition. "You have consulted your husband?"

"Of course," I lied.

My father sighed and regarded the heavens. He had reasons to be reluctant. After all, his track record was questionable at best. Ages ago, Papa's love potion made my ex fall in love with my cat instead of me. Imagine my surprise when I woke up in the middle of the night to find my beloved at the foot of my bed, caressing poor Mr. Snuggles as he whispered, "There is no remedy for love but to love more . . ." Most recently, I asked him to bring Mama back from the dead; she returned to us as a cranky, flatulent baby and we didn't know what to do with her until she was adopted by a happy couple from Poughkeepsie. In spite of these troubling outcomes, I was desperate for supernatural aid.

"You may regret this, foolish one," he said. "I certainly will."

Papa knew his daughter was a stubborn creature; he preferred to aid in my destruction rather than leave me to my own devices. And so, he disappeared to his basement laboratory. I put a hand on my stomach and gazed at the overgrown grass in my father's rented yard. After a while, he returned with a bottle of green lotion. He sprinkled a few ladybug wings and a slice of summer squash into the mix and shook it up. He told me to rub the lotion all over my body and contemplate the pain it brought me and soon it would all be gone.

"You must be certain," he said. "There will be no going back to how things are."

"And good riddance," I said, making him wince.

I ran home as fast as my aching legs could take me, and then I slathered on the lotion and thought of the physical indignities I had faced. First, there was being born, then passing gas, then hunger, then teething, and, skipping ahead some years, there was menstruation and hangovers, and being attracted to men who were not my husband and so on, but my body's latest series of disappointments was so awful I could not bear to think of them, and yet I did, three separate half-formed children rushing from my nether regions like bloody waterfalls, hot and furious, taking with them my final shreds of faith. I rubbed every last drop of the lotion all over myself, hesitating only slightly when I covered my erogenous zones.

I was becoming a touch translucent by the time my husband came home, dropping a sack of ungraded composition essays on his feet.

"First you buy those hideous curtains. Then the new car that we never use. And now this," he said.

He was laughing because he did not understand my condition was permanent. It dawned on him slowly. He knew I had been suffering, but he still believed in our future as parents and did not fathom the depth of my pain or know that I had given up, three strikes and I was out. Well, what could he do? He put a record on, opened our only nice bottle of wine, and we stormed the porch. The wine was pure ecstasy, an explosion of cherries and earth. The evening light was wondrous. But when I sipped my second glass, the wine flowed through me, all over my chair. My husband lowered his head in his hands.

"Look, I know it happened to your body, but it hurt me too. I just wish you'd let me know that you ran out of hope."

"But I am letting you know," I told him, and he sighed in exasperation.

"Why couldn't you just tough it out like the rest of us?" he said.

He stalked out into the darkness and I let him be. I stood before the bathroom mirror, watching my body fading until it contracted into an orb of light, a sun the size of a baby's fist. This fine glow would never let me down. I was flawless, the pinnacle of efficiency and splendor. I could move quickly too, did I mention that? I could float, and flit, and flutter about. It was far better than driving my new car down the open roads, trying to forget myself as the wind flitted through my hair. I was beauty and perfection.

My husband begged to differ. When he returned, I found I could communicate telepathically, and I tried to convince him our marriage would only improve with our new arrangement. I pointed out that he could, for example, revert to the old curtains. I would no longer steal the covers at night, or hog the bathroom, or wake him when he snored. Furthermore, we would save money on clothes and groceries, not to mention health insurance. Looking to the future, he would save thousands on my burial costs, did he know how much coffins alone were going for these days? It was simply outrageous.

When this did not take, I added, "I thought you married me for my mind."

"I'm not so fond of your mind right now, either," he said.

Then he lumbered up the stairs. I followed him to bed, but I recalled that I was a transcendent orb that did not need sleep for fuel like some base human creature, so I explored the woods behind our house all night long, hovering above the ground and then levitating to the leafy treetops and their dark, lush beauty—and, when I grew bored with that, I zipped right up to the heavens and bounded around the fiery planets and glowing stars and their endless imperturbability. When I floated back in the morning, I found that my husband had pulled out a chair for me at the breakfast table, and in that manner our marriage resumed.

THINGS WERE great for a while. In fact, they were better than ever. Every evening my husband and I sat on the porch comparing his composition students to my woodland creatures. He drank wine and sprinkled it in my direction and I said I could taste it, though I couldn't and no longer needed alcohol for transcendence. I could transcend anything I wanted now, quite literally, and spent most of my time orbiting the dark, lonely moons, as well as the bright stars that were set like diamonds in the velvet of the all-knowing night.

Sometimes Papa would join us for dinner. Though he was wistful when he gazed in my direction, he did not berate me for what I had done.

"Your car runs like a dream," he told me, and I was pleased he could go anywhere he wanted and did not gloat about how much better my peregrinations were without a car weighing me down. My husband resented my father for transforming me, but he did not tell him to leave. He was pleased to have company. We lived far from the university and had few friends.

One day, though, I was the one he asked to leave. We were having dinner. Or rather, my betrothed was devouring a bowl of spaghetti and meatballs, one of my favorite meals, taking his time with the rich saucy dish just to tease me, no doubt.

"I can't take this anymore," he said. "I did not marry a ball of light."

"But we've been getting along splendidly. I don't feel pain any longer. Plus, you have already saved a small fortune on wine," I tried. When he put down his fork and glared, I added, "Don't you want me to be happy?"

His jaw hardened. "I have needs, Yulia."

"You are a base, physical creature."

"I never denied it."

"You could always join me," I said, desperately, though if I thought there was any chance he would join me, I would have asked him to begin with. He lowered his head into his hands but I stubbornly pressed on: "I can talk to Papa."

"Don't be a fool."

"Just the other day, you said you'd rather die than grade another composition essay," I reminded him gently, but this failed to win him over.

He returned to his meaty repast, and for a moment I wanted to have a bite, in spite of the digestive problems and guilt I would have felt after eating it as my former physical self. I orbited around him and could have sworn his hair stood up from the electricity I generated. I was stunned by the sight of his rogue strands of golden hair in the dusk light.

"You are beautiful," I told him.

"So were you," he said, wiping sauce from his chin.

I floated off after that. But I could not help myself. I was no longer thrilled by the breathlessness of the heavens, and wanted to float closer to earth. More specifically, I floated near the treetops by my former home, so I could keep track of my husband, and it did not take long to yield results. When a low, vulgar-looking woman arrived at his door, I did not hate her. I only felt sorry for her, for the weary flesh under her eyes and how her legs must have ached in her high, high heels.

After that, I hung out at Papa's. I watched him dine and fumble with his basement machines and heard stories of his Kyiv childhood and entertained him with tales of my nocturnal expeditions, most of which kept me closer to the earth now, grazing icy mountains and traversing over the blue, beguiling ocean, and the deserts with their hunched, resigned camels, and the heavy, low-flying clouds. Sometimes, I even floated above Papa's bequeathed car when he drove down the long gravel roads outside of town, singing Soviet ballads and thinking of Mama, and I thought maybe it wasn't such a bad escape after all, pressing the gas with abandon as you felt your wheels shuddering over stones on a dark lonely night.

But after a while, I knew it was time to leave Papa. I could see how much it hurt him that he could not stroke my hair. One day, his eyes glazed over when I was raving about how I joined a flock of birds in migration, upsetting their purposeful geometry, and I told him I understood.

"I wish you could accept the natural state of things," he said, turning to the window.

"The natural state is short and degrading."

"Indeed," he said, watching two squirrels chasing each other around the base of a tree. "But it has its moments, little one."

I flew far, far away without looking back. I began spending most of my time near the ground. I raced with wild horses and antelope and slowed down to observe shameless necking teenagers and gorgeous bird mothers tending to their flocks and, on one occasion, a fisherman who sang the most beautiful song in a language I did not recognize in the early dawn. I did not think of my desperate husband rutting on his high-heeled whore or my widowed father fussing over lab equipment that would never salve his pain.

I only returned years later, when I sensed that Papa was fading. I was just in time for his funeral and was not sad I did not get to say goodbye, because I knew seeing my glowing aura would only bring him pain. I did attend the funeral, where two Soviet cousins and a handful of graduate students spoke of my father's hard work in spite of a lack of results.

Only as I floated off did I see my husband in the distance, crouching behind a mausoleum with a bouquet in his hands. His hair was thinned and gray, but his mouth was as crisp and lovely as it was when he kissed me on our wedding day. He did not see me, which was for the best. He crept off toward his getaway car, which was driven by the same vulgar woman from before, who was a dignified redhead now. And in the back of the car there were two somber teenagers who had my husband's eyes.

Papa was right. There was a natural order of things, and by the time I reached what was supposed to be old age, I did crave oblivion. I craved it hard. It had been years since I had roamed the galaxies or grazed the treetops, learning that ecstasy had its limits. My floatations had been limited to the ground for years. I raced graceful deer and breathless gazelles and brushed over wildflower fields, trying to delight in the earth's flora and fauna. I wondered if I would have felt better if I could touch those living creatures, if I could feel the earth crunching beneath my feet like Papa felt the gravel below his car. But Papa was dead and there was no way I could revert to being a person. I did not know how my nonlife would ever end.

I took to the galaxies once more. I flew into space for weeks at a time, hoping the thinning air would do me in, but it had no effect. I flew all the way to the moon, but it did not chill me, and then I recalled the ancient warning about flying too close to the sun, and I did just that, I tried to melt into the hot ball of fire, but it turned out that was a lie. When I floated down to earth, I must admit that for a second, our unruly planet with all its imperfections held a certain beauty and logic.

Logic would tell me that fire could be quenched, like the children in my womb, so I tried soaking in the ocean I had grazed for so long. I went down to the bottom of the sea, to barnacles and shipwrecks and coral reefs and electric fish, so luminous and unloving, but it did not drown me. The lakes did nothing for me either, though I did encounter droves of bug-eyed snails who beheld me with wonder. The light I cast on the bottom of the lakes was a glory. But nothing would do me in.

Around this time, I sensed that my husband was expiring. As I floated toward home, I had conflicted feelings. I did not want to be a nuisance, to complicate his passage to the abyss. But even my lack of humanity had its limits. My darling was in the hospital and I had to see him. I tried not to linger as I passed our former home to the place where my husband was convalescing.

I floated in the room slowly. There he was, my beloved in bed, in the most degrading state, hardly the size of a child, collarbones protruding, eyes retreating, the mouth I had loved creased with folds, his head as smooth as my surface.

Beside him sat the same wife in her dotage, white-haired with a tipped-down head, and two children not much younger than I had been when we parted. How I pitied them! These sad, saggy humans watching their patriarch dissolve into the ether while knowing that they were all destined to meet the same fate. I must have been thinking aloud, because his eyes popped open as I hovered over his horned feet.

He reached toward me and said, "I hope you're happy after all."

My non-heart purred; he remembered our last conversation after all these years. Was I happy? Would I have traded my worldly adventures to be decaying beside him, holding his hand? I was at a loss for words. I hadn't spoken to anyone in years. I hovered closer, brushing against his cracked lips. His wife whispered to their children, saying they should go tell the nurses their father was hallucinating.

"I wish I had tasted that spaghetti," I told him, and he laughed softly.

He was still the man I loved, after all. I wanted to rest beside him for eternity. As he fell into slumber, snoring gently with his mouth open, I knew what to do. I floated between his lips. I slipped past his tongue and squeezed down his throat and pushed and pushed through slime and gastric juice until I was inside his warm and primordial stomach.

It would not take much longer for him to die, I knew. There was nowhere else I wanted to go, so I stopped my manic movements and listened to the faint beating of his heart. I waited for my beloved's body to shut down and prayed I would be smothered, just like our non-children had been, snuffed out within the blameless body of someone who loved them. The darkness and quiet embraced me and filled me with warmth and something resembling hope. I was perfectly still and certain that if this did not kill me, nothing would.□

LITHIUM

by STEFAN MANASIA

from ANOTHER CHICAGO MAGAZINE

I shaved my inguinal area
and placed around my neck
the silver necklace
as if she could see me
I checked myself in the mirror:
sadder and more handsome
than ever
I put on my shorts
I went out on the balcony
        the wind carries
        vortices of petals & dust
& like some amber worms
my energetic fields
draining through my wrists
through my Adam's apple
right there where she so often
placed her forehead
and, adjusting
her breath,
she fell asleep,
my poor bipolar Amazon.

translated from the Romanian by Clara Burghelea

FROM HEDGE TO HEDGE

by WENDY WILLIS

from OREGON HUMANITIES

The Poetry of earth is never dead:
When all the birds are faint with the hot sun,
And hide in cooling trees, a voice will run
From hedge to hedge about the new-mown mead;
That is the Grasshopper's—he takes the lead.

—John Keats
"On the Grasshopper and Cricket"

1. THE PEOPLE

"How're the people?" my husband asks as I hand him a now-lukewarm cup of coffee. I shrug: "Fine, droopy, acting like a diva." I get up early—alarm set for five, but often up at four due to a vivifying cocktail of middle-aged insomnia, lifelong anxiety, an early-rising (and boisterous) neighborhood robin, and existential panic. David and Senator—our six-year-old border collie mix, who is greeted with his own ritual "Good morning, Senator"—come downstairs at 7:00 a.m. sharp, regardless of how long they have been awake. (David, reading; Senator, dozing on my pillow.) Before they appear, I write or catch up on email or doomscroll, but I also spend a good lot of time fussing over the fifty or so houseplants pressed up against every source of natural light in our otherwise tree-shaded house. I spray-mist them, study new shoots, google for the millionth time why the ficus—diva that it is—continues to drop leaves despite getting at least twice as much attention as any other plant in the house.

We started calling them "the people" sometime last spring after a transplanting frenzy. Once they were watered and settled onto their new shelves and windowsills, I called David in and asked, "Do you want to see where the people live now?"

"The people?"

"Yes. The plants, you know. The people."

And that was it. From that day forward, they joined the ranks of *the people*, and they have been referred to as such ever since.

2. A TAIL

During normal daylight hours, I work with and for other kinds of people. Specifically, I direct a statewide community engagement program that connects Oregonians—particularly those that have been excluded from public decision-making—to the decisions that affect them.

Not long before the early morning christening of the plant people, my colleagues and I did some work that explored Oregonians' hopes, concerns, and ideas about water and water use. Near the end of the project, I was called to present the results to the Oregon Water Resources Commission. Sitting there in my late mother-in-law's garnet necklace, which I wear to channel her confidence and I-mean-business countenance, I listened to some of the usual sparring about in-stream versus out-of-stream water use—people need water to drink, to make a living, to grow the food we eat. And also, the fish. The turtles.

When it was my turn, the presentation went to plan, and the commissioners asked a few polite questions. But just before I got up to leave, one commissioner looked past me, up and to the left, not really talking to me so much as thinking out loud: "But what about the rivers themselves? How do we hear from the rivers on their own behalf?"

I felt as if a fissure had opened in my brain and a burst of light had poured out. *Wait, what?* I grasped at a thought just out of reach. And then it was gone—the seam closed. I gathered my things, and I walked out into the cold, bright afternoon.

The closest experience I can compare it to is the time when my husband and I went for a hike along an old logging road in the McKenzie River Valley on the day after Thanksgiving. A few miles in, our aging goldendoodle started zigzagging back and forth across the road, nose down. Every minute or two, she tore off into the bracken. We called her back—for at least the fifth time—and I grabbed her by the collar. As I bent to put her leash on, a snarl or growl or some throaty sound I'd never heard before bounced off the basalt cliff, and we turned to see a tawny tail disappear into the heavy ferns. We heard it, glimpsed it, yet did not quite see it. It read: cougar. But really, it was the tease of a cougar. And it kicked off a longing that I haven't yet satisfied.

A similar dissatisfaction keeps niggling around the edges of my mind as I return to that interaction with the commissioner. It's not that it was a new question, exactly. An oft-repeated axiom in our work is: "Nothing about us without us." In other words, those most affected by a decision should be centered in making that decision. Mostly, that guidance has been applied to communities of humans that have been excluded or ignored. And rightly so. But sometimes others ask: *Who represents the other-than-human world in elections, in lawsuits, in public decision-making?* I have asked myself such questions. I have asked others.

Typically, environmental and conservation advocates raise the profile of animals and waterways and mountain ranges in the public discourse, but ultimately, those advocates are still human stakeholders representing *their* values and interests. And there are people who have explored more direct ways of including nonhuman beings in significant decisions, including initiatives like Animals in the Room, founded by a group of scientists, philosophers, and democratic theorists who have set out to "devise and test models for representing nonhuman animals in decision-making."

3. HONEY AND WOOL

But what about the rivers themselves?

As I have chased the tail of that question, I have found myself chest-deep in bracken and blackberries, headed into wilder, less human-built terrain. Though I'm still not quite sure what I'm bushwhacking after, the questions have inverted themselves—rather than asking whether or how we can include animals and plants and other nonhumans in the democracy we have built, fortified, and defended, I find myself asking questions like: Is democracy capacious enough to include *what is*? Because if we stray off the well-trodden path of presidential politics and Supreme Court rulings and try to orient ourselves to our surroundings, it becomes clear that *what is* includes a lot more than the institutions of late capitalism or even the most progressive liberal democracies apprehend. It is as if *what is*—an amalgamation of star dust and red plateaus and black sand and wolverines and earthworms and glacial lakes and skunk cabbage and horsehair lichen and grackles and dry riverbeds and butter lettuce and, yes, cougars and border collies and humans and ficus trees—is no longer a backdrop to the human drama but is the main character, and it is now up to democracy to contend with it.[3]

I want to give democracy a chance. I love democracy. I love the word. I love the idea—*demos*: people; *kratia*: power. Where else can we find the intertwining aspirations of individual sovereignty, equal rights, and the common good? As the political scientist Danielle Allen puts it, we have to "lov[e] democracy all the way down" because the practice of democracy asks a lot of its adherents.

Maybe a bigger and wilder conception of democracy is what loving it "all the way down" looks like. For years, I have carried around a quote from the Potawatomi botanist Robin Wall Kimmerer: "If citizenship is a matter of shared beliefs, then I believe in the democracy of species. If citizenship means an oath of loyalty to a leader, then I choose the leader of the trees. If good citizens agree to uphold the laws of the nation, then I choose natural law, the law of reciprocity, of regeneration, of mutual flourishing."

At first, I think I was attracted to the poetry of Kimmerer's vision, and of course, to the escape valve of voting for the tallest and strongest western red cedar rather than one of the craven apparatchiks who present themselves to us each election cycle. But what if Kimmerer is not speaking in metaphor at all? What if she is telling us that democracy really does encompass the whole of *what is*? What if the democracy of *what is* is infinitely more pluralistic than we have ever imagined? And what if the full pluralism of *what is* requires more than including prairie dogs and redbud trees in our lawsuits and public processes? When we talk about "inclusion," it often has a patronizing flavor to it. Yes, "inclusion" in public decision-making—in democracy itself—broadens the circle of care, but it also suggests that the "includer" is the actor and the "includee" is the recipient of that action. Even if the proposed action is at least putatively beneficial—rather than explicitly harmful—the conception of inclusion suggests that the includee has no agency in the matter and the includer doesn't have to change anything besides adding an extra chair.

---

* And a teaser for next time: If, say, Hobby Lobby is a "person" for the purposes of the First Amendment, surely the mule deer can't be far behind. In that spirit, the Yurok Tribe has adopted a resolution granting the Klamath River and its ecosystem "the rights of personhood" and the standing to enforce the right to "exist, flourish, and naturally evolve," as well as the right to a clean and healthy environment.

But democracy is not an autonomous machine that spits out benefits and burdens. Rather, it is a complex and ever-changing network in which each person—however that is defined—is sometimes the actor and sometimes the acted upon. Sometimes we pay taxes, and sometimes we receive benefits. Sometimes we build roads, and sometimes we call the fire department at the first sign of smoke. Sometimes we give CPR to a stranger on the street, and sometimes we receive it. In a democratic culture, we both contribute to and receive from the whole, depending on the needs of the moment.

Let me offer another example, one that explicitly explores the edges of the relationship between humans and other animals. I have been a vegetarian for more than forty years, and for the last few, I have been a near-vegan. When people ask why, I say, "Ethical reasons." But the ethics of the question are messier than they first appear. Many vegans avoid the use of any products that come from other animals—not only meat, dairy, and eggs, but also silk, wool, and honey. As one advocate explains: "The goal of veganism is to reduce and finally end the exploitation and cruelty of [using] animals . . . for human sustenance."

On the surface, this conception of the relationship between humans and other animals seems to have only upsides for those other animals. And sure, the elimination of slaughterhouses and factory farming and other cruel practices will reduce the amount of suffering, deprivation of dignity, and painful death inflicted upon many animals. But characterizing the use of any animal product as ipso facto "exploitation" denies the notion that there can be—that there is—reciprocity between humans and other animals. It denies the possibility that humans might offer a garden filled with bee balm and aster and hyssop or a bale of alfalfa hay in exchange for a honeycomb or a bag of wool.

This, of course, is not to suggest that anybody should use any animal products they are not comfortable with—and I am certainly not going to run out and start eating meat anytime soon—but it does raise the question of whether, by defining exploitation so broadly, we vegans are replicating the commodification and lack of agency that we oppose in the mainstream treatment of nonhuman animals. It also calls into question the ethics of our relationship with plants that provide food and other products for human sustenance.

A true "democracy of species," as Kimmerer calls it, would require that we humans not only expand the circle of care to protect other beings, but that we discern, recognize, and respect their agency and their contributions to the whole.

If we consider agency in its simplest terms—the ability to initiate action or even express preferences—nonhuman beings demonstrate their own agency regularly, both on their own behalf and on behalf of others. Senator, the aforementioned border collie, barks both when I've forgotten to feed him dinner and when someone comes up on the porch. And, among the plant people in our home, the peace lily in the guest room seems to need water about three times as often as anyone else. After a day in the south-facing window, it droops dramatically, playing dead. But after a quick dose from the watering can, the leaves and stems stand right back up, ready to start the cycle all over again.

There are expressions of will and agency all around us, even among beings that are unfamiliar or almost imperceptible to most humans. Writer and visual artist Jenny Odell suggests a practice she calls "unfreezing in time" to train ourselves to notice the agency all around us. She suggests we pick a point somewhere in our close-enough but not immediate world—a branch, a section of sidewalk, anything—and that we return to it repeatedly. We should look at it daily, or at least regularly, and notice how it changes. She argues that through close and repeated looking, we will see more subtly and more dynamically, freeing the place and the beings within it from both the Western conception of time and the human habit of treating a tree or a tulip or a patch of grass as a backdrop or a symbol rather than as an actor in its own right.

4. A THING WITH FANGS

And even if it starts with a houseplant, once we begin to notice and take seriously what other beings both offer and need, the enterprise of living in community becomes something else entirely. It changes who and what we consider to be the *demos*—the people—and what we see as an expression of power. And once we decide to more fully apprehend the dizzying intricacy of the web we are entwined in, democracy reveals its other faces: The ones with fur and fangs and vines and needles. The one that shape-shifts between the wizened and the just born. The one that is fearsome and the one that is placid. The one that is housebroken and the one that is feral. The one that shatters and the one that mends. The one that rattles with thunder and stills on a breezeless afternoon. The one that breathes in our tame old stories and breathes out a burst of blue flame. The one that shimmers with the truth of *what is*.

A BLACK MOTHER'S CHILD CONSIDERS HIS LOST DREAM OF IMMORTALITY

by IAIN HALEY POLLOCK

from AMERICAN POETRY REVIEW

I.

What was she hoping I'd learn? What lessons
when my mother, who taught Greek
at the college on the hill, read their old stories
to me? To be ready one night for hooded snakes ss
to crawl into my cradle? To leave a trail of twine
behind me as I walked the labyrinthine corridors
of my country? Not to raise the wrong sail
whenever I came home to her? Not to dive
as the swan and plummet into a woman bathing
in the seclusion of high reeds, not to be the shock
and awe of white wings? For me though, the truth
in the myth was this: power transforms
into life, and life forever. And when my mother
was finished, all I wanted was to live
as those changing but unchanging gods.

II.

The White man who taught me Greek
hated me. He thought I was lazy. I admit
that I often slept through his morning class,
often stumbled through his translations as a boar

through deep, sudden snow. My mother cried when
she left me in the parking lot of that place. Cried
harder than I'd seen since the week after her father
died. I think she had learned that no Black mother
can save her children. Save them, as you have proven
(and are still proving), America, from your primitive,
bullhorned violence. And so, more days than not there,
her son stood beside an aluminum keg, fermenting
himself, pouring into his gullet a river,
not of forgetfulness, but of an urgent forgetting.

III.

My mother wanted to learn Latin on her way
to Greek, but the teachers had her pegged
to cook and sew. Short but thickset,
the school's own former football hero, her father
traded on his glory, the scars earned for it,
on his hobbled knees, the slight slur of his speech
to demand a place for her in a room of primers
and chalkboards. They thought she should scurry
about the rooms of your house, America, picking up
what you had dropped. But she overcame to stand
at the front of a room, professor of language
and myth. I told a version of this story to Black children
at a school in Philadelphia. When I came to the end—
my mother teaching Greek at the college on the hill—
they rose from their chairs and applauded her
through the proxy of me. I think now I lied to them.
Lied to them while standing in a room across town
from where you firebombed a city block to save
yourself. America, you have eaten your children
to keep your place on the honeyed mountaintop.
If you have not already, you will consume those children
too. And still you will come, with wild, ravenous hunger,
for more. And why do you keep doing what you do?
And what will you do one day when, instead of a child,
you swallow a stone?

WHISTLING PAST THE GRAVEYARD

by TED KOOSER

from NEW LETTERS

I live in the aftermath of cancer, the green reforestation period after the great fire, the brown high-water line drying to dust on the siding after the hundred-year flood, one lane now opened on the mountain-side highway, a sheer drop to the sea on one side, cluttered by tons of broken concrete, a few chunks with sections of bright yellow centerline leading out into the blue.

I'm not alone. My wife is at the wheel of our life together, wind in her full, lovely gray hair. I'm on the passenger side, giving myself my mid-day tube feeding, trying not to spill into my lap. I live on cartons of a prescription formula for diabetics, with ample washes of water. Medicare picks up the tab for my feedings. We're on our way into the rest of our lives.

I don't think I've ever before used the word aftermath in something I've written. Something awful that has happened to one little old man, however seismic he may have felt it to be, scarcely merits the use of the word. But the etymology tells me that "math" comes from Old English and describes a meadow that has been mowed. So an aftermath is what's left after some kind of crop has been harvested, and I am what's left, a meadow now dusty stubble. The crop was malignant, like the black mold that ruins a whole stand of corn. Once smut's in the soil it can keep coming back, and I've had three oral cancers over twenty-five years, most recently nine hours of surgery during which the right half of my jaw was removed and replaced with a section of bone from my left fibula—one of the two bones below the knee, not the shinbone but the one behind it—not necessary for walking or bearing weight. I can both walk and bear weight and only yesterday I wrestled a forty-pound bag of sunflower seeds into a garbage can with a tight lid that keeps the raccoons from eating the food for the finches, the grosbeaks and cardinals, bright creatures of my reforestation.

My new jaw was at first held in alignment by a titanium plate that had been computer-designed to match the profile of the original. The plate was left screwed in place for about a year until the bone had healed into position, then it was removed because of a persistent infection it had been sheltering. Whistling past the graveyard, I asked my surgeon if the screws were Phillips head or slotted. He said that the screws, terribly expensive, come from their makers with their own bespoke screwdrivers.

My healed face is now as symmetrical as it ever was, my nose a little crooked from a drunken fall in my thirties, my eyes positioned on either side of my nose as they should be, framed in trifocals, my ears where they've always been, fitted with hearing aids. My face is partly numb on the right side and around to my chin, which feels as if it might be carved out of wood, like the hinged chins of Charlie McCarthy and Mortimer Snerd.

The floor of my mouth is a drink-coaster-sized patch of skin carefully lifted away during the leg surgery, then fitted into the floor of my mouth, and since I'm an old man with bald legs I don't have any hair growing there. Some patients do. One of the many small blessings for which I am thankful.

My tongue is limited in motion, right and left, in and out, and my swallowing apparatus has stiffened from the radiation I had twenty-five years ago. With three-quarters of my teeth still in place, I should be able to eat normal meals, but my swallowing problems prohibit that. Thus the tube in my belly.

That's not as bad as it sounds. For one thing, it's efficient, no chewing and chewing and chewing. No dirty dishes from my side of the table. I don't really long for those roast pork, sauerkraut and dumpling dinners I once so loved, but I can savor them in memory. I have all of those tastes in my head. No need for Alka Seltzer. I'm not in any pain as a person might think of pain, just a persistent dull ache on that side of my jaw. I have thick, syrupy saliva and sometimes I'll blow a bubble when I open my mouth to speak, which would have been great fun in fourth or fifth grade.

I nearly always surprise myself with the sound of my voice, which is unpredictable, ranging from near normal to the squeakiness of Saturday-morning kids' TV cartoons.

Between the original tongue-and-neck surgery and radiation in 1998—which gave me more than twenty very good years as husband, father, grandfather, uncle, friend, poet and professor—and my jaw replacement in 2022, I had a small cancer removed from the right side of my lower lip that left an almond-sized gap that embarrasses me, as I'm likely to drool and I can't tell when I'm doing it. So I periodically dab at my mouth with a bandana I keep balled in my fist. The more I speak, the more drooling, so I'm better off keeping my mouth shut. My wife and my friends have already heard all my good stories anyway, sometimes over and over again. I limit my everyday conversations since I have difficulty making myself clear. I carry a card with my name on it so I don't have to try to spell it out for the clerk who wants it to record my awards points. I never answer the phone, so don't call. I'm best with email.

I've had a course of speech therapy sessions, which were helpful, but no longer would I dare rise to the challenge of reading in public. Getting through just one poem aloud can get messy. I could get through a short poem like "The Red Wheelbarrow" and you'd be able to understand me, but any poem longer than that is beyond my capabilities. I'm shy and I never much liked getting up in front of audiences anyway. I spent a lot of time as U. S. poet laureate being scared of my audiences, but I'm done with that, and now I'm afraid of a tumor recurrence instead.

I've been very lucky to have had one very fine doctor overseeing me since my first run-in with cancer, a specialist in head and neck oncology and an excellent surgeon, teacher and mentor of residents. He was in his mid-thirties when we first met and he's now in his early sixties. At our first meeting, now twenty-six years ago, as he prepared me for the possibility of having a sizeable piece taken out of my tongue, he asked if I did any public speaking, and I said none that I couldn't do without, and my wife said, "Well, he IS a poet and sometimes does poetry readings." By our next appointment he had gone to the library and checked out some of my books. That's the kind of physician and person he is.

Every few weeks I have a session with a psychologist who helps me with bouts of anxiety. "Are those thoughts that you're having in the wee hours being helpful?" Well, no, they're not helpful at all. I've taught myself that if I wake and begin brooding obsessively about illness and death it's time to get up and do something, to sit under a lamp with my notebook and write down whatever I'm given. While I'm writing I lift away from my body, have no discomforts, no ominous little pinches of pain. I pass into my words.

I've moved myself into the words you've been reading, though writing about cancer frightens me, as if by doing it I might inadvertently tilt something out of balance, and the experience of writing the few paragraphs you see here has stirred up some worry. Yet while I'm writing I'm almost always invincible, indelible. I'm not going to die today, or tomorrow, and I'll probably live through this week and the next week, and I might not die this month, or six months from now.

So what can I do with today? A road crew has shown up to repair the mountain highway, and down on the flood plain a woman in galoshes is standing out in her puddled front yard scraping mud from her coffee pot. All around the black, still smoldering mountain, little green pine trees are beginning to show.

WHAT MY FATHER WISHED FOR

by PATRICIA CLARK

from PLUME

I could never say anything about my father
except he was quiet, and next to Mother
he receded like a hermit crab into its shell.
Is that an excuse, at seventeen, for raising
my voice against him, trying my best
to goad him to anger? "How can you just go
to work, drive downtown, day after day
arriving on time, leaving at five? Don't you
ever start asking yourself what it all means?"
Someone should have slapped me. I see
the kitchen at Browns Point, a round table where
we sat, high cliff light over the bay
smoky stink of pulp mills, a madrona tree
by the deck sickened by sewage. He's about
to drive me to Stadium High, down Snake Hill,
across Tacoma's tide flats, drawbridges opening
and closing like jaws for tankers heading
out west to Japan, stacked high with lumber
or salt, later, jeeps and tanks for Vietnam
And then I badgered him, too: "Why can't you
take a stand against the war?" This, hurled
at my father who'd enlisted after Pearl Harbor
with his favorite brother, a brother who didn't
come home from Germany. Did someone
call regret "permanent remorse"? After my father's

diagnosis, he refused to talk about death. "I've had
everything in life I could have wanted." When the priest
came to the house, Dad sat up in bed, talking
as though he'd be around weeks, as the sunset
turned salmon, then mauve over
Commencement Bay. Later, he leaned in, close
to me, to say, "One thing, though. I wish
I'd had a sister." He told me this, sotto voce,
when I sat alone beside him, holding his hand
through the metal rails.

TIME OF THE PREACHER

fiction by BRET ANTHONY JOHNSTON

from VIRGINIA QUARTERLY REVIEW

Holland spent Wednesday building a privacy fence for a tiresome academic couple in Barton Hills. Pressure-treated posts, horizontal cedar boards, stained and sealed, it was his third that week. He had another scheduled tomorrow, then a set of deck stairs on Friday, plus bids out on a tree house, a couple of pergolas, and too many fences to count. Now that everyone was marooned at home, they were dumping money into their yards, walling off their neighbors.

Holland was still getting acquainted with being in demand. He was forty-two, living in a gooseneck trailer out by the airport, divorced. He'd started Good Fences right before the world skidded to a stop. Well shit, he'd thought, and figured he'd soon be back working the paint counter at Home Depot. In those early months, when folks were only buying toilet paper and hand sanitizer, he occupied himself by building elaborate coops for the chickens he'd found pecking along the gravel shoulder of the interstate. Now almost a year in and the price of lumber near quadrupled, he turned away more jobs than he took.

While Holland was ripping cedar planks on his table saw in the Barton Hills front yard, a man stood on the opposite sidewalk trying to get his attention. When Holland finally clocked him, the man asked if he built skateboard ramps. "Wouldn't know where to start," Holland said with considerable relief. The man seemed skeptical, possibly insulted. He had two poodles on retractable leashes. Liberals, Holland thought.

When he finished the fence, he pinged the academics inside the house. He knotted his bandana around his nose and mouth despite knowing they probably wouldn't venture outside. Every aspect of the job had been negotiated by text.

And like that, they appeared in the bay window, reminding Holland of meerkats. The husband pointed at the fence and pumped his fist like he'd sunk a difficult golf shot. Beside him, the wife laid her hands on her heart and mouthed, *Thank you*. Holland waved, then felt ridiculous for having raised his bandana. The husband made a show of brandishing his phone to send the payment. Holland set to loading his table saw into the truck bed and soon felt his own phone vibrating in his pocket. He used a leaf blower to clear sawdust from the manicured lawn.

It was January, warm even for Texas. The day's light was giving up. When he climbed into the truck, he fished out his phone to check traffic and found his screen stacked with notifications: the academics' payment, news alerts about case numbers and vaccine trials, a request for a bid on a patio deck, a message asking when he could start work on the tree house. Holland hardly registered any of it because there was also a text from Mandy, his ex-wife.

Snake at preachers, help?

It had been almost three years. He dragged his palms over his hair and his patchy beard, couldn't recall when he'd last trimmed either. A churn in his bowels. His thoughts firing too fast. He was tired and hungry and read the text again. He dropped the truck into gear.

Mandy had been the preacher's landlord for a decade; her parents owned rentals all over Austin and employed her to manage them. Before she and Holland went bust, he'd done the handyman work. The preacher's house was well south of the river, tucked back on a street with ditches instead of sidewalks. A few lots had never been developed, dense with twisted mesquite and waist-high bluestem grass. At night, deer stalked into the neighborhood to tear up gardens and tug clothes off the lines. The preacher had once told Holland about seeing a buck with a woman's red teddy hanging from its antlers. Holland could still readily summon the pride he'd felt upon refraining from a joke about racks.

Snakes didn't bother him. He liked catching them and feeling them slip from one hand to the other, as if he were letting out rope. He liked watching them vanish in the brush afterward, liked happening upon the sheaths of their shed skins, featherlight and lace soft. Mandy knew he was partial to them, which was undoubtedly why she'd invented the snake tonight. Driving toward the rental, Holland clocked a certain surprise that this was the first time she'd baited him like this, then beneath that, the deeper surprise that she'd stoop to invoking the preacher. Mandy wasn't a believer, exactly, but she wasn't a nonbeliever either, so whatever had occasioned the lie had her in a corner. When she'd contacted him a couple years back, she was just of a mind to start some static. They'd met at the Little Darlin' and fought about midterm elections, property taxes, their past transgressions. Holland gathered she was arguing with him because the stakes of arguing with her husband were too high. Mr. Tech Boom, Holland thought. Mr. Start-up.

Holland passed a food-truck court illuminated by a sagging canopy of string lights, then a bible church with a digital sign that read: TEXT YOUR PRAYER REQUESTS!!!! Rush hour traffic. Bleating horns. Cars blocking intersections. A mobile testing site had taken over the parking lot of a dead mall, and Holland got stuck behind the line of cars stretching out onto the street. He tried to fix his hair in the rearview mirror while waiting to change lanes. On the radio, hotheads debated stimulus checks and mask mandates. The sky purpled.

When he arrived, Mandy's Tesla was in the driveway where the preacher's hatchback should have been. The front door was open and spilling light onto a doormat: Bless This Mess. The scene had the upending air of aftermath. Like someone had fled. Like medics hadn't had time to close the door after wheeling the preacher out on a gurney. Holland's body flushed with the abrupt, radiating heat of panic. He parked behind the Tesla and bounded across the clumpy front yard, trying to remember the shortest route to the closest hospital.

But then Mandy appeared in the doorway, framed in light. Holland halted, embarrassed she'd caught him rushing. At the house less than a minute and he'd already lost ground.

Mandy wore yoga pants, her favorite chambray shirt, a floral mask. She pointed to her face, somberly. He raised his bandana.

"Those don't do squat," she said. "You'd be better off wearing a paper bag with eyeholes."

"I can turn around," he said. He sensed neighbors watching between window curtains. "I've got chickens to feed."

"Sorry," she said, regrouping. "I've had a day."

"Where's the preacher?" he said.

"Exactly," she said.

Holland followed Mandy through the house. It was all but cleared out, and yet smaller than he remembered, more cramped. The air smelled like the inside of a dust-bloated vacuum bag. In the den, the preacher's ratty leather recliner sat opposite the wall where a TV had been mounted; now only the stubble of protruding cables remained. A single wire hanger dangled in the coat closet. In the kitchen, cupboards were open, a can of peaches on one shelf, a box of instant rice on another. Mandy's sleek leather purse hung by its strap from a cabinet knob. The overhead lights were garish, the kind of despairing brightness Holland associated with police stations.

"He's under the fridge," Mandy said, and it took Holland a beat to understand. He'd already forgotten the pretense of the snake. And now he remembered how Mandy referred to all animals as males. He wondered if she was still in therapy.

"What color?" he asked.

"Brown," she said. She opened the back door and posted herself beside it, keeping distance. "Or gray. I didn't get the best look. I screamed and ran outside."

"Any black and white stripes on the tail? Any red or yellow?"

She lidded her eyes, a pantomime of recollection, then shook her head. "He's all the color of mud."

"That's the right answer," he said. He kneeled woodenly; his muscles had seized up on the drive. He used his phone's flashlight to look at the bottom of the fridge: a plastic grille near flush with the Saltillo tile.

"You smell like outside work," she said. "You could bottle it and call it Eau de Labeur."

"You saw it go under here?" he said. "How big?"

"Brides would buy it for their husbands by the boatload," she said. "You could retire early."

"I like my job," he said.

"Good for you," she said. "Good for fucking you."

The preacher—midsixties, eyebrows as wild and white as toothbrush bristles, the slightest suggestion of a lisp—had been two weeks late on rent. He didn't use a cell phone and hadn't replied to emails. He usually paid early, so Mandy assumed his payment had gotten lost in the mail or, with the world gone to pot, he'd just lost track of the date. She waited another week. She logged into her bank account to confirm *she* hadn't forgotten depositing his check. She did entertain the possibility he'd gotten sick but talked herself out of it; Sunday services had been online since March. And weren't preachers prone to cautiousness? Preternaturally wise? Driving to the rental, she'd rehearsed how to strike a disarming tone—*I near forgot my own birthday this year! Who can remember anything right now? Not this lady!* She stopped and bought the Bless This Mess doormat as an excuse for dropping by. Even pulling into the empty driveway, she told herself he'd started parking in the garage. She rang the doorbell. Knocked. Checked her phone. Knocked again, harder, with the heel of her fist. When she finally turned the master key, she was already berating herself for not checking on him sooner, already convinced she'd find him stiff on the floor.

"But, no," she said, pacing the kitchen. "The only things left were that ugly-ass chair and the goddamned snake."

Holland was laboring to move the refrigerator. It was wedged between the counter and hallway wall. Each side would only scoot an inch at a time.

Mandy hopped up to sit on the kitchen island and started swishing her feet like a girl on a pier. Still, she kept her distance. She said, "So that's the situation. The world's on fire, and preachers are skipping out under cover of darkness."

"If you had to estimate the size of the snake, shoelace or belt or—"

"You don't find that, like, blasphemous?" she said. "That a man of God would just up and disappear, shafting his landlord? What's to keep me from logging into his Sunday sermon and outing him in the chat?"

"He's been in the wind for two weeks, maybe more. I guarantee he took more from the church than from you," Holland said. A kind of doubt was accruing form and ballast. "Right now I need to know how big of a snake I'm liable to find when we lift this fridge."

"Average size," she said.

"Average of what?" he said.

"He wasn't too big. Or small," she said. "Maybe on the smaller side. Maybe a youngster. He's probably not dangerous, but I don't want him making a guest appearance when I'm showing the house."

Holland was stretching over the counter to see behind the fridge. If there was a snake, and if Mandy had startled it, the most likely place to slither for shelter would be under the fridge. It wasn't impossible.

"Younger snakes are more dangerous," he said. "They can't control their venom. They shoot more in."

"Like I said, I didn't get a good look," she said.

Back in March, when it became clear the madness was only beginning, he'd expected Mandy to check in. Each day he thought: Tomorrow. Each week he talked himself out of calling. Borders closed. Field hospitals were set up. College students were throwing parties, trying to catch it, and Holland knew Mandy had rentals by the university. Before long he got spooked enough to drive out to the gated community on Bee Cave Road. If the gate wasn't open, he'd wait to tail a Land Rover in; the drivers never balked. The Good Fences logo on his truck made it easy for them to think he was building a gazebo for a neighbor's pool. He parked out by the stalled new constructions and watched Mandy's house through field binoculars he'd ordered to sight planes and birds of prey. He listened to the radio, Willie and Waylon, and hotheads saying convention centers might be converted to morgues. Eventually, he spied her mulching a flowerbed while her husband cleaned their gutters. Occasionally he allowed himself to believe Mandy had done her own furtive wellness checks, but he knew better. He'd just about broken the habit of hoping to hear from her when she texted about the snake.

And now she was standing on the kitchen island, poised to tip the refrigerator back so Holland, sprawled on the tile, could see underneath. Her palms were flat against the freezer. He was actively avoiding looking up her chambray shirt.

From the floor, he said, "If I say, 'Drop it,' just let it go. Don't worry about me, I'll move."

"You already said that," she said. "Just tell me when to tilt it back. I feel like I'm being frisked."

"Okay," he said, bracing, ready to spring to his feet if he saw anything he didn't like.

"Okay, tilt? Or okay you'll tell me when?"

"Tilt," he said.

"Now?"

"Now," he said. "Yes. Go."

Dust bunnies and dead cockroaches. The bottom panel was solid sheet metal, nowhere for anything to slip in. Holland said, "You can let it down."

"He's gone?" she said. She lowered the fridge but stayed on the island. Like they were castaways and she'd sought higher ground in hopes of flagging a helicopter.

"You're sure it went under here?" he asked. "You're positive?"

"Hundred percent," she said.

Holland sidled between the counter and refrigerator, squeezed behind it. The space was so tight that his only option was to squat straight down, as if being lowered into a well, and graze his hand over the backside of the fridge near his boots. He shut his eyes to picture what he was touching: six tiny screws fastening a vented panel, the slits thin and tight. To slip inside, the snake would have to be the circumference of a drinking straw. Assuming Holland could even remove the panel, he'd have no room to scramble if the snake struck. A rush of claustrophobia, a sense that the walls of the well were constricting, pressing in from every direction, that water was rising. His bandana made it hard to breathe.

"And there's zero chance of it being red and yellow?" he said, leaning back to rest his head against the wall, eyes shut. "I need you to be real certain on that count."

"I'd recognize a coral snake," she said. He heard her jump down from the island and pad in the opposite direction. "You think I'm dumb, but I'm not."

"I've never said that."

"You say it without saying it." Her voice had gotten louder, clearer, but also farther away. He envisioned her sitting on the threshold of the back door, unmasked, inhaling clean night air. She said, "That was always your method. You're an insult ventriloquist."

"I don't think you're dumb," he said, and it was true. He thought she was selfish and impatient and made a habit of grinding his heart into dust, but not dumb. She ran circles around salespeople, convinced judges to dismiss speeding tickets, and on a lark one summer, she learned passable Spanish by watching Mexican soap operas. Since the divorce, he'd measured every woman against her and enjoyed a surge of futile, misbegotten pride when each came up short.

"But then again," she said, "a preacher left me holding the bag, so maybe I am stu—"

"There's a vent," Holland interrupted, feigning discovery. "He might've gotten inside."

"That sneaky little shit," she said. "I knew it."

Holland opened his pocketknife and used the tip of the blade to loosen the screws. Tedious, halting work. The blade kept slipping, and it took concentration to find the slot again. He imagined Mandy scrolling through her phone, texting Mr. Startup or searching for the wayward preacher. Chambray shirt, he thought. Yoga pants. How she believed brides would buy his bottled scent. He wanted to squirrel away every detail that would animate this evening in his recollection. He wanted Mandy to offer up something she missed about the old times. There was only the metallic hum of the refrigerator, the blood marching in his ears.

When he undid the final little screw, he held the panel in place. Sweat in the corners of his eyes, tracking through his whiskers. He reminded himself that Mandy had conjured the snake from thin air, that it was imaginary, a ploy. To what end, though? To call him an insult ventriloquist? With his shoulders lodged between the fridge and the wall, it seemed feasible he'd misjudged the situation, that he'd maybe never trusted her enough, and for that, he'd soon find himself inches from the dull gaze of a pit viper. He wiped his face on his sleeve.

He had to work to get eye level with the vents in the cramped space, finally rolling half onto his back, chin pressed to his chest like he'd fallen down a stairwell. His breath was coming quick and shallow. The image of the snake striking: the pink flash of its diamond-shaped mouth, the rifle-fire snap of its recoil. He could almost feel the slow boil of the venom in his veins. He slid the panel up slowly, incrementally. If he was lucky, he might be able to slam the edge back down like a guillotine. He was overcome with thirst, sandpaper in his throat. He considered refastening the panel and telling Mandy he'd been mistaken, the vents were too tight after all. When the panel was high enough for him to squint inside, what he saw reminded him of a glove compartment in an old Cadillac—black and spacious and empty. He closed his eyes, just then realizing he'd been forcing them open. He was sapped, awash in humiliating relief.

Now who's dumb. Now who's left holding the bag.

When Holland squeezed out from behind the fridge, he found himself alone. Now Mandy's purse lay on the island like a curled-up animal. She'd snuck off to the bathroom, he figured. Or the preacher had returned, or her husband, and she'd intercepted him at the front door. He felt useless, besieged by the seasick awareness of standing alone in someone else's house. The urge to hide. To bolt. On his phone was a text from the Barton Hills woman saying she'd given his information to a neighbor who wanted a skateboard ramp. Holland deleted the thread. He listened for Mandy's voice, for a flushing toilet. He tried to think of anywhere else a snake might hide. He pulled down his bandana, then pushed and slid and rocked the fridge back into its place. Eventually he went out the back door, stepping down onto the rough concrete slab that served as a patio.

The backyard was bigger than he recalled, and darker. The preacher had once told him that Mrs. Salazar, the sickle-backed widow in the corner house, had shot the streetlamp out with her husband's rifle because the light shone directly into her bedroom. Holland had repeated the story many times. He hoped she was still there, armed and ornery. The stars were splotchy and dim, the weak splatters of a near-empty can of spray paint. And yet there was light enough to see the yard had gone mostly to dirt. Either the deer had defeated it, or the preacher had never run the sprinklers Holland had installed.

"I left the door open in case he slithered out," Mandy said. Holland had to squint to find her under the live oak across the yard. She was in a folding lawn chair. "I'm sorry I abandoned you."

"Do what?"

"In the kitchen," she said, too quick, lest her apology evoke past disappearances. "I started feeling panic attack-y. I carry chill pills these days but left my purse inside."

"I can grab it," he said. Still in therapy, he thought. "Water too?"

"He took all the cups," she said. "I'm calmer now. I just keep thinking this is the end of the world. A snake in a house previously occupied by one of God's servants didn't exactly help."

"Maybe the snake was raptured too," he said.

"Or maybe I'm just mourning not making enough bad decisions when I had the chance."

Holland couldn't tell if she was hinting, setting a snare, or saying the first thing in her mind. His eyes were adjusting, and she was coming into focus. Maybe she'd undone a button at the top of her shirt. Years ago, when she'd started static about the midterm elections, they'd wound up at the Deluxe Inn.

"So far," he said, aiming to sound unfazed and open a door, "my worst decision has been adopting chickens somebody dumped out by the airport. It took me a day to catch them. Brahma, they're called. Show chickens. Prize winners. They have feathers down to their toes. I guess their owners couldn't afford to feed them and couldn't bear to eat them."

"That's some depressing shit," she said.

"The chickens might disagree," he said.

"You built them a chicken mansion is my bet."

The stomach-jump of being known. He looked at his work boots in case he couldn't suppress a smile. He said, "Special chickens deserve special accommodations. They deserve towers connected by a covered bridge. They deserve ramps and balconies."

"And I bet you still make your spaghetti sandwiches," she said.

"Everything tastes better between two slices of bread," he said.

A flotilla of clouds skimmed over the sky from the east, pulled or pushed by secret wind. Then, the sucker punch of memory: a decade prior, another backyard, Mandy sitting in another lawn chair while he cut her hair. He'd never done such a thing and was convinced he'd botch the job, but they were trying to save money for—what? Just then he couldn't remember wanting anything beyond her. The next morning they drank their coffee outside and watched a wren deliver wispy clippings of Mandy's hair to its nest.

"Why did I cut your hair? What were we saving for?" he asked.

"Speaking of bad decisions," she said, but fondly. "I spent twice whatever we saved the next day at the beauty shop. I don't know what we wanted. I think you were mad about taxes."

"So you didn't lure me here for a haircut?" he said. "That's not the next bad decision."

"I lured you here to catch a snake. 'Comes with king cobra' isn't a selling point in today's market."

"If you'd actually seen a snake, you'd call the exterminator. Or your husband."

"Exterminators charge for their services, and Wade appreciates snakes less than I do," she said, then shuddered, as if hit by an arctic blast. "He moved so fast! I'm sure I'll have nightmares about him coming—"

"Up through the toilet when you're trying to pee," he said. "It'll never happen."

"And saying that will never be reassuring," she said.

"Snakes can't breathe under wat—"

Mandy started swiping tears from her cheeks. Then she just crumpled and was crying in her hands. Holland wanted to rush to her but knew she'd fumble for her mask and retreat across the yard. It wasn't a reality he'd be able to bear. He surveyed the dirt and rotting fence, then realized the haggard clouds had disappeared without his noticing. The murmur of faraway traffic.

"Fuck, Holland," she said. "I was already worried before I knew you were just wearing a bandana. Real masks aren't expensive. I'm sure they make sizes to fit libertarians."

"I'm getting by," he said. "I'm doing all right."

"I'm worried you'll get it, obviously, but also that you'll get it and not tell anyone," she said. "And by anyone, I mean me. You're all the way out in the sticks. You're all alone."

"You're really underestimating my chickens," he said. Insects trilled ceaselessly in the dark, a throbbing chorus he now realized he'd been hearing all along.

"You think you're protecting people, but really you're just scared," she said.

"Scared of what?"

"I never figured it out. If I had, maybe we wouldn't have parted the sheets."

"Things can be simple," he said. "Not everything needs figuring out. Not everything is a mystery that needs—"

"What I need is for you to swear you'll tell me if you get it."

"Scout's honor," he said, quick and easy. When she started crying again, he said, "I've got bottled water in the truck. I can fetch your purse and you can take a—"

"It's like everything was on a solid glacier for our entire lives," she said as she blotted her eyes with the cuffs of her shirt, "but now it's breaking apart and we're on our own little pieces of ice and floating away in different directions. Soon I'll be gone or everyone else will. I mean, if you can't count on a preacher to stick it out, who's left?"

"I am," he said. "I'm right here."

"You are," she said. "And you're sweet to rush over even if you think I'm lying about the snake."

"I want you to feel better," he said.

"Maybe I hallucinated him. Maybe mirages are a symptom they haven't announced yet. Maybe I *did* invent him to get you over here and seduce you one last time, but the shitty preacher took the bed. Who knows? Nothing feels true anymore."

The feeling was constant lately, fortitude being corroded from the inside out, but in her presence, he knew some things were still true. Like, he'd already spent a week in July coughing up blood, his sheets so sweat-sopped that he'd rolled onto the trailer floor but found no relief. Like, he was convinced that's where someone would eventually discover him, and he'd spent hours imagining Mandy getting the news but couldn't figure what he hoped her reaction would be. Like, he'd told himself that if he recovered, he'd vie for another chance, that he'd find a way to approach her without suspicion or wariness, that he'd suggest lighting out for Mexico or Canada, just them and the chickens, but now here they were and he was the same old coward.

"I have a drywall saw in my toolbox," he said.

"English, please."

“I can cut into that wall behind the fridge and look for the snake,” he said. “No one’ll know once it’s pushed back.”

Mandy leaned forward in the lawn chair, pondering something. A breeze expanded the branches of the live oak, as if the tree were drawing a great breath. A barred owl called from somewhere nearby: Who cooks for you? Who cooks for you?

“People need home offices right now,” she said.

“English, please.”

“I’ll list it as having space for an office, and someone’ll rent it, snake or no snake.”

“Or I can cut in behind the bottom shelf of the pantry, which might flush him out the way he came in,” Holland said. “If he’s not there, we can take the house down to the studs until we find him.”

“You’re as stubborn as a scar,” she said. “Maybe just help me drag that awful chair to the curb on our way out?”

And like that, the night was over. They listened to the owl for a while, then donned their masks and sulked into the house. For no reason beyond extending their time together, Holland dipped into each room as though doing one last pass for the snake. They tried a couple of different approaches at moving the recliner before pulling out the footrest and stretching the chair to its full length, which made negotiating the doorway disappointingly easy. Mandy carried the front end with her back to Holland. He was tempted to crack a social distancing joke, but instead suggested they hoist the chair into his truck bed in case the garbage collectors wouldn’t take it. “I’ll give it to the chickens,” he said. “Or I’ll leave it in the truck and put my feet up when I go fishing.” Really, he just wanted to offer her a little more help, wanted that memory to ambush her at some point. Mandy thanked him and promised updates on the preacher. Holland promised to call if he got sick. They took a rain check on hugging goodbye and pledged to grab lunch when life returned to normal, the bald and courteous lies their parting required.

Holland reversed from the driveway, then she did, and he followed her to the stop sign. Even after the Tesla glided silently through its turn and her twin taillights faded, he lingered at the corner. He knew the chickens hadn’t eaten since morning, knew he was due early at tomorrow’s job site, knew she wouldn’t text or hook a U-turn, but his boot stayed on the brake. No other cars on the road. The night pressed against the truck’s windshield; the temperature was dropping. He needed to remember anything he’d said to make her smile, anything that might serve as a seed for some future encounter. His thoughts could gain no purchase. His turn signal clicked and clicked. The engine idled. The exhaust purled like smoke from a downed plane.

From behind trees and the darkest corners of the undeveloped lots, the deer watched the blinking red light. All twitching ears, flicking tails, delicate ankles. A buck nibbled delphinium, then, still chewing, raised his top-heavy head to scan the area and check on the red light. A doe scratched her neck with her hind foot. Then she froze. The buck's jaw locked. A tremor beneath their hooves, a rumbling motion somewhere. They swung their heads in unison toward the blinking light as it advanced slowly into the dark. In the truck bed, the old recliner jostled, swayed. There, deep under the seat's cushion, the snake—a copperhead, hungry, still gray at five months old—lay coiled and alert. The world was reverberating from every dark direction, a chaos that frightened and confused her, so she curled tighter, made herself smaller. She stared with unblinking eyes into nothingness. She flicked her tongue, trying to decipher the numberless threats in the cold air.

NASHVILLE, 1999

by JOHN OKRENT

from PLOUGHSHARES

David Berman 1967–2019

"What's for you won't go by you," he told me, the great, recalcitrant songwriter so heavy-browed with doubt and kindness. I was eighteen and had taken a Greyhound from New York to Nashville to find him, my corduroys indistinguishable from my self. That whole wolf-on-skates year his music had saved me, made me feel something like head-over-heels for the world, the one he gestured to always lurking there just underneath this one, or just beyond it. *Water looked like jewelry coming out the spout. The jagged skyline of car keys.* I looked for his name and found it in the white pages in the phone booth in the bus station and I called him and left a voicemail. This was before cell phones. I called my hero's home. Maybe I reached his wife, Cassie, who people blamed for ruining the band but who really saved it, or saved him, for a while, at least, which is forever while it lasts. I don't really remember. Why did I zap my brain with so much pot and booze when I was young? Diversion was the rage. But wasn't being eighteen high enough? I remember I found a motel room for $19.99 and called him again and got him, the man himself, and told him I'd travelled from NYC, told him how I loved his poetry, really loved it, and would he meet me? We made a plan. I probably watched hours of Sports Center, smoked a million cigarettes, I don't know. I have no memory of that afternoon or evening. But that night at 2:00 a.m. the phone in my room rang and it was him, and he said, "John, let's push it back tomorrow. I'm still out and I won't be in good shape. Can I pick you up at one instead?" And when I wrote to him twenty years later, less than a month before he killed himself, I reminded him of that, how he called this random eighteen-year-old kid at two in the morning not to cancel, just to reschedule, just to give himself a bit more of a cushion the next day. And in his letter back to me, which was only five lines long he wrote, "thank you for reminding me I was a decent guy at my worst." Anyway, next day, he picked me up in an old brown Volvo station wagon and took me out for a burger and a Coke. I asked him all my questions, which mostly had to do with unrequited love and he was patient with me and wise and must have been so terribly hungover and depressed, and he told me how he sometimes got so bad—he told me this as he was driving me back to the bus station—that he'd wind up in the hospital for a few weeks, and when I got out of the car he said, "God bless you, John." And no one has ever said that to me before or since and really meant it, as I felt he did. He was younger then than I am now but I doubt I will ever be that old. We were in touch briefly after that meeting and then not again for twenty years, just before he hung himself, in Brooklyn, where he'd been rehearsing before beginning a tour for his new album. "Why don't you write more about love?" I had asked him. "I try to write with love, not about it," he'd replied.

CONSIDERING TOP SURGERY AT THE END OF THE WORLD

by REBECCA MARTIN

from BRINK

I'm tracing a line: object becomes
subject. Trajectory of a body under
the pool of streetlight, of a deer choosing
salt over two-lane road and living another
night. Salt is the object and I wake up
feeling my hair for antlers. The worst
I can imagine is a treeline, flooded
bright and clinical. Instead, I live
in my old neighborhood and spend hours
walking around looking for me.
You offer to record yourself cooking,
and I'm sunburned on the coast
with you, sand in my mouth
collecting in my blanket
which I shake out for months after.
I think about the shape
of a keyhole, what it means
to have tissue, more or less,
and what locked door I'm
staring so hard at. Subject becomes
object again, becomes pliant under
a surgeon's hand, antlered
with waiting.

CAIRN

fiction by CLINT BENTLEY

from THE IOWA REVIEW

James Perkins had just killed his goats. Forty-seven in all. But for the two bulls, every one had been born right there on his property, and even though he was a rancher and they were stock, he loved them—as he would later tell me—as much as anyone loves their pet.

The day I met him he was digging a hole in his pasture to bury them.

I had gone to his property to interview him for an article in the local paper in Brennan, Texas: *The Brennan Eagle*. More of a community bulletin really, but my life had quite derailed by that point and so I took what I could get.

I had been writing for the *Eagle* and building their "social media presence" for about three months. As long as any relationship can last before it must either turn serious or start to die a slow death.

I moved to Brennan from New York, where I had spent about eight months living in a friend's stairwell in Brooklyn, trying to write some great, spacious novel, but instead inadvertently developing a not-so-mild chemical dependency, spinning into a deep depression, and eventually limping out of the city with just three half-finished short stories and a fresh scar up my left wrist.

I woke up in a detox facility with my mother at my bedside, saying *how? how?*—a question I still find myself asking in quiet moments.

I don't even remember how I got to Texas.

But about that article.

Apparently one of Perkins's long-dead relatives had fought in a battle or two in the Texas Revolution. Perkins even had some family heirloom to prove it, I guess. I was tasked by Geoff—the editor and owner of the paper, who had penned no fewer than three "anonymous" op-eds trumpeting support for the sheriff's office campaign for a new jail—to write a charming and subtly patriotic story about Perkins's great-great-whoever.

"Something everyone can get behind," Geoff said.

"What about the folks in town whose ancestors were on the other side of that land grab?" I asked. "Maybe we interview some of them too? Let the article itself be a conversation."

But Geoff had lost patience for ideas like that. He faked the same pitying half-smile I got when I was overexplaining why I missed another deadline and said, "Let's see a draft by Thursday."

Perkins was hacking at the ground with a long-handled mattock when I got there. When he finally noticed me coming across his pasture, he stopped his work and squinted toward me, hunched and holding the tool crosswise in the open field like some old fairy tale creature.

"You from the county?" he yelled at me even though I was close by then.

"Huh?"

I had popped a gummy on my drive there. They tended to define my afternoons back then. This one was starting to vibrate a little earlier than expected.

"I don't need a permit to dig a hole on my own land. And I ain't starting no fires, I don't care what Doc Hathaway told you."

I didn't know who Doc Hathaway was, but that didn't seem worth clarifying. I reminded him why I was there.

"Oh," he said and dropped the mattock head to the ground. "That was today?"

"Yeah, but I can come back another time. If that'd be better."

"No, you made the drive all the way out here. How long you think it'll take?"

"Doesn't have to be long. I just have a few questions that can give me the bones of the story. Then we can do a follow-up after I have a draft."

"Well, it's a pretty long story. But OK." He wiped his face with a dusty rag from his pocket and suddenly seemed very frail in his sun-bleached shirt, his brittle hair quivering in the wind.

I looked at the ground he had broken up. An area about the size of an apartment kitchen.

"Gonna be a pretty big hole, huh?"

And so he told me about his goats. Like he had been practicing the story, just waiting for someone to come along and ask.

Two weeks earlier, Perkins found three of his goats dying in the pasture.

"Laid right out in the open. Away from any tree or brush," he told me. "That tells you an animal don't care about living no more. Not even trying to hide itself. I figured the rest of the herd took it to mean the same thing because they had left them there and moved on across the hill to graze."

When he approached these three, they just sat there with their legs curled under them, staring at the ground and coughing like old men.

Perkins brought them into the barn and laid them in a stall together. He then called Dr. Julian Hathaway, the veterinarian in town, who promised to stop by in the next day or two.

But by the time Dr. Hathaway got there the next afternoon, those three were dead and four more had similarly wilted in the fields.

"It went on like that for the better part of a week," Perkins said. "Every day, a couple more sick. Two days later, dead as a doornail. Doc Hathaway tested them for all types of things. Were they eating something? Was there something in the water? But my water's clean, I told him that. This ain't the Higgins ranch. Then he said it could be some kind of African virus that came over in pigs. But I knew it wasn't that. How do you get a African pig virus if you ain't been around any African pigs?"

He waited even though the question seemed to be more of a statement, so I said, "Right."

"Some of these doctors they get so educated they don't know anything anymore. That's half the trouble these days. Well, if not half of it, a good portion."

"Did he ever find out what it was?"

"Yeah," he said slowly. He looked around as if to find the memory somewhere. "Some kind of virus. Got in their brains I guess. Like that old, uh, chronic wasting disease that deer can get."

I wrote the words *chronic wasting disease* in my notebook.

"Doc said that the whole herd was now exposed. Needed to be got rid of. Exterminated, he said. Over and over he said that. Exterminated. Like they were just things. Someone's supposed to come out from the state in a day or two. But that didn't sit right with me. Somebody else doing it. They're my goats. I'm supposed to take care of them.

And I know the doc sees a lot of animals, but the way he talked about it . . ."

His voice trailed off.

I started to ask him how it was done. Had he shot them? Poisoned them? How did the goats respond to the others being killed? But it felt wrong to ask.

"So you have to bury them?" I said.

"I could burn 'em, Doc said. But of course there's a burn ban in the county right now."

I had a dozen other questions but the gummy was really kicking in. My whole body felt numinous.

Perkins looked out across the land. The autumn grass swayed in the chilly breeze. His property was a wide bowl of rocky pastureland lined on three sides by hills. The south end sloped away as if carved out by some ancient flood and the land dropped off across counties named after both genocided indigenous peoples and after the men who had engineered their killings.

"Doc said they had probably had the virus for months before they started showing signs," he said, somewhere far away. "Just cooking in them."

I started to make a note of that but my pen just skated across the page. My penmanship was magnificent, but I couldn't make the shapes into letters.

"Welp," he finally said. "I better get back to it. It's getting dark."

"Oh yeah, of course, sorry. I'll uh. . . . Maybe I'll come back another time and we can talk about your grandpa. Your great-grandpa, I mean."

"My great-uncle Maynard. That sounds good. Just call me in a couple days. Make sure to shut that gate on your way out. If you don't mind."

Driving away under a ragged purple sunset, my busted Corolla hummed over the faded two-lane road and I soon found myself at Buford's Smokehouse—a bar run by a taxidermist just across the county line. Brennan is in a dry county, so everyone has to drive two towns away to get a drink.

I tried to write a piece about the liquor ban when I first got to the paper. I wanted to correlate the number of drunk driving incidents against the passage of the law, juxtapose it with interviews from both sides. But Geoff killed it, said that's not what this paper is for.

I was two mezcals deep by the time my burger arrived. At the end of the bar an old woman played a casino machine. Mashing buttons for a quarter. Losing over and over. A mounted deer head hung above her, looking just as bored as she did.

The glow of the gummy had worn off, replaced by a distant numbness from the liquor. I needed someone to talk to and so I found myself bothering the bartender. I told her all about Perkins and his goats and his funny way of talking that seemed like he was chewing his words on their way out.

Apparently she was familiar with the man. She called him "half nuts three quarters of the time." Said he claimed to have been hired by NASA for a spell in the eighties, though he never would share the details of his assignments. She said, "I bet you two had a lot to talk about," then said she needed to check on something in the kitchen.

I laughed. Then I started to overanalyze what she said.

Was she making fun of Perkins with me?

Or making fun of me?

I found myself in the faded bar mirror, surrounded by liquor bottles of every color and hue. I started to drift into a familiar spiral: feelings of worthlessness, then more liquor, then some kind of upper to counter it, then some cough syrup or pot to get me to sleep, then a deep dread the next morning that would be treated with more liquor.

I couldn't stop thinking of Perkins. Out there all alone. What was I doing? Just using his stories for other people's entertainment? Was my need to be liked by every stranger truly that deep?

Nighttime and I stumbled out of the bar. I bumped into a cardboard cutout of a cowboy who then turned and glared at me. I said excuse me cowboy and he said what the hell do you think you're doing. His wife was all fried hair and big earrings and seemed very disappointed in me too. She said my name but I was halfway back to my car before I could figure how I might have met her.

Driving was then an exercise of supreme focus. *Am I between the lines? What's my speed? Anyone in the rearview? Am I between the lines? Don't touch the radio.* Repeat until you reach your destination.

The trees crowded up next to the road as if they gathered there at night to commune. The fluorescent eyes of the night animals flashed out from among them—orange and green and ancient as the moon.

Then I was stopped at Perkins's gate. I shut the car off. Killed the lights. Out in the field he had hung a little lamp on a pole and he lay under it on a pile of dirt. I watched him a while and he never moved.

I stumbled through the grass and sat down next to him. He hadn't made much progress on his hole. A plastic milk jug filled with water lay nearby and I pulled down half of it.

He woke up, mumbling. Took him a minute to recognize me.

"I was just closing my eyes." He groaned as he sat up. "Did you shut that gate behind you?"

"What's left to keep in?"

He didn't answer.

I didn't mean it sarcastically, but I was worried it came off that way. "You've got a ways to go, don't you?"

"Seemed like I had made a little more progress before I drifted off."

We stared at the broken ground.

"Well. If you've got an extra shovel. I don't have anywhere to be."

Perkins broke the topsoil with the old wood-handled mattock and I piled it to the side with the shovel. The soil came up in dark clods that got heavier with every scoop.

We talked not at all.

After a couple hours we hit the hardpan. Like finding a buried layer of pavement. The hole was only knee-deep.

We climbed out and sat on the piled dirt, catching our breath. Perkins handed me the jug of water and walked out of the lantern-light. His truck door opened and shut again somewhere in the dark and he came back with another jug and sat next to me.

"I can fill these back up at the barn if we need more."

I lay back on the soil. It still held some warmth from the earth. My head was swimming from the mezcal.

"Look there," said Perkins. "A shooting star."

I found it. Blinking a lazy transit across the stars.

"I think that's a satellite," I said.

"Oh . . ."

We sat in silence and watched it arc toward the eastern hills.

"I saw Sputnik when I was young," he said. "That very next Sunday the pastor read to us from Revelations and told us we better be right with Jesus. He had us all thinking they'd be shooting missiles down on us within a few months. But I guess they didn't."

"Yeah, I guess not."

The stars were draped across the whole of the sky. Too many to pick out any constellations. The smudge of the Milky Way ran like an infinite river above us.

"You think there's anybody else out there?" I said.

"Out where? Like aliens?"

"I guess."

"Hell how would I know. If there is, it probably ain't like in the movies. They're probably just stuck in their little world like we're stuck in this one. Getting behind on bills. Trying to make it work with the missus. Looking out and saying, you think there's anybody else out there?"

I laughed.

"What?" he said.

"I find that kind of comforting."

We took turns busting into the hardpan with the mattock. Like breaking up a buried street. We only made the hole two inches deeper before we had to take another break.

My whole body trembled from exhaustion. I could barely open my hands. I asked him how deep he thought we should go.

"Let's break up as much as we can in the center. Make a bowl. All we can do."

Any drunkenness I had was evaporated. In its place, a distant vagueness and the need to vomit.

I had no idea what time it was.

I eased back down into the hole.

Sometime late in the night the dark hardpan gave way finally to reveal white stone that rang when we struck it. I cleared away the soil and chipped at it some more.

Perkins looked down into the hole. "Limestone. We won't get any deeper without a machine."

I picked up some of the chipped stone. Mixed in were tiny mollusk shells from some long-extinct ocean. I began to fathom it and I got dizzy all of a sudden.

I said, "I'm dizzy all of a sudden" and dragged myself out of the hole to lie on the dirt. It had lost all its warmth and my insides felt dried up and dead.

Perkins handed me the jug of water. One sip and I threw up everything inside me. Then the whole world started to tilt. I cradled my head, silently begging it all to be still.

"Just sit there a minute," he said. "Catch your breath. I'll clear the rest of the hardpan."

I could see lights from the cars out on Highway 84, miles away, tracing the horizon before disappearing behind the hills. Like a procession of ghosts. A train moaned somewhere out there and then I was asleep.

I dreamt of my mother. She was a child—as I had seen her in old family photos—but by some dream logic I knew she was her adult self. She was knelt praying at her bed and I stood watching her. I was so happy to see her and I told her so. I told her a lot of things I never had the courage to say in real life. But she couldn't hear me. After a while I stopped talking. She looked up at me with that mix of pity and disappointment and love that only a mother can manage. The same look she gave me when she saw me in the hospital, gaunt with a bandaged wrist. I started to cry and she faded from the room and then I woke up as the sky was lightening to gray. Some planet hung golden and solitary in the western sky like a little jewel. The last light from the night.

And there was Perkins: crouched, making a fire, blowing the little blue flames to life.

"Come here," he said. "Get warm."

I did. I ached all over from mezcal and the cold and everything else.

"Sorry about that," I said.

"You don't have anything to be sorry for."

The fire popped to life across the stringy wood. Its warmth loosened up my hands.

Perkins looked out across the scraggled land. "Pretty morning," he said.

And it was.

A little stock tank gleamed, reflecting the first light like pooled metal. Whispers of birds shuffled out into the sky and large stones in the grass stirred and then stood on four legs to stretch and take the form of deer and browse away toward the tree line.

Perkins fed some more sticks to the fire then walked away. His truck coughed to life and came back dragging a clanging metal trailer. He swung the truck around and backed the trailer to the pit: piled high with the dead goats—all lying in deranged intimacy with bloated bellies and boney legs protruding at every angle. Some with heads bloody and caved in, mouths aghast, while others seemed to have just drifted off to sleep.

Perkins stepped around and handed me a pair of leather gloves.

"That pair's brand new so they'll be a little stiff." Then he looked at me. "You alright?"

I nodded.

"You don't have to help with this next part. If it's too much."

"No, I'm OK. Any particular way to approach it?"

"Whatever gets them in there."

I grabbed one by the leg to pull it down—heavier than I expected, like a small child. My stomach turned as I swung it down into the hole. It landed with a groan, as if hurt by the fall.

Perkins let out a half-whimper and looked away.

"I'm sorry. I didn't mean to . . ."

"Naw, it's just that she was. . . . Ah they're just goats. I shouldn't get so sentimental."

He took one from the trailer, cradled it, and let it slide awkwardly down into the hole. Then he stared at the goat a while.

"Why don't I just hand them down to you?" I said.

"That might be better."

The hole was not as big as it seemed in the night. The goats filled it entirely and still lay piled and spilling out of it.

"That's alright," Perkins said, staring at the pile of bodies. "I'll cover them with stones to keep the coyotes from them. Then set a fire over them, if they ever lift that burn ban."

I didn't really have the words to say goodbye after all that, so I made a joke about cleaning up my puke, then we shook hands and that was that.

By noon I was back at my apartment. I stood in the shower a long time. Watched the grime wash down the drain. My whole body ached. Somehow, for the first time in over a year, I felt a peace I had no words for.

I decided to take a different approach on the Perkins article. I would make it a long profile, tell his story and the story of his family in the area. It could grow and maybe come to represent the story of the area as a whole. Maybe Geoff could dedicate the back half of the issue to it. And we could profile a new person every week. The possibilities just kept unfolding. I forgot to even be hungry.

I got out of the shower to outline it and found I had missed three calls from Geoff, which I took as a sign.

When I got to the newspaper office, Denise was there at her desk like she always was and I said Morning Denise like I always do, even though it was late in the day, but she just shrugged her eyebrows and looked at her desk like someone who knows something about your fate that you don't yet.

Geoff stepped out of his office and stared at me.

"Tell me about the Perkins interview," he said. "How did it go?"

"Well, Geoff, it's funny you ask because I was coming in to talk to you about it." I started to explain the whole thing about Perkins's goats and the strange virus and I was trying to convey my excitement about the possibilities for this piece but Geoff cut me off.

"I saw you last night," he said.

And immediately I remembered. The cowboy outside the bar.

I thought of explaining myself, but I recognized his look. Had seen it many times from many people. I was a lost case in his eyes and there was no chance for recovery.

"Nothing?" he asked. "All of a sudden, nothing to say?"

There's so much to say, Geoff. So much that it starts to weigh you down. Like a dark cloak that someone placed on your shoulders. One that gets thicker and heavier as the years go by until you can barely stand on your own. Can barely speak to put words to it. Can barely breathe.

But all I could get out was, "I'm sorry, Geoff. I didn't recognize you."

Thus ended my career as a newspaper man.

Late afternoon and I was back at my apartment. I stared at the walls and the day turned heavily into night. Hard to know how much of a fuckup you are until you try to stop being one.

I pulled out every bottle I had to drink. Every container that rattled with pills. I lined them all up on the kitchen counter and stared at them a long time. Thought of taking them all into the bathtub with me.

But something pulled me away.

I found myself again at Perkins's place. His gate was locked so I hopped it, went back to the grave.

He had already piled it high with stones and it stood in the field like a monument to something forgotten. I sat beside it and wrapped my coat tight against the wind. I thought if I could just make it through the night, I might be worth something.

Soon there was a rustling in the grass and Perkins was standing over me with a long-barreled shotgun.

"Oh, it's you," he said and sat down next to me. It was too dark to see what he was looking at.

The wind had turned out of the north and rushed through the grass and between the stones and into our jackets. As if it was trying to get down close to our hearts.

Something cried out in the night.

"Listen to those old bobcats," he said. "They always sing for a new moon."

MORDIDA

by EDUARDO MARTINEZ-LEYVA

from FOGLIFTER JOURNAL

God came down the valley one dust-covered day.
Told you to gather His flock. He spoke slowly
and carried a passport. Rounded his shoulders to get closer
to you. His speech was low and raspy like a headmaster's
or the hot wind that capsizes rowboats on summer nights.
The one that makes widows out of wives. He was looking
for two just men who had fallen off the wagon again.
Asked you to roll up your sleeves. Asked if you had ever shot a gun.
If your conscience was clean. Asked if you spoke English.
If you paid off your loans. Asked for your credit score.
¿Caballero, cómo nos arreglamos? To enter into this kingdom,
he said, you must pay the toll. He folded up your documents
and smacked the palm of His hand with them, waiting impatiently
for your response. Where is your brother, He asked?
What is the circumference of your wound?
What can you do with your mouth? Let's see it.
Show me what's under your tongue.
Do you own anything that isn't your shadow?
Why are you shaking? He scooped you up like a yearling.
His hands were soft but firm.
He could break you like morning bread.
What can you tell me about the rooms you've ruined?
I'm going to touch you now.
Are there any areas that are tender, sensitive?
What else besides your body do you carry

that is illegal? Will your body also carry bullets one day?
What other type of dark alphabet do you know?
Write it down. You keep shaking.
I'm only going to ask you this one more time.
How is it you keep going
when so many who look like you are dead?
Keep dying. Tell me, how many more elegies
do you still have left inside you?

PLATE SPINNER

by FRANCINE WITTE

from NEW WORLD WRITING QUARTERLY

I was probably eleven when my father started spinning plates. He'd been watching *The Ed Sullivan Show* and in between Petula Clark and Sergio Franchi, there was a man, all tuxed-up, spinning fifteen plates, five in the air on spindly sticks, five on the table, as he ran back and forth to keep everything going at once. The orchestra, trumpet-heavy, behind him, the audience's rippled applause.

My father hadn't been out of his armchair, leather and patched, since the accident. The accident being our twelve-year-old neighbor, Jimmy, on his ten-speed, knocking the briefcase out of my father's "coming home from his crappy job" hand and hurling him to the ground. My father's leg breaking like it was made of cheap china. I always hated Jimmy a little because of how he told all the kids I had Lemon Pox, which isn't even a thing, but after the accident, I hated Jimmy even more.

My father sat in that chair for months, even after he healed, even after the doctor said he was fine and could walk again and go back to work. Instead of doing either of those, my father seemed to sink even deeper into his chair. "This accident," he said, "was the best thing that ever happened." My mother didn't agree. She was at work all day at the flower shop. "We're not gonna starve," she said, "but a man has got to *do*."

"Do," my father scoffed, "I *do* all day for a punk half my age always telling me call this client, go make a sale." He shook his tired head. "Enough," my father said. "It's enough." And that's when he saw the plate spinner. "God," he said, "if I could only move like that". The plate spinner eased back and forth, twirling the sticks with the plates on top,

making sure this one twirled and then that one. And as soon as they were all in play, he'd set the plates on the table in motion. One little wrist flick and they were, all of them, turning in the same direction at once.

The next day my father got up out of his chair. When my mother said, "ohhhh how wonderful, now you can get back to work," he said, "no, this is not work." He went to our china closet and took out five plates, bone white, with tiny little flowers along the edge. He set them up on the dining room table. He wasn't ready yet for the sticks, but he seemed convinced he could handle the plates on a flat surface. Certain he could make them dance.

And he did. My mother and I held our breath as the plates, and he, came to life at once. My father was able to find a rhythm in those plates that he had lost everywhere else. They seemed to love his touch. My mother didn't seem very concerned about the china. "Oh we never use it," she said. "And if it makes him DO something, I'm glad."

From then on, every night after dinner, we were eating together as a family again, my father would clear everything off the table. He'd lay down a linen tablecloth (the linen, he said, kept the plates from sliding off.) Then he took the plates out of the china closet and set them nicely in a row. He looked them over and put his finger under the rim of the first one, then the second, just as the man on TV had. He moved on his leg, which seemed like it had never been broken, as if he were leading his own line of ballerinas, all tutus and pirouettes, and my father waiting for the trumpets to come up, followed surely by the applause.

ANA

by KENDRA SULLIVAN

from REPS (Ugly Duckling Presse)

A story about a waterbirth
A story about the ways water is not
exactly its location, source, or destination
not its surface, depth, or volume
not its contents or a tissue stretched
          between continents
A story about how water exceeds identification
          how its soul is "circulation"

A story about vital needs being ignored by nuns
A story about crowning in a toilet
A story about a family forged at a crowning
A story about being sovereign not royal
A story about bypassing the crown
of circular narrative by marrying the church
A story about how an institution
          cannot reproduce biological life
A story about how institutions can and do
          reproduce bare life
A story about how the museum
as an institution is always
about itself (William Pope L.)

A story about a nun
and another single mother named Pilar

A story about a midnight waterbirth
in a convent bathroom
how the nuns' habits gathered like damp
curtain swag beneath the bathroom stalls
A story about the preponderance of blood
        and afterbirth that gladdened
the paving stones by the drain

A story about a dried caul
        to protect against (dry) drowning
A story about birthing coworkers
A story about a vocation
a calling
A story about a convent education
A story about the contents of convents
        subduing the heart
or its heat, about the arterial sounds
of rushing water in a rusted pipe
about crocheting pillow covers to smother
the needling question of so many remains
A story about children
A story about what makes some nuns
        such hardy bursars
        of so many small burials?

A story about the role of unwed women
        in colonialist expansion
A story about who can counter nunwork
        if not mothers
A story about how nuns make it hard
        but moms make it work
A story about how moms who don't have help
        help each other out
        help themselves

A story about being a child eating dinner
late at night in another's mother's kitchen
A story about neighbors raising
        my mother's child
        me

A story about Patricia Hill Collins'
othermothering and accepting
the fundamental workability
    of asymmetrical love
    that it doesn't have to be reciprocal
    or nothing

A story about sleep
is like water
a dream of disidentification
with the self

a hatch is another
word for a passage is . . .

A story about an earlier, ongoing pandemic

A story about how my mom
gave birth to navel genres

submerged her story
in a sub-sub genre
she called "crush depth"

A story about how "passage"
    is another word for para
graph begins and ends with a break
in sense, because submarines
    also breach
when they go too deep

A story about asking future generations
how to soften the blows
A story about ceding power
so we can heal

A story about the way male
    seahorses carry a couple thousand
babies in their abdominal pouches
A story about how some males give birth

and take life with abandon
without recourse

A story about how queer
nature is

A story about the way floating suspends
            storyforms
like location, migration, and belonging

A story about how motile we become
after birth

cruising straight down
into "crush depth"

DON'T BLEED ON THE ARTWORK: NOTES FROM THE AFTERLIFE

by WENDY BRENNER

from OXFORD AMERICAN

I've been dreaming, I've been
paying dues
I'm not one for the glory
And I've been falling, won't be landing soon
It's not the end of the story

—*The Revivalists, "Good Old Days"*

I don't want to hold back
I don't want to slip down
I don't want to think back to the one
thing that I know I should have done

—*Cake, "Love You Madly"*

Months into my new art-framing job, the stacks awaiting me on the worktable each day still feel like a miracle, a surprise party just for me. The art is piled neatly between empty frames, matboards, sheets of glass, foamboard, giant vinyl portfolios. I turn the pieces over one by one, each a puzzle. Glass, paint, wood, canvas, paper, ink, cardboard, silk, wire, tape, staples. Dog hair. Legos. A golf ball. A recently filed legal brief—just a little stapled booklet—for a federal case about protecting immigrants' rights. (The young attorney who brought it in explained when I asked, his face full of pride.) A century-old studio portrait of a small boy in a sailor suit, smiling out from under his bangs, taken the year before he died, a faded note handwritten on the back: *The brother I never knew*. I use my phone to take a snapshot of these words. Later on my computer I'll enhance it, print it out, then slide it into an acid-free sleeve to be taped onto the finished piece's back, as the customer requested. The original note will remain, too—sealed safely and invisibly inside the frame. Maybe for another hundred years.

We are not a museum, just a tiny, scruffy, neighborhood frame shop in Evanston, Illinois, a Chicago suburb known for Northwestern University and the Mitchell Museum of the American Indian, for its commitment to social justice and the arts. As in most places, that commitment often fails when it meets reality, but still, Evanston is fierce and beautiful where you least expect it.

At my job, for instance. The art is unrelenting.

Landscapes and dreamscapes, towers, harbors, mountains, forests, icebergs, beloved anonymous houses, beloved anonymous pets, psychedelic visions and graffiti, diplomas, hockey jerseys, vintage bicycle parts, photographs of every possible object or being, doing every possible activity. A little pencil line drawing of Warhol's famous Absolut vodka bottle, his signature scrawled at the bottom. A dentist's certificate of appreciation for his work caring for "the oral health of Holocaust survivors." An orange cartoon brontosaurus riding a tiny scooter through downtown Chicago. A pack of fierce-faced bicyclists racing along a cliff, in an advertisement for the 1953 Tour de France. Director John Waters grinning in his favorite pink Comme des Garçons jacket ("that looks like your aunt's bedspread with the little balls on it," he told *GQ*). A tasseled table-runner from Turkey, a Dave Chappelle poster, a disintegrating page from a 1904 Chicago newspaper found under someone's bathroom floor during a renovation. Lots of Phish posters. An anonymous, headless female nude painted all in rich, egg-yolk yellow. An 1871 textbook illustration of a uterus embellished with flowers. A Japanese golfer painted in broad calligraphic black brushstrokes. A cowboy in full dress, rodeo number pinned to his back, standing on a diving board over a swimming pool. A child's felt-scrap collage. Autographed photos of Billie Jean King, James Brown. An Alaskan indigenous formline hummingbird, a Hebrew mandala, a Frank Lloyd Wright window. An aerial view of Machu Picchu, glowing gold and black against a bright orange sky, as if the whole world is on fire.

When I get home at night, I collapse in a chair, mute and unable to move. The art feels like a tornado whooshing through me. I feel euphoric and empty, cleaned out. Words and thoughts blasted away. My eyes scoured clean.

I love the art so much I sometimes weep. I try not to let anyone see. My boss works in the basement building frames, and the only other employee works mostly on days I don't. When customers come in, I can't look up at them right away anyhow because I'm handling glass or razor blades or using some sharp tool I never knew the name of until now. (For the first time in my life, I own an awl, a sleek little wooden-handled model sheathed in clear vinyl. My boss gave it to me, said to keep it secret, write my name on it. This felt ceremonious, initiatory, though I think he just wants all our awls to quit disappearing.)

I have no training for this work. I got the job by bringing in my posters to be framed, things I bought in the 1980s at Chicago's famous Wax Trax record store, now closed: David Bowie's *Lodger* album cover art; a Roxy Music concert poster from the band's 1973 German tour; Tom Tom Club's Tina Weymouth standing naked in a swamp, strategically smeared with mud, electric guitar strapped across her chest.

I got the job by asking the frame shop guy—my boss—if he needed an assistant.

My life has gone off the map, it seems. Possibly also off the rails.

In 1989, in my early twenties, I fled Chicago and moved to the American South, where I hoped to spend my entire adult life, writing and teaching and teaching writing. I planned never to return. Chicago was cold. My parents were difficult and made mistakes. In North Carolina, I lived at the actual beach. I won awards, I published books, I got tenure—I showed everybody, didn't I? I got cancer; I recovered, surrounded by friends. I survived hurricanes.

Back home in Chicago, my parents grew old. I didn't see this happening and neither did they. They were busy birdwatching, attending new plays, trying new restaurants. Our relationship had mellowed and warmed with time. But then my father, my sweet, strong, and only father—he began to die, and then he died. Words that still don't sound true five years later, as I type them here.

I stopped caring so much about words. In Chicago, my mother, now alone, began to lose hers. She fell, and didn't remember falling. She said she never fell, and if she did, she certainly wasn't going to tell anyone.

She had no family left in Chicago. She agreed to move into Memory Care. I decided to move back north.

Why? Why did I leave you many years ago? wrote the artist Marc Chagall in the 1940s, in a letter to Vitebsk, the Russian city of his youth. He imagined that the city understood and forgave him: *Maybe the boy is crazy, but crazy for the sake of art . . . he is still "flying," he is still striving to take off . . .*

I had flown. Now it was time to migrate back.

I did not yet know what else it was time for.

At the frame shop there is so much beauty, it can't be real. Maybe this is the afterlife, I think. Or purgatory.

The work is taxing. I stand all day, or walk around and around the worktable. I carry huge sheets of glass to a cutting machine and cut them. I smash unusable pieces loudly into a metal bucket, then tote the bucket to the dumpster out back. My hands grow strong and scarred.

A few blocks away, my mother dreams, awake or asleep. She plays Uno with an aide or naps in her wheelchair, wearing one of my old sweaters. *Hand-me-ups*, we joke. She can still joke. But I don't understand how she can forget so much of her life so quickly. Or where a life goes after you forget most of it. She hasn't forgotten me yet. Not yet.

The assignments on the worktable each morning have been set aside for me because they're easy and I'm a novice, or because they're complicated and there's a skill I need to learn, or practice. Or because my boss knows I will love them—though maybe I'm imagining that.

Once, early on, I drilled a screw into the back of a frame and it came out through the front, a bad mistake. The frame had to be rebuilt. I arrived at work the next day to find twenty identical manufactured frames from Target or Walmart, allegedly brought in by a customer who wanted only new hangers installed on the backs. A strange order. I spent the day drilling forty holes, installing forty screws, twisting forty wires. My hands hurt for a week.

I work six or seven hours without breaks. I can't seem to explain this to my friends. Momentum, focus. While I'm cleaning glass, inspecting endlessly for specks of dust or lint, using a marker to cover a flea-sized chip on a frame, time falls away. Everything outside the moment falls away, like a blurred background in an Impressionist landscape. No, I don't want lunch, no I don't want to sit down.

My boss is in the basement building frames. Sawing or chopping long pieces of wooden moulding, joining corners with a compressor-powered pneumatic machine that seems to breathe on its own. It's dark and dungeony down there, cement floor and cinder-block walls, accessible only by rickety wood plank stairs. The basement runs the length of the building, filled with machinery and racks upon racks of uncut wood, organized in a system only my boss understands. Ash, oak, pine, eucalyptus, ramin. Finger-jointed wood, wood made of milled scraps. Narrow, wide, flat, scooped, beveled, painted, stained. My boss knows them all. He knows what each wood will do, and what it won't. One crumbles so easily he calls it "cornflakes." Others are impossibly hard. He hates maple.

(Why? Because it builds like shit, he says. Maple is hard. Plus its shade varies and might not match the sample the customer viewed. Whenever maple is mentioned, my boss starts giving everyone dark and desperate looks.)

He has been making frames since the 1970s. He sort of *is* the 1970s. He's Wolfman Jack, WKRP's Johnny Fever; he's Oscar the Grouch with the worst smoker's cough I've ever heard. He keeps smoking anyway, even inside the store, though none of his legions of customers seem to notice. He's a rebel, an old hippie, or maybe a young one? A long-hair, not a suit. No framers are suits, he tells me.

He once hoped to become a comic book artist. He loves vintage sci-fi comics and Robert Crumb and Lichtenstein and Dali and Hieronymus Bosch and has adorned the store's walls with samples of their work and lots of other dark and strange images, showing off our frames. My boss quotes randomly and significantly from *Dune*. (It's best just to nod.) When he's in the basement, thumping bass and psychedelic reverb waft up the stairs into the store from his beloved Hawkwind CDs, faint behind the blare of our workspace boombox.

Yes, we have an actual boombox, its radio dial set to Chicago's WXRT-FM, the alt-rock soundtrack of my youth—how does this station even still exist? (And why is it still playing Warren Zevon's "Werewolves of London"?) Soon I'm humming along with Black Pumas, Tame Impala, Teddy Swims, Cold War Kids, the Revivalists. Also Cake, and Beck: *Things are gonna change, I can feel it.*

And yet, here in our shop, they haven't. Our customers seem to love this about us, our indie small-business vibe. We are falling apart in so many ways—our bodies, our tools, the glass-cutter's blade holder. Our two-sided tape gun is held together by one-sided tape.

The store's front room is no bigger than my apartment's living room, an open space with high whitewashed ceilings and bright track lighting to illuminate the worktable, around which everything, and everyone, revolves. Our picture window directly overlooks the sidewalk and busy street, nothing but glass between us and the pedestrians rushing by or stopping to look in. Lots of people know us. Customers love to tell us how long they've known my boss. It's not that they want special treatment. It's like they want to be part of us in some way.

When my boss works in the "cellar," as he medievally calls it, he stays down there as long as he can, because of his knees, because stairs. He leans heavily on counters and tables just to walk around a room. Descending the steps, he literally yells in pain.

Ascending a couple of hours later, he carries newly constructed frames so perfect, so beautiful, that I feel I've never really *seen* frames before. They are just squares and rectangles, pieces of wood holding air, empty space. Once fitted onto the artwork, they become necessary, almost invisible, essential as a body part.

Sometimes customers actually gasp when I show them their finished framed piece, or even when they see a frame sample held against some artwork. Maybe the art doesn't look like much, or even like art. Maybe it's a mass-produced postcard or a child's crayon scribble. The frame changes everything.

When my boss stomps up from his frame-building cellar and sees me, he always barks: *Are you still here?* Which is literal, because I'm new and only working part time, but also existential because how *am* I still here—or back here? It's been a year since I returned to Chicago, but it still doesn't feel like real life.

My boss is laughing, of course. His long gray mustache covers the corners of his mouth, so it takes me some weeks working there to realize he's smiling. Later I learn where on his face to look.

Get back to work, chop-chop! he yells. He talks to himself all day, even in the restroom, not that I'm listening on purpose. The glass cutter is right outside the bathroom, so close it's necessary to shout a heads-up before going in or out. *Glass always gets the right-of-way,* says my boss. He sounds like William S. Burroughs, that lazy ironic drawl. Other times he sounds exactly like *Mystery Science Theater,* erupting into rapid-fire joyously sarcastic commentary on everything. When I run to answer the store phone, I hear him in the background: *She's running!*

It's just hard not to be happy in this place.

Are you still here? My mother doesn't remember I now live in Chicago again. So she is always surprised and happy to see me, happier than I've ever known her to be. *Is this your last day?* she asks, beaming up from her wheelchair. *Let me know when you're coming back.* She has forgotten all her grudges. Well, most of them. When I sign in at her facility's front desk, the receptionist says, *Oh, you're Mrs. Brenner's daughter? Are you the good one or the bad one?*

I never thought you would turn out so well, my mom tells me. Her formerly sharp face is soft and full of light. Her dated mom perm is all grown out, thanks to COVID, and she is actually beautiful.

No matter what time I visit my mom, I end up helping her in the bathroom. But that's okay. I know these days won't last forever.

Other ladies who live on my mom's hallway sometimes cry at the breakfast table, or yell for help from their rooms. Often ignored by overburdened nurses. One woman's eyes look like they're bleeding. In Memory Care, one sees and hears many things one wishes to forget. But my mom says she feels safe here, says there's nowhere else she'd rather be.

When winter comes, I drape my long wool scarf around her neck because she's always cold. *That's how you can tell we're sisters,* she says, her eyes shining. My mom doesn't even have a sister.

On my drive to work, I pass my old high school, which I'd hoped never to see again. Across the street from my apartment, improbably, stands a perfect half-scale model of the Leaning Tower of Pisa, built in 1934 by an American guy who evidently just loved the Leaning Tower of Pisa. In the 1980s, my mom and I often swam laps at the Leaning Tower YMCA—now closed and slated for demolition. The Tower itself still stands tall.

Well, leans tall.

My apartment is beautiful to me, with its ten-foot ceilings and original recessed canister lighting from 2007, and the floor-to-ceiling red silk living room drapes the previous tenant left behind, far too dramatic for my mismatched old furniture. I'd planned to take the drapes down, but after I move in they seem perfect. They make me feel like I'm at the ballet, or possibly a puppet show. They give my old furniture a weird new beauty.

Like putting an ordinary postcard or snapshot into a giant gilded frame—ironic but also not. Everything transformed and elevated. The whole greater than the sum of its parts.

The frame shop is housed in a rundown mid-century brick two-flat, its purple-painted front door decorated with Andy Warhol photos and quotes: ART IS WHAT YOU CAN GET AWAY WITH, and THE IDEA OF WAITING FOR SOMETHING MAKES IT MORE EXCITING. Some previous employee did this decorating, my boss tells me. Not that he has anything against Andy.

Inside are multitudes of everything: the rainbow of four hundred frame samples on the walls, those upside-down V's we all recognize; a long side counter covered with tape guns, staple guns, spray bottles, glass gloves, art gloves, rolls of brown kraft paper and plastic bags and hanging wire, labeled and unlabeled drawers of hardware, hangers, screws, tools—and everywhere, littered about the store like ballpoint pens on every surface: razor blades. (In fact, we frequently run out of ballpoint pens, but we never run out of razor blades.) Soon I am grabbing blades casually, as all framers do, to pop a speck out of a mat, shave off excess paper or tape. Soon I have Band-Aids on all my fingers.

Our store is not yet computerized, so work orders are done manually on paper forms, which become crowded with numbers and notes in different colors and handwritings as each piece moves through the framing process. In the margin, we always add a quick description of the art, so we don't accidentally put something in the wrong frame. The artwork's title is not enough, as many pieces are untitled, or their title is unrelated to the image itself. Our descriptions are quick and literal: BIRD ON BRANCH. HEBREW LETTERS IN A CIRCLE. DANCERS. WOMAN PASSED OUT IN CHAIR.

This last was for an exquisite realistic painting of a woman, possibly a model, in a sleek black minidress and matching stiletto heels, sitting in a straight-back chair with her head thrown back, her slim knees knocked together. Her face isn't visible, just her elegant neck and jawline. But she is clearly not unconscious—her hands grip the edges of the chair, as if she's just taken a wild ride. The room is Edward Hopper dim around her. Only when I look closely do I see the glass tumbler, a half-finished drink, set on the floor before her, and the bar in the background, behind which a bartender works, his back turned, business as usual.

There ensues a lively debate between my boss (who wrote the description) and everyone else who sees WOMAN PASSED OUT IN CHAIR as to whether the woman is indeed "passed out." (I later learn she is one of artist Nigel Van Wieck's famously and ambiguously sexual characters, hanging out at the edges of the dark, just before some kind of wanton act, or just after it. Predator or prey, unclear.)

Once, early on, when I was feeling discouraged by how slowly I was learning, how many mistakes I made daily, I arrived at the shop to find a work order for TALKING POTATOES. (This was also written in my boss's cartoonist hand, all caps and somehow funny. Can handwriting be funny?) TALKING POTATOES made me decide to stick around a little longer. Literally, I did not quit my job because my boss wrote TALKING POTATOES on a work order form. I wonder if he knows that.

Although there are rumors we will soon abandon these antiquated forms and move to a computerized workflow, my boss's big desktop Dell in the store's back room goes mostly unused for now. We clock in and out on it, or when his knees force him to sit, he smokes and plays virtual solitaire, or reads trippy articles in online science magazines and leaves all his tabs open. *What was it like when no stars yet existed? After the hot Big Bang, it took minutes for atomic nuclei to form and then hundreds of thousands of years to make neural atoms, but the first stars wouldn't form until nearly 100 million years had passed.*

Reading this, I picture our customers, generation upon generation of people floating through the ages with their infinite torrent of saved stuff, their evidence of life, the photos and flags and newspapers, their kids' drawings and baby teeth, their dead pets, their flower crowns, their diplomas and vintage candy wrappers. I love them so much, these people.

Framing is alchemical, but it's also just a series of steps, straightforward as a recipe. First, you measure, cut, build, and join the four sides of the frame, using an electric saw or manual chopper, and a joining machine or miter vise to attach and secure the corners. Then you cut the chosen matboard, glass, and backing to fit, unless the art will be framed with no mat or glass, as is customary when framing paintings on canvas, so that the canvas can "breathe." Then you putty the frame—i.e., smooth and mask dings or irregularities in the wood, and fill, or *appear* to fill, any visible gaps in the frame's corners using special putty that exactly matches the frame's color and texture (which you may have to custom-mix in advance, no big deal, just keep an ice cube tray full of blobs of every possible hue stored under your worktable, and be careful to keep your putty *away from the art,* best to set up a kind of paper-covered putty station as far away from humanity as possible, where you can work in peace and safety, making sure to check and wash your hands, clothes, and body before re-joining your coworkers). Now place your finished frame face down on the worktable, clean the glass with non-ammonia spray and microfiber cloth—always wear glass-handling gloves for this step, *do not bleed on the artwork*—and then, finally, making sure you have the correct side of the glass facing outward, place the pane gently into the frame, brush it free of lint, then place the artwork in there (which you've attached securely and not crookedly to its mat with acid-free tape, which might take more than one try, or maybe the mat is off by one or two sixteenths of an inch and needs to be recut). Finally, place the backing foamboard on top, and use your point gun to secure everything in place with framer's points, so that you can turn the whole thing over and inspect for lint, specks, hairs, or other glitches you may have missed, and, when you find these, open the piece back up by removing the framer's points with pliers or your fingers—you may choose to open only one side or corner of the work if you're optimistic—and slide your finger or a special eraser or a razor blade in under the glass to remove the debris, wear gloves or not, *just don't bleed on the artwork*, then close up the entire thing with the point gun again, roll a two-sided adhesive tape gun over the outside back borders of the frame, cut and attach brown backing paper, shave off the excess paper with a razor blade, then drill holes for the hardware that holds the hanging wire, making sure to first assess the width, depth, and weight of the entire work and the length of the screws you're planning to use, measure where you want the hardware placed, and make starter holes with an awl or a manual hand-drill before using your power driver to drill in the screws. When your drill slips and punctures your backing paper, use brown paper tape to cover the hole, and it's a good idea to put matching tape on both sides of the frame back even if you only fucked up one side, thus giving a symmetrical, intentional look. And then you just attach and twist the hanging wire. Use needle-nose pliers or brown paper tape to tamp down any errant wire so the customer doesn't puncture a fingertip. *Don't bleed on the artwork.*

I've omitted some steps, above. Like chefs, framers never share all their secrets.

After my father died, my mother chose only two pieces of art from our old house to move to her new room in Memory Care. Both are mid-century modernist prints, by Marc Chagall and the Bolivian artist Graciela Rodo Boulanger. Neither is rare nor particularly valuable. I don't recall either having any special meaning to my mom. They were just always *there*, in the background of my childhood.

Both are full of color and movement and light. In the Rodo Boulanger print, dated 1977, a young girl holds a long horizontal pole on which six large flapping birds are precariously balanced, three on either side of her, in an explosion of patterns and colors. In Rodo Boulanger's work, children are often aloft: riding bicycles or animals, leaping after balloons, sitting on high ledges, their feet always dangling above the ground.

The Chagall lithograph, from 1960, is titled *La Jongleuse* (The Juggler). A woman in a bright flowered dress—a circus acrobat—appears to be dancing in air, the audience, animals, and other performers all falling away around and below her. Chagall famously loved the circus, and the theme of flying. In his vision, our sky is never empty, but always full of men and women and horses and angels, all swooping and soaring about up there amidst waves of color, in ecstasy, in love, in a dream.

When I ask my mom why she chose these two pictures in particular, she smiles and says she doesn't know. She says, *They just make me happy.*

My boss calls me down to the basement one afternoon and asks me to carry up a bunch of newly built frames. *Take as many as you can,* he says. When I think my hands are full, he tells me to hold my arms out straight like branches, and starts hanging more frames on them. I can hold about twelve or fifteen—they're not terribly big, or heavy, or even fragile. Still, I move gingerly, not wanting to do any damage. The frames clank a little against each other, but I don't drop them. I look back and see my boss right behind me, grinning under his mustache as we make our unsteady way up the dark steps, ascending into the light of day.

When he takes the frames off my arms, I feel like I can fly. ▲

APRIL 2020

by MIHAELA MOSCALIUC

from THIS BROKEN SHORE

"Let no love poem ever come to this threshold."
—"Quarantine," Eavan Boland

Which incidence of body shall I leave you?
Below the tallow sun, gannets eviscerate sea life
to sustain their sky life. Same thought courses
everyone's morning, *death, please not today.*

I soap off chinolas, holding the shore within sight.
You sweep the runny yolk under a bread crust.

I've slipped on a flouncy dress and lipsticked
though there's no place we can go.
We whisk ourselves away from news
and practice breathing on mirrors.

I breathe into your nape and call it kissing.
You breathe out and out and out.

When needles consecrated our love
with Brâncuşi's "Kiss," we didn't know the artist
had sculpted the lover's embrace to shape
the letter M in Moarte/Death.

If you're to harvest the inked skin from my arm, love,
dry and stretch it in the Caribbean sun before you frame.

When you parcel out the rest, remember
a synecdoche of bones for my ancestral plot,
a fistful of ash as mulch for what I failed to grow.
The rest, our children should add to your remains
under that oak tree, in the season of chanterelles,
so we may bring one mouthful of earth to ecstasy.

REFUGE

by SHEEMA KALBASI

from SPOON & SHRAPNEL: VERSE & WARTIME RECIPES: (DARAJA PRESS)

We hid in the mouths of closets,
Under the ribs of stairwells,
Bomb shelters like coffins in waiting.
Some of us surfaced, gasping—
Some, the earth swallowed whole.

THAT

by CHRIS DOMBROWSKI

from NARRATIVE

That we have tea to drink. That late-winter sunlight streams through the living room windows, through the slats in good blinds. That the dog has a bed to sleep on or a couch if he prefers or a warm spot on the rug. That there are books by friends on the shelf beneath pictures of my beloveds. That one of the pictures is a black and white of a woman of surpassing beauty smashing a kiss into the young poet's smile-tightened cheek. That she still throws her arm around his older-now shoulder and repeats the gesture. That the ponderosa out back around which the kids' tree house was built is waving its branches in a variable wind. That the baby swing Mary and I hung and long ago left out to weather is rocking ever so slightly. That the kids who swung there are teenagers. That it is early March again, manifestation season for Pisces like me. That the dog wants out and the slider doesn't catch. That there are five sturdy red Gerber daisies in a jar on the dining room table. That some years ago a man named Dan Gerber, a poet friend of a poet friend, looked on me with concern and sent me books I needed to read. That Gillian Welch is on the stereo singing an acoustic version of a song that buoyed me through those dire days when Gerber checked in on me with his handwritten, calligraphic letters. *The days were rough and it's all quite dim / but my mind cuts through it all / like a wrecking ball*. That the dog who had a tennis ball–size cyst removed from his spleen last March just hung his chin on my knee and left a line of slobber on my jeans on his way back into the living room. That we have a living room. That we are living.

LESSONS OF THE LINE

by DANA LEVIN

from THE YALE REVIEW

1. 1988

I was learning how to breathe (line vs. sentence); I was interrogating syntax but I did not know it. I thought I was building images in an open field.

I pored over two versions of William Carlos Williams's poem "Young Woman at a Window" (1934), which differed in their line breaks. Both poems were originally published together in *The Westminster Magazine*, but only one version—what I'll call "version two"—was subsequently reprinted.

Why did I prefer version two, in which line breaks obscured understanding?

(version two)

She sits with
tears on

her cheek
her cheek on

her hand
the child

in her lap
his nose

pressed
to the glass

I liked how stable each block felt. Stable, yet—disorienting: the puzzled mind stymied in its work, which was to swiftly find a pattern it could name, *a story*—

Every time I read the poem, I lingered over stanza two: the drama of its suspension outside the whole poem's sentence, how defamiliarizing it was, though the diction was completely accessible—the way it sounded like birdcall if you said it out loud:

her cheek
her cheek on

I imagined Williams walking down a city street, passing a diner window, behind which a woman sat with her child in her lap—I imagined him glancing and seeing her through the window, seeing her through the ghost of his own sun-reflected body in the glass.

Was it this double-exposure that made him first take notice? A trick of light—and then realizing he was walking by a plot—

Years later I would learn that he published version one only once, in that obscure university journal. Why didn't he ever republish it, as he did version two? Because what he had *seen* was obscured, here, by what he had *thought*?

(version one)

While she sits
there

with tears on
her cheek

her cheek on
her hand

this little child
who robs her

knows nothing of
his theft

but rubs his
nose

Stanza by stanza, version one moved inexorably toward diagnosis, with its poker tell of diction: *robs*—the child an oblivious vector, but still to blame.

Version two was like standing in the light, outside a window.

As if the *poem* were the window—every time I finished reading version two, I could feel a feeling trying to press through.

Years later I would think of his famous motto: "No ideas but in things." I would think: the child's robbery in version one is an idea; the young woman's tears are the thing.

2. 1988 (JOURNAL)

January

Simic doesn't think "Young Woman at a Window" is a bad poem, but he doesn't like the prosody: "Y'know, couplets are tricky—they really must stand on their own." But thinking about it on the way home, I realize that I never *looked* at them as couplets—more as a flow with a flow in between—

So, now I must defend myself: Why do I see it this way? Why am I impelled to design the poem this way? Why do I not see couplets the way Simic sees them? And what does Simic think about e. e. cummings? And what does prosody *mean* anyway?

Dangers of line breaking too much: melodrama; broken glass.

February

Charlie and me with our surgical gloves, in the cold objective classroom of poetry, using a scalpel, a compass, a magnifying glass—

*

But if the poem is a process, if it is the other side of a conversation, then every time I balk at revision I am cutting the poem off mid-sentence—

*

Questions for Charlie:

Do you *enjoy* revising?

Is there some sort of emotional frustration behind the birth of free verse?

What about punctuation?

March
"Well, you know Williams used to say that he could revise a poem twenty different times just by changing the line breaks."

They taste good to her
They taste good
to her. They taste
good to her

3. GREEN BUDDHA

Charles Simic! My teacher. Maybe you know his watermelon poem:

Green Buddhas
On the fruit stand.
We eat the smile
And spit out the teeth.

He said to me once, advocating a cut in a poem I showed him, "*But* is the word of hair-splitting, not very interesting." He leaned forward, resting his elbows on his knees, clasping his hands and looking down at them, as he often did when making a point. "A thinker, a 'civilized' man, would say, 'Farmer Joe had the loveliest pig and cared for it like his own child *but* slaughtered it for dinner,' while the simple man, the peasant, says, 'Farmer Joe had the loveliest pig that he cared for like his own child, *and* he slaughtered it for dinner.'" He looked up at me, to make sure I was getting it. "*And*," he said, "is more interesting than *but*."

Was I getting it? Something about being civilized being a lie? And how that was "more interesting"?

Later I would see that Simic practiced this philosophy of *and* in all his poems, a metaphysics of radical inclusion: brutality and death were everywhere in life, and they were ordinary. They didn't arrive hitched to that conjunction of turn and exception, *but*. We were at their mercy and their call: meat-handed humans, driven to eat and fuck and be safe, willing to kill to do it. "That's life," a Simic poem shrugs, about all this drive and death. You can see this attitude even in his most whimsical poems, like "Watermelons": a laughing Buddha fruit, our smile-eating an act of innocuous metaphor—until the last line.

He never mentioned to me his childhood in Belgrade, in what was then Yugoslavia, under Nazi occupation during World War II, but he later wrote about it. Indelible image: young Charlie playing with a lice-infested helmet swiped from a dead soldier's head. Here was *and:* a child making a toy of catastrophe's debris. We eat the Buddha and spit out teeth.

When I first met him, in January 1988, I had recently graduated from Pitzer College in Southern California and had followed a few college friends to Portsmouth, New Hampshire, to try out a new life. Simic, meanwhile, had recently been awarded a "Genius Grant" from the MacArthur Foundation. In 1990 he would win the Pulitzer for a book of prose poems; in 2007, he would be named U.S. Poet Laureate. But in 1987, as I was finishing college, I only knew him as the author of a *Selected Poems* (1985) that my college lover, a divorced professor, had gifted me at graduation. This "Charles Simic" wrote poems about shoes and forks and brooms in a matter-of-fact tone and plain diction that was at effective odds with his dark-humored sensibility: awake to life's absurdities, attentive to the uncanny, cynical about human nature, always aware of the hooded friend with the scythe loitering offstage, waiting for his cue. In one of Simic's poems, the protagonist is a little lump of ashes; in another, a zero.

In the divorced professor's kitchen, I opened the book to the first poem, reading the first stanza:

> *Sometimes walking late at night*
> *I stop before a closed butcher shop.*
> *There is a single light in the store*
> *Like the light in which the convict digs his tunnel.*

This was a poet for me.

At the bakery where I worked, that winter in Portsmouth, counter staff took turns leaving early if it seemed that the cold and the prospect of early-falling dark were keeping afternoon customers at bay. One day in January that liberation fell to me, and I turned to Cher, one of the bakers, and said, "What should I do for the rest of the day?" And she said, "I think you should go see Charlie."

Charlie. I couldn't imagine addressing the poet—whose name I had seen only in print—in such a familiar way.

Warm Cher, her brown hair pulled up into a messy bun, flour dusting her temple—she had been on a gentle, persistent campaign for months, once I had told her I wrote poems: You should go see Charlie. By complete chance, this poet—the author of the *Selected Poems* I had brought with me when I'd moved across the country—taught nearby, at the University of New Hampshire. Cher had taken a class with him once; she had found him to be a wonderful teacher. I would like him. Charlie.

"What would I even *say*?" I protested. She smiled her wide smile with its one crooked tooth and surveyed the mound of dough before her. Then her strong hands plunged in and began kneading. "Show him a poem."

4. 1988 (JOURNAL)

May

Simic compares my poetry to a sort of geometry, "lyrical shapes."

Because I used to be
a boat
without sail
or anchor
now I am
a fish
without the ghost
of a treasure

September

"Why do you always do this? It astounds me how you dissect the music of your voice, the incredible slowness of the prosody—so difficult and distracting, when the poem *has* such a beautiful voice—let yourself sing!" He confesses he too composes thinly and slowly, two words to a line, but then he fits them all together. "It's as though you are extracting the intestines of the poem, seeing how it works—so it's good to start this way, but not to finish. Ultimately," he says, “you have to make a body,” and then he begins to laugh, “Maybe you were always *meant* to write long lines—” and he keeps laughing, he seems to find this hilarious—

*

Because I used to be a boat without sail or anchor,
now I am a fish without the ghost
of a treasure

Too dense—

The ear and the eye in constant battle, the lyre trying in vain to sing through a microscope—

The long line bores me and the short line is not true to the music—is there not a way to present music to the eye, diversity of visual form to the ear?

October

The *Paris Review* interview:

Interviewer: (picking up a copy of *Paterson V,* from which some clippings fall to the floor): These opening lines—they make an image on the page.

Williams: Yes, I was imitating the flight of the bird.

Interviewer: Then it’s directed—

Williams: To the eyes. Read it.

Interviewer: “In old age the mind casts off . . .”

Williams: In old age
the mind
casts off
rebelliously
an eagle
from its crag

5. READING: AN INTERLUDE

At twenty, I worshipped a narrow pantheon: a Doctor, a Prophet, and a Mad Girl. By the time I graduated college at twenty-two, Williams, Blake, and Plath were joined by a revelation of poets from Eastern Europe: Popa, Holub, Herbert. I didn’t know it then, but I was being introduced to contemporary poetry largely by men whose own revelatory experiences had come via Robert Bly and the Deep Image school. None of these men taught me a serious lick of prosody; no one assigned deep engagement with the incredible range of the mid-twentieth-century American greats: Bishop, Lowell, Hayden, Brooks, the entire New York School. Ginsberg, still alive, was referenced with reverence, but no one suggested I read "Howl." A fellow student gave me a peek of Berryman; he'd been carrying *The Dream Songs* (1969) everywhere—how had he found it?

In the early 1980s, the revelations and follies of L=A=N=G=U=A=G=E poetry were most alive, producing some of its crucial works—Michael Palmer's *Notes for Echo Lake* (1981) and Lyn Hejinian's *My Life* (1980) come immediately to mind—but my professors, to a man, were creatures of a particular kind of 1970s vibe. We read Merwin. Kinnell's *The Book of Nightmares* (1971). Calvino's *Invisible Cities* (1972). Laura Jensen. The recently deceased local poet hero Bert Meyers, master of image and metaphor. The lit-mag *FIELD*. One professor handed me *Another Republic* (1976), which featured a heady mix of Eastern European and Latin American poets; another, Jerome Rothenberg's *Technicians of the Sacred* (1968), which surveyed a range of indigenous poetry from across the world. What I did read was formative and intoxicating; it was also, in retrospect, partial and eccentric.

I didn't realize, until I started teaching seriously myself, in my thirties, that in college I had received an incredibly narrow education in twentieth-century American poetry—even by the somewhat rudderless standards of the undergrad poetry classroom of the 1980s. One reason for this was that twentieth-century American poetry was still happening. In 1984, when I started college, many literary survey courses, where most English majors are introduced to historical and cultural contexts of literary works, stopped at 1945. Confessionalism—one of the great literary liberations of midcentury—seemed the last codified school of poetry, mainly because its pioneering practitioners—Lowell, Berryman, Plath, and Sexton—were dead and their great poems were cementing into history. Some poets and critics had just begun to blow up the established canon, but I wouldn't know that until grad school in the early 1990s.

As an undergrad, I never took a class called Contemporary Poetry; I don't think one was ever offered. Living poets swam into my ken through conversations in office hours and the campus café, through other students, and through texts assigned in creative writing classes. There, my assigned reading was largely designed by instructor passion, prejudice, and whim, with no obligation to breadth or background.

The aesthetic preferences of my professors became mine. Their blinders became mine, for a long time, with a few exceptions. None of my poetry professors, who were all male, straight, and white, taught me Sexton, Rich, Lorde, Shange, or the Black Arts writers. I found L.A.'s Wanda Coleman myself, on a visit to the Beyond Baroque bookstore in Venice Beach, in a thin collection I still have, and which has survived to this day, ragged and intact (thank you, Black Sparrow Press). Plath I'd smuggled in from adolescence (the love abides); I knew Lowell mainly as the guy who wrote the forward to *Ariel* (1966).

Yet, in fairness to my teachers, I must also say: no one gets a comprehensive education in literature, contemporary or otherwise, by the time they get their bachelor's degree. And it was marvelous to find contemporary poetry on my own, via the magic of serendipity: in used bookstores, spreadeagled on the floors and beds of my college friends, and on the bookshelves in the Bert Meyers Poetry Room at Pitzer's Grove House, the old Arts and Crafts bungalow that served as the college's de facto student union. Besides, why would I, a young woman at a hippie-groovy school in southern California in the 1980s, want to read a book called *For the Union Dead* (1964)?

As for craft: I had arrived on campus as a sophomore in 1984 with a love for the music of T. S. Eliot, from his *Practical Cats* (1939) to "Prufrock," but then I took a poetry writing class with Miroslav Holub, our Spring Visiting Writer. Holub was a major Czech poet and he was also a doctor—he introduced me to another doctor, an American one, and my poems would never be the same. Immersed in William Carlos Williams, I forsook fusty Eliot and embarked on a prolonged Imagist tear. I associated poetic music with the evils of rhyme and, for one unbearable semester, with the tortures of class exercises in meter with Professor Robert Mezey at Pomona College, Pitzer's stately sister school. My new mission was image. Image was all!

That was how I graduated in 1987: metrically deaf, scarcely conscious of pacing and the line, despite all the poems I had read, despite all the poetry workshops I had taken, despite my own, new, heavily enjambed poems—as I walked into Simic's office, this was my state.

6. CHARLIE

It is shocking to me now to consider myself at twenty-three, showing up unannounced at a famous poet's door. These days I am mostly uncertain and afraid, an overthinker, acutely aware of the potential thorns embedded in any idea's rosette. Hedged by experience, I cast these lines back to that brave fool, thinking: who is rescuing who.

Cher suggested I call the UNH English Department to see if Charlie had office hours later that afternoon; by luck, the secretary on the phone said he did. I ran for the little bus that ferried students between Portsmouth and Durham (where the campus was located) several times a day.

I gazed out the window as the bus chugged between icy marshland and pockets of evergreen, past saltbox houses and white colonials—gray, white, winter green: New England, exotic north. Only a few months earlier I had left southern California, where I had lived my entire life, and moved to the other side of the country. I had told my parents that I would be home in September; then at Thanksgiving; then for New Year's; and then, in December, on the phone with my weeping mother, I said I didn't know when I would come home.

Hatted and scarfed, my face pressed to the cold glass of the bus window, as if to merge with the snow and marsh flashing by—

"Charlie." What would I say.

I found Simic's office down a dark hallway, upstairs in a very large building with a broad curving stair.

I sat down in a chair that had been set up across from his door and waited. At one point a young man advanced down the hall and I must've given him a look because he stopped and stammered, "—are, are you—?" and gestured in the direction of Simic's office. When I silently nodded he backed away and fled.

I watched him go, feeling bristly and braced and—*not budging*. Then self-consciousness set my face on fire, my heart clanging with alarm. I was a complete impostor with no real right to be there, scaring that boy away: I wasn't even a student!

Then a man, a little thick-set, came down the hall. He stopped at Simic's door and stuck a key in the lock, while looking up at me: "Hello." He pushed the door open and vanished behind it, leaving it open the barest crack.

A moment passed. I could see a thin slice of him through the cracked door, sitting at a desk. He had drawn a thin brown cigarette from somewhere and started furiously smoking. I hauled myself up, thinking: *You have come all this way, and so—*

I knocked, and he told me to come in. As I opened the door he gestured to a chair across from his. I sat down and blurted: "My name is Dana Levin, and I don't go to school here, and I don't want to go to school here, and I was wondering if you would work with me on my poems."

He looked down. "Mmmm," he said. And then, with a tone of consideration, in an English marbled by the thick r's and guttural vowels of his native Serbian: "Why don't you take Intro to Creative Writing with Mekeel McBride?" Then he suggested another class. And another. He leaned forward, elbows on knees, hands clasped, his demeanor increasingly magnanimous, as he rattled off the many classes I could take—none taught by him.

When he finished his catalog of options, I said: "But what if I want to work with you?"

He sat back, silent. We studied each other. I think we were both surprised by this turn in the conversation. Then, without asking me why, without asking to see a single one of my poems, he said, "Okay."

He didn't want to know why I wrote what I wrote.

He didn't want to know my dreams, my family, or any news from my life.

Later, he would learn what I was reading as a by-product of coming to rent movies at Atlantic Video, where I worked after quitting the bakery. At checkout, he would glance down at whatever book was open on my desk: one day, the diaries of Anaïs Nin, another day, D. H. Lawrence, *Women in Love* (1920). On seeing the Nin, he offered a studied look but no comment; "Excellent," on seeing the Lawrence. Then he would pay, gather his rentals—comedies, mainly—and walk out of the store.

A few times he gave me jazz mixtapes, mostly bebop, after hearing me play Thelonious Monk over and over at the store for weeks. You could tell he had recorded them long ago, from their frayed, half-faded labels.

I worked with him every week for a semester. Then every few months. For two and a half years, whenever I had five or six poems to show him, I'd make the mini-bus pilgrimage and climb the broad stair to his office.

When I showed up, there were no niceties, no chitchat. "Whaddya got?" he'd ask and motion to a chair.

I would hand him the thin stack, and he would bend over it, scanning each poem, flipping pages with a grunt. Then, stabbing a thick finger at a page, "Let's talk about this one."

Just this was a lesson: his scanning and flipping and not choosing—and then, what he chose—

One day he sent me home with a stack of literary magazines and told me to check them out. When I returned the next week he said, "What did you think?"

"I dunno," I said, hedging, not wanting to hurt his feelings. "I didn't like them very much."

"Good!" He exclaimed with delight. "You *shouldn't* like them!"

We didn't really converse extensively about anything. I'd listen to him talk about my poems, about poetry, with braced attention, and then later, in my journal, I would argue with him.

He rarely looked me in the eye. He talked to me with his head down or facing me with his eyes focused a bit to the left of my head.

He never hit on me.

7. BOUNDARIES: AN INTERLUDE

In high school, I had encountered older men, mentor types, would-be mentor types, who would come on to me, with more-than-mild flirtation. In college, I had been taken to lunch and propositioned by the editor of a venerable literary magazine. Even at twenty, I had had the sense that this was the editor's habit when on the road: a "writer girl on every campus" seducer. I had also encountered older men, teachers, who had not behaved this way at all. Having been a woman now for over half a century, having never—yet—been raped nor assaulted nor harassed beyond the pale, I think I have lived an extraordinarily lucky life in this world of men—even if the first twenty years of my life were anviled by the jubilations and plummets, by the stomping rages, by the daily tyrannies, of my bipolar father.

She sits with
tears on

But I didn't yet know I was writing about my father. I was sitting without tears in Charlie's office, showing him a poem about becoming a fish.

Simic was clearly a sensualist. From his poems, you knew he loved food, and women, and all the earthly pleasures. Here too his philosophy of *and* was in play: death and brutality were everywhere, yes; and so was "the sweet speech of trees." Most of his poems barely made it to the top of page two, but in the *Selected Poems* I found a three-page, sixteen-stanza ode to breasts that began with an announcement: "I love breasts, hard / Full breasts, guarded / By a button." At mid-point, the poem declares:

I spit on fools who fail to include
Breasts in their metaphysics

Star-gazers who have not enumerated them
Among the moons of the earth . . .

They give each finger
Its true shape, its joy: . . .

And the poem ends:

I will tip each breast
Like a dark heavy grape
Into the hive
Of my drowsy mouth.

For a lover of breasts, by the still-fungible standards of 1980s academia, where it was not uncommon for teachers and students to depart the classroom together for cafés and bars and, for some, the backseat or bedroom, Simic held to impeccable boundaries with full-breasted me. When I was in his office, along with never letting an eye stray beyond that area to the left of my head, he always kept his door ajar; this was long before doing so became the advice, the convention, and then the policy at campuses nationwide. During my time in college, teacher-student relationships could be quite personal and intimate even without sexual entanglements: each semester I was there, I had something called Independent Study with my beloved mentor Barry Sanders, which took the form of showing up at his office to tell him dreams, gripes, current intellectual and literary passions and, occasionally, to show him a poem I had written. Thus, I received academic credit for being a person.

Pitzer's intimate and personalized environment had been incredibly nurturing and formative for me, especially coming off twenty years of a deeply oppressive home life. But this intimacy made boundaries porous. I had gotten to know my college lover, the divorced professor, through poetry readings and gallery openings and hanging out at the Grove House café: we were engaged in the intimate life of a very small, progressive liberal arts college community, which flourished in part because of the relaxed standards of academic protocol and convention. Our relationship naturally developed, within a context that made it easy to feel like peers.

I never took a class with him until after we started sleeping together. The power dynamics of being a student sleeping with my teacher were complicated in no small part because we genuinely cared for each other.

I cannot subscribe to any reading of myself being a victim in this relationship. He was clearly attracted to me, and I was attracted to him and to his attraction: it was completely novel for me. Maybe if I could see myself through his eyes, I could stop torturing my body with judgment and self-loathing; maybe I could see what he so valued in my brain. I actively pursued him; he demurred for all the correct reasons; and then he consented. He was thirty years older than I was. He loved poetry, and so did I.

Still, the very fact that our positions outside the bedroom were not equal affected the class I took with him. How could I really be learning when I was so engrossed by my erotic secret? It was not even a secret, not really: half the students knew. *He* knew. It was the subtext for all of us in his classroom.

I was not aware of this then, but now I think that the impersonal atmosphere of my work with Charlie served as a tonic after the dramas of my undergraduate life. He wasn't interested in me; he was interested in my poems. This was a first lesson in learning the difference between poems and personality, which would prove crucial if I was to see the poem as material to be worked rather than as an extension of self. There was nothing precious about a poem, in Charlie's office: stretch it, poke holes in it, dismember it, knife it in its failing heart.

8. YOUNG WOMAN AT A WINDOW

For months, all we talked about was the line. Explicitly, implicitly. One time we talked about jokes, which amounted to the same thing: pacing, dramatic accrual. Simic did not teach me formal prosody, and he did not attempt to define how prosody worked in contemporary poems. For that he handed me Charles O. Hartman's *Free Verse: An Essay on Prosody* (1981).

Half the time I did not understand what I was reading. I did not have the poetics background or the patience to wade through the craft jargon and academese of Hartman's writing style, especially in this "class" with Simic I was taking for no credit. Maybe this was also why Simic, who was conducting this "class" for free, did not ask me about the book beyond, "How's the Hartman?" I shrugged. He chuckled. We turned to my poems.

In Hartman, I read:

> "What the Image does among things, form does among words.
> The imagist poem imitates nature."

How did this work, exactly? How did version two of "Young Woman at a Window" "imitate nature"? I think now that one problem I was having was that I thought "realism" and "nature" were the same thing.

She sits with
tears on

This did not seem realist. It was as if tears here were some kind of accoutrement, the glinting accent of a fashion ensemble. As if this young woman were not the one crying—

Was this why I preferred the shape that obscured understanding? The distance at which she sat from the tears she wore—the open space of the stanza break like a moat around feeling—

Soon, my powers of dissociation and compartmentalization would fail me, and I would feel, as if for the first time, a childhood that had made me crave no feeling at all. I would start psychoanalysis, where I would have to contend with becoming the woman with tears on, instead of the child pressed to the glass. But before that, for a few years, Charlie and I sat in hard chairs in his untidy office, trying to find out what made my poems break.

READING "YOUNG WOMAN AT A WINDOW" now, more than thirty years after I first encountered it, I can finally see: version two tracks materialization—

her cheek
her cheek on

as the result of the friction between line and sentence—

her hand
the child

as the result of the friction between child and mother. Look at stanzas three and four, how they rely on each other to make a body! And yet, by the end—*pressed / to the glass*—a yearning for autonomy, escape—

Williams out walking, glancing at a window, the economic and psychological ramifications of the era flashing up through the glass—

To be a young woman with a young child: under certain conditions, it could pose acute problems, as it did in 1934, the year Williams published the poem, in the depths of the Great Depression.

In his preference for version two, had Williams finally decided to put away version one's diagnosis in order to try to build with words what he had simply *seen?* A realization, perhaps, that the real task, for him, was not to chronicle the development of knowing but to enact, via enjambment, the struggle of seeing—and so to find himself asking the reader to participate in that struggle too, to work with him in empathy?

Isn't that what I was trying to do, at twenty-three—struggling to see?

Now, at fifty-nine, after a long apprenticeship in poetry, I can finally tell you what I had no language for back then: that my boredom with long lines in poems was really boredom with lines that moved like ordinary sentences. The fascinating defamiliarization, the nuance and drama, the quality of revelation offered by the hard enjambment of version two of "Young Woman at a Window" broke open my seeking mind. This was the difference between prose and verse! Verse, the art of turning! And then, an ensuing problem: How could a fragmented sentence sing?

Here is the confession of this essay: I did not learn much about the line from Charlie. But he directed me to start paying attention to this foundational tool, to start paying attention to poems as made things—products of decision, as much as magic. And as he divined, long lines found me. They were in the poetry of Jorie Graham's *The End of Beauty* (1987), a book that became my obsession as my time with Simic drew to a close. In it, I discovered the play of long and short lines, the play of text and open space, which I'd been seeking but had not known how to describe. Graham's line could parse and annotate and end-stop syntax all in a single poem; sometimes rushing, sometimes stopping, sometimes slaloming through a stanza, her lines felt *mimetic*, enacting hesitations and urgencies of thought and feeling. I could feel the movements of her lines *in my body*. It was thrilling; it was what I wanted my lines to do! And I had only discovered this because Graham's book had been reviewed in one of the lit-mags Charlie had sent home with me. Long lines found me too in the long avenues of New York City, where I started a master's program in creative writing at NYU in 1990. "Every poet should live in New York City at least once," Simic had advised. Writing poems in New York, my lines started to venture across the page.

Simic never effused much over my poems, never made pronouncements about an illustrious fate awaiting me. Twenty-five years after our work together ended, I would find out that his confidential grad school recommendation for me began, "Dana Levin is a big talent!" when a fellow grad student who had worked in the director's office in those years confessed, over drinks, that she read everyone's files.

I was utterly surprised by this declaration. So impersonal had been our engagement, it had never occurred to me that he had ever had strong feelings about me, beyond the usual obligations one expected from a teacher. What a fool I was. He had given me, an uninvited stranger, free of charge, the two most precious gifts he had to give: his time and his attention. He had taken my art seriously, and it had transformed me. Why should I be surprised that he had had feelings about it?

One evening in 1992, as I was finishing grad school, I went to the 92nd Street Y to see Simic read with Tomaž Šalamun. I had not seen him in two years. In the restroom, as I came out of a bathroom stall, I spied his wife, Helen, at the mirror. When had I met her? I recognized her, and she me: when she saw me, she rushed up and took my face in both her hands, exclaiming, "Dana! Charlie will be so happy to see you!" I stood speechless in the surge of Helen's enthusiasm and warmth. She greeted me as if I were family, as if I were a daughter, returned from a long journey. She pinched my cheeks and stood back, exclaiming with feeling, "You've come for your Charlie!"

My Charlie! So I had.

LETTER TO JD VANCE

by TORLI BUSH

from ANTHOLOGY OF APPALCHIAN WRITERS

JD,

In some ways, our stories are alike. I was also raised by my white grandparents in Webster Springs, West Virginia, from the time I was seven years old. I'm black. Before your mind trails off too far: dad's white, mom's black, she died in the after of childbirth, brain aneurysm from having sickle cell anemia. Dad was in the Navy at the time, going with his parents was eventually the best option. I had a good life, I can admit that. I had some kind of anomalous privilege of growing up well off cause James Lee Bush, Sr., my grandfather, worked and retired from coal mining. I wanted to believe that your book wasn't that bad, that it was a feel good story that got misconstrued; I'm sorry no editor checked your ego at the door. If you had stuck to memoir, the worst would've been you outing your grandmother as crazy enough to cap a man with a six-shooter; even that would've been too much 'cause everybody who's anybody who's Appalachian knows you don't paint your grandmother like that, JD. Like "hillbilly" was the only word that could define her, like she wasn't a "homemaker" like my grandmother Xanna, keeping you fed and clothed and getting the sense of needing an education into you.

You couldn't even bring yourself to admit what good you had, how it advantaged you. *Even being black and out of place I can see what I had.* I saw my classmates too. Here's some people I graduated with: Tyler Neal didn't come from much but started his own timbering business and has a family, doing well for himself. Cassandra Clevenger lost her mom as a young woman; she's a pharmacist now. Aerial Lake had her house burn down our senior year; she pushed and pushed and did her undergrad in three years and became a Physical Therapist. Cameron Clutter became a barber, and can play a mean electric guitar. Samuel Canfield, a biologist, trying to help the changing environment. There's so many others in my class who went into a trade or healthcare or just outright working, *we ain't fucking lazy*.

I was the only black kid in my grade for most of my time up through high school but I know that I ain't the only black person in the whole of Appalachia; where were people like me in that white monolith you wrote, JD? Tucked behind your ranting & raving on "welfare queens?" You just gonna pretend like we don't exist? Like we're all just rustbelt ghosts and magnolia tree ornaments? You ain't been to the core of Appalachia where the wild magic is: the hollars know every skin tone, it's kinda Christian, kinda queer, kinda folk, kinda soul food and moonshine; it's perfect dirt, fishing, hunting, and playing basketball into the nighttime 'til we bond around bonfires. There's an empty wicker chair and a mason jar with your name on it; come find me, learn who *we* really are.

THE LAST THING THAT HAPPENED BEFORE I BECAME A MED TECH

fiction by DAVE NEWMAN

from NEW WORLD WRITING QUARTERLY

I ran into Dawn Reedy at the Big Lots in Beckley. We'd dated when we were teenagers but I hadn't seen her since high school. I was buying canned pasta. I was buying fish sticks and bread. I'd just blown my nose into a napkin and stuffed the napkin into my pocket. It all sounded louder than I'd intended. Dawn was a lawyer with two kids, both young—one on hip, the other holding her hand. I saw them and recognized her and tried to bolt but she said, "Hey," and waved so I smiled and changed direction. Adulthood is mostly lies and mistakes until the lies and mistakes become something else. I don't know how I knew she was a lawyer. This was dinnertime but I'd just woken up. I was hungover and pretty sick with dope.

She said, "I thought that was you," but more like handling her kids.

She wore a camelhair jacket or mohair or something in beige I couldn't name. It looked like someone put a needle in her neck, removed all the fun, and replaced it with responsibility. I was jealous and wanted the same shot.

I breathed and imagined success and presented my face as such.

Dawn didn't wait for me to start lying.

She said, "My mom watches the kids," and paused. "I pick them up after work." She said, "Work is up in Charleston. Our office. It's near the DMV."

"How is your mom?" I said.

"Still my mom," she said, hiking one kid higher on her hip.

The older kid said, "Can I get this?" and held up an unblown punching balloon. His hair was long and styled with bangs like the wing of a blonde bird.

Dawn said, "What?" Then, "No." Then, "Don't touch things."

The kid returned the balloon to the shelf without complaint.

I coughed into my hand and the cough sounded like a drowning victim.

She said, "You okay?"

"Wrong pipe," I said, straightening the inside of my throat.

I picked up the punching balloon.

I said, "I could buy this for him."

She said, "He'd kill his little brother."

I put the balloon back. I mostly said stupid shit when I wanted to say the opposite. Trying to buy a balloon for a small child whose parent can obviously afford balloons and has rejected balloons is a rude offer. It was another reason to tilt my head to sobriety.

Dawn said, "But thank you. That's sweet."

I looked at the kid and nodded an apology.

The kid approached tears but still quiet.

The little one snuggled in, almost asleep.

I was trying to get clean and wanted to become a med tech. One of my pals moved to Pittsburgh to study nursing but I knew I wasn't that smart.

Some of this involved the community college and some involved still doing drugs.

Dawn said, "Don't have kids," and faked a smile.

I nodded, not considering kids.

I probably wasn't going to eat the fish sticks I clutched to my chest.

I liked to pick at the canned pasta, even if it stayed out on the counter.

She said, "You ever see . . . ?" then she couldn't think of a name we shared.

Dawn used to be a cheerleader. I wrestled but it was different. I rode a ten-speed bike I'd pieced together from parts. Dawn knew she'd get a car for her next birthday. She drank beer in bottles. I stole rotgut gin from the bar where my mom worked and mixed it with Doctor Thunder, Wal-Mart's version of Dr. Pepper.

Once the games finished, after she ditched her cheerleading outfit for jeans and a rock t-shirt, Dawn reached out to older kids to find ways to get loaded.

If she couldn't score oxy or xanax or molly or weed, she huffed glue.

If no glue, she huffed gas.

If no gas, she huffed paint.

When she slurred, it was a love affair, and I put my ear into whatever she said because her words always sounded better than mine, the way she owned everything by telling.

When she huffed paint, a goatee of color formed around her mouth and chin. I never minded the paint on my shirt, the paint on my neck. Sometimes she fell asleep while we kissed and woke up and said, "Why aren't you kissing me?"

I never wanted to be popular, let alone date a cheerleader, but I won on the mat and people I'd never noticed suddenly noticed.

It was like money you couldn't spend, a bottle without an opener.

At the beginning of wrestling season, we attended the Sadie Hawkins dance, the one where the girl asks the boy. Dawn's mom dropped her off. I lived close enough to the school and walked backroads to the tree where we planned to meet. My mom worked nights and drank. My dad lived in Alaska on a fishing boat. I'd bought a flower at the gas station, a single white rose. Dawn said, "How sweet!" She wore an oversized flannel she belted like a dress and checkered leather boots that looked expensive. I wore what I always wore.

Deeper in the trees, in a patch of dying jaggers and dead berry bushes, Dawn reached around until she found two six packs of beer. She dusted off the bottles and pulled a joint from her purse. We smoked. We drank. The beer was so warm. The taste broke my tongue so I kept swallowing like my mouth was a tunnel. We stopped to kiss then smoked and drank some more. Alcohol helped with weight loss, how it dehydrated you. The whole wrestling team loved to get loaded and run around in plastic garbage bags, sweating, trying to shrink without shrinking. I hoped I didn't get the munchies. The munchies were a problem when I smoked. I often dreamed of corn chips and woke up with crumbs on my tongue.

Dawn said, "I can read your mind."

"Yeah?"

"You won't get the munchies."

"I will," I said, but I hit the joint again.

Dawn apologized for the temperature of the beer.

She said, "I tried to get my mom to stop for ice."

"We should have gone to my place," I said, knowing my mom always kept ice and mixers and occasionally eggs but not much else.

I sometimes lived on ice water and eggs.

I sometimes stirred sours mix into my ice water and called it lemonade.

Dawn said, "That woman is the devil," about her mom, but not seriously, or teenage seriously, or maybe seriously, while I nodded and drank and smoked and tried not to dream about French fries dipped in milkshakes from McDonalds.

I said, "I dig your mom."

She said, "You want to bang her. All the boys do."

I didn't want to bang her mom. I'd just learned to bang Dawn. The pressure of banging an older woman, one with money and confidence, ached in my stomach until I remembered it wasn't my responsibility. I worried Dawn thought I fucked poorly.

I said, "Your mom is pretty."

Dawn said, "Try living with her."

I pictured Dawn's kitchen, her refrigerator. I wanted a refrigerator like that, not brushed nickel or whatever the color, but one with Boar's Head lunchmeat and leftover soup and cheese in blocks and cheese by the slice. I would have eaten it all and wrestled heavyweight and I would have been happy to lose every match.

Food matters when you're poor.

A sandwich is a dream.

Dawn had two older sisters. One had an abortion when she was a senior. The other one attended rehab down in Florida and their family called it college. Her dad never looked at me. Once he said, "You the guy?" and I shrugged, embarrassed. He walked off before I could say something humiliating. But her mom fed me and gave me hugs and asked about wrestling, if I hoped to get a scholarship. I shrugged and thanked her and waited until she slept so I could go down on her daughter. Dawn pulled a pillow over her face when she came, muffling the sounds.

Once, after sex, she said, "We fuck like adults."

I hoped she was right and I trusted her experience.

It was weird growing up around kids with rich parents, kids who could pass through mistakes and phases without consequences, because their future always looked like a starting line. I only knew how to shoot and take down and force boys onto their backs, hoping I made it cool, hoping I looked less poor because I finished on top.

Standing in Big Lots, even with her kids, even exhausted from arguing cases, Dawn looked rich as a castle, a place you'd see in a picture but never visit.

I coughed again, less wet.

I didn't care that she had stuff.

I cared that I didn't.

She said, "It took a couple seconds but I was pretty sure that was you," a repeat from earlier.

"It's me," I said, thinking of a lie, some career I could pull off.

Once, later in high school, after we'd drifted, she said, "You need to bury my soul."

I said, "What's that mean?" but sweetly, intimidated by her even when she sounded the opposite of intimidating, even when she sounded like she'd matured in reverse, even when she wanted me to love her or tell her she deserved love. I hugged her and wanted her to kiss my neck.

Now she looked at her kid, the older one, still eyeing the balloon.

I looked towards the door, planning.

I turned back to Dawn.

The kid looked away.

Dawn sighed.

I said, "My fish sticks are probably melting."

She said, "You still eat fish sticks?" sounding shocked and grossed out, then caught herself and added, "This one," meaning the sleeping kid, "loves fish sticks."

I said, "I didn't think I'd see you here," which was not an answer.

She said, "I didn't think I'd see you here either," but friendly.

Near the flour and the off-brand sugar she looked like a successful lawyer too busy to consider a drink, let alone a bag of glue. But she looked the same too. A lot of guys took what they learned from wrestling and headed to college. I took what I learned on the mat and headed to parties and got loaded and sometimes took down men who were years older than me then bashed their faces until they quit saying whatever was meant to be an insult.

You can't imagine how many rich young people love drugs and live in dumpy apartments and need to be punched in the head.

Dawn said, "You were a really good wrestler."

I said, "You still cheer?"

She laughed and caught the laugh to not startle her son.

"Yes," she said, "I pompom." She said, "In the mirror." She said, "Cheering for myself."

I said, "I'm glad your mom is doing well."

She adjusted herself while adjusting the sleeping kid. She looked at the shelves and picked up the balloon and handed it to the older son who muffled his excitement to not wake his little brother. She shooed him towards the front of the store.

She said, "Meet mommy at the counter. I'll be there in a second," and waited while he walked away, clutching the punching balloon. Then she turned back to me and said, "It's good to see you," and made her face curious.

I knew not to speak.

Then she said, "Honestly, I heard you were dead. This was a while ago, I think." She paused. She said, "I may have heard it a couple times. I may have heard you killed someone." She said, "I didn't believe it."

I replayed her lines in my head, my head which was filled with needs and dreams and leftover whiskey and a couple lines of crushed oxycontin. I looked at her purse, dangling, and imagined all the textbooks I could afford. Then I imagined drugs. Then textbooks.

Then I stopped imagining.

I wanted to help people.

No one anywhere, not high school or the community college or my drug addict pals or even my parents, mentioned that helping was a way to go into the world.

Now I wanted to be a med tech, to lift and comfort.

I was sporting a Nirvana t-shirt, jeans, and old Converse sneakers.

I dressed like I forgot to grow up.

Dawn adjusted the collar on her coat.

I touched the snot rag in my pocket.

Dead would have been more expensive but I would have paid for it if I had the money.

She said, "I forget who I heard it from, but it was definitely dead." She said, "I'm glad you're not." She said, "I never believed you killed someone." She clutched the back of her sleeping kid's head with great love or maybe great protection, which made me feel worse. She said, "But whoever said it made it sound exciting. The dead part."

"It's not," I said.

"What's not?"

"Dead. It's not exciting."

She said, "Where do people even go around here?"

I think she meant for drinks. I think she may have been asking other things. I think she may have thought I was still a good fuck or remembered that I listened more than I talked. I looked at her purse again, dangling, and imagined all the textbooks I could afford. Then I imagined drugs. Then textbooks. Again and again, every millisecond. It's an addiction, imagining money. But also survival. So I stopped imagining. I bet her husband came home exhausted and furious and never wanted to talk, let alone listen.

I said, "Are you really a lawyer?"

She said, "Really am," and smiled.

I said, "Then why are you shopping at Big Lots?"

She looked like I'd said something mean and I had.

I'd hoped to hurt her then thought of all the people I'd hurt.

The thing with hurting people is it's always too many or not enough.

I ran into lots of people when I was failing at being sober, which is much different than being an addict who doesn't realize their addiction. I ran into those people less once I became a med tech and moved away but I came home often, mostly to help my mom who decided she wanted to get sober after forty years of drinking. I never minded seeing the people who'd fallen or who had lost what little they started with, mostly because I saw my face on their faces and wanted to provide comfort and some respect.

Prayers don't work until they do.

The thing about wrestling is the rules, which look a lot like facts as you get older.

The rest is blurry and you usually have to cheat.

I'm still not religious.

Sometimes. I kiss the dead on their foreheads.

Sometimes, I hold their loved ones up when they hear the bad news.

RANSOM NOTE

by LAUREL ANDERSON

from ECOTONE

We have your planet.
If you want it back, gather

blue wheels of chicory flowers
from the edge of the highway,

a white egret mirrored in black
water at dusk, pink curves of petal

tongues from an orchid's soft
mouth, smooth cold damp

of salamanders under wet leaves,
smooth dry glide of a snake

in sand, glitter-flash of comb jellies
in midnight oceans. Wrap them

unmarked in the weave
of your skin as you fissure

down to your molten core.
Go to the desert. Go alone. Come

to a valley carved by a long-dead
river with great mesas on each side.

See herds of clouds grazing
the sky to the horizon. Spread

everything you have on the red floor
of the valley and wait.

When the rim of the world is gold
in the west and cobalt in the east,

when bat wings flap against stillness,
when cacti open their pores to sigh at last

in coolness, you will feel your planet's breath
warm the stones as it rises up behind you.

BAM, APOCALYPSE

by PATRICK WHITFILL

from THE SOUTHERN REVIEW

I read somewhere that what the secular
cultural growth industry did most
was rob us of our reason to meet at regular
times with somewhat like-minded, OK folks.

Make snacks together. Rise in unison.
Sing some hymns. That's why, some say, the uptick
of massacres, droughts, shootings. Imagine
a universe like that: a few groups skip

meetings and, bam, apocalypse. But I'm
like that, eager, maybe close to zealous,
about a good End Times. It's why I like flying.
Lax dress code, booze, gas masks, and the long, precious

unair-conditioned minutes as the pilots
taxi out. Everyone gathered at last.

QUICK THINKING

by NATALIE SHAPERO

from SOUTHERN INDIANA REVIEW

I mean it. I don't want to be called a SURVIVOR.
I don't want to be called a SURVIVOR so much that I just
went ahead
and died: problem solved. That's called
QUICK THINKING. That's called WOMEN'S INGENUITY.
Everyone wants to know if I now miss the world
or at least its insensate components, such as the pulling apart
of Parker House rolls or the clarity that comes
with knowing that pull-apart Parker House rolls
are named for the Omni Parker House, formerly the
Parker House
hotel located on School Street in Boston and notable for briefly
employing in the kitchen both Ho Chi Minh
and Malcolm X, who share—and now we're getting to the part
of the world that I do miss—a May 19 birthday. I love
a good fact. I love how Mark Rothko's brothers
truncated ROTHKOWITZ to ROTH, while he went weirder.
I love how *No. 1 (Royal Red and Blue)* exceeded by forty million
dollars
its pre-sale estimate of thirty-five. I love knowing
that suicide is less like a choice and more
like being sucked out of the open door of an airplane. Is it
selfish
to be sucked out of the open door of an airplane? Is it weak
to dignify the world, a world no longer mine? Its markets

and its solvents and its tyrants always talking
about how they're redoing their windows, how they're shifting
to extruded aluminum with the rot-resistant
cladding? I WOULD LOVE TO KNOW MORE
ABOUT THAT, I purred. Love was of course the wrong word.

AFTER THE FIREWORKS

by JESSICA R. GORDON

from THIMBLE

On one side of the fork in a bend on the Tuckasegee river, nine
 geese
sit in a loose "V"—the river is low and they're close to the rocks—I
 keep
counting the large grey-brown river rock a goose—want to make
an even ten—and I don't want to confirm
what I know—why these Canada Geese sit bobbing
over inches of water and smooth stone on July 5—they dip, pop up,
formation unbroken even when families on red and blue tubes
and floaties glide past—one shakes its tail only slightly—Listen,

the signs aren't good. I don't need to type in keywords to know
Canada Geese shouldn't be in a river bend off the Smokies
when it isn't snowing in Ontario. But I too
have lingered on in seasons when I should have gone
and made myself a home
in shifting waters. The connecting "V" flips
under the surface completely—got to get cool, this heat
so sticky, so pressing—back upright again—black eyes on
the laughing, floating family headed downstream—

I take my sandals off at the bank, creep in—shallow water
spills over my toes—so cool—a dream, to linger.
All water rushing past, all patterns with it.

CIRCUS FIRE

by CIARAN BERRY

from AMERICAN POETRY REVIEW

The big cat act was over, and The Great Wallendas were getting ready to work on the high wire. Not yet Arthur Konyot and his Hungarian Riders. Not yet Ludwig Jacob emerging from the cramped quarters of his clown car. And let's say you and I have just wandered in from the midway with a red balloon, a monkey sewn from rabbit fur. Let's say the circus has arrived a day late from Providence, the big top coated in paraffin wax to keep out the rain.

Not yet the cigarette dropped outside the men's toilets, or the match struck by a razorback livid over late pay, or the schizophrenic who would confess later to setting the blaze at the behest of a ghost in a headdress. Not yet the stench of burning flesh in this, another century of needless death, setting off the vet who remembers Okinawa, where an enemy soldier burns at the end of a flame thrower. Instead, we're in the year of Liz Taylor in National Velvet and Bing Crosby asking "Would you like to swing on a star?" And my father, two days after this not-yet-fire, slipping out between the legs of his mother, which means, of course, we can't really be there, in the third row of the grandstand, waiting for Emmett Kelly to hang his tattered coat on the tightrope and beat himself at a game of solitaire, for Dolly Copeland to slip from her slop shoes on the sawdust track that circles those three rings before taking to the air. Yet there we are, among the families of those men from Travelers Insurance and Royal Typewriter, and, by the bleachers, the ex-servicemen in their wheelchairs, all of us come to see the elephants, which in the parlance of the place means to lose your innocence. Not yet the mahouts afloat on their howdahs, the horses testing the length of their lunge lines, and Kelly's 'Weary Willie' chewing a cabbage on the sidelines, or, with a broom, sweeping up the spotlight. Not yet my father's father come back from Egypt and the war with a deep tan, my father's father back from the South of France singing "It's a Long Way to Tipperary" or "We'll Meet Again." Not yet, but soon, Karl Wallenda in San Juan falling to his death between the penthouse suites of the Condado and the Flamboyan, and the heat that pops your red balloon, the heat like wasp stings on the skin as the tent takes flame like a zeppelin over the city of our dreams. And the fire like the last blast of a sunset, and the fire like the onset of a full moon.

SPECIAL MENTION

(The editors also wish to mention the following important works published by small presses last year. Listings are in no particular order.)

FICTION

Mark S. Bailen—Bears Discover Time Travel (Ecotone)
Adam Warren—Literal Spit (Mississippi Review)
Joan Murray—The Wreath (Five Points)
Diane Williams—The House For The Casanovas (Bomb)
Molly Giles—Celebration (ZYZZYZA)
Leslie Pietrzyk—F-I-N-E (Iron Horse)
William Pei Shih—Amsterdam (Joyland)
Joy Lanzendorfer—The Bear (Chicago Quarterly Review)
Dave Eggers—Keeper Of The Ornaments (American Short Fiction)
Anne-E. Wood—Losing It (Colorado Review)
Danny Ramadan—The Elusive Mrs. Omram (Consequence)
Ruhani Chhabra—Recycling (Berkeley Fiction Review)
Sarah LaBrie—Tender (Electric Literature)
Rosalind Margulies—The Super Villain (Epoch)
Sahil Mehta—The Silent World of Jordi Soto (Tint)
Nicole Simonsen—The Last of His Kind (Chicago Quarterly Review)
Kate Tighe-Pigott—Neighbors (American Short Fiction)
Samuel Kolawole—Portland Cement Food Canteen and Bar (Five Points)
Iyesatta M. Emeli—The Better Person (Examined Life)
Susan Minot—The Rooms (Narrative)
Miriam Ho Nga Wai—Growing Tomatoes (Ecotone)

Katelyn Pike—Prison Guard Blues (Another Chicago Magazine)
Lily Scheckner—The Things We Don't Talk About (One Teen Story)
Imad Rahman—Ed Thinks of Everything (New England Review)
Shanteka Sigers—Come To A Good End (Adroit Journal)
Joanna Kavenna—Otternes (Zoetrope)
Daniel Seifert—Vultur Gryphus (Bellevue Literary Review)
Emma Cairns Watson—The Dissection Question (One Story)
Andrew Nickerson—Belle Epoque (Chestnut Review)
Jonathan Gleason—Guardians (Indiana Review)
Ashleigh Bryant Phillips—Pallbearers (Southwest Review)
Vi Khi Nao—Slingshot (Noon)
Andre Dubus III—The Collector (Ploughshares)
Erika Krouse—Jude (Colorado Review)
Danielle McLaughlin—Sanctuary (Yale Review)
Miles Harvey—Four Faces (Failbetter)
Allegra Hyde—Diluvian (Orion)
Morgan Talty—The Prepper (Narrative)
Christine Sneed—Scavenging (Chicago Quarterly Review)
Joe Wilkins—The Brothers' Fire (Missouri Review)
Molly Anders—A Straightforward Matter (One Story)
Jeffrey Wolf—A Good Living (Conjunctions)
Elizabeth McCracken—Howard Johnson's, Late Spring (Story Quarterly)
Matt Jones—The Fisherman (Wrath Bearing Tree)
Jake Maynard—Take Me Home (Hopkins Review)
Reginald McKnight—1967 (Sewanee Review)
Jeneé Skinner—Mother Goose (Pleiades)
Matthew Neill Null—In the 301 (Florida Review)
Tara Ison—My Ahab (Coppernickel)
Gordon Lish—Already With the Matinal Colloquy Again? (Litmag)
Sarah Starr Murphy—Clever Girls (River Styx)
Lucy Tan—Falling Action In Hoboken (The Sun)
Michelle DuBarry—Staying Tender (The Sun)
Sarah Anderson—Take Me To Kirkland (Joyland)
Eliza Gilbert—Mama Don't Let Your Babies Grow Up To Be Cowboys (Litmag)
Andrew De Silva—Emotional Labor (Missouri Review)
Judith Sanders—The Adventures of Freydel the Meydel (Jewish Fiction)
Nikki Ervice—The Pilot (Virginia Quarterly Review)

Andrew Furman—Not Everyone Gets To Go To Tennessee (Grist)
Monona Wali—Love Thy Monster . . . (Santa Monica Review)
Jennifer Maritza McCauley—Black Planet (Boston Review)
Theodora Ziolkowski—A Hospital Man (The Normal School)
Dustin M. Hoffman—Rosie The Riveter's Résumé (Arrowsmith)
Helen Anderson—Career Opportunities (Black Warrior)
Naoimh O'Connor—Porcelain Children (Ragaire)
Lisa Allen Ortiz—The Vault (Chicago Quarterly Review)
Zanny Fran—Candyland (Iowa Review)
Ginger Pinholster—Jumping off (Prime Number)
K. D. Walker—Tourist Attractions (Hopkins Review)

NON FICTION

Hugh Martin—Shooting A Dog (American Scholar)
Miko Yoshida—Into The Fold (Consequence)
Allyson McOuat—The Call Is Coming From Inside The House (ECW Press)
Lane Scott Jones—Creation Of Woman . . . (Longreads)
Amela Skinner Saint—Breaking Kayfabe (Reed)
Albert Goldbarth—Danae (Willow Springs)
Jay Rogoff—Race, Taste, And Fred Astaire (Salmagundi)
Lindsey Drager—The Kepler Story (Alaska Quarterly Review)
Benjamin DuBow—The Sabbath Stew (Longreads)
Judith Hannah Weiss—Not Screwed Up Enough (Examined Life)
Jenn Scheck-Kahn—Coyotes (Ecotone)
Maribeth Fischer—Writing Happiness . . . (Lit Hub)
Brenda Miller, Julie Marie Wade—Sea Of Troubles (Fourth Genre)
Torrin A. Greathouse—The Crooked Child (Copper Nickel)
Benedicte Boisseron—Off-The-Grid (Transition)
Tariq Maqbool—Being Human (Santa Clara Review)
Jenna Hammerich—Ground (River Teeth)
Faith Shearin—My Ghost Fleet (The Sun)
Renata Golden—The Gift of A Greyhound (Columbus State University Press)
Patrick Hunt—The Backpack (New Letters)
Brigitte Fielder—Zenaida Doves And Audubon's Black Sisters . . . (Transition)
Sarah Minor—The Voicer of God (River Teeth)
Steve Stern—Kafka and The Uncannny (Salmagundi)

Eric Wilson—For The Young Writer (samfiftyfour.com)
A Memory, And Sorrow. . . . Ricard Bausch (River Teeth)
Elvis Bego—Mother's Hands: On Grief In 33 Beginnings (Agni)
Ann Linder—Regrets Of A Snake Handler (Alaska Quarterly)
Jehanne Dubrow—Red Monsters (New England Review)
Alisa Slaughter—The Sacrifice Blur (Santa Monica Review)
James K. Boyce—Return Of The Puffin (The Common)
Michelle Donahue—Moon Jump (Shenandoah)
Victoria Blanco—Corn-Yellow Light (Water Stone Review)
Shantell Powell—Saddles In The Kitchen (ReDivider)
Liza Minno—Unspeakable Home And The Settler Uncanny (Washington Square)
Naomi Gordon-Loebl—Lost Uncle (Florida Review)
Elizabeth Hall—Waiting With The Bar Rats (Pleiades)
Paul Crenshaw—The Butterfly Girl (Litmag)
Julia Kolchinsky Dasbach—Zombie Tag (Michigan Quarterly Review)
Chloe Garcia Roberts—Timesmiths Assemble (Ecotone)
Lia Purpura—My Deaths (Terrain)
Char Gardner—Stuck At Siple Dome (ReDivider)
Nikki Nojima Louis—Father, I Hardly Knew Ye (El Palacio)
Michael Ramos—41:A Meditation (After, University of North Carolina Press)
Hannah Bae—The Girls In The Boat (Indiana Review)
J.D. Mathes—On The Origin Of Time : A Meditation (Ploughshares)

POETRY

Bertha Crombet—Tonue Mother (Florida Review)
John E. Stintzi—International Pillow Fight Day (The Fiddlehead)
Danusha Lameris—Nothing Wants To Suffer (Blade by Blade, Copper Canyon)
Sarah Ghazal Ali—Theophanies (*Theophanies*, Alice James)
Luisa A. Igloria—When You Sit Down To Write . . . (Caulbearer, Black Lawrence)
Melissa Kwasny—The Apple Tree In Blossom (Copper Nickel)
Linda Gregerson—Is There Intelligent Life on Earth (Revel)
Catherino Barnett—Still Life (American Scholar)

Rita Mookerjee—Ode To Bathroom Mirror Altars . . . (Calyx)
Lisa Marie Oliver—Linea Nigra (Birthroot, Glass Lyre)
Lisa Badner—Always Playing The Boy Circa 1977 (Fruit Slice)
Rick Barot—Pine (Under A Warm Green Linden)
Martha Collins—If I Lived (Lily Poetry Review)
Angie Estes—Solstice (Revel)
Beth Ann Fennelly—One Line Shy of A Sonnet (Smartish Pace)
Nick Flynn—A Wall of Honey (Superpresent)
Majda Gama—All My Life I Never Once (Terrain)
Rose Solari—Inheritance (On The Seawell)
Jianqing Zheng—Jumping Mind (San Pedro River)
Sheila Black—Acequia Madre (Trace Fossils)
Murray Silverstein—In The Matter of Paternity (Red Studio, Sixteen Rivers)
Sarah Emmett—Yankins The Veil (Irreantum)
Jan Freeman—Single Helix (North American Review)
Vincent A. Rendoni—Weenies Con Huevos (Pleiades)
Rosa Lane—Paire de Corps—*Called Back* (Tupelo Press)
Christina Lloyd—Esperanza of Manila (Women Twice Removed, Sixteen River)
Stephen Ackerman—Let Her Sleep . . . (Mudfish)
Ricky Ray—Digging A Hole . . . (Honey Literature)
Janan Alexandra—Open Letter to A Politician (Sixth Finch)
Gail Mazur—Couplets (Salmagundi)
LaWanda Walters—The Flamingos Instruction . . . (Southern Review)
Sherman Alexie—Two Rivers Calling Me (Limberlost Review)
brittny ray crowell—On Groceries (Swamp Pink)
Llya Kaminsku—Reading Dante in Ukraine (Asymptote)
Stephare Dickinson—Corso in North Dakota (Midwest Review)

PRESSES FEATURED IN THE PUSHCART PRIZE EDITIONS SINCE 1976

A-Minor
About Place Journal
Abstract Magazine TV
The Account
Adroit Journal
Agni
Ahsahta Press
Ailanthus Press
Alaska Quarterly Review
Alcheringa/Ethnopoetics
Alice James Books
Ambergris
Amelia
American Circus
American Journal of Poetry
American Letters and Commentary
American Literature
American PEN
American Poetry Review
American Scholar
American Short Fiction
The American Voice
Amicus Journal
Amnesty International
Anaesthesia Review
Anhinga Press
Another Chicago Magazine
Anacapa Review
Antaeus
Antietam Review
Anthology of Appalachian Writers
Antioch Review
Apalachee Quarterly
Aphra
Aralia Press
The Ark
Arkansas Review
Arroyo
Artangel
Art and Understanding
Arts and Letters
Artword Quarterly
Ascensius Press
Ascent
Ashland Poetry Press
Aspen Leaves
Aspen Poetry Anthology
Assaracus
Assembling
Atlanta Review
Autonomedia
Avocet Press
The Awl
The Baffler

Bakunin
Bare Life
Bat City Review
Bamboo Ridge
Barlenmir House
Barnwood Press
Barrow Street
Bauhan Publishing
Bellevue Literary Review
The Bellingham Review
Bellowing Ark
Beloit Poetry Journal
Bennington Review
Bettering America Poetry
Bilingual Review
Birmingham Poetry Review
Black American Literature Forum
Blackbird
Black Renaissance Noire
Black Rooster
Black Scholar
Black Sparrow
Black Warrior Review
Blackwells Press
The Believer
Bloom
Bloomsbury Review
Bloomsday Lit
Blue Cloud Quarterly
Blueline
Blue Unicorn
Blue Wind Press
Bluefish
BOA Editions
Bomb
Bookslinger Editions
Boomer Litmag
Boston Review
Boulevard
Boxspring
Brevity
Briar Cliff Review
Brick
Bridge
Bridges
Brown Journal of Arts
Burning Deck Press
Butcher's Dog
Cafe Review
Caliban
California Quarterly
Callaloo
Calliope
Calliopea Press
Calyx
The Canary
Canto
Capra Press
Carcanet Editions
Caribbean Writer
Carolina Quarterly
Catapult
Caught by The River
Cave Wall
Cedar Rock
Center
Chariton Review
Charnel House
Chattahoochee Review
Chautauqua Literary Journal
Chelsea
Chicago Quarterly Review
Chouteau Review
Chowder Review
Cimarron Review
Cincinnati Review
Cincinnati Poetry Review
City Lights Books
Clarion
Cleveland State Univ. Poetry Ctr.
Clover
Clown War
Codex Journal
CoEvolution Quarterly
Cold Mountain Press
The Collagist

Colorado Review
Columbia: A Magazine of Poetry and Prose
Columbia Poetry Review
The Common
Comstoot Review
Conduit
Confluence Press
Confrontation
Conjunctions
Connecticut Review
Constellations
Copper Canyon Press
Copper Nickel
Cosmic Information Agency
Countermeasures
Counterpoint
Court Green
Crab Orchard Review
Crawl Out Your Window
Crazyhorse
Creative Nonfiction
Crescent Review
Cross Cultural Communications
Cross Currents
Crosstown Books
Crowd
Cue
Cumberland Poetry Review
Curbstone Press
Cutbank
Cutthroat
Cypher Books
Dacotah Territory
Daedalus
Dalkey Archive Press
Daraja Press
James Dickey Review
Decatur House
December
Denver Quarterly
Deep Wild Journal
Desperation Press
Dogwood
Domestic Crude
Doubletake
Dragon Gate Inc.
Dreamworks
Dryad Press
Duck Down Press
Dunes Review
Durak
East River Anthology
Eastern Washington University Press
Ecotone
Egress
El Malpensante
Electric Literature
Eleven Eleven
Ellis Press
Emergence
Empty Bowl
Epiphany
Epoch
Ergo
Evansville Review
Exquisite Corpse
Faultline
Fence
Fiction
Fiction Collective
Fiction International
Field
Fifth Wednesday Journal
Fine Madness
Firebrand Books
Firelands Art Review
First Intensity
5 A.M.
Five Fingers Review
Five Points Press
Fjords Review
Florida Review
Flyway
Foglifter
Forklift
The Formalist

Foundry
Four Way Books
Fourth Genre
Fourth River
Fractured Lit
Frontiers: A Journal of Women Studies
Fugue
Gallimaufry
Genre
The Georgia Review
Gettysburg Review
Ghost Dance
Gibbs-Smith
Glimmer Train
Goddard Journal
David Godine, Publisher
Gordon Square
Good River Review
Graham House Press
Grain
Grand Street
Granta
Graywolf Press
Great River Review
Green Mountains Review
Greenfield Review
Greensboro Review
Guardian Press
Gulf Coast
Hanging Loose
Harbour Publishing
Hard Pressed
Harvard Advocate
Harvard Review
Hawaii Pacific Review
Hayden's Ferry Review
Heat
Hedgehog Review
Here
Hermitage Press
Heyday
Hills
Hobart
Hole in the Head
Hollyridge Press
Holmgangers Press
Holy Cow!
Home Planet News
Hopkins Review
The Hopper
Hudson Review
Hunger Mountain
Hungry Mind Review
Hysterical Rag
Iamb
Ibbetson Street Press
Icarus
Icon
Idaho Review
Iguana Press
Image
In Character
Indiana Review
Indiana Writes
Indianapolis Review
Intermedia
Intro
Invisible City
Inwood Press
Iowa Review
Ironwood
I-70 Review
Jam To-day
Jewish Currents
J Journal
The Journal
Jubilat
The Kanchenjunga Press
Kansas Quarterly
Kayak
Kelsey Street Press
Kenyon Review
Kestrel
Kweli Journal
Lake Effect
Lana Turner

Latitudes Press
Laughing Waters Press
Laurel Poetry Collective
Laurel Review
Leap Frog
L'Epervier Press
Liberation
Ligeia
Linquis
Literal Latté
Literary Imagination
Literary Matters
The Literary Review
The Little Magazine
Little Patuxent Review
Little Star
Live Mag!
Living Hand Press
Living Poets Press
Logbridge-Rhodes
Longreads
Louisville Review
Love's Executive Order
Lowlands Review
LSU Press
Lucille
Lynx House Press
Lyric
The MacGuffin
Magic Circle Press
Malahat Review
Manhattan Review
Manoa
Manroot
Many Mountains Moving
Marlboro Review
Massachusetts Review
McSweeney's
Meridian
Mho & Mho Works
Micah Publications
Michigan Quarterly
Mid-American Review
Milkweed Editions
Milkweed Quarterly
The Minnesota Review
Mississippi Review
Mississippi Valley Review
Missouri Review
Montana Gothic
Montana Review
Montemora
Moon Pie Press
Moon Pony Press
Mount Voices
Mr. Cogito Press
MSS
Mudfish
Mulch Press
Muzzle Magazine
n+1
Nada Press
Narrative
National Poetry Review
Nebraska Poets Calendar
Nebraska Review
Nepantla
Nerve Cowboy
New America
New American Review
New American Writing
The New Criterion
New Delta Review
New Directions
New England Review
New England Review and Bread Loaf
New World Writing
Quarterly
New Issues
New Letters
New Madrid
New Ohio Review
New Orleans Review
New South Books
New Verse News
New Virginia Review

New York Quarterly
New York University Press
Nimrod
9×9 Industries
Ninth Letter
Noon
North American Review
North Atlantic Books
North Dakota Quarterly
North Meridian Review
North Point Press
Northeastern University Press
Northern Lights
Northwest Review
Notre Dame Review
O. ARS
O. Blk
Obsidian
Obsidian II
Ocho
Oconee Review
October
Ohio Review
Old Crow Review
Ontario Review
Open City
Open Places
Orca Press
Orchises Press
Oregon Humanities
Orion
Other Voices
Oxford American
Oxford Press
Oyez Press
Oyster Boy Review
Painted Bride Quarterly
Painted Hills Review
Palette
Palo Alto Review
Paper Darts
Paris Press
Paris Review
Parkett
Parnassus: Poetry in Review
Partisan Review
Passages North
Paterson Literary Review
Pebble Lake Review
Penca Books
Pentagram
Penumbra Press
Pequod
Persea: An International Review
Perugia Press
Per Contra
Pilot Light
The Pinch
Pipedream Press
Pirene's Fountain
Pitcairn Press
Pitt Magazine
Pleasure Boat Studio
Pleiades
Ploughshares
Plume
Poem-A-Day
Poems & Plays
Poet and Critic
Poet Lore
Poetry
Poetry Atlanta Press
Poetry East
Poetry International
Poetry Ireland Review
Poetry Northwest
Poetry Now
The Point
Post Road
Prairie Schooner
Prelude
Prescott Street Press
Press
Prime Number
Prism
Promise of Learnings

Provincetown Arts
A Public Space
Puerto Del Sol
Purple Passion Press
Quadermi Di Yip
Quarry West
The Quarterly
Quarterly West
Quiddity
Radio Silence
Rainbow Press
Raritan: A Quarterly Review
Rattle
Red Cedar Review
Red Clay Books
Red Dust Press
Red Earth Press
Red Hen Press
Reed
Release Press
Republic of Letters
Revel
Review of Contemporary Fiction
Revista Chicano-Riqueña
Rhetoric Review
Rhino
Rivendell
River Styx
River Teeth
Rowan Tree Press
Ruminate
Runes
Russian *Samizdat*
Saginaw
Salamander
Salmagundi
San Marcos Press
Santa Monica Review
Sarabande Books
Saturnalia
Sea Pen Press and Paper Mill
Seal Press
Seamark Press
Seattle Review
Second Coming Press
Semiotext(e)
Seneca Review
Seven Days
The Seventies Press
Sewanee Review
The Shade Journal
Shankpainter
Shantih
Shearsman
Sheep Meadow Press
Shenandoah
A Shout In the Street
Sibyl-Child Press
Side Show
Sidereal
Sixth Finch
Sky Island Journal
Slipstream
Small Moon
Smartish Pace
The Smith
Snake Nation Review
Solo
Solo 2
Some
The Sonora Review
Southeast Review
Southern Indiana Review
Southern Poetry Review
Southern Review
Southampton Review
Southword
Southwest Review
Sparks of Calliope
Speakeasy
Spectrum
Spillway
Spork
The Spirit That Moves Us
St. Andrews Press
St. Brigid Press

Stillhouse Press
Stonecoast
Storm Cellar
Story
Story Quarterly
Streetfare Journal
Stuart Wright, Publisher
Subtropics
Sugar House Review
Sulfur
Summerset Review
The Sun
Sun & Moon Press
Sun Press
Sunstone
Sweet
Sycamore Review
Tab
Tamagawa
Tar River Poetry
Teal Press
Telephone Books
Telescope
Temblor
The Temple
Tendril
Terrain
Terminus
Terrapin Books
Texas Slough
Thimble
Think
Third Coast
13th Moon
THIS
This Broken Shore
Thorp Springs Press
Three Rivers Press
Threepenny Review
Thrush
Thunder City Press
Thunder's Mouth Press
Tia Chucha Press
Tiger Bark Press
Tikkun
Tin House
Tint
Tipton Review
Tombouctou Books
Toothpaste Press
Transatlantic Review
Treelight
Triplopia
TriQuarterly
Truck Press
True Story
Tule Review
Tupelo Review
Turnrow
Tusculum Review
Two Sylvias
Twyckenham Notes
Undine
Unicorn Press
University of Chicago Press
University of Georgia Press
University of Illinois Press
University of Iowa Press
University of Massachusetts Press
University of North Texas Press
University of Pittsburgh Press
University of Wisconsin Press
University Press of New England
Unmuzzled Ox
Unspeakable Visions of the Individual
Vagabond
Vallum
Verse
Verse Wisconsin
Vignette
Virginia Quarterly Review
Volt
The Volta
Wampeter Press
War, Literature & The Arts
Washington Square Review

Washington Writer's Workshop
Water-Stone
Water Table
Wave Books
Waxwing
West Branch
Western Humanities Review
Westigan Review
White Pine Press
Wickwire Press
Wigleaf
Willow Springs
Wilmore City
Witness
Word Beat Press
Word Press
Wordsmith
World Literature Today
WordTemple Press
Wormwood Review
Writers' Forum
Xanadu
Yale Review
Yardbird Reader
Yarrow
Y-Bird
Yes Yes Books
Zeitgeist Press
Zoetrope: All-Story
Zone 3
ZYZZYVA

THE PUSHCART PRIZE FELLOWSHIPS

The Pushcart Prize Fellowships Inc., a 501 (c) (3) nonprofit corporation, is the endowment for The Pushcart Prize. "Members" donated up to $249 each. "Sponsors" gave between $250 and $999. "Benefactors" donated from $1000 to $4,999. "Patrons" donate $5,000 and more. We are very grateful for these donations. Gifts of any amount a welcome. For information write to the Fellowships at PO Box 380, Wainscott, NY 11975

Founding Patrons

Michael and Elizabeth R. Rea
The Katherine Anne Porter Literary Trust

Patrons

Marist University
Charitable Trust
Carter C. Chinnis
Margaret Ajemian Ahnert
Daniel L. Dolgin & Loraine F. Gardner
James Patterson Foundation
Neltje
John Sargent
Charline Spektor
Nelson S. Talbott Foundation
Ellen M. Violett

BENEFACTORS

Anonymous
Russell Allen
Barbara Ascher & Strobe Talbott
Hilaria & Alec Baldwin
David Caldwell
Ted Conklin
Bernard F. Conners
Richie Crown
Cartherine and C. Bryan Daniels
Maureen Mahon Egen
Loraine Gardner
Joyce Carol Oates
Warren & Barbara Phillips
Stacey Richter
Olivia & Colin Van Dyke
Dallas Ernst

Cedering Fox
H.E. Francis
Diane Glynn
Mary Ann Goodman & Bruno Quinson Foundation
Bill & Genie Henderson
Bob Henderson
Marina & Stephen E. Kaufman
Wally & Christine Lamb
Dorothy Lichtenstein
Glyn Vincent
Kirby E. Williams
Margaret V. B. Wurtele

Sustaining Members

Anonymous
Agni
Lisa Alvarez
Barbara Ascher & Strobe Talbott
Jim Barnes
Ellen Bass
Bruce Bennett
John Berggren
Wendell Berry
Binswanger-Charlton Fdn.
Rosellen Brown
Ethan Bumas
Phil Carter
David Caldwell
Patrick Clark
Suzanne Cleary
Martha Collins
Linda Coleman
Pamela Cothey
Richie Crown
Dan Dolgin & Loraine Gardner
Jack Driscoll
Maureen Mahon Egen
Alice Friman
Ben & Sharon Fountain
Robert Giron
Diane Glynn
Alex Henderson
Bob Henderson
Lynne C. Hiller
Hippocampus
Jane Hirshfield
Helen Houghton
Don and Renee Kaplan
John Kistner
Peter Krass
Edmund Keeley
Ron Koertge
Wally & Christine Lamb
Linda Lancione
Jessica Leitner
Maria Matthiessen
Alice Mattison
Robert McBrearty
Rick Moody
Joan Murray
Joyce Carol Oates
Dan Orozco
Thomas Paine
Pam Painter
Barbara & Warren Phillips
John and Donna Potter
Elizabeth R. Rea
Stacey Richter
Diane Rudner
John Sargent
Sharasheff-Johnson Giving
Schaffner Family Fdn.
Sybil Steinberg
Jody Stewart
Donna Talarico
Andrew Tonkovich
Elaine Terranova
Upstreet
Olivia & Colin Van Dyke
Glyn Vincent
Maryfrancis Wagner
Rosanna Warren
Michael Waters
Diane Williams
Kirby E. Williams

Sponsors

Altman / Kazickas Fdn.
Jacob Appel
Jean M. Auel
Jim Barnes
Charles Baxter
John Berggren
Joe David Bellamy
Laura & Pinckney Benedict
Binswanger Charlton Fdn.
Wendell Berry
Laure-Anne Bosselaar
Kate Braverman
Barbara Bristol
Kurt Brown

Nelson DeMille
E. L. Doctorow
Penny Dunning
Karl Elder
Donald Finkel
Ben and Sharon Fountain
Alan and Karen Furst
John Gill
Robert Giron
Beth Gutcheon
Doris Grumbach & Sybil Pike
Gwen Head
The Healing Muse
Robin Hemley
Bob Hicok
Lynne C. Hiller
Hippocampus
Jane Hirshfield
Helen & Frank Houghton
Joseph Hurka
Christian Jara
Diane Johnson
Janklow & Nesbit Asso.
Edmund Keeley
Thomas E. Kennedy
Wally Lomb
Sydney Lea
Stephen Lesser
Gerald Locklin
Richard Burgin
Alan Catlin
Mary Casey
Siv Cedering
Dan Chaon
Andrei Codrescu
Linda Coleman
Ted Colm
Stephen Corey
Tracy Crow
Dana Literary Society
Carol de Gramont
Thomas Lux
Markowitz, Fenelon and Bank
Elizabeth McKenzie
McSweeney's
Rick Moody
John Mullen
Joan Murray
New York Community Trust
Thomas Paine
Barbara and Warren Phillips
John and Donna Potter
Hilda Raz
Stacey Richter
Diane Rudner
Schaffner Family Foundation
Sharasheff—Johnson Fund
Cindy Sherman
Joyce Carol Smith
May Carlton Swope
Andrew Tonkovich
Glyn Vincent
Julia Wendell
Philip White
Diane Williams
Eleanor Wilner
David Wittman
Richard Wyatt & Irene Eilers

Members

Anonymous (3)
Stephen Adams
Betty Adcock
Agni
Carolyn Alessio
Dick Allen
Henry H. Allen
John Allman
Lisa Alvarez
Jan Lee Ande
Dr. Russell Anderson
Ralph Angel
Antietam Review
Susan Antolin
Ruth Appelhof
Philip and Marjorie Appleman
Linda Aschbrenner
Renee Ashley
Ausable Press
David Baker
Catherine Barnett
Dorothy Barresi
Barlow Street Press
Jill Bart
Ellen Bass
Judith Baumel
E. S. Bumas
Richard Burgin
Skylar H. Burris
David Caligiuri
Kathy Callaway
Bonnie Jo Campbell
Janine Canan
Henry Carlile
Carrick Publishing
Fran Castan

Mary Casey
Chelsea Associates
Marianne Cherry
Phillis M. Choyke
Lucinda Clark
Suzanne Cleary
Linda Coleman
Martha Collins
Ted Conklin
Joan Connor
J. Cooper
John Copenhaver
Dan Corrie
Pam Cothey
Lisa Couturier
Tricia Currans-Sheehan
Jim Daniels
Daniel & Daniel
Jerry Danielson
Ed David
Josephine David
Thadious Davis
Michael Denison
Maija Devine
Sharon Dilworth
Edward DiMaio
Kent Dixon
A.C. Dorset
Jack Driscoll
Wendy Druce
Penny Dunning
John Duncklee
Nancy Ebert
Elaine Edelman
Renee Edison & Don Kaplan
Nancy Edwards
Ekphrasis Press
M.D. Elevitch
Elizabeth Ellen
Entrekin Foundation
Failbetter.com
Irvin Faust
Elliot Figman
Tom Filer
Carol and Laueme Firth
Finishing Line Press
Iliyas Honey
Susan Indigo
Mark Irwin
Beverly A. Jackson
Richard Jackson
Christian Jara
David Jauss
Marilyn Johnston
Alice Jones
Journal of New Jersey Poets
Robert Kalich
Sophia Kartsonis
Julia Kasdorf
Miriam Polli Katsikis
Meg Kearney
Celine Keating
Brigit Kelly
John Kistner
Judith Kitchen
Ron Koertge
Stephen Kopel
Peter Krass
David Kresh
Maxine Kumin
Valerie Laken
Babs Lakey
Linda Lancione
Maxine Landis
Lane Larson
Dorianne Laux & Joseph Millar
Sydney Lea
Stephen Lesser
Donald Lev
Dana Levin
Live Mag!
Gerald Locklin
Rachel Loden
Radomir Luza, Jr.
William Lychack
Annette Lynch
Elzabeth MacKieman
Elizabeth Macklin
Leah Maines
Mark Manalang
Norma Marder
Jack Marshall
Michael Martone
Tara L. Masih
Dan Masterson
Peter Matthiessen
Maria Matthiessen
Alice Mattison
Tracy Mayor
Robert McBrearty
Jane McCafferty
Rebecca McClanahan
Katrina Roberts
Judith R. Robinson
Jessica Roeder
Martin Rosner
Kay Ryan
Sy Safransky
Brian Salchert
James Salter
Sherod Santos
Ellen Sargent

R.A. Sasaki
Valerie Sayers
Maxine Scates
Alice Schell
Dennis & Loretta Schmitz
Helen Schulman
Philip Schultz
Shenandoah
Peggy Shinner
Lydia Ship
Vivian Shipley
Joan Silver
Skyline
John E. Smeleer
Raymond J. Smith
Joyce Carol Smith
Philip St. Clair
Lorraine Standish
Maureen Stanton
Michael Steinberg
Sybil Steinberg
Jody Stewart
Barbara Stone
Storyteller Magazine
Bill & Pat Strachan
Raymond Strom
Julie Suk
Summerset Review
Sun Publishing
Sweet Annie Press
Katherine Taylor
Pamela Taylor
Elaine Terranova
Susan Terris
Marcelle Thiebaux
Robert Thomas
Donna Talarico
Ann Beattie
Madison Smartt Bell
Beloit Poetry Journal
Pinckney Benedict
Karen Bender
Andre Bernard
Christopher Bernard
Wendell Berry
Linda Bierds
Stacy Bierlein
Big Fiction
Bitter Oleander Press
Mark Blaeuer
John Blondel
Blue Light Press
Carol Bly
BOA Editions
Deborah Bogen
Bomb
Susan Bono
Brain Child
Anthony Brandt
James Breeden
Rosellen Brown
Jane Brox
Andrea Hollander Budy
Susan Firer
Nick Flynn
Starkey Flythe Jr.
Peter Fogo
Linda Foster
Fourth Genre
Alice Friman
John Fulton
Fugue
Alice Fulton
Alan Furst
Eugene Garber
Frank X. Gaspar
A Gathering of the Tribes
Reginald Gibbons
Emily Fox Gordon
Philip Graham
Eamon Grennan
Myma Goodman
Ginko Tree Press
Jessica Graustain
Lee Meitzen Grue
Habit of Rainy Nights
Rachel Hadas
Susan Hahn
Meredith Hall
Harp Strings
Jeffrey Harrison
Clarinda Harriss
Lois Marie Harrod
Healing Muse
Tim Hedges
Michele Helm
Alex Henderson
Lily Henderson
Daniel Henry
Neva Herington
Lou Hertz
Stephen Herz
William Heyen
Bob Hicok
R. C. Hildebrandt
Kathleen Hill
Lee Hinton
Jane Hirshfield
Hippocampus Magazin
Edward Hoagland
Daniel Hoffman
Doug Holder

Richard Holinger
Rochelle L. Holt
Richard M. Huber
Brigid Hughes
Lynne Hugo
Karla Huston
I-70 Review
Bob McCrane
Jo McDougall
Sandy McIntosh
James McKean
Roberta Mendel
Didi Menendez
Barbara Milton
Alexander Mindt
Mississippi Review
Nancy Mitchell
Martin Mitchell
Roger Mitchell
Jewell Mogan
Patricia Monaghan
Jim Moore
James Morse
William Mulvihill
Nami Mun
Joan Murray
Carol Muske-Dukes
Edward Mycue
Deirdre Neilen
W. Dale Nelson
New Michigan Press
Jean Nordhaus
Celeste Ng
Christiana Norcross
Ontario Review Foundation
Daniel Orozco
Other Voices
Paris Review
Alan Michael Parker
Ellen Parker
Veronica Patterson
David Pearce, M.D.
Robert Phillips
Donald Platt
Plain View Press
Valerie Polichar
Pool
Horatio Potter
Jeffrey & Priscilla Potter
C.E. Poverman
Marcia Preston
Eric Puchner
Osiris
Tony Quagliano
Quill & Parchment
Barbara Quinn
Randy Rader
Juliana Rew
Belle Randall
Martha Rhodes
Nancy Richard
Stacey Richter
James Reiss
Andrew Tonkovich
Pauls Toutonghi
Juanita Torrence-Thompson
William Trowbridge
Martin Tucker
Umbrella Factory Press
Under The Sun
Universal Table
Upstreet
Jeannette Valentine
Victoria Valentine
Christine Van Winkle
Hans Vandebovenkamp
Elizabeth Veach
Tino Villanueva
Maryfrances Wagner
William & Jeanne Wagner
BJ Ward
Susan O. Warner
Rosanna Warren
Margareta Waterman
Michael Waters
Stuart Watson
Sandi Weinberg
Andrew Wainstein
Dr. Henny Wenkart
Jason Wesco
West Meadow Press
Susan Wheeler
Mary Frances Wagner
When Women Waken
Dara Wier
Ellen Wilbur
Galen Williams
Diane Williams
Marie Sheppard Williams
Eleanor Wilner
Irene Wilson
Steven Wingate
Sandra Wisenberg
Wings Press
Robert Witt
David Wittman
Margot Wizansky
Matt Yurdana
Christina Zawadiwsky
Sander Zulauf
ZYZZYVA

CONTRIBUTING SMALL PRESSES FOR PUSHCART PRIZE L

(The following small presses made nominations for this edition)

Abandoned Mine, PO Box 3782, Albuquerque, NM 87190
About Place Journal, 4520 Blue Mounds Trail, Black Earth, WI 53515-9719
Abstract Magazine TV, 124 E. Johnson St., Norman, OK 73069
Academy of American Poets, 75 Maiden Lane, Ste 901, New York, NY 10038
Accents Publishing, 250 S. MLK Blvd., #116, Lexington, KY 40508
The Account, Ayers, 712 W. Huron St., #104, Ann Arbor, MI 48103
Acorn, S. Antolin, 115 Conifer Ln, Walnut Creek, CA 94598
The Adroit Journal, 1223 Westover Rd., Stamford, CT 06902
AFM, 100 Hilton Ave., #402, Garden City, NY 11530
After . . . , M.A. Owen, 57 Thorpe Gardens, Alton, Hampshire GU34 2BQ, UK
After Dinner Conversations, K. Granville, 2516 S. Jentilly Lane, Tempe, AZ 85282
After Happy Hour Review, 599 Blessing St, Pittsburgh, PA 15213
After the Art, RB Noble, 3000 Connecticut Ave. NW, #233, Washington, DC 20008
Agni Magazine, Boston University, 236 Bay State Rd., Boston, MA 02215
Aim Higher Press, 1693 State Route 28A, New York, NY 12491
Al-Khemia Poetica, 6028 Comey Ave., Los Angeles, CA 90034
Alaska Quarterly Review, ESH 208, 3211 Providence Dr., Anchorage, AK 99508
Alice James Books, 60 Pineland Dr., New Gloucester, ME 04260
Allium Journal, Columbia College, 600 So. Michigan Ave., Chicago, IL 60605
Alocasia, 11 Sprague St., Providence, RI 02907
Alta Journal, B. Spotswood, PO Box 14666, San Francisco, CA 94114
[Alternate Route], M. Starr, 741 Katydid Ct., Martinez, CA 94553-2221
Always Crashing, 823 Burch Ave., #A, Durham, NC 27701
American Poetry Review, 1906 Rittenhouse Sq., 3rd FL, Philadelphia, PA 19103

American Scholar, 1606 New Hampshire Ave., NW, Washington, DC 20009
American Short Fiction, 203 W. 32nd St., Austin, TX 78705
Amplicon Press, 71-75 Shelton St., London, Wc2H 9JQ, UK
Anaheim Poetry Review, Van Camp, 1882 N. Garland Ln., Anaheim CA 92807
Anamcara Press, PO Box 442072, Lawrence, KS 66044-2072
And Other Poems, 31/6 Royal Park Terrace, Edinburgh, EH8 8JA, UK
Anhinga Press, 1812 Skyland Drive, Tallahassee, FL 32303
Another Chicago Magazine, 1301 W. Byron St., Chicago, IL 60613
Anthology of Appalachian Writers, Appalachian Heritage, Shepherd University, S. Bailey Shurbutt, PO Box 599, Shepherdstown, WV 25443
Antiphony, 1534 Plaza Lane #191, Burlingame, CA 94010
Apostrophe, Jan Lee, Hong Kong Writers Circle, www.hongkongwriterscircle.com
Appalachia Journal, Woodside, 41 Bridge St., Deep River, CT 06417
Apparition Literary, Robinson, 1220 Johnson Dr., SPC 81, Ventura, CA 93003
Apple Valley Review, 88 South 3rd St., #336, San José, CA 95113
Arachne Press, 100 Grierson Rd., London, SE23 1NX, UK
Arizona Authors Association, 1119 E. LeMarche Ave., Phoenix, AZ 85022-3136
Arkana, UCA, Thompson Hall 324, 201 Donaghey Ave., Conway, AR 72035
The Arkansas International, 333 Kimpel Hall, Univ. of AR, Fayetteville, AR 72701
Arts & Letters, Georgia College, Campus Box 89, Milledgeville, GA 31061
Asian American Writers' Workshop, 112 W. 27th St., #600, New York, NY 10001
Asian Arts & Letters, RC Short, 39 Eastview Court, Sag Harbor, NY 11963
Asimov's Science Fiction, 6 Prowitt St., Norwalk, CT 06855
Assignment Literary, Rose, 267 Port Augustine Cir., #102, Ocoee, FL 34761
Aster Literary, Z. Seldon, 12614 Greene Ave., Los Angeles, CA 90066
Aster(ix), Cruz, English, U.P., 609-F, 4200 Fifth Ave., Pittsburgh, PA 15260
Autumn House Press, 5614 Elgin St., Pittsburgh, PA 15206
Autumn Sky Poetry Daily, 5263 Arctic Circle, Emmaus, PA 18049
Awakenings Review, PO Box 177, Wheaton, IL 60187

Bainbridge Island Press, 4704 NE North Tolo Rd., Bainbridge Island, WA 98110
Ballast, 18335 Amberly Ln., South Bend, IN 46637
Baltimore Review, 6514 Maplewood Rd., Baltimore, MD 21212
Bamboo Dart Press, 112 N. Harvard Ave., #65, Claremont, CA 91711
Barrelhouse Magazine, 1400 N. 80th St., #501, Seattle, WA 98103
Barstow and Grand, 3315 Nimitz St., Eau Claire, WI 54701
Bath Flash Fiction, 6 Old Tarnwell, Stanton Drew, Bristol BS39 4EA, UK
Bauhan Publishing, PO Box 117, Peterborough, NH 03458
Bay to Ocean Journal, E. Rich, 3828 Leonard Cove Lane, Trappe, MD 21673
Bear Review, M. Myers, 4211 Holmes St., Kansas City, MO 64110

Bearskin Lodge Press, L. Wright, 501 S. Crouse Ave., #713, Syracuse, NY 13210
The Believer Magazine, S. W. Mao, 362 W. 116th St., #2B, New York, NY 10026
Bellevue Literary Review, 149 East 23rd St., #1518, New York, NY 10010
Bellingham Review, WWU - English, MS 9053, 516 High St., Bellingham, WA 98225
Beloit Fiction Journal, Box 11, 700 College St., Beloit, WI 53511
Beloit Poetry Journal, PO Box 450, Windham, ME 04062
Bennington Review, 1 College Dr., Bennington, VT 05201
Berkeley Fiction Review, 2465 Bancroft Wy, 312 Eshleman, Berkeley, CA 94704
Beyond Words, (Gal Slonim) Hermannstr. 230, 12049 Berlin, Germany
Big Table Publishing, 632 Santana Rd., Novato, CA 94945
Bindle Rag, 7151 Cold Water Court, Dayton, OH 45459
bioStories, 225 Log Yard Ct, Bigfork, MT 59911
Birmingham Poetry Review, UAB-English, Birmingham, AL 35205-4250
The Bitter Southerner, 524 Hill St., Athens, GA 30606
BKMK Press, 5 W. 3rd St., Parkville, MO 64152-3707
Black Bough Poetry, 19 Hendrefoilan Rd., Tycoch, Swansea, SA29LS, UK
Black Fox, R Henry, 3019 Edgewater Dr., PMB A1048, Orlando, FL 32804-3719
Black Lawrence Press, Goettel, 279 Claremont Ave., Mt. Vernon, NY 10552-3305
Black Warrior Review, Box 870170, Tuscaloosa, AL 35487-0170
Black Widow Press, 9 Spring Ln, Boston, MA 02109
BlacKat Publishing, 18835 Curtis St., Detroit, MI 48219
Blink Ink, PO Box 5, North Branford, CT 06471
Bloodroot Literary Magazine, 71 Baker Hill Rd., Lyme, NH 03768
Blue Heron Review, N66W38350 Deer Creek Ct., Oconomowoc, WI 53066-6303
Blue Light Press, PO Box 150300, San Rafael, CA 94915
BOA Editions, 250 N. Goodman St., #306, Rochester, NY 14607
BOMBS Publishing, 1221 Edenham Way, Greensboro, NC 27410
Booth, Butler University, 4600 Sunset Ave., Indianapolis, IN 46208
Boudin Press, MSU, 4205 Ryan St., Lake Charles, LA 70605-3465
Boulevard, D. Freund, 2702A Ann Ave., St. Louis, MO 63104-2224
Bourbon Penn, PO Box 7764, Myrtle Beach, S 29572
Box Turtle Press, J. Hoffman, 184 Franklin St., New York, NY 10013
Bracken Magazine, Deimling, 167 Bainbridge St., Brooklyn, NY 11233
Braided Way, 8916 Shank Rd., Litchfield, OH 44253
Bravura, C. Rolens, 5375 Adams Ave., San Diego, CA 92115
Brevity, Moore, 128 Campbell Ave., Havertown, PA 19083
Brick Road Poetry Press, 341 Lee Rd. #553, Phenix City, AL 36867
Bridge, 2858 W. Belle Plaine Ave., #3, Chicago, IL 60618
Bright Flash Literary Review, 12520 Caswell Ave., Los Angeles, CA 90066
Brigids Gate Press, 9232 Kessler Lane, Overland Park, KS 66212

Brilliant Flash Fiction, 3B Bent Grass Ct., Black Mountain, NC 28711
Brink, 450 Hwy 1 W., #126, Iowa City, IA 52246
Broadstone Books, 418 Ann St., Frankfort, KY 40601-1929
Broken Tribe Press, W. Lawrence, 6006 Cobridge Sq., Raleigh, NC 27609
Bronze Bird Books, D. Pring-Mill, 145 Tyee Dr., #30972, Point Roberts, WA 98281
Brooklyn Poets, 144 Montague St., 2nd Fl, Brooklyn, NY 11201
Brownstone Poets, Carragon, 8785 Bay 16th St., #B-8, Brooklyn, NY 11214
Burningword Lit Journal, PO Box 52945, Lafayette, LA 70505

California Quarterly, CA State Poetry Society, PO Box 4288, Sunland, CA 91041
Calyx, PO Box B, Corvallis, OR 97339
Candid Review, S. Sahoo, 3594 Sunnymead Ct., San Jose, CA 95117
Cape Cod Review, 61 Lily Pond Dr., S. Yarmouth, MA 02664
The Caribbean Writer, UVI, Box 10000, RRI, Kingshill, VI 00850
Catamaran, 1050 River St., #118, Santa Cruz, CA 95060
Cave Wall, PO Box 29546, Greensboro, NC 27429-9546
Celestial Echo Press, 7919 Heather Rd., Elkins Park, PA 19027
Centaur, L. Mundell, 736 Santa Fe Ave., Albany, CA 94706
Central Avenue, 254-1582 Guilford, Point Roberts, WA 98281
Chapter House Journal, C. Wilcox, 36 Vista Montana Loop, Placitas, NM 87043
Charlotte Lit Press, 933 Louise Ave., Ste 101, Charlotte, NC 28204-2299
Chautauqua, UNC-W, English, 601 S. College Rd., Wilmington, NC 28403-5938
Chestnut Review, 213 N. Tioga St. #6751, Ithaca, NY 14851
Chewers by Masticadores, 233 N. Desmet Ave., Buffalo, WY 82834
Chicago Story Press, 2754 Ridge Ave, Evanston, IL 60201-1720
Chiron Review, 522 E. South Ave., St. John, KS 67576-2212
Choeofpleirn Press, 1424 Franklin St., Leavenworth, KS 66048
Cholla Needles, 6732 Conejo Ave., Joshua Tree, CA 92252
Cicada Creative Magazine, 355 The Preserve Dr., #428, Athens, GA 30606
Cincinnati Review, English, PO Box 210069, Cincinnati, OH 45221-0069
Cirque Press, S. Kleven, 3157 Bettles Bay Loop, Anchorage, AK 99515
Citron Review, A. Brommel, 291 Walnut Village Ln, Henderson, NV 89012
Cleaver, L. Murphy, 1675 Woodbine St., #2R, Ridgewood, NY 11385
Cleveland Review of Books, PO Box 181424, Cleveland, OH 44118
Clockhouse, J. McConnell, 1031 Highland Dr., Columbus, OH 43220
Cloudbank Books, PO Box 610, Corvallis, OR 97339-0610
Club Plum, T. Swanson, 6534 N.E. Plum St., Suquamish, WA 98392
Coachella Review, UCR, 75080 Frank Sinatra Dr., Palm Desert, CA 92211
Coffin Bell Journal, T. Grisanti, 11950 Clifton Rd., Savannah, TM 38372
Cold Moon Journal, Jacobson, 405 S. Jefferson Way, Indianola, IA 50125

Collapse Press, PO Box 3016, Easton, PA 18043
Collateral Journal, A. Murray, 616 N. Prospect St, Tacoma, WA 98406
Colorado Review, CSU, English, Fort Collins, CO 80523-9105
Columbia Review, 415 Dodge Hall, Columbia Univ., New York, NY 10027
The Common, Frost Library, Amherst College, Amherst, MA 01002
Commonweal, 475 Riverside Dr., Rm 405, New York, NY 10115
Comstock Review, UW-English Dept., 800 Algoma Blvd., Oshkosh, WI 54901
Conjunctions, Bard College, 30 Campus Rd., Annandale, NY 12504-5000
Connecticut River Review, 9 Edmund Pl, West Hartford, CT 06119
Consequence Forum, PO Box 60036, Las Vegas, NV 89160
Constellations, N. Alonso, 127 Lake View Ave., Cambridge, MA 02138-3366
Cool City Review, English, University of Kansas, Lawrence, KS 66045
Copper Nickel, UC-D, English - CB 175, PO Box 173365, Denver, CO 80217
Cornerstone Press, UW, 1804 Fourth Ave., CCC 127, Stevens Point, WI 54481
Cowboy Jamboree Press, A. Van Winkle, 712 Ottawa Dr., Rock Hill, SC 29732
Crab Creek Review, J. Hands, 15327 SE 45th St., Bellevue, WA 98006-2593
Cream City Review, UW-Milwaukee, PO Box 413, Milwaukee, WI 53201
Creation Magazine, 105 S. Westland Ave., Tampa, FL 33606
Cresheim Press, 1717 Arch St., #4020, Philadelphia, PA 19103
Current, CC-English Dept., 14049 Scenic Hwy, Lookout Mountain, GA 30750
Cutleaf, 272 Marys Pond Rd., Rochester, MA 02770
Cutthroat, 5401 N. Cresta Loma Dr., Tucson, AZ 85704

Dactyl & Co., 425 Texas Ave., Las Cruces, NM 88001-3644
Daraja Press, PO Box 99900, BM 735 664 Wakefield QC J0X 0C2 Canada
Dark Thirty Press, A. Roncaglione, 1951 Terry Rd., Durham, NC 27712
Dashboard Horus, M. Lecrivain, 6028 Comey Ave., Los Angeles, CA 90034
Dawn Review, G. Lin, 2115 Stonebridge Dr., Ann Arbor, MI 48108
Daxson Publishing, E. Castro, 6625 Northside Dr., Los Angeles, CA 90022
DBS Press, T. Christine, 2724 Berwyn Rd., Bensalem PA 19020-1406
december, P.O. Box 16130, St. Louis, MO 63105-0830
Decolonial Passage, PO Box 35238, Los Angeles, CA 90035
Deep Wild Journal, 2309 Broadway, Grand Junction, CO 81507
Delete Press, B. Vogler, 400 E. Olive St., #2, Fort Collins, CO 80524
Delmarva Review, PO Box 544, St. Michaels, MD 21663
Delta Poetry Review, 11955 SW Cheshire Rd., Beaverton, OR 97008
Denverse Magazine, 1001 N. Logan St., #109, Denver, CO 80203
descant, Texas Christian University, TCU Box 297270, Fort Worth, TX 76129
Dewdrop, PO Box 74, Upton, WY 82730
Dialogist, 5461 S. Cornell Ave., #2W, Chicago, IL 60615

Dipity Literary Magazine, J. Kaur, 403 Pyramid St., Henderson, NV 89014
Dirt, W. Gleen, 589 Carlton Ave., Brooklyn, NY 11238-3431
Dirtbag Magazine, M. Itaya, 808 Lisa Court, Mobile, AL 36695
Disappointed Housewife, Brennan, 2819 Cauchoo Ct., Cool, CA 95614
Disturb the Universe Mag., S. Evens, 804 Parapet Rd., Chesapeake, VA 23323
Dithering Chaps, 11 Bakers View, Corfe Mullen, Dorset, BH21 3JS, UK
DMQ Review, S. Ashton, 16393 Bonnie Lane, Los Gatos, CA 95032
Dodge (formerly Artful Dodge), M. Starr, 1189 Beall Ave., Wooster, OH 44691
Does It Have Pockets, 23907 7th Ave. So., Seattle, WA 98198
Dogwood Alchemy, 1139 Maple Stream Dr., Indianapolis, IN 46217
Door Is A Jar, 77 Linden Blvd., #3B, Brooklyn, NY 11226
Dreams & Nightmares, Merket, 10055 Goodwood Blvd, Baton Rouge, LA 70815
The Drift, PO Box 75, New York, NY 10113
Driftwood Press, 14737 Montoro Dr., Austin, TX 78728-4320
Dust Poetry, C. Redford, 13 Blanquettes St., Worcester, WR3 8BN, UK

EastWest Literary Forum, 19-22A 22 Rd., Astoria, NY 11105
Eclectica Magazine, 5114 Aspen Ave NE, Albuquerque, NM 87110
ecotone, UNCW- Creative Writing, 601 S. College Rd., Wilmington, NC 28403-5938
805 Lit & Art, S. Katz, 507 Bayview Dr., Holmes Beach, FL 34217
eMerge Magazine, C. Templeton, 15 Eugenia St., Eureka Springs, AR 72632
The Engine (idling, 124 Rockwood St., Monroeville, PA 15146
EPOCH, 251 Goldwin Smith Hall, Cornell Univ., Ithaca, NY 14853-3201
Essay Press, M. Wilson, 1106 Bay Ridge Ave., Annapolis, MD 21403-2902
Ethos Books, 28 Sin Ming Lane, #06-131, Midview City, Singapore 573972
-ette review, Maynard, 230 E. 59th St., #4, New York, NY 10022
Etruscan Press, Brady, 334 Tod Lane, Youngstown, OH 44504
Eucalyptus Lit, PO Box 390261, Mountain View, CA 94039
Exposition Review, PO Box 48542 Los Angeles, CA 90048
Eye Publishewe, 201 Harrison St., #828, San Francisco, CA 94105
Eye to the Telescope, PO Box 6688, Portland, OR 97228

Fahrenheit Books, 42 Water St., #222, Guilford, CT 06437
Fallen Tree Press, T. Simon, 330 Marganza South, Laurel, MD 20724
Fence, L. Mead, 449 37th St. #2, Oakland, CA 94609
Fiction Week, 887 S. Rice Rd., Ojai, CA 93023-9417
Fiddlehead, 11 Garland Ct, UNB, PO Box 4400, Fredericton NB E3B 5A3, Canada
Fifth Wheel Press, 404 S. Eaton St., Baltimore, MD 21224
Final Thursday Press, 815 Slate St., Cedar Falls, IA 50613
Finishing Line Press, POB 1626, Georgetown, KY 40324

First Matter Press, 10948 E Burnside St., Portland, OR 97216
Five Fleas, R. Jacobson, 405 S. Jefferson Way, Indianola, IA 50125
Five Points, Georgia State Univ, Box 3999, Atlanta, GA 30302-3999
Flapper Press, 4400 West Riverside Dr., Ste. #110, #115, Burbank, CA 91505
Fine Print Press, PO Box 64711, Baton Rouge, LA 70896-4711
Five South, 1850 Industrial St., #714, Los Angeles, CA 91102
Florida Review, UCF-English Dept., PO Box 161346, Orlando, FL 32816-1346
FlowerSong Press, 1218 N. 15th St., McAllen, TX 78501
Flying Island, IN Writers Cntr, 4011 N. Pennsylvania St., Indianapolis, IN 46205
Flying South 2024, 546 Old Birch Creek Rd., McLeansville, NC 27301
Foglifter Press, 3490 Downey Ave., Reno, NV 89503
Forge Literary, Haggerty, 4018 Bayview Ave., San Mateo, CA 94403-4310
Forgotten Ground Regained, 183 Millerick Ave., Lawrenceville, NJ 08648
Fork Apple, 390 Broadway, Apt. 55, Somerville, MA 02145
42 Miles Press, IUSB- English, 1700 Mishawaka Ave., South Bend, IN 46615
Foundation for Light Verse, CPU Box 274499, Rochester, NY 14627
Four Leaf Collective, 360 Vernon St. #303, Oakland, CA 94610
Four Windows Press, 321 N. Hudson Ave., Sturgeon Bay, WI 54235
Fourth Genre, English, 4198 JFSB, Brigham Young University, Provo, UT 84602
Fraidy Cat Press, R. Helfst, 6340 Shelbyville Rd., Indianapolis, IN 46237
Frazzled, L. Cooney, 8 Parkgrove Neuk, Edinburgh, EH4 7QT, Scotland
Frozen Sea, POB 33143, Los Gatos, CA 95031
Fruitslice Magazine, 2306 Effie St., Los Angeles, CA 90026
Fugue Journal, Univ. Idaho, 875 Perimeter Dr., MSC 2282, Moscow, ID 83844-9803
Full Bleed Press, MICA, 1300 W. Mt. Royal Ave., Baltimore, MD 21217-4134

Garden of Neuro Institute Publishing, 73 Peach Rd., Poughkeepsie, NY 12601
A Gathering of the Tribes, 151 1st Ave., #220, New York, NY 10003
Gemini Magazine, PO Box 1485, Onset, MA 02558
Georgia Review, 706A Main Library, Univ. of Georgia, Athens, GA 30602-9009
Genrepunk Magazine, A. Heffers, 1101 Ekstam Dr., #208, Bloomington, IL 61704
GigaNotoSaurus, L. Wanak, 441 Bay Hill Dr., Madison, WI 53717
Gival Press, PO Box 3812, Arlington, VA 22203-0812
Glass: A Journal of Poetry, 1667 Crestwood, Toledo, OH 43612
Glass Lyre Press, POB 2693, Glenview, IL 60025
Glassworks, Rowan University - Writing Arts, 260 Victoria St., Glassboro, NJ 08028
Gnashing Teeth, 242 E. Main St., Norman, AR 71960-8743
Gold Man Review, 9730 Flourish Dr., Redding, CA 96001
Golden Bridges, S. Hendess, 344 Aldrup Way, Lake Mary, FL 32746-2383
Golden Dragonfly Press, A. Maldonado, 87 Colonial Village, Amherst, MA 01002

Golden Foothill Press, 1438 Atchison St., Pasadena, CA 91104
Gone Lawn, 2207 Anthem Ct., Brentwood, TN 37027
The Good Life Review, S. Shehan, 13644 Seward Circle, Omaha, NE 68154
Good Printed Things, L. Ramos, 6 E. Chaucer Rd., Greenville, SC 29617
Good River Review, Spalding Univ., 851 S. Fourth St., Louisville, KY 40203
Gorko Gazette, C. Gee, 1923 Hawkinson Rd., Oregon, WI 53575
Grady Miller Books, 1236 1/8 N. Cahuenga Blvd., Los Angeles, CA 90038-1655
The Gravity of the Thing, 17028 SE Rhone St., Portland, OR 97236
Great River Review, 310 Pillsbury Dr. SE, Minneapolis, MN 55455
great weather for MEDIA, 253 Warren St., Hudson, NY 12534
Green Linden Press, 208 Broad Street South, Grinnell, IA 50112-2583
Green Silk Journal, 228 N. Main St, Woodstock, VA 22664
Green Writers Press, 34 Miller Rd., W. Brattleboro, VT 05301
GTB Publishing, getthatbookpublishing@gmail.com
Gunpowder Press, 1136 Camino Manadero, Santa Barbara, CA 93111

Half Mystic Press, T. Winters, 240 E. 2nd St., #B, New York, NY 10009
Halfway Down the Stairs, 3117 E. 33rd St., Minneapolis, MN 55406
HamLit, R. Robinson, 227 S. Forest St., #301, Bellingham, WA 98225
Harvard Advocate, 21 South St., Cambridge, MA 02138-5906
Harvard Divinity Bulletin, McDowell, 45 Francis Ave., Cambridge, MA 02138
Harvard Review, Lamont Library, Harvard University, Cambridge, MA 02138
Hayden's Ferry Review, ASU, English, P.O. Box 871401, Tempe, AZ 85287-1401
Headlight Review, KSU-English, 440 Bartow Ave., MD 2701, Kennesaw, GA 30144
Headmistress Press, 4 Corley Loop, Eureka Springs, AR 72632
Healing Muse, SUNY- Bioethics & Humanities, 618 Irving Ave., Syracuse, NY 13210
Hedgehog Review, Univ. of Virginia, PO Box 400816, Charlottesville, VA 22904
Heliotrope, 99 East 4th St., #3J, New York, NY 10003
Here, D. Donaghy, ECSU-English, 83 Windham St., Willimantic, CT 06226
Heterodox Haiku, 4329 Minnehaha Ave., Unit 2, Minneapolis, MN 55406-4076
hex literary, 28 Rich St., Worcester, MA 01602
Highland Park Poetry, 1690 Midland Ave., Highland Park, IL 60035
Hillfire Press, C. Craig, 100 Academy Drive, Mercersburg, PA 19236
Hindsight Creative Nonfiction, J. Ellis, 4440 Whitney Place, Boulder, CO 80305
Hippocampus, 210 W. Grant St., #104, Lancaster, PA 17603-3707
HNDL Mag, 1317 Old Farm Dr., St. Louis, MO 63146
Hominum, E. Wang, 130 Cambridge Rd., King of Prussia, PA 19406
Honey Literary, 908 S. Barstow St., #2, Eau Claire, WI 54701
Hong Kong Review, T. Huang, 2306 Proper Commercial Bldg., 9 Yin Chong St., Kowloon, Hong Kong

Hopkins Review, 3400 N. Charles St., 81 Gilman Hall, Baltimore, MD 21218
The Hopper, 4935 Twin Lakes Rd., #36, Boulder, CO 80301
Hotch Potch, G. Schwartz, 5-45 Ella St., Ottawa, ON K1S 2S3, Canada
Howl, 17 Waterpark Green, Carrigaline, Co. Cork, P43 DC85, Ireland
The Hudson Review, 33 West 67th St., New York, NY 10023
hunger button books, 33 Dexter Av., Redwood City, CA 94063
Huizache, UC-Davis, Chicana/o Studies, 1 Shields Ave., Davis, CA 95616-5270
Humana Obscura, B. Bruce, 1554 Meadowridge Rd., Corralitos, CA 95076
Hypertext, C. Rice, 1821 W. Melrose St., Chicago, IL 60657-2001

I-70 Review, 5021 S. Tierney Dr., Independence, MO 64055
iamb, M. Owen, 57 Thorpe Gardens, Alton, Hampshire GU34 2BQ, UK
The Icarus Writing Collective, 50 Eden Way, Roslyn Harbor, NY 11576
Identity Theory, M. Borondy, 413 Opal Dr., Henderson, NV 89015
IHRAM Literary Press, 4142 73rd St., #5M, Woodside, NY 11377
Ilanot Review, K. Marron, 75-54 113th St., #3-F, Forest Hills, NY 11375
Illuminations, CC-English, 66 George St., Charleston, SC 29424-0001
Image, 3307 Third Avenue West, Seattle, WA 98119
Imposter, L. Camiolo, PO Box 63549, Philadelphia, PA 19147
In Short, S. Liberatore, 6412 Brandon Ave. PMB 105, Springfield, VA 22150
Indiana Review, English Dept., 1020 E. Kirkwood Ave., Bloomington, IN 47405
Indianapolis Review, N. Solmer, 2635 Vinewood Dr. Speedway, IN 46224
Ink, 2413 Elm St., Guntersville, AL 35976
Inklings, J. Bates, Miami University, Harris Hall, 500 Harris Dr., Oxford, OH 45056
Inner Child Press, W. Peters, Sr., 3280–1 Zion Rd., Bellefonte, PA 16823
Inner Worlds, S. Jackson, 50A Worsley Rd., London E11 3JN, UK
Inquest, 23 Everett St., Cambridge, MA 02138
Interstellar Flight, A. Klein, 451 S. Harvard Blvd., #342, Los Angeles, CA 90020
Intrepidus Ink, 40580 Los Robles Rd., Fallbrook, CA 92028
Iowa Poetry Association, M Baszczynski, 16096 320h Way, Earlham, IA 50072
The Iowa Review, University of Iowa, 308 EPB., Iowa City, IA 52242
Irreantum, T. Jepson, 115 Ramona Ave., El Cerrito, CA 94530
Italian Americana, M. Terrone, 3556 77th St., #31, Jackson Hts, NY 11372
IX Studios, PO Box 45501, Westlake, OH 44145

J Journal, English, 524 West 59th St., 7th Fl, New York, NY 10019
JC Studio Press, 56 Alder Rd., Milton of Campsie, Glasgow, Scotland, UK
Jabberwock Review, MSU-English, Drawer E, Mississippi State, MS 39762
Jacar Press, 6617 Deerview Trail, Durham, NC 27712
James Dickey Review, RU-English, 7300 Reinhardt Cir., Waleska, GA 30183-2981

Jawbone Collective, 1 Manor Farm Ct, Walditch, Bridport, Dorset, DT6 4LQ UK
Jelly Bucket, R. Szabo, EKU-English, 521 Lancaster Ave., Richmond, KY 40475
Jerry Jazz Musician, 2538 NE 32nd Ave., Portland, OR 97212
Jet Fuel, Review, S. Muench, 1508 W. Erie St., #3, Chicago, IL 60642
Jewish Book Council, B. Kantor, 520 8th Ave., 4th Fl, New York, NY 10018
Jewish Currents, PO Box 130049, Brooklyn, NY 11213
Jewish Fiction, N. Gold, 378 Walmer Rd., Toronto, ON M5R 2Y4, Canada
jmww, 2306 Altisma Way, #214, Carlsbad, CA 92009-6311
The Journal, OSU- English, 164 Annie and John Glenn Ave., Columbus, OH 43210
Joyland Publishing, M. King, 168 Prospect Pl. #2, Brooklyn, NY 11238-3838
June Road Press, PO Box 260, Berwyn, PA 19312
Juniper, L. Young, 47 Robina Ave., Toronto, ON M6C 3Y5, Canada

Keeping the Flame Alive, C. Dean, 9382 W 525 S, Columbus, IN 47201
Kelp Journal & Books, 1491 Cypress Dr., #475, Pebble Beach, CA 93953
Kelsay Books, 502 S. 1040 E, #A119, American Fork, UT 84003
Kelsey Review, MCCC, 1200 Old Trenton Rd., West Windsor, NJ 08550
Kestrel, Fairmont State Univ., Humanities, 1201 Locust Ave., Fairmont, WV 26554
Kitchen Table Quarterly, 4622 Prospect Ave., Los Angeles, CA 90027
Kitty Wang's Mambo Academy, PO Box 5, North Branford, CT 06471
Kweli Journal, POB 693, New York, NY 10021

LAdige, A. Ovanesian, Via Generale Giacomo Medici 12/3, 38123 Trento, TN, Italy
Last Leaves Magazine, 507 Airey Ave., Endicott, NY 13760
Last Syllable, S. Cornwell, 3900 Lomaland Dr., San Diego, CA 92106
Latin@Literatures, 1267 Wensley Ave., El Centro, CA 92243
Laurel Review, NWMSU, 800 University Dr., Maryville, MO 64468
Leon Literary Review, 2 Saint Paul St., #404, Brookline, MA 02446
Libre Magazine, Sellers, 2004 Walden Place, Brandon, MS 39042
Like a Blot from the Blue, 75 High St., New Pitsligo, AB43 6NF, ABD, Scotland
Lily Poetry Review Books, 223 Winter St., Whitman, MA 02382
Lincoln Review, English, Univ. of Lincoln, Campus Way, Lincoln LN6 7TS, UK
Lips, 141 Madison Ave., Clifton, NJ 07011
Listen To Your Skin Press, 9868 W. 74th Place, Arvada, CO 80005
Literary Namjooning, 233 Windham Dr., Exton, PA 19341
Literary Revelations, 2901 Research Forest Dr. #400, The Woodlands, TX 77382
Literate, W. Meiners, 1422 Meadow St., Mount Pleasant, MI 48858
LitMag, PO Box 476, Bedford, NY 10506
Litt Magazine, 56 Kratz Rd., Callicoon, NY 12723
Littoral Books, PO Box 4533, Portland, ME 04112-4533

LiveMag!, PO Box 1215, Cooper Station, New York, NY 10276
Livingston Press, J. Taylor, Stn 66, Univ. West Alabama, Livingston, AL 35470
Loch Raven Review, 1306 Providence Rd., Towson, MD 21286
Lone Stars Poetry, M. Rosebud, 4219 Flinthill Dr., San Antonio, TX 78230
Lonesome Press, PO Box 155, Salt Point, NY 12578
Longreads, C. Rowlands, 1228 Evelyn Ave., Berkeley, CA 94706
The Loveliest Review, PO Box 132, Greenwood, MS 38924
Loving Healing Press, V. Volkman, 5145 Pontiac Trl, Ann Arbor, MI 48105-9238
Lowestoft Chronicle, 863 Penfield Rd., Rochester, NY 14625
Lunch Ticket, 1699 N. Terry St., #167, Eugene, OR 97402

The MacGuffin, Schoolcraft College, 18600 Haggerty Rd., Livonia, MI 48152-2696
MacQueen's Quinterly, PO Box 2322, Kernersville, NC 27285
Mad Swirl, C. Calle, 10018 Woodridge Dr., Dallas, TX 75218
Madville Publishing, PO Box 358, Lake Dallas, TX 75065-0358
Main Street Rag, 12180 Skyview Dr., Edinboro, PA 16412
Mama's Kitchen Press, 10301 Ranch Rd. 2222, #638, Austin, TX 78730
Manhattan Review, P. Fried, 440 Riverside Dr., #38, New York, NY 10027
Manifest Station, 34 Porter Rd., Andover, MA 01810
Mánoa, University of Hawaii - English., 1733 Donaghho Rd., Honolulu, HI 96822
Many Nice Donkeys, J. Davis, 145 Washington Ave., Bellevue, KY 41073
Many Worlds Press, 720 Adams St, #8, Davis, CA 95616
The Margins, AAWW, 112 W. 27th St., #600, New York, NY 10004
Marsh Hawk Press, PO Box 206, East Rockaway, NY 11518-0206
Masticadores USA, B. Leonhard, 204 East Parkway, Columbia, MO 65203
The Massachusetts Review, Photo Lab 309, 211 Hicks Way, Amherst, MA 01003
matchbook lit mag, 16 Jersey Ave., Suffern, NY 10901
Mayday Magazine, N. Palladino, 2 Elizabeth Ct, Medford, NJ 08055
Mayari Literature, Phynne-Belle, 1617 17th St., San Pablo, CA 94806
McNeese Review, MSU- English, Box 92655, Lake Charles, LA 70609
The Meadow, TMCC - English, Vista B300, 7000 Dandini Blvd., Reno, NV 89512
Meadowlark Press, PO Box 333, Emporia, KS 66801
Meat for Tea, Valley Review, 282 W. Franklin St., Holyoke, MA 01040
Mercer University Press, 1501 Mercer University Dr., Macon, GA 31207-1515
Metaphorosis, PO Box 851, Neskowin, OR 97149
The Metaworker Lit Mag, 12133 Mitchell Ave., #111, Los Angeles, CA 90066
Miami University Press, J. Bates, Harris Hall, 500 Harris Dr., Oxford, OH 45056
Michigan Quarterly Review, 435 S. State St., Ann Arbor, MI 48109-1003
Micromance Magazine, G. Brown, 3316 Timber View Lane, Cookeville, TN 38506
Mid-American Review, Bowling Green State - English, Bowling Green, OH 43403

Middle Creek Publishing, 9161 Pueblo Mountain Park Rd., Beulah, CO 81023
Midnight Mind, PO Box 536, 1461 Main St., St. Helena, CA 94574
Midsummer Dream House, 4833 Santa Monica Ave. #7341, San Diego, CA 92167
Midwest Review, University of Wisconsin, Stevens Point, WI 54481-3897
The Militant Grammarian, H. Smart, 31 Riviera Dr., Hattiesburg, MS 39402
Military Experience & the Arts, PO Box 4101, Morgantown, WV 26504
Milk Candy Review, 3145 Grelck Lane, Billings, MT 59105
Milk House, R. Dennis, 9444 North Hill Rd., Arkport, NY 14807
The Minnesota Review, Virginia Tech -English, Blacksburg, VA 24061
Minutes Before Six, 2784 Homestead Rd., #301, Santa Clara, CA 95051
Minyan Magazine, Marlow, 7683 Cross Village Dr., Germantown, TN 38138
Mississippi Review, USM, 118 College Dr., #5144, Hattiesburg, MS 39406-0001
Missouri Review, 453 McReynolds Hall, Univ. of Missouri, Columbia, MO 65211
Mobile Data Mag, 3422 N. Broadway, Los Angeles, CA 90031
Mobius, Journal of Social Change, 149 Talmadge St., Madison, WI 53704
Mocking Heart Review, 2783 Iowa St., #2, Baton Rouge, LA 70802
Modern Language Studies, English, 514 University Ave., Selinsgrove, PA 17870
Mom Egg Review, MER, POB 9037, Bardonia, NY 10954
Monday Mag, C. Cole, 1227 N Fuller Ave., West Hollywood, CA 90046
Monkfish, 22 East Market St., Ste. 304, Rhinebeck, NY 12572
Moon City Review, MSU-English, 901 S. National Ave., Springfield, MO 65897
Moon Park Review, PO Box 87, Dundee, NY 14837
Moon Tide Press, 6709 Washington Ave., #9297, Whittier, CA 90608
Moonshine Review Press, A. Kaylor, 4218 Abernathy Pl., Harrisburg, NC 28075
Moria Literary, Woodbury Univ., 7500 N. Glenoaks Blvd., Burbank, CA 92504
Moss Puppy, M. Martini, 961A Village Dr. West, North Brunswick, NJ 08902
Mukoli Magazine, SCMPD, 3201 Campus Loop Rd., Kennesaw, GA 30144
Muleskinner Journal, 3427 Paraiso Way, La Crescenta, CA 91214
Multiplicity Magazine, H. Parton, 148 Wildwood Ct., St. Paul, MN 55115
MUTHA Magazine, 304 18th St, Brooklyn, NY 11215

Narrateur, 500 Hofstra Way, Hempstead, NY 11549
Narrative, C. Burke, 1313 SE Spokane St., #409, Portland, OR 97202
Nassau County Poet Laureate Society, PO Box 4104, Farmingdale, NY 11735
National Flash Fiction Day, 2 Pearce Close, Cambridge, CB3 9LY, UK
Naugatuck River Review, 45 Highland Ave., #2, Westfield, MA 01085
Nelle, UAB-English, 1402 10th Ave S., Birmingham, AL 33294-1241
Neshaminy, 56 S. Main St., Doylestown, PA18901
New Delta Review, 1509 Highland Rd., #204, Baton Rouge, LA 70802-7073
New England Review, Middlebury College, Middlebury, VT 05753

New Flash Fiction Review, V. Fox, 2440 Princeton Pike, Lawrenceville, NJ 08648
New Generations Beat Publications, D. Kilday, 54 Tosun Rd., Wolcott, CT 06716
New Greek Voices, H. Mitsios, 20 East 9th St., #8H, New York, NY 10003-5944
New Letters, 5101 Rockhill Rd., Kansas City, MO 64110-2499
New Ohio Review, OU, 201 Ellis Hall, 45 University Terrace, Athens, OH 45701
New Territory Magazine, K. Foster, 304 N. 8th St., Oskaloosa, IA 52577
New Verse News, J. Penha, 107 Laurel Hill Dr., Westtown, NY 10998
New Verse Review, Knepper, 155 Robinson Ln., Lexington, VA 24450
New World Writing Quarterly, 33 Southwood Dr., Tonawanda, NY 14223
Next Page Press, 118 Inslee Ave., San Antonio, TX 78209
Nightboat Books, 310 Nassau Ave., #205, Brooklyn, NY 11222-3813
Nine Muses Review, 1918 Liberty Dr., Liberty, MO 64068
Nine Sisters Press, 2401 St. George St., Los Angeles, CA 90027
No Tokens Journal, T. Madden, 72 Countryman Rd. Voorheesville, NY 12186
Nobody Thoughts, B. Booker, 532 Barry St., #1/2, Stroudsburg, PA 18360
Nomad litmag, 329 W. 3500 S., Bountiful, UT 84010
Noon, 1392 Madison Ave., PMB 298, New York, NY 10029
Noor Magazine, 540 2nd St., Brooklyn, NY 11215
North American Review, UNI, Cedar Falls, IA 50614-0516
North Carolina Literary Review, ECU Mailstop 555 English, Greenville, NC 27858
North Carolina Poetry Society, Griffin. 131 Bon Aire Rd., Elkin, NC 28621
North Meridian Press, 711 Oak St., Anniston, AL 36207
Not a Pipe Publishing, 898 Morning Glory Dr., independence, OR 97351
Not Quite Write Press, PO Box 9067, Wyoming NSW 2250, Australia
Notch Magazine, 110 Thompson St, $4B, New York, New York 10012
Noyo Review, 267 Divisadero St., San Francisco, CA 94117
Nude Bruce Review, A Mobbs, 941 SW 15th St., #206, Corvallis, OR 97333
null pointer press, 86 Silver Sage Cres., Winnipeg MB R3X 0K2, Canada

Obsidian, Illinois State Univ., Box 4241, Normal, IL 61790-4241
Ocean State Review, URI, 60 Upper College Rd., Kingston, RI 02881
Off Assignment, 1802 Massachusetts Ave., #32, Cambridge, MA 02140
The Offing, PO Box 22022, Seattle, WA 98122
Ogham Stone, ER3019, University of Limerick, V94 T9PX, Ireland
Old Mountain Press, 85 John Allman Lane, Sylva, NC 28779
On the Seawall, R. Slate, PO Box 179, Chilmark, MA 02535-9800
One Art, M. Danowsky, 219 Sugartown Rd., I-304, Wayne, PA 19087
One Day, Bernstein, 320 Carrera Dr., Mill Valley, CA 94941
One Story, 232 3rd St., #A108, Brooklyn, NY 11215-2708
Only Poems, J. Payton, 1178 Amber Pines Dr., Leland, N 28451

Orange Blossom Review, D. Fagan, 22586 205th Ave., Paris, MI 49338
orangepeel literary magazine, 312 4th St. SE, #32, Charlottesville, VA 22902
Orca, J. Ponepinto, 6516 112th Street Court, Gig Harbor, WA 98332
Orchards Poetry Journal, Kelsay, 502 S 1040 E, A119, American Fork, UT 84003
Oregon Humanities, 610 SW Alder St., #1111, Portland, OR 97205
Origami Poems, 1948 Shore View Dr., Indialantic, FL 32903
Osiris, 106 Meadow Lane, Greenfield, MA 01301
Outcult.id, 18 Office Park Bldg., 12th Floor, Unit A&H, Jl. TB Simatupang No. 18, Kebagusan, Kec. Ps. Minggu, Jakarta Selatan 12520
Oxford American, PO Box 3235, Little Rock, AR 72203-3235
OyeDrum, 99 Wall St., #1138, New York, NY 10005
Oyster River Pages, PO Box 706, Lewes, DE 19958

Paddock Review, 452 General John Payne Blvd., Georgetown, KY 40324
Pangyrus Lit Mag, A. Lewis, 6 Wilson St., Winchester, MA 01890
Parlyaree Press, 2309 Melante Dr. NE, Atlanta, GA 30324
Passager Books, 7401 Park Heights Ave., Baltimore, MD 21208-5448
Passages North, English, NMU, 1401 Presque Isle Ave., Marquette, MI 49855-5301
Passengers Journal, A. Winham, 180 Sterling Place, #11, Brooklyn, NY 11217
Paterson Literary Review, PPCC, 1 College Blvd., Paterson, NJ 07505-1179
Pelekinesis, Givens, 112 N. Harvard Ave., #65, Claremont, CA 91711-4716
Pen in Hand, 13A E. Patrick St., #1, Frederick, MD 21701
Periwinkle Pelican, I. Grey, 906 Hill St., Hastings, NE 68901
Persea Books, 90 Broad St., Ste 2100, New York, NY 10004
Perugia Press, PO Box 60364, Florence, MA 01062
PGN Publishing, 2001 S. Calumet Ave., #202, Chicago, IL 60616
Philadelphia Stories, 1167 West Baltimore Pike, #267, Media, PA 19063
Phoebe, GMU, Mailstop 2C5, 4400 University Dr., Fairfax, VA 22030
Pictura Journal, A. Wright, PO Box 355, Belmont, WV 26134
Pineberry Literary Magazine, E. Kraft, 5480 Crestridge Ter., Dublin, CA 94568
Pink Trees Press, 8237 61st Rd., Middle Village, NY 11379-1420
Pioneer Works & Pioneer Works Broadcast, 159 Pioneer St., Brooklyn, NY 11231
Pithead Chapel, B. Terwilliger, 6865 Kirkville Rd., East Syracuse, NY 13057
Pleiades, Box 800 (MAR 366,) English, UCM, Warrensburg, MO 64093-5069
Ploughshares, Emerson College, 120 Boylston St., Boston, MA 02116-4624
Plume, D. Lswless, 740 17th Ave. N, Saint Petersburg, FL 33704
Poem-A-Day, Academy of American Poets, 75 Maiden Ln, #901, N. Y., NY 10038
Poet Lore, 4508 Walsh St., Bethesda, MD 20815
Poet Heroic, T. A. O'Brien, 1550 NW 14th Avec., #306, Portland, OR 97209

Poetose, 655 Centre St., #302268, Boston, MA 02130
Poetry, 61 West Superior St., Chicago, IL 60654
Poetry As Promised, 2135 James Way, Saylorsburg, PA 18353
Poetry Box, 3300 NW 185th Ave., #382, Portland, OR 97229-3406
Poetry Center, CSU, 2121 Euclid Ave., Cleveland, OH 44115-2214
Poetry Daily, MS 3E4, 4400 University Dr., Fairfax, VA 22030
The Poetry Distillery, 1693 State Route 28A, West Hurley, NY 12491
Poetry Society of South Carolina, PO Box 1090, Charleston, SC 29402
Poetry South, 1100 College St., W-1634. Columbus, MS 39701
Poetry Super Highway, R. Lupert, 24203 Mentry Dr., Newhall, CA 91321-3950
Poets Online, K. Ronkowitz, 97 Yorkshire Dr., Cedar Grove, NJ 07009
Poets Wear Prada, Hoffman, #2, 533 Bloomfield St., #2, Hoboken, NJ 07030
Ponder Review, 1100 College St., W-1634, Columbus, MS 39701
Pony Express, G. Whitmore, 1125 Methodist Rd., Hood River, OR 97031-8768
Porter House Review, English, TSU, 601 University Dr., San Marcos, TX 78666
Posit, 237 Thompson St, New York, NY 10012
Post Road, Boston College, 140 Commonwealth Ave., Chestnut Hill, MA 02467
Postcard Lit, 3 Parkwood St., #1, Albany, NY 12208
Potomac Review, MT 212, MC, 51 Mannakee St., Rockville, MD 20850
Preservation Foundation, R. Loller, 313 Pennington Bend Rd., Nashville, TN 37214
Press 53, PO Box 30314, Winston-Salem, NC 27130-0314
Prime Number Magazine, 560 N. Trade St., #103, Winston-Salem, NC 27101
Prism Review, University of La Verne, 2230 1st St., La Verne, CA 91750
Prolific Pulse Press, 5921 Waterford Bluff Ln, #1418, Raleigh, NC 27612
Propelling Pencil, A. Niven, 32 South Lodge Crescent, Enfield, EN2 7NP, UK
Prose Poem, 2 Pearce Close, Cambridge, CB3 9LY, UK
Pulley Press, 5626 University Way NE, #B, Seattle, WA 98105
Pure Sleeze Press, 1915 McConnell Ave., Evansville, IN 47714
Purple Ink Press, 24 NE 23rd Ave, #5, Pompano Beach, FL 33062

Quarterly West, English, 255 S. Central Campus Dr., Salt Lake City, UT 84112
Quartet, Blaskey, 10613 N. Union Church Rd., Lincoln, DE 19960
Quill and Parchment, 2267 Lambert Dr., Pasadena, CA 91107

Racket Journal, N. Sanders, 2045 Grahn Dr., Santa Rosa, CA 95404
Radar Poetry, 19 Coniston Ct., Princeton, NJ 08540
Radon Journal, 2671 Avalon Court, #301, Alexandria, VA 22314
Ragaire Lit. Mag., 182 Gort na Coiribe, Headford Rd, Galway, H91R5C2, Ireland
Rainy Weather Days, 109 Hotts Lane, Madison, AL 35757

Ran Off with the Star Bassoon, Kelly, 69 W. Hanover Ave., Morris Plains, NJ 07950
Rattle, 12411 Ventura Blvd., Studio City, CA 91604
Raw Earth Ink, PO Box 39332, Ninilchik, AK 99639
Raw Lit, 10 Miniati, 11636 Athens, Greece
Read or Green Books, 261 Burma Dr. NE, Albuquerque, NM 87123
Reckon Review, PO Box 1280, Flat Rock, NC 28731
Reckoning Press, 206 East Flint St., Lake Orion, MI 48362-3225
Red Branch Review, 5221 Horsestall Dr., Knoxville, TN 37918
Red Penguin Books, 27 Ontario Rd., Bellerose Village, NY 11001-4112
Red Rock Review, 6375 W. Charleston Blvd., Las Vegas, NV 89146
Red Wheelbarrow, De Anza Coll., 21250 Stevens Creek Blvd., Cupertino, CA 95014
Red Wheelbarrow Poets, 90 Kennedy Rd., Andover, NJ 07821
Redfern Ink, 219 Cummins St., Franklin, TN 37064
Redhawk Publications, 2550 US Hwy 70 SE, Hickory, NC 28602-8302
Redivider, Emerson College, 120 Boylston St., Boston, MA 02116
Reed Magazine, SJSU- English, 1 Washington Sq., San José, CA 95192-0090
The Rejoinder, M. Colbert, 27 Greenleaf St., Apt. 2, Portland ME 04101
Renaissance, WCC-English, 3000 Wayne Memorial Dr., Goldsboro, NC 27534
Revel, P. Campion, 1293 Grand Ave., #303, Saint Paul, Mn 55105
Revolute, 158 Westbrook Dr., Clifton Hts., PA 19018
Revolution John, A. Smith, 1659 48th Ave. NE, Willmar, MN 56201
Rhino, PO Box 591, Evanston, IL 60204
Ribbons, S. Weaver, 127 N.10th St., Allentown, PA 18102
Rinky Dink Press, 15552 N. 156th Lane, Surprise, AZ 85374
Riot of Roses Publishing House, 11435 Marquardt Ave., Whittier, CA 90605
Rising Phoenix, 4421 Clover Hollow Rd., Slatington, PA 18080
Rivanna Review, 807 Montrose Ave., Charlottesville, VA 22902
River Heron Review, PO Box 12, Fountainville, PA 18923
River River Books, 10 Linganore Pl., Durham, NC 27707-2971
River Styx Magazine, 7112 Idaho Ave., St. Louis, MO 63111
River Teeth, English, BSU, 2000 W. University Ave., Muncie, IN 47306
Roadside Press, 519 N. Coal St., Colchester, IL 62326
RockPaperPoem, A. Perry, 18473 69th Place N., Maple Grove, MN 55311
Rogue Agent, J. Khoury, 5441 Covode Pl., Pittsburgh, PA 15217-1914
Room, Box 46160, Station D., Vancouver BC, V6J5G5, Canada
The Rumpus, 704 Leona Drive, Ann Arbor, MI 48103
Rust + Moth, PO Box 2450, Fort Collins, CO 80522
Rusted Radishes, S. Wisenberg, 1301 W. Byron St., Chicago, IL 60613-2818
Rye Whiskey Review, Robbins, PO Box 3, Knotts Island, NC 27950

Sagging Meniscus Press, 115 Claremont Ave., Montclair, NJ 07042-3705
Saginaw, D. Horton, #4-1812 Baihuan Jiayuanm 66 Guangqu Road, Chaoyang, Beijing 100022, China
Sailors Review, 701 Copperline Dr., Unit 306, Chapel Hill, NC 27516
Salamander, Suffolk U., English, 8 Ashburton Pl., Boston, MA 02108
Salvation South, 3563 W. Hill St., Clarkston, GA 30021
Same Faces Collective, D. Whitlow, 1164 N. Dearborn St., #211, Chicago, IL 60610
San Antonio Review, A. Fee, 2170 Sulky Trail, Beavercreek Twp., OH 45434
San Pedro River Review, Alfier, 5403 Sunnyview St., Torrance, CA 90505
Sand Literature & Art, Bellini, Dunckerstr. 37, 10439 Berlin, Germany
Sans.Press, 17 Rice's Cor., High Rd., Thomondgate, Limerick, V94 KT51, Ireland
Santa Barbara Literary Journal, 444 Los Feliz Dr., Santa Barbara, CA 93110
Santa Clara Review, SCU, 500 El Camino Real, Santa Clara, CA 95053
Santa Fe Literary Review, SFCC, 6401 Richards Ave. #225B, Santa Fe, NM 87508
Santa Fe Writers Project, 4916 Edgemoor Lane, Bethesda, MD 20814
Santa Monica Review, S. M. Coll., 1900 Pico Blvd., Santa Monica, CA 90405
SAPIENS, C. Weeber, 655 Third Avenue, 6th Floor, New York, NY 10017
SARKA Publishing, F. Kritikos, 4701 N. Talman Ave., 3rd Floor, Chicago, IL 60625
Saturnalia Books, 2816 N. Kent Rd., Broomall, PA 19008
Scaffold, S. Gergley, 65 Wickham Dr., Warwick, NY 10990-2134
Scapegoat Press, B. Furnish. PO Box 410962, Kansas City, MO 64141-0962
Scoundrel Time, Bender, 221 E. 18th St., #4A, Brooklyn, NY 11226
Send Me Press, PO Box 165, Hartland, VT 05048
Serving House Books, W. Lawrence, 6006 Cobridge Sq, Raleigh, NC 27609
Seven Kitchens Press, 2547 Losantiville Ave., Cincinnati, OH 45237
Seventh Wave, 1213 SW 174th Pl, Normandy Park, WA 98166
7th-Circle Pyrite, 4201 Hubbard Rd., Charlotte, NC 28269
Shadelandhouse Modern Press, PO Box 910913, Lexington, KY 40591
Sheila-Na-Gig, 203 Meadowlark Rd., Russell, KY 41169-1539
Shenandoah, English, W&L Univ., 204 W. Washington St, Lexington, VA 24450
Shine, S. Terrell, 4 Hi Over Rd., Binghamton, NY 13901
Shö Poetry Journal, PO Box 4410, Chino Valley, AZ 86323
The Shore Poetry, 611 Irene Ave., Salisbury, MD 21801
Short Reads, S. Knezovich, 155 Fairview Ave E., Pittsburgh, PA 15237
Short Story Long, 41841 E. Ann Arbor Trail, Plymouth, MI 48170
Silhouette, Virginia Tech, 344 Squires Student Center, Blacksburg, A 24060
Silkworm, T. Clark, 30 Berkshire Terrace, Florence, MA 01062
Silverfish Review, PO Box 3541, Eugene, OR 97403
Sine Theta Magazine, 24 Pearl St., Provincetown, MA 02657

Sixteen Rivers Press, PO Box 640663, San Francisco, CA 94164-0663
Sixth Finch, 95 Carolina Ave., #2, Jamaica Plain, MA 02130
Skipjack Review, J. Huff, 2751 S. Wallis Smith Blvd., Springfield, MO 65804
SLAB, English, 114 SWC, Slippery Rock Univ., Slippery Rock, PA 16057-1326
Slag Glass City, DePaul Univ., English, 2315 N. Kenmore Ave., Chicago, IL 60614
Slapering Hol Press, 300 Riverside Dr., Sleepy Hollow, NY 10591
Slippery Elm, Univ. of Findlay, 1000 N. Main St., Box 1615, Findlay, OH 45840
Small Beer Press, 150 Pleasant St., #306, Easthampton, MA 01027-1875
Smartish Pace, 2221 Lake Ave., Baltimore, MD 21213
SmokeLong Quarterly, C. Allen, 2127 Kidd Rd., Nolensville, TN 37135
Smoky Blue, 36 Louisiana Ave., Asheville, NC 28806
Sneaker Wave Magazine, J. Levine, 1165 5th Ave., New York, NY 10029
So to Speak, MS 2C5, The Hub Ste 1201, 4400 University Dr., Fairfax, VA 22030
SoFloPoJo, O'Mara, 1014-E1 Green Pine Blvd., West Palm Beach, FL 33409-7005
Solstice, 38 Oakland Ave., Needham, MA 02492
Sontag Mag, 6095 Wurtenburg Ln, Stone Mountain, GA 30087
Soundings East, English Dept., Salem State University, Salem. MA 01970
South Dakota Review, 414 E. Clark St., Vermillion, SD 57069
South 85, L. Pietrzyk, 2580 Country Club Rd., Winston-Salem, NC 27104
South Shore Poets of Long Island, 62 East Olive St., Long Beach, NY 11561
Southeast Review, English, FSU, 405 Williams Bldg., Tallahassee, FL 32306
Southern Indiana Review, USI-Orr C., 8600 University Blvd., Evansville, IN 47712
Southword, Frank O'Connor House, 84 Douglas St., Cork, Ireland
Southwest Review, PO Box 750374, Dallas, TX 75275-0374
Spartan Press, 1136 Saint Christopher St., Columbia, MO 65203
Spectrum, UCSB, Bldg. 494, 1 UCEN Rd., Santa Barbara, CA 93106
Spiritus, M. Burrows, 8 Central St., Camden, ME 04843
Spit Fire Review, C. Harris, 1219 Ansley Ln, Mentone, CA 92359
Split Lip Magazine, W. Oleson, 409 E. Cherry St., Walla Walla, WA 99362
Split This Rock, 1301 Connecticut Ave. NW, #600, Washington, DC 20036
Spoon River Poetry, ISU, Campus Box 4241, Normal, IL 61790-4241
Stackfreed Press, 634 North A St., Elwood, IN 46036
Stanchion, 281 W. Lincoln Hwy., Unit 402, Exton, PA 19341
Star*Line, 61871 29 Palms Hwy, Joshua Tree, CA 92252
Still: The Journal, 89 W. Chestnut St., Williamsburg, KY 40769
Stone Circle Review, 306 Steel Rd., Havertown, PA 19083
Story Magazine, 312 E. Kelso Rd., Columbus, OH 43202
Story Circle Network, PO Box 200, Idledale, CO 80453
Story Quarterly, RU-English, Armitage 4th Fl, 311 North 5th St., Camden, NJ 08102
Storylines Press, 1Erie St., #202, Stratford, Ontario, N5A 2M3, Canada

Storyteller Poetry Review, 4270 N. Elephant Butte Rd., Queen Valley, AZ 85118
Strange Horizons, R. Stott, 408 Highland Ave., Winchester, MA 01890
Strange Matters, J. M. Colon, 5205 Congress Ave., #627, Boca Raton, FL 33487
Streetlight Magazine, 56 Pine Hill Lane, Norwood, VA 24581
Sugar House Press, PO Box 13, Cedar City, UT 84721-0001
The Summerset Review, 25 Summerset Dr., Smithtown, NY 11787
Summit Journal, M. Levy, 225 W. 106th St., #3G, New York, NY 10025
Sundial, Murphy, 5932 Valley Forge Dr., Coopersburg, PA 18036
Sundog Lit, 51209 Canal Rd., Houghton, MI 49931
Superpresent, 2122 Whirlaway Dr., Stafford, TX 77477
Suspect, 3W 122nd St., #5D, New York, NY 10027
Suspended, J. Sweezer, 1510 Heather Dr., Aurora, IL 60506
Susurrus, M. Champagne, 3809 Cotswold Ave., #C, Greensboro, NC 27410
Swamp Pink, College of Charleston, English, 66 George St., Charleston, SC 29424
Sweet Lit, 83 Carolyn Ln, Delaware, OH 43015
Swimming with Elephants, W. Gibson, 3872 Lissa Dr., Eureka, CA 95503
Swing, 245 Running Knob Hollow Rd., Sewanee, TN 37375
SWWIM Every Day, J. Karetnick, 301 NE 86th St., El Portal, FL 33138
Syncopation, N. Welsh, 4 Shady Glen Crescent, Bolton, ON L7E 2K4, Canada
Synkroniciti, 7603 Rock Falls Ct., Houston, TX 77095
Systemic Dreaming, 3422 N. Broadway, Los Angeles, CA 90031

Tab Journal, Chapman University - English, 1 University Dr., Orange, CA 92866
Tadpole Press, 2770 Arapahoe Rd., Ste. 132-620, LaFayette, CO 80026
Talon Review, Hargrove, 102 Hawkeye Ct., #216, Iowa City, IA 52246
Tampa Review, Univ. of Tampa Press, 401 W. Kennedy Blvd., Tampa FL 33606
Taos Journal of Poetry, 615 Sakai Rd., Taos, NM 87571
Tar River Poetry, ECU, MS 159, East 5th St., Greenville, NC 27858-4353
10x10 Flash Fiction, 15 Eliot St., Chestnut Hill, MA 02467
Tenebrous Press, 10003 N. Buchanan Ave., Portland, OR 97203
Terrapin Publishing, 4 Midvale Ave., West Caldwell, NJ 07006
Thimble Lit Mag, 47 Pleasantdale Rd., Rutland, MA 01543
Thirty West Publishing, 518 Wilder Sq., Plymouth Meeting, PA 19462
This Broken Shore, 15 Sandspring Dr., Eatontown, NJ 07724
3: A Taos Press, P.O. Box 370627, Denver, CO 80237
3 Elements Review, M. Collins, 198 Valley View Rd., Manchester, CT 06040
Three Rooms Press, 243 Bleecker St., #3, New York, NY 10014-4438
Threepenny Review, PO Box 9131, Berkeley, CA 94709
Tilting at Windmills Press, 13224 W. 132nd St., Overland Park, KS 66213
Timber Journal, U.C. Boulder, A. Sheffer, English, 226 UCB, Boulder, CO 80309

Tin House, 2617 NW Thurman St., Portland, OR 97210
Tint Journal, info@tintjournal.com, Graz, Austria
Tiny Wren Lit, 99 Tabilore Loop, Delaware, OH 43015
Tipton Poetry Journal, 642 Jackson St., Brownsburg, IN 46112
TL;DR Press, Penfold, 213 Heady Lane, Fishers, IN 46038
TopTweetTuesday, 19 Hendrefoilan Rd., Tycoch, Swansea, SA29LS, UK
Torch Literary Arts, 5540 N. Lamar Blvd, #39, Austin, TX 78751
Touchstone, Poetry Society of New Hampshire, PO Box 1118, Amherst, NH 03031
Trace Fossils Review, 3475 Shagbark Circle, Mount Pleasant, SC 29466
Trampoline Press, 324 12th St., New Orleans, LA 70124
trampset, J. Kruft, 2519 36th Ave., Astoria, NY 11106
Transcendent Zero Press, 16429 El Camino Real, #7, Houston, TX 77062
Transition, Hutchins Center, 4R, 104 Mt Auburn St., #3R, Cambridge, MA 02138
Trash Cat Lit Magazine, 7 Hasell St., Carlisle, Cumbria, CA2 4HB, UK
Trestle Creek Review, NIC, 1000 W. Garden Ave., Coeur d'Alene, ID 83814
Trio House Press, 2615 Emerson Ave S, Minneapolis, MN 55408-1223
TRP—University Press of SHSU, PO Box 2146, Huntsville, TX 77341-2146
TulipTree Publishing, J. Top, PO Box 133, Seymour, MO 65746
Tupelo Press, 60 Roberts Dr., #308, North Adams, MA 01247
Twenty Bellows, 3344 W. Walsh Place, Denver, CO 80219
The Twin Bill, 3778 Burkoff, Troy, MI 48084

Unbound Press, 1293 Grand Ave., #303, Saint Paul, MN 55105
Ugly Duckling Presse, 232 3rd St., #E303, Brooklyn, NY 11215
Umbrella Factory, A. ILacqua, 838 Lincoln St., Longmont, CO 80501
Under Review, 1536 Hewitt Ave., MS-1730 c/o CWP, Saint Paul, MN 55104
Under the Gum Tree, 3768 4th Ave., Sacramento, CA 95817
Under the Sun, PO Box 332, Cookeville, TN 38503
underscore_magazine, E. Weidner, 101 Loetscher Pl., #303, Princeton, NJ 08540
Undertaker Books, R. Cuthbert, 27 Wright Park Dr., Dunkirk, NY 14048
Undertow Publications, 1905 Faylee Crescent, Pickering, ON L1V 2T3, Canada
University of Tampa Press, J. Aja, 401 W. Kennedy Blvd., Tampa, FL 33606
University of Texas Press, PO Box 12866, Austin, TX 78711-2866

Vagabond City Literary Journal, A. King, PO Box 300552, Austin, TX 78703
Valley Voices, MVSU-7242-English, 14000 Hwy, 82 W, Itta Bena, MS 38941-1400
Vast Chasm, 1302 Hillview Dr., Norfolk, NE 68701
A Velvet Giant, 951 Carroll St., #3A, Brooklyn, NY 11225-1924
Vestal Review, D. Galef, 65 Edgemont Rd., Montclair, NJ 07042-2304
Viewless Wings Press, 5424 Sunol Blvd, #10557, Pleasanton, CA 94566-7705

Vincent Brothers Publishing, 8502 Seawell School Rd., Chapel Hill, NC 27516-9245
Vine Leaves Press, Parsens, 1458 Sequoia Circle, Toms River, NJ 08753
Virginia Quarterly, 5 Boar's Head Ln, PO Box 400223, Charlottesville, VA 22904
Vita Poetica Journal, 2105 Linden Ln, Silver Spring, MD 20910-1706
Vox Veritas Vita Press, 4446 Battlecreek Way, Ave Maria, FL 34142

Wallstrait Literary Journal, D. Judge, 2549 E. Marion St., Des Moines, IA 50320
Wandering Aengus Press, PO Box 334, Eastsound, WA 98245
Washington Square Review, NYU, LVCWH, 58 West 10th St., New York, NY 10011
Washington Writers Publishing House, 8908 Cold Spring Rd., Rockville, MD 20854
Water~Stone Review, MS A1730, 1536 Hewitt Ave., St. Paul, MN 55104-1284
Waxwing Lit Journal, 3540 Pleasant Ave., Minneapolis, MN 55408
The Way Back to Ourselves, 4535 Cozzo Dr., Land O Lakes, FL 34639
Wayne State University Press, 4809 Woodward Ave., Detroit, MI 48201
Weird Lit Magazine, S. Herrin, 609 NW 191st St., Shoreline, WA 98177
West Branch, Bucknell University - English, 1 Dent Dr., Lewisburg, PA 17837
West Trade Review, 12701 Moores Mill Rd., Huntersville, NC 28078
West Trestle Review, 84 Scenic Ave., Apt. B, Point Richmond, CA 94801
West Virginia University Press, PO Box 6295, Morgantown, WV 26506
Westchester Review, 2 Willow Ave, Larchmont, NY 10538
Wet Cement Press, 1908 Yolo Ave., Berkeley, CA 94707
Whale Road Review, 3900 Lomaland Dr., San Diego, CA 92106
Whiptail Journal, Lehmann, 134 White Birch Dr., Guilford, CT 06437
Wigleaf, MU-English, 114 Tate Hall, Columbia, MO 65211
Wildhouse Poetry, M. Burrows, 8 Central St., Camden, ME 04843
Willow Springs, 601 E. Riverside Ave, #400, Spokane, WA 99202
Willows Wept Review, 17517 County Road 455, Montverde, FL 34756
The Winged Moon, R. Quintas, 6759 Kawula Ln, Sobieski, WI 54171
Winning Writers, 351 Pleasant St., PMB 222, Northampton, MA 01060
Woodhall Press, 81 Main St., Unit 25a, Branford, CT 06405
Workhorse, 3030 Breckenridge Ln, Bldg. #1, Apt. 110, Louisville, KY 40220
World Inkers, 16429 El Camino Real, Apt 7, Houston, TX 77062
World Literature Today, 630 Parrington Oval, #110, Norman, OK 73019-4033
Worlds Within, E. Jones, 699 Waggoner Rd., Reynoldsburg, OH 43068
Wrath-Bearing Tree, Yeager, 155 Sullivan St., Brooklyn, NY 11231
Write or Die Magazine, 29 Alden St. #1, Plymouth, MA 02360
Write Volumes, 728 W. Sheridan Rd., Chicago, IL 60613-3244
The Write-In, 2 Pearce Close, Cambridge, CB3 9LY, UK
The Writer's Workout, PO Box 76, Columbia, KY 42728
The Writing Disorder, C. Lukather, PO Box 3067, Ventura, CA 93006

Xray Lit Mag, J. Greidus, 7610 W. Comet Ave., Peoria, AZ 85345-0730

Yale Review, Yale University, PO Box 208243, New Haven, CT 06520-8243
Yalobusha Review, C128 Bondurant Hall, PO Box 1848, University, MS 38677-1848
Yearling, c/o Workhorse, 3470 Castleton Hill, Lexington, KY 40517
Yellow Arrow Publishing, PO Box 65185, Baltimore, MD 21209
Yolk, 2031 av de Verdun, Montreal, QC, H4A 3NZ, Canada
Your Impossible Voice, 4972 Farview Rd., Columbus, OH 43231

Zephyr Press, 400 Bason Dr., Las Cruces, NM 88005-3717
Zibby Media, G. Tito, 121 E 71st St., #2, New York, NY 10021-4275
Zoetrope: All Story, 916 Kearny St., San Francisco, CA 94133
Zone 3, APSU, Box 4565, Clarksville, TN 37044
ZYZZYVA, O. Villalon, 57 Post St., Ste. 708, San Francisco, CA 94104-5025

CONTRIBUTORS' NOTES

STEPHEN AKEY is the author of two memoirs and the essay collection *Culture Fever.*

LAUREL ANDERSON is a plant ecologist and poet living in Delaware, Ohio.

RICHARD BAUSCH won the Rea Award for the short story. Knopf will soon publish his story collection, *The Fate of Others.*

CHARLES BAXTER's fiction, essays and poetry have appeared in thirteen previous Pushcart Prize volumes.

BRUCE BEASLEY is the author of nine poetry collections, most recently from Orison Books and BOA editions.

CIARAN BERRY's *Liner Notes* is available from The Gallery Press. He grew up in Ireland and now teaches at Trinity College, Hartford CT.

CLINT BENTLEY is a writer and film maker. He was nominated for an Academy Award for best adapted screenplay.

LEONE BRANDER lives in Saskatchewan, Canada and holds an MFA from Boston University.

MARK BRAZAITIS, the author of nine books, teaches at West Virginia University.

TORLI BUSH's *Requiem for A Redbird* is published by Pulley Press.

CYRUS CASSELLS, the 2021–2022 Poet Laureate of Texas, won the 2025 Jackson Poetry Prize.

CHEN CHEN is the author of two poetry collections and has appeared in two previous Pushcart Prize volumes.

SUZANNE CLEARY's *The Odds* was just published by NY Quarterly Books. She teaches at Converse University.

PATRICIA CLARK is the author of *O Lucky Day* (Madville, 2025). She lives in Grand Rapids, Michigan.

ANDREI CODRESCU has a new substack. His most recent book is *How To Live Under Fascism* (Black Widow Press).

JANE DELURY is the author of the novels *Hedge* and *The Balcony*.

CHRIS DOMBROWSKI is the author of three poetry collections and two books of nonfiction. He teaches at The University of Montana.

SARAH GREEN teaches at St. Cloud State University. Her books are *The Deletions* and *Earth Science*.

JESSICA R. GORDON served as poetry editor for *Qu: A Literary Magazine*. She lives in North Carolina.

JAMES ALLEN HALL's most recent publication is *Romantic Comedy* (Four Way Books, 2023)

SARAH C. HARWELL teaches at Syracuse University. Her poetry collection is *Sit Down Traveler.*

CHRISTIE HODGEN is the editor of *New Letters* and the author of *Boy Meets Girl* and three other books.

ALLISON HUTCHCRAFT is the author of *Swale* (New Issues, 2020). She teaches at the University of North Carolina, Charlotte.

BRET ANTHONY JOHNSTON directs the Michener Center for Writers in Austin, Texas. His latest novel, *We Burn Daylight* (Penguin Random House), is just published.

JANE KALU's stories have appeared in *Best American Short Stories* and the *O' Henry Prize*. She is at work on a novel.

SHEEMA KALBASI is an Iranian–American poet, translator and researcher. Her work has won many humanitarian awards.

JOANNA KAVENNA novels include *A Field Guide to Reality, Inglorious* and *Zed*.

TEN KOOSER is a former United States Poet Laureate and a Pulitzer Prize winner. He lives in rural Nebraska.

MARIA KUZNETSOVA teaches at Auburn University in Alabama. Her novels are *Oksana, Behave*! and *Something Unbelievable*.

DORIANNE LAUX's most recent collection is *Life On Earth* (W.W.Norton). She lives with her husband Joe Millar and their bunny Odin in Richmond, CA.

AMY LEE LILLARD won the 2022 BOA Short Fiction Prize. Her next book is forthcoming from the University of lowa Press.

STEFAN MANASIA lives in Romania. He has published six volumes of poetry and a collection of essays.

MICHAEL MARK won the Rattle Chapbook Prize and has been published by Atheneum.

ANTHONY MARRA won the National Magazine Award for fiction in both 2016 and 2025, and two previous Pushcart Prizes.

REBECCA MARTIN lives and works in Pittsburgh. She is poetry editor for *45th Parallel.*

EDUARDO MARTINEZ-LEYVA's poetry collection is forthcoming from The University of Wisconsin Press.

LOU MATHEWS won a previous Pushcart Prize. His selection here is from his new novel *Hollywoodski* (Turner Publishing).

SHARA McCALLUM's latest poetry collection is *Behold.* She teaches at Penn State University.

MELISSA McKINSTRY is working on her first poetry collection. She lives in San Diego.

KEYA MITRA teaches at Pacific University. She won the 2024 Perkoff Prize and the Prairie Schooner Nonfiction Prize.

TOMMY MOORE was selected for the PEN Emerging Voices fellowship in 2013. He lives in Los Angeles.

MIHAELA MOSCALIUC's *Heartmoor* is out soon from Alice James Books.

YXTA MAYA MURRAY is a writer and law professor from Studio City, CA. Her books are available from Cornell University Press and New Oeste.

ANGELA NARCISO TORRES is the author of two poetry collections and a Chapbook. She won the Yeats Poetry Prize.

RANDY NELSON's first story collection won the Flannery O'Connor Award. He teaches at Davidson College.

DAVE NEWMAN was a finalist for the Rattle Poetry Prize. His work has appeared in publications around the world.

JOHN OKRENT is a family doctor at a community health center in Tacoma, WA.

JESSICA PETROW-COHEN is the winner of *Kenyon Review*'s Short Nonfiction Contest. Her substack is "Claiming Writerhood."

ROGER REEVES teaches at the University of Texas. He has received four previous Pushcart Prizes plus a Guggenheim Fellowship, and the Kingsley Tufts Poetry Award.

ERICA REID won the Donald Justice Poetry Prize from Autumn House. She lives in Fort Collins, Colorado.

NATHAN CURTIS ROBERTS lives in Utah. His fiction has appeared in *The Atlantic, Best American Short Stories* and elsewhere.

CAREY SALERNO's books include *The Hungriest Stars, Tributary* and *Shelter.* She is Director and Publisher of Alice James Books.

KIM SAMEK is a comedy writer and TV producer. She lives in Los Angeles.

GRACE SCHULMAN received the Frost Medal for Distinguished Lifetime Achievement in American Poetry. She is Professor Emerita of English at Baruch College, and the author of nine poetry collections and a memoir.

NATALIE SHAPERO's new book is *Stay Dead*. She lives in Los Angeles and teaches at UC Irvine.

AVIGAYL SHARP's first novel, *OFF Season*, and a story collection, *Animal After Dark*, are forthcoming from Astra House (US) and Weidenfeld & Nicolson (UK).

MAURA STANTON's book of stories is due soon from Slant Books. She lives in Bloomington, Indiana.

KENDRA SULLIVAN is a poet, public artist, and activist scholar. She directs the Center for the Humanities at CUNY Graduate Center.

M.H. TSE is the Inaugural Postdoctoral Fellow in Animal Law at the University of Toronto.

RYAN VAN METER is Associate Director of the program in creative writing at the University of Chicago. His essay collection is *If You Know What I Know Now*.

WENDY WILLIS is a poet, essayist, textile artist and national leader in community engagement and democratic governance.

PATRICK WHITFILL's chapbook is *Curiosity*. He lives in Spartanburg, South Carolina.

FRANCINE WITTE has authored eleven books of poetry and flash fiction. She is editor of *Flash Boulevard* and *South Florida Poetry Journal*.

INDEX

The following is a listing in alphabetical order by author's last name of works reprinted in the *Pushcart Prize* editions since 1976.